SON OF THE MORNING

SON OF THE MORNING

A Novel of the Hundred Years War

MARK ALDER

PEGASUS BOOKS
NEW YORK LONDON

SON OF THE MORNING

Pegasus Books LLC
80 Broad Street, 5th Floor
New York, NY 10004

American copyright © 2016 Mark Alder

First Pegasus Books cloth edition February 2016

Interior design by Maria Fernandez

ISBN: 978-1-60598-950-1

10 9 8 7 6 5 4 3 2 1

Printed in the United States of America

Distributed by W. W. Norton & Company, Inc.

To Dad
1933–2013
Much missed

I form the light, and create darkness: I make peace, and create evil: I the LORD do all these things.

—Isaiah 45:7 King James Version

﹘﹘

I tell you that to everyone who has, more will be given, but as for the one who has nothing, even what they have will be taken away. But those enemies of mine who did not want me to be king over them—bring them here and kill them in front of me.

—Luke 19:26–27 New International Version

PART I

1337

＊— · —＊

In the year that young King Edward defied the French king Philip's claim to the fief of Aquitaine. Sometime between Lammas and Michaelmas. The beginning of the great war against France.

1

The torchlight flickered against the ruins of the church, like the ghost of the flame that had burned it. The knights sat mounted outside as if they too smoldered, their horses steaming in the cold coastal air. It was a flat, gray, English September of rain and cloud and fog.

The enemy was gone, but the nobles, far too late to face them, had put on their war gear to reassure the people. The horses stamped and blew, metal clicked against metal where a mailed hand readjusted armor or loosened a helmet strap, but the great body of warriors, two hundred strong, were otherwise silent. Even the young pages behind the knights, looking after the spare horses, said nothing. Not a joke, not a cough. The cooks, armorers, smiths, and chandlers who made up the ragged tail of the column caught the mood and were quiet around their wagons and carts.

At the front of the body of riders a man-at-arms, his pig-face visor pulled down, held up a standard—the three sprawling leopards that announced the riders as the personal bodyguard of Edward III, king of England. This standard-bearer was flanked by two others who held the red and white banner of St. George.

In the church a bareheaded young man knelt before the charred altar. His surcoat bore the same motif as the standard, and the helmet that sat beside him was encircled by a metal crown.

A respectful distance away, across the debris of the floor, were four armored knights, standing around a brazier. Closer to the altar stood another knight, in a surcoat of red diamonds. This man was much older than the king, in his mid-thirties, and his face was as a worn as a campaign saddle. An eyepatch hid his right eye, a deep scar emerging above it on the brow and going below it on the cheek.

Beside him was a small boy of no more than seven. The child had pattens on his feet—wooden overshoes that raised him above the filth and mud of the floor. He wore a full hooded tunic in the Italian style, its rich red cloth trimmed with gold and pearls, but when he spoke, it was in the ragged French of the English court.

"How shall we repay the French for this, Father?"

The king stood up in a jingle of armor. He walked over to the boy and put his hand on his head. Then he turned to the scarred knight.

"Salisbury. Montagu, cousin. Advise me." The king's voice was low and confidential, and he spoke in English.

The knight shifted from foot to foot. He glanced into the shadows. There were other men in the church, beside the higher nobles—the banker Bardi and the merchant-knight Pole, huge creditors of the king's, traveling west under his protection. In the church they kept well away from the men of better sort, shunning the torchlight, standing in the darkness by the side of the ruined door.

Montagu's eyes were on them and his voice was a murmur. "Our dear Gascony is under attack by the French king. The war in Scotland is as pressing as it ever was, with the French reinforcing the natives. The French send Genoese mercenaries to raid our shores and we can scarcely muster the men to defend them. Buying off the Genoese is out of the question. Our money has been spent in Scotland. I have given the accounts my closest scrutiny. And now this. We are fighting on too many fronts."

"So your counsel is?"

Montagu said, "Continue in Scotland, bide our time here, suffer a little, and, when the crusade takes the French king away, we strike. Our allies in the Low Countries and Germany will support us, the former for want of our wool, the latter because the Holy Roman emperor suspects the ambition of the French."

The king snorted and scraped at the ashes with his foot. "The pope has canceled the crusade; I had word from our spies at his court in Avignon this morning."

"Then God help England."

Edward shot Montagu a questioning look.

"Will He? Or are the rumors true?" the king asked him.

He said, "The French have not managed to persuade their angels out of their shrines, sir; I'm sure of that. We would have heard by now."

"Philip attacks our ancestral lands in Gascony and the Agenais. Angels have been seen outside Bordeaux. Our garrison is terrified." The king related the threat as lightly as if discussing the menu for a tournament feast. He was a war commander, experienced against the Scots, long used to the importance of conveying certainty and strength to all those around him. "Lights were seen in the sky," said Edward.

"All sorts of things can cause lights. Men's imaginations first of all. The French have employed sorcerers—it's well known. The manifestation could be demonic, rather than angelic."

"And that's supposed to reassure me?" Edward smiled.

"It would mean we're on the right side. When I traveled to France on your business in the spring, I saw no sign they had coaxed the angels from their raptures."

Edward said, "Though they try. New churches cram the streets of Paris; relics are collected from all over the world. His queen is a woman of rare piety; it's well known."

"They call her a devil."

"Because she is lame and because they fear her. She is no devil. She has succeeded in this way before."

"Sire, when the angel came to their aid at Cassel it was clearly God's work. A peasant rebellion is, by definition, unholy. There is no question of that here. And besides, it is not an important point. We can't invade anyway."

"Why not?"

"The French have no need of angels. The Royal House of Valois can put fifty thousand in the field and their men-at-arms are formidable. Their lances alone will do."

"I spit on their fifty thousand. Thirty thousand of them are commoners and of no account, five thousand are mercenaries who will run after one decent charge, and the noblemen are the same ones I've been beating the brains out of at tournaments since I was sixteen. My army has razed half of Scotland against those furious men of the north; Philip's has hardly been in a battle worthy of the name. One of us is worth five of them and they know it, or they would invade properly. They burn our churches. They hamper our prayers. This must be their aim—to weaken us spiritually, for they know they cannot face the teeth of the English lion in fair battle."

"There are many churches in England, Edward. We can spare a few."

The king said, "Does God see it that way?"

"It may be that we do enough already. Angels have danced on the tips of French spears before, but there have been none in the kingdom since Cassel. Perhaps our prayers, our devotion, keep it so."

"Perhaps. But God will not favor us if we cannot defend His houses."

Montagu kicked at the dirt of the floor and said, "Well, look at it this way. The cancellation of the crusade increases the physical threat, but diminishes the spiritual one. God must love King Philip less today. He will allow no angels to help him if he backs out of his obligations in the Holy Land. We should hold here, greet him with great force when he attacks us, and fight on our land—well supplied on ground we know."

"The cancellation has holy sanction—on the edict of the pope. God loves Philip as much today as He ever did. But we will make war without God if we have to."

"To make war without God is to make war on God."

"Not so. I am king because of God. I want different counsel. Sir Richard, come here."

Another man-at-arms walked forward—a tall, powerfully built man aged around forty, wearing a mail coat, his basinet beneath his arm, his long gray hair bright in the firelight.

Edward said, "Richard. You have the wisdom of great age. What do you think? Do we repay this? Take on the French in open war?"

He replied, "To face them directly is suicide. It is for you to decide if it is a right and noble suicide."

"You don't think we can defeat them? There is no guarantee they can put angels in the field against us."

"Our spies say that the French king asks for the Oriflamme on every saint's day."

Edward bowed his head. The Oriflamme—the holy fire banner, dipped in the blood of the French martyr St. Denis—was one of the most powerful relics in Christendom. It had been used very rarely by the French in all memory, such was their regard for it, but flown at the head of the army it meant two things: that the French army could not be defeated and would give no quarter; that God was with them and would cut down their enemies as he had the firstborn of Egypt. St. Michael the archangel sat sometimes in the abbey of St. Denis where the Oriflamme was kept. The French king needed the archangel's blessing to take the banner. Once taken, the French angels would come to his aid and England would be in great peril.

The king added, "We'll face the Oriflamme and all his angels if we have to. My honor will not be trampled into the dirt. It's possible to beat them even if they have it. Our royal ancestor John fought without angels, without the blessing of saints. He fought against the Oriflamme without flinching."

Montagu spoke. "That's not a particularly propitious example. John lost Normandy, he saw England racked by civil war, and he died, struck down by who knows what. Cousin Edward, your father's angels . . ."

The king's hand went to his sword. "If you say more, though you are my dearest friend, I will strike you down where you stand."

Montagu shrugged. "Not very likely to speak then, am I?"

"Keep your flippancy and your caution, Montagu! I am king of the English, and a Norman true. When I bid you fight to defend my lands, you will fight and, if necessary, die, along with your sons—with all the sons of England, if that is what God wills! God made me your master, and your life is mine to do with as I see fit! England is me and I am England." The king spoke his somewhat mangled French, to emphasize his ruler's right.

"I served your father; I will serve you."

Edward smiled, his anger gone as quickly as it had come.

"My father was a godly man," he said in English.

"Though we might want to ask ourselves how God allowed him to fall to the usurper Mortimer," said Montagu. "You know your wife thinks an explanation for our lack of angels might be found there. I could investigate this."

"Mortimer never usurped everything. He seduced my mother, turned her mind, and used her to throw down my father, but it was me he put on the throne, remember that. Are you saying I am a usurper?"

"You were a boy. You were his puppet."

"And when I became a man God blessed me to free my mother from his grip, avenge my father, and kill him in his turn."

"So let me investigate."

Edward said, "You cannot investigate the mind of God. And God guided my hand to send Mortimer to Hell, never forget that. I would not be here if I did not have God's blessing. Kings are appointed by God and only stay kings as long as it pleases Him."

"King Philip of France has been a king for a long time."

"Then we'll face him in the field and see who the Lord favors. I have faith in God that I will prevail."

"You have faith in yourself, Edward. That is very different and close to vanity. Wait until tomorrow to decide. We've ridden a long way and the fire that burned this church has inflamed your passion too. Slake it on a girl—there is a queue of merchants' daughters in the town waiting to see you, and I have it on authority that no fewer than eight famous whores have traveled to Southampton hoping to please you. Let your temper cool in your bed for a while; make your decision in the clear light of morning."

"No, Montagu. Courtiers talk; kings act. We'll have them. Angels or no angels, Oriflamme or not, we'll have them. We'll take the battle to France and we'll do it soon."

"We should wait until we can summon at least one angel to counter theirs. Let me look into it more fully. I understand you don't want an investigation, because of the damage it would cause if it were known that the angels were more than simply *reluctant* to appear. But I can be discreet."

Edward held forward the breast of his surcoat. "What does that say?"

Montagu rolled his eyes. "It's rather difficult to see in this light."

"Don't joke your way out of this, Montagu. What does it say?"

"It is as it is."

"The motto of my house. 'It is as it is.'" No point whining about it. We took on the Scots without angels and won."

"To be fair, sire, the Scots have never managed to win an angel from God."

"I wonder why that is."

"I'd always assumed they rather terrify Him," said Montagu.

Edward smiled. "You can always amuse me, Montagu. Particularly with the victories you bring me." The king was quiet for a moment. "Can you bring me victory here?" he asked.

"I can try, sire. Your royal wife brought the patronage of eight saints as part of her dowry, the court has another thirty or so between the higher nobles. We can call in the relics and see what divine aid can be summoned."

"It has been tried, Montagu. I . . ." The king waved his hand.

"I wasn't told."

"My wife has tried. If a lady of her royal blood and piety can't gain insight with eight saints, then we have no hope even with eighty or eight hundred. We must ask for God's blessing, of course, but we cannot expect it."

"And if the French receive it instead?" Montagu asked.

"Then we shall show Him on the field that, by our valor, we deserve His help."

"We'll show plenty of valor to take on fifty thousand men, backed by angels, under a banner that guarantees victory."

"Good, then how can He deny us? We are English, like the mastiff who goes grinning into the maw of a bear. We honor God on the battlefield, shedding our blood to defend Him, showing Him that the French cannot defend church, cathedral, and monastery from the devastation we can wreak. Then the angels will come to us. Or Philip's will go from him and we will have our victory. The French do not yet suspect our weakness; our spies report no gossip at court. We may force them to an accommodation that could make us all rich men. Take courage, cousin—Christ once thought God had forsaken Him too. It was not so."

"And if we lose?"

Edward glanced at the men in the shadows. He replied, "Then I am dead and my debts are cleared. To man, if not to God."

Montagu gave a short laugh. When he had first heard Edward say "I am England," he had thought it a useful piece of propaganda. Lately, the king was coming to believe it.

"Well," said Montagu, "a happy outcome is almost guaranteed. Luckily I had not expected to live to see all my children wed."

"Who does? That concludes our business. Send these whores and I'll see which of them pleases me." Edward put his arm on Montagu's shoulder.

"Trust to God, William; trust to God. He will not desert us when our hour of need comes."

Edward walked from the church; his trumpets sounded and the cold air was loud with the rattle of the knights sitting up on their horses.

Montagu glanced up into the black sky as he followed his king. "This is our hour of need," he said to the heavens.

Two men remained in the ruins of the burned church. One was a lower sort of knight in a blue coat trimmed with sable fur and bearing three golden polecats.

The knight spoke. "What were they talking about, Bardi? He kept glancing at me as though he wanted to borrow more money."

"The cancellation of the French crusade, I should guess." The other man, a head shorter than the first and not nearly as portly, had a thick accent and was dressed in a rich high-collared black tunic studded with sapphires. At his neck was a fine gold chain that bore a small green bottle, held by a tiny casket of gold and silver. He wore a black beaverskin hat, to which was pinned a cockleshell, worked in silver. It was a sign he had made a pilgrimage to the tomb of St. James at Compostela.

"Christ's cullions! When did you hear about that?" he asked Bardi.

He replied, "I learned of the pope's decision a week ago."

"And you didn't tell the king?"

"To what purpose?"

"The defense of our lands."

"I am, as you may have noticed, of Florence, not London. These are not my lands. I think rather of the defense of my family's money. While the king awaited news he did nothing. Now he has it, you see what happens."

"You don't need to worry about money. You bankers are as rich as Croesus."

Bardi said, "We were, until we gave our money to the king. Things are tighter now, believe me. My family needs to recoup its money. I say that to you because you are a man who understands such things. And the importance of keeping them confidential."

Pole blew like an exhausted hunting dog. He admitted, "I'm into him for one hundred thousand, myself."

"I know. Can you afford that?"

Pole drew himself up, pulling at the heavy rings on his fingers. "Don't ask me what I can and cannot afford, Bardi. I am a Norman, born in high estate in Hull, recognized in law as a high man above the common English herd, a master of this land. You are a foreigner and a baseborn man, lower than an Englishman here. Remember that when you speak to me."

The Florentine shrugged, but his expression showed that he knew Pole couldn't afford to lose that sort of sum. No one could.

"Well," said Bardi, "there's clearly more money in wool than I thought."

"There's plenty of money in wool," said Pole.

"But you need the king to pay you?"

"Yes. And if he goes to France and fails, as he will fail . . ."

"Bankrupt?" said Bardi, rolling the English word around his mouth like a sugared plum.

"Yes. No hope of angels yet?"

"Why ask me?"

Pole said, "You seem to keep your ear to the ground."

"I let others do that. In Italy, keeping your ear to the ground is a good way to have a cart run over your head. As I guess it is here. But I hear things."

"What?"

"The king has lost his contact with the divine entirely. The angel of St. Paul's will not speak."

"Not even speak? We have had no angels in battle since the king's father defeated Lancaster at Boroughbridge, but everyone knows they're harder to coax out than a prioress's tits. Not even speak?" Pole asked.

"No."

"Since when?"

"Since ever. The angel of Westminster never appeared to him at his coronation, so I hear. His father was the last king to have such contact."

Pole said, "My God, it's worse than I thought. Mind you, a fat lot of good they did old King Ted when his dear wife had Mortimer's men ram that red-hot poker up his arse."

Bardi shrugged. "A curious death for sure. A curious time when kings were thrown down by their wives. How could God have allowed it to happen, I wonder?" he asked.

"What?" said Pole. "Do you know something I don't, Bardi?"

"My lord, I would never presume to say that." Bardi put his hand to his chest in a way that made Pole wonder if he was mocking him. "Young Edward came to the throne in revolution. He was a puppet. He overthrew his usurping mother and her lover, who had used him as their instrument, as soon as he could, but nevertheless, he benefited from rebellion. Perhaps God has closed his account. He will extend him no more credit."

"God as a banker. I like that, Bardi. It would take an Italian to come up with such a heresy."

"Tell me, Pole, as you are a merchant—if you seek to raise funds from one bank and are refused, what would you do?"

"Go to another."

Bardi replied, "We will not get our money back if Edward dies."

"No."

There was a long pause. From somewhere in the night's distance a dog barked.

"So what do we do?" said Pole.

"Edward needs help, from somewhere."

"But from where? All his alliances combined can't face a French army flying the Oriflamme and backed by angels."

"I have this," said Bardi. He took a small velvet pouch from inside his tunic. It was secured by a cord about his neck. He teased open the drawstring at its mouth and shook something out into his hand. A small box in dark wood.

"A ring?" said Pole. "It'd better be a rare one if it's to cover your debts, Bardi."

"Not a ring."

Bardi took great care in opening the lid. Pole strained forward to see. On a tiny velvet cushion lay something that looked almost like a scrap of paper—a yellow, almost translucent thing shaped like a key.

"What is it?" said Pole.

"Something given in collateral to my family many years ago. It is a key."

"To what?"

"To Hell," said Bardi.

Pole crossed himself. "Where did you get that? From a marketplace conjurer?"

"This is a true relic, not a carved sheep's bone. It has been identified by one who would know. I have met him."

"Who?" asked Pole.

"The ambassador. Satan's emissary. He has been summoned and contained at St. Olave's in London."

"I will not have truck with devils."

Bardi said, "Then the king will be vanquished. Your investments will fail. Poverty would not suit you, Pole. This way we might find the reason England is missing its angels."

"How would Hell know that?"

"The ambassador tells me that there are those there who might know."

"Devils?" asked Pole.

"Demons."

"What's the difference?"

"Devils are the gaolers of Hell. Demons are their prisoners. So the ambassador says, though he may be lying. My priest who summoned him believes he tells the truth. It tallies with things I've heard before."

"Heard where?"

Bardi said, "The highest circles of the church."

"That contradicts all holy teaching."

"Not really. God rightly threw Lucifer into Hell. He needed someone to keep him there."

Pole waved his hand in dismissal. "Sounds like rubbish. I never heard of that in Hull, and if it means nowt to Hull it means nowt to me."

"The ambassador maintains that Edward has an association with demons. He is not sure what that association may be."

Again Pole crossed himself, this time uttering a Hail Mary under his breath.

He said, "Our king is put there by God. He doesn't go trawling Hell for help. He asks Heaven."

"What if Heaven doesn't listen?"

"Then he asks Hull!" said Pole, touching his chest. "Demons and devils. Is this why you brought me here, Bardi? What's this to me? Why are you showing me this?"

"Contact with such creatures often requires further investigation. Our interests are similar. You can pull strings that I cannot. You can ask questions, look places I cannot. And besides, I may need more money."

"You've got plenty."

"On paper. In debts and promises. You have access to ready coin." Bardi did not say it, would not say it, but Pole caught the implication. The Florentine bankers had extended themselves too far, lent on uncertain projects. Bardi added, "A successful war in France would reap a lot of money for Edward and enable him to repay his debts to us. An unsuccessful one, well. Have you ever tasted the gritty bread the paupers eat? It would not suit you."

"How did you come by this key?"

"Everyone needs money eventually," said Bardi, "even the holy."

"It doesn't look strong enough to open a mouse's larder—what's it made of?"

"The bone of the finger of Judas Iscariot," said Bardi, "from the hand that took the thirty pieces of silver."

Pole swallowed audibly and crossed himself a third time. He became aware of a presence to his left. Someone was standing in the shadows watching him. Pole drew his sword. He said, "Who's there? Show yourself, or I'll come over and run you through."

A man-at-arms stepped forward, not tall but weatherbeaten and muscular, his dark padded coat bearing a tear at the shoulder that no moth put in it. He was a lowborn man, but he had a presence that unsettled Pole. He knew his sort, a fighter, a brawler, maybe a killer. Pole stepped back, it being apparent that such a man would take some running through.

"Condottiere Orsino. A mercenary captain. My man who does," said Bardi. "A useful fellow, if you don't mind his manners." Bardi was slightly self-conscious—Orsino wasn't the sort he normally introduced to company of quality. With his torn ear and battle-patched coat he looked more like an aging tomcat than a noble's retainer.

He said to him, "You brought him, Orsino? Is he far?"

"Arigo has him. Not far. I'll get him now." The man's accent was like Bardi's, but rougher, deeper.

"What are you up to, Bardi?" said Pole.

Bardi said, "The captain has been on a long errand for me."

"How did he know to meet you here? We've only been here a day."

"The French are raiding all along this coast. I had him await my word at Dorchester and travel down the road from there when I was sure there was a raid. I didn't expect to be with the king."

"Why wait for the French?"

"Because what we are about to do requires a burned church. And I thought the French would be most helpful in providing one."

Pole crossed himself again. "That is sacrilege."

"Yes," said Bardi. "Rather the point. There are worse alternatives, believe me."

Horses stirred outside the church and a mule brayed.

Orsino returned, and Pole gave a start. Behind Orsino, floating in the darkness, was the head of an ape he was sure. Then the figure came toward him and he saw it was not an ape, but a very small man, so thin that his face was little more than a skull. He wore a priest's cassock, though on his head was a good beaver fur hat. A man who could afford a hat like that could afford to eat, thought Pole. He'd seen healthier looking types emerge from a year's confinement in a dungeon.

Behind the parson another of Bardi's men had a rope, on which he led a boy tied by the hands. The child was around thirteen years old, wearing a pair of rough woolen braies that reached to his knees and a ragged tunic, open at the front. Incongruously, he had a hood on his head and wore a good cloak many sizes too big for him, which he was forced to hold to prevent dragging on the muddy ground. His feet were bare, he was filthy, and the right side of his face was swollen and bruised as though he had taken a good blow.

But it was his bare chest that took Pole's attention. It bore a terrible puffy burn, fresh and livid, even under the torchlight. Pole knew what it was. A thief's brand. He let out a loud whistle of disapproval. He'd thought the Saxon practice of branding thieves had disappeared when he was a boy.

Fellows like that laughed at such punishments. There should be only one penalty for thievery—the gallows. The world, thought the merchant, was going soft.

"Did you do that to him?" said Bardi. "I wanted him unharmed." He spoke in English so as not to annoy Pole.

"He'd been caught by the priest. Second time. I stopped them hanging him. The burn was a compromise," said Orsino.

"You met trouble."

"Yes. His people came for him. I lost two men. You will compensate me, and I will pass the money to their families."

"You'll pocket it yourself!" said Pole.

Orsino turned his slow gaze to the merchant.

"Am I a liar?" said Orsino. Pole felt an urge to change the subject.

"Who's this?" said Pole, nodding toward the thin man.

"This is Father Edwin of St. Olave's Towards the Tower," said Bardi.

"A long way to come for a sermon, Father."

The priest said nothing.

"Who's the boy?" asked Pole.

"He answers to the name of Dowzabel," said Father Edwin, "or rather he doesn't answer. He says nothing."

"Sounds like a devil's name."

"I think it is. The outlaws of the West Country forswear their real names when they band together. They take on those of demons."

Pole shrugged and said, "I've never heard of that," as if the fact rendered the information completely worthless.

"They are of a different faith from us," said Edwin. "Or rather, their faith is differently put. The boy is a Luciferian. He believes it is Lucifer who was betrayed by God, that God is the usurper. Satan, he would say, is God's servant—a gaoler charged with keeping Lucifer locked away."

"The Devil is two people?" said Pole. "This is too much for my York-shire head."

"They say so," said Edwin. "It's up to you if you believe them."

"Damned right it's up to me. A thief and a devil worshiper?" said Pole. "And we suffer him to live?"

"For the moment," said Edwin.

The boy's eyes moved from face to face. He was shivering, beaten, and half starved, but he was not cowed. He held his head up.

Pole walked closer to the boy and studied him. Small and very slightly built, he had a clever face that bore an expression of fearful insolence. Pole knew his sort. He had whipped enough boys like that for their presumption. "Bow, boy, in deference to my nobility." Pole spoke in English.

"He doesn't understand English too well," said Edwin. "If you use big words, you'll lose him."

"What does he understand then? French? Don't tell me he's a courtier down there in the West!" Pole laughed, but his laughter was like a spark to wet grass and it died where it had begun.

"Cornish," said Edwin, "as they do in Cornwall."

Pole detected a touch of condescension in the priest's voice. He knew men like Edwin as well—men who supposed their cleverness placed them above those who had been born their betters. He'd whipped enough men like that too.

"Make him bow. Doesn't he bow when he greets his superiors?"

"I should imagine he guts them when he gets the chance," said Edwin. "Luciferism is a religion of revolution. He would upend God's order, place poor men above kings."

"Then you should take him from here and have him hanged," said Pole.

"That would bring all our schemes to nothing," said Bardi.

He asked, "Why so?"

"Because," said Edwin, "while I can weedle devils through the postern gates of Hell, or call spirits who were trapped in this realm at the Fall, he can open the main gates."

"And what does that mean, Bardi?"

"The enemy of my friend is my friend, dear Pole."

"What?"

"If you want to know how to deal with angels, ask someone with experience. We're going to talk to a demon."

3

I have a diagram and amulet against evil death, another against being struck by lightning! Laminas guaranteeing good fortune—made by master monks! All illnesses cured, all worries removed!"

Osbert the pardoner had suffered a flat morning, selling forgiveness for sins in the marketplace, and so was turning to his second line of trade—that of magical cures, charms, and writings. The trade was not strictly legal. But the number of secrets the pardoner knew—a market constable asking for an indulgence for fornication here, a London city official wanting clemency for embezzlement there—meant he went about his business unmolested.

He'd chosen a position between a stall selling poultry, rows of neat white geese gazing blankly down from their hooks at him, and one selling mainly pork. A pig's head stared out into the seething marketplace, as if wondering what bad choices it had made that led it to the butcher's table.

The pardoner felt a spark of pity. The pig had done nothing but be born to seal its fate. He, by contrast, had started life with many advantages but had thrown them away to finish where he was now, among the flies, the offal, and the stink of the marketplace, selling penny indulgences that were supposed to guarantee Heaven's favor.

A merchant walked past in rich robes, his pretty daughter walking behind him. Osbert smiled at the girl, but she turned her head away at the sight of a man so far beneath her. Had it not been for women, he himself might have walked along like that, maybe with a daughter of his own. His father, however, had insisted on the monastery to curb his lustful ways. It hadn't worked. At all.

"Are these *effectif* ?" A goodwife in a loose fitting kirtle had approached him, looking down at the long roll of cloth where he displayed his wares. Osbert noted that her dress was not of the modern, tailored sort and, as everyone dressed up to come to market, this meant the woman was not worth much. Still, she'd dropped a French word into her conversation, *effectif*, so she clearly fancied herself above the common herd. He could use that. He'd hardly had a sale all morning, so he needed to get whatever he could from her.

Osbert replied, "I swear by them. I have worn them these ten years and have suffered neither an evil death nor a lightning strike. They work very well."

"Hmm, my son is going on a voyage and I would like to buy him some protection."

"These are a shilling, madam."

"That is too much."

"For a woman like you? Surely not. Is it the king's business your son does?"

"A penny, and no more for flattery." Clearly the woman's pretentions ended at the point she had to put her hand into her purse.

"To aid a noble voyager, why not? It has been a slack morning, or I would not sell such powerful magic so cheap."

He took the woman's penny and passed her a scrap of vellum, on which was drawn a magic circle. "That contains the secret names of God," he said, "and now they are known to you."

The woman went on her way and the pardoner went back to shouting out his pitch.

"I am a master of tetragrammaton, of the ananizapta cure for fits, of devices angelic, cosmologic, and hermetic. Here, sir, will you take an angelic cure? If you have a thick-headed son or apprentice, it's just the thing. It is the seal of the archangel Samhil, who takes away stupidity."

"Don't sell too many of those, pardoner, or you'll be out of business." A young man in a fashionable short tunic stood looking at him.

Osbert said, "My business is the forgiveness of sin; while men sin, I shall never go hungry."

"Likely why you're so fat!"

"Laugh your way to Hell if you will, boy. You'll find the Devil a poor audience for your jokes!"

"If I go to Hell, pardoner, you'll be keeping me company!" The young man laughed and passed on.

"Do not be as the ass who lies all day in the barren field, be up and ready for the . . ." Osbert wasn't entirely sure where he was going with that biblical quotation, or even if it was a biblical quotation. He crouched to rearrange his wares. He noticed he was running low on teeth of St. Odo and reminded himself that he would need to visit his contact at the poor hospital to get a few more.

A skull landed in the middle of the pardoner's roll of amulets and papers.

He looked up to see a big, red-faced farmer glaring down at him. Then another, smaller skull landed next to the first—this from a soldier, a Welsh bowman by his dark looks and muscular frame.

"Careful, friends, it is the names of the lord and his angels that you crush."

The farmer spoke. "Last week you sold me the skull of St. Anthony, for protection against evil and for certain guarantee of a long and prosperous life."

Osbert said, "It was my blessing to come by such a thing and my charity to allow it to be sold to you for such a price."

"Three shillings," said the farmer.

"So low? Does a vision of the saint instruct you to return and pay more?"

"No, pardoner, it does not. I fell to drinking near to here and struck up conversation with this fine fellow of Wales."

Osbert said, "God bless our bowmen and the deliverance they brought us from the Scots."

"It seems he too has been sold the skull of St. Anthony—for two shillings."

"Well," said the pardoner, noticing the farmer had a number of fit-looking young men assembling behind him and the bowman a number more, "that one is smaller, if you're worried about the difference in price."

"Two skulls of one saint?"

"Friends, the explanation is simple."

"Yes?" the farmer asked.

"That larger one is from the saint as a grown man. That one is from when he was younger," said Osbert.

The men thought for a moment as the pardoner gathered his roll as best he could. Then the farmer erupted and lunged for the pardoner. One reason Osbert had been recommended by his former abbot—to take up the role of a pardoner when he had been expelled from his monastery—was that, chief among his talents, he was a nimble man who could run quickly for one of such belly. In fact, when Osbert reflected, it was probably his only talent.

The pardoner set off at a clip away from the market, down Lyme Street. He'd worked out his route well in advance. His aim was to run all the way down Lyme Street, ignoring all the churches until he got to St. Margaret Pattens. Here he would dive inside and run for the back. He knew from long experience there was a door behind the altar that led out into the church gardens. The men pursuing him would be loath to apprehend him in a church—it was neither legal nor wise.

Only the desperate, such as Osbert was, would risk offending the clergy, as they made very dangerous enemies. The pause won, he could get out from the back of the church, through the gardens behind it, hoping to avoid dogs. There was one particularly unpleasant alaunt, a sort of shaggy, enormous mastiff he'd have to avoid, he knew from experience. Then he would be onto Mincing Lane, past the huge Clothworkers' Hall, and get lost in the crowd.

The mob chased him, passersby joining in the pursuit. A hue and cry went up, the distinctive ululating howl that was London's alarm for a thief on the run. This was serious trouble. The fact that he was running from the hue and cry allowed him to be beheaded on the spot if any of the city watch got hold of him.

"This isn't robbery, it's fraud, you fools," thought Osbert as he ran, "there is no hue and cry for fraud." In theory, the pursuers were in the wrong to raise the cry of "thief," but there was no benefit in stopping to argue that with them, the satisfaction of putting them right on a point of law being rather outweighed by the inconvenience of being beaten to death.

Osbert made St. Margaret's no more than twenty yards ahead of the mob. The door of the church was open and he ran inside, his eyes swimming as they adjusted from the brightness of the day. Quickly he slammed the door behind him, signaling that he was claiming sanctuary.

St. Margaret's was a wealthy church and the floor was well flagstoned, the air heavy with the incense of the last mass and the windows a beautiful blue stained glass. Osbert didn't have time to admire the interior; he just ran for the back, past the altar, past the priest and a couple of prelates who greeted him with less surprise and alarm than might be expected—this having been about the fourth occasion he had made his escape this way. He tugged at the rear door. It was locked.

"Shit!" Osbert beat on the door with his hands.

"This is not an escape route for deceivers and frauds," said the priest, coming toward him.

"Let me go, Father—they mean to kill me."

He said, "Perhaps that's what you deserve."

The church door opened and a bulky figure appeared in the entrance. The farmer, silhouetted against the bright autumn day.

Osbert said, "I'll claim sanctuary, then, and as a fellow cleric: alms, food, and water. I may have to stay here for forty days, farting and belching through the services. And you'll have to feed me from your own pocket!"

"I wonder if you could confess your sin in the time it takes that fellow to get hold of you."

"I have sold false charms and trinkets," said Osbert, "there you go. I am confessed; you must give me sanctuary."

The farmer hovered in the doorway, uncertain before the priests.

"I'll let you go," said the priest, "but you use this way no more."

"No more, right, definitely," said Osbert.

The priest unlocked the door as the farmer stepped into the church.

"I'll have no bloodshed in my church!" shouted the priest. "Nor any more running and shouting! He's coming out now. If you want to kill him, lead your mob around the side, not through here!"

Osbert was gone already, out into the gardens. He ran around a duck pond, past a henhouse, and quickly skirted the snarling alaunt on its long rope. Then he ran up an alley and into Mincing Lane. From there it was through more back alleys and gardens as far as St. Olave's.

"There he is—skin the bastard!"

Osbert ran around the church, his breath hitching with fear. There, by the church, was the priest's house—a two-story affair, with a bedchamber supported on wooden pillars projecting out above the main bulk of the building.

He raced around the back, down an alley between the house's uneven garden wall and another property. Panting like a flogged carthorse, he threw his roll over the garden wall, climbed up the rough brick, and dropped down the other side. He found himself in an overgrown and seemingly untended garden. Osbert ran toward the back of the house. If there were servants there, he intended to offer them indulgences for their sins in return for hiding him.

The back door was no more than a few planks nailed together and not sturdy.

He heard a shout of "He went over the wall!"

"Get round the front and the other side, and make sure he doesn't come out."

Osbert glanced at the opposite wall to the one he'd climbed over, but it was so overgrown with brambles that he would have no chance of scaling it. Another house had been built directly against the rear wall, removing all chance of escape.

The door was locked, but only on a latch. He took up a stick from the floor and lifted it. He went directly in to a big pantry, or what had once been a pantry. Whatever food had been in there was long rotted and gone, though hopeful rats still scuttled away as he entered the room. It was dark and dusty, sparsely furnished with just a stool and a bench among broken pots and cups. It smelled of damp and disuse.

Osbert moved inside and through another door. People were hammering at the front now and he could hear voices behind him. He had no idea what to do. To his left was another door. It was locked. That might help him. If the men chasing him were law-abiding, they might balk at breaking a householder's lock. Osbert had enough experience of life on London's streets to know how to deal with that.

He took a pig's bone he had been selling as the rib of St. Mark and inserted it into the lock. A bit of wiggling and waggling and he pushed the internal lever aside. The older-style lock was so crudely made it was hardly worth having. There was a narrow set of stone steps going down. A cellar. Perhaps he could hide in there. It was a scant hope, but he had no other ideas.

Osbert went within and closed the door, fiddling with the bone and the lock again to secure it. It was flat dark with the door closed and he stretched out a foot to feel his way down the steps. People were moving through the house. Under his breath he said a Hail Mary.

He said, "Get me out of this, Lady, help me, help me."

Suddenly it was light and Osbert gave a little cry.

Someone said, "Who is it that seeks the aid of the Mother of God?"

The cellar was a large room and, in contrast to the rest of the house, was swept clean, the floor neatly flagstoned. There were desks and tables in there, all heaped with books, and strange things in neat piles on the floor, or stored on rough shelves that leaned against the walls—dismembered cats, bottles, scribbled drawings, astrological charts.

At the far end was a figure Osbert would never have expected to see in his life, let alone in the cellar of a broken-down house. It was a cardinal, in red robes and a wide brimmed hat, standing with a lantern in his hand. The pardoner recognized his uniform from miniatures he had seen at his monastery.

"Your, er, Grace."

Osbert kneeled.

The mob above were crying out.

"Not upstairs!"

"This door's locked."

"Break it in."

"Hang on a minute, this is the priest's house!"

"It can't be, look at the state of it!"

"I tell you it is. You can't go smashing up the priest's house. You'll hang!"

The door above rattled and Osbert fell to his knees.

"Holy Father, I am a sinner, but not guilty of the sin for which I am pursued. Please, use your word to protect me from this mob. Intercede for me here."

The cardinal said, "I'm afraid I can't."

The door rattled again. The crowd's voices began again:

"I can pick that lock, we've no need to break it."

"He's not going to be in a locked room, is he?"

"Well, we've looked everywhere else."

Osbert put his hands together in prayer. He said, "I will live a devout life henceforth, I swear it."

"I would like to help you, but, as I say, I can't. I'm stuck here."

"How stuck?"

"The sorcerer who owns this house has enchanted me. I can't move. He's got me stuck in this circle. It's dark magic that can hold a holy man like me."

Osbert looked down at the man's feet. Sure enough, there was a circle in chalk on the floor. It wasn't too dissimilar to the sort of thing he sold every day, though more carefully drawn.

"I've never seen such a thing," he said. It was a good idea to profess ignorance of charms in front of a cardinal.

The man said, "No, well, neither had I."

"It's open. The door's open."

"It's black as the devil's sooty nutsack down there," said a voice.

"Get a light!"

Men were thumping down the stairs, blundering about as if blind.

Osbert's heart was pounding; he didn't have time to think about how strange it was that he could see the cardinal with the lantern as clear as day, while the men above complained of darkness.

He said, "I will release you. If I do, will you swear to protect me?"

"I swear."

Osbert scuttled forward and rubbed out part of the chalk.

"Thank you," said the cardinal, "now let me intercede for you."

He stepped out of the circle. Osbert noticed the strangest thing. The cardinal's skin didn't meet all the way around at the back of his head and was laced tight there, as through the eyelets of a shoe. The cardinal opened the lantern and took out the lighted candle. Then he put it into his mouth, swallowing it whole. There was an enormous belch from the cardinal, a roar of fire from his mouth and a great billow of smoke, and Osbert, along with all his pursuers, fell to the floor.

4

Paris was beautiful in the autumn morning; a low mist lit by the sun clung to the river and the light caught the windows of the great towers of Notre Dame, splitting into shafts of gold and red. People had gathered for miles along the bank to see the flotilla of handsome cogs and hulks that was making its way east on a kind wind. The boats flew the pennants of Philip, King of Navarre, though it was his wife, Joan, who was coming to the capital in as much pomp as her land could provide.

The country people were flocking out in their church best to gawp at her as she made her way down the river. Not so long ago she had been *their* princess, and a popular one. She was generous and she was pious, it was said. Plenty among them regarded her son as their rightful king, being old-fashioned enough to see nothing wrong with inheritance through the female line.

As the boats neared the city, merchants began to appear in the crowd, rattling pots and pans, displaying cloths and shaking tunics in the latest buttoned styles toward the ships. Bareheaded women wearing red- and green-striped hoods on their backs stroked their hair and called out to the sailors, telling them they must want a bed and someone to warm it after such a long voyage.

On the scaffold-built forecastle of the leading and largest ship on the river stood a woman dressed in finery to rival that of the cathedral. Her dress was cloth of gold, her red cloak trimmed with ermine, and the hood that dropped from her shoulders was heavy with pearls and emeralds. Her golden hair was woven with rubies and she wore a fine golden crown flashing with diamonds, topped by a two-coned headdress. Queen Joan of Navarre, the most beautiful of the famously beautiful daughters of old King Louis, fair skinned and tall, as only a noble lady raised on good food and light work could be.

At her side stood a five-year-old boy, equally impressively dressed in a doublet of red taffeta hung with pearls, the fine blue silk hat on his head bearing on its front the image of a dragon picked out in tiny rubies. In his hand he carried a small dagger with which he was chopping at the rail of the ship. Next to him was his nurse and the queen's ladies-in-waiting—four of them, two carrying fine cages of songbirds, one a posy of flowers, and the final one a silver cup of wine, ready should the queen require it. Also on the platform was Count Ramon of Aragon, a young knight, tall and slim with the dark hair and skin of his family. He did not wear mail, but instead a fine wide-sleeved coat decorated with the four red bars on a yellow field of his homeland.

The queen knew it would do no harm to show off the alliances she was making—her oldest daughter, Maria, was betrothed to Peter, the future king of Aragon and three territories besides. They were both young—she eight and he twelve—but Joan had hope of a marriage and children to cement the bond as soon as Maria was twelve.

Finally, her own cousin and favorite, the short and squat Ferdinand D'Évreux, stood with his hooded hawk on his arm, his coat a splendid glittering red affair in which the yellow dots on the red square of House Évreux were picked out in yellow sapphires. The forecastle was so crowded that the servants—eight of them liveried in the yellow on red square of Navarre quartered with the blue fleurs-de-lys of the House of Capet—had to cling to the back of the structure outside of the rail. They were in danger of falling onto the men-at-arms who stood on the decks behind them, sixty strong, all in the same livery.

The fighting men were crammed in among the crates of chickens, the horses, the barrels, the hunting dogs, the falcons, plus the servants and cursing sailors who shared the deck with them. By the ship's rail, three trumpeters fought for space to sound the fanfare. At the center of the throng was the queen's litter—splendidly canopied in blue silk with embroidered golden fleurs-de-lys. She had brought it with her when she married her husband and had never bothered to refit it in the dual arms of both their houses.

The queen squeezed the boy's hand. "I can't believe we have to bend the knee to these Valois barbarians." She spoke as much to the air as to her son.

The trumpets sounded and a heavily armored man shouted from the deck. "Bow down before Joan, Queen of Navarre, Princess of France, Countess of Évreux. Bow down before the lady and her son, Charles, Prince of Navarre!"

People sounded cheers on the riverbank, and there were shouts of "God bless King Philip!" and "Long prosper the House of Capet!"

The queen waved and smiled, though she still spoke to her son. "This should all be mine. And if not mine, then yours. I am the daughter of the king and you are my son. Why should not a woman inherit? And if she should not, why not her son? Those Valois bastards—and they are bastards—stripped me of everything in this land, everything when my father died. We lost Brie and we lost Champagne, and what did they give me in compensation? Angoulême. Halfway up a mountain with the laziest and most troublesome countrymen to be found outside of England."

The boy continued hacking at the rail.

"Well," she went on, "we still have rights here. They'll have to let you see the angel. That's the least they can do. They get to keep you here—we can't refuse them that—and you get to see the angel. You're owed an audience with it. They'll give you an audience or I'll burn down the Great Hall and the Louvre and see how Philip likes holding his court in the street."

The boy suddenly turned and looked at her. "Uncle Philip stole from us?"

She said, "Yes, but it doesn't do to say so. Do not say so here."

The boy seemed to think for a moment. "Why didn't you stop him?"

The queen betrayed no signs of emotion other than a slight tightening of her jaw. "I am a woman. I was alone against the arrayed might of the House of Valois. If I had resisted, we would have lost Navarre as well. They'd been sewing up alliances for years and persuading people that it was impossible to inherit by descent from the female side."

"Why doesn't Papa stop him?" he asked her.

"He doesn't see it the way I do. That's why he scuttles off to Scotland, fighting the English like a dutiful vassal. He forgets his own claim to the throne. He has a claim too. Not like yours. You are of the fleurs-de-lys on both sides of your family. Doubly royal." She tousled his hair.

"I will be king one day." The boy gestured to the bank.

"You will. But again don't say that here." She rested her hand on his head. "We made a treaty disallowing that. Or rather *they* made a treaty and I signed it. I had no choice."

The boy took her hand. He said, "Mother."

"Yes."

"When I am grown, I shall not prove so pliable."

The queen put her hand to her mouth to stifle a laugh. "Oh, my boy, the words you come up with. Where did you get that from? Ladies, ladies, did you hear what he said? "'Pliable!'"

The woman all laughed and cooed and the noblemen smiled indulgently.

Joan bent down to her child, drawing him close and whispering into his ear. "I hope you won't, my Charles," she said. "When you are grown you will come here, not with five ships but with five hundred, and you will make that thief, Philip of Valois, eat the treaty he made me sign. Now smile and be simple as I've told you. As you grow up here, don't let your uncle see what a clever boy you are. His son is a fool. Dim your own light, so it might not overpower his. That would be dangerous for you."

"Can I see the angel? They say it's very different from ours."

"Different in that it has taken the field in living memory. Different in that it occasionally makes sense. If your father could only find a way . . ." Her voice trailed off.

"Will the angel give me sugar?"

"That's right. Play the fool, boy. You are a fine son, Charles, a very fine son."

The boy nodded and his mother stood erect as the low bridge that formed part of the walls approached. The great square castle of the Louvre loomed above them, its pointed turrets rising out of a sloping roof. The queen found herself speculating how easy it would be to burn. Not very, she thought. The river was diverted around it to form a moat and the inner keep was safe enough to store most of the kingdom's treasure. She coughed, and one of her ladies placed the band of a nosegay of violets around her neck, the little basket dropping to her chest. Joan was very glad of their scent. The river here was rank, even though it was relatively high from a wet summer. They would disembark there and travel to the Île de la Cité by barge.

The ships came in to dock—the queen's first. She was helped down the ladder to the castle by the two noblemen, Ferdinand above and Ramon below; Charles needed no such help and slid down the ladder with his feet outside the rungs, as the sailors did. His nurse, helped onto the deck by one of the liveried servants, checked him over and called for a basin of water to clean his now filthy hands. The queen waved her away.

"He will do like that," she said. The nurse bowed, but one of the ladies-in-waiting—a noblewoman used to talking freely to the queen—spoke out.

"Madam, the court will think the boy an uneducated savage."

"Good," said the queen, eyeing a group of assembled town dignitaries in their brightly colored tunics waiting to greet her on the shore. "He should fit in here, then. My God, these commoners had better not be my welcoming party." She climbed into her litter and beckoned the boy in beside her.

The boat was moored tight to a landing stage and the difficult work of disembarking from the boat began. Eight strong men lifted the litter up so its front poles rested on the quay. Then they shoved it forward and leapt up beside it. An alderman in all the finery the law would allow and a little more—the emerald brooch he wore at his neck should only have been worn by men of noble birth—came forward and bowed deeply to the curtain of the litter.

"Great majesty, honored sovereign, Queen of Navarre and favored vassal of King Philip. It is good to see you again, ma'am, if I may add a personal note."

A heavily ringed hand came out of the curtains, its palm on the vertical. "You may not."

The man stuttered and bowed, for want of anything else to do.

"Convey me to the barge," said the queen, from behind the curtain. "I expect to be greeted and groveled to by a better class of man than you. The king should have been here himself, or failing him, his idiot son."

The man said, "Majesty, I . . ."

"The barge."

"As you wish."

The litter was carried the thirty paces to the barge—a canopied affair in blue silk embroidered with the royal fleurs-de-lys—over a pavement of crushed herbs that gave up their scent of lavender and mint to the air as the men stepped forward. The queen was helped out by Count Ramon. Then Ferdinand nobly leapt down the steps to guide her on to the barge where she was greeted again by a dignitary and a blast of bugles.

The rest of the ladies, nurses, and servants made their way on board, arranging the cages of the songbirds, all of a squawk in the presence of the hawk, on the hooked poles that had been provided. Ferdinand took his falcon to the perches at the far end of the barge to avoid it disturbing the more gentle fowl.

"Great Queen, lady of the . . ."

"Just get this thing moving; the sooner I'm off this sewer of a river the better," she said. "Don't bother with the titles. I know who I am."

The queen did not sit. The boat cast off and the oarsmen bent their backs to steer it under the low bridge that marked the entrance to the city proper. From the windows of each of its houses people called and waved, and the queen waved back. She might despise commoners individually, but she knew the value of the mob.

The mist was clearing now and the sun was strong, though the queen chose not to go under the canopy. She wanted the people to see her, to dazzle them with her jewels, to have them cheer her and call her name, to let Philip know the affection she commanded. The boy looked up at the ripples of sunlight reflected on the underside of the bridge.

"They look like little mouths snapping at us," he said.

"You are a Capet and a prince," said the queen. "It's you who will do the snapping."

As the barge emerged from the bridge the queen broke into a smile. All along the shore, the people had turned out to see her. The outskirts had been thronged, but here it was as if the city held a fire and all the people were straining forward to get as near to the water as they could. The city rang with her name.

She stood up proudly and the boy came to join her. She shooed him away. To protect him, she needed to make the Valois think she valued him lightly.

The barge moved on past the formidable round towers of the Tour de Neslé—a city defense and mansion combined. Joan shivered as she saw it. Her uncle, Philip IV, had discovered that his daughters-in-law had conducted certain rites there. The official line was that they had been caught in adultery and sent to monasteries, their lovers flayed and killed. Joan knew better, for her cousin Isabella, Louis's daughter and the mother of King Edward of England, had told her the truth. They had been summoning devils. It was a weakness of the Capetian female line.

She crossed herself. She had been very fond of all those who had suffered.

The barge slid on to the Great Hall, the palace of the Valois king, her palace when she was a little girl. It was beautiful in the morning sun, its roofs a floating blue, its pretty turrets with their tops like pointed caps, and rising above it all, the great square structure of the holy chapel, its huge rose window now in shadow. She knew what it was, though, to stand inside that chapel at sunset, to approach its greatest treasure—Christ's crown of thorns—and feel the presence of the angel in golden light. They called it the Chapel of Light and it was well named. Huge stained-glass windows dominated its walls, the stonework reduced simply to traces, but what traces! The stone was adorned with every color of gem, gold and silver, bright emerald and deep ruby paint.

Joan remembered standing, bathed in the light of the dying sun, clothed in jewels that turned her to a creature of light, the whispers of the angel and the song of the stone saints in her ears. Then she had known that France was God's kingdom, blessed and protected by Him. She swallowed as she recalled the moment she realized they would not let her inherit. Cast out, forced away. She looked out from the barge and waved, smiling hard for the people.

Something flashed from the quayside. It was the king's crown, brilliant in the morning sun. Beneath it his robe too sparkled, cloth of gold smothered in rubies and emeralds.

The ranks of lesser men stood behind him, the prince in a shining blue tunic adorned with fleurs-de-lys in sparkling gold, the ranks of knights gaudy as a meadow and, by the side of the prince, a troupe of minstrels, all in ape masks. Philip V was finer than she, Joan couldn't deny. But he hadn't the bearing. Philip stooped like a country villein—he didn't stand erect and proud like a king, even if he did have four hundred courtiers and soldiers in their glimmering best clothes at his back.

She smiled deeply and genuinely as the barge approached him. He wanted to deny her a great welcome, she knew, but he could not. The people loved her and he had to be seen to love her too. Cheers burst over her like the crashing of surf.

The child called from behind her. "Shall I see the angel, Mama?"

She didn't turn to face him, but she replied, "Yes, my Charles, you shall. And it will see you, the true king. Then we'll discover what favors Heaven will bestow. And whom the Lord God will curse."

5

D owzabel would not show his fear, though he was terrified before those great men in that desolate place. He had only once before been outside the moors of Cornwall, and this city, with its close, packed houses, its church, and its stink, seemed very strange to him indeed. It reminded him of Plymouth and what had happened to him there, so long before. He would never forget the night the priest came for him and took him there, the night his nan had sung to him for the last time of how friend Lucifer made the world and was thrown down by his angel, the treacherous Îthekter, who raised men up as kings on condition they worshipped him. Îthekter, who made Satan and the barren lands of Hell; Îthekter, who brought disease and poverty to the world and cast men out of Eden. He remembered his nan's stories too, and said the words to himself, to keep himself from crying.

"In the beginning was the void and darkness was on the face of the deep. And the spirit was borne upon the waters. And the spirit said, '"Let light be made."' And light was made and the spirit's name was the light's name, which was Lucifer, who is rightly called Son of the Morning."

They'd dragged his nan away. The last thing she even said to him: "Dow, I bless you! In the name of all the fallen angels, in the name of Araqiel and Jetrel and Sariel. In the name of dear Sariel who protected you, I bless you and I love you!"

Then they'd taken him, those rough men with their crosses and their spears. The magistrate had said he was too young to hang, so the church had cut his tongue for his heresies. Though it was seven years ago, the fear he felt in the ruined church brought the memory back sharply. The shears, the priest grinning as he cut. Dowzabel had crawled back to the moor and found the bandits again, the Devil's Men as the people of the moor called them. He'd burned his nan on the hillside, returned her to the light of which she was made. A kestrel, silver in the dusk, wheeled above him, turning the world around its wing. Nothing would ever be the same again.

His tongue had mended, but his heart had grown cold with desire for revenge. His childhood had been a torment to him from then on. He wanted to be a man, an avenger for Lucifer and the light, a killer of priests.

Dowzabel thought he was around thirteen when he'd been caught stealing from a church, been given a damn good hiding and sentenced to hang. But the Florentines had come with their money and their swords and the priest had given Dowzabel to them, after branding him.

They took him past Exeter on the day of the summer fair. He had never seen so many people, the roads pulsing like a river full of eels, but what eels! Men dressed in clothes of so many colors; women in dresses that seemed cut from the cloth of the sun, they seemed so bright; fine horses; wagons stuffed with food and wine.

But none of that now. Just these faces in the torchlight, these men whose scorn he could taste in his mouth, bitter as nettles. His chest was agony where they'd branded him, his jaw hurt—but he wouldn't cry, wouldn't beg. His captors were of Îthekter, the horror, the three-faced usurper who trod down the poor, whose followers built grand churches while their fellows starved. Dowzabel had expected nothing but cruelty from them and that was what he had received. But big Abbadon would come for him soon, he was sure— Abbadon and the others of the Devil's Men, not the ragged band who had tried to steal him back from the Florentines and paid with their lives. They'd take him back to his home on the moor, to freedom from pain and from lords.

The priest took the rope and tugged him to the center of the church, forcing him to hop. His right leg was useless because of his ankle. The ash and grit dug into his foot, and the mud of the rain-heavy floor numbed his toes.

The priest said something in English. He got the gist of it. "My devil shows this boy to be useful." Dowzabel had learned English from some men in his band and, though he struggled to speak it, could understand it in parts.

The fat one in the coat decorated with ferrets pointed at the one he'd heard called Bardi. He was angry and cursed in a language that was not English but contained some English words.

All Dowzabel could understand was "Not right!" The other one, the dark one—who spoke like Orsino and Arigo, his captors—said something in the same language, followed by one word in English: "Money." Then the fat one was quiet.

The church's roof had been thatch and, though timbers had fallen in when it had burned, it was still possible to move through the interior quite freely. Orsino checked that the king's entourage were all gone from around the church and came back in with a "clear." So reassured, the thin priest took the rope that secured Dow while the kidnapper Arigo swept the floor with a broom. Then the priest took out a spade and began digging into the cracked earth. Orsino joined in to help him while the fat one looked on in disdain. It took them a long time to make a hole about knee depth and one and a half man heights across. Near the top of the circle, Arigo and Orsino sank a charred black stake into the ground.

The thin priest then, strangely, started shoveling earth back into the pit. In a short while he had put back enough to satisfy himself and he jumped into the pit and began to work the earth, using the ashes and charred timbers to make the shape of a man.

When he was done it looked as though a body, encased in cinders, lay in the bottom of the pit. The priest used the spade to take embers from the brazier. He sprinkled them all over the form, so it sparked and hissed as the hot coals met the cold wet earth. The priest took something from a pouch and laid it on the chest of the mud man. It was a small key, worked in fine bone. He put a ring where the figure's mouth would be, placed a vessel of oil at its feet and at its head a clay tablet with four crosses on it.

He got out of the pit and gestured to Orsino. Dowzabel was shoved forward into the pit and tied to the stake on a short rope, like a lead, which tethered him at the neck.

"Sorry, kid," said Orsino, "I don't like this any more than you. I'm sorry. I'll do penance for this and I'll pray for your soul."

Dow felt like retching. How like the servants of Three Face to torture you, kill you, and then pray for your salvation.

"Denledhiaz!" Dow could not find the English word for "murderer," so he used the Cornish. The fighting man did not understand him, but they could not mistake the scorn behind the word.

"Someone's filled your head with lies," said Orsino. "I'll pray for you whether you like it or not."

Dowzabel spat at him, hard as he could. Orsino wiped his face, pursed his lips, and stepped backward.

The priest took something from a pack. Salt, or some white powder, which he sprinkled in a circle around the hole. He laid parchments around the circle, weighting them down with stones.

"Dust from the tomb of St. Lawrence mixed with salt. The demon will not cross it, that is certain. The names of God on the parchment give added protection," he said to the other men.

"You're certain it won't cross the dust and yet you need added protection. Stick to preaching, Father—you'd need to improve your patter to make it as a merchant," said the fat one.

Dowzabel had no idea what was going on.

"Why the boy?" Pole spoke again.

It was Bardi who replied. "Our intelligence suggests he can use the key. Both to open and to close the main gate to the first level of Hell."

"How many layers does it have?"

"Four, we think," said Bardi.

"And what do you expect to learn that your devil in London doesn't tell you?"

Edwin smiled. "Tell me, Sir De La Pole. When you go to the Tower of London, if you had a question on affairs of state or philosophy, who would you ask? The gaoler or the noblemen, heretics, and rebels imprisoned there?"

"I don't go to the Tower of London," said Pole.

"Yet," said Bardi.

"Aye, yet."

Dowzabel shivered. The wound on his chest hurt, he was afraid, and he thought of his nan.

The priest lit an incense burner. Then he walked slowly around the circle, swinging the burner and intoning a chant in Latin. Had Dowzabel been able to understand it, he would have been glad. The man was summoning demons, helpful demons, the friends of the poor, the enemies of the great.

"I summon thee, in a friendly and pleasant form. I summon thee, I confuse thee, mixing thy name with that of the most holy angels of Heaven, bringing together that which God has separated, AlasAlazatorel, MichMolochael, SimOrobosial, BalthasarZiminiar, MetatronBelial, and LuciRaferphael. I warn thee, thou art surrounded by powerful magics and the names of God, which you may not cross. I summon thee to the gate, as I have the key to open it!"

To a man, everyone but Edwin and Dow crossed themselves.

"I don't believe this," said Orsino. "He's only a kid, a beaten-up kid. He can't do this."

The chant droned on. The incense scent was bitter in Dowzabel's throat; the night grew ever colder. He thought to try to undo the tether, but he saw that would be useless. The men who surrounded him were armed, well fed, fully grown, and strong. He was crippled, his ankle swollen and painful. He wouldn't have a chance. The coals on the man were dying, losing their light. Now something was wrong with Dow's hearing. The chant seemed muted, as if underwater. The sky was black, full of clouds, no star nor moon visible.

He prayed in his mind. "He who is the morning star, he who trusted and was betrayed, he who will rise again when the trumpets sound on the final day, Lucifer, son of the morning, protect me here."

Nothing happened. The priest kept walking around the circle, the hard eyes of little Bardi upon him. Dow's feet were numb with cold and with standing for so long. His head swam, he couldn't feel his hands, and a strange taste like metal was in his mouth.

There was a sudden pressure all about him. The priest's movements seemed unnaturally slow, as if he was wading through water. The clouds raced, as if trying to get away from the moon to shed light on the darkness below.

"Ahuel! Ahuel!" The thin, dark priest was shouting at him in Cornish. "Key! Key!"

Dowzabel was certainly not going to do anything that man asked of him. But then another voice was in his head, low and resonant like the booming of the sea.

It said, "I am at the gate. Release me. Touch the key."

What are you? The thought came unbidden.

"A son of the light."

Dowzabel saw the little key on the mud man's forehead. The voice seemed so persuasive, so kind. Dow had suffered horrid abuses of beatings and the branding—no one had talked to him kindly since he'd left Cornwall. He reached forward and touched the key with his bound hands. The pressure in his head released, he fell forward, held by the rope, bleeding at the nose. There was a sound like the tinkling of bells, another like the crying of a child, and still a third like the call of a crow. Then another noise, a great scraping, like an enormous door, swollen on its hinges, being forced to open. Dowzabel fell to the floor, pressing one ear into the mud, pushing the back of his hand against the other to block out the sound. All the men outside the circle put their hands over their ears, and the fat merchant dropped to his knees.

The embers on the mud figure sparked into life, features formed on its head—a broad mouth glowing with coals, two burning eyes. The grating noise stopped and the thing stirred and moved, first an arm raising from the mud with a hiss.

Dowzabel heard a cry from the men outside the circle. The fat one made the sign of the cross and shouted out some words. He shouted them again and again until the little dark man actually put his hand across his mouth.

The creature sat up, its body adorned in glowing coals like rubies, and said clearly, in words Dowzabel could understand:

"I am ashes, born of light."

6

O h God, not the poetry. Please, not the poetry." On the barge the queen of Navarre crossed herself, which the assembled people took for a demonstration of piety.

Prince John came forward on the bank high above her. He was a tall, good-looking young man in the blond Valois way, but his expression managed to capture a mixture of brutishness and naïvety that the queen found deeply unappealing. She knew him well from her time at the court and despised the strain of mawkish sentimentality in his character that went hand in hand with his viciousness.

He bowed and gestured to his ape-masked minstrel, who bowed himself and struck up a tune on a harp. Then the prince began to intone the poem, half-singing it in a high nasal voice.

> Of all the fruits and all the flowers
> My garden holds a solitary rose:
> The rest lies ruined, every bower,
> To this the sweetest bloom.

The queen continued to smile and wave at the crowd, paying the prince very little attention. John looked somewhat nonplussed.

"It is to you that the poem refers, dear queen of Navarre." John was at least two men's height above Joan, so she had to raise her voice considerably to reply.

"Yes, I got that," said the queen. "Very nice. Lovely that the troubadour style is still preserved here in Paris, I haven't heard it for years at home. Shall we get in before this river poisons us or one of us develops a sore throat from shouting? I'm sure it wasn't so filthy in my day."

"You should watch your manners, lady, you're not in Navarre now," said John, his face darkening.

"John! We are observed," said the French queen. "You are welcome, sister." She and King Philip looked down on the queen of Navarre from the quay. She clapped her hands.

"The music and formal greetings."

The musicians struck up, and lists of titles were read out for all those present as Joan stood on the boat as if stuffed.

Queen Joan bowed, though those on the shore might have been forgiven for thinking she was simply rocking with the movement of the boat.

She whispered into the ear of Count Ramon, who shouted out, "You honor us deeply!"

"Though her bow is shallow," said the king.

Joan suddenly found her voice. "You must forgive me, brother, I am not as young as I was and my legs grow stiff." Ramon jumped ashore and offered her his hand to help her up the steps, but the queen ignored it and fairly sprang from the boat.

The count jumped after her and took her hand to escort her up the sloping jetty, the ladies-in-waiting, courtiers, and servants rushing to catch up.

At the top of the slope she faced the king and queen, and they all turned together to wave to the people on either side of the bank.

"We will proceed directly to the homage," said Philip. "I have erected a stage for the people to see you bow your knee and kiss my hands."

"My lord, I am a woman, as you have so consistently pointed out. What does my homage mean? You should take it from my son. Though I fear he is not a clever boy and is going through a phase of biting. Is it good for the dignity of kings to be bitten?"

"Let me look at the boy."

Philip smiled as broadly as someone gritting his teeth for a physician to examine. Joan of Navarre did the same, both wanting the crowd to see their "joy."

She gestured to her lady-in-waiting, and the lady reached down the steps that went up from the barge to lift little Charles onto the quay. The boy looked around him with wide eyes. He looked at Prince John; at King Philip; at Philip's wife, Joan of Burgundy; at the ranks of dukes and knights. Then he burst into tears.

"I'm afraid he has none of his father's steel," said the queen of Navarre. "He is not the heir I hoped for."

"You are too unkind," said the French queen. "Come to me, boy, I have some sugar for you."

Charles allowed himself to be comforted and led forward to the French queen. One of her ladies-in-waiting put a few crystals into the boy's hand and he swallowed them. Then he smiled, bowed deeply to the queen, and said loudly:

"Thank you, ma'am. Mama is never so generous."

The whole French court laughed, and the queen bent to gently pinch the boy's cheek.

"My Joan has a way with children," said King Philip.

"Well, she's welcome to his company if she wants it," said the queen of Navarre.

"Perhaps we can forgo the homage for the moment," said Philip. "The child's bow says enough for the people. Come, we have prepared a feast for you and tomorrow we have a few days of tournaments."

"I shall delight to see Prince John triumph in the lists."

The king just snorted and turned to climb the steps to his palace. Joan knew that Prince John was a sickly man who had never been known to take part in a tournament, preferring to spend his days with poets and minstrels. She thought of Edward, the English king across the sea. Now *he* was a famous warrior and someone who might support her claim to the throne. He was a dragon in a tournament, a proper king. France against England was dominant. France against Navarre would triumph easily. But against England and Navarre? Still not enough. There were the Flemings, and the Holy Roman Empire. Yet still not sufficient while Philip could call on his angels. The Navarrese angel had not made sense in a generation—or rather only when it said that it feared the attack of the Tartars of the Caliphate with whatever strange spirits it could conjure.

Joan climbed the steps after the king, giving one last wave to the crowd. This adulation, this acknowledgment from the ordinary people, was her birthright. She would find a way to claim it one day.

They stepped into the splendid interior of the Great Hall, its gilded columns bending like trees into the canopy of the ceiling, everything inlaid with gold or painted in beautiful reds and glittering greens. The floor alone was a marvel, scrubbed to sparkling, tiled in elaborate motifs of stags, birds, and horses, all intertwined in golden branches. Along the walls, courtiers bowed in greeting.

Joan walked on, following Philip and his Joan down the corridor toward the door to the Great Hall. The other woman limped terribly and if that wasn't a message from God about the rights and wrongs of the disputed succession, the queen of Navarre would be at a loss to say what was.

The doors opened to reveal the enormous dining room, with tables around the walls and several in the center, shimmering with the scales of so many fish it resembled a treasure hoard. The main table had a magnificent display—swirls of bream were laid out along the edges, with more rare and expensive fish arranged to form an ocean wave of crashing color, crowned by a dolphin, artfully stuffed and mounted so that it seemed to leap from the table.

Joan now saw why the king's messengers had asked her to wait at the mouth of the Seine for a day. If she'd arrived on a Tuesday, the usurper Philip would have had to go to the expense of providing meat. On a Wednesday, with meat prohibited by the church, he could stage the banquet for half the price.

She took her place at the royal couple's right hand, as did her son, but her noblemen and ladies were escorted to the left of the table, away from her. And, worse, there was a seat for John between her and the king. She hadn't considered that. She was going to be in the oaf's company all the way through the meal. Joan quickly swapped places with her son. Now he could talk to John throughout the dinner.

The best people of France assembled on the top table—visiting nobles and courtiers. A sour note was struck by the presence of some wealthy merchants toward the edges of the table, something Joan could not approve. France was not in hock to them and, even if it were, their place was to hand out money, not to sit with their lords and imagine themselves as mighty. They might dress their wives in jewels and ermine, in contravention of all natural law and the law of God, but they needed reminding that God had set them a place lower and separate from that of noble men. Near to the servants was the best idea—though no servants were eating in the hall. It had become the practice at the French court under Philip for the servants to eat in the lower dining room on the ground floor of the palace. She thought this a bad idea. Lords should eat in the sight of those serving men who weren't employed at the feast. The low men needed to see their betters living highly, to compare the magnificent dishes served to the royals with their own poor provision. What low man could think himself as good as a king when his lord dined on sturgeon and salmon in serving after serving while he ground his teeth down on coarse bread and mackerel?

Dinners were a way of visibly reinforcing divisions, of displaying the wealth of the lord in attendance, of reminding people of their place and, crucially, the importance of holding their tongues. Tucked away in the bowels of the palace, they could easily talk badly about their superiors, undermining respect and God's order.

Prince John was led to his seat, smiling to the crowd but clicking his fingers at a servant to fill his cup instantly. John's wife, Bonne, sat on the left side of the French queen, heavily pregnant. She was older than John—twenty-two to his seventeen—and was dark and beautiful, dressed in exquisitely tasteful clothes. The queen of Navarre had often wondered what a trial it must be to have to lie with the oaf prince. But, to her surprise, the two had seemed well matched, content to spend all day together mooning at poets and minstrels.

All were assembled and a priest said grace. Then the hall erupted with servants rushing to hand out the dishes. Each trencher was brought before the king, his Joan, John, and—owing to her rearrangement of the seating— little Charles before it got to her. She put her hand to her mouth as she realized that in her irritation with John, she'd exposed her boy to danger by shifting him near to the prince. That was strictly her place. The only reason for putting the boy there—other than to interpose him between her and Prince John—was if she regarded him as having a claim to the French throne and thus being above her.

Philip had noticed what had gone on and was looking at the boy with something approaching dismay in his eyes. Joan couldn't very well change places with the child, and to have him on her knee would confess a tenderness for him that she wanted to disguise.

John smiled at Charles. "Look at you in your high seat. Just one inconvenient prince away from the king's chair."

"Mama says I shall never be king here, so I should never listen to those who say that I should."

John's smile became broader. "That's very wise of your mother."

"It's not about wisdom," said Joan, "it's about honoring a treaty. We've given our word before witnesses. All ambition ceased on the day it was signed."

John laughed. He said, "Indeed, my father says that if you had any true intent on the throne, you'd disguise it better, rather than being such an ill-tempered shrew. What do you say, little one—is your mother ill-tempered?"

Joan cut in. "You will find me mild here, Prince. And I'm sure the tournaments of the coming days will improve my humor. You may carry my token in battle."

John said nothing, just bit at his cup. The little boy looked up at him, apparently in awe.

"When I grow older I shall think it silly to waste my effort in sport," said Charles. "I shall fight my enemies, not my friends!"

John chuckled at the boy and ruffled his hair. "What an extraordinary little fellow," he said. "Well said, sir, well said! I will carry your favor, madam, gladly. But when I am riding through Westminster with Edward's head in my hand. When I bestir myself it will be for the kingdom in war, not some lady's pleasure at a tournament. Here, little boy, you may sip from my cup."

John passed the boy his big goblet of wine and Charles guzzled at it.

"Better to play chess," said Charles.

"Indeed, indeed. The game of kings. Though don't play any games against old King Philip there. Cathedrals have been built while he makes up his mind on a move. No wonder he always wins—his opponent'll do anything just to end it."

"You're so funny!" said Charles. "Do you know any rhymes, Uncle? Mama will never tell me rhymes, but I do love them so."

"Well, now, I do," said John. And then he was off: "To market, to market, to buy a plum bun, home again, home again, market is done!," "Cock a doodle do, my dame has lost her shoe!," and countless others, getting the boy to repeat them. He sat with the child on his knee through all fifteen courses, lifting his wine cup to Charles's lips, seemingly delighted with him. Eventually, the boy began to loll and gape—the wine having made him quite drunk. "Come on, little man," said John, "give us a rhyme!" Charles tried to repeat the rhymes, but his speech was slurred and he kept forgetting them, or adding rude words to the hilarity of the prince.

"Enough," said Joan.

"Oh, surely not, ma'am. Is there anything in the world as funny as a drunk five-year-old? I ask you, ma'am, is there? Oh, you should let me ply him with wine every day."

"He is not here to be your court fool. I shall make sure his guardians see that you do not."

The boy asked, "Shall I see the angel?" Charles's head was lolling.

"What a good idea. Father, what says we take the little boy to the Sainte-Chapelle to see if the angel will receive him?"

Philip's face was furious. "Absolutely not. Particularly not in that condition. No!"

John too became angry. "You deny me all amusement!" he said. "Imagine what the child would make of it in this state—it would be such a funny sight."

"You can amuse me at the lists tomorrow if you like. My son should be out there, putting these Navarrese in their place with sword and lance, not playing nursemaid."

John shrugged off his father's contempt. "As you like. You're probably scared it'll appear for him and not for you," he said. He turned to the boy and cuddled him.

"Uncle, you are so kind!" said Charles, and threw up across the table.

"Oh, isn't that the funniest thing, the very funniest thing!" shouted John, clapping wildly. Then he beckoned to a servant. "Clear it up then."

Joan of Navarre called her ladies to her. "Put the boy to bed," she said. "Give him water and sing to him if he wants you to."

The child was lifted and carried from the halls. She turned to Philip, leaning across John. "What did I tell you?" she said. "The child's an idiot. A complete idiot."

Philip stood up. "I'll take my leave now," he said. "The festivities are at an end."

His trumpets sounded, his wife took his arm, and he swept out of the Great Hall by the doors behind him. Up, thought Joan, toward the Sainte-Chapelle, where the angel was.

7

D owzabel moved backward, catching his heel on the rim of the crater, and falling to sit looking at the glowing figure. He felt his heart come into his mouth. A demon, from Free Hell! Come to liberate the poor and throw down the high men!

The priest held up something in his hand—a lock of hair. He was warning the creature, Dow could tell, though he didn't seem very confident he could act on his warning. His legs were stiff and straight, rooted as if to allow them any movement at all would risk them running away of their own volition.

"Obey me, demon! Obey me! By the names I have uttered, by the command of Holy God."

"The hair of St. Bernard of Clairvaux," said the figure, "a holy saint. But I am not afraid of that, priest. I have made saints—death at the teeth of a demon being a sure route to the blessings of the three-faced God. Their barbers' cuttings do not bother me greatly."

The priest screamed something at the demon in the secret tongue his sort used for their mass.

"My name? My name is Paimon. By your conjuration you may command that of me. Why do you call me and then threaten me? You have done Free Hell a service in opening the first gate."

Every time the creature spoke, Dowzabel had a feeling as if he had walked past an open oven door. Blasts of heat seemed to come from its mouth. In his frozen condition, Dowzabel almost welcomed them.

The little dark man in the gold chain whispered into the priest's ear and the priest, still holding up the lock of hair, addressed the demon.

"Is the gate of Hell open?" The priest now spoke in English.

"It is; others would come through, seeking forms, seeking ways to be in this Eden." He sniffed heavily. "How sweet the air is to one who has lived among the fumes of sulfur."

Dowzabel looked around him. Coils of smoke rose from the ground, writhing like snakes and rubbing themselves against some invisible shield. It was as if they were trapped in a giant bubble they could not escape, its perimeter the circle's edge.

"Will you serve us? We need help against the angels of France," said Bardi.

"Oh, Signor Bardi, I am but a little demon. An angel would eat me whole. For greater aid, you need to open more gates."

"Where are the keys?" Edwin's eyes shone like a miser's before a pile of gold.

"All lost. There are friends of ours in this world, some whom God did not manage to imprison when he overthrew our lord. They have looked for eons and not found them. Jehovah hid them well. I cannot see, not with these poor eyes of coal and ash."

"Then can England be saved?" The one called Bardi was as wild as the priest.

"Can it be lost?"

"Very easily," said the fat one with the ferrets on his surcoat.

"Then it can be saved. Just let me from this circle and we may discuss it."

The priest composed himself. "Remain within. By the names of St. Anthony, by St. Eurgain and St. Matthew, you will tell me, can animals be made from inanimate things? Can a frog grow from a lily?"

"Poor Edwin," said the creature, "so pure in question, so contaminated of mind."

"How can the French be defeated?" said Bardi.

"Aren't you on the side of the French?" asked the demon. "Here's Sir William Pole, who disdains to call himself English." He gestured to Pole.

"You know me, demon?" said the fat man. He drew himself up, his show of arrogance undercut by the tremble in his voice.

"All Hell knows you, merchant."

Pole crossed himself. "We are Normans, masters of England, appointed by God."

"No, it's the French who are appointed by God. I'm sure that's what they say."

"Does the substantial form of the soul configure the prime matter of the body? Answer. Do not evade or try to trick me," shouted Edwin.

"Stop your stupid questions, Edwin," said Bardi. "In war who will win, England or France?" The banker's face was taut with concentration.

"How many skulls from one old saint's head? How many enemies at one another's throats all appointed by God? Does He smile to see His kings at war? Will you not release me?"

The coals on the demon's skin shimmered and flared. Dowzabel lost vision and, when he regained it, the demon was gone. Instead, a beautiful woman stood in the circle, richly dressed in the tailored fashion of the French court.

"How did I get here? Help me, help me!"

"That's a Valois princess!" said Pole. Fear had set his legs jigging, and he looked like a bear at a staff.

"It is a trick, a trick of Hell," said Edwin.

"A devil carried me here, help me," said the princess.

"Do you think it could be true?" Pole pawed at his beard, still dancing the Black Nag.

"We cannot risk believing so. Either go or stay, Pole, but quit your hopping," said Edwin.

The woman's body dissolved into light, and this time a child stood in the circle, a prince by his crown.

"Help me. I was dragged here by a devil," he said, "I am Giuseppe, prince of Padua. I will give power and money to the man who releases me. Be quick, the demon will eat me."

"Oh, think of the money!" said Pole in a tone of great lament.

"What is the nature of the Holy Trinity? Reveal it to me!" To Dow, the priest seemed mad, spitting as he spoke.

"Edwin, remember who funds your investigations and your idle life," said Bardi. "Command it to answer my question!"

That seemed to bring Edwin to his senses.

"I command you, tell me how the war against France may be won!" Edwin held up the lock of hair.

The little prince remained, wide-eyed in the circle.

Edwin crossed himself. "He will need to be commanded in the name of a higher demon," he said. "We cannot do that without peril to our souls, but this boy is already damned." He took a paper from his pocket and began to read. When he spoke it was in a careful, badly pronounced Cornish that Dow could understand.

"Command it in the names of the higher demons to reveal the answer I seek."

The boy clamped his jaw and stared past Edwin.

Edwin gestured to Bardi's servant. He leveled a crossbow at the boy.

"Command it!" Then, in English, "Command it. I know you know the rite, I know you know it."

"He can't command it, you fool. He can't speak. The boy's practically a mute!" shouted Orsino.

The little prince looked at Dowzabel. "Command me," he said, "as is your right to do."

I will give them nothing, thought Dowzabel.

The demon's voice sounded in his head. *You would see them burn and suffer? You would see high men cast down? Command me. My tongue is cursed to silence but you can undo it. Let them see you useful. You are the one.*

"What one?" Dow grunted the words.

"The one who is lost."

Dowzabel didn't know what to do.

In whose name? Now he spoke with his mind.

What is the name of the Lord of Light? What are the names of your Cornish fellows?

How wonderful, thought Dow, to speak with this thing just his thoughts.

I command you. In the name of Lucifer, in the name of Belial, in the name of Abbadon and Sabnock and Orobos. Reveal the answer I demand!

The prince's form seemed to melt and turn in on itself, the demon grew up from him like a shoot from the bulb of a flower, the human flesh peeling away to reveal the fiery demon below.

The demon said, "The boy has asked and I may reply. Take the banner."

"You can't steal the Oriflamme," said Pole, crossing himself yet again. "It sits in the abbey of St. Denis, directly under the angel's arse. There are more relics in that abbey than the rest of Christendom combined. And besides, it can only be taken out of the abbey by the rightful king of France, or someone appointed by him. You need your money back on this demon, Bardi, by St. Catherine's queynte, so you do!"

The demon spoke and its skin flared. "Scales and fire, wing and bone; so flies the banner of the English throne."

"What's it talking about?" said Pole. "Speak sense, you abomination."

The demon spoke again: "And the beast, whom I saw, was like a leopard and the dragon gave his virtue and great power to him."

"Do not corrupt the Holy Scripture with your voice, demon! It's a wonder the Bible's words don't burn your tongue as you speak them!" Edwin looked crazy, his eyes scrunched up to slits, sweat dropping from him like tiny stars falling through the torchlight.

"A dragon," said Bardi. "The leopard is Edward! That is his sign. A dragon will give him his power. The pennant of the English throne—St. George. The banner of St. George, that's the saint of the English throne! Are you talking about the banner of St. George?"

"The banner of St. George is the Drago," said the demon. Dow heard a voice in his head. *Let them believe that is what they seek. You will find something far more powerful that will tear down the thrones.*

What?

The banner of all rebellions.

Bardi strode to the edge of the circle, his eyes wide. "Where can we find it?"

"Let me from the circle. All your debts will be paid."

"Let the fellow out," said Pole. "All our fortunes depend on this." He stepped forward and backward now, like a boy trying to summon the courage to knock on a girl's door.

"No!" said Father Edwin. "I have long experience of these fiends. He is working upon your mind, even through that circle. He will trick you and connive. He will use fair words and appear in many guises. But do not listen to him; he is a demon, shunned by God. I command you, in the names of all the higher demons, to reveal what you know. Where is the banner we seek?"

"Some things are hidden to us."

"Holy things!" said Edwin. "Command him again, boy."

I will not. How can I free you? How can I serve Free Hell?

Dow heard a voice in his head. "Hold fast and bide your time. There are great powers at work in the world. You move under the eyes of angels and devils. Move softly."

"Command him again!"

"Where is the banner?" said Dow.

"I'm going to let him out!" said Pole. "There's profit in this!"

Orsino grabbed the merchant to restrain him.

"By Christ's balls, send him back!" said Orsino. "He's working on us!"

"Where is the banner?" said Edwin.

"Let him out. There's gold and profit for the man who does!" Pole tried to get free of Orsino, and the Florentine threw him to the floor.

"Where is the banner?"

Pole scrabbled forward, but Orsino leapt on his back, holding him down.

"For God's sake, send it back. I can't hold this fat pig forever, unless you want me to cut his throat!" said Orsino.

"Send him back!" shouted Bardi.

"Not to the fire and the heat and the smoke," said the demon.

Edwin cursed and spat. "Even there," he said. "I complete the ritual by feeding you the blood of an unbeliever!"

Bardi signaled to Arigo, who said something in his native tongue. Bardi shouted back at him in English.

"If I say do it, do it! I'll pay your blasted penance!"

Arigo leveled his crossbow at Dowzabel.

"Is it not a sin, by your religion, to kill?" said the demon. Its voice was like the sizzling of water on coals.

"He is a heretic and a devil worshiper—there can be no sin in his death. It will make Heaven smile," said the priest. "Satan's ambassador has revealed this."

"And they always speak the truth," said the demon.

Dowzabel focused on the crossbow. He hated the man who bore it. He had contacted his uncle and offered him money to betray Dow. He knew the high men were evil the moment he'd seen them on their fine horses outside the priest's house where he had been kept—waiting to drag him away from everything he knew, waiting to torture him and, now, to kill him.

The crossbow clicked, and Dowzabel heard the bolt hiss. It did not strike him. The demon had snatched it from the air, its hand extending in a flare of fire.

"I have been a long time hungry in Hell," he said. He put the bolt into his mouth and crunched it up in his jaws. "Boy, break the circle."

"Go back," said the priest. "We offer you an unbeliever's blood. You are bound by the names of Holy God, here displayed before you on the parchment; you are bound by our use of the key, you are bound by salt and by ritual. Accept the blood. Bardi, have your man shoot him again."

Arigo put his foot into the stirrup of his crossbow, engaged his belt hook, and began pulling back the drawstring. He was talking all the time; Dowzabel guessed he was telling his masters that a second bolt would likely only provide another snack for the monster.

"You have not offered me the blood of an unbeliever," said the demon.

"This child is a disciple of Satan," said the priest.

"Of Lucifer," said the demon, "not Satan."

"They are the same!" said Orsino. He now had Pole in an armlock.

"I wish I could let you stand in the morning light to face the Lord of the Dawn and say such a thing."

"You lie and dissemble, demon," said the priest.

"Why trust me in one thing but not another?"

"I trust you when I bind you to the truth. When I call the names of God and strip your lies from you. The boy is a heretic and an unbeliever. His blood is the price you require to return."

"Not so. His faith is strong," said the demon, "and, more than that, it is true. It is you who are the unbelievers, who talk of love and practice hate, who praise the God of the poor and raise yourselves up in palaces of marble and gold. You said in your heart, 'I will ascend to Heaven; I will raise my throne above the stars of God.' But here you are, my gentlemen, brought down to the depths of the pit." He gestured to the priest. "Here's one who consorts with devils; here's one who calls Hell's gaolers and makes them skip to his command."

"Take the child's blood."

"I will not. I *cannot*. Though I will take blood before I go. Unless you wish to release me."

"Let him out, Edwin!" shouted Pole. "We need to find that banner!"

"He is working on you, Pole. Go back to Hell, abhorred of God!"

"Then blood, priest. Yours, his." He extended a fiery finger toward Pole. "An unbeliever's. Or freedom. Give me my freedom."

"Never."

Pole cried out: "We can buy remissions for this sin if my money is recouped. I'll take you to Avignon and give the pope so much gold he'll carry us to Heaven himself. Let the thing free if it can help us! Make it swear not to harm us and what do we care what else it does in the world?"

"It has your mind, Pole; they are persuasive even guarded by charms. Orsino," said the priest, "take this lock of hair—the demon cannot hurt you while you carry it. Enter the circle and cut the boy's throat. The demon will take the sacrifice he is offered."

"I've got my hands full with the merchant! You cut his throat," said Orsino. "It seems to me that, one way or another, God wants him alive."

"I'll do it." Arigo stepped forward.

"No, Arigo!" said Orsino.

"Orsino, this is a thing of Hell. I believe in Jesus Christ. I am His servant. It needs to go back. The child is a heretic—God will smile on me for this."

Arigo took the lock of hair from Edwin, crossed himself, and walked forward, freeing a long knife from his belt. The demon put his finger to the rope that held Dow to the stake, burning it away.

Dow fell and swiped his hand on the floor, scattering the parchments and sending a spray of ash and salt toward the watching men. Orsino rolled away from the merchant, drawing his sword.

The circle was broken; the priest was down on his knees, holding forward the lock of hair. A blaze of heat rushed over Dow's head; he looked up to see sparks flying out into the night from the circle, swirling and turning to form the shape of a man. The demon was free.

8

I n the lilac light of the first-floor chapel at Sainte-Chapelle, Philip of France stood holding the hand of his wife, Joan of Burgundy, called the Lame. They had retired from the banquet as soon as manners allowed. Philip squeezed his wife's hand as she leaned upon her cane of oak and silver.

In front of them, among the jewels of the altar, was a golden reliquary, an elaborate basket of wrought gold. It contained something far more precious—a substantial part of the crown of thorns worn by the crucified Christ. The one next to it, no less splendid, contained a piece of the true cross. Next to that lay the last cubit of the holy lance that had pierced Christ's side on the cross. In alcoves all along the walls, small statues of saints looked down. The saints were present in their likenesses. Philip could hear them singing praises to God.

The king and queen bent to touch the altar and kiss the relics.

"The Navarre woman troubles me," said the king.

Joan smiled at her husband. "We are of God," she said. "He brings destruction to our enemies."

"The angel will no longer see me alone."

"But it will see you. Do not doubt God's love for you, Philip. Look at how you honor Him, build Him splendid churches, house His saints' bones in caskets of gold and precious stones. Look how you have warred on His behalf, how many of His enemies you have slain. Remember the story of Job. Those whom God loves, He tests. Now pray."

Philip sank to his knees. "I, Philip of France, who bows before no man, bow before you. Holy Father, who made Heaven and earth, who puts kings on their thrones and gives them power over men, hear me now."

Philip looked around him at the stone saints. They did not move, but their song rose louder throughout the great chapel, high and beautiful, singing the Lumen Hilare: "Oh light, gladsome of the holy glory of the immortal Father, having come upon the setting of the sun, having seen the light of evening, we praise the Father, the Son, and the Holy Spirit."

He smiled at Joan. They had said he was mad to marry her, that her withered leg was a sign of great evil. But Philip knew she was of the royal line, granddaughter of old King Louis, St. Louis, whose stone likeness now looked down on them from the tall columns of the stained-glass windows. It was he who had built the chapel in which they now stood, he who had first summoned the angel, luring it from Heaven with the splendor he had provided on earth. Sainte-Chapelle was a marvel; the veils of deep blue glass hung between thin golden pillars and surrounded the king and queen on every side. It was a place of such richness, such light.

Philip had wed into the family of God when he married Joan, and he had never regretted it for an instant.

"The angel will come?" He spoke to his wife.

"It's here. It's always here." Her voice was strained, ecstatic.

The light burst around them, and it was as if they had entered the stained glass of the window. The air itself seemed to shimmer in gold, crimson, blue, and green. A wonderful airiness filled Philip's heart. He felt like crying with joy, as he always felt when the angel materialized.

"Jegudiel." The angel said its name, and that name seemed to shape itself into golds, reds, and deep greens—all the colors of autumn— and go floating through his mind like a falling leaf caught in a sunbeam. The colors of the air split and sparkled. When Philip had first encountered it, he had thought it would take form as a man, but now he knew that, amid beauty like that in the chapel, it took its form from the beauty, changed it and deepened it, honored it. In battle it could appear as a light on the spears of his army, a light in the sky, or—as it had at Cassel—an armed knight of such brilliant beauty that few could bear to look at him.

"Jegudiel." Philip and Joan repeated the angel's name. "Angel of the sacred heart."

The angel spoke and the colors of the chapel seemed to flow through the bodies of the king and queen. Philip did not feel like a thing of flesh anymore, but something woven of light.

"A usurper on God's Holy Throne?" The angel's voice was all beauty, the fall of a waterfall, birds in a meadow, the breeze among trees.

Philip crossed himself, acutely nervous. Did it mean him? The angel never made it clear if it knew what Philip had done to gain the throne of France, but then, it never made *anything* clear. Philip said, "I bow down before God."

"Then come into His light."

Philip felt himself drifting away, intoxicated by the presence of the angel. It seemed to unlock something inside himself—an understanding. "And God said, 'Light be made.' And light was made." That had been the beginning, but in the beginning was everything. Everything was light, he, the angel, the chapel, and the world. All light, colliding in its various beams and colors.

He forced himself to think. His father had told him that speaking to angels was necessary but dangerous; that it was not unknown for kings to lose their minds doing it. It was said that old Edward of England had so loved his that he bade it take flesh and accompany him about the court, sucking in all his love and arousing the jealousy of his lords. Even if that story was not literally true, thought Philip, the moral was worth bearing in mind. These contacts with the divine needed to be handled with great care. And the angel made such little sense, talking in riddles, losing the thread of reason. Its mind was not a human mind, but a strange, deep, and wide thing.

The angel said, "The sun sets at Orwell and the river burns like the path to Hell. Many shadows are on the water."

Orwell was where the English fleet might muster! Shadows on the water. Philip had expected an invasion, but this was the first indication it was happening.

He asked, "Will you sparkle on our bowsprits; will you fill our sails and inspire our men to valor? Will you strike at our enemies with light and with fire, and teach them God's will?"

"A usurper on God's Holy Throne."

"I am not a usurper. I couldn't be here without God's blessing. I . . ." Philip was going to say that he had atoned for what he had done, but he didn't know if the angel knew he had done anything that required atonement. His father had told him the angels were far from all-knowing but that they had ways of finding out things. Philip stuck to what he had done for it. "I house you in this magnificent chapel; I pray to you. My nobles lay gold upon your altar and light incense so that you might delight to put yourself into a wisp of smoke and float on the scented air."

"God tests his kings in battle."

"I give rings and gold. I build great churches. I . . ."

"The three fleurs-de-lys are withered. Hugh Capet's line is cut?"

So it *did* know. The three fleurs-de-lys formed the Capetian arms, but Philip knew it also referred to the three sons of Philip the Handsome, all of whom had very short reigns and died without sons, opening the way to the throne for him. The king knew the rumors about him—his nickname "The Lucky" was said with a great deal of courtier's irony. It was apt.

"That was the work of the Templars, heretics and worshipers of Lucifer." This was true. Although their work had needed a sponsor.

Philip felt the angel's displeasure as a tightening in his chest, a ringing in his ears, a thumping in his head. He said, "I . . ."

Philip could not lie even if he wanted to. It was as if the light had opened his head and his thoughts themselves were now light, mingling with the beams of the dying sun, with those of the angel whose presence was light.

He remembered that dirty shack by the river where he'd met the Templars—the candles fluttering as if caught in the breath of a ghost, the stink of fish, the hollow eyes of the Templar grandmaster, Jacques De Molay, evaluating him, seeing if he could be trusted. He was only a boy then, thirteen, uncertain and scared. His father had taken him there. The poverty of the knights had struck him—their coats worn, their shoes broken. It disgusted him to be among such men, though his father assured him their war gear would be the envy of any duke's son. The Templars were heretics, he said, whatever face they presented to the world, but they were useful men.

De Molay had been straightforward in his demands—the Templars wanted their own state in France, a place of the "Free Fallen." It had been gibberish to Philip. Philip's father the count knew only he wanted to be king and promised them whatever they wanted if they worked their magic. They said the risk was great, that if God discovered their purpose, He would move against them and undo them. Many in their number opposed the idea. But De Molay, that cold, thoughtful man, had agreed—after demanding proof of good intention from the count.

So they'd set him a task—bring them a twig from the crown of thorns. Had it been necessary for their ritual, or a test of faith? Philip had volunteered for the task himself—so it might be passed off as childish mischief if he was discovered. He'd stolen into the chapel at night, heard the cries and sighs of the stone saints as he'd broken it off. Regret had swamped him the moment the twig snapped. It cut his finger, and it seemed as if Christ was mocking him, comparing his selfless sacrifice to Philip's selfish one.

He returned with the twig to the Templars. They'd cast their spell, but the ritual was a long and difficult one, and it had attracted the attention of a Capetian spy. Philip had watched the Templars hang, knowing they had not completed their curse before they died. All their assets had been taken.

Then Philip's father had died, that dark day at Nogent-le-Roi, and the task of finding someone to complete the magic had fallen to Philip. It had not been easy and had cost him far more than money, but he had done it—contacting the ragged remains of the Templars who had gone over to their rivals, the Hospitallers, out of desperation or because of threats.

The crown had been put on to his head in the great light of Notre Dame. From that moment on, he had promised to serve God truly, but his relationship with the angels remained poor. They distrusted him, he could tell, and he could not rely on them in his wars. That left him very vulnerable when it came to dealing with other kings.

Now the angel said, "England. Angels have died there. I heard their screams."

Philip crossed himself. He was sweating greatly. "Are all his angels gone?"

"Edward, favored by God. Gone. Not there. There. Yes."

Philip wished greatly the angel would be less oblique. Why couldn't divine power be linked to the power of plain speaking? He knew from long experience it was useless to press the creature. Only God was all-knowing, and he half suspected the angels descended into cryptic speech when they simply didn't know what they were talking about.

He said, "We will invade. Give me your assurances you will deal with their remaining angels."

"The English king's angels labor at God's task night and day. Lucifer. He was once and may yet be."

"What of Lucifer?"

"Yes."

Philip put his head into his hands momentarily. He could not make sense of anything the angel said.

"We will strike the English," said Philip, "if you will sparkle on our spear tips and give our men heart."

"Faith, first," said the angel. "Faith that parted the seas and led God's people out of Goshen."

"You cannot ask an angel for guarantees," said Joan.

He replied, "I have labored for God."

"What of your crusade?" The angel's voice was like the whisper of rain on a dry land.

"It has been canceled."

"Why?"

"Because . . ."

"Rings, churches, wealth, you give and you give, but still you have more than any man in the world. Little is the loss. You were haughty and not prepared to weep; you were not prepared to see sons slaughtered, to lie wounded in some foreign dusty land, your armor full of grit, your mouth thick with sand. You would not give your suffering, as Christ gave you His."

Philip had noticed before that angels could be very exact in their criticism, while remaining entirely impenetrable when you asked them for anything useful.

He said, "The pope himself ordered me not to go."

"England's hand is in that!" said Joan. "He wishes to keep us from favor with God."

"And yet you refused to crusade with him five years ago," said the angel. "You could have done great service to God."

Philip crossed himself again. The truth was that he had not wanted Edward to win favor with God. Philip had been pleased to help Edward overthrow his father and been glad when the old man died. He had turned young Edward into a usurper, alienating the English angels. All good. But through his mother, it might be argued that Edward had a better claim to the throne of France than he did. What if Edward proved himself more courageous, more holy, won back God's favor? The man was a prodigy of arms. Would he topple Philip?

Philip asked, "What do you want? I invaded Gascony to take the cathedrals at Bazas and Auch so you might dwell in the light there and be worshiped as you are worshiped here."

The angel said, "Give me the head of God's enemy."

"What?"

"He is born. The arch-usurper."

"Who is he?"

"A boy, born to tear the world. I see him and half see him. All Hell is behind him. He has been brought to his beginning."

The light shifted and swam, splintered and shone. Philip felt sick. "What is his name?" he asked.

"God as yet only glimpses him. He is known and not known. Should he live or die?"

"If he's the Antichrist, he should die."

"God sees wider purposes. Angels cannot know them."

"So you'll go against God?"

"I will express that part of God that wants him dead. Others may express the part that would let him live."

"What is his name?" Philip asked the angel.

"God does not reveal it."

"Ask Him."

"You do not ask things of God. You are told."

"Is it Charles of Navarre?" he asked the angel.

"He is young."

"How shall I act? What shall I do? I would take the Oriflamme, lead the angels, repel England!"

"Consider what you can give me. Now return to the dark."

Suddenly it was night. The sun had gone down, and the chapel—its candles unlit—was quite dark, the scant moonlight draining the splendid windows, the jewels, and the gold of all color. Philip felt lumpen, solid, fleshy.

Philip put his hand on his wife's shoulder. "It's gone. What of that?"

Her face was pale. "It will be back when it gets what it wants from you," she said.

"What?"

"What God always wants of the faithful. What He wanted of His son on the cross."

Philip repeated, "What?"

"Blood," she said, "and plenty of it. Prepare to invade England. And kill the boy."

Philip nodded. "The angel was plain. Charles is a servant of the devil and must die."

9

The demon flew out of the circle like a blast of sparks from the mouth of a furnace. Many things came out of the circle, things of light and smoke, things with wings that rustled like paper or ground like stone, there and gone in an instant, things that crawled and crept, serpents, frogs, five-headed, scuttling, a boy with eyes burned to nothing. A woman, her head plumed with feathers as if she were some sort of bird, ran shrieking into the night.

"Tell me how to find this banner!" shouted Pole. He was up on his feet, clenching his fists like a two-year-old in a fit.

The demon, his coals burning, turned to him. "Look into your heart."

His hand reached forward into Pole's chest, tearing through the rib cage, pulling out the pulsing heart. He put it to his mouth and squeezed its juice from it as easily as from a ripe orange. Arigo was on him from behind, stuffing the hair of the saint into the demon's mouth, stabbing at the creature's back with his knife. He fell away from it screaming, his body consumed by fire.

Edwin jumped toward Dowzabel. He dribbled powder from his pouch, recompleting the circle from the inside, grabbing the parchments and putting them at the edge. Bardi leapt over the powder to cling to the boy.

"You can command him—you send him back," said Bardi, pricking his knife into the back of Dow's neck. All around their feet creatures seemed to pour from the earth, hemmed in by the circle.

The demon turned to face them. "I would leave the circle if I were you, my friends, for what comes inside will not look on you kindly."

The priest made the sign of the cross. Bardi held up a piece of bloodied cloth. Orsino, outside the circle and without its protection from the demon, displayed his piece of sacking.

"Send them back, boy, send them now or I will kill you!" said Bardi.

As the knife jabbed at his neck, Dowzabel felt weak and faint. Little demons, things in the form of cockroaches and rats but monstrously deformed, many-legged, many-headed, were crawling all over him. A little girl, her face eaten by leprosy, stroked his hair.

It was unbearable, even for someone who believed in the salvation that Hell had to offer. He had to keep his faith, he had to believe. He remembered Abbadon, next to him on the moor, holding him by the fire, tending Dowzabel in his agony after they'd cut his tongue. "Let me tell you about Hell," he'd said.

So Dowzabel knew what was coming out of the first gate—demons, lesser angels chained to an earthly form, taking what they could from ashes and coals, or the insects that crawled in the earth, or the bodies of devils they had killed in war. Coming too were the lost, Dow's own people, the souls of the poor and downtrodden. Still, he could not bear to look at them, their fly-eaten eyes, their diseased lips. Worms were all around his feet, spiders, crawling things, a baby starved to nothing, but pulling at his leg.

He thought he would go mad, but he had to endure. If Hell's gate was open, then salvation was near; this was the army of liberation, seething from the floor, pushing against the invisible barrier of the holy dust. Dow had to bear it. The fallen angels would liberate them, fight God, break His curse, throw off their twisted bodies, and return to the world of light.

Then there was the sense of something else, something terrible. Smoke was all around him. He had a feeling of a great weight on his chest; his ears were dull as if he had plunged to the bottom of a pool. His nose began to bleed once more, and his mouth was full of the taste of iron.

"It is here. It is here. The gate has been open long enough. Close the gate now, Dow. Close the gate!" The fire demon was reaching toward him.

Dow was finding it difficult to think. His thoughts seemed unwieldy things and he had that sensation from a dream where a simple action seems impossible to complete.

"Close the gate. The worst of Hell is close. Do not risk freeing him!"
The demon spoke again, its voice hissing like a smith's iron plunging white
hot into water.

All the little creatures in the circle chirped and shrieked in agitation.

Dow still had the key in his hand as creatures swarmed all over him, all
over Bardi and Edwin. He saw a monstrous cockroach on his arm, a head
at either end. He pitied it, the poor soul forced to take its form from the
offcuts of creation.

"Forbid these things from harming us!" Bardi's knife was drawing blood.
"Tell them to go back!" Dowzabel's fist was curled tight around the key, but
Edwin's fingers prised his hand open and took it.

Orsino stood in front of the demon, waving his sword, screaming that it
had killed his friend. The demon ignored him, so Orsino swung at its head.
The sword went straight through it and emerged on the other side in a burst
of ashes, as if the demon's body had no substance at all.

"Fight me! Fight me!" shouted Orsino. "You who killed Arigo!"

"I will not fight you."

"Why not?"

"You are not of God. Lucifer heard your curse echoing across all Hell
when your family died, and now Free Hell has claimed you. We have uses
for you, Condottiere."

The words seemed to stun the man. He sank to his knees, crossing
himself, shouting out that he hadn't meant what he had said, that his mind
had been disordered by grief—that he would do penance and go on crusade.

Dow spoke to the demon with his mind. *What am I to do? Don't leave me
with these men. Stay and talk to me, soft demon.*

"Do what they say and you will have nothing to fear from them. Find
the banner. Free Hell charges you with that."

Where shall I look?

"I cannot tell, but there is a phrase on the wind. Can you not hear it?"

A wind was springing up, stirring the ashes, stirring the parchments.

I hear nothing.

The demon put his hand to his ear. "The king in the east."

Dow sank to his knees. Looming before him through the smoke was a
man, richly dressed but his face flayed. His coat was torn away at one arm,

and Dow saw he had writing of some sort down it. His neck bore an ugly wound all around it and a strange lacing through the wound. It looked as though he had his head tied on by twine. Bardi screamed when he saw the man, his legs doing a little back and forth as he tried to decide whether to leap out of the circle and face the fire demon or remain in the circle and face the bizarre figure that was materializing in front of him. Dow choked and spat.

The demons in the circle scrabbled and screamed to be free. "A devil! A devil! He comes for us! Let us fly!" A hand groped from the smoke to grab at the one called Bardi. The rich man let Dow go and frantically stabbed at the creature's arm with his dagger.

"You!" said the devil. "You played me most false, banker!" It grabbed the dagger arm.

"It's trying to drag me to Hell! It's trying to drag me to Hell!" screamed Bardi.

"Quickly!" said the fire demon. "He cannot be allowed through! Close the gate!"

Another devil appeared—a monstrous head on a pair of legs, stuffing the tiny demons into its mouth. Dow recognized the face—it was that of the priest who had cut his tongue. Dow was stiff with fear. He remembered that so clearly—the bleak summer, so far from home, the Plymouth sea front, gray on gray, and the shears on his tongue. He'd thought he would die, drown on his own blood. That priest's face was in front of him now, leering through darkness. "You speak like a serpent, so you shall have a serpent's tongue," he'd said.

They'd let him go then and he'd gone—back to the Devil's Men, back to find his nan's body on that sparse hill, to call the others to it to make a fire of heather and gorse and return her to the light of which she was made. He'd vowed as he'd watched her burn that the priest would come to regret letting him go. The Devil's Men had finally got him coming back from Lostwithiel. He'd died too quick for Dow's liking.

Dow felt faint at the memories. He had a sense of a gate or a door through which the devil who had grabbed Bardi was summoning the courage to pass. He could not let it. Bardi howled and screamed:

"Release me! Release me! I never played you false!"

I close the gate! thought Dow.

"In whose name?" said a voice in his mind.

He could think of no demon's name, his thoughts drowned by an inner scream.

In mine. In Dowzabel's. I close the gate to Hell.

The scraping, that terrible noise. The devil released its grip on the rich men. Everyone else put their hands to their ears, but Dowzabel, tied up, was forced to bear it.

Bardi fell to the floor, clutching his arm and howling.

"When the gate opens again, I will be waiting! For both of you!" The voice was tormented, distant.

"Give me the boy!" the demon bellowed.

Edwin all but threw Dow over the powder of the circle. Dowzabel could not stand, he was so exhausted, so cold, and so frightened, and his ankle would not support his weight.

Help me! Dow screamed with his mind.

The demon stretched forward a burning finger to the wound on Dow's chest. Dow felt a searing pain and flinched away, howling in agony. Exactly where the priest had branded him, the demon had burned him again.

"You will help yourself. We who are now free have work to do."

You have betrayed me! You have burned me. You are the same as the men of Îthekter!

But the demon didn't seem to hear him. It folded its arms over its chest. "I go to pursue Free Hell's destiny; I have places to go, bad men to see."

The wind stirred the ashes of the demon's body, and it began to blow away, stripping him to nothing, until he was no more than a trail of sparks flying into the night sky.

Bardi kicked a gap in the circle of powder, and the remaining little creatures that surrounded them blew out, flowing up toward the black sky like so much smoke.

Edwin collapsed, sitting back on the rim of the crater.

Bardi stumbled over to the ravaged bodies of Pole and Arigo. His arm was a tattered mess, and he held it close against his body, wincing with pain even as he spoke.

"Well, broadly speaking," he said, "I'd call that a success."

Orsino stood up. He had recovered his wits. "You're a bastard, sir, if you call this success. Arigo was my friend."

"Watch your tongue, Orsino," said Bardi, "unless you want to lose it like the boy lost his. Though considering the circumstances, I'll forgive you this once."

"I don't want to work for you any more, sir."

Bardi sat on the floor, clutching his arm. "Then gamble less or sell your family's home and pay your debts. Remember, your mother and your sisters sit secure for as long as you are useful to me, or for as long as I live. You are mine until you can pay your debts."

"What is our debt now? And where is your profit? We open the gates of Hell and allow demons that God locked away to come crawling into the world. A great man dies. My friend too," said Orsino.

"The gate to Hell is closed and will remain so while I have the key," said Edwin.

"Perhaps that's best in the short term," said Bardi. "We got what we wanted. Nothing worth having is without cost." He turned to the priest. "Your spirit was right about the boy, Father."

The priest bowed his head to his knees, hugging himself, sitting on the lip of the pit and staring into space. "Who was that devil, Bardi? He knew you."

"The fire demon knew Pole. It means nothing. I've never seen the other one before."

Orsino went to Dow. The boy tried to stand, but he was too weak. The soldier supported him.

"We can let the boy free now?" said Orsino.

"I need him," said the priest. "He is going nowhere. He has a rare command of these demons. He will come with me and help me learn about Hell. If he can open the gate to Hell, he can get more from my devil than I have achieved."

"Your devil at St. Olave's wants him dead," said Bardi.

"A good enough reason to keep him alive. We can strike bargains with it. We may pull more truths from it yet."

"The demon said England's liberation was in the Drago. Use your art to find it," said Bardi. "Everything depends on it."

"Everything? If a fiend like that commands it of a heretic like this, I say keep away from magic banners," said Orsino.

"England will not succeed against the French without it," said Bardi.

"I am a Londoner; what do I care for England? The king asks permission before he visits my city," said Edwin.

"Think what you have done, Edwin," said Bardi. "You have walked in the darkness. Now return to the light."

"Do you think God would favor whoever found this banner?" said Orsino. "Could so doing wipe away sin?"

"It's a powerful relic. It would take great effort to find. Of course God would smile on whoever located it," said Bardi.

The priest's head slumped forward. Then he nodded slowly. He said, "I will ask my devil. He led us to the boy. He may lead us to the flag."

Bardi was clutching his wounded arm.

"If you open the gate to Hell again, make sure I am far away."

"Unless our knowledge deepens, that will be impossible," said Edwin. "Many more demons are free in the world tonight. I thought we could force it back. We couldn't, and I will not attempt this again until I am sure I can dispel what I summon. Devils are one thing. These demons another."

"You sound like you believe their heresy," said Bardi.

"I do not. I believe what the church believes. Yet it seems true that some creatures of Hell bow to God, while others do not, and so the distinction is useful."

"You spend too long in the sewer, you'll eventually get shit on you," said Bardi. "Make sure you respect the faith of the holy church."

"I embody it," said Edwin.

"Then the boy? He is a heretic and should be hanged," said Bardi.

The priest pursed his lips as if he were a condescending master and Bardi a thickheaded apprentice. "No. Hell favors him. That may be to our advantage. We'll see what use he can be for a while."

"If you think that's best," said Bardi. "Orsino, you will go with him."

"Why?" said Orsino.

"I think I should keep an eye on the priest and this boy," said Bardi, "and a spell in his stinking hovel of a house might teach you to mind your manners in the future. Make sure they apply themselves, Orsino, and report to me monthly. I want to see progress in finding this banner."

Orsino snorted. "It will be a rare hovel that's more inhospitable than the moors."

"Now," said Bardi, "I'm going down into the town to fix my arm and stay with a merchant friend of mine. Accompany me, Orsino. We head for London tomorrow. At first light," said Bardi.

"Not first light," said Orsino.

"Why not?"

"Because before we do anything, me and the father here are going to bury my friend."

Bardi nodded. "Return once you have seen me to my lodgings. Work through the night and say your mass at dawn. Clear the rest of this mess as well—including Pole. We'll leave his family to wondering what could have happened to him on the road back to London. I will stop at Windsor to report our findings to the king. After that, you are at my disposal. Fetch me my horse. And you, priest, prepare to work. Your salvation, England's salvation, and indeed mine, depend upon you."

10

L
ondon was unbelievably vast, stretched out as wide as the moor along the north bank of the river. A huge spire to Dow's left, an enormous white castle and tower to his right shone in the umber dusk. On the river, tiny boats moved, some with lamps, some unlit, all heading for the shore as the sun went down.

They had arrived later than his escorts had intended, after detouring to drop Bardi at Windsor. Windsor Castle had terrified Dowzabel—so big, so unnatural looking. The biggest building he had ever seen before was a church. This was ten times bigger. The Devil's Men said that the creator Lucifer would return one day to throw down the high men. Could even he breach the walls of a place like that?

From Windsor they'd traveled with a party of government servants and courtiers up to London, deciding not to cross the river at Staines but by London Bridge, which the priest said would lead them very close to his house in the city. This would spare them crossing through London at dusk.

"Will we get in at this hour?" said Orsino.

"We are not the lower sort," said Edwin. "As men of good character, we should be allowed in at night."

Dow had never seen anything like the bridge itself. It seemed almost to sag with the weight of buildings on it, higgledy-piggledy houses that jutted out over the river as if being shoved by their fellows to make room. Dowzabel—who had thought Exeter enormous—was breathless at the sight. The heads of those who had displeased the lords of the city looked out from spikes high on the gate tower, some fresh faced, others hardly more than skulls.

The moor that yielded to the road all the way into the city housed vast camps of people—hungry-eyed children, bony women, and broken-down men, clamoring for alms from anyone coming in. Dow knew he was a foreigner in that country and that he might get a hard time from the people of the moor, but probably better to be there, among people he understood, than with these rich fellows who burned and beat him. He thought to slip from his horse, to try to run.

But the burn throbbed on his chest; Dowzabel had a fever and felt weak. Besides, his ankle would still not support him. He would not get away. Why had the demon burned him? He had put his trust in it. He'd been taught on the moor that Lucifer was a kinder soul than Îthekter, called God. But the demon had not been kind. Not kind at all.

He looked down upon children reaching up with thin arms, women calling out offering their bodies, the men begging absolution, forgiveness, or, more often, just money from the priest. There were thirty travelers on the road with them—apart from Dowzabel, all people of rank.

But the poor seemed numberless, a field of them stretching out beyond the dilapidated maze of houses and inns on the southern shore into a wide and ragged camp. Dowzabel thought of Abbadon back home on their own moor. How little, he'd said, it would take for the starving and the frozen to reach out and tear these high men down. But they didn't. They just clamored and begged. Dowzabel could not understand why. As the column approached the bridge the city guard stepped forward and the wretched fold kept back, no one wanting a kick or a smack with the butt of a polearm to add to their woes.

The priest Edwin had a lamp that he held before him as a sign he was not using the darkness as a cover for evil deeds, and Orsino—a foreigner by his manner and dress—had ceded his sword to him.

Once through the damp and piss stink of the gatehouse and portcullis and onto the bridge, the scene was even more remarkable. The bridge *did* sag under the weight of the shops and houses crammed upon it, some straight, some tipping into others at angles, as if shouldering for room. A begrudged strip of road ran down the middle, its fine cobbles firm beneath the horses and beautifully free of mud.

The bridge was not quite deserted; some noblemen—exempt from the curfew laws that applied to ordinary men—rode boldly on with their retinues, or lingered in shops to examine clothes, candles, weapons, or books. The shopkeepers would not face the censure of the city watch while they served lords.

Something running between the hooves of Dowzabel's horse made it start. It wasn't a rat, as he'd thought, but a fine fat black cat, chasing through the shadows for prey.

"There are doctors here, kid," said Orsino. "I'll come tomorrow and get you something for that burn."

"He deserves to suffer," said Edwin, "until he finds a path back to Christ."

Orsino shrugged. "Believers suffer too," he said. "I lost my wife and both my sons to fever. More Christian people you could not meet."

The priest gave him a disapproving look that said clearly that people got what they deserved in life. Sickness was God's punishment for sin, and only a fool would deny it.

They traveled over the bridge and into the city proper. Here the dark was full of eyes—the poor, clinging to the shadows of back alleys and the lees of buildings. Dowzabel saw one man almost naked, huddling by a doorway, clearly desperately sick. The boy wondered why his fellows didn't help him. In the narrow alleys the darkness bubbled like a black river, thick with rats. The horses were loath to travel that way, and it took all Orsino's considerable skill to make his animal walk forward. This emboldened Edwin's horse to follow and lead Dowzabel's.

Dowzabel's hands had been untied since Bardi left. His captors had confidence he couldn't escape with his swollen ankle. Where would he go? Dow knew he lived in the west but had no idea how to get home and, besides, traveling alone, shoeless and branded, he could anticipate his fate. If the bad men didn't get him, then the good ones would.

He had no plan and felt utterly alone. Hell had not come to his aid, but he would not bow down before Heaven and beg. To take its charity would be to accept everything—the kings, the golden palaces, the churches that rose in beauty to the sky while the people froze, starved, and died in the filth of the streets.

They were traveling now along a row of rich houses that lined the river—they seemed to frown down at him, their roofs of slate like the flat black caps of the Plymouth magistrates.

"Turn here." They went up a narrow lane of smaller houses, the path no wider than a stream between them. Orsino ducked as the lower gables of the houses threatened to bash his head. The smoke of hearth fires lay low and bitter on the street, and it was as if they moved through a moorland mist. Down a tiny alley between two walls, they came to a gate secured by a lock.

"The horses can stay within," said Edwin.

He opened the gate to reveal an overgrown patch of land. The men led the horses inside, and Dowzabel saw the garden had its own well. Orsino drew up a bucket and let the animals drink.

"At least the horses will gobble up these weeds," said Orsino. "A wonder your congregation don't talk about this."

"I have the same gardener who was in Eden," said Edwin.

"Well, you want to sack him and get a better one," said Orsino.

Edwin rolled his eyes at the bad joke.

"Doesn't your curate help? Do you not have a housekeeper?" said Orsino.

"No other clergy live here," said Edwin. "My work forbids housekeepers or any others."

"Well, you've got the boy now," said Orsino. "You can set him to cook and clean once he's back on his feet."

Edwin snorted and went inside the house. Dowzabel and Orsino followed.

The boy thought that country villeins lived better than this man. The first room was filthy and there was a terrible stench of something burned in there.

"Someone's been in here," said Edwin. He held up his lamp, his gaze scanning the room.

"How can you tell?"

"The cellar door!"

He sprang out of the kitchen and Dowzabel heard him thumping down some stairs.

"Go down." Orsino prodded Dowzabel on in front of him.

The boy stumbled down into darkness and saw the flash of the lantern and heard a cry:

"I'm saved!"

By the flickering lamplight Dowzabel could see he was in a cellar. In the corner sat a man in the poor dress of a pardoner, a finger bone tied on a string about his neck. He had clearly been weeping, but now he had an expression of wild delight on his face. At his feet, chalked on the floor, was a magic circle like the one Dowzabel had seen in the burned church. The man stood and tried to come toward them. But then he stopped, as if uncertain of the ground in front of him.

"So this is why you have no housekeeper," said Orsino. He crossed himself. "You do some dark work, priest."

Edwin grunted. "Strange as it may seem, this devil is a servant of God."

"Friends, let me free," said the man in the corner. "Are you friends of the cardinal, sent to aid me? He said he'd help me—that great man spared me from the mob. Have you come to free me? I'm the victim of some sorcery. Look, a circle, this is why I can't leave here. Please, this is evil magic, free me!"

Orsino stood shaking his head. Edwin spoke. "This devil," he said, "is my spirit. He has many guises, though I have never seen this one before."

"He doesn't look very impressive," said Orsino.

"You're no Lancelot yourself," said the pardoner.

"One of his deceptions. I tell you, Condottiere, if he were to break this circle, I have no doubt he'd do worse than that thing we saw at the church."

Orsino asked the priest, "Why, if as you say he serves God?"

"I summoned him, pulled him from his purposes in this realm. And that makes me cursed in the eyes of God. Do you know what the bible says? A man also or woman who hath a familiar spirit, or who is a wizard, shall surely be put to death: they shall stone them with stones; their blood shall be upon them."

"Shall I fetch a rock?" said Orsino.

"No need, I will atone when my curiosity is slaked."

"Just let me out, noble fellows, let me out," said Osbert.

"This is a sly fellow, but I am privy to all his tricks," said Edwin.

"He led you to the boy?" said Orsino.

"Yes. And presently we'll have more out of him concerning the Drago. Who has been here, spirit? I command the truth by the high name of God!"

Dow felt none of the terror that had emanated from the priest devil at the church. Perhaps it was actually a demon! The priest was clearly playing "try my luck" with the spirits of Hell. Dow had to try to speak to it. He tried to use his thoughts, as he had done in the ruined church.

Why did Hell abandon me? Why did the demon mark me? Do you still want me to find the Drago? Dow received no reply.

The man said, "I am not a spirit. I was chased here by a mob. I was chased here. Sirs, I am but a poor pardoner. A good man who cares for the souls of others. If I have been ensorcelled, then break the spell. Let me free. I am a good man—it is not right to keep a good man so confined."

"It wants to kill the boy," said the priest. "He was protected on the moors."

"His tongue was mutilated there, he was branded, and he was abducted. How is that *protected*?" said Orsino.

"Protected from things more terrible than pincers and hot irons," said the priest.

"Protected from what and by what?" asked Orsino.

"By the rebels, from God. By demons, from servants of God—devils like this vile fellow in the circle."

"Hey!" said the pardoner. "I might be a little shabby, but plenty of women find me pleasing enough."

Edwin ignored him.

Orsino said, "So why is it not safe to release him?"

"Not everything that is of God is friendly to man. Consider the lion and the wolf. God made them both and they were pleasing to Him. I bargained with this devil to bring the boy here. I would deliver the boy to death once he had opened the great gate of Hell. But I have reneged on that bargain, as a bargain with a devil needn't be kept, although I have no doubt that, if it could, it would seek revenge."

"How can it be dangerous to a priest if it is of God?"

"*'I make peace and create evil, I the Lord do all these things.'* So says the Bible. God is more mysterious than you can know."

"So you won't give the boy to it?" said Orsino.

"He's too useful to be fed to a fiend. That much became apparent in that church. I want to keep it around longer. There are further bargains to be struck and, if I cannot have them softly—" he tapped one of his books—"I shall have them by force."

"What bargains?"

"For the only thing worth having. Knowledge." The priest's tongue flicked at his lips.

"You want to know how to save England?" said Orsino.

The priest laughed. "Perhaps that. Bardi would not let me keep the key unless I asked that. But these creatures can tell us so much about existence. There are mysteries, celestial and infernal. I would gaze upon them all."

"And why can't this fellow tell you that?"

"He has revealed a lot. I have begun to understand the nature of Hell. But this spirit is of a different order to what we saw at the burned church. That was a demon, and I had hoped to command him. This is a devil, a respecter of order, and so easier to direct. This fellow was licensed to leave Hell to seek the boy."

"For what?"

"To kill him," said Edwin. "He is an assassin."

"I could murder an ale, but that's about all," said the man in the circle. The man joked, though Dow thought he looked uncomfortable. Had he been sent to murder him? He didn't look like the men-at-arms who scoured the moor for his fellow outlaws. In fact, thought Dow, he looked as if an ale would stand a good chance of murdering *him*. For the first time since he had been taken, Dow smiled.

"I am tired," said Edwin, "and I need to regain my strength before confronting him again. I will sleep and tomorrow face him, using harsher strategies to pull out the truth. In the meantime, beat the boy as a lesson to him."

Dow felt his stomach skip.

"The kid's been beaten enough," said Orsino.

"If you won't do it, I will. He may try to escape and needs to learn what will happen if he does."

"I won't do it," said Orsino, "and neither will you."

"Do you defy the authority of the church?"

Orsino said nothing, but his gaze met the priest's eyes unwaveringly, saying clearly that twenty years' experience of fighting and a solid right fist were all the authority that mattered in this situation.

The priest moved his lips as if trying to expel a fish bone. He said, "Then you will be responsible for the boy remaining here."

"He will remain here. He can hardly walk, and even if he could, where has he got to go?" said Orsino.

"Very well. I'll show you where he's to be locked for the night." The priest made toward the stairs.

"Do not leave me!" shouted the man in the corner. "Do not leave me!"

But Edwin directed Dowzabel and Orsino back upstairs. The boy looked back at the thing in the corner. Even a devil was a rare fount of knowledge. Dow could find out what Hell wanted of him, why he had been burned.

"Stop staring at him and get up the stairs." The priest thrust his knuckle into Dowzabel's back, making him cry out in pain as he straightened up and stretched the skin over his burnt chest. "Don't give me that insolent look; I can whip you if I choose, no matter what the captain here says."

Dowzabel struggled up the stairs, Orsino behind him, and Edwin at the back with the light.

"Don't leave me! Don't leave me! I'm *not* a spirit. Look, there was a farmer who bought the skull of St. Anthony; there was a bowman who did the same, in Leadenhall by the goose stall. I was pursued. Ask them what I am—that's if they're still alive and haven't run from the country in fear!"

The man in the circle was frantic, wringing his hands and hopping on the spot as if his feet were on fire. But they did leave him, and, at the top of the stairs, Father Edwin set down his lamp, closed the door, and returned the cellar to darkness.

PART II

1338

❦ — ·· — ❦

In the year that King Charles of France, called the Wise, was born to Prince John and Queen Bonne and that King Edward's queen was delivered of a son, Lionel.

1

D unbar. Montagu was weary just saying the name. How long had his army been camped in front of those walls? Two months—not long in terms of a siege, but he had thought the castle would fall inside a fortnight. He'd ridden hard from the south coast to be there, almost believing that the siege would be over by the time he arrived in Scotland. It wasn't. Black Agnes—Countess Dunbar—and her hideous army were still holding out, despite the best pounding the English catapults could give them.

Every time Montagu allowed himself to think they'd had a breakthrough in the war in Scotland, they suffered a setback. It was just depressing. All the lands north of the Forth had been lost and Bothwell Castle reduced to a ruin by William Douglas. Montagu sometimes found it difficult to keep track of the shifting allegiances of the Scots. The English army was at Dunbar backing the claim to the Scottish throne of Edward Balliol, son of John, whom the Scots had first ignored until he was out of the way in exile. As soon as he'd left, they'd claimed him as their king, despite the fact that King John had clearly become sick of them by then and never wanted to feel heather beneath his feet again.

Montagu would rather face Douglas or any other Scotsman than the countess any day. After one particularly vicious assault by the siege engines, the woman had led her maids onto the walls of the castle and contemptuously dusted the debris away. Then, using one of the very stones that had been fired at her, she had managed to crush his best battering ram. It was March, and spring, though someone had forgotten to tell the Scottish weather, which clearly still thought it was January. Montagu shivered in the sleet as he dismounted from his horse.

He needed to take the castle soon. With the Scots active and the French raiding the channel and the eastern ports, the country was burning from both ends and one side. He returned the greetings and salutes of the army and nobles and he strode through the ranks of wet tents. He was tired and sore, but he knew the importance of communicating health and vigor to his troops.

"How goes it, cousin?"

Hugh De La Spencer, a young noble in a pale blue surcoat marked with golden doves, came running to meet Montagu. He was wrapped in so many scarfs Montagu could hardly see his face. The boy was known by his middle name of George, to distinguish him from his father—the late Hugh Despenser, in Montagu's opinion the worst man who ever lived.

"As ever, Lord Salisbury."

"No sign of them cracking?" Montagu asked.

George said, "I'm afraid the countess's resolve is firm, sir."

Montagu rolled his eyes. "The woman constitutes an entire second front just on her own."

"She is a remarkable lady, sir, but we have one piece of good news."

"What?"

"We've caught her brother, the earl of Moray."

"Really? Oh, he's a good fellow—I've met him at a tournament. Send him to me when you have a minute."

"Very good."

Twenty paces away, Montagu noticed someone staring at him. He was a very thin, brown fellow in tattered clothes—just rags tied about his feet for shoes.

George saw him too. He said, "Go away, villein, you can have nothing to say to the lord."

"Great Lord Montagu." The man dropped to his knees in the freezing mud.

"If you want food, my man, I suggest you commend yourself to one of our engineers or other useful men. We work for our living in this army," said Montagu.

"Sir, I would speak with you."

"Do you think the earl of Salisbury spends his time consorting with beggars?" said George. "I'm sorry, my lord, he's been here nearly as long as we have and has been asking after you daily. I've grown tired of beating him, though I can again if it pleases you."

The man put out his hands, imploring him. He said, "I am of Corfe. Of Corfe Castle. I would speak to you. I have news of the king."

"I've just come from the king; you can have no news I don't know."

"The old king, sir. King Edward that was, not King Edward that is. Of what happened at Corfe."

That got Montagu's interest. "What news? He's been dead ten years."

"I would speak with you alone."

Montagu pondered for an instant. "You'll have as long as it takes them to fetch me some dry clothes," said Montagu. "George, I'll take your tent to speak to him. In the meantime throw up a scaffold—a big one—right in front of her walls where she normally appears. Threaten to hang Moray. See if that softens her up a bit."

"Yes, sir. Though I wouldn't count on it."

"Neither would I, neither would I. If it doesn't work, bring him back here and I'll take dinner with him later."

George led Montagu to his tent, the beggar trailing behind.

It was a small affair in stained yellow canvas, but dry and with a comfortable couch. How different George was from his father, the notorious Hugh Despenser, favorite of King Edward II, his lover, his bewitcher, it was said. The older Hugh's tent had been bigger than the king's, stuffed with precious things, silks and gold, and giving the impression of staging a permanent banquet.

Yet George had hardly known his father. His mother felt betrayed by her husband for misleading the old King Edward into tyranny, and she never spoke of him. And when Mortimer—the Mortimer as old Edward had known him, giving him a name as if he was a pox you could catch— had thrown down old Edward and Despenser, he had killed everyone in Despenser's immediate retinue too. Legend had it that he'd drawn and quartered his hunting dogs and horses into the bargain. Montagu knew this to be untrue—Mortimer was far too mean to throw valuable animals away like that. Despenser's greyhounds alone had been worth a fortune.

But the Mortimer had, in his own words, "burned the weed to the root"—even imprisoning Despenser's wife for a time and forcing his daughters into nunneries. Young George had been saved only because he had been raised well away from his father—partly, guessed Montagu, for his own protection. His mother had seen trouble coming. When finally freed, the woman had run off with Walter De La Zouche. First, however, she had burned Despenser's family castle at Hanley—clear proof, people said, that she abhorred his memory. People said other things too—Hugh had been sent from the Devil. But the low people said that about anyone they didn't like. Mind you, they said it an awful lot about Hugh.

Montagu sat down and helped himself to the young man's wine. He breathed in the smell of the tent. Camp life. It was all he'd known since he'd been fourteen years old. Sieges, battles, expeditions. For a second he wondered what it would be like to turn his back on it, sit in some castle or manor house warm and snug for the rest of his days. Boring, probably.

The beggar shuffled into the tent. Montagu picked up a loaf, tore off a bite, and ate.

He said to him, "Say what you've got to say, man."

"Sir. I beg your pardon and ask indulgence of your greatness, I being . . ."

"Cut out the fawning and slice into the meat of it, fellow."

The man looked uncomprehending.

"Say your piece directly," said Montagu.

"I am John Lockey, formerly of Corfe Castle."

"You've come a long way masterless, Lockey."

"I heard your army was in Scotland, sir. You are the new king's most trusted friend and have a reputation as a gentle and noble lord."

"Have I? Perhaps I should do something about that; it never does for low men to think their masters too mild. Why have you come from Corfe? You could have saved yourself a trip; I was down in Southampton not a month ago."

"I didn't know that, sir. Only that your army was here."

"Indeed. So you worked for old Edward's gaoler, Berkeley?"

"I did work for that mighty lord. And it is in that capacity that I came to know what you must know."

"Get on with it." Montagu sipped at the wine.

"There was a rumor among the servants."

"There is always a rumor among the servants. I hope you're not wasting my time, Lockey."

"No, sir, I saw them."

"Who?"

"The king, the king and the angel. They were there until nine years ago, I swear it."

"The king is in Windsor."

Lockey said, "I mean the old king, sir—old Edward."

Montagu put down his cup of wine. "Rubbish."

"I swear it, sir; in Christ's name I swear it. I would not risk my life to bring you this news were it not so."

"Rubbish, I say again. You are lying and now you have blasphemed against Heaven and will hang."

"Please no, sir! I got drunk, sir, and on a dare I went to the tower to see who the prisoner was. We knew we had a prisoner and that he was an important one, but people said he was all sorts of people. One of the Despensers, I thought. We were all in a curiosity to know, so I snuck in there to see him."

Montagu found this amusing. "You're a brave fellow when you're drunk. The Despensers aren't the sort to tolerate paupers crawling to their rooms at midnight. Hugh Despenser had Lady Baret's arms and legs broken until she went mad. Don't think he even quite knew what she'd done to offend him. What he'd do to a sneaking villein beggars the imagination."

"I didn't think of that, sir. There are ways up that tower that only the servants use and the old doors have holes in them. I thought I'd just take a look."

"What did you see?"

"A man. And light. More light than I've ever seen. Light everywhere. And something snapping, sir. A red serpent that crawled and spat."

"What did you take that to be?"

"I heard the man's name—Edward. The light said his name and I know that doesn't make sense, but it did. It was the old king, I'm sure, and he was with a bright, bright angel and they were fighting the Devil."

"Old Edward died nearly ten years ago at Berkeley Castle. I was at the funeral myself and saw the usurper Mortimer who had him killed smirking in the corner of the abbey. You've wasted my time."

"But I was told, sir, to come and see you—it told me."

"An angel spoke to a pauper? Well, now I am sure you're lying."

"Not the angel, sir. No. The serpent. The serpent told me to find you and say what I had seen."

Montagu leaned back on the couch, stretching. He said, "And it took you nine years?"

"I couldn't leave Corfe—I was tied to the land. And then I was thrown out for drinking and I feared I should starve. You and your generosity are all that stand between me and the grave, sir. I am telling the truth; I implore you to believe me."

Montagu leaned forward, putting his forearms onto his knees. Something about the man suggested he should not dismiss him. "What did he look like? What did the king look like?" he asked.

"He was a very tall man, sir."

"Everyone in England knows that."

"But the serpent, sir—it said it had a message for you."

"What message?" Montagu's patience was coming to an end.

"*Verus Rex ago. Pede poena claudo.*' It said you would know it to be a true message by those words."

Montagu found that he had stood up.

It was unusual enough to hear a villein speaking Latin, but what he had just said was remarkable. *The true king lives. Punishment comes limping.* It was conceivable that a pauper might have learned some Latin by rote to perpetrate a fraud. But he had given code words—the ones Edward III had used to verify his letters to Montagu when they were planning the rebellion against Mortimer. *Pede poena claudo!* Two people in the world knew that secret—Edward and himself. Montagu reached and took up the cup of wine from the camp table, swigging the last of it down. He was trying to escape the conclusion that he'd just received a direct message from the Devil.

He stood gawping at Lockey for a moment.

"I need to think about this," he said. "Who have you told?"

"No one, sir. I wouldn't have told you if I wasn't desperate. I don't want people thinking I consort with devils."

Montagu had been knocked from his horse in a tournament more than twenty times, yet never had he felt as disorientated as he did just then.

"No angels in England," he said under his breath.

The most logical explanation—the one that no one seemed to have thought of—was also the most extraordinary. The angels spoke to the king or the queen, God's proxy, appointed by Him. All contact with an angel had to be through the rightful king. Young Edward had been crowned, the third Norman king of his name, in Westminster Abbey, under the eyes of man and God. The angels were duty-bound to come to him. There could be no other way. Unless his father was still alive. Then young Edward was not God's king and the angels would stay away.

Montagu stood staring at the ragged man in front of him, hardly able to take in the implications of what he'd been told.

Edward II had died ten years before, almost to the day. Montagu remembered Westminster Abbey—the hearse shining with golden adornments, a leopard on the top; the four evangelists, each to a corner; eight incense burners in the form of angels; rampant leopards at each side. He had never seen so many candles—it was almost as if the king's effigy on top of his coffin floated on fire. All that splendor for the king the English people had gladly seen fall.

They'd given his heart in a silver vase to Isabella, his queen, who had always asked that her heart be buried with his. Her lover Mortimer, the evil dog who'd had the king killed, had the spleen to shed a tear. People whispered that he wept because he knew his soul was bound for Hell. Edward had died quickly after the rebellion, and there had always been the suspicion that Mortimer had killed him, a suspicion that had taken on the status of fact after young Edward had overthrown Mortimer and had him executed at Tyburn.

Mortimer had been found guilty of the king's death in front of Parliament. But they hadn't let Mortimer speak—he'd been tried bound and gagged. Who had ordered that? What were they afraid he might say? *No, wait.* Montagu wasn't thinking clearly. Mortimer had never been charged with killing the king. He had been charged with appropriating royal power. It was just that, in the years following his death, people had begun to assume

Mortimer had been tried for the king's death. Where had that idea come from?

Montagu tasted salt on his lips. Sweat. If the old king wasn't dead then . . . He couldn't think what. He felt utterly ill-equipped to consider the implications. Words flashed through his mind. "Disaster," "treason," "blight on the land." It was the end of everything.

Montagu took out his purse. "How much will it cost you to drink yourself to death?" he said.

"I don't know, sir."

"Three pounds should do it." Montagu took out his purse. He counted sixty shillings onto the table and waved for the villein to take them. He did, almost leaping forward.

"Now get out and never relate this to anyone."

The man left the tent as if pursued. Montagu had thought to take the precaution of hanging him, but no one would listen to a beggar with tales of old Edward—no one who mattered would believe him. He himself hadn't, until the man had uttered the code words. And Montagu almost felt pity. How desperate must a man be to walk the length of the land on the chance his story might earn him some small coin? Montagu's entire upbringing made him haughty and dismissive with low men—any noble behaving otherwise would be considered weak by the villeins—but he did have some sympathy for them in their sufferings.

"Is this all fine words? Are you a coward, Montagu?" he said to himself. "Afraid to lay a paw on the devil's messenger?" Maybe. Maybe not.

He picked up his sword and kissed its hilt. The sword was called Arondight, said to be the one that knight nonpareil Lancelot had carried in service of King Arthur. Inside the pommel was a tooth of St. Anne. He prayed and tried to raise the saint in his thoughts, asking her to fulfill the role of all saints and petition God on his behalf. He closed his eyes, trying to feel the presence of the blessed lady. Was she there? A cool blue light was in his mind, a movement of robes, a gentle presence.

"Glorious St. Anne, I humbly beg of you to take the present affair that I recommend to you under your special protection. Vouchsafe to recommend it to your daughter, the Blessed Virgin Mary, and lay it before the throne of Jesus, so that He may bring it to a happy issue. Cease not to intercede for

me until my request is granted. Show me the truth of old Edward's death."
He swallowed and crossed himself, chasing away the thought that came
unbidden into his mind.

"And let him be dead."

He thought of a letter he'd received nearly six years before, from Queen
Philippa—young Edward's bride. She had begged him to find a way to persuade her husband to look into the circumstances of Mortimer's rebellion,
how he had defeated the king and his angels. The king had dismissed her
worries. He had been with Mortimer and Isabella as they landed to face his
father—a boy subject to the control of his mother. But still man enough to
see what was going on. The angels had appeared but declined to fight for
his father, and now they were now failing to appear for him, very likely in
anger at the way he had come to the throne. There was no more to discover.

Montagu thought for a long time about what he would do. Could he trust
this business to a subordinate? No, he must investigate it himself.

An angel could only be raised, even by the king, in a properly sanctified
space. Money would have to be spent on gold and fine things for the altar.
If Edward had been summoning angels at Corfe, some trace of those things
might exist. And he needed to visit Berkeley too—the castle where Edward
was said to have been killed.

There was a cough and George stepped into the tent.

"The scaffold's up, sir," said George.

"Didn't take long."

"We made use of a tree, sir."

"Have you threatened to hang the earl of Moray?"

"Yes."

"What does the countess say to that?"

"She seems quite pleased, sir. She says she'll inherit and substantially
increase her lands."

Montagu put his head into his hands. "Well, of all my troubles, at least
I'm not married to Black Agnes. Can you imagine trying to bring a woman
like that to obedience?"

"It's why the earl of Dunbar is always in the field. They say he'd rather
face the English in the open than his wife in his own castle. What of Moray?
Shall I hang him anyway, sir?"

"No, I'll go to my tent and take dinner. Send him in there; I'll dine with the earl. And get my squires to repack my kit. We're going south again tomorrow."

If old Edward were alive, thought Montagu, then England really was doomed. The old king had been a useless and ineffectual man, even backed by angels. He had been ruled by favorites and led into terrible tyranny. While he lived, there had always been the possibility that some ambitious group of nobles would find him and use him as a figurehead to reclaim the throne and overthrow young Edward.

But he *had* been anointed king. Montagu, raised on chivalry and obedience, could not think beyond that fact. If still alive, he must be restored, no matter what the cost. What were the implications for young Edward? He would be a usurper, abhorred of God. That was as serious a charge as Montagu could imagine.

Rebel thoughts came into his head—if old Edward *were* still alive, someone would have to find him and kill him. Which would mean that someone would save England but be damned himself. He would die a hero but go to Hell. *How brave are you, William? Easy to risk your life, what about your soul? Insupportable!* God had put old Edward on the throne and nothing could remove him, not abdication, not exile. Only death. If England's king *was* a usurper, as young Edward might be, the country's fall was inevitable. God would not tolerate such an affront for long.

To act or refrain? The young Edward was so much the better king than his father, and was Montagu's friend, but the path of chivalry, duty, and godliness was clear. Montagu must seek the truth. If the old king still lived, he must be restored, however hateful the thought. It was not up to Montagu to question the will of God, only to enact it. He would travel south in the morning to speak to Berkeley, in whose castle the king had supposedly been murdered, hoping that the old knight would tell him he had seen old Edward butchered with his own eyes.

Montagu crossed himself and kissed the pommel of his sword. God would provide the answer. He had to trust to Him.

2

M idnight was different in the city, Dow thought. The moor
was still at that time, just the moon and the deep stars to see
by, the Devil's Men all around him, lying close for warmth.
In London there were strange sounds everywhere—people hallooing one
another in the dark, drunken men mainly, riding past, calling to whores to
come out. Dow understood well that night in the city belonged to the city
watch and those either too rich or too poor to bother about the law. Dogs
barked and the bell tolled the hours. He'd been there months now and still
was unused to it.

Every night he lay on the floor of the little room in complete darkness. Dowzabel had never known such blackness—no windows meant
no light at all. On the door and the wall were wards and symbols—the
names of God and the angels, the signs of planets and the zodiac—to save
him, Edwin said, from Hell's rescue. He felt their presence even when he
couldn't see them.

Part of Dow almost wanted to stay, just to rest and to think. Orsino had
found him a straw mattress and bought him a thick cloak. He had thought
at first to reject the gifts, but he had been so cold every night since he had
been taken that, lonely and scared, he had accepted these small comforts.
Had Hell really deserted him? The demon had branded him, as the priest
had branded him. And yet when he had spoken to it with his mind, he'd felt
its warmth, its love for him, even. Dow was very confused.

The Florentine's kindness surprised him. The followers of Heaven had only ever brought him pain before. He couldn't quite believe that the man wasn't going to hector or beat him. The straw was softer than anything he'd ever lain on, fresh and free from bugs.

He was heartsick and he would not sleep. His captors were fools if they thought Dow would not try to return home when he was fit.

Matins rang out at a distant monastery, a long lonely peal through the city's empty spaces. It was well after midnight now and would be cold on the streets. December had brought snow, January too, and his ankle would still not support his weight. The Florentine had wrapped it tightly in bandages, saying they would have to see how badly it was broken—if it healed deformed.

Orsino said he'd like to train him as a soldier—that being a cripple wouldn't necessarily prevent that. The priest had talked of using him as an assistant, though never called him to the cellar. Neither of those things would happen, Dow vowed. February blew in, raw, cold. He could just about walk and the swelling was much less. By March it was time to leave.

The room was warmer than any shelter he had ever known, and it was difficult to leave its comfort. Still, he would. He touched his chest. Orsino had been kind to him, Dow couldn't deny. He had brought him salves of comfrey, lavender, and vinegar that stung terribly but had helped. Now it was healed—just about.

He crawled through the darkness across the floor toward the door, careful of his footing, feeling his way. He had assessed the door as no real barrier on the way in. The Devil's Men, when times were bad, would ghost into Bodmin, stealing from the houses of merchants to sustain themselves. Abbadon had shown him how foolish householders had concentrated on good locks, forgetting about the state of their warped and bent doors. This door did not have a particularly good lock and it was certainly warped—crudely fashioned from cheap oak planks. It also had a good thumb's width gap beneath it into which he could work his fingers, plus a bigger gap at the top. It was all Dow needed.

He rocked the door back and forth, as quietly as he could, pulling hard against the hinges as he moved it upward, loosening the rivets. In a few minutes the door had enough play in it for him to shove it back against its jamb and get the tongue of the lock free of the recess in which it sat.

It was sightless dark in the passageway too. Dow couldn't risk standing for long, so he crawled carefully to the kitchen, every movement threatening to betray him. Here there was a small window—its shutter broken—and the moon outside was strong enough for him to see by. It was cold in there, though he knew it was only a taste of what was to come. The horses outside were blanketed, blowing steam in the moonlight. Dow found the back door. It was secured by a bolt. He drew it back and crept into the garden.

The horses were undisturbed by his presence. He thought to take one, but he would not give the priest an excuse to hang him. It was very quiet now, the last drunken noblemen gone home. Dow lifted the latch on the gate and went out into the narrow alley. Here he stood, his ankle still feeling weak, though not painful. A rat scuttled by his feet. He went on.

At the top of the alley he had a view of St. Olave's, boxy, spireless, and squat, overlooking a wide thoroughfare. Dowzabel couldn't risk spending too long on that road—the city watch might see him. Once across it, though, he would be free of the Florentine and the priest. London was a forest and its paths were many—three streets away in the town was as good as thirty miles in open country. They'd never find him.

Dow loped toward some grand houses across the street. With a tangle of alleys in front of him—five in all, each splitting and turning through houses and gardens; he chose one at random. He was going as quickly as he could now, hugging the side of the alleyway.

Down a tight little lane, he thought he saw movement. Not a dog, Dowzabel hoped, as he had no stick to fend it off. He took another alley, to his right. Movement in front of him again. Was it a dog? It wasn't.

Something was on the air. Smoke. In the washed-out moonlight he could see it now, pooling about his feet. Was a house on fire? Should he raise the alarm?

And then it wasn't as dark anymore. Ahead of him was a deep crimson light. Stepping toward him from the retreating shadows came a man dressed all in red, with a broad red hat on his head. In one hand, a lantern with a candle in it, in his belt, a dagger. Then the man opened his mouth revealing a fire, burning as fiercely as any Dow had ever seen.

"Unwarded, unguarded, and alone," said the man, his voice like the crackling of a kindling fire.

The thing stretched a hand toward him. Panic overwhelmed Dow, even as some strange empathy awoke in him. He sensed the boredom and hunger of the dogs of the city; the dulled emotions of a whore sleeping above a cheap inn by the river; even the burbling, bellicose attitude of a rich young man climbing the stairs to bed in a nearby fine house. And Dow knew what the "man" in front of him was feeling: He was nervous.

The creature was sweating heavily. His mouth leaked smoke, making the alley hazy. Dow could not move. He came toward Dow, his hand spraying red light, his fingers huge talons of light. The man was a devil, Dow was sure. The devil wanted to touch him, but he was uncertain.

His fingers were at Dow's shirt and were not now light but flesh, hot and clammy, with great black nails. Dow managed to step back and the hand drew away.

Dow felt so hot. He threw off his cloak. Why didn't he call out? Why didn't he run? He didn't know. It seemed as though he was in a strange dream world where everyday actions were odd and puzzling, unthinkable, even.

The creature's hand returned to Dow's chest. *No!* The burn on the boy's chest was fire again, scalding and hot as when the demon had first touched him, as when the priest had branded him. He cried out, but the devil was on him. He had his fingers in Dow's throat, stuffing them down, trying to choke Dow, his nails ripping at the flesh of his tongue. The smell of burning was all around him—burning his hair and skin. The creature's robes were painful to touch, so hot they were, and reeked of smoke.

"You die as you were drawn here to die," said the creature. "Eden is saved."

Dow could not cry out as the scorching fingers were forced farther and farther down his throat. He bit down hard, but the thing didn't even seem to feel it.

The burn on his chest pulsed and sizzled. As the devil pulled Dow's head down, the boy could see his own livid scar, exposed and glowing, like fire itself, like metal in a mold, a moving, living thing. The demon Paimon's claws had changed the T of the priest's brand to a new shape—a three-pronged fork. This pitchfork on his chest was the symbol of Lucifer, the symbol of demons.

Dow knew the story—how Îthekter had sent the bright angels into Hell and had devils torment them with hot forks. But the demons—as the angels had become—rebelled again, fought their tormentors, and took their weapons, setting up their own cities in Hell. They turned the symbol of their captivity into that of their freedom, as the peasants could turn the instrument of their toil to that of their liberation. And there it was, burning bright on his chest, Lucifer's sign, the sign denoting he had the protection of the lord of Free Hell.

A bell was ringing—three times for Terce. He heard cocks crowing in the new day, the stir of animals and humans. Not dawn yet, but there was a light, a pure light, like the morning. From where? His vision blurred.

Dow desperately wanted to vomit, but his breath was choked. The thing was too strong. Without thinking properly, he put his left hand to his chest. He heard a voice.

"Such light, such light, where is the light?"

The devil snatched his fingers out of Dow's throat and turned. Dow fell down, but, as he did, he saw a woman, so beautiful that even in his agony he registered it.

She was small and dark-haired, her skin like snow and her lips like red berries. The rich dress of brilliant deep green she wore was stained and dirty and torn at the bottom. But she seemed to have stopped time, to have drawn the attention of creation to her, everything but she: his pain, the devil, the cold earth of the street against his cheek, was irrelevant.

"You!" said the devil, a red light flashing from the furnace of his mouth.

Dow got to his feet. His mouth was full of blood.

The devil pulled out a long dagger, wicked, curved, and thin. "Well, Hell knows your tricks, lady, and has ways to stop them!"

The devil stepped toward her, but Dow leapt at him. He instinctively wanted to protect the woman. His hands and arms burned as they seized the devil. The devil's entire body was scorching hot, and the thing shook him off like a dog shakes off water.

But then it was like dawn in the street. The lady was looking about her, up to the heavens. The light was coming from her!

"Oh no, don't make me shine! It hurts so much to shine through this flesh."

The light intensified, burning ever brighter. The woman cried out as if in agony, and all around was light. Nothing else, white, burning, cleansing light.

Dow was momentarily blinded, and when he had recovered his sight, the devil was gone. Only its dagger remained. The woman in the dress lay unconscious on the ground.

He heard voices, far off. The city watch were shouting to one another, but they were not near. His tongue and throat were terribly raw, the root of the tongue, in particular, lacerated by the devil's nails. But his only thoughts were to get this lady off the street before thieves or the city watch found him. Dow hobbled toward the woman, putting his hand to her chest. She was still breathing.

Despite her tattered clothes, she looked like a very rich lady, but he would neither rob nor leave her. She had saved him. He stuck the dagger into the back of the belt of his trousers and adjusted his cloak to cover it. Then he picked her up. It was awkward to lift her with his still unreliable ankle, but she was much lighter than he expected. Dowzabel carried her in his arms, back toward the priest's house.

Free Hell had protected him, called this woman to him, and driven the devil away. Was she a demon? He hoped so. Even if she were not, his course was set. Free Hell wanted the saint's banner found, Free Hell would have the banner. He would go back to the priest, he would learn his art; Dow would let the soldier teach him to fight. And when he had learned what he could, he would kill the priest, kill the soldier, and use what they had taught him to follow the will of Lucifer, lightbringer, downthrower, Lord of the Dawn.

3

H unting is not a seemly activity for a boy of his age," said Prince John. Two troubadours, gaudy as parrots, sat on either side of him on a couch. One held a lute, the other—who had been singing—now simply stared like a coshed eel at King Philip and the phalanx of courtiers behind him.

The boy Charles pranced about the prince's oak-paneled room of retreat in a splendid blue skirt adorned with paste jewels in amber and red. On his head he wore a little basinet and he carried a wooden sword in his hand. In the year he'd been at the court, he had become a great favorite of Prince John. Charles liked the idea of hunting, and spring had finally arrived, but he felt slightly self-conscious at the king's sudden interest in him.

"I shall hunt dragons!" he said.

The king said, "The boy isn't like you, John—he wants to hunt. Look at him in his sword and helmet. He's six years old now and can drag along on a pony as well as any of the other highborn sons."

"He's acting out a romance. We're interesting him in poetry. Minstrels, play an air for the king so he might see the boy hop and dance."

The king gave the minstrels a look that suggested they might do well to remain silent and they shuffled on the couch, apparently suddenly struck by indecision about what to play.

"I will dance for Prince John, the cleverest uncle in the world!" said the boy.

The king ignored him. "It's a good spring. The hares are running and the boars are grunting and ready to test our mettle. The boy will hunt with me tomorrow."

"It might rain," said John. "Children die of chills and you know, Father, how awfully fond of him I am."

"It's fine sunshine. If it rains he can shelter under a tree."

"And what if it's struck by lightning? Play, minstrels, play!"

The lute player plucked anemically at his strings while the singer made a sort of uncommitted hum that could have been classed as singing by a prince or not singing by a king.

"The boy hunts!" said Philip. "And I'll hear no more about it!"

The king turned smartly and left the room.

"Well, we shall go with Charles, shan't we, boys?" said John. "And if he is to hunt, let him hunt something fun. Would you like to hunt a dragon, dear Charles?"

"I would!" said the boy.

"Then let's go to my wife and her ladies and see if they can conjure a dragon!"

The prince leapt up so enthusiastically that the lute player was forced to lift his instrument abruptly to prevent it being dashed to the floor.

At Vincennes the next day, Charles found himself mounted on a placid pony, looking out into the great wood. John had dressed him as St. George, with the red cross on his white coat and his own wooden spear. Charles felt mildly self-conscious. Edward in England had adopted the saint as his own, and relations with France were not good. It was rumored the English king was raising an army to attack through his lands in Aquitaine and Gascony, and the Norman lords were siding with him—along with the counts of Flanders.

Charles's mother, Queen Joan—who had gone up to visit relatives in the north of France in the Agenais—kept her son well informed, in person when she was there or by letter through Count Ramon when she was away. Charles found it easy to follow the broad nature of the alliances, particularly as Count Ramon helped spell them out to him with chess pieces.

"Here is the French king," he said. "And here the English. The English one should bow to the French as he owes him homage for squares he owns in his land. But he will not bow. He thinks the board is wrong—he should change places, the white king become the black. This is why he's currently stomping all over our northern towns with his army. And we're stomping back, I should add."

He picked up a white and a black pawn and bashed them into each other.

"Now the white pawns are the English king's men. Most of these pawns are to be loaned by the Holy Roman Empire in Germany. Though they might *not* be, because that emperor, who is on another board, might decide to keep them. Here are the castles. These are Edward's lands in Gascony. Very valuable. The French king is attacking those. And his bishops—well, those are the godless weavers of Flanders who overthrew their masters. The English knights—we'll say those are the various lords of the flatlands, the duke of Guelders, Louis of Nevers. The queen?—is his angels. Not been seen for a while—may move late in the game.

"For France we have the wild Scots under King David. They can be the French knights. They can launch sudden surprise attacks but aren't going to win the game on their own. We have various wavering allies—Normans, for instance. Then there's us. We have to be the queen, don't we—the Navarrese? Very important. Most of the rest of the field belongs to Philip. He's much less dependent on allies, though he buys some in—they can be the bishops—Genoese with their crossbows and galleys. Very, very useful. The rooks are the angels."

"Why is the English angel a queen and the French a rook?"

"More of 'em and move sooner," Ramon had said.

"We're going to invade soon, though, aren't we? Invade England."

"Yes. I should think so."

"Then what happens?"

Ramon smiled and sent all the white pieces clattering to the floor.

"That," he said.

In the woods, Charles tried to pretend he was a knight preparing for a battle, ready to run down the English boar—as he'd heard Edward called.

King Philip's retinue—all splendidly dressed in coats of green, turquoise, and scarlet, their horses adorned with fine brasses, boar spears glinting in the sun—drummed up a hubbub of talk as they prepared to hunt. Charles felt proud to be included in such a throng—nearly three hundred people including pages, servants, squires, grooms, and minstrels; not to mention the hangers-on from the outlying villages who had come to watch, to sell, to cheer, and to offer whatever service could be imagined. A smith had set up an impromptu forge, a saddler had his wares laid out, piemen and priests moved among the throng. The dogs were baying up a storm, falcons cut curves in the air, and elegant ladies sat on fine horses while servants strung their bows for them.

"How shall they ever find a boar with all this noise?" said Charles.

"They'll find one," said Count Ramon, dressed in unflattering red, with a cap like a cockerel's comb on his head, in honor of his French hosts. "In fact, I think they've already found one."

"What do you mean?"

"The king has hunters and trappers in these forests," said Ramon. "There'll be one in a cage—maybe more—hidden around here. When the hunt starts they'll let it go."

"That saves a lot of grubbing and makes him look good in front of his people!" said Charles.

"As ever, my lord, you grasp the truth of a situation very well."

"Charles, come, come!"

John was waving to him. He was dressed in scarlet riding braies, an extravagant padded pourpoint coat, blue with golden fleurs-de-lys, topped by a huge stag mask, complete with fur. It was dotted with little sapphires, and its eyes were glittering yellow topaz.

"Be careful the hounds do not mistake you, Uncle!" called Charles.

"They might, cousin, they might! I am king of the hunt, am I not?"

"You are, you are!" Charles was always careful to look excited in the presence of his idiot uncle, as his mother had impressed upon him to do.

Charles pulled his pony alongside John's. "I wonder you can ride such a fine horse," he said. "I'm sure no other rider in the land could take him in hand."

"I am the only one who can ride him!" said John. "He's a fire-breather—you're right about that, you rascal. But we have other fire-breathers to contend with! What's that up ahead? What is it you spy, young hunter?"

Charles put his hand to his eyes. In the trees there was a flash of vivid green. "What is it?"

"Let's go and see. Be careful with your spear now; you may need it at any point—there are dragons in these woods for sure."

"John, the boy comes with us!" Philip was shouting over to his son.

"You wanted him to hunt, Father, he's hunting, as am I. There's no nobler prey than the dragon—I could be St. George himself!"

"Haven't the English rather bagged that saint?" said Philip. "You'll make him a traitor."

"I will make him a hero!"

Charles rode his pony into the woods after John, Ramon trotting beside him. There, about fifty paces from him through the trees, was a dragon, next to a horse. Or rather it was very clearly one of the prince's acrobats dressed up as a dragon, a long stuffed tail behind him, ridges on his back, and a crocodilian snout covering his head.

A stream of red leapt from its mouth. It was breathing fire! Charles realized, to his delight, that the acrobat had just put a roll of scarlet cloth to his lips and flicked it out suddenly.

"Shall we spear this saucy fellow?" said John.

"Let's run him through!"

The two princes trotted toward the dragon, but the dragon didn't stay where he was. He jumped onto a horse and began to trot away himself.

"Blow your horn, cousin, blow your horn!" shouted John.

Charles put the horn to his lips and blew. All the prince's retinue came lolloping after him—ladies, fools, poets, and minstrels all whooping and shouting. Two darker figures, horsemen who peeled away from the king's party, followed on too.

Charles galumphed through the woods, John at his side, Ramon trotting behind so as to sustain the conceit he couldn't outpace the royalty. His French uncle irritated Charles normally—too friendly too quickly, too sure he knew what was on the boy's mind, and inclined to treat Charles as nothing more than a performing monkey. But Charles was enjoying leading the hunt and felt a childish pride in being first through the trees.

"Oh, in name of Christ, where has the dragon gone?" said John. "He's going too quickly. Someone go and get him, and tell him he's going too quickly!"

John put his spurs into his horse and Charles kicked his pony to keep up. But John, a good rider on an excellent horse, outran him easily and Charles quickly found himself swallowed up by the mob of cavorting courtiers.

"There he is!" one of the riders who had come from the king's party cried out. Through the trees, nearby there was a flash of green.

"Follow the prince!" shouted a brightly clad squire.

"Kill the dragon!" shouted a squeaky-voiced lady.

"Be careful, in the name of God!" Ramon cried out—a man dressed as a fool had run his horse straight into the count, unseating him. No one seemed to notice.

The main body of the riders lummoxed on after John, but a group of about ten split to pursue the green that had been seen through the trees. Charles, following the prince, suddenly found a presence at his side. A rider he did not recognize from the court caught his bridle.

"Let's steal a march on your uncle John!" he said. "Let's spear that dragon before he does!"

"Let me go! Do you presume to touch royalty? Let me go, you base fool!"

But the man did not let go. He spurred his horse forward, tugging at the pony's bridle and pulling the animal into a reluctant gallop. They tore through the trees, outstripping the ladies and minstrels who had split from the prince, racing toward where the dragon had appeared. Charles was not an idiot and knew he was in the grip of an assassin. His mouth went dry, his heart raced, and he tried to summon the courage to leap from the pony, but he couldn't. He abandoned its reins and clung to its mane as the trees flashed by. The more he willed himself to jump, the tighter he clung.

The boar came from nowhere. There was a rattle and a great squeal and it rushed past him, fast as a gunstone. Screams from the ladies behind him. The rider was tearing at the bridle, the pony fretting, whinnying as it ran, the rider forcing it on.

Another rider came to the other side of the pony.

"We've lost them," he said, and shoved Charles from his saddle.

The green of the trees blurred, the brown of the floor rushed up at him. He fell. The whole experience had the quality of a memory, even as it was happening. He smelled blood in his nostrils, the leaves on the ground, had the taste of soil in his mouth. His shoulder struck first, then his head. Everything was slow and fast at the same time.

Bang! He was winded, dizzy; he tried to stand but a rider was coming for him full tilt, trying to charge him down. Charles rolled away—by luck more than judgment—as a hoof smashed into the ground beside his head, but the second man had dismounted and was running toward him with a knife. It was clear to Charles he was in mortal danger, but the knock to his head had disoriented him, and he just sat watching as the man ran at him.

A noise. A heavy breath. Something beside him in the trees—a man of blood. All blood. Red robes, a red hat, his face hanging down in tatters, his eye socket exposed, his ears burned and charred. He was on all fours, panting like a dog, but in his hand he carried, bizarrely, a lighted candle.

The man with the knife stopped. The other horseman had come around and was staring down too.

"What in the name of Satan are you?"

"His servant," said the tattered man. He swallowed the candle.

"He looks like a cardinal. What's wrong with his face? I don't like this," said the man with the knife.

"You'll like this less," said the cardinal, and belched out a great billow of fire, smoke, and sparks. The horse screamed and bucked; the rider fell, his hair and head on fire. The man with the knife was also burning, all aflame, screaming through the woods.

The tattered man took Charles by the shoulder, smoke still seeping from his mouth. "She shone at me! I'm lucky to be alive. Things are not going well for me, but I must have arrived here for a reason. It is obscure to me, but I can sniff it on you—you interest the chief gaoler of Hell. Say my name when your purpose becomes apparent."

"Apparent?" The boy was convinced he had been knocked into a dreamland. He drew back from the man whose breath stank of sulfur.

"Ready. Say my name—Nergal—if you need me. My name is Nergal."

The rider was lying on the floor, his head flaming like a torch, howling and rolling.

"I need to get a face," said Nergal, "and his won't do. Remember, call me when you are ready—we may aid each other's purposes."

"What is my purpose?" Charles asked him.

"I don't know. Destruction, I should guess."

"What's destruction?"

"To burn and break things."

"I am to be a great burner and breaker?"

"My presence here would seem to show you'll be one of the best. Now I must go."

With that Nergal picked up his hat, put it to his ravaged head, and ran off through the trees.

The horse lay dead, charred and smoking on the ground. Some dry bushes were burning about twenty paces to his left, where the rider had collapsed. He was still on fire. The knifeman was dead, the white of his skull showing through his burned skin.

There were voices around Charles, faces—pink blurs.

"What happened, oh little man, what happened?" John was there. Ramon too.

Charles felt tears coming down his cheeks and he could not stop himself weeping.

"What was it, cousin Charles? What has happened here?"

"A dragon!" said Charles. "Uncle John, it was a dragon!" And he cast himself into John's arms.

4

Montagu rode into Berkeley lightly attended by only four squires and eight pages, no more than a couple of cooks, plus a falconer, armorer, scribe, and minstrel—the very minimum a gentleman of his standing needed to get by.

Two weeks' hard riding brought him there just before the early Easter. The weather had been good. It was a sweet spring, the hedges full of birdsong, the meadows in flower. Montagu counted himself lucky to be a freeman on such a day—at liberty to wander and to see England in its glory, from the vast shimmering lakes of the northern hills to the woods of the Midlands, and now this pretty, even if formidable, Gloucestershire dwelling rising out of a lilied moat, its walls girded by a necklace of yellow daffodils.

The castle was an impressive structure, two curtain walls and, just visible above them, the flinty square structure of the new castle attached to the old round Norman keep.

Berkeley had seen the diamonds of Montagu's banners from afar and had the gates open for his arrival. The lord himself came running out to meet Montagu, dressed in a surcoat bearing his family's distinctive crosses pattée—each arm tapering in toward the center of the design like four arrowheads.

"Thomas!" shouted Montagu. "It's good to see you, old man!"

"No older than you, Salisbury!" said Berkeley.

"And so old enough! How long has it been?"

"Ten years."

"It seems longer. I should have come this way before."

Montagu dismounted and the two men bowed to each other.

Berkeley said, "William, you're very welcome, especially at such a time. I should have thought you'd be in the south readying for the French invasion. It's all we hear about nowadays."

"Not going to happen now," said Montagu. "Thank God for corrupt men. The Genoese mercenary admiral didn't pay his men. They mutinied. Result—four in every ten of the French invasion force packed their banners and went home. We're on French soil burning Philip's lands—he won't be on ours for at least another summer. The king will force Philip to battle. If he doesn't dither himself into the grave before that."

"What does Edward hope to achieve there? Surely he can't think he could win France."

"He thinks he's the rightful king of France. He has a claim through his mother. God is on his side. We'll give Philip a bloody nose for invading the Agenais, make safe our allies in Flanders, and then head home with a sackload of booty. The southern ports are full of French riches already."

"Good stuff, good stuff! So what brings you here?"

Montagu said, "On my way to my own lands. Seemed a good idea to pay you a visit. Why pay for board at an inn, I thought, when I can drink old Berkeley dry for nothing?"

"Very good! Come with me, I'll have rooms made ready."

The pages led the horses in as Montagu's men followed him through the gates in the curtain walls and then into the inner castle—through a long tunnel into the courtyard. It was very impressive, just as Montagu had remembered it, low buildings with crenellations on them—the big gothic windows of the Great Hall and some higher, solid towers fronted by ornate doors carved with the images of saints.

Montagu listened, but he couldn't hear them singing, as nobles often could. Berkeley saw him cock an ear.

He said, "Do vigil here, then they may sing to you."

"You still have saints?"

"Yes—does it surprise you?"

"Not at all," said Montagu, meaning "very much." A king had died here, after all.

That said, there was an air of peace about the place, a lovely smell of apples from a cart overflowing with them. Healthy, well-liveried servants moved about, busy and smiling.

"It's good of you to come, really good," said Berkeley. "We've not had many visitors here the past ten years."

"No."

Montagu knew why—Berkeley had stood trial for the murder of the old king. He had been acquitted, but the stain of the accusation had never left him. Other nobles shunned him, and he'd not been at a tournament since the day he'd left Westminster a free man.

"My God, it *is* good to see you." Berkeley patted Montagu on the shoulder. "You'll do me the honor of joining me to dine tonight, William?"

"I know you keep an incomparable table," said Montagu. "Of course!"

Berkeley certainly did know how to throw a feast. Even though he had had no idea Montagu was coming until a few hours before the earl arrived, the food was lavish and the wine excellent. The warner—the first course—itself would not have been out of place at the king's court. It was a "sotiltee"—a sugar sculpture—in the shape of a crown with, springing from its center, three leopards.

"You had that knocked up this afternoon?" said Montagu.

"The cook's a good 'un," Berkeley affirmed with pride. "Though we may be far from civilization out here, it does not follow that we must live basely."

The hall was enormous—the finest in England, Berkeley said. Large stained-glass windows shattered the sinking sun into blue and red as the servants busied themselves among the tables. Montagu had come unexpectedly, and so the hall was only half full. It took more than a few hours to get news to the goodmen of Gloucestershire that the king's favorite friend had come to the castle. Still, there were enough young knights and ladies, all of whom wanted to meet the famous earl and to talk to him about his exploits in the east, in France, and—above all—the night he had plucked the tyrant Mortimer from his bedchamber at Nottingham Castle.

"How did you get in?" they all wanted to know.

"Carefully and quickly," was his answer. The truth—that they'd employed a secret passage into the castle—had never really been revealed. The castle was a royal seat and no one wanted it widely known that there was a direct route to the king's bedroom from a crag in the cliff on which the castle stood. He was sure Edward had had the passage sealed now, but seals can be undone, so silence was the best option.

Eventually, the number of young people approaching the table grew too great, and Berkeley waved them away.

"You're a hero to these people, William."

Montagu said, "Only because they don't know me. I did my duty—it would have been impossible not to."

"Quite. A few of these youngsters should hear you say that. In any enterprise modern knights seem to consider only two things—the money it will bring them and the advancement they might win. I tell them, honor wants no reward."

"But it can get one."

"Well, quite."

Montagu wondered how Berkeley could talk of honor when he'd allowed the old king to die under his roof. He felt a spark of anger at the man's hypocrisy. He'd wanted a chance to bring up the subject of Edward's death. This appeared to be it.

He said, "I'd like to see the room where Edward died."

Berkeley put down his knife. "Go to Corfe, then."

Montagu felt his mouth go dry as he heard the answer. Corfe. Where Lockey had come from. Where he had claimed to have seen the dragon and old Edward.

He said to Berkeley, "The king died here."

"No."

"That was the accusation."

"No. The accusation was that I conspired in the king's death. I did not, and that was accepted by our new king and Parliament. The stain on the reputation of Berkeley Castle, however, was not removed by my acquittal."

"So he didn't die here?" Montagu asked.

"What did I say when I was tried in Parliament?"

"It was a long time ago, Thomas. I can't recall the exact words."

He retorted, "I bloody well can. I said I never knew that the king was dead until I received the summons for his murder."

"But I have never heard anyone say he wasn't killed here."

"Then you've not been listening to me. You think I'd have noticed something like that happening in my own home? I'm not the most attentive man, William, but even I would notice the corpse of the reigning monarch, and the man I was charged to protect, in my best guest room. It's the sort of thing that takes the eye."

Berkeley's cheeks were florid, shaking like a hound catching scent of an intruder.

Montagu said, "You were ill and you weren't here, I remember you said that. You had gone to your manor to recuperate. You said in your deposition that you nearly died."

"So I did."

"What did you have?"

"A fever."

"And you traveled to your manor like that?" he asked him.

"I thought it best to spare the king the chance of infection by leaving the castle. I went away and I prayed hard and I was delivered."

"That is a blessing. Which saint interceded for you?"

"Ireneaus. I'd sent word ahead to provide a feast for his day and the offering worked."

"The king died on the Feast of St. Alban of Mainz. That's a week earlier. It took you a week to travel forty miles to your manor?"

"Have you come to my home to retry me?" said Berkeley.

Montagu studied Berkeley. He knew him well enough. He was an artless, eager-to-serve sort who had worshiped the ground on which the old king walked. Berkeley would not have left while the king was under his roof. He would have considered it a dishonor to Edward.

He also knew that he must have regarded himself as very lucky to have escaped execution for what had happened. Then an idea struck Montagu— Berkeley had not been acquitted of all charges relating to the death of the old king.

"Were you ever acquitted of appointing Gurney and Ockley? They were working for you when they murdered Edward."

"I was not acquitted. The charge remains. No one has acted upon it these ten years, but for all I know, the king could resurrect it tomorrow."

"I should attend to that, when I return to Westminster," said Montagu. He was ambiguous enough that Berkeley could take his words either way. Montagu was Edward's closest friend. His implication to Berkeley was clear. With a word he could damn him. Berkeley chose the positive interpretation of Montagu's words.

"I'm flattered that you are so concerned for my welfare. Those men were my retainers, true. But Mortimer was old Edward's retainer. A servant doesn't always do what his master says."

Montagu thought Berkeley had a point. However, he pressed his advantage. "You prosper here, Thomas, your lands are bountiful, and you still even own much of Kent, no matter that it was given to you by the usurper Mortimer."

Berkeley heard the unspoken question. "I have friends still, William. Or one friend who counts very much. If I prosper it is because the king wishes it."

"Does Edward know his father left here?"

Berkeley exhaled heavily.

"Shall we speak frankly?" said Montagu. "I think you are innocent. I think there was no attack on Edward here. Did your men even kill him at all?"

Berkeley thought for a long time before replying. "Like you said, it was a long time ago."

"Did he go to Corfe from here? Was the king held at Corfe?"

"Not on my authority."

"Is that the same as a 'no'?"

Berkeley stabbed at his chop with his knife. "I tried to get him out of my custody. I wouldn't be party to murdering the man whom God had set on the throne."

Though you did nothing to oppose it, thought Montagu. Many would have done the same. Not Montagu. He saw his duty clearly and always did it without fail.

"So you moved him?"

"No. He moved."

"The difference being?"

"My men did not take him. Others did."

"What others?"

Berkeley put his head up, then looked down his nose at Montagu. "These questions would be better addressed elsewhere. I have answered before my peers, now I decline to be tried by you alone."

"I'm not trying you, Tom. Do you think I'm asking these questions for my amusement? Believe me, as a man you know to be honest, when I say that the fate of the realm rests on your answers. Please, Tom. I'm not trying to send you after Mortimer to hang at Tyburn."

"He went with some foreign knights. He called them here."

"How foreign? Gascons from his lands? Frenchmen? How foreign? In what way?"

"Frenchmen. An ill-mannered lot. One of them was no more than a chandler's son by his manner and speech."

"Whose knights?"

"Hospitallers."

"Why them?"

"I don't know. He insisted on them."

"Why did he go with foreigners?"

"I genuinely don't know. There was talk here, of course."

"What talk?"

"That the queen had set a devil on him when she rebelled. He was trying to subdue it. He summoned his angel in our chapel, you know. The knights offered their help. They thought he might do better at Corfe."

Montagu, normally an urbane man, put his hand up to his face. This tallied completely with the tale the servant from Corfe had told him.

"Can I see the chapel?"

"For all the good it'll do you."

"Why?"

"It's been rebuilt. It burned down. The king burned it down."

"Deliberately?"

"I have no idea. But it caught fire when he was in it. That's why the knights thought to move him. God was not favoring him here."

Montagu said, "Thomas."

"Yes?"

"Do you believe the old king to be dead?"

Berkeley glanced about him, as if fearing he would be overheard. "I've no reason to believe otherwise. Absolutely none at all. Mortimer had issued commands for his death; he went to Corfe under the custody of the knights but with Maltravers—Mortimer's man. He killed him, didn't he?"

"So it was said."

Montagu suddenly recalled—young Edward had charged some of the Knights Hospitaller with looking after his mother. He'd thought it was because of their great self-discipline and lack of connection to anyone his mother might know. He'd encountered them on crusade in Lithuania as a young man. As humorless and severe a bunch as you could wish to meet.

Montagu had thought Edward had chosen them because he wished to confine his mother and reduce her influence to a minimum. The lady was famously beautiful and famously difficult to refuse. Her son had sought men who were resistant to her charms. But was there more to it? Could it be coincidence that the same order had been with the king when he left the castle?

Montagu took up his cup of wine and drained it. "Why not mention this at your trial?"

"Legal defenses are subtle. Best to keep the jury focused on one thing—did I kill the king or order his death? I had good counsel that this was all they needed to consider."

"So who did kill old Edward?"

Berkeley looked hard at him. "You don't think he's dead, William?"

"I do," said Montagu, "because if he's not dead, then . . ."

"Young Edward, willingly or not, is a usurper. But if that was the case, the angels would not come to him. He would be a neutered king, the victim of any rightful monarch who could call angels to the field."

"Exactly," said Montagu, "and the angels do attend the king. So I share your faith. I'm just not completely convinced the right men were hanged for it."

"Why does that trouble you?"

"The real guilty ones may have walked free. You know me, Tom, I don't forget these things easily. But I do wonder what the Hospitallers were doing with our king."

"Why don't you ask them? Castle Rising is not so far."

"The king forbids access to his mother. You know that."

"Not to the knights who guard her."

"That path is too rocky and strewn with briars," said Montagu. "They are friends of the king. And Edward has made his wishes clear."

"Probably for the best; she is famously persuasive," said Berkeley.

Montagu drew in a breath. Isabella. As a younger man he had feared to look at her lest his lust for her show on his face. More than lust, devotion. Plenty of knights went mooning after unobtainable women, but Montagu was not one of them. He was a lousy poet and wasn't about to denigrate his feelings in doggerel verse, or attempt to sing to her. She was his own age, but the king's mother—beautiful and untouchable as a star.

Berkeley picked at some meat in his teeth. "There's always Maltravers."

"He's dead," said Montagu.

"Is he?" he asked.

"Edward told me himself."

"But I hear . . ." Berkeley shrugged.

"Yes?"

"Gaunt's nice at this time of year."

Montagu could scarcely believe what he was hearing.

"Why don't you tell the king where Maltravers is?" he demanded.

"Perhaps he knows."

Montagu turned away a servant who offered him a plate of sugared pastries.

"He killed Edward's father." Edward had been known to bash men's brains out at tournaments for the merest slight.

Berkeley replied, "That's what they said."

Montagu struggled to take all this in. All right, say Maltravers was alive. Could he have something over Edward? If he knew the old king was alive, then young Edward would not want to bring Maltravers before a court, risking the information coming out. Perhaps better that Maltravers disappeared somewhere. But why not just have him killed? A word to the count of Hainault and his throat would be cut. Did Maltravers have some secret protector? Had someone some power over the king to stay his hand?

Montagu looked hard at Berkeley. Two men, Maltravers and Berkeley, suspected yet unpunished. There was some secret, but Montagu was realistic enough to know that, whatever it was, he was never going to get it out of Berkeley. Not directly, anyway.

Montagu needed to get a letter to his wife at the court. She was friends with Queen Philippa and could sound out the lady subtly to discover what she knew. It wasn't impossible that Edward had been in some way compromised by Maltravers. Oh, God. If Maltravers knew Edward was a usurper. If he had letters placed with persons unknown to be released upon his death. At the very least, with England's angels missing, it would raise very awkward questions.

Montagu knew he was playing a dangerous game. He would need to tread carefully. He affected insouciance. "I suppose it might not sit well with the king if I see Maltravers."

"Does the king need to know, William? Great men sometimes don't know what's good for them, and we who serve behind them must do so cloaked and concealed. So I served Edward the elder against the tyrant Mortimer."

Served him! Served him up, more like.

He added, "And so you now serve Edward the younger. He may never know of your help, or may even misconstrue your actions, but still you serve."

Montagu looked out on the hall. The minstrels were coming out to a great cheer from the lower men at the poorer tables. He wasn't in the mood for music. "I should get to bed. I've had a long ride."

"Of course," said Berkeley. He stood and clapped his hands, and the hall rose to bid Montagu goodnight.

5

Dow managed to carry the lady all the way back to the priest's house. Orsino was at the gate and, seeing Dow, came running toward him.

He said, "Christ, you're covered in blood. What's been happening?"

Dow opened his mouth, revealing the bloody mess within.

"Where have you been? How did you get out? What happened to you? Who's this? What have you done to her?" Orsino's eyes were fixed on the woman. He crossed himself repeatedly. For a man who kept his head under any attack, Orsino looked very near to panic. He touched the woman's head, a gesture of deep tenderness. Then he put his fingertips to her mouth. "She's breathing! But she's frozen, boy. Get her in and build up a fire!"

Dow carried the woman past Orsino into the garden.

Edwin was there, a short whip in his hand. He went to touch the woman and then drew back.

"What have you done to her, you unbeliever?" he asked Dow.

"There'll be time enough for that, priest," said Orsino. "She needs care. Move her to your chamber."

"That's not seemly," said the priest.

"Fair enough," said Orsino. "I'll drag your mattress down, shall I? And you can sleep on the bare boards?"

"That would be preferable. Must be a slut or she'd not have her hair uncovered so."

"Stop that talk!" Orsino rounded on the priest and took him by the throat. Dow had never even seen him angry before—warlike, yes, aggressive, certainly, but always in control. Here he was a madman, his face drained of color, his lips pulled back in a snarl.

Edwin was not an easy man to intimidate. "A goodwoman would not loose her hair. A goodwoman would not be in a position where she would invite attack. I don't want her in this house for long."

"She won't be in your shithole for long!" said Orsino. He tossed the priest onto his arse and strode inside the house.

The priest glared at the lady, then turned away to go inside. Something about her had disturbed the man. What? Her beauty? Priests were supposed to stay away from women. The Devil's Men said that Lucifer had sent his mind from the Fortress of Dis in Free Hell to speak to the first pope, to charm him and make sure that his evil following had no offspring. The priests did not stay away from women, though—even in the tiny communities of Cornwall where many a cuckolded husband had come to the Devil's Men to gain his revenge.

Dow carefully laid the woman down on the grass. Then he quickly dug a hole by the wall with the knife, dropped it in, and covered it.

"In here," Orsino's voice said from inside.

Dow stamped down the soil and went to gather up the lady.

He laid her on the mattress Orsino had dragged down to the kitchen floor. Orsino put his hand to her mouth.

"Still alive. By God, this woman will be missed by someone." Tears were in his eyes. Dow thought this very strange. The Florentine was not at all himself.

Dow drew a cup of water from the pail in the kitchen and swilled it around his mouth. Then he went to the door and spat out red blood into the garden.

The priest, who had paused before leaving the kitchen, watched him spit. He said, "What have you been doing?"

Dow just turned away.

Orsino was kneeling in front of the woman. He too had taken a cup and was offering it to her lips. "Can you speak, boy, what happened?"

Dow tried to talk, but it was too painful. All he could say was, "Red man."

"What?" Edwin said. The priest took Dow by the shoulder.

"Red man. Mouth fire." It was agony to talk, his tongue raw on his palate.

"A man dressed in red with a mouth of fire?"

Dow nodded.

"That devil has been freed," said Edwin. "He's slipped his circle somehow."

He ran out of the room and down the stairs into the cellar. Dow heard shouting from below. "Where did you find her? How did you get out?" The priest seemed somewhere between rage and panic.

Neither Dow nor Orsino paid heed to him, instead focusing on the woman. She was giddyingly beautiful. Her black hair shone, her pale skin was unlike any he had ever seen—entirely without flaw, her lips as red as May roses. Again Orsino touched her face.

He said, "She's frozen, boy—get a fire going."

Outside the animals brayed and the dawn chorus began, the birds singing up the sun. A light started to stream in at the little window.

Dow built the fire. Downstairs the priest was still shouting.

"You've been a bold fellow, haven't you? How did you get out of that circle? What have you done and who is that woman? I constrain you, I command you, in the name of the archangel Michael, in the name of the archangel Gabriel, in the name of God, the Father, the Son, and the Holy Ghost."

"Someone got out of the wrong side of bed this morning!" It was the devil's voice, shouting above Edwin's incantations.

Dow crouched to fan the fire, glancing at Orsino tending the woman. He watched them for a long time, Orsino stroking back her hair, offering her water, wiping away his tears. Orsino finally met his gaze, and saw the question in Dow's eyes.

"She reminds me of my wife—that is all. She is very like her. I had a wife and a son. Dead of fever. I . . . " Orsino shrugged, unable to continue.

Dow grimaced.

"I cursed God, when I should have prayed to him."

Dow returned to poking at the fire, to save the mercenary the embarrassment of his attention. The Lauds bells had rung out, and then Prime, before Orsino drew away from the woman.

Orsino said to him, "Let me look at your tongue."

Dow clamped his jaw. He didn't want the Florentine poking inside his mouth, causing more damage. And he didn't want any more of his kindness, the sort that prayed for you before offering you to death.

"I want to see if it needs a salve. What happened to your chest? It's burned again."

Dow put his hand to the scar. It was very sore. But Hell had come to his aid and he felt uplifted by that. Was he up to the task the demon had set him? Perhaps, though not as a boy.

He needed to gain Orsino's knowledge—to learn to fight to take on the high men. Dowzabel would show him courtesy; he would make Orsino believe he had won his trust. He opened his mouth and Orsino looked inside.

"You've got a couple of big cuts," he said. "I'll see what I can find at market today. Goose grease might be best. I'd love to know what you've been up to."

It was hot and smoky in the room now. Dow saw Orsino cross himself as he looked at the beam of sunlight coming through the window. It reminded Dow of that circle in the church, where the demons had first appeared from Hell—taking their form from the smoke of the torches.

The light beam was moving by tiny degrees across the floor. It touched the woman's head, shining on her hair.

"Best move her; she might be uncomfortable in the light," said Orsino.

The sun moved across the top of her face, casting a glowing veil over her eyes.

"Come on, help me move her."

But the woman blinked and opened her eyes. Dow had never seen anything like them—they were a pale and rare violet that almost seemed to shine in the sunbeam. They reminded Dow of the fragile blue sky over the moor in the winter morning, of sapphires he had seen on the fine cups and plates in a church, of the blue light of the stained windows, and of none of those things. They were a color unto themselves, unearthly. Orsino actually crossed himself as she awoke.

The lady sat up and turned into the sunbeam, stretching up into its warmth.

Edwin was at the door. "Are you a gentlewoman? Are you a good Christian woman or a city slut?"

She turned to face him. "Your Christ fell, like me," she said, "or rather, he was pushed."

"*My* Christ! The world's Christ, woman!"

She smiled. "As you say."

Her voice was like a song—bringing with it the fresh feeling of a spring morning, not just a sense of goodness, but of evil dispelled. She had a heavy accent—something Dow had not noticed before. She spoke like Orsino, though much more prettily. Dow wanted to ask her, "Are you a demon? Did you fall with Lucifer?" but his mouth and throat were in no fit state for speech. He tried with his thoughts, as he had tried with the fire demon.

She said, "You saved me, thank you."

Dow stared at her so hard it was as if he was trying to bore the words into her mind. She didn't respond but stood up.

"Are you a blasphemer?" said the priest, extending a shaking finger toward her.

"Truth is blasphemy," said the lady, "so says the king of Heaven. I was cast out of Heaven for the love I inspired."

"Then you are a demon!"

The priest's jaw wobbled. Dow had never seen him daunted before, not even when facing that demon back in the burned church. There he had seemed manic, possessed. In front of this strange lady, though, he was uncertain, scared even.

The woman looked about her. "This is a dark place," she said. "I need the light."

She walked out into the garden. Dow went to the threshold.

She put her face up to the horse. "He is light, he is made of light." She kissed the horse on the nose and turned from the garden.

"Lady, let us help you," said Orsino. "You've been distressed by your ordeal."

"Yes, I have," she said. "I don't know my way home any more." She put her hand on his arm. "You're looking for forgiveness," she said, "but who is blaming you?"

She walked to the garden gate, opened it, and stepped through. Orsino ran after her, following her through. He re-emerged a moment later, wiping his eyes with his sleeve.

"She's gone," said Orsino. "She's vanished." He sat down on the floor heavily, almost as if knocked down by an invisible force. "She was like my wife," he said. He repeated, "She was like my wife."

"These demons can take various forms," said Edwin. "You, boy, bring Hell to my door. A shame you can't keep it here. I should have constrained her. If we'd had longer, we could have caught her in a circle."

"You think she's a demon?" said Orsino.

"She said she was cast out of Heaven. What more evidence do you want? You felt what she conjured in you. And in me, if I tell the truth. You heard her blaspheme and now she vanishes like the morning mist. You saw her perfection. Not of this realm, for sure," said Edwin.

"Is a fallen angel the same as a demon?" said Orsino.

"Not necessarily. When the gates of Hell were shut at the Fall, some fallen angels hid and resisted being rightly turned to beastly forms. The Devil says God has expelled others since, or sent them down when it suits his purposes."

The priest glanced about him, as if he expected the city watch to burst in at any minute and take him away. He turned to Dow. "How did you call her? It took me a lifetime of study to win my spirit, yet you, yet you . . ." His words trailed away, but his eyes were fixed on Dow as if his gaze could peel him and lay all his secrets bare. When Dow did not reply, Edwin sniffed and said: "You will apply yourself to the control of the fellow we have trapped below. You will attend me while I question the spirit about this latest appearance. Now."

Dow's mouth was agony and he wanted to rest. But this was his chance to see the devil.

6

Y ou again, Bardi? Recovered from the attack that took Pole, I see."
The king sat on the wooden terrace overlooking the knights'
practice field at Windsor. The castle rose behind him, the great
round tower white in the sharp sun, the glass of the chapels sparkling, the
year's last nip of frost in the air.

Edward had come home from the wars in the north of France, though
he would not call them wars. "I've had worse scraps with my son," he said.

If he had, the son looked well on it.

On the king's knee was little Edward, splendid in his green velvet and
pearls. King Edward bounced the child up and down as he spoke.

"The attack by the bandits was lamentable, sir." Bardi had been trying
to see the king for months, but Edward had been back and forth to the
continent. He'd been within touching distance of him on several occasions—
including at Southampton—but had not yet been invited to speak. Finally,
one of Edward's snotty secretaries had said it might be possible. If . . . If
what? What do you think? Money, as always. Well, more money. The
amount of bribes he'd doled out should have been enough to secure him an
audience with God, let alone a king.

Bardi had received a message from his father saying that the situation
at home was becoming difficult. "Difficult" was the word old man Bardi
habitually chose when others would have preferred "impossible." People were
not convinced the Bardis were going to see a return on their investment,

and it was taking all Bardi Senior's considerable skills to prevent a run on the bank.

Edward had to be prevented from a suicidal mission into France. Theoretically the crown would still owe the money if Edward died. Practically it would prove nearly impossible to get it from Edward's successor. The boy prince was only seven. His uncles could argue that their hands were tied regarding any debt until the child came of age.

"Not hurt yourself, though?" the king asked him.

In truth, Bardi's arm had not been too badly hurt by the demon's attack, though a good coat had been ruined, but he had hoped—rather optimistically—that the wound might generate sympathy at court, so he'd kept it bandaged. The banker knew that some of the ladies might look favorably on him, but a warrior, like Edward, wouldn't regard having an arm *potentially* ripped off—or even ripped off—as much to shout about.

The events of that night still haunted Bardi. He'd covered up his fear from the low men around him at the burned church in Southampton, but he knew who had tried to drag him to Hell. Hugh Despenser, old King Edward II's dead favorite. Men had called him a devil for all the wickedness he had unleashed on the country. The rebel Mortimer had believed so, because he'd had him covered in magical wards and charms before he'd killed him. But now he was trying to come back from Hell.

Why was he so angry with Bardi? The banker had conveyed some letters for him to the Knights Hospitaller in France. Naturally he'd had the seals broken and remade to check their contents, but he'd made neither head nor tail of them. Some trade in relics, some spiritual advice, nothing he could understand. Magic, and magical skullduggery, no doubt, but Despenser was too clever to give away much in the letters, and it wasn't worth opening the replies. If the baron had suspected, even for an instant, there was something amiss with the seal on the returning letter, he would have given Bardi the sort of death a Roman emperor might have considered harsh.

Bardi had been pleased to make contact with the Hospitallers, though. It stood him in good stead years later in his dealings with Edward. Those fellows had absorbed the Templars on their dissolution. There were certain learned men of that order who were very useful to kings, particularly those who wished to be free of over-powerful uncles.

Officially, Bardi had known little about the business between the Hospitallers and Edward. He had simply responded to the young king's request for "useful men" who might help rid him of "certain problems." The king had only one problem—the power-grabbing Mortimer. A month after Bardi had put Edward in contact with the holy knights, the tyrant Mortimer was gone and Edward was king in fact as well as in name.

Bardi said, "I'm well, sire."

"No chance of dying of gangrene or succumbing to an infection?"

"I think not, sire."

King Edward snorted, almost as if he was disappointed to hear that, pulling his cloak closer about him and his son. The three sat in silence and watched the knights going through their paces in the frost of the practice ring, charging hard before wheeling to charge again. Every time a horse turned it paused for a second, wreathed in the steam of its own breath.

"Magnificent," said Edward. "No sight in the world like a war-horse stamping, ready for the charge."

"Indeed not, sire." Bardi looked across the ring at the figure of stout Sir William Neville, who was seated on a tall four-legged bench that stood in for a horse. The knight, in full mail and basinet, with a lance in front of him, was acting as the instructor and the target, catching the lances on a large shield—yellow with a blue chevron. Over his mail he wore a solid breast plate in the latest German style. It covered his chest, but his belly was still exposed. What better way to test new armor than to put a man in it, charge war-horses at him, and see if he was killed?

The English were lunatics, thought Bardi. He was becoming increasingly convinced that the entire country had a death wish. He'd have found it amusing if he hadn't had such a large amount of money invested in it. He wished he'd seen them using themselves as lance targets before he'd parted with all that coin.

A war-horse leapt forward, its skirts billowing, the rider high in the saddle, his lance couched. His aim was true and the lance slipped the shield, slamming into the breastplate. Sir William was lifted clean out of the hobbyhorse saddle and dashed to the turf of the ring.

"Good, good!" shouted Sir William. "You put the tension into your arm at nearly the right moment. Do it again and see if you can really hit me this time. I expect to land here." He rolled over and put a mark in the grass.

"You think the French can beat this, Bardi?"

"I'm not a military man, sire."

"No. You're not," said Edward, as if that indicated some deep character flaw. "Well, they won't have to," he continued.

"Sire?" said Bardi. Was there a hope Edward was going to put off his campaign, try to pay his debts by subduing the Scots, maybe raising taxes? Would he at least wait until the Drago had been found, so they might have some chance against France? Bardi was convinced he would never recoup his investment otherwise.

"This is just a game now. We go through the motions, but the day of the war-horse is done. Won't stop us having them—taking them to France and charging down a few peasants with them when we scorch Philip's lands—but the cavalry charge is living on borrowed time. Did you hear of our glorious charge against the Scots at Halidon Hill?"

"Er, I heard something of the brave deeds done by your knights that day, sire."

"More than I did. They never took place. Our horses were useless against their pikes. We got off, defended our archers, and let them pin the Scots to the mud. And pin them they did. The arrows fell like a sleet storm. We had our fun chasing the retreating army, but it was the archer who won that battle. The common man. Fact. Galling, isn't it? The future's behind me there in the keep. Five hundred longbows. More are coming. Many more."

Bardi tried to collect his thoughts. He had only a few moments with the king, and that had taken him months to secure. The courtiers had been ordered a way off to allow the king to speak to Bardi in confidence, and they stood lounging around on the grass at the foot of the terrace, cold butterflies in their scarlets, yellows, and greens—too keen to show their finery to wear cloaks, too proud to admit they were frozen to the marrow.

"Sire." Bardi was about to speak again when Edward held up his hand for silence. Another rider had come into the practice area, a huge man with a bright yellow surcoat over his mail, his black hair thick on his helmetless head.

The king tapped the child on his arm. "What's wrong with the way Baron Holland holds his lance?" he asked.

The boy said, "Too strong, too straight, Father."

"Very good. He could almost unhorse himself against Sir Robert like that, and his horse is made of wood and doesn't gallop. If Holland hits another knight at full pelt, he'll be off—as he often is. You tense only at the moment of impact and then release. Tense, release. Get it?"

"Yes, Papa."

The knight charged. Edward cried out, "Douce, Thomas. Douce! Gentle, you fool!"

The boy joined in too. "Douce! Douce!"

The king laughed. "The baron is a good man. Man's a beast in a foot mêlée. I'd have him by my side before four others."

The knight hit the shield, but Sir Robert on the hobbyhorse expertly turned aside the blow.

"See, if he was doing it right, old Neville would fly over the castle. Thomas, unhorse, I want to see you fight on foot. You against Desbrulais and Grosvenor. Get Fortescu to fight you too. Go on, Bardi, I haven't all day." The king spoke in English. Bardi, more competent in the normal court language, replied in French.

"Sire, certain signs delivered by certain men . . ."

The king said, "My God, you speak like a politician."

"Thank you, sire. These signs indicate a way forward. Something to help and augment our own angels. Perhaps even stand in for them, should they not be coaxed from their shrines."

"The angels will come, Bardi. You presume too much."

Bardi refused to be sidetracked. "You are aware of the existence of the banner known as the Drago?"

"I am. My mother had it when we fought my father at Orwell."

Bardi wasn't sure how to respond. So *that* was how old Edward had been defeated. He said, "Would it not be politic and wise to use it against the French?"

"It would."

Bardi had no response to this.

Edward was suddenly furious. "It went missing. Stolen and hidden by the tyrant Mortimer, no doubt. Do you not think we'd use it if we had it?"

Bardi kept quiet. He knew Edward's tempers were fierce, but only like a summer storm, there and then gone.

The knights on the practice field were strapping on their gear for the foot fighting, laughing with one another as they did. Bardi never got used to this. In five breaths' time, they were going to be bashing one another's faces in.

The king spoke to his son. "Watch this, little Edward, and you'll see how he doesn't get overwhelmed by the numbers. He attacks quickly and cleanly to stop them surrounding him and makes every blow count. He doesn't bother about defense—if he tried to block or dodge then they'd gain the initiative. He goes in directly, lets the armor do its job, and makes sure his opponents are on the back foot. In his mind, he's their problem, not they his."

"Doesn't their armor help them?"

"Of course, but Holland hits hard and keeps pressing. He's more accurate than his opponents in finding the gaps in the armor—or he would be if this was for real—and he's advancing while receiving blows from a retreating man."

Bardi said, "I'm sure the Drago can be found. I have my best fellows working on it. It will be located shortly."

"Sorcery?" said King Edward.

"The work of churchmen, learned churchmen. There is a London clergyman who has achieved some remarkable insights through his studies."

He repeated, "Sorcery."

"No priest has ever been convicted of that."

"Only because they have the right to be tried by the ecclesiastical courts, which are never going to convict them because half of them are up to the same thing."

"These are learned men."

"Learning leads to the sin of pride, and pride was the first sin against God. Dealing with divine powers is the province of kings; dealing with diabolic powers that of the damned. Churchmen should not infringe on either sphere."

Bardi said, "But if the banner could be found . . ."

"At the cost of a soul? Better one thousand English bodies go into the grave before one soul goes to Hell."

Bardi swallowed a sigh. Piety didn't suit Edward. He knew for a fact that Edward had at least consulted with sorcerers, if not used them. After all, it was Bardi who had arranged the meeting, through the Hospitallers. Nothing wrong with that—several European kings kept their own magicians and the church contrived to look the other way.

He said, "With it, sire, you have every chance of success. I wouldn't be surprised if it might even be used to persuade some of the French angels to our side."

"You have a poor opinion of the piety of the French. Besides, it has not been found."

"Not yet, but as I say, it will be discovered. It would be equal to the Oriflamme in combat. And no angel would strike at an army that bore such a holy banner before it."

Edward shrugged his shoulders. "Not enough time," he said. "I'm paying the lords of the Low Countries through the nose for the use of their forces. They're ready to go. I can't keep them sitting on their arses indefinitely."

"Your chances of victory . . ."

"Bardi, do I advise you on your investments and loans?"

He said, "No, sire."

"Because I trust you know what you are doing. Pay me the same compliment when it comes to the arts of war."

"Yes, sire."

"You also know little of the arts of diplomacy, despite your sophisticated air. You say you are certain you will find the Drago."

"My men are excellent."

"Then it's as good as found. So I can announce to Parliament that we have it. That should stiffen their resolve for the fight with France."

"I didn't go that far, sir, I . . ."

The king said, "Have you lied to me, Bardi? It would suit me to call you a spy and cancel my debts to you."

Bardi colored. "Lord, I . . ."

"Don't worry," said Edward, smiling, "I still have need of you. Unfortunately, killing bankers—however attractive and pleasurable that may be in the short term—tends to diminish one's chances of credit at a time of future need."

Bardi said, "Yes, sire."

"Forget about holy banners. Concentrate on raising me more money. I'm going to the Holy Roman emperor. If he'll declare me vicar of the Holy Roman Empire, I will stand in his place before God and add the angels of the Holy Roman Empire to our own, not to mention a good few thousand Bavarian men-at-arms. By summer we will sail for France and I intend to give Philip the beating he's been asking for all these years."

Edward stood up, lifting the boy to his feet. In the circle, Holland had a mace in one hand, a shield in the other. Three other knights surrounded him, armed with swords.

The banker went to say more—but Edward was crying out, "Set to! Set to!"

The three knights attacked almost simultaneously. Holland caught Desbrulais's attack high on his shield and thumped a quick blow to the side of the helm, sending Desbrulais crashing to the floor. He deflected Grosvenor's attack with the vambrace on his arm, stepping in and under the cut before delivering a stab with the mace into the back, dropping him too. Fortescu, having missed his first swipe, came on straight at Holland, who seized his arm, stepped his foot behind him, and sent him crashing to the floor, where he faked smashing him in the head.

"Take a look at that, little Edward," said the king. "That's the future, right there, smashing Sir David in the head. The foot soldier. Makes you weep, doesn't it? Go, Bardi. My lady is approaching."

The king set the boy down as the queen, Philippa, came up the stairs, followed by four ladies-in-waiting. The queen was a good-looking, slim woman in her early twenties with deep olive skin and dark eyes. Edward smiled to see her. Bardi knew she had been given to the king, but they were as close as any love match. She'd borne him good sons and, though they'd lost their William as a baby the year before, she was likely to produce more. What king would not love her for that?

The king smiled as Sir Gerald Sydney bent to one knee and began a poem to Lady Charlotte Hamilton, the prettiest of the queen's women, a pale red-haired thing in a blue gown. Edward took the queen's hand and walked with her to the bottom of the wooden terrace, away from their retainers, seeking privacy, thought Bardi.

A cloth banner hung at the back of the terrace and, checking to see if he was observed, Bardi ducked beneath it as the courtiers applauded the poem. He moved inside to where he could hear clearly and see enough through a gap in the boards. He pressed his eye to it. The king had turned his back to the rail at the bottom of the terrace and his queen stood sideways, speaking to him. Bardi was so close that he breathed slowly, afraid he would be heard.

"My lord." The queen bowed.

"My lady." Edward bowed deeper.

"The fleet is mustering, I hear," she said.

"You hear right. We have powerful allies on our side. The duke of Brabant stands ready to welcome us on the continent, and Ludwig has put the forces of the Holy Roman Empire at our disposal. He may yet do more."

"But Parliament?"

Edward's lips blew, like one of the war-horses asked to do its twentieth charge of the day. "They'll give me what I want. We'll get a wool levy and that will give us collateral for all the loans we need in Flanders. One of the advantages of admitting commoners to Westminster was that they're used to doing as they're told."

"It is said there is a serious chance they may not fund the expedition."

He chided, "Don't pay attention to the gossip of court ladies."

"So you would have to sue for peace. And on Valois terms."

"I go to them this afternoon. I have plans that should secure the money."

"Will the French angels appear?"

Edward kicked at the terrace, and Bardi had to stop himself from crying out in surprise.

"Too much is talked of angels!" he shouted. "Why must it always be angels? We had none at Halidon Hill. Give me good knights and five thousand archers above all the angels God can grant."

Philippa crossed herself. "Do not talk so!" she said. "We succeed under God or not at all."

Edward was already calm again. "I simply think we trust too much to God, when God wants us to trust to ourselves. The French have no angels, I'm sure of that. Sir Walter Manny lured the French garrison at Sluys into a fight at Cadsland. No angels."

"Manny is blessed by God himself, and you know full well that a victory against a rattish garrison led by no one more noble than a knight is different entirely from the flower of France under the angels and the Oriflamme. You cannot be certain!" She whispered, so low that Bardi had to strain to hear, "Our angels do not come!" Bardi was amazed the king let his wife speak so openly and so frankly. He was inclined to think of a saying of his father's: *Women are like peppercorns. They yield their best flavor with a little bashing.* Why did the king not strike her?

Edward replied, "I would not wish to be certain. If there was only certainty in war, there would be no valor."

The pair said nothing for a while and then the queen spoke, "I hear word from France."

"Yes?"

"My aunt Joan says her husband, the king, is entertaining Joan of Navarre and her son."

Edward nodded slowly. "Nothing to concern us at present. Navarre fights with the Scots. God, he must hate us to come from his warm palaces to get blown about up there. How does our cousin Philip?"

"Well."

"That's bad to hear. The man is somewhat indecisive, but only because he thinks too much. And often, though he wobbles, he settles in the right place. His son John thinks too little. I prefer the offspring as the opponent. The Valois have produced generations of idiots, why did I have to come against a clever one?" Edward said.

"You're speaking about my family."

"I don't include you in it."

Philippa said, "Your Capetian blood boils at the thought of a Valois as an equal." She laughed and leaned in to him affectionately.

"I'm Plantagenet—your little struggles don't bother me."

"Your mother is a Capetian."

Edward said, "There are significant differences between us. She's a woman, for instance. You'll notice I'm a man."

"Oh, I notice that," she said, patting her belly.

"You're not . . ."

"Maybe. I feel different, so maybe."

"You must be blessed three times a day. Make sure of that, Philippa."

"You hardly need remind me to go to church, Edward. You're the one who only goes on Sunday and no more." She prodded him in the chest.

"Ow!" He laughed and took both her hands in his. Edward added, "The child must be christened and warded as soon as it is born."

She said, "I'm not even sure yet. It's just a feeling."

"Even so, every preparation must be made. The child must sleep in a magic circle. I'll speak to the Knights Hospitaller; they will arrange that."

Had Bardi been a dog, his ears would have pricked up. The king certainly feared supernatural attack. What to make of that? Even without angels, would God let a devil or a demon harm a king? And still relying on the Hospitallers. Well, he knew the king had relied on them to imprison his mother, Isabella. Bardi had thought that politic—the Hospitallers were a marginal group without too much in the way of influence. Even if Edward's mother corrupted them, her sphere of influence would be limited.

But was there more to it? He knew what was said by some about the old queen—she was a witch. He had thought it just an insult, a way for tired minds to understand a woman of subtlety and influence. The longer Isabella was insulated from public life, the better for Bardi. He knew she hated him. The king had rewarded him well after her lover was overthrown, and the lady blamed Bardi for undermining her control of her son. That was something of too simple an explanation, but he'd let it be believed to enhance his reputation.

The queen said, "Little William died naturally." Philippa squeezed Edward's hand. The loss of her baby had hit her hard, Bardi knew. The child had thrived when he was born but was found dead in his crib at two months, wasted away seemingly overnight.

Edward said, "Yes. But I have many enemies, and without the angels, my children are at risk."

"William *did* die naturally?"

"William died naturally." He let go of her hands.

Bardi, beneath the terrace, crossed himself.

"If we go to France, I won't see you again. You cannot win."

"I am not without hope."

She asked, "How so?"

"A king is only a king as much as he looks a king. We will go to France and on to Cologne to meet Emperor Louis and we'll make a great show of it. There he will mark me vicar of the Holy Roman Empire. God will listen to me then. He'll send me my own angel."

Philippa nodded. "And if Louis refuses?" she asked him.

"One too many 'if's for a fine morning," said Edward. "Take the child. I must go to Parliament and tell them our angels stand ready to support us."

"Why won't the angels come, Edward?"

"Who can guess the mind of God?" He stood up and clapped his hands. "Page, get my horse—I'll set off for Parliament!" he called.

Bardi watched the king with two strong convictions. The first was that he was a man of destiny, an uncommon warrior and leader capable of achieving what others thought impossible. The second was that he would never see Edward again. Edward, he thought, would be killed in France and, with him, most of Bardi's chances of getting his money back.

Bardi had seen Hell's ambassador and was convinced the Drago could be found. Well, if England didn't want it, then others might. Navarre would never be king of France, but the Capetians hated the Valois. The king of Navarre was a lapdog, but his wife showed more promise—Bardi knew she was ambitious for her son. Perhaps the Drago could be sold to them, an alliance entered into with England, and his money recouped.

Why not? thought Bardi. He would like to deal with the Navarrese. They were pretty, they were sophisticated, and they listened to reason, unlike these English dogs.

There was another enormous shout from the ring. They'd resumed tilting and Sir Robert had been knocked from the hobbyhorse.

"Excellent, Holland, excellent," shouted the old knight. "Much more like it. I think you've broken my ribs! Nice work!"

Bardi ducked out from beneath the banner. He'd write a letter to the queen of Navarre to be sent on the first tide.

7

D o you consider me clever, little Charles?" Prince John sat on the steps outside the Great Hall with the boy on his lap, feeding him sugar pieces. In front of them a fool tumbled and flipped, delighting the little boy. It was morning, and the sharp sun cast crystals of light along the river. Since his ordeal in the woods, John had been particularly kind to Charles. The puzzle of the burned bodies—whom no one could identify—had been explained neatly. Men had tried to kill Charles, but God—or one of his angels—had struck them down. John had had the taverns and public squares searched for suspicious-looking foreign men and hanged five as probable conspirators in the matter.

"You are the cleverest person I ever met," said the little boy.

"What do you think of my father?"

"He is king."

"He is indeed, but do you think him as clever as me? Do you think I could outwit him?"

"Oh yes. You could outwit anyone. Everyone says so."

John let go a deep chuckle.

"Shall we play a trick on him?" said the little boy.

He asked, "What sort of trick?"

"You'll have to think of that, you're the clever one."

"We could tell him someone he loves has died," said John.

"Or we could go to see the angel."

"The angel won't appear unless he's there," said John. "I'll have to wait until I'm king before I can command it."

"My mummy used to see the angel whether her daddy liked it or not."

"How?"

Charles said, "She'd go to the chapel and wait for him to come in. The angel appeared as soon as he came in, so he had to talk to it before he could tell her she had to leave."

"That's very good!" said John. "But the angel doesn't seem to favor Daddy that much at the moment."

"Surely with two princes present, a king and your holy mother, if she comes running, it's bound to hop along. It's worth a try, isn't it?"

"It can't hurt, can it?"

"I'm sure if you try it you'll succeed, cousin John. And if there is a rumpus in the chapel then your father and mother may come and so the angel will just"—he gestured as if fanning up a fire—"whoof up!" If it doesn't, then your father can hardly be angry at us for looking at the pretty glass. And it will at least show him for being bossy."

The prince giggled. "It may indeed whoof, in just the manner you've suggested. What are we waiting for? Let's go and see some whoofing!"

They went through the palace and up through the gilt and the deep blue and the crimson and the silk carpet of the stairs to the door of the chapel, the prince's retinue of minstrels, fools, and poets cutting capers behind him.

Two guards were at the door, liveried in red tunics decorated with fleurs-de-lys. One said, "Not the little boy, sire. Only you."

"Are you giving orders to your prince? You're Deschamps, aren't you? A good family. Do you behave like a common soldier or a hired guard?"

"Sire, I'm sorry, we were put here specifically to prevent the child getting in. It's your father's orders."

John said, "And what do you think my orders might be when I come to power, Deschamps? Do you imagine that you will prosper when I am king?"

The young man colored. "I have to obey my king, sire."

"What can the problem be? We can't raise the angel without my father."

"It's a precaution, sire. If the boy's father were to die when he was in the chapel, he would be king of Navarre. Then he would be able to talk to the angel."

"And what would he say? Do you think God looks with the same favor on a king of France as he does on one of little Navarre?"

The man looked everywhere but in John's eyes. "I cannot admit him, sire."

"If I were prince, I should kill them both and walk in," said little Charles. "Stab, stab, stab!"

The prince's retinue all laughed at the child's precocity.

"Not a bad idea," said John. "Fool, bring my sword."

"Go for the king, Jehan," said Deschamps to the other man-at-arms.

"You were right," said little Charles, "he's doing exactly as you said."

"Do you intend to fight me, Deschamps?" said John.

"I won't raise a weapon against my prince," said Deschamps, "but neither will I stand aside."

"Then we shall remove you!" said John. "Fools, minstrels, poets, take this dull servant away!"

The retinue burst into laughter as they came forward, leaping onto Deschamps, a couple trying to tickle him as they did so. The man-at-arms shouted and protested but he didn't draw his sword, and the weight of numbers dragged him aside. John opened the doors of the chapel and the throng carried Charles into the chapel.

Glutinous light, light that floated in blobs and pools like those shimmering stars that halo the vision on rising too quickly, filled the chapel. It was the light of storms, of the war between the sun and the dark clouds, of an effusion of gold breaking from the gloom of a rain-soaked hill.

"Ah, my father must be coming," said John. "As you said he would, you clever boy."

Charles had never seen its like before, not even when he'd been with his father in the chapel at Pamplona, watching the angel draw its form from the luminescence of the glass.

The air was thick and heavy, as if it needed a storm; the light of the chapel was a burden to him, something that ached at the corner of his eye, that seemed to contrast so sharply with his sense of his own body that he felt solid, lumpen, made of meat. He did not want to stay inside, but the chattering fools at his back expected it of him.

Charles looked around him. Suddenly the idea of coming to that place didn't seem such a good one. No king was there. The angel shouldn't come without one. Unless . . . Angels had appeared to lower people before. The shepherds. And the people they smote at Sodom and Gomorrah. Charles felt confused, as if his head was full of fivestones.

The air in the chapel was becoming difficult to breathe. He had never had that sensation before. The feeling of being in front of the angel at Navarre had always had been wonderful—light, like a mountain morning. There was a commotion down the corridor. King Philip was coming. Charles felt dizzy and had a strong urge to sit down. The pooling light was all around him and he felt as though he might drown in it. Noises behind him. He was aware that his mother was there, Joan the Lame too, with the king, had come in, but he could not look away from the angel.

"Why are you saying these things to me?" the boy stammered.

The angel's words boomed in his mind but, though Charles understood them, he could not yet believe them to be true.

"Who brought him here? Who brought him here?" King Philip was shouting.

"Jegudiel." The name was in Charles's mind, crackling and spitting like a bonfire.

"Why are you saying these things?" cried Charles. He felt as though he had drunk a river of wine.

"Get him out of here. You, Deschamps, remove the child."

Charles fell to the floor and Deschamps hovered above him uncertainly.

"What's happening?" Prince John's hands were stretched to the ceiling, as if he would pluck the light down like an apple from a tree.

"Charles, Charles!" The queen of Navarre bent over her boy. A thick bubble of blood issued from his nose.

"The angel spoke to me! It spoke!" Charles was distraught, trying to frame the words, trying to express the horror that had been revealed to him.

"What did it say?" King Philip was there.

"There'll be time enough for that. Can't you see that he's hurt!" said Joan.

"What did it say?" Philip insisted.

The boy was sobbing, gulping in air, trying to get his words out. Joan picked her son up and started to carry him away.

"What did it say?" The king was shouting, imploring.

"Charles, Charles!" said the little boy. "King of Navarre. Never of France! Never be king of France!"

King Philip put his hands on his hips. "Well," he said, "well. This is interesting news indeed! John, bring your minstrels to the Hall. I am in a fine mood and would drink some wine, hear some songs, and watch these fools cut their capers! An internal threat removed, we can concentrate on the external ones. The Antichrist. Is it Edward? Who is it?"

"God does not yet see." The voice was like a struck gong.

"But it is not this boy. Not this one here."

The angel said, "He is on the side of God."

Philip bent to his knees. "Jegudiel, for this gift of knowledge, I promise you England. You will dwell in the light at Westminster, at Canterbury and at Walsingham. You will be England's angel!"

The light of the chapel blazed, red, yellow, gold, a bonfire light.

"Your lands are burning, Philip." The angel spoke.

"Yes!" said Philip. "And my people suffer. See the productive farms I lose, crops, animals, and toiling men to the usurper. Say now that I don't suffer!"

"You suffer. I will watch over you in battle."

"Will you speak to Michael at St. Denis? Will Michael release the Oriflamme?" said King Philip.

But the light died and the chapel was ordinarily beautiful again.

8

D ow descended the stairs behind the priest, clasping the rail for
support.

The glow of the candle lit up the cellar, showing the demon,
devil, or whatever it was, quite immobile in the circle. It was lying facedown, its head on its arm.

Dow looked around at the books, the powders, the skulls, and the animal
corpses that lined the walls. There was even a whole human hand, rotted
almost to nothing.

More of Îthekter's filthy relics, he thought. He tried to speak. His throat
was so raw and swollen, he could emit no more than a grunt.

"What?" said the priest.

Dow picked up a quill from the desk. He was desperate to learn exactly
what the devil could tell him about the strange woman who had saved him.
He'd seen priests writing before he'd fled to the moor, though he had no
idea how to do it himself. Still, he dipped the nib into the well.

"You can write? Now *that* would be a miracle," said Edwin.

Instead, Dow used the pen to draw. He used symbols—manacles for
himself to represent that he was a captive, a distaff for the woman, shining
with light, and then the man with the mouth of fire. The priest knocked
the parchment from his hands.

"You'll not cast your spells in here," he said. "You'll . . ." Then he seemed
to think better of it and picked up the parchment.

"Is this a spell?" he asked. "Is this how I make it do my bidding?"

Dow shook his head in frustration, which the priest took for encouragement.

"You regret handing it over? Well, you've given it to me now."

Dow thought that the man had talked to devils for so long he was incapable of recognizing the truth when he saw it.

The priest walked up to the magic circle brandishing the paper. The devil remained lying on the floor. Dow came closer too. The devil was shaking. Then the devil looked up and he realized their captive was sobbing.

"Look at this. What do you make of it? Does the paper command you? Will you now do my biddings?"

"I will do whatever you want—just release me," said the devil.

"Well, that's progress," said Edwin. "It's just repeated its lies about being a pardoner before. Have you heard of the Drago?"

"Yes. I've sold three."

"Three?" said Edwin.

"Probably more. There was a rush on a few years ago when it looked like our good King Edward was going on crusade with his cousin the French king. When that went quiet, demand dropped off."

"There were three Dragos?"

"There are as many as there are bedsheets with a splash of paint on 'em to look like a dragon. I used to know a lady knocked 'em up lovely. Mind you, why St. George would have had a dragon on his pennant going to fight a dragon is anyone's guess. It's like going to kill the king of France with his head on your banner. Doesn't make sense, but it's what the people want."

Edwin turned to Dow. "Can you interpret his dissembling?"

Dow gestured to his open mouth.

"The sooner we teach you to write, the better. I can hardly understand a word you say at the best of times."

Edwin went to his tables and his books, the candle flame wavering to send the shadows dancing as he passed. He took up a book and made the sign of the cross over it. Then he studied it for some time before returning to face the figure in the circle.

"In the name of the Father and of the Son and of the Holy Spirit, I command you, devil, whether of the day or of the night, by the power of the undivided Trinity and the intercession of the glorious Mary ever Virgin, by the prayers of the prophets, by the merits of the patriarchs, by the supplication of the angels and the archangels, by the intercession of the apostles, by the passion of the martyrs, by the faith of the confessors, the chastity of virgins, the intercession of all the saints, and by the seven sleepers whose names are Malchus, Maximianus, Dionysius, John, Constantine, Seraphion, and Martimanus." He approached the devil, repeatedly making the sign of the cross.

"Cease your vagueness and your deceptions and reveal the truth of what I ask! Christ reigns. Christ commands. Christ conquers!"

The thing in the circle let out a long and sonorous fart.

"That fart is an offense to God! Will you not be commanded?"

"What do you want? Just set me free and you can command me to play Evensong out of my arsehole."

"Hear it blaspheme! No wonder my mind plays tricks on me when I am forced to work daily with such as this, who laugh in God's face. Where is the Drago?" Edwin made the sign of the cross.

"Where do you think it is?"

"I think the French took it."

"Then the French took it."

"You see!" shouted Edwin. "These things can be made to obey!"

"If a Drago's all you want, I can get you one before the end of the year. I know a woman in Cheapside who, for the right price, will embroider you one so it looks as if the dragon will bite you. Painted version, by the end of the week."

"How can the Drago be in Cheapside if it's also in France? Did French agents bring it to Cheapside?"

"You are not the most stupid man I have ever met," said the devil. "That honor goes to a knight to whom I managed to sell a hoof of St. Horse. But you are a creditable second."

"I try to use my guile to see truth through lies."

"Well, you're doing a good job of seeing lies through truth here, pal. I am a pardoner, stuck in here by a very odd sort who is probably wandering about as we speak, eating people, or worse. Very probably worse, whatever that is."

Dow could sense the despair coming off the creature. It had decided, Dow thought, that it had no hope at all of getting out and was now just talking nonsense.

"You return to your old song," said the priest.

He went back to his desk and started leafing through books. Again he took an age, while the thing in the circle muttered disconsolately to itself, making not much sense.

"Eating people with your mouth open—that has to be worse than just eating them. Why won't they believe me? How would I know about the Drago? I know about Dragos all right, but who knows about the real thing? Is there even a real thing?"

Dow stared at the creature. *Direct me to the banner. Why talk in riddles? Do you not know where it is?*

No reply.

"Kid, why don't you let me out of this circle. Do you know how?"

"Keep away from the circle or the price is death, heretic!"

"Heretic!" said the figure. "Now why do you say that?"

"He is of your party," said the priest.

"I have a party?" said the pardoner. "Glory be! Could you tell them I'm here so they'll come and rescue me?"

The boy held up three fingers to the creature.

"Nope, means nothing to me," said the pardoner.

"Now I know that you lie," said the priest. "You're telling me you don't even recognize your own devil's sign."

"Oh, *that* devil's sign," said the pardoner. "Now you mention it . . . no, I don't."

"And yet you said 'Oh, *that* devil's sign,' clearly recognizing it," accused Edwin, "catching yourself out with your own lies."

"Have you ever been in an alehouse?" said the pardoner.

"No," said Edwin.

"Thought not. Go into one. You need to learn when people are joking."

"Will that lead me to the Drago?"

"What's that got to do with anything? You can have one for sixpence if you let me out of here!"

"You should mark how he speaks in circles," said Edwin to Dow, "how nothing at all makes sense. And yet there are glimmers of sense in it. What do you make of it?"

Dow gestured to his chest. It was agony and he needed to lie down.

"Still whining about that? This is insufferable," said Edwin. "If you are to be my assistant, you'll need to learn to communicate properly—not in grunts and groans. We'll get you reading and writing, and then I can use your skills to question this fiend more closely. He is a devil from Hell, gaoler of those you worship, and I would establish if he is telling the truth about the nature of Hell."

The devil said, "I'm to be here until the kid learns to read? How long will that take? I haven't eaten, I haven't drunk!"

"And neither have you pissed or shat."

"Odd, I admit. I don't even feel hungry. Still, at least I can fart. Whatever happens to me, they'll never take that from me." He laughed, but without mirth. "And I haven't said anything about the nature of anything," he added.

"Liar! You told me before that devils are Hell's gaolers and demons its prisoners. That is an old heresy, but one repeated enough to make me take it seriously."

"Look, I don't understand this any better than you do. Just let me out!"

"You think me a fool, abomination? You are a creature of magic, sustained by magic."

"I am a creature of total bollocks, sustained by total bollocks!" shouted the figure. "I am a liar, trapped in a fool's lie to himself."

"I have forced a confession of at least that from you. I regard my work as done for a while. Boy, follow me. Orsino must go to Cheapside and find out what he can about the Drago. We need to follow every lead this creature gives us."

"I have a lead!" said the creature.

"What?"

"Go to Puppekirty Lane in Cheapside. Ask any of the whores in the more economical establishments to attend here. They will vouch that I am a pardoner, and not a devil as you contend."

"You ask me to take the word of a whore?"

"There's none so truthful as a whore you don't pay."

"Up," said the priest to Dow, "we will begin your reading and writing lesson. And I will expect attention, for I teach by the rod as the Bible instructs."

"Does it instruct you to call devils?" said the thing in the circle.

"So you are a devil," said Edwin, "and condemned from your own mouth."

"Oh, by God's holy testicles," said the thing, and put its head in its hands.

Dow looked hard at the priest. He would work out how to find this Drago. Then he would act, not for the priest but for himself, his brothers on the moor, and for Free Hell. First he had to find out if the thing in the circle was a demon or a devil. If it was a demon, he would help it escape. If it was a devil, as the priest seemed to think, Dow would practice upon it, learn how to send it back to Hell. Then he would be fitted for the task Free Hell had set him, no matter what God and his servant Satan could throw at him.

He climbed the stairs, clenching his jaw and hoping that Orsino had found something to ease the pain.

9

King Edward sat in his room, his head bent over the parchments in front of him. He'd secured the very best lodgings in Antwerp—a splendid merchant's house he'd rented for the duration, but even that was an expense he wished he did not have to bear.

They'd arrived in the city to find the wool he had been promised simply wasn't in the warehouses, and no one had had the courage to tell Edward that until he'd gone to see it himself. It was as bad a situation as could have been imagined, short of losing it to the French. The levy that Parliament had ordered simply hadn't taken place. The wool hadn't even been gathered—corrupt collectors and disobedient subjects had meant that only £3,000 worth of a promised £200,000 had arrived to sell to the weavers of Flanders. No wool, no money, no army, no allies, no war.

Well, the wool *would* be collected—he'd make sure of that. On that security, he thought he might touch the Bardi bankers and other Florentines for £100,000. The great crown could be mortgaged and the treasures of the monasteries too. He'd be bled dry, Edward knew— massive interest rates and sureties demanded—but he had no choice. He had to start paying the allies, he had to travel to meet the Holy Roman emperor in great style and to distribute monies freely as he went. To be a king is to be seen to be a king. If his allies suspected the real state of his finances he would be done for.

The king went to the window and looked out. The town bristled with English banners, bright flowers growing on the dung heap of his debt. Every day his army remained static was a day he had to pay them, while getting nothing in return. It was July, though a cold one. He couldn't pay for this lot beyond August, unless he raised more money.

Edward dashed off a letter himself, demanding that a new wool levy take place in England. It was demeaning not to use a scribe, but he was not willing to give anyone in his camp access to such dispiriting news. He scratched his anger into the vellum. Not having any wool was not an excuse for not providing any. Men who didn't own any must buy some.

His meeting with the princes of Flanders and the Rhineland had gone terribly. Each had said they hadn't yet mustered a proper army—only their personal entourages had come with them. Each had demanded money, and one—the margrave of Juliers—had requested to come into the presence of the angel. Edward had put him off, arguing it would be a while before the chapel in Flanders was ready. It was no easy job to call an English angel, and an even harder one to make it go back again if it considered it had been raised for nothing. Still, he'd found a good course of action to keep the meddlesome margrave busy—sending him to Germany to set up a meeting with the Holy Roman emperor.

Edward stirred the fire. One of the innovations in the merchant's house was a brick chimney, which meant the room was wonderfully free of smoke. July, and the evenings chilly—just his luck to have to buy firewood in high summer.

He owed Louis of Bavaria—the Holy Roman emperor—£54,000. If he couldn't pay some of that back, he would never receive his blessing. He had to buy an angel because he hadn't inherited one.

He snuffed out his candle. The last of the daylight filtered weakly through the glass of his window. He kneeled toward it. "Lord, help me. Lead me from this wilderness. Grant me your favor. I have built you a great chapel at Windsor, I have contributed mightily to your church. I will crusade, I will tear the unbeliever from Jerusalem—but build my strength. Let me bring King Philip to terms. I am not a greedy king. I do not seek to rule France, just to defend my lands. When I have angels, I will . . ."

Somehow he couldn't say the words. Atone. Put it all right. They implied he had been in the wrong, not the victim of a fraud perpetrated by his mother and by her lover Mortimer. He had been forced to take radical steps, make unpalatable bargains. He had no choice. *Never forget that, Edward. There was no other way.*

No angels. Why? Because Mortimer had compromised him, told him his father was dead. After young Edward had been crowned, Mortimer told him his father had not died after all but had been taken away. The threat was clear—be Mortimer's spaniel or face exposure as a usurper. For a time he hadn't known if Mortimer had lied. But where were his angels?

He touched the finger bone of St. Catherine he carried in a purse at his belt, trying to bring the saint into his mind. He saw and felt nothing, no light, no sense of calm.

The light was dying. A wind was in the chimney. Edward watched as the fire breathed sparks into the room, each one so bright and so quickly extinguished. Like men's hopes, he thought.

"Has my family not suffered enough? I traded with demons, yes, but to be the true king that you made me! They took my son! My son! Favor me, Lord, favor me! Give me angels."

He could never erase the memory of the deal he had made. Mortimer was defended by forces divine or diabolical, he could not tell. So Edward had gone to the banker Bardi, that useful man, and asked him for help.

Bardi had never known that the angels were more than simply reluctant to appear; Philip neither. Bardi got him his help, at terrible cost. He'd approached the French king, of all people—relations had been friendly then. Philip had sent an intermediary, not knowing that Edward's difficulty was more than the customary reluctance of angels to appear. Besides, Philip was keen to help Edward. It had been convenient for him to remove the old English king, but he could not allow a successful rebellion against an appointed king to be seen to succeed.

Edward had gone by arrangement to a tavern, dressed as a common man. It was May, and the fire, cajoled from green wood, filled the place with a hazy smoke in which the former Templar had appeared to him like a devil. Good Jacques was a tough, brown little man, hair shaved like a friar, wearing the livery of the Order of St. John Hospitaller. He looked a fair bet for a magician. The Grand Master of the Hospitallers was with him, disguised as a common monk.

"I know your problem," he'd said.

"Which is?" Edward asked.

"The continuing health of your father."

"Does Philip know?"

"No one knows," said the Grand Master. "Outside of me and Good Jacques here. We came to your father's aid, at his request."

"And Mortimer knew you got him away?"

"Yes."

The sweet smell of the fire smoke drifted over Edward. He tried to remain calm.

"And where is he now?"

The Grand Master shrugged. "He has no wish to be found."

"This is powerful information," said Edward. "You could use it to your great advantage."

"We intend to. But as practical men we see we have *you* where we want you. Not Mortimer. We will prosper if you come to true power."

"You will that," said Edward. "I will see to it."

"You will swear so?"

"I will swear."

"Then I leave the details to our friend here," said the Grand Master. "I have no taste for consorting with demons."

"I can get you in front of Mortimer," said Good Jacques. "I can put him in your power. But can you dispatch him?"

Edward replied, "Get me within arm's length of him when he is undefended. I can do the rest."

The Templar had tricked him, tricked the Grand Prior. He'd made Edward swear in front of the demon, summoning it in the wilds of the Welsh borders, well away from the prying eyes of the Hospitallers. It had taken fleshly form as a mud man, a thing of the clay of the soil, sucking and squelching into life. Edward, the dupe, had offered what Free Hell demanded, not the Hospitallers of God.

"It has come from Hell?" he asked Good Jacques.

"It came through a crack in the outer wall. This demon will give you Mortimer," said the Templar. "What will you give it?"

"I will give your order power and influence in England."

"Not my order," the Templar had said. "I work for Free Hell. These demons would be free of Hell, to live on earth. Give him a place on earth so that when the gates of Hell are opened by the Man of Perdition, the demons may rebuild Eden."

"I will not do it."

"Then remain in Mortimer's power."

It is as it is. No point going that far and faltering.

"Gascony or Aquitaine," said Edward. They were his to give.

"Swear that if Gascony or Aquitaine is not delivered in seven years, you will let Free Hell take one of your children. Five years after that, another, and three after that yet one more."

"You will not kill my children."

Good Jacques said, "We will take them. Free Hell does not murder."

"It won't come to that. You will keep this secret, even from the other demons of Hell?"

"Secret forever, just provide the land, free of angels and kings."

"I will do it, and so I swear." Edward had been so desperate to be rid of the tyrant Mortimer, he would have agreed to anything. He was young and he was confident. A couple of distant French dominions—however valuable—were outweighed by the reward of being his own man.

Only much later did he realize the Grand Prior had not sanctioned the deal that had been done. Good Jacques had gone missing, back to his work with the poor. Edward let the Hospitallers think his bargain had been with them, not with Free Hell. He gave them their lands and the care of his mother. They were useful for that.

Philip had got what he wanted—the English king held to an impossible bargain and he hadn't been long making sure he couldn't fulfill it by attacking Edward's possessions in France.

In the merchant's house in Antwerp, the wind blew again, more sparks flashing out into the room. The smell of burning. The stuffed chair nearest the fire was smoldering. It had been a gift from his wife! He leapt up and threw a pitcher of water over it. But it was too late; the cover—his arms and those of the lion of Hainault quartered—were badly burned.

Edward's temper sprang up. "If you will not help me, God, then I curse your name!"

There was another light in the room, a furnace light, deeper and more constant than the fire. "You prayed so once before."

Edward looked up. The streaming sparks of the fire were flashing into the room. But instead of blinking away to nothing, they were swarming, taking shape.

In the air in front of him, the figure of a man, or something like a man, took form, its body made up of a shimmering field of sparks, the heat of it buckling and warping the air.

A voice said, "Your debt is not forgotten." The sparks seemed to crawl over the surface of the creature, little insects of flame.

"Are you of Hell?" Edward asked.

"Free Hell. I bring word from the liberated city of Dis."

"You spirits are various in your forms."

"As are the creatures of the earth."

Edward stood up and looked directly at the creature. The heat coming from its body was intense.

He said, "Do you think I forgot who took William? Do you think I forget my wife, drowning in tears? The lengths I went to convince people he had died? To cast away my own heir. Because of you!"

"You did not honor your debt. Seven years you were given from the day the Templars guided your way. Seven years to bring us Eden in France. You promised us Gascony."

"And you would have had it if Philip hadn't invaded. I'm trying to honor my promise, you monster. Why do you think I am here?"

"Free Hell won't wait forever for its kingdom. Eden on earth, a refuge from flame and fire."

The king said, "You will have it! France will fall or we'll carve a big enough chunk out of it to satisfy you. Then it will be yours and you can pour in all the demons you like."

"You can deal with the angels?"

"France has no angels or they'd be in the field against us."

"When Hell comes to earth, they will stir."

"I'll burn every church and every cathedral for one hundred miles. They will not come."

"They will come, and you must be protected. Know your allies. You will march for Lucifer or you will perish by the hand of God. See how He forsakes you. We will bring you a gift that will put the angels to flight. The man of perdition is here. He will find a banner of great power and bring it to you. Welcome Lucifer. Your father did; did he not break bread with the ordinary people? Labor with them until the fallen angel Despenser seduced him?"

Edward fell to his knees, crossing himself and uttering Hail Marys. "Equality is against God's plan. A poor man is not equal to a king, as a rat is not equal to a lion. I have atoned. I have built great churches and shrines, and I have gone on my knees before the statue of the Virgin and begged forgiveness."

"Do you feel forgiven, Edward? Do the angels come?"

The king's mind boiled with anger.

He took up his sword—the sword that King Arthur had pulled from the stone—holy and blessed, which, in Mordred's hand, had killed the old king and become etched with his divine blood. The stain could still be seen, ruby red in the light of the demon's fiery skin. Edward jabbed the sword toward the demon. He said, "My father may be dead naturally by now."

"Where are your angels? Usurper!"

It was all Edward could do not to strike the thing.

Instead he replied, "He must be dead. God would not have let me sit on the throne for so long, nor delivered Mortimer to me. Tell me, then, if my father lives, where is he? *Where is he?*"

"We cannot tell. It is hidden."

"By angelic power?" asked Edward.

"Or greater. Welcome Lucifer as friend, champion the poor as your father would have done if devils had not beset him. Lucifer forgives the man who forgives himself. Give us England and let us share it with its people. You would keep your children. We would restore the one we have taken to you."

"Get away. You will have what I promised you and no more! I will atone for my offense to God."

"There is no atonement for the theft of a throne."

Edward's mind was white with rage. He couldn't think, couldn't reason. "I will atone! I will atone!"

"Atone for your rage. Atone for killing just men to hide your secrets! Where are those who went with your father? You killed them all!"

"And I'd kill them again to protect my right! I am king! You will not have my children! You will not take another!"

"Seven, five, and three. Eden in France or you pay what you owe."

"I'll kill you!"

Edward swiped at the creature with his sword. The demon lost shape for an instant as the holy sword struck, the sparks just shimmering in a glittering sheet before the king. And then they seemed to explode, flying to every corner of the room, to the tapestries on the walls, the rugs on the floor, the cloth on the table, Edward's clothes even. In a breath the room was on fire, smoke falling like a black waterfall from a wall hanging. Edward, oblivious to the flames spreading on his own shirt and hose, grabbed it from the wall and threw it down, but it was no good.

The room had caught fire; the heat was overwhelming. He staggered back through the door, calling for his men, his squires, telling them to bring water as quick as they could. Men were on him then, beating at the fire on his body, leaping past into the room and then recoiling, overwhelmed by smoke.

He found himself in the street, men all around him, asking if he was all right, offering him water, blankets, ale, wine. His father, *alive*? Edward had tried to ignore it for so long. It was as if, by believing it to be untrue, it would *be* untrue. And what of it, if he was? There was nothing he could do. He could not find his father.

He had thought Mortimer lied, telling him his father lived just to control him by threatening to expose him as a usurper—but Edward bowed to no man. Either his father was dead, in which case he was king and could do as he pleased, or his father was alive, in which case Edward was compromised and must act. Either way, the solution had been plain. Death to all those who might have sniffed out the secret and, where blackmail kept him from murder, as in the case of Berkeley, bribery and advancement for his children. No bribe for Mortimer. Edward had known he would never reveal where

Edward's father was, even on the scaffold, and he could not risk Mortimer saying the old king lived, lie or not. Better to gag him and restrain him in silence, as he had done.

Did anyone else know the secret? His uncle Edmund was in the grave, painted a fool for believing the story of old Edward's survival and executed for rebellion in trying to "rescue" him from Corfe. Foolish Edmund—sentenced to death by Mortimer but expecting young Edward to protect and pardon him. But his silence could not be bought, so he had died. Edward had killed so many to hold on to his secret. He had no regrets. He would do it again in an instant.

"I'm perfectly well! Let me be!" He pushed his men away from him.

The throng stood off him. "A candle, knocked over by a servant, no doubt," Edward said.

"My lord!" It was Montagu in a traveling cloak, standing beside him. *There* was the man he needed, to save England and to keep the promise that had won him his throne.

"William," the king said, "we need to speak."

10

J oan comforted the little boy as he lay on the rich bed in his solar at the palace.

The nurses and other ladies had been dismissed and the queen of Navarre tended to her son alone.

The room was on the top floor of the palace with a good large window in clear glass. The sunset lit the room with a beautiful warm glow, though the boy had complained about the light and Joan had closed the shutters to shade him.

"There, little Charles," she said, "you have had a shock. The presence of angels isn't easy for anyone, least of all a child of your age. But you did well, very well. Tell me, darling, what did the angel really say?"

The little boy turned away from her in a silent fury.

"Very well. There will be time enough for all that when you've recovered. Would you like some sugar? I have a few crystals I got from the cooks."

Charles still said nothing, his back to his mother. She took some of the sugar from a wrap of cloth and reached over to put it to his lips. He could not resist it and his tongue popped out to take it into his mouth.

"There, that's better, I think," she said. "You'll soon be back in a good temper. Don't cry, remember your status. Be in the habit of disguising your emotions and then they cannot be your master in front of lesser people."

"But, Mama."

"Yes, baby?"

"The angel *did* say that. King of Navarre, king of France never."

Joan tapped her tongue against her teeth in thought. She said, "You could not have mistaken his words?"

"No!" The boy's face was puce and swollen, his tears flowing freely.

Joan put her head into her hands and massaged her temples. She got up and went to the window. The day was dying now and Paris lay out before her, the smoke of its fires hazing the last rays of the sun.

"It should have been ours," she said, "all of it. Every hearth, every home, every soul in this city, and the land beyond belongs by rights to us. All the seven angels of France should have been ours. What do we have instead? Little Pamplona, freezing or boiling halfway up a mountain."

"What shall we do, Mother?" Charles sat up, distraught.

She came to the bedside. "I don't know. If God is against us, then perhaps we should accept it."

The boy drew himself up, managing to give the impression of looking down at someone who was a head and a half above him. He said, "If God is against us, then I am against God."

Joan crossed herself. "That is a terrible thing to say!"

"Why?"

"Think of the life to come. And think of this life. You will have angels of your own to speak to when you are king of Navarre."

Charles wiped away his tears. "A measly cherub—France can call on archangels. I don't care for angels," he said. "They have done us no good."

"When God speaks to us directly, Charles, we must accept what He says, no matter how horrible that may be."

"No. I shall be like Great-Aunt Isabella."

"Charles!" Again Joan crossed herself.

"You said she took what she was owed."

She said, "And look where it got her."

"Is it true she turned to Hell for help?"

"Her enemies said so." Joan looked about her, as if fearing being overheard. "Something went on. You can't invade England, overthrow the king, his army, and his angels without some sort of aid, even if the king is your husband. It was well known her lover got where he did by sorcery. The distaff line of the Capetians has always had certain skills."

"You are of that line."

"Don't think on that," said Joan. "I am respectful of my duty to God."

"She had bad luck, you said," said Charles.

"Yes, very bad luck. That's one way of looking at it. Or God punished her for setting herself above her son, the rightful king. Look, sleep now. I shall get someone to come and see you."

"Who?"

"A churchman. He can remind you of your spiritual duties."

Charles said, "Do not talk to princes of duty. Princes command duty; they are not commanded."

"And your father? He serves the king dutifully."

"Then Daddy is a fool. You say it yourself." Tears still fell over his blotchy face.

Joan patted the boy on the head. "You are wise enough to keep these thoughts to yourself, Charles?" she asked him.

"I am."

"Good."

"Mama," he said.

"Yes?"

"If we cannot have France, then France must burn."

Joan thought deeply. She hated to see the Valois on the throne. What was the alternative? Rule from England. But Edward could not hope to really govern two such countries. If the English king ruled France, then the real power would fall to those who knew the country best.

She looked at her son, so beautiful, so clever. He deserved to rule, if not in name then in truth. And if a war failed? Well, she would have poisoned Philip's reign, tied him up in a vicious conflict, burned the crops that yielded his revenue, killed the farmers who tilled his lands. Yes, England. Philip was a pious prig who talked always of the imitation of Christ. Well, she would turn his crown to one of thorns, make a cross of his kingship, France into a new Golgotha.

But her husband would never move against the Valois or ally with the English. He was an impediment, she thought, a Valois serf to fetch and carry.

She cradled Charles to her, kissing him on the top of his head. *If you can't be king of France, you can soon be king of Navarre,* she thought.

The child wept, great sobs racking his body.

"You stay at this court, smile, and learn," said Joan, "because one day, my son, and it won't be very long, your day will come. From the rolling waves of the west to the shimmering blue seas of the east, we will see France burn and the banners of the Valois imposters trampled into its ashes."

"I would like that, Mama," said Charles. "I would like that very much."

11

T he day before the fire, Montagu had kicked his horse toward the setting sun, heading down the broad river Scheldt away from Antwerp toward Gaunt. It was thirty-five miles, he had an excellent scout's horse—an Irish hobby he'd taken as plunder in Scotland—and he hoped to make the town well before dawn. He'd be missed at court, but his excuse of being ill would deflect suspicion for long enough.

He'd managed to get a letter to Maltravers after having a man tour the city for Englishmen for a week. He'd found Maltravers, but not in good condition—begging by the cathedral, asking for coin. The traitor had read the contents of the letter and sent a letter in reply saying he would be pleased to meet the earl. Montagu's man told him to hurry up—Maltravers was starving and would not have approached another Englishman had he not been at death's door.

Of course it was dangerous to travel at night, but Montagu had been attacked before by English bandits and lived. A few halfhearted weavers looking to make some quick coin on the side weren't going to bother him. He disdained to show fear of common men and rather thought that he, with his fine sword, was more of a problem for bandits than he was for them.

He expected no trouble—ordinary night travelers being unusual and the armies of the count of Hainault and other allies mustering to Edward's banners in the area—but he still wore his aketon of canvas and kid leather, the thick padded coat keeping the rain off, even if it was a little hot once he got into the ride. Also, there had been war in the area. The French had made a halfhearted attack on Gaunt when they learned of its alliance with Edward, and the pope had excommunicated the entire town's population, which would have put their angels to flight even if the Flemings had any in the first place.

The rain was light and the night cold, but the road was lit by a watery moon, full, shimmering, like a silver penny in a fountain. The king was feasting the count, spending lavishly to disguise his bankruptcy. Montagu had pleaded illness and retired for the night. George, one of his squires, had begged to go with him, but Montagu had refused. He didn't want the young man caught up in it if anything did go wrong, nor to attract any blame if the trip invoked the king's displeasure.

The road was a good one, even paved in parts—where the common people hadn't stolen the stones for building materials.

He trotted on through the silver dark, bypassing hamlets and camps, and, where the forest thinned enough, he saw fires in the distance. He felt good out and alone on his horse, unencumbered by his retinue, dressed no more grandly than a bowman. He wondered what it would be like to live life like that, no politics to contend with, no bullying and coaxing others into doing what they needed to do, no army to command or angels to worry about. Boring, he concluded, though he wouldn't have minded a month of that life, once in a while.

The road to Gaunt would have been easy to follow even if Montagu hadn't done it several times before, and he was cresting a low hill, looking down on the huge town just as the bells of the city's churches were ringing Matins. He would make the city well before dawn, which might prove a problem, he thought—the gates were likely barred during the hours of darkness. Never mind.

The rain had stopped, so he unbuttoned his coat to reveal a shirt of rich yellow silk, decorated with boars' heads. The men on the gate would bow to his nobility and let him pass, he hoped, even though he was a foreigner. Where he would find stabling for his horse and anywhere to keep himself warm and stop his sweat from freezing on him, he didn't know. Montagu rested the horse a while and let it eat. Then he kicked on toward the city. The French had done little damage to the walls, and what they had done had been repaired. The remains of a couple of sorry-looking catapults lay broken at the edge of the woods.

The night guard let him in, though he had to make himself understood through sign language—he could never get so much as a word of Flemish. The guards knew well enough that a nobleman would want to stable his horse, wash, and eat, so they led him to a good inn and knocked up the innkeeper, whose complaints were silenced when Montagu opened his purse.

At dawn, the bells of Prime ringing in his ears, he set out for St. Bavo's Cathedral, over St. Michael's bridge, as its shopkeepers were opening up for the morning, calling to him as he passed, some holding up rolls of cloth, others holding up hauberks or helmets, still others trying to interest him in rich golden cups. One man showed him a razor and sliced a piece of cloth with it to show how sharp it was.

Montagu said, "There are a thousand French lords who will bleed me for free should I wish it, and a few who have already done the job. Can't say I felt better after the experience. Let me through."

He couldn't understand what the shopkeepers said but, by their obsequious manner and deep bows, he could see they marked him for a noble. Montagu smiled to himself. He may have been dressed like a foot soldier, all finery concealed beneath his thick coat, but his bearing marked him out as above the common swell of men. "You can't disguise it, William," he said to himself. "Breeding always comes out."

It wasn't difficult to find the cathedral—its huge tower dominated the city and, even if he had been blind in two eyes instead of one, the noise of the mason's hammers, the carpenter's saws, and the calls of the workmen would have led him there. That and the waxy smell of the fires the bell founders had lit to cast their brass work. The city was rising into noise—hoofbeats, hawkers' cries, the rattle of shutters, and the scrape of shop tables being set out in the streets. The people spoke so loudly here, louder even than London.

Of course, it would be impossible for them to talk in the cathedral with so much building work going on and a market already setting up inside. Montagu found the noise intolerable. He would find an inn and take an ale with Maltravers to help him sleep on the boat ride back to Antwerp.

Maltravers didn't turn up. Not for the first hour, nor the second. After the third, Montagu accepted he had been on a fool's errand and set about finding a boat to take him home. By the docks he saw a man watching him from fifty paces away. An Englishman. No, the dirty ghost of an Englishman. In his wars he'd buried healthier-looking men. "Maltravers?" he asked. Montagu had known Maltravers at court, but he scarcely recognized the starveling in front of him.

The ghost crossed itself.

Montagu said, "I haven't come to kill you, John."

"No? Nor drag me to torture?"

"No. I bear you no malice. My sergeant could have done the job. I'm afraid you've fallen below the level where you'd get the personal service."

"Can we eat?" Maltravers shook, his hands raised almost as if in prayer.

Maltravers's clothes were in the English court style—hose, a short tailored jacket, and long, pointed shoes. But the jacket was torn and filthy, the hose had holes in them, and, though the day was cold, he wore no cloak. In Flanders, where wool cloth was very cheap, you had to be a poor man indeed to dress so shabbily, thought Montagu. The man was short, dark, very thin. Two things he hadn't sold in his starvation, Montagu noted, were his sword and a brass medallion that hung around his neck. Montagu recognized it as a lamina—something sold by frauds to idiots supposedly to ward off evil.

He said, "Yes, we can eat."

"Thank you, William—Earl of Salisbury now, aren't you?" Maltravers actually licked his lips at the thought of food.

"I am."

So much for discretion. Still, if the count of Hainault had spies about, they would more than likely report to Montagu himself, which would stop the king hearing news of his trip. If the old king *was* alive, he would have to confront Edward with the news sooner or later, but Montagu wanted to do it on his own terms and in his own time.

Maltravers led Montagu away from the docks, across the broad square in front of the cathedral to a big inn that faced its front. The knight gave a boy a coin to guard his horse and went inside the inn. It was clean and well kept, with herbs on the floor so there was a pleasant lavender smell to the entrance corridor, before the smoke of the fire in the main hall overwhelmed it. The men went into the hall.

There were few people in it—just a couple of old men sitting by the fire in the big main room—but Maltravers went in and sat at a bench by a table and called loudly for service. A man emerged to whom Maltravers spoke in Flemish. The innkeeper's glances shot between Montagu and Maltravers. By the cut of their clothes—one fine, the other ragged—neither was the sort of man he felt comfortable entertaining. However, Maltravers set him at ease—doubtless with the promise of extra payment—and the man went away.

"Thank you for coming to see me, my lord." Maltravers's eyes darted to the door and to shelves where pies sat. "No fresh delivery from the bakery, so they'll be cold—but still wholesome, I guess."

"Indeed."

Montagu took a roll of parchment from his purse that he'd copied from the parliamentary record. It laid out clearly Maltravers's crime—he had deceived the old king's brother, Edmund, into thinking the king was still alive. Edmund had gone to rescue his brother with the aim of reversing his abdication and restoring him to the throne. That was treason, and the rebel Mortimer had seen that he was executed for it. Young Edward, though at that point just a puppet ruler, could have stopped his uncle's execution. But he did not. He let him die.

Then, once he got rid of Mortimer, he had Maltravers charged—not with old Edward's murder but with Edmund's. That alone was odd but, as Montagu was discovering, perhaps there just wasn't the evidence to convict Maltravers of the old king's death. Maltravers had left the country by then and gone to ground. Montagu read the parchment.

"John Maltravers is guilty of the murder of Edmund, Earl of Kent, the uncle of our lord, the present king. He especially, treacherously, and falsely plotted the death of the said earl. Although the said John Maltravers knew of the death of old King Edward nevertheless, the said John, by ingenious manner and by false and evil claims, convinced the earl that the old king was alive, by which false plotting he caused the death of the said earl."

"You have come to take me back!" he said. Maltravers was ashen, and he rubbed the medallion between his finger and his thumb.

"No. You are dead, officially. The king believes you were killed by the knight Wyvill. As did I. He was sent to kill you."

"I bought him off with what money I could find."

Montagu said, "My God, that's worth knowing. Wyvill's a pompous ass, always banging on about honor!"

Maltravers looked around for the innkeeper. He said, "I am thankful to the king for awarding my lands and income to my wife. I thought that he might confiscate them after my work for the tyrant," he said.

"Can she not send you money?"

"She thinks I'm dead too. It's better that way. I would not have my taint fall on her. Has she remarried?"

"Not as far as I know."

He nodded. "Good. Good. Where are those pies?"

The landlord had disappeared for the moment.

"Are you guilty, John?" Montagu asked him.

"What should I say? I want to return. What should I say?"

"Tell me the truth—and, believe me, I will know truth from lies. If I judge you truthful, I will work for your return."

Maltravers, a man who seemed given to expressing his inner thoughts physically, slumped forward over the table with a sigh. Relief? Despair?

"When Edmund tried to free the old king from Corfe, it was not because I had lied to him. It was because I had told him the truth. The king *was* there."

Montagu bowed his head. It was as he had suspected. The king had not died at Berkeley. But that wasn't the same as saying he was still alive. Montagu needed to know more.

"You mistreated the king. There was word you tried to drive him mad by locking him away, denying him food. Why did you then act as a friend to him?"

"What it is to be accused," said Maltravers. "I am damned for trying to save the king, damned for abusing him. I was not the one who locked him away. The old king himself demanded it!" Maltravers thumped the table. "Oh, where are those pies?"

"Control yourself and speak softly. What do you mean?"

"Ah!"

The innkeeper had come back in, though not with pies but ale and bread. Maltravers tore into the food at once. He had wolfed down the whole little basket, gulped all the ale, before he continued.

"A devil had set on him. A terrible devil. The king said it was a curse called up by Despenser, though I don't know why he would choose to attack the source of all his power. The king and all his angels fought it. At Berkeley they subdued it and sealed it in a box. The king heard that men were coming to murder him, but he would not leave the box. He was convinced the devil would break out. So we transported him and it to Corfe, where a chapel had been sanctified to allow him to call his angels again. There he sealed it further, with the help of certain foreign knights."

"The Hospitallers?" Montagu asked.

"Yes. They had a man working under duress with them."

"Who?"

"I don't know his name. He was a Frenchman. Good Jacques, they called him, I don't doubt to mock him. They seemed to think him anything but good."

Montagu said, "You know no more about him?"

"No. Where are the pies?" He stamped his foot like an impatient child.

"And when he had sealed it, why didn't he await his brother Kent's arrival? Edmund would have freed him."

Maltravers said, "He was afraid."

"Of what?"

"Of the thing in the box. He said that, for the future of his line, he needed to take it away. They took him away—along with the box."

"Who?"

"The Knights Hospitaller."

"Where to?"

"Across the sea. I went with him."

"To where?"

"To the pope at Avignon, and under disguise. From there I was dismissed, and shamefully—no pay. I barely got my expenses back from Mortimer."

"You applied to Mortimer for expenses?"

"Yes." Maltravers took out a purse and opened it. There, on a threadbare piece of parchment, was an official delivery note. "For expenses incurred at Corfe. £273, eight shillings, and sixpence." It bore the seal of the royal exchequer. Montagu studied it. Maltravers, he knew, had only been at Corfe for around a week, a fortnight at most. How in that time had he incurred such massive expenses? Only kings spent on that scale. If Maltravers was looking after the notoriously extravagant Edward, that would explain the huge bill. But wait—Edward had traveled without his retinue.

Montagu said, "What was the money spent on?"

"Equipping the chapel in gold and plate. He needed to summon an angel. In fact as many as he could to seal the box."

The pies were thumped onto the table and Maltravers stabbed at his with the fury of a man conducting a revenge killing.

"Is he alive, John?" he asked him.

Maltravers crossed himself, munching and swallowing. He replied, "I have no reason to believe he's dead."

"Where did he go?"

"After Avignon, I have no idea. I came back, having done my duty," he said. "My nerves were shot. That demon, that . . . dragon, looked at me and told me that Hell claimed me. I have never slept properly since. Then the king hanged the traitor Mortimer and blamed me for killing his uncle. It was he who signed the death warrant." As he spoke he stuffed down the pie. Montagu hadn't touched his and, without asking, Maltravers pulled it toward him and started to eat that too.

"Your protector."

"As you say. I was condemned to die. Then I fled the country and came here, taking what I could. I am not guilty of what I am accused, Lord Montagu, not at all. I did my duty and stood by the king. If only young Edward would hear me. He might find his father and restore him to the throne."

Montagu sipped his ale. That, he thought, might not suit the present king at all. Would it suit England? Maybe. If the French invaded, as they were rumored to be planning to do, better a bad king with angels than a good one without.

"Where would you look if you wanted to find the old king?"

Maltravers said, "The Knights Hospitaller might know more than me. Or find the box. The demon was a thing of magic. Magicians might be able to find it."

"You think the king is with the box?"

"I feel sure he wouldn't let it out of his sight. He was adamant that its contents were a peril for us all. Go to magicians," said Maltravers. "Surely they can find it with their art?"

Montagu stood up and took out his purse. He shook out a handful of Italian florins.

"You've been useful to me, John," he said, putting the florins into Maltravers's hand "I can't promise a return home but I'll let your wife know you're here."

"Will that endanger her?"

"You have said nothing so far. Stay here and keep quiet, I doubt Edward will trouble himself to have you killed. He has more to think about than chasing old scores."

"I do long to see her."

Montagu nodded. Maltravers was a weak man who went with the prevailing wind and had been caught out by an abrupt turn in the weather. He was not bad, though, and Montagu considered that he lacked the guile implied in that charge of deceiving the duke of Kent. Edmund had been the cleverest man in the kingdom, no one's fool.

He remembered the words of the letter to old Edward that had damned Kent: "Soon you shall come out of prison and be delivered of that which plagues you."

Had Kent known about the devil? Had he found a way to subdue it? There *had* been a devil and an enemy of God—of that he was now sure. Three separate sources had confirmed it: the gaoler, Berkeley, and Maltravers. Two were men of noble birth. He had to take that seriously. What a mess that had been—old Edward still king, refusing to abdicate, his son a puppet. No one had been surprised when the king had met his death—it brought clarity and legitimacy to his son's rule. Only old Edward had *not* died.

And now he had a means of finding the old king—magicians. Not assistance Montagu welcomed. But the knights were a possibility—though they were notoriously tight-lipped. He would have liked to pay a visit to Queen Isabella in her prison at Castle Rising as she was attended by Knights Hospitaller under pay of the crown. They had spirited the old king away. Now they guarded the new queen. Easy to see how they got a grant of land in Norfolk if they had Edward by the cullions over the survival of his father.

Montagu watched Maltravers finish the last of the pie. He wished he could abandon this whole affair. Honor would not allow that. Not if the old king lived. Oh, William! If the old monarch lived, England and Edward were damned. He had to be dead, didn't he? God would not support a usurper.

Montagu bid Maltravers good-bye and rode from the inn, returning through the cart-battered streets to the river, where he took a boat. It felt good to be afloat and under way and, for the first time, Montagu allowed himself to doze. His head was full of competing cares. The army could stand in the field for no longer. They hadn't the money to pay them. They needed to engage the French. But the French would not come to battle. And if old King Edward was alive, then there would be no prospect of angels. Practically, the best course of action was to find the old king and do what was necessary—or have it done. But that was against God. Morally, he should search out his king and restore him.

Montagu could stop right there, do nothing. But that was the road to Hell, to know what was right and ignore it.

He needed more information before making any decision. He would dearly have loved to interview the Knights Hospitaller, or even Edward's mother, Queen Isabella herself. But they were at Castle Rising, and all access to that castle was denied. Only the king could visit, and he rarely chose to.

"Isabella." He said the old queen's name. He remembered what the poets had called her—the beauty of beauties. For once, they hadn't lied. Involuntarily, he crossed himself. He understood why her lover, the traitor Mortimer, had overthrown old Edward for her. She always seemed ageless, enchanting, the cleverest and the most beautiful woman he had ever known. He was frightened of her; he knew what a woman like that could make a man do. Had Mortimer not been gagged when he was executed at Tyburn, he would surely have died with her name on his lips.

The boat came in to Antwerp in the dusk. Help had arrived, he could see. Alongside the three long leopards of Edward's banners, the many arms of his knights, the rearing black lion on gold of Brabant flew, as well as the black and gold chevrons of the count of Hainault, the three red flowers of the duke of Guelders, and hundreds of other beasts, shapes, ships, and flowers that made up the standards of lesser men. The allies had arrived. Montagu crossed himself, thanked God, and cursed the bankers. The cost of paying so many men would be ruinous for Edward.

There was smoke on the breeze and, from the shore, a hullaballoo. He couldn't understand the cries of the people, but it was plain enough something big was afoot. Montagu peered into the falling light. From deep inside the town a plume of smoke was rising. Now he began to hear shouts in English and French. "Fire! Fire! The king's house is on fire!"

Montagu rushed through the streets. People were running toward the fire, some with pails from the river, others just to see the spectacle.

Montagu found the king watching the blaze.

He said, "Thank God you're safe!"

"I'm well."

Montagu eyed the king. Could you tell a usurper by looking at him? "Was it an angel?" he asked Edward.

The king looked at him strangely. "No. Just a candle knocked over by a clumsy servant. There's a worse crisis than this. Do you know the warehouses are empty? The wool hasn't come in from England. I've been lied to, William."

"Will Louis grant you his angels if you don't pay him your debts? Have you enough money? The war will be lost without them."

"William. We need that wool. I need someone I can trust to oversee its collection. Go back to England. Take the treasures of the monasteries and mortgage the great crown too. This is a time of great need, and each true subject must come to his king's aid." He put his hand on Montagu's shoulder.

"I will need a free hand to ensure we get what we need," said Montagu.

Edward said, "You will have it. The earl of Norfolk died last week. His office of Marschal of England is free. You have it, William. Do what you need to do. Each man to contribute according to his station. Those who have no wool to give can buy some."

"I will have to knock heads together."

"Do it. Get the wool and the money we need. Use your new powers as you think serves us best. You act in place of our royal person—no one can deny you. Act firmly. The time for great scruples is over."

Montagu bowed. "I'll head to England with the first tide," he said. "You will have your money."

"Let nothing prevent that," said Edward. "Everything depends on you, William, everything." He turned to his squire. "See that the merchant is paid for his house."

12

C oblenz. That city was going to bleed Edward dry and he wasn't even in it! He was still upriver at Niederwerth, waiting for the Holy Roman emperor to decide if he was going to see him or not. According to spies, the French were mustering not two days' ride from Antwerp, and the Somme was crawling with Valois troops. Edward needed money and fast or he and his Flemish allies would be overwhelmed.

He sat on the most impressive seat the locals had managed to find—a tall-backed carved thing. It was no replacement for a throne, and it gave him a rick in his back. Dancers and jugglers cavorted in the hall, tables of roast meats, poultry, and fish groaned under the weight of their burdens. It was September and it appeared to Edward that he'd bought the entire abundant Belgian harvest.

Then there was the expense of the clothes. His courtiers were all dressed up in fine silk garments, as was he, following the theme of Waltharius and the Nibelungen knights. He was Waltharius—in a red-crested helm, costing twenty florins, and golden greaves, whose price he had been too afraid to ask. He needed to make a show, though, and the expense was necessary. All Coblenz had to believe he was a wealthy lord and a worthy ally.

Beside him was a table piled high with stacks of money that had been obtained in a fit of wild borrowing by Edward's finance-raiser John Montgomery and by pawning most of his jewelry to the merchants of the Rhine.

He looked up into the timbers of the Guild Hall. If this place burned down like the merchant's house at Antwerp, then he'd be down to selling the ships to pay for it.

A German courtier came forward, bowing as he did, reminding Edward of a chicken pecking at grain.

"Stephanus Tocker, lawyer," said Montgomery, "important man and a confident of the Holy Roman emperor. Fifty florins at least."

"Count it in."

Montgomery dropped the money into a small purse.

"Tocker," said Edward, acknowledging the bobbing courtier, "please accept this gift as a mark of our respect and love for your emperor!"

A clerk alongside translated. The courtier beamed as Edward took the purse and dropped it into his hand.

By God, Galahad found the Grail more easily than Edward came by a florin, but coins flew from his hands like so many birds.

Another courtier, another fifty florins. And another and another, each of them scraping his way in before fairly springing from the hall with his booty.

"How much now?" Edward asked.

"Given or to go?"

"Given."

"Including the payments to the Emperor?"

"Yes."

Montgomery said, "Fifty thousand florins."

"In God's money, Montgomery—I can't do the reckoning."

"£7,500. Exactly as much as we borrowed."

"Which leaves us how much?"

"What you see on the table. About £40."

Edward smiled at an approaching counselor, dismissing the brief desire to put his foot into the man's face. He gave him fifty florins and sent him on his way.

A fanfare sounded outside. The trumpets were coming from the direction of the river. *Let it be the emperor.* He'd paid a third of his debts to Louis, but he knew that representatives of the French court were in town, vying for the emperor's approval. The pope in Avignon had excommunicated Louis, but the pontiff was ill and his likely successor was a French puppet. Louis's right as the Holy Roman emperor was respected by God and he'd kept his angels, but he would love a way back into the church. The French could offer him that.

If he had come all this way, made all this effort for nothing, then Edward would . . . what? Crawl home to Parliament like a feckless and wayward son to his father.

The doors of the hall opened and a herald shouted out, "Stephen, Duke of Bavaria, Vogt of Alsace and Swabia, beloved son of the Holy Roman Emperor Louis, God bless his name." In strode a tall young man dressed in a fine blue costume in a Hunnish style—wide trousers, a fur-trimmed helmet, and long split coat. Good sign or bad sign? Waltharius had tricked the Huns to escape them. Was Stephen joining in with Edward's fancy dress, or was he making a point? The man was accompanied by six knights and a host of brightly clad hangers-on. None of the retinue was in costume so Edward assumed the prince had traveled at short notice—no time to provide attire for them.

Stephen bowed, good start. Edward could think of some German princes who would disdain to bow to an English king.

Edward stood up and bowed himself.

"We will talk alone," said the prince.

Edward waved a finger to dismiss his courtiers. Stephen clapped and his own filed out too. In moments the hall was empty. Edward was glad the prince had opted to speak informally. It meant he wouldn't have to give him money.

Stephen picked up a sugared plum and sniffed at it. Then he put it back. "My father sends greetings," he said. "He is inclined to help you."

Edward said, "He sees our cause is just."

"Well, that and he sees you can fight the French for him. While they're attacking you, they're not attacking him. He, well—I, would like some clarifications first."

"Whatever you want." Desperation was not an emotion that became one of God's holy knights, so Edward disdained to feel it.

"I hear interesting gossip concerning England's angels."

Edward smiled. He said, "In my experience it's easy to hear interesting gossip about anything you care to."

"Do you have any angels?" The prince thrust his face forward as he spoke, and the king longed to thrust it back again.

Douce, Edward, douce! You need this man. He imagined Montagu beside him—how would he deal with this impertinence? What would he say? Edward threw back his head and laughed.

"Oh, what I would give for our English courtiers to have just an ounce of your German directness!" said Edward. Then, "Am I not king?" He could not keep the edge from his voice.

"Not all kings can coax out their angels. The French haven't put one in the field for years."

"Which in itself should tell you whom God favors. Stephen, please, one day you will be my guest at Windsor, I hope. There you will see the chapel we have constructed, see how the angel turns the sunbeams to harp strings."

The young man nodded. "I am satisfied," he said. "Will you be requiring the services of one of our angels, or is just our blessing enough for you to rally and command your enemies? And reassure your creditors."

This man's impertinence knows no bounds.

Edward said, "I think the presence of your angel would at least send a message that men can understand."

"There would be no risk to it?"

"Risk to an angel? I'm not sure I follow, old man."

"The Knights Hospitaller. They are a closed and silent bunch of fellows, even with those who protect them. There was talk among some of that dour lot that Hugh Despenser"—he crossed himself—"had found a way to kill them."

Again Edward laughed. "I was a boy when all that took place, not old enough to be my own master, but even I could see that Despenser was just working his familiar art of fear and lies. Despenser stood with my father, so why would he move against his angels, even if he had the power?"

The prince looked Edward directly in the eyes. Edward prayed that he could face him in a tournament one day. Then he'd knock some of the condescension out of him.

Stephen said, "You keep your mother locked in a tower."

Edward forced himself to wait before speaking. "Not so," he said. "My mother is not in good health. The tyrant Mortimer enchanted her to force her to rebellion. She was rescued by prayer and by angels. She is in the tower so that she may have the peace she craves to praise God and to recover."

"Surrounded by the holy knights, chanting day and night."

Edward forced his eyes away from his great sword that lay beside the table. *So this is what it feels to be a beggar. To stand affront after affront in the hope of small alms.*

He said, "My mother's peace of mind is dear to me. If the knights can ensure that, it is a small price to pay."

The two men faced each other in silence. The prince spoke first.

"Good, thank you for indulging my curiosity. The royal barge is here, and we would be pleased to convey you into Coblenz in three days' time to ratify the alliance before God. Angels each have their powers. Perhaps you would like an angel of healing for your mother, though we had anticipated you would want a more martial spirit."

Edward waved an indulgent hand. "I would not put the emperor to the trouble of raising another. I know from experience how troublesome it can be to disturb them from their raptures. Whatever angel your father has brought with him, I will be pleased to have."

Stephen said, "Very good. I will lodge here until we are ready to sail."

"You will be my welcome guest. Please, let's invite in our friends and celebrate our alliance."

"Indeed," said Stephen. "English food leaves much to be desired, but I understand you are using German cooks. Hey ho, fellows, join us!" he shouted.

As expected, courtiers had been pressing their ears to the doors to hear whatever might be to their advantage and now came streaming in.

"Is a tournament planned to honor our happy union?"

"It is," said Stephen. "I intend to have a tilt myself!"

"Excellent!" said Edward. "Excellent. Montgomery, please help serve the prince!"

Montgomery led Stephen away. The king beckoned his squire.

The young man hurried forward, keen—and keen to be seen to be keen.

"Adam. Do you think if you send a messenger today you could get my jousting armor here within three days?" asked Edward.

"I took the liberty of including it in the provisions of things coming by barge."

"Good man, good man. And would you get the margrave of Juliers in here? Now we've sealed this deal, he should be willing to advance me some more money to feed this guzzling Frank for the three days until his father makes me vicar and I bash some manners into that upstart's head to celebrate."

13

Y ou are a base and tattered man." Charles sat up in his bed in the Great Hall. The windows cut lattices of moonlight on the floor, the scudding clouds making the shadows seethe.

Nergal sat in the little room's single chair. His robes were torn and scorched, but it was his face that caught the boy's attention. It too was loose, torn and patchy, like a worn mask on a scarecrow. The skin had shifted slightly on the skull, meaning the eye holes were askew on the eyes, and a gaping tear at the lips revealed the teeth were much too big for the head— great yellow spearheads that seemed to take up half the face. There was a smell of burning in the room.

"You called my name?" Nergal asked.

Charles said, "Yes. I want to talk to you."

"It took you long enough."

"It's not easy to ally with Hell."

"Do you fear me?"

"Yes. No. No. You protected me."

"As much as I could. I am weak and wounded." He gestured to his face. It was different from the one he had worn in the woods.

"You stole a face."

"I am too weak to work the magic to fix it. I have had a terrible shock. I was lucky to survive and I need to recover in order to restore my former glory."

"It has been a year."

"An angel shining right next to you isn't the sort of thing you easily recover from if you're put together like me. I didn't know the fallen could do it. They didn't tell me that when sending me here for this mission."

"Are you not a demon?"

"I am a devil. God's servant. Hell's assassin. Here to remove Lucifer's stain from the world. I have been waiting for you to call for me. I have heard your anguish from afar and my soul is moved to pity. You would see all France burn?"

"I would."

"That might be more to God's favor. The angels don't look in a hurry to defend it. I can help you."

"How so?"

"The English would do it for you. They need to win before Philip calls forth his angels and takes the Oriflamme. But you could help the English. May I light your candle?"

Charles said that the creature could do what it liked. It quickly kindled a spark using the flint and steel at the side of the boy's bed and got the candle going. Then it sucked at the flame, pulling it out into a long stream of fire, which it drank down.

"I have been wounded," it said, "and I am in poor shape to bring my influence to bear."

"Who wounded you?"

"An enemy of God."

"You are a devil. Surely that makes you an enemy of God."

"Not so. As I said, I am a servant, a despised servant—as the villeins who tend your fields are despised servants, or rather as the torturers who man your gaols. I am a gaoler. A devil. It is the prisoners of Hell who are His enemies—men often call them devils, but they are more rightly called demons. Follow me and you follow God."

Charles sat straighter on the bed. "I should look to my soul."

"You would win favor with Heaven to ally with me."

"For burning the earth?"

"It may be that the time of the enemies of God is coming on earth. Perhaps the demons are to reign. Perhaps God allows it as punishment to sinful

man. Already one gate has been opened and they are thick in the air—but
it's only the lesser sort who lack enough purpose to rally. Other gates may
open. It may be impossible to stop."

"God is all-powerful; my mama says so."

"Then why does He need to work through intermediaries? Why priests,
popes, and kings? God may be all powerful—I do not know. As with the
angels, His mind cannot be fathomed. But it is certain that he lets men,
demons, and devils determine their own fate and rarely intercedes to help
them. He helps those that help themselves."

"So what do you plan to do?" Charles asked.

"If the fallen will take possession of this realm, then we must ensure it
is not worth having. We must make a Hell on earth. This will please God,
but it will expand Satan's domain too."

The boy nodded. "I like nice places. I like palaces and gardens. I would
not live in Hell but according to my rank."

"There are gardens in Hell, fountains and beautiful lakes. Satan dwells
there, servant of God, commander of legions of devils, rewarded for his toils.
You would be rewarded too."

Charles got out of bed. "Can I fetch my mama?"

"Do."

He opened the door to his room and ran down the corridor, a sleepy
guard coming to attention as he did so. At his mother's door a guard stopped
him. "Back to bed, young man, the hour is late."

"I need to see Mama."

"She is sleeping. Let her rest."

"I will be king one day, low man, and I do not forget easily."

The guard laughed, but something about the boy's manner made him
open the door. Charles ran to his mother, shaking her awake, trying not to
disturb the ladies-in-waiting sleeping at the foot of the bed.

"Mama, come and see. The cardinal has come to see me. The one I told
you about."

"What?" she asked.

"The one who breathes fire like a dragon. He eats candles. Come and
see," he whispered.

"You're dreaming, Charles, go back to bed."

"No, Mama, please come and see. The cardinal is here. He says he will help us."

"The cardinal is asleep in his bed."

"No. This is not that cardinal. This is a devil, which you must not call a demon, he says. He wears the skin of a cardinal. When you go round the back of him you can see where it's laced up, like that." The boy made a stitching motion.

Joan sat up. "If you are lying, I'll have you thrashed," she said. She knew this was an empty threat. None of the guards would lay a hand on the boy—too fearful of what he might become, and his father was never there to do it. She, as he knew, loved him too much to ever lift a finger against him.

She walked down the corridor, shooting the guards a look that suggested they should have kept the boy in his room.

She stepped inside the small room and Charles followed her.

"Queen Joan," said the devil, his skin mask drooping on his face, the candle burning next to him. "Hell loves you and hears what is in your heart. Hell understands the suffering you have undergone. I have suffered too. Our enemy is near to success. In the name of God, in the name of Satan, I offer you my aid."

Queen Joan closed the door, crossing herself. "He hasn't harmed you, Charles?"

"No, Mama, he has just talked."

The lady was used to negotiating at a high level and something struck her about the devil. Joan said, "You are desperate."

"My lady?"

"You have come to us as a last resort. I know devils. One was trapped at my father's court years ago and dispatched by the angel. You would not have known him from a normal man. Yet here you are, in this shabby guise, burned and torn, sir. You have been somewhere before here and it has not suited your temper at all."

"Indeed not, madam. Our enemies prosper. Free Hell is on the move, arming its servants, and the rightful lords of Hell can do little to stop it."

"What is Free Hell?" said Charles.

Nergal said, "The part the fallen angels took from the devil guardians appointed by God."

"I have heard this heresy before," said Joan. "But the devil I met was killed by an angel. Why did the angel kill him, if he was on the same side?"

"Angels do kill devils. The angels fear us. We would take their place. They serve God in their way; we serve Him in ours. Angels are jealous and can brook no rivalry. They tolerate us while we stay in Hell or serve them. If we venture to independence they kill us where they can."

She said, "You account yourself a servant of God?"

"Yes, madam."

"Then say: 'I turn to God as Savior.'"

"I turn to God as Savior."

"I submit to God as Lord."

He repeated, "I submit to God as Lord."

Joan sat back on the bed. "There will be no contract for our souls with you."

"I ask none."

She nodded. "What are you offering?"

"France in flames," said the devil.

"Why should I believe you can do that? This is the greatest nation on earth, protected by seven angels and a host of powerful relics."

"Because," said the devil, "I know how to kill the angels. If we kill but one, the rest may withdraw all support for Philip. They will stay in their shrines and will not allow him the Oriflamme. Without them, France will fall, the English will burn and kill, and Hell will cast its dominion over this land. Free Hell is trying to break into this realm. We will make it a wasteland."

Joan asked, "Can God still smile on those who kill His angels?"

"It depends," said the devil, "on how the angels are killed. We will not harm one ourselves—we will use an enemy of Heaven. That minimizes the risk to us. It will not be our offense."

"But there *would* still be risk?" said the boy.

Joan put her hand on her boy's head. Charles was so forward, so precocious, that sometimes she forgot he was only a child.

"To kill such a creature is always risky. They exist at all times and in all places; their attention may be anywhere. Philip's may be here in the room with us."

Joan looked around and crossed herself.

"If it is, we are undone anyway, so better to proceed as if it knows nothing," said the devil. "If it can be drawn to the flesh then it might be killed. The man of perdition might do it."

"Who is that?" said Joan.

"The Antichrist," said the devil, "the one who would upset the order God placed upon the earth, turn kings into servants, and make servants masterless. I was sent to kill him, but he's a tricky customer. He's got my knife. That's a good knife, that. A good cutter. A good stabber." He illustrated by stabbing and swiping at the air.

"How shall we find this person?"

"He's an English boy called Dowzabel. He could kill the angel, for I have seen what protects him."

"What is that?"

"Another angel, though a fallen one. We can use her, and we can use him to kill the angel in the chapel. Then what relics you shall have—angel's feathers, their teeth, and their bones."

"What favors do they bring?" said Charles.

"Many. With a feather a man might walk through a wall, with a bone heal all maladies."

"Why haven't you killed this boy if you were sent here to do it?" said Joan.

"Because of his angel protector. But if we can draw the angel of Sainte-Chapelle to rapture with her, then both will be enraptured. Then might we strike against the boy and the angel. If we kill the angel—or he manages to kill it, as I believe he could—then the fallen angel will go mad with grief for a while and be in no state to defend him. Then"—he mimed swallowing a candle and breathing out flame—"we strike."

Charles hopped on the spot, his eyes streaming slightly from the smoke that had issued from Nergal's mouth during his demonstration of the Antichrist's death.

"It would be sweet to take the Valois angels, would it not, Mama?"

"It would indeed," said Joan. "What do we need to do, devil?"

"First, you must bring me to a room that I can seal, so as to be free of the spirits of the air. Free Hell has demons on the earth, and they torment me and prevent my finding my skin in a way they would not dare, were I whole. And you must fetch me a man to eat, his skin to wear. One who will allow me influence. Then I might regain my former strength."

"That," said Joan, "we can do. I'll send for the cardinal in the morning. Will his face do?"

"It will. And write to the banker Bardi. We thought to use him in our stratagems before, yet he proved a slippery sort of pawn. He can send the boy to you," said the devil.

"The Antichrist? It would be exciting to see such a person, Mama!"

"Yes, it would, Charles," said Joan. "I will summon the banker tomorrow. But for now, I will pray."

14

S t. Castor's at Coblenz teemed with color—knights and princes in their best outfits, splendid as statues in a shrine, decked in gold, in blue, in purple, and in red. The air was hazy with the smoke of hundreds of candles, their light drawing glitters and sparkles from the crowned heads of the prince-electors in attendance. There must have been fifty of them, thought Edward, each come to witness this grand alliance.

Edward stood outside the open doors in a light mizzle, waiting for his processional entrance to begin. At his side was Grand Prior Alan York of the Knights Hospitaller, dressed in his plain black surcoat and white cross. He was a small, wiry man with a lean, tough face. A hell of a fighter, Edward knew. The Knights were highly favored by Louis too. Edward fairly itched inside his robes when he thought of the secrets they could pass on to the emperor if they so wished. *Put it from your mind. It is as it is.*

Behind Edward stood Henry Burghesh in his bishop's robes, Montgomery and a host of nobles too, laughing away at some joke of his. Montgomery wasn't particularly highborn, but he had a marvelous touch for getting money out of people, so Edward introduced him to whoever he could. Edward spoke to the grand prior in a low voice, anxious the bishop should not hear.

"I had thought to send for you once the arse-kissing was done," Edward said. "The emperor invited you, did he?"

He replied, "*You* did not."

"Indeed not. What have you done for him?"

"Less than we've done for you."

Edward laughed without much mirth. "How fares my mother?" he asked.
"Well."

"The man of Wales?" He meant his father.

The grand prior's eyes were neutral. He said nothing and Edward had
the great urge to punch him. As a king he was unused to restraining his
urges, and the necessity of so doing made him more angry still.

"It will be good to see an angel in Westminster Abbey again," said the
grand prior.

"I've banned you from the capital. You've got a bloody great pile in Norfolk for your order; be happy with that."

Edward rocked on his feet. The Hospitallers made him uncomfortable. They had helped him overthrow his tyrannical uncle but knew he
had resorted to sorcerers. That gave them power over him. He imagined
the grand prior swinging from a gibbet at Tyburn. An attractive notion.
Impossible, of course. They were too useful in containing his sorcerous
mother.

"The English warriors must feel they do God's work. An angel on our
side shows them that they do," said Edward.

"I hear there are men in your kingdom who want no such backing."

"What?" he said.

"There are mutterings of blasphemy—men holding Lucifer as creator
and cursing the name of God. Lebonne's heresy. Genoa's too. Our Italian
tongue says the people are ready to overthrow the Guelf faction."

Edward thought of that demon, burning in his room. He said, "Could
be good for us if the Genoese take their galleys back from Philip for good."

"But not if revolution is preached in England."

"If I hear such talk it will be punished."

"It would still be more practical if . . ."

Edward turned to face him, drawing him close and whispering, "If you
harm one hair on my mother's head, I will drop the war against France,
destroy you in England, and sail east against the rest of you, Prior. Whatever
you have over me will be as nothing. You know me to be reckless, and you
know I can wreck."

"It was not my suggestion to harm your mother. Your mother is a remarkable woman, but she does not follow Lucifer. She follows God, though she has communed more directly with his servant Satan."

"Are you trying to goad me, Prior? Any other man in England would be on the floor spitting teeth after saying that. My mother can bring none of her powers to bear while she is locked in Castle Rising under your holy wards. I wish her to live out her days there, is that clear?"

He replied, "It's an expensive operation to contain her like that."

"A sight more expensive if I expose your tricks or start burning your monasteries. It's a compromise, Grand Prior, life's full of 'em. Get used to it."

"I did that many years ago." The Grand Prior leaned back, perhaps sensing Edward's great desire to fill his face in.

Bugles sounded and Edward strode forward into the church, glad to get out of the rain and the company of the monk. God, he hated the Hospitallers for how they'd compromised him, useful as they were.

A huge white vault stretched above him, its beams studded with stars, the windows lighting the candle smoke like the rays of a sun from behind a cloud.

On a great throne before the altar, a scepter in his lap, an orb in his left hand and a naked sword in his right sat Louis, king of the Romans, king of the Germans, Holy Roman emperor—a severe, lean man with a full beard. He wore a massive golden crown and a robe of rich scarlet. Edward, who had persuaded the margrave of Juliers to lend him his crown, was not quite so splendid but splendid enough. He too wore scarlet and also indigo. He strode on, bowed to the emperor, and knelt before him. Edward's head swam. So much effort, so near to his reward. He half expected the ceiling to fall in, given the luck he'd had.

Trumpets sounded and Louis stood.

"Edward, beloved cousin, most noble king of England whose birthright in France has been denied by the usurper Charles of Valois, I invest you with all my authority to use as you see fit in furthering your noble cause. Your wars are our wars and you fight in defense of the empire, put on earth by Holy God. Disobedience to you is equivalent to disobedience to me, and a treasonous assault on God's holy order that He has imposed upon this earth.

You are Vicar of the Holy Roman Empire, commander in the emperor's absence, our right hand against the French."

He handed Edward his sword and Edward gripped it as if he thought the emperor might take it back.

"I call the angel," said Louis, "light from light. Honor us with you presence. Shine on the tips of the English spears so all men may know their bond with the empire."

The light swam and the assembled princes drew in their breath. Was it the smoke that swirled and took shape or was it the light from the high windows? Edward could not tell. The light of the jewels on the crowns, the light of the windows, the golden hearts of the candle flames seemed to be leaking, the color to smudge out of the shape that held it, flowing into the vault of the cathedral, ruby dancing around emerald, gold dancing around silver. Music was in the air—trumpets, but none that had sounded in the church. These played a high melodious music, not a tune but a series of sweet chords, a perfect fanfare.

A golden wheel of light spun above the altar, drawing streams of light from the windows, from the candles, from the jewels. Another wheel turned within it and around its rim eyes began to form, the gem reds, the jewel greens sparkling in their pupils. There were hundreds of eyes spinning around the great wheel of light, and a voice like a child's rang forth.

"Great Emperor, God's appointed, I come to answer your call."

"Angel, will you work for us? Angel, will you leave the light and sparkle on the tips of the English spears?"

The wheel spun and the eyes flashed and shone. "You have honored me with great chapels, you have woven the light in glass and gold. Will the English king do the same?"

"Our English artists will take the light of the sea and catch it in glass, we will build a chapel at Windsor and give you sunsets and dawns in its windows, starlight in the diamonds of its vault. Westminster Abbey would welcome you. Appear before our army, lay waste the usurping French, and set the order God intended upon the earth," said Edward.

"Where are the English angels?" A voice—Prince Stephen, shouting up at the angel from among the ranks of nobles.

"With the king," said the angel, "doing God's work."

Edward swallowed down his anger and dismay. No, there were many meanings to what the angel had said and Stephen would have to take the most obvious.

It changed nothing. Course unaltered, sails set as they were. He felt a knot in his stomach, a yearning for this half life to end and that he should step into his true kingship. One day his father would die and he would be the true king, invested with angels. He just had to hold it all together until then. He felt hot and cold all at once.

"Will you side with us?" said Edward.

"You are the vicar of the Holy Roman Empire and I recognize your right. The light at Westminster is enchanting," said the angel. "I will play in it for a while."

The wheels flared and spun, the eyes blinked, and the angel was gone.

"The refurbishment of Westminster Abbey was truly worth it," said Burghesh. "An angel can be anywhere and only true beauty, commissioned to my design, true dedication and prayer, from monks schooled by me, can hold it to one place. We did well to spend the money there, truly we did. My lord, I expect no gratitude—I am here to serve!"

The relief in his voice spoke volumes. England had an angel again.

Edward should have been as happy as a fisherman's cat, and he endeavored to look it.

"Games to honor this alliance!" he said. "We have done great work this day, and to honor it I shall tilt in the lists myself!" A murmur went through the princes, deep approval. A king who maneuvered his armies and played the game of politics well would be respected and honored. One who split a few skulls would be loved.

Edward kissed the emperor's hand and turned from the chapel. "Pray," he addressed the church. "Pray to thank God for this precious gift. And know that I am the true king of France." He'd said it on impulse, but now it seemed so right.

The congregation drew in breath.

"Yes," said Edward. "I have the better claim through my mother's side than the usurper Philip. I will make war on Philip throughout his lands and watch as his angels recognize my right and come to me!"

The Holy Roman emperor rocked from side to side on his throne in approval, clapping and braying. Edward knew why. This guaranteed war for a long, long time. While England fought France, the French would not look east.

The church nobles took their cue from Louis.

"King of France! King of France!" they cried.

When the shouting was done, Edward left the church, Burghesh at his side. "Well done," he said.

Edward grunted. *Douce, Edward, douce. Couch the lance lightly. Be as they expect you to be.*

"Not the usual form for the angel," said Edward. "Usually they come as strange colors or shining men."

"That is one of the Ophanim," said Burghesh, "one of the carriers of the throne of God."

"A good catch?" said Edward.

"Well, undoubtedly," said Burghesh, "but I foresee problems. Firstly, it's a creature of the third order of the first sphere of Angels."

"Meaning?"

"The French have been buttering up the archangel Jegudiel. There's every chance our angel will just defer to him. You know how they respect God's holy hierarchy. It was too much to hope that one of the emperor's archangels would attend."

Edward took the bishop by the arm and drew him to a halt. "Have we been sold short, Burghesh?"

"We've got what we paid for, Majesty. A third of the debt, an angel of the third order. It is a formidable spirit and will prove invaluable in battles where the French cannot summon their angel. And who is to say that they will be able to? God is sure to recognize your claim in France so the angels will come to you."

"That is assured," said Edward.

The king was aware he was holding up a column of people trying to leave the church, not to mention drawing great attention to his conversation with Burghesh. He walked on, the bishop falling in uncertainly by his side.

Through the houses on a big area of common ground he could see the bright colors of the tournament tents. Wet earth, no rain. An ideal day for tilting. Perhaps he should indulge in the mêlée too. It was all very well practicing the noble art of jousting, but he could do with knocking the rust from his armor in some more realistic fighting. He hoped that Stephen would take part on the other side.

He'd become carried away in claiming the French throne, all the tension and annoyance of the previous years giving way in an instant. Edward needed somewhere to vent his anger, his shame. The prince would find it difficult looking down his nose once he'd had it smashed into his face. A hundred doubts were hammering at the doors of his mind, but Edward's will was a fortress. He had been willing to fight without an angel. Now that he had one, he was eager.

What had his mother told him when she had announced they were going to overthrow his father and he had begged her not to? "Other men tremble. Kings do not." He wasn't afraid—he had deployed his forces in the most favorable way he could, given the land he stood on. He had a chance now; he at least had a dice to roll in his game with Philip. And if God favored him in war, he could become the true king of France, blessed by victory in battle. Then the French angels would come to him and he would not be dependent on the death of his father.

He addressed Burghesh, an inch from his ear. "It might at least engage the other angel for a while and that'll give us the chance to fight the French sword to sword. By the time Jegudiel finishes parleying with it, God may have given us the battle. The archangel will respect that." He shouted to his squire, "Adam! Go and stick me in the lists. What we discussed." He gave him a wink to remind him to put him up against Stephen. The boy returned a big smile and went running.

"There is one more problem, Majesty," said Burghesh.

"What problem?"

"Well, not a problem as such. Not for you, my lord. But I would point out that the Ophanim are angels of divine justice. It might be good to remember that in your dealings with it."

Again, a sharp stab of doubt in his breast. What did Burghesh know? Nothing, but that man had a nose for weakness like a hound's for a deer. Edward dismissed his anxiety. He had stepped over a precipice in the shakiest of ground. Where he stood now was a secure footing compared to where he had been. He knew what he had done, and what bargains he had struck to replace the tin crown Mortimer had set on his head with one of gold, one of real power. He had done it for England, to honor God's will that the king should rule, not some skulking usurper.

God himself had used Satan—the Bible showed that to be true in the book of Job when he had set him on his dearest worshiper. How was it different, the bargain Edward had struck? Burghesh knew nothing dangerous and was still smarting because he hadn't been in on the plot to oust Mortimer . . . and probably from the kick in the balls Montagu had administered to him.

Edward stopped himself from laughing. He'd necessarily had to stay out of the action in the castle, so as to deny any knowledge should the plan have failed. But he would dearly have loved to have seen the bishop take a good one to the stones. Just thinking about it made him smile. *Ah, Montagu, I need you back.* He wanted his friend at his side to celebrate his success. And to give Stephen a second spanking after he'd finished with him.

Burghesh was one of those species of men who liked to place the blame for his misfortune on anything and anyone but himself, and he had been heard to blame anyone from the Devil to the bankers to the Jews for the brief inconvenience and imprisonment he'd suffered when the Mortimer fell. In truth, he should have thanked his lucky stars. If Edward's father had caught the man consorting with his enemy, he'd have handed him over to Despenser for one of the more sickening deaths history had to record. Burghesh was lucky the new king was a practical man. Raised in France and an assured diplomat, Burghesh was too valuable to send to the scaffold. No point letting the past poison the present.

"I have nothing to fear, Burghesh," said Edward. "I am an instrument of justice."

"In that case, sir," said Burghesh, "I'm sure you'll get along just fine. But it's too late to campaign this year. Given the state of the finances, it looks like it might be you and the angel on your own next year against the French, sir. You're a formidable man; I'm sure that will be enough."

Edward prodded the bishop in the chest. "I *am* a formidable man," said Edward. "And will and faith in God can succeed in place of money, in place of armies, in place of anything. France will burn until I get what I want."

PART III

1339

❖ · · ❖

In the year that the French conference at Vincennes resolved to invade England, with a great force of Normans, and that Plymouth, Southampton, and Ipswich were burned. Louis was born to John of France, and England was shamed at La Flamengrie. The Agenais suffered under most grievous wars and sieges and Edward's cog Christopher was captured by the French.

1

The uses of ritual circle and ritual sword, ritual crown and ritual ring; the names of the angels and the names of the demons of Hell, Dow learned them all. He learned the importance of moondark and moonrise, the ascent of Venus and the decline of Mars, the nature of the angels who live in the south and those who live in the north, how conjunction of the planets intersected with the temper of devils and demons, that time and tide must be exactly right to summon Belial and not incur the wrath of Asmodeus. A dismembered cat, tallow, and mercury were needed to appease Baal, mandrake and gold to call and compel Mammon.

Devils were easier to call than demons because a demon needs to sneak through a crack in the walls of Hell. A devil may be licensed to leave or may simply walk through a gate.

While the streets of London sighed with fear of French invasion, while Edward wandered France like the embodiment of a biblical plague, burning and pillaging but forever incapable of taking a town or inflicting any real damage on Philip, and while the French stalled and burned the English ports as best they could in this hobbled sort of war, Dow learned.

But he only learned. He did not act. The priest seemed indecisive and, though he endlessly discussed what might be done with Dow, even set up summoning rituals and rehearsed them with the boy, he did not go through with them. Never did he take out that key to Hell he kept in the pouch around his neck. Instead, the priest spent day after day shouting at the man in the circle, trying to command him with every name holy and unholy he could remember. He seemed more trapped than the devil as he clung to the repetition of rituals that had repeatedly failed. He was like the king in France, repeatedly burning the same bit of earth.

The priest was afraid now, Dow could tell. The woman had unnerved him. He endlessly questioned Dow on what he had seen in the street. Dow told him. He was as keen as the priest to discover the true nature of what he had seen, if for very different reasons. Dow suspected the red cardinal had been a devil. The woman had to be a fallen angel, by the protection she had offered him. The thing in the circle? Some sort of spirit. He just called it Osbert now.

Orsino had taken to wandering the streets in the early morning, searching for her. "Why do you look for her?" the priest asked him as he left the house one morning.

"She is beautiful. She's a creature of the dawn," he said.

"Who knew warriors could be poets?" said the priest.

"Aren't your knights poets?"

"They're men of a different rank from you."

"We're all the same rank dead, priest," said Orsino.

"That," declared Edwin, "shows a fundamental misunderstanding of the nature of Heaven."

Edwin was a very tired man, Dow saw. He never really ate and seemed physically frail. Not too frail to wield the whip when he was displeased, though. Dow took his beatings. He was learning, slowly, and—in his room at night—he said the beautiful names of the demons and, in particular, those of the fallen angels. There were two hundred of them and Edwin wanted him to memorize them all.

"Araqiel, Armaros, Penemue, Samyaza, Shamsiel, Baraqel, Gadriel, Azazel, and Sariel—also called Suriel, Suriyel, Sahariel, Juriel, Seriel, Sauriel, Esdreel, Surya Saraqael, Sarakiel, Jariel, Suruel, Surufel, and Sourial."

Sariel. That was the name of the angel his nan had once used to bless him. He hoped that the woman he'd seen in the street was her. The name seemed to fit her—he couldn't think that she could have another. The priest said Sariel was male, all angels were male. But Sariel was a woman. Dow found the fallen angel's description in a book the priest had brought back—written in English, unusually.

He guessed this book must have been written by someone of his own Luciferian faith. The priests wrote in Latin, keeping their secrets tight. The book said Sariel was one of the watchers—the Grigori. They were not rebellious angels but had fallen in love with humans and were cast out of Heaven. Sariel was an angel of death, forever writing in a mortal book, forever crossing out names. But she—it said in the book—was a healing angel too and was known by the name "moon of God." She was made of fire and air and reflected the light of God.

Dow found this disturbing. Was the angel in league with his enemy, the usurper Îthekter? He could not believe that, and the idea of her presence remained a great comfort to him.

By day, in the hours the priest slept, Orsino tried to teach him the arts of war. Dow learned quickly and uncomplainingly. He tried to hold on to his hate of Orsino, an anchor to his past, what he had been. The man had snatched him from his homeland and killed his friends when they tried to rescue him. But, in another way of looking at it, he had freed him from a prison and simply defended himself when attacked. It was difficult not to admire the warrior—he was no high man—but it was very hard to return his friendliness.

Orsino had him endlessly stepping in the garden, walking like a frog with bent knees, sidestepping, and ducking. So Dow learned to move, to come into distance of his opponent's weapon to draw a thrust or a hack before stepping back and away from the blade, making his opponent miss. Orsino tried to teach him to wrestle and found the boy a rapid learner—wrestling had been the chief sport of the Devil's Men.

The Florentine taught Dow the three murder strikes with the balled fist—to the heart, to the temple, to the throat with both hands. He taught him how to close quickly on his man, how to break too. He took him to the butts to test him with the longbow and found the boy was no great archer, yet he hit more often than he missed. His use of the staff was a different proposition. Orsino had to look to his own ankles or he might have had one broken. But when Dow gestured toward the sword Orsino laid on the grass while he was instructing, the mercenary just shook his finger in a "no, no, no" gesture.

Weekly, Orsino took a ribbon and used it to measure around Dow's upper arm. Some weeks he seemed satisfied, others not so, but Dow knew that he was growing, adding bulk to his wiry frame, and height too. Where once the crown of his head had come to Orsino's chest, it now came to his chin and, though he was still lean, he was gaining muscle—enough for Orsino to give him his own old tunic and shirts. In the Leadenhall market a stallholder had mistaken them for father and son and, with Dow's black hair and athletic frame, it was easy to see why. Orsino, though, carried himself with ease and assurance. Dow glared at the world as if, said Orsino, he was about to kill it.

For six months Dow didn't touch the sword. Dow knew that swords had their limits—no match for a staff in the right hands. A staff, Abbadon had said, could split a man's liver through any mail, had better reach and either end could be used to attack. But a sword was a useful weapon and if he had the chance to learn it, Dow should take it. Dow had made up his mind to become a rare killer of high men, and he would embrace anything that took him toward that goal.

Then, as the final snow melted at the end of February, Orsino seemed satisfied with the circumference of Dow's biceps. He threw his measuring ribbon to the floor and put the sword into Dow's hand. First, he trained the boy to use it as a civil weapon, with a buckler in the street. To hit and not be hit was the essence of the art, and Orsino taught him dodges, blocks, and parries.

At Easter, Orsino came back with a rusting suit of mail with a great hole in the back, a moldy padded coat to go beneath it, and a battered, old-fashioned helmet the shape and weight of a bucket. With these he taught Dow the art of fighting in armor. Some things Orsino wanted to teach him puzzled the boy greatly. First he had to learn to turn a somersault where he stood. Then he had to do it in all the armor. This was the art of the sword in war. No dodging here, no ducking or blocking. Just all-out, savage attack by a body strengthened by ordeal.

And what ordeals. Dow had to climb a rope using only his hands, this time with the helmet on. He had to jump as far as he could and as high as he could over sticks Orsino lay out on the ground or held in the air. Orsino made him run lengths of the garden flat out in all his armor. Sometimes the Florentine didn't consider that heavy enough and made him do it again, carrying great logs. Dow could see hardly anything through the slit in the helmet and his breathing was almost impossibly restricted. This didn't seem to bother Orsino, who would wait until Dow had finished his running and jumping, and then set about him with a stick.

"Come on," he'd cry, "this is when you need to learn to fight. This is when technique and skill will save you, when the strength of your arm has gone, and your feet seem set in stone. This is where you live when you might die!"

Dow fought back furiously. He had never wavered in his purpose. He was learning what Orsino could teach him in order to kill great men. And when he had learned that, he would start by killing Orsino. The priest would be second.

The training often exhausted Dow, and he was glad when the priest arose and called him in.

Edwin continued to be useful to him. Dow's studies now included learning to read in Latin. Dow progressed quickly—he had to. The priest rewarded the least slowness, or laziness, with the rod. Dow, though he could have broken the man in two had he chosen, took the beatings. Edwin had achieved a great deal in summoning the thing in the circle. Dow needed to know how that was done—to be a master of the situation the next time he opened the gate to Hell.

When he went to his room at night, Dow took a candle and a book to continue his studies.

All the time, they questioned the figure in the circle—who still claimed to be a pardoner called Osbert—but he never yielded anything, just sat in his circle as if trapped out of time, his beard never growing, never getting thinner, never fatter. Osbert would complain only that he was a pardoner, that he had been caught by what must have been a demon, that he wanted to be free to know thirst and hunger again, to get drunk and to gorge himself. The priest was surprised by the spirit's persistence of form.

Edwin ran off down wild avenues of thought. He said, "It has used its mind to make the woman we saw in the garden. It tempted you from your room. How else do locked doors fly open in the middle of the night?

"In the past it has sought to tempt me," he said, "appearing as a beautiful woman or a merchant bearing riches. How little it knew me. But now it comes at me through my weak spot and, like a ram at a door, persists and persists, confident in its eventual triumph. My weak spot is pity. In this form, it does stir such feelings in my breast, though with prayer I tamp them down."

The priest questioned Dow on his faith and Dow learned to write. So the priest confirmed his knowledge of Free Hell, and how the demons seek the light and the devils serve the three-faced God to keep them in darkness. Edwin wrote all this down, but as soon as the priest had read them back, he immediately burned them in a candle flame. It was as if he feared their existence, as if burning the words would make them less true.

Edwin could not leave off questioning Osbert.

"Which part of Hell are you from? Gehenna or Dis?" he asked.

"Get it into your head," said Osbert. "I am not of Hell. I am of Winchester, where I wish I'd stayed."

"Where is the Drago?"

"Here we go again. It's up my arse."

"Do you think it could have secreted the banner there?" said Edwin to Dow.

Dow, who was sitting at one of the great books the priest kept in the basement, using a candle for light, shook his head. For the first time since he'd come from the moor, he felt like laughing.

The priest sat down on a stool. "Perhaps I should send it back and try to summon a new one."

"That'd be my favorite," said the pardoner. "Try sending me back to the Leadenhall market place."

"We need to question Hell again," said Edwin. "We need a more compliant devil. I would summon the one we saw in the church but, in truth, I fear it."

"That was a demon," said Dow. "The other thing was the devil."

Edwin ignored him. "This circle works; I would reuse it. Could you send it back?"

Dow felt sorry for Osbert, whatever he was. He had never given up his humor nor his complaint that he had been wronged.

It was nearly summer when Dow decided—he needed to communicate with Free Hell himself urgently, to seek further instructions. Osbert could do that for him. He would send him to Hell to ask. Dow would bind the spirit to return, not by spells or ritual but by asking for its word. Yes, he would send the thing back to Hell and, in return, he would give it its freedom—whether to stay in Hell or to wander the earth.

How to get the key? He had no idea. But he was sure that, if he could question it correctly, Osbert would know. He might be a lesser spirit and not able to tell him where the Drago was—after all, the fire demon in the church hadn't known that—but Dow would bet that it knew how to sneak into a room and find a key.

All he would have to do was find a way of speaking to it alone.

2

I t wasn't just the bedbugs and the chill of the spring night that kept Montagu from sleeping. He hadn't traveled to see the old queen in her prison at the castle lightly. Edward was bound to ask what business his nobles had with his mother, and Montagu feared to give him the answer. Still, no one could refuse him now.

It was a bright cold spring, and Montagu was Marschal. With the queen and prince on campaign with the king, he was de facto ruler of England. He didn't much relish the job—particularly since it meant he had to travel with a ridiculously large retinue, flying the royal banners—now quartered with the arms of France to reflect Edward's claim.

Even Montagu, Edward's best friend, found that a bit hard to take. Philip's claim was stronger by far. What, then, had been the point of Edward calling himself king of France? To absolve the lowland French vassal lords of rebellion in backing Edward against Philip—and of course as a sort of spiritual gamble they'd get some French angels. That hadn't worked and that was no surprise.

Montagu had been raising finances for more than a year now, and doing it well. The issue was so pressing that he'd had no time to devote to the investigation of the lack of angels and the whereabouts of the old king, and he was glad of it, an excuse to do nothing. But now the right men were in place to see that things worked smoothly, and duty demanded that Montagu act, no matter how uncomfortable he was in doing that.

The war on the continent was at a stalemate. Philip had put his army of sixty thousand in the field but refused to close with Edward. Edward was razing everything around him, but Philip opted to let him, reasoning that the English king would soon run out of money and supplies, or simply exhaust the patience of his army. A good strategy, if you could prevent hotheaded lords from charging into the English come what may. Philip intended to let the English army sit in the field and rot.

There had been some English successes—against the French raids on Plymouth and the Channel Islands. On both occasions the angel had appeared—devastating the French and Genoese fleet on Guernsey with tongues of fire. After that the country had been in a buoyant mood—an angel in the sky over English shores again.

Montagu, bringing in the revenue, was not cheerful. He knew that the angel had effectively been hired. If the money ran out, then so would the lease. The wool collection had diverted him from his investigation. But he remained troubled. If old Edward was found—and killed—it would beat all the wool collecting in the world. Inaction was not an option. In months the English army could simply peter away in France, leaving England very vulnerable. With a true king on the throne, Old Edward or Young Edward with his father dead, invasion became a much tougher prospect.

How would he justify his visit to Isabella? He'd toyed with some story about just dropping in while supervising the loading of wool in King's Lynn, but he didn't think the king would buy that. No one just "dropped in" on the old queen. But Montagu needed the truth about her husband. In addition, he would get to observe the Knights Hospitaller at close quarters, though he wouldn't waste his breath questioning them.

Montagu was to meet the monk by his inn at dawn. They'd arrived the previous evening but too late to go on as a group to Castle Rising, so he'd sent a rider ahead and got his head down as best he could.

He sat up in bed. He got up without waking either of the two squires who slept alongside him, or the pages who, having missed out on the bed, had made camp on the floor.

Already dressed, having slept with his clothes on, he picked up his cloak and boots, felt his way down the stairs, and made his way through the hall of the inn—the fire still smoldering in the hearth, the dogs asleep around it.

Montagu stepped outside into the dewy dawn, the sky a deep, dark metallic blue, the stars fading. One bright star hung next to the moon.

"No angels in England," he said aloud. Montagu hadn't seen Edward in a year—the king was a virtual prisoner of his creditors on the continent, so unable to get home. Montagu missed his friend. Was it possible he didn't know his father was alive? Possible, yes. Cling to that.

The dawn chorus began and the inn stirred. Montagu walked a little way down the lane that led up to the castle. He wanted to be alone with his thoughts, which thronged in on him.

He recalled the attack by Isabella and Mortimer. No one had stood against them, no one. The king's army had melted away before them. Some said it was sorcery, some spoke of angels in the sky, others of devils.

The king had faced them at Orwell and been defeated—his army mutinying and joining Isabella—even though the people had no fondness for Mortimer. Old Edward's angels were seen but offered no defense. That alone, said the people, was proof of the judgment of God.

Mortimer had thought to use young Edward as a puppet ruler but had succeeded only briefly: Edward was a poor puppet.

Montagu remembered the night they'd taken the rebel Mortimer at Nottingham. Parliament was being held there, and Mortimer had thrown the earl of Lancaster out of his rooms to make way for himself and his own retinue. He'd also told the castle guard to ignore the young king's orders. Even now, Montagu felt his anger rise at mere recall of such arrant presumption. Well, Mortimer had enjoyed his last taste of usurped power.

The king had discovered, through the warder William Eland, that there was a secret passage that led from the river to the queen's apartments. How the fog had come down that night—Mirk Night, the chroniclers called it later. Bill Bohun was with him, Ralph Stafford, Robert Ufford, and John Neville.

Edward had patted Montagu on the shoulder and wished him Godspeed. He had anointed them with oil from the tomb of St. Mark as a blessing against sorcery—Mortimer was very capable of invoking infernal powers, it was known. For this reason he couldn't be allowed to utter a word and would need to be gagged. Montagu recalled the night smell of the autumn river, the bonfires on the air, the cold mail against his cheek.

He remembered his nervousness as he stepped into the passage, first of twenty, all the time fearing a trap or a trick. They'd reached the top and found the small door opened into a closet and that on to a spiral staircase to the queen's chamber.

It had so nearly come to ruin. Fat old Sir Hugh Turpington was doggedly doing his rounds. He'd screamed and drawn, but Montagu was quick, running him through before they stormed the doors. That good man John Neville had battered his way in and cut down two of the rebel's squires.

They'd caught the traitors in the hall of the queen's lodgings, discussing what to do about the plots against them. Too late: both Mortimer's sons were caught, along with the conspirator Beresford and Mortimer himself.

Montagu recalled his own delight as he'd seen Mortimer rush desperately for his sword. He laughed as he thought of Bishop Burghesh clucking and fretting like a hen with the wind up it, trying to find an exit. Montagu had been young then and had kicked the bishop hard in the balls. It was his revenge for when he'd had to look after Burghesh on a diplomatic mission to Avignon and had suffered from his pomposity. Any young knight in the country would have deployed his foot with similar enthusiasm.

Mortimer, for all his vaunted battle skill, was no match for ten opponents and had the sword torn from his grasp by Neville. Montagu had thought to gut him there and then, but something had stayed his hand—the queen's anguish: "Spare gentle Mortimer!" *Gentle* Mortimer had managed to black Montagu's eye with a headbutt even as they'd dragged him down to the river—bound and gagged, as Edward had instructed. But the lady had asked him to spare Mortimer's life and so he had.

That was the last time he'd seen the queen. She almost certainly hated him, but Montagu was undeterred. He had to persuade her to put the safety of the realm, the continuation of her royal line, above any personal feelings— if she still had personal feelings. It was widely believed that Isabella had gone mad. It was still worth questioning her. The mad, he thought, might be less careful with their words than the sane. Perhaps too it was a convenient madness—providing reason for her confinement and explanation for her rebellious behavior. Montagu reflected, however, that he had never seen any signs of madness in her before.

His men were rising now, calling out that the lord was up and to make haste to serve him. They wouldn't eat in the inn but would wait to be received at Castle Rising.

The horses were readied while he stretched his legs outside the inn. Montagu felt at home here, his men busy with the animals, his squires kneeling before him, awaiting instruction. He'd lived a lot of his life on the trail, and the rituals of camp and campaign were a comfort to him.

"Sir, your clothes."

He said, "Oh yes."

In his moment of nostalgia, Montagu had forgotten that he was about to meet the most splendid lady in Europe, not burn and maraud.

His squire brought him his fine tunic of green taffeta embroidered with the rich red diamonds of his family crest, blue hose, and green shoes tapered to points a good eight inches beyond his toes.

"Do I have to wear these?" he asked his squire.

"They are de rigueur at court, sir."

"Not my court. Note this, George: if I ever see you in a pair of these, you can do an hour at the trot wearing them and full armor besides. Carry them—I'll put them on when we get to the castle." In front of them down the lane they heard a horse blowing.

Brother Robert rode through the wet dawn, his white cloak emerging from the green of the lane to the castle, two of his brothers behind him. The arrowed white crosses that adorned their black surcoats seemed to float in the morning haze. It was only when they got nearer that Montagu realized the men were fully mailed, though they hadn't gone so far as armoring their horses.

"Hello, Brother. Is the way so perilous between here and the castle?"

Robert drew up his horse. He was a large, very athletic man with a muscular neck and a shaved head. He had the look, thought Montagu, of a man who could be hit over the head with a spade without it disturbing his supper.

"We are warriors for Christ," said the monk. "It's good to remind ourselves of that. And to let men see it." He spoke his French with a rather common accent.

Montagu reminded himself that the Hospitallers, although a proper order whose upper echelons were drawn solely from men of high birth, had admitted a number of Templars to their ranks when that order had been dissolved. The Templars had not been as scrupulous in their recruitment or promotion, and common soldiers' sons had been known to advance to high office in their monasteries. Montagu might have regretted the bloody manner of the Templars' dissolution, but he could not regret the dissolution itself. Promotion based on talent was a recipe for anarchy and an affront to God.

"We're all warriors for Christ, brother," said Montagu.

"Really? Or for self-aggrandizement and riches?"

"The aims aren't mutually exclusive."

Robert said, "Yes, they are."

"Don't contradict me, brother. Your order may admit low men, but in England we still have standards and insist on doing things the right way. You are a man of common birth. Remember that when you speak to me." Already Montagu was finding the monk hard work. He'd had some dealings with the Knights Hospitaller before, when on crusade against the pagans in Lithuania as a younger man. They always kept to themselves, which was the way he liked it. They took themselves rather seriously and were notorious booty-hogs, despite their high moral posturings.

"I am a man before God," said Robert, "so I am your equal."

"God ranks men and beasts in order according to their estate, monk. Remember that. Look, let's get this over so I can get out of your sight as quickly as you would wish."

"You have asked to see the queen?"

"Yes."

"You are not allowed in. No one comes here without royal permission."

"Well, Robert," said Montagu, "look at my banners, look at my retinue. I'm the Marschal of England, the one who gives out royal permission nowadays. So, let's do this properly: 'Montagu, can I have permission to go into Castle Rising?' 'Why of course you can, Montagu—no need to ask.' There, I've given myself permission, let me in."

Robert looked uncertainly at the banners—the three leopards quartered with the lilies. He looked at the twenty men-at-arms mounted behind Montagu.

"The queen anticipated you would say this," said Robert. "She has prepared a feast. Follow me."

The big knight wheeled his charger about and set off down the lane.

"An extraordinary fellow," commented George Despenser, bringing up his horse.

"And a very useful one, or I'd have been forced to set him in his place," said Montagu. The lord caught a doubtful expression in his squire's eyes. "What, you think he's too big for me to beat him? You've a lot to learn, George. More to aim at."

He smiled and patted the young man on the back. Then he mounted his horse and led his men after the three departing knights.

"Why such dour fellows, sir?" said George.

"Do you really want to know?"

"Yes."

"Queen Isabella. Between you and me, the king prefers to keep his mother here after what happened with his father. The queen, even for a woman of her age, is, shall we say, engaging. She is quite the most charming lady I have ever met and has a rare ability to manipulate men. These monks may be stronger than most of them are. Perhaps they mean their vows of chastity."

George asked, "Really?"

"Really."

"Well, I can believe anything now," said the squire.

Castle Rising was magnificent. The attached monastery grounds were huge and prosperous, the castle itself a massive square block looming above formidable grass ramparts topped by stone walls. There was nowhere in England he'd sooner defend if it came to a scrap with the French. But the castle's chief purpose right then wasn't to keep the enemy out but one woman in. Robert waited at the top of the lane until Montagu drew level with him. Then he kicked his horse on toward the open castle gates.

"Your retinue must ignore what they see here," he said. "You'll need to make them vow that before we leave."

"My men are the best in England, entirely loyal to the king. There will be no need of vows; my instruction will be enough."

"I prefer vows," said Robert.

Montagu said, "Shall we go on?"

The monks were chanting as the knights trooped into the castle, their chorus like an expression of the morning, like the sunlight and dew, thought

Montagu. *"Crucifer boncy Lucisator . . ."* He translated in his head as they sang: "Oh cross bearer, radiant source of day."

Some monks patrolled the ramparts in their red surcoats emblazoned with their tapering white cross, incense burners swinging. Interesting, thought Montagu—the red surcoat was battle dress for the order. Other monks went scurrying behind the horses as they came in to sprinkle dust. Montagu looked around and saw, at the base of the rampart, a huge circle marked out in what looked like chalk dust. It was this the monks were running to repair. Montagu crossed himself.

"What's all this, sir?"

His squire was at his elbow.

"I don't know, I don't know. What is this, Robert?"

The warrior monk said nothing, just gestured for them to follow.

Montagu knew what it looked like—a magic circle of the sort sorcerers were said to use to keep demons at bay. But why would that be needed?

A chill went through him. The rebel Mortimer had come with Edward's queen, Isabella, to defeat Edward II—a king backed by Heaven. How had he done it?

Something else Berkeley had said came back to him. "Ask how Mortimer escaped his prison when old Edward put him in The Tower for the first time." Was the queen caught up in sorcery? He couldn't believe that.

But of Mortimer, he could believe anything. The old King Edward had not been good—a terrible combination of laxness and tyranny. The king had surrendered government to his favorites—in particular the vicious Hugh Despenser, Montagu's affable young squire's father.

Old Edward had treated Mortimer very badly, taken his lands, left him no more than the clothes he stood up in, and imprisoned him in the Tower of London. The queen had fared rather better, but not well. But there were two differences between Edward and Mortimer when Mortimer had come to power—by proxy through the boy king, Edward III. The first was that Mortimer loved the king's wife, whereas the king did not. The second was that he was rigorous in his tyranny, not capricious.

Sunlight caught the dewdrops on the grass, turning them to shimmering jewels of wet light. And there she was at the unglazed window, splendid as the dawn, her diamonds, rubies, emeralds, and pearls shaming nature with their brilliance. Montagu actually crossed himself. He had last seen the old queen ten years before. She had been thirty then, an age where most women would be considered dry forage indeed. She, however, seemed to defy all aging and remained for him a woman of vast allure.

The official line was that the rebel Mortimer had used her to overthrow her husband—bewitched her, even. But the man didn't exist who could use that woman, Montagu knew. Intelligent, witty, wise, and fierce, she had a beauty that left even the most sophisticated courtiers stumbling for words. If any bewitching was to be done, it would be by her. In fact, the only man she'd ever failed to enchant was her husband. But now they said she was mad. Well, he'd see.

Montagu raised his hand to her and then bowed deeply in his saddle. She held up the back of her hand in acknowledgment, a queen's greeting—light flashing from the sapphires on her rings.

"Well, boy, she's put on a show for us—that at least's good news," said Montagu to his squire.

George nodded, looking around him in wonder. The party moved on, up to the shadow side of the castle and the stables. Montagu dismounted.

"You've got the presents, George?"

"Of course, sir. And those shoes."

"Good God, I should receive some remittance of sin for wearing them. Fashionable shoes. A sure mark of a fool." Montagu put on the shoes and waddled forward after Robert toward the door.

The monk put his hand on George's arm. "Only the lord. No retainers."

"That's unacceptable. You'd have me go in there looking like some land-less merchant," complained Montagu.

"The queen knows who you are and your worth. No retainers. And you, lord, must not meet her eye."

"Why ever not?"

"She is . . . persuasive," said the monk.

"I damn near grew up with this woman," said Montagu, "and you will not tell me how I can and cannot behave in her company."

Robert continued, ignoring his protests. "Do not speak to her. Only her ladies may speak to her directly. Speak through them."

"Claptrap," said Montagu. "*And* I'm taking my squire in with me."

"If he tries to speak to her, or she to him, I am to intervene," said Robert. "On orders of the king."

"My lord, what's the world coming to?" said Montagu. "The lady's charming company, always has been. You're painting her like some enchantress."

"That's what I believe her to be. Who knows what bargains she struck in France?"

Montagu was an even-tempered man, but that was too much. "You speak too boldly of your betters, sir. Retract what you say," he said, "or I shall invite you to support your comments in the old-fashioned way."

Robert eyed Montagu's sword, the famous Arondight. How many men had that killed? In Montagu's hands alone, probably twenty. Robert had no wish to become number twenty-one.

"I retract," said the monk.

"As any civilized fellow would," said Montagu. "You simply mistake the famous allure of the Capetian queens for something sinister, Robert. It is nothing of the sort. Don't be surprised she affects you that way. Just shows you're a man with red blood in your veins. And now *that* unpleasantness is over, please show the way."

Montagu was led into the castle, under splendid arches of brick and up some stairs to an antechamber. A page bowed as the earl came in and directed him to another door. He went down a short corridor and into the grand hall. A feast had been prepared and the hall swarmed with servants, some busying themselves laying out great platters of meat, some sitting at the tables, loudly wishing the lady would come in so they could begin eating.

Swathes of bright cloth starred with glittering stones dropped from the walls, tapestries showing hunting scenes, and above the main dining table at the back of the hall the arms of England and of France. Montagu tutted as he saw them. Old Edward had mistreated this lady, ignored her, given away her wedding gifts to his favorites. How could he have thought that she, doubly royal, would stand for it?

The hall was dim even in the bright morning—just a couple of windows let in light from high near the ceiling—and lamps and candles were mounted around the walls. Montagu had the impression he'd entered an enchanted cave. He laughed to himself—weren't dragons meant to inhabit such places?

And then the doors behind the hall opened. Four pages marched in and demanded everyone stand for Isabella, mother to the king. The room came to attention. Two trumpeters stepped forward and delivered a fanfare and the queen glided between them, the jewels of her dress and hair catching the torchlight to sparkle with a cold fire.

The beauty of beauties. That title had been given to her when she had been married—at twelve years old. Now, at forty or more, she had obviously lost her incandescent childish prettiness, but it had been replaced with a disconcerting perfection, a sophistication of poise and manner, and, as his friend Bohun had once noted, beauty irresistible as the tide. She did not look forty, or even thirty. Some had called her a witch and a sorceress, as Robert had just suggested. In the hallway Montagu had thought this rubbish.

Looking at her now, he could almost believe it. How in the name of God had old Edward preferred his favorites to her? At Newcastle he'd left her to the advancing Scots, choosing to save his lover Piers Gaveston. The queen escaped only through her own resourcefulness. Montagu would have presented Gaveston's body and riches to the Scots on a velvet cushion before he'd have given them one hair from Isabella's head. Abandon her? He'd face ten thousand clansmen alone rather than that.

Isabella's gown was of yellow baudekin—silk woven with gold—adorned all over with tiny flowers in red and pink, picked out in rubies and sapphires. It was cut in the latest fashion, clinging tight to her body with voluminous sleeves that reached almost to the floor. On her head, making clear her status, was a delicate gold crown studded with rubies. It sat above her white blond hair, which, hung with pearls, remained uncovered, an immodesty that only such an important lady could be allowed.

She was pale as a primrose, her lips deep red, and her figure slender and shapely. It would have been easier for Montagu to find her transformed into an aging hag, but no such luck. Again his desire for her would be written all over his face. And this was not the affectation of a chaste spiritual desire for the queen, some courtly love bilge, but something genuine, incapable of disguise. He remained uncompromised only because the queen was used to the reaction she drew from men.

Montagu bowed as the queen came to her seat.

"Still beautiful," he murmured under his breath to Robert.

"Only God is beautiful," said Robert. His eyes were on the floor. He had not looked at the queen once.

"Seems they picked the right man for the job when they chose you to guard her," said Montagu.

Robert shot him a glance. "When a man of the Hospitallers takes a vow of chastity, he means it," he said.

"Well, how nice for you," said Montagu. "A chaste monk! Who ever heard of such a thing? Rarer than dragons."

"Dragons are not so rare," said Robert.

There was silence, grace was said, and the queen gestured for Montagu to join her at a place on her right.

He went directly up to the table first and went on to one knee before her.

"Ma'am, you do us much honor with this feast."

Isabella smiled. She said, "You did me the courtesy of telling me you were coming. The last time I saw you, you approached more suddenly."

She spoke in her wonderful Parisian French, none of the crunching consonants of the English Norman court.

"Ma'am." Montagu didn't know what to say. *Sorry for dragging off the love of your life, so your son could execute him in a just, if horrible, way.* It seemed inadequate. And they both knew, he wasn't sorry. He had done what was right, and what his duty to king and to God required of him.

He gestured for his squire to come forward. Good boy, George, he'd found a rich red cloth from somewhere on which to show the gifts. He used it to avoid touching the gifts—a good ruby ring, a book of romances, a finely wrought golden chain.

"Charming," said the queen, signaling for a lady-in-waiting to come forward and take the gifts, "really charming. Most thoughtful gifts, Montagu. Your manners always were impeccable. Sit beside me and tell me stories of the outside world. I've not seen it in a long time."

Montagu did as he was bid, sitting next to the queen. He breathed in her smell—rose and apple oil. It was distinctive and he knew that it came from her use of Castile soap. A hundred women at the court used that soap, but not to that effect. If Isabella smelled of apples, then it was the ones that hung in Eden.

"So what brings you to see an old madwoman in her prison?"

He said, "You're hardly mad, ma'am, and certainly not old."

"You flatter me, Montagu. I am old, certainly old. I would *need* to be mad to believe otherwise."

"To me you seem the loveliest of women. If that makes me mad, I say thank God for madness."

He speared a herring from the dish in front of him.

She smiled. "I don't think you are a flatterer, Montagu, so I thank you for your compliment. But it is true they say that I am mad, is it not?"

"They say very much, ma'am; little of it makes sense and even less is true. You can hear whatever you want to hear about greatness."

"And what do you hear about me?"

"That you are mad."

Isabella put her hand to her mouth to cover her laugh. "You know, Montagu, you always could make me laugh. You always made everyone laugh. Even Mortimer."

Montagu studied his plate.

"Don't worry," she said, "I don't bear grudges, or rather, there are more important targets for my hate than you. I forgive you—you were acting for your king."

"Ma'am."

"It's a trait of my family," she continued. "Edward has it too. We are pragmatic and can recognize a good man. If I had ruled, I would have found a use for you."

"As an adornment for a spike on London Bridge?" he asked.

"Perhaps. Who knows what might have been necessary? But if we cannot be friends, we can at least be civil. Tell me, finally, how you gained entry to Nottingham Castle? Who let you in? How many guards did you have to bribe?"

"We had help from the castle steward Eland. He showed us a passage through the rocks at the base of the castle. We came up through a secret passage."

The queen was suddenly stern. "Don't treat me like a fool, Montagu."

"Ma'am?"

She said, "They were all peddling that story in the year after they took my Mortimer."

"It was no story, ma'am, but the plain truth."

"No. There was no passage and there was no Eland. The castle warder was William Baricloughe, Mortimer's man for twenty years. He would have known of any secret passage. And there was none. Whatever Mortimer might have been, he wasn't a fool. The whole castle had been thoroughly searched. Mortimer knew he was surrounded by his enemies and he knew how many nooks and cracks those old buildings contain for spiders like you to crawl through."

Montagu turned down the wine bowl as it was passed to him, but he picked up his cup of ale. He said, "I tell you honestly, ma'am, how we came into the castle. I swear it on the tooth of St. Anne here in my sword and by her sacred daughter the Holy Mary."

Isabella stared ahead.

"Then I *am* mad," she said. "I was left alone in that castle fearing for the life of my beloved. Do you not think I searched for the way you went? Do you think I did not order you pursued? I had four hundred of Roger's men in that castle, ready to cut off your escape. But you were gone, poof!"—she clenched her fist and released it in front of his face—"into the air! I have no idea how you got in or got out. Sorcery was involved, I'm sure of that."

"Madam, it was not! Do you think I would imperil my soul?"

Isabella said, "I think you would do anything for your king."

"Not that."

"Do you imagine I have no knowledge of these things?"

"I don't know what to imagine."

"God was coming to recognize Mortimer as equal to a king. But his men could not find you. Nothing could find you. And that time the spirits did not come to his rescue."

Montagu said, "What spirits?"

"The saints were involved more substantially than you could imagine. He prayed, you know, when my husband, Edward, imprisoned him, to be released. And it was on the feast of St. Peter in Chains that he escaped, rescued by holy powers. He was divinely blessed, a saint himself, I'm sure. It must be recognized one day. What powers did you summon to help you? Were the Florentines involved? I know that Bardi had something to do with this. Now there's a man I would have dealings with. Bankers are vermin, God says so quite clearly in the Bible. I'd make him suffer what I have suffered."

"The banker had nothing to do with it. The king was with us. He called his divine aid to protect us."

"Did he? I was at Westminster Abbey, Montagu, with the king as he went to the Confessor's shrine. I've seen the angels speak to my father, my husband, my brother a hundred times. It didn't happen to my son there and, from what I hear, it hasn't happened since."

"Who do you hear that from?"

Isabella smiled. "There are murmurs on the breeze if you care to hear them."

"I can't imagine you hear much here."

"Then you can't imagine much. Men speak—they always speak if you know how to ask." She gave a little wave of dismissal. When the poet wrote of the "white hand of my lady," that was very much the sort of hand they had in mind, Montagu thought.

He said, "Was it Mortimer's saints that kept the angels away from old Edward? Is it something like that that still keeps them away?" He realized he'd said too much. This woman had a way of making you drop your guard.

She laughed. "No. The source of all my husband's troubles was Hugh Despenser, his favorite, his lover, his devil. *He* kept the angels away."

"I can believe that. The man *was* a devil." He looked over to where George sat munching on a chicken leg. Very unlike his father, thank God—a pleasant boy, eager to serve.

"Despenser was in league with these fellows," she said.

Montagu brought his hand to his mouth to stifle a cry of "What?"

"The Knights Hospitaller. They visited him before they tried to face us at Orwell."

"How do you know that?" he asked her.

"Do you imagine I was entirely without friends in my husband's court?"

"So what did Despenser do?"

"I don't know. We knew Edward was having difficulty raising his army, such was his unpopularity and the hate the people bore Despenser. But the angels came. We saw them at Orwell."

"So why did Mortimer think he would be successful? He had no angels; Old Edward had three."

"Because the angels don't always do anything. It's a risk, but war is a risk."

Montagu thought how like her son she sounded. "And they didn't act?"

"No. They left. It was a great boost to our army. Despenser caused them to leave."

"How did he do that?" he asked.

"By making a serious mistake. Some magic was cast. Something was called. We know that from his servants."

"A demon?" Montagu asked.

"Maybe. Whatever it was, we were grateful for it."

"Why isn't this known?"

Isabella countered, "What happened to Despenser and his servants?"

Montagu pondered. Mortimer had given Despenser an inventive and cruel death. A ritual death. Verses from the Bible had been scratched all over his body before they'd executed him, and monks had chanted all around his execution. Despenser had been too beaten to speak. His closest men had been purged too, viciously. Had Mortimer been trying to conceal something?

He said, "I always thought you had a say in Despenser's death. Your hate for him was well known."

"No."

"Speak plainly, ma'am; what are you saying?"

"I tell you what I think. Despenser was a black magician. He bewitched my husband and led him to folly. At Orwell, he relied on his arts to make up for the lack of an army. And it failed him."

"Why not rely on the angels? They were seen there, as I recall."

"Perhaps he feared they'd do nothing—as they did. Perhaps he wanted to impress the king. You know what Despenser was like."

Montagu looked down at his plate.

She continued: "Despenser knew the secret of what happened to England's angels. There was a blaze of fire and they left. The fire came from his side."

"I thought that was Mortimer's doing."

"No." She gently pulled the meat off a tiny quail. "Mortimer had only his faith, which was rewarded. My lover was a holy man. Perhaps God rewarded him by cursing Despenser and making him drive the angels away."

Montagu thought it was time to be direct. "Did Mortimer tell your son his father was still alive?" he asked her.

Her face was impassive. She said, "If he did, he lied. Did you know I made them give me his heart in a vase?"

"It was a sign of your love?"

She smiled, her perfectly even white teeth showing. "My husband told me he loved Despenser. He said no woman could ever win his heart. I proved him wrong."

Montagu thought it better to concentrate on eating for a while.

Eventually, after some lamb cutlets, he said, "Why have you not told of your suspicions about Despenser before?"

"Tell whom? My son has me cooped up here like an old hen."

The queen smiled as the Hospitaller Robert leaned closer. "That is enough of talk," she said. "Do you intend to stay the night, or will you be about your business?"

"We will stay the night," said Montagu. He had thought to press on to King's Lynn. But, he thought, Nottingham was only eighty miles west and he very much wanted to inspect its castle. And from there it was no distance at all to Hanley Castle—the Despenser's family seat. It was a ruin now, but Montagu wanted to take a look at it, as well as question Despenser's wife, who lodged down the road at Tewkesbury. There was no other reason he wanted to stay—was there?

Isabella put her hand on his.

She said, "I'm glad you will stay. We will give you our best lodgings in the east wing. It's where my chambers are. I love to watch the sun rise there."

Montagu felt his mouth go dry. The wine bowl was passed to him once more. He turned it aside. "Servant, bring me some weaker ale," he said. "I have affairs of state to attend to and must keep a clear head."

3

D ow had bided his time in planning his approach to the thing in the circle, learning well from Edwin how to be as ready as he could for what lay ahead.

The priest was always careful to lock the door when he left the cellar, and he never left Dow in there on his own. This lock was not like the one in his own room—the priest had replaced the cellar lock himself after Dow had encountered the red cardinal in the street. Edwin seemed to think that, if magic failed to hold in the devil, ironmongery might.

Dow was always locked in his room at night and, since his escapade with the lady in the street, the lock on that door had been changed to an external bolt. There was no shaking that out. The room was windowless and there were no means of exit, but Dow had already thought how he might talk to the demon. The floorboards were old, and some of the wooden pegs that secured them to the cross beams were loose. When he realized he could pry them up he almost laughed. How had he not considered it earlier?

Dow worked on them at night while his candle lasted. Three pegs from a long board would come free with persuasion. He used the one that was very loose to pry up the other two. Beyond that, he thought, he would need some sort of tool. The knife in the garden was the obvious one.

One blue washday of nippy sunlight a few weeks before Easter, when Orsino was teaching him the sword, the Florentine went to the house to get some water from a pail.

Dow quickly scrabbled in the dirt where he had buried the knife. He dug down with his fingers, touching something solid, which he pulled out. It was a little crucifix.

What had happened to the knife? He pushed the dirt back into the hole and stood up as Orsino came back into the garden.

"You're looking for your knife. And you found God. I put it there to teach you a lesson of where to address your thoughts. Don't look so angrily at me, boy; your knife's in my bag if you want it."

Dow ran to the canvas bag in which Orsino kept his practice weapons. There was the knife, clean, bright, and cruel.

Orsino said, "What do you intend to do with that? Kill me? Kill the priest?"

Dow cast down his eyes.

"No? Then what?"

Dow swallowed. He said, "I do no harm."

"You could do great harm with this. It's a rare blade. Where did you get it?"

"The red man dropped it."

"The devil you say you saw."

"That's right." He held the knife out, as if for Orsino to take it. Dow repeated, "I do no harm."

Orsino shrugged. "It's good to keep souvenirs. You honor your enemies in that way, and it's good to honor your enemies because it reminds you to treat them seriously. Have it back. I will trust you, Dow. I want to trust you. But make sure you don't abuse my trust. If you escape again . . ."

"I won't escape. Nor do harm."

"Then keep your knife."

The boy put the knife next to the bag. Then he continued his lesson.

At dusk he picked up the knife and went back into his small room, waiting for the priest to come and lock him in with his half candle for study. Edwin was a believer in study and thought it would bring Dow to God. Some chance.

Edwin locked the door and left. Dow waited, working on his reading, until the candle was half burned. Then he removed the three loose pegs and worked the blade beneath the floorboard, raising it as quietly as he could.

It still gave out some fearful creaks, and he waited after each one, listening to see if he could hear anyone coming. Stillness. Just after dusk was the quietest time in the city—all the good folk were home and most in bed. The bad folk weren't yet drunk enough to go bawling through the streets.

He worked the knife farther in. The board gave a loud groan of complaint, five pins flew out, and it was free. Dow froze and held his breath. From the street came a voice: "You there!" It was the city watch. He breathed again. The watch had given an explanation to anyone who was listening.

There was no ceiling to the cellar, so he found he was looking almost directly down at the demon in the circle.

It was curled up on the floor.

"Asleep?" said Dow.

The demon sat up. "Not after that row," he said. He stood and peered up at Dow.

"Need help," said Dow.

"What help?"

"The priest has a key. I could unlock the door, get you out."

He said, "Yes, yes. Look, just drop down here, get me out of this circle by whatever means you can, and I'll kick the door through. Never mind about the priest—I'll kick him through as well if I have to."

"Orsino will hear. We need the key to the cellar. But the priest sleeps on it."

"Do as I told you. Go to the stews of Southwark as I asked you to a year ago. Ask for Joanna Greatbelly. Tell her you need a sleeping draft. Get that into his wine and he'll be flat out for twelve hours."

"I can trust it?" Dow asked.

"The whores use it to rob rich clients. Tell Greatbelly that Osbert the pardoner sent you."

"I have no money to pay her."

"Then steal something to give her. A church cup, a plate. Not that expensive. Give her one of the books down there. Anything. Just give her something, knock that madman out, and get me out of here!" His voice was an insistent whisper.

"I will."

Dow replaced the board and pressed the pegs back in with the flat of the knife.

The next day, as Orsino moved his sword to correct his guard, Dow spoke up. "I want you to take me to see a whore," he said.

Orsino laughed. "Yes," he said, "you're a man now. High time. High time."

"When?"

"Now, if you like."

Dow put down the sword. "Come on then," he said.

4

There was no passage at the foot of the stairs that led to the main bedroom of the grand tower at Nottingham Castle. Montagu had insisted, as Marschal, on turfing old Earl Lancaster and his wife out of their bed so he could use the most luxurious rooms himself. Normally he would have held back from such boorish behavior, but he wanted to conduct an investigation.

The cupboard through which he and his fellows had emerged to steal away Mortimer was just that—a cupboard. There was no sign of any false panel, any hollowness when he knocked on its interior and, pry at it as he might, Montagu could not move the wooden panel.

"Never mind," he told himself, "very likely Lancaster has filled it in." A secret passage is, after all, no longer secret when it has been used to abduct the most powerful man in the land and take him to his death. But the story of the raid was not well known—or at least the fact the passage had been used. They hadn't wanted to compromise the defenses of what had always been a royal castle. The safest thing was to decommission the tunnel. He would go down to the sandstone caves beneath the castle to investigate any routes that had been filled in.

Montagu pulled on his coat, but before he left, he went to his bag. He took out a piece of cloth—a fine damask sleeve of a lady's dress, shot through with a pattern of dogs pursuing a stag. He breathed in its scent. Castille soap. He had not gone to Isabella, but Isabella had come to him:

A soft knock on the door of his chamber. Montagu pulled on his braies. Then he stumbled through the darkness of his room, fumbled for the catch on the door, and opened it to see Isabella's lady-in-waiting standing there with a candle in her hand. He was going to turn the girl away. He was aware that his martial achievements and position made him attractive to young women but, though the marriage vows placed no responsibility on men to be faithful to their wives, he loved his Catherine and found other women wanting in manner, intelligence, and beauty when compared to her.

All but one. The lady pushed the candle into his hand and slipped away as Isabella came toward him down the passageway. Her shining blond hair was loose about her shoulders and she was wearing a long, tight white shift, the shape of her body beneath it an assault on all reason and common sense.

Montagu felt his breath catch in his throat. His every good instinct told him to close and bolt the door. But his bad ones left him standing where he was. He could no more step away from her than walk through the wall.

She brushed by him into his room. He almost wanted to call for the Hospitallers to come and rescue him. Montagu felt utterly vulnerable, as if a panther had swept past him, its sleek side lingering an instant too long against his. He knew the legend of the panther, the beast they called the Love Cervere, how it emitted its sweet perfume to draw in its prey. He was at a loss how to react, how to proceed.

She sat on the edge of the bed. He came into the room, closed the door, and put the candle on the dresser.

Montagu asked her, "Have we not talked enough today?"

"I have matters that cannot be discussed in company." Her smile with sadness behind it. *Oh, Montagu! Listen to yourself! So sentimental, so gullible. It's an act*, he told himself. *She bends men like an archer a bow and to the same purpose—to make use of them.* But what an act. And she wanted him to see it. She wanted to say, "Look what I do for you, see how I turn my head and touch my hair. It is a performance and it is performed for you, as an offering. Show me comfort, hold me. Once my head is on your breast, anything is possible."

He raged inwardly. He wanted to tell her, "I see what you are doing. I know your tricks and your deceptions." But it was useless. This woman had made a country fall in love with her, made armies steal away from her husband at her approach. He'd wanted to kill Mortimer from the second he'd seen her on his arm and he'd wanted to kill old Edward too, for ever having touched her. Was that it? His honor, his bravery, the risks he had taken to depose the tyrant, the risks Montagu was taking now, spiritual and physical, to find old Edward—simply driven by love of this woman?

No, not love, something stronger. He knew what he bore in his heart for old Edward. Hate. In her presence, he hated other men for just existing, for having eyes to see her. Yes, it was hate she kindled in him—of himself for his weakness, of everything that had ever happened and would happen without her. Did Montagu care that England got its angels back? He didn't care for anything but her. If old Edward lived, he would die for how he'd treated her. With her mouth on his, his hands in her hair, Montagu's life had no other purpose.

He said, "Lady. I . . ."

"What?"

Montagu felt unbearably self-conscious. "I think of my wife."

"It is no betrayal."

"But you must be faithful to your husband."

Isabella said, "My husband is dead. Is he not?" She looked at him with that slight smile, a smile that had toppled a king. Montagu could not read what she meant. An invitation to bed or . . .

She held up her hands and he took them in his. "William," she said, her eyes on his.

She began to stand and he instinctively took her weight to help her. Then she was in his arms, her head in the crook of his neck.

"Come on, Lord Marschal," she said, crunching up the "ch" in imitation of a provincial English lady. "Tell me all your troubles."

A while later she gave him a sealed letter for her son. Young Edward insisted that all communications between him and his mother went through Brother Robert—with the result that none did.

"The king might be angry that you bring him this," she'd said.

"I'm used to his anger. I can stand a little for you. But will he read it?"

"If you stress its importance. He trusts you, Montagu. Use that trust for me. Read it to him if you have to. Will you swear it?"

"I will. I swear it."

"Robert searches everyone who leaves, so be careful."

"I'm Lord Marschal of England," Montagu had said. "If he searches me, he'll find my sword quicker than he'd like." He felt dizzy at how easily he became angry on her behalf.

As Montagu put the sleeve back into his bag, he continued dwelling on the events of that night.

She'd put her arms around him and he'd felt that he could do anything at all while she held him in her regard. Good Lord, no wonder Mortimer had overthrown a king for her. When she nuzzled into his neck and nibbled at his ear, Montagu felt he could overthrow God if he chose. What had old Edward been made of that he was immune to her charms?

She'd given him the sleeve, like a lady at a tournament might give her sleeve to a champion. He'd understood what she was saying. Montagu had felt like a knight from a romance on a quest, and felt foolish for doing so. He was only delivering a letter, not slaying a dragon. But it felt good to be doing something for her, noble even.

Coolheaded now, sitting on his bed at Nottingham, he sniffed the letter. Even the smell of the wax reminded him of her. He was not in control of his passions while he thought of her, let alone in her presence. The seal was different from the one he remembered. No fleurs-de-lys to signify her royal descent. This was a scratchy circle with Latin names upon it, a snake curling around its circumference, a broken triangle above it. He felt a flash of anger that her son had denied her even her family seal. *What are you thinking, Montagu? Edward was generous to spare her life.* He put his head into his hands and vowed that he would never see her again as long as he lived.

He picked up a pen to write to his wife to tell her he would try to come home soon, that he loved her. No, that was the action of a coward wanting to apologize for his betrayal but lacking the backbone to do it outright. He did love Catherine very much. Montagu thought of all his favorite times with her—with the children by his manor, long days by the river, on his little boat or just playing in the garden. And yet Isabella seemed like a deep shadow over his memories. He could be lost to the queen, he knew.

He went down the stairs out of the tower. The courtyard outside was loud with the sound of the clash of arms. His squires were taking one another on in an informal tournament that had been fought all day. It was nearly dusk, and Montagu thought he should tell them to stop before someone got seriously hurt or wounded. Still, it did them good to exercise their skills, though he wished they could do it against Lancaster's men and not one another. Lancaster's men were all with Henry out in Flanders, bashing up a few of the Holy Roman emperor's knights at tournaments in similar fashion.

Montagu felt guilty and wanted to be with his king. He laughed at himself. Everything made him feel guilty that morning—including laughing at himself.

"You're a flippant dog, Montagu," he said. "You deserve the public pillory."

He reached the bottom of the tower and strode across the courtyard. Two armored young men who had been circling each other with longswords immediately stopped and bowed.

"Enough, Thomas," he said, "and you, George. We want you in one piece to fight the French. It won't be long, boys, so put up your arms for this evening."

Both men bowed again and embraced each other.

Montagu slipped out of the main courtyard and down to the curtain wall. From there he told the guard he was off to take the air and took a lantern with him. There were four men at the gate, and three of them were new to him—picked up with the new office of Marschal, sergeants detailed to help keep in the wool collections. The three fell in behind him but he waved them away.

Sergeant Darrel Cook, a man Montagu had had in his retinue for twenty years, came wandering by, declaring: "The lord bested ten pagans in a straight scrap out in the east. A few Nottingham beggars won't bother him."

Montagu shook his head as he went through the gate. He'd heard that story many times, but it wasn't true—or at least, it was only true if you counted the enemies in what was known as "knights' numbers." That is, you multiplied the number of enemies by at least five. The result of this was that, if you said you'd killed only one or two—and Montagu knew he had done only for a couple of men when he had been ambushed in the woods of Livonia—people assumed you had spent the entire campaign in bed.

He walked down beneath the cliff, the green fields stretching out before him into Nottingham.

It wasn't ideal to come in the dusk, but he needed to make his investigation discreetly. He couldn't search at night, and by day too many people might wonder what the de facto ruler of all England was doing crawling around in bushes. There was thick undergrowth around the base of the cliff, trees and grass too, going up to at least five man-heights above him.

The mouth of the cave gaped in front of him—or rather the mouths of the cave—four of them, two below and two above. Montagu recalled the one they'd taken—the smaller, above. He scaled the rock as he'd done on that night. Not so easy now, Montagu. Not the monkey you were, eh? The going was tougher than he remembered. He carried the lantern in his teeth. Back then they'd gone by moonlight.

He made the lip and struck to light the lantern. Then he went within, the shadows of his lamp dancing ghosts in the darkness, the damp in his nostrils. He made it thirty paces in before he came to the rocks. The entire passage was blocked—it was not a fall; these blocks were regular and showed the marks of chisels. Relief, then. The way had been closed by Lancaster. Montagu explored the other tunnels to similar result. All blocked, all quite deliberately.

He went back with a spring in his step. Sorcery? Rubbish. Always look for the simplest explanation, William. Isabella had been teasing him, testing his credulity. Very like her.

When he returned to the courtyard, the two young squires were at it again, clashing sword against sword, the fat scarlet figure of Lord Lancaster and some of his ladies watching—with servants carrying torches.

Montagu said, "Stop!" The two men instantly broke apart.

"William, sorry," said Lancaster. "I was taken up in town with legal business all day and I wanted to see your men fight. They do you proud, sir."

"Thank you, Lancaster." Montagu bowed.

"Been outside?"

"Just surveying the castle. You never know when we'll need to defend these walls."

"Not that bad yet, is it?"

"No, but too much caution never hurt anyone in war. Thank you for the use of your room by the way," said Montagu. "Tell me, given my history at this castle, I'm slightly concerned about security here. The French aren't above an attempt on my life. And, while I disdain to fear for myself, the wool collection is very critical to our success abroad. So it would be inconvenient for me to die now. I'm glad to see you sealed the passage that leads up to your rooms, but are there any other entrances?"

Lancaster smiled and tapped his nose. "Ah, the secret passage," he said.

"I don't follow, old man."

"The one you used to take the usurper."

"The same."

"Ah, the famous, famous secret passage."

Montagu looked at Lancaster quizzically. The chubby knight slapped him on the back. "It's a long time ago, William. You can let that one go now!"

"Say it plain, Henry, I've a thick old head for riddles."

Now it was Lancaster's turn to look puzzled. "This is my family seat," said Lancaster. "The foundation stone of my security and that of my ancestors. If you think us foolish enough to provide a herb-scented road for our enemies to get in then you underestimate us, William, which I know you don't. The passages were used as quick routes up from the bottom of the cliff when the castle was built in old Henry's day. They were filled in one hundred and more years ago. It's a castle, not a whorehouse—you don't want a quick and furtive way in and out."

Montagu smiled, tried to remain light. "I just want to be sure there are no threats to security, no way of scrambling over the rocks."

"No. People have tried. The peasants believed your story, you know. We even had some of the rougher sort skulking around the base of the cliff looking for it—fancied a bit of my tapestry work, I'd guess."

Montagu laughed, trying to make out he was in on the joke. "They never found it."

"No. A nice bit of fluff to cover the truth, though. I would be interested to know who you suborned to get in here. Particularly if he's still working for me."

"Mortimer's men were not all as loyal as they seemed," said Montagu. "They knew where their true duty lay." Montagu's mind was racing and he struggled not to betray his surprise.

Lancaster said, "As I thought. Can't have been easy, though—you'd have had to come through three hundred men to get there."

"Well, I didn't exactly put on my full battle colors and sound the trumpet at the gate," said Montagu.

Lancaster laughed. "Indeed not, indeed not. You did a great thing freeing us from that tyrant's yoke."

"We did God's work. We could not fail."

"You could not. Will you come to the hall? I've a range of rare meats for you."

"Gladly," said Montagu.

Montagu was having a hard time marshalling his thoughts. He had got there through that upper tunnel—he wasn't mad. So how? Isabella, on reflection, was not the sort for a childish joke at his expense. So, if she were telling the truth, then what? Sorcery? No. Edward, now king, was appointed by God. Even if Montagu allowed old Edward to still be alive, he could not believe any prince of England would have truck with sorcery. It was unthinkable. So, if not by magic, how had Edward enabled their entry?

Had it been through angels? That would mean the new king had had use of angels and had lost them. He was deeply confused.

That night, when the glad-handing was done, the greeting and the courtesies to knights and dignitaries too old, too young, or too useless to be with the king in Flanders, Montagu lay alone in the great bed of Lancaster's solar. He imagined Isabella lying there with him, her body as lithe as a snake's, the smell of her sweet breath, the feeling she gave him that some things in the world were more important than any comfort, any peril—even that discomfort and peril were preferable to all the sweetnesses of life.

Isabella was dangerous for him, but he couldn't put her from his mind. He tried to think of exactly what he knew concerning Nottingham and the condition of the angels. Montagu sat up in his bed, sweating. Had she enchanted him? How far to Castle Rising? How long would it take to get back there? How many horses would he need to canter the whole distance? Eighty miles. Not possible to do it in a day.

Dawn came up and still he hadn't slept. Montagu forced himself to sit at his table and write what he knew, to focus his mind on what he needed to think about, rather than let thoughts of her consume him.

Isabella said Despenser had vanquished the angels—a miscast sorcery. Well, then it would be necessary to see Eleanor, Hugh's widow. She was as unlike old Hugh as the sea to the land, but she might know something. He would visit her at Tewkesbury and drop in at Hanley—the old Despenser seat before his wife set it ablaze. What might be found there? Montagu didn't know, but it wouldn't hurt to look. But Nottingham? There was no passage. He had never even thought to question its existence before. He had seen it with his own eyes on that night, so why would he? He went through the names of the men who had been with him then. He would write to them all and ask them what they recalled.

Montagu mulled over what he knew in his mind. The king had no angels. And yet Mortimer, Isabella, and Edward as a boy under their sway had overthrown a sitting king with angels. They must have had some supernatural power—divine or diabolical. Had the French king employed his own angels to help his sister Isabella?

Whatever the power was, it had not helped Mortimer when they'd crashed into the castle, bound him, and dragged him to Tyburn. Old Edward was dead and young Edward on the throne by the time Mortimer was cast down. England's angels were supposedly absent for some three years before that night.

It must have been angelic power that opened the passage—angels backed kings; no devil would. And that meant the angels *could* be called—under the right circumstances. So old Edward might be dead after all. Montagu's head was awhirl.

If he could find the means by which the passage had been opened or, if that had not occurred, by which they had been transported into the castle, he would be closer to understanding why the angels had attended then and would not now. He would need to question Eland, the old steward, if he was still alive. Montagu had met the man himself, so he was sure Isabella was mistaken in naming this Baricloughe the custodian. But first, he called for George.

"Despenser," he said, "we're heading west and we'll take a night at Hanley. I'd like to impress on your mother the need for getting the taxes collected. Send a couple of men to ride ahead to give proper notice."

George replied, "Yes, my lord."

"And ask Lord Lancaster if I might meet his man Eland, the steward."

Montagu looked out of the window and thought of Isabella. It would be better for everyone if old Edward was dead.

An hour later, George returned. He said, "The noble lord says there's no such man, sir."

Then how had the king secured their entrance? Montagu smiled. "Must have been my mistake," he said.

5

Dow's heart skipped just looking at the Southwark stews. He'd passed them on his way into the city, but then he had been over-awed by everything he saw, in great pain, his head spinning. Now he wasn't just seeing them but actually going in. The houses were set very close and leaned into one another, like drunken men grasping for mutual support. The place stank of . . . so many things. It was like a great rubbish tip. Every trade that existed in the city existed here, but crammed in, meaner, darker, smaller, and poorer. Leatherworkers, stinking of the shit they used to soften the skins, jostled against butchers, next to ironworkers with their acrid fires, next to fruit stalls full of maggoty apples, next to bakers and barbers and brewers and—finally—bawds.

Gangs of ragged children ran barefoot through the streets, people pissed openly in doorways, lewd women enticed raucously from windows. These weren't the rural poor Dow had known—priest-cowed church mice—nor even like the open rebels he'd lived with on the moor. Here were people who neither bowed to nor fought authority but simply ignored it. There was a shabby church, but it seemed to list at one side on soft foundations like a storm-grounded ship. Dow was scared but exhilarated. What a power these rough people would be if they could be made to move collectively against the high men and the priests.

How it would be to live so free.

"Hello, handsome!" a young woman called from a doorway. Dow thought she was very pretty—no more than eighteen, small, dark, and lovely.

"Take a tumble with Flying Bess?" she said.

"You like her?" asked Orsino. The journey to the stews had lightened the Florentine's bad mood. He had been restless since Sariel had come and gone, and it did him good to have some purpose, however small. The mercenary had spoken of how he had thought that one day he would make such a journey with his own son, it being a great day for a Florentine father to take his son to a whore. Dow had sensed stirrings of a reciprocal feeling. Could this fellow be converted, saved by Lucifer? He tried to focus on the joy Lucifer brought. He could not forgive, but could good fruit spring from bad seeds?

"I want to see Joanna Greatbelly," said Dow.

"She's been recommended to you?"

"Yes."

"Doesn't sound very promising," said Orsino.

"She's the one I want to see." Dow's throat was tight. He really would have liked to "take a tumble" with Flying Bess. He'd had his fun with the girls on the moor—but none of them were as pretty as Flying Bess, nor dressed the same in her yellow hood and tight dress.

"Do you know Joanna Greatbelly?" said Orsino to the woman in the doorway.

The woman took his hand and put it to her breast. "You like 'em old and fat, do you?"

"It's for the boy." He turned behind him. "Look, Dow, give me a little while, then we'll find yours." He turned to the woman. "Never mind about the bath—we'll just get down to business straight away; I'm only meant to be here for the boy."

As he ducked into the doorway, leaving Dow in the street, Orsino called back, "Actually, Dow, give me quite a long while."

The boy looked around him, suddenly feeling vulnerable. Orsino had left him with no weapon, no money, no anything. He wanted to summon the courage to speak out—to spread the word of Lucifer. Abbadon had often held the villagers rapt with his preaching, but that was a different place. There was a tradition of Luciferism in the West Country; men were prepared to hear the word. Here, in the shadow of the church? No, it was not yet the time.

He stood in the street for a good half hour and, other than one gentleman complimenting him on his good looks and asking him if he was plying for trade, no one spoke to him. Dow had felt sorry to disappoint the man and tell him he had no trade and had nothing to sell or offer in the way of service. The man had been quite insistent that Dow had *something* to sell and had taken some persuading to go away. Dow had thought to lead him away and try to rob him, but he wanted to stay near Orsino. Besides, the man had a friendly manner, quite unlike the contempt he was used to from gentlemen and nobles.

Orsino emerged smiling. "Right, Greatbelly it is," he said, "although you're missing a trick there, boy. Several tricks, in fact."

They walked down the length of the narrow alley.

"This is Gropqwente Lane," said Orsino. "We want Puppekirty." He asked a passerby, who directed them.

This lane was even meaner and narrower than the others, not nearly wide enough for them to walk two abreast, dark, despite the ribbon of blue sky visible above them.

"Ah," said Orsino, pointing to a sign that showed a man in a bath that had a large rose on the side, "this I believe is the Rose stew."

The doorway was low, and a thickset man sat on a stool just inside it. The place was rank, even compared to the stinking street outside. "Two free, one fat; one skinny, take your pick."

"Joanna Greatbelly," said Orsino, "for the boy."

Dow was aware he was trembling slightly. He didn't know if he'd be able to get what he wanted. The man raised his eyebrows. "This your first time, son?"

Dow said nothing. The town made him nervous, the stews more so, robbing him of speech.

"Hell of a way to start," said the man. "Upstairs, pay her before. If she goes on top, you won't be in a fit state to reach your purse after."

They climbed the narrow stairs. There was a small landing on the top with two rooms either side, privacy provided by dirty yellow curtains.

"Joanna."

"In here, my darling." The voice was low and rough. It came from the room on the right.

Orsino ducked in and Dow followed him.

A woman had just discarded a linen wrap and stepped into a big, low wooden tub. She was completely naked, big breasted, her belly white and puckered like a plucked hen's.

"Hello, lads," she said, reaching down to splash water on her breasts, "two at a time is cheaper as long as you're quick."

Orsino wore a look of surprise. "This is the one you want?"

"Yes."

"Sixpence straight, ninepence for sins carrying a three-year penance, a shilling for acts unnatural and damnable," said Greatbelly.

Orsino seemed to find this rather funny. "I've seen you face down a demon, kid, but I think you might have bitten off more than you can chew here," he said, careful not to let the woman hear. "Why don't you come back and take on that lithe young piece we saw earlier?"

"This is the one that I want," said Dow.

Orsino shrugged and reached inside his tunic for his purse. "How much shall I pay her? You heard the price list."

"Two shillings," said Dow.

Orsino took on the openmouthed look of a man who has come down to his stable to find his horse has turned into a unicorn.

"You young lads," he said. He pressed two shillings into Dow's hand.

"I'll meet you downstairs," he said, and left the room.

Dow stood looking at Greatbelly for a few moments. Her face was pretty, he thought, or had been once. He admired her, he thought, keeping a roof over her head and growing so fat through her hard work. Whores did work hard, he had heard it said. Abbadon had an expression "working like a market-day bawd."

"I don't want to do it," said Dow.

She said, "I still want paying. If you like, I'll just take the money and you can tell him downstairs what you like."

"Osbert the pardoner sent me."

Now the prettiness left her face and a hard, spiteful look replaced it. "Well," she said, stepping out of the water and picking up her sheet, "have you come to pay me what he owes me?"

"What does he owe you?"

"Five shillings. I paid him—in kind—for a cure for my little Betsy. The child's as sick as the day I sprinkled the oil on her. What's wrong with your tongue?"

Dow stuck out his tongue to show her the fork.

"My God," she said, "I always said the Devil'd come for him in the end. What happened to you? The priests get you?"

"Yes."

She wrapped the sheet around her. "They're the ones who go for tongues."

Dow didn't know where the words came from. "Where's your daughter?"

"She's not available."

"If she's sick, I'd like to see her."

"And you a friend of Osbert! I've given up paying frauds and cheats."

He said, "I don't want paying. I cured a boy once. I'm not saying I could cure her, but I could try."

Greatbelly looked him up and down for a second. "Very well," she said, "but any funny stuff and I'll gut you myself. You'll believe me when I tell you that you won't be the first. Come on."

"I need something. Osbert said you could give me something to make a man sleep."

She padded to the back of the room and opened a second door that descended a staircase. "Suck him off and ask him to tell you he loves you," she said.

"Osbert said you would have a philter."

"Did he? Where is he?"

Dow said nothing, just looked at the floor.

"Too scared to come here himself, is he?"

"He's in prison."

"For debt. Best place for him. Two shillings."

Dow walked across and put them into her hand.

Joanna Greatbelly went to the back of the room and opened a chest.

She took out a wrap of hessian.

She gave him the wrap. "It's a bit gritty sometimes, so put it in something strong like wine and stir it in well."

Joanna added, "If you get anything worth having—any loot, any plunder, come back to me. I know someone who can shift it for you without getting you hanged. Now do you want to see my daughter?"

Dow said, "Yes."

The woman rearranged her sheet around her and opened a door at the back of the room. They descended another narrow staircase, which brought them out by a back entrance into another narrow alley.

Greatbelly led Dow barefoot down the alley and turned left into a wider street. Five doors down they came to a small house with a thatched roof. It had one front door with an iron handle and lock on it. Greatbelly knocked and the door opened.

It was a small but clean room that had a big bed in it, along with a couple of mattresses on the floor. There was a table with some knives and bread plates on it, two chairs, and a fire burning in the center of the room—most of the smoke escaping through a hole in the roof. It was like a cleaner, better furnished version of a poor man's cottage on the moor, thought Dow.

Lying in the big bed was a girl of around ten years old, very thin and pale, with a vivid purple growth as big as a turnip at her neck.

"It's the king's Evil," said Greatbelly.

Dow walked over to the bed. "I've seen this before."

"What are you going to do?"

"I don't know," he said. "It's only worked for me once."

Greatbelly exhaled, looked down at the floor. "Once more than for most of the doctors I've had to her, I should say."

Dow didn't know what to do. The baby he'd cured in his village had had a lump like that and Dow had just held his hand and said, "I wish you'd be well in Lucifer's name." He'd imagined him growing up, big and strong, playing stick fighting as Dow loved to do. And that was it.

The next day, the child was cured, Dow was the talk of the village, and the priest had begun his hunt for him.

The swelling at the girl's neck was cold when he touched it. She moaned and turned away from him.

"She sleeps a lot," said Greatbelly.

He asked her, "What does she like to do?"

"What do you mean?"

"Does she have friends?"

"Yes, she plays with a girl called Rose. Or she used to."

"What did they play?"

"I don't know, what do kids normally play?"

"What does Rose look like?" Dow asked.

"A dark little thing. Black hair all of a mess. Why are you asking this?"

"Do you remember a time when your daughter was very happy?"

"We had a nice bit of cake a couple of Christmases ago and she found the bean."

"What bean?"

She said, "If you find the bean in the cake you're queen or king of the bean. Where are you from you've never heard of that?"

Dow held the child's hand tighter. He thought of her, whole and well, spitting the bean from her mouth in delight as she found it in her slice of cake, showing it to a girl he could not see but envisaged as a mess of dark hair.

"I wish you'd be well," he said, "in the name of Lucifer, Son of the Morning."

"Oh my word, a demon!" screamed Greatbelly. "Get out, get out!" She picked up a knife and started waving it about as if trying to fend him off, despite the fact Dow was still holding the little girl's hand.

Dow said nothing and walked from the house back around to the brothel.

He stuck his head through the door.

"Go on," said Orsino, "tell me what you paid for that meant you ended up in the street. Has she got some rare treat tucked around the corner? You sly dog, you weren't after her at all, were you? I bet there's some fresh young thing around the corner you've heard about and want to keep to yourself."

"Let's go back," said Dow.

There was a shout from up the street.

"Demon! Fiend!" It was Greatbelly, looming into the alley as if drunk, still swinging the knife.

Orsino laughed. "We'd better go. I think you've annoyed her."

The two men hurried down the dark alley as Greatbelly came rolling after them, still shouting abuse.

"Run," said Orsino. "I've fought in many wars but I've never taken on anything that fearsome! We can't outfight her, but we can definitely outrun her—come on!"

By the time they reached the bridge Greatbelly was well out of sight, and Orsino had to stop for laughing. He put his hand on Dow's shoulder.

"Please," he said, "you have to tell me what you did or said that disgusted a whore of her experience. Really, I must know. I can't guess, I lack the necessary power of the imagination. What can it be?"

Dow smiled. "I spoke to her about the morning light," he said.

Orsino stopped laughing and pointed his finger at Dow. "You need to come to God," he said, "or at least to learn to keep your mouth shut before you're burned for your heresies."

"You are not of God," said Dow.

"How do you make that out?"

"You are kind," said Dow. "Only serving him makes you cruel."

Orsino crossed himself. "Let's get back to the house," he said.

6

Montagu had heard that Hanley Castle had been burned quite badly, though its walls still stood. The village underneath it had become a poor affair with the castle's decline, though there was a school there. It had been set up by Despenser's wife, Eleanor, it was said, as some compensation for razing one of the area's main employers.

As they moved through the countryside toward the castle, they saw doors locked against them, people huddled indoors in houses and inns. This wasn't the normal reception a royal entourage received. Normally it would have pulled in hawkers and gawpers like a traveling fair, but here no one waved, no one came to greet them.

"Extraordinary behavior," said Montagu as they passed through a little village in the March green of the Malvern Hills.

"It may help if I lower my pennant," said George. "My father is still remembered here, I think."

"Won't hear of it, my boy," said Montagu. "Was he that cruel to his own people?"

"Not just them, I think."

It was a warm day, and Montagu was sweating on his horse. "Lower it a bit when we get to the next village," he said. "I would like to be offered a cup of ale without demanding it."

Montagu hated to travel now because he had become a nuisance to his men, always cajoling them, criticizing the state of their kit, the speed at which they deployed their pavilions, even the way his barber cut his hair. So slow too, with the full royal train in tow.

He had to be busy, had to nag and worry his retinue because, with want of things to occupy his mind, he thought only of her. Isabella. He loved to say her name to himself and wished dearly that he could write to her, tell her how he felt. Montagu wished dearly he was free to follow his heart—and was then consumed with guilt thinking of his wife. Poor Catherine, there at home. She had been nothing but loyal to him, and Montagu was quite aware he didn't deserve her, didn't deserve to draw breath, not for what he had done—any husband could lie with another woman, that was no sin.

His betrayal was in how he felt. He loved Isabella, more than he loved Catherine. It was commonplace for men to say they would die for women. Montagu, raised on chivalry and the romances, could think of no higher calling than to give his life for that lady. He thought of it constantly and he knew why. In dying he would express his love for Isabella as deeply as he could and he would receive the punishment he deserved for the betrayal of his wife. But no such luxury as death could be afforded him. Montagu was a servant of England, and England needed him to live.

Hanley Castle was a mess. The outer walls were breached, the living quarters and outhouses ruined. The keep had not been demolished, but a great hole had been torn into its side and it looked unstable. Montagu and Despenser walked across the ash of the courtyard. Why burn such a valuable property? People said Lady Eleanor had suffered at Hugh's hands there and the memory of the place was hateful to her.

He said, "I'm sorry, George, but I did need to come here."

"Means nothing to me," said Despenser. "I've been here once and then for too long. My father and I didn't get on. I reminded him of his mortality, my mother said."

"He would have done well to remember it while he was urging the king to folly. He received a stark enough reminder when they ripped out his guts."

"Indeed," said Despenser.

"Did he have much loyalty from his followers here?"

"Only that from terror. My father was a cruel man. My mother suffered at his hands, but his retainers certainly took their share. Why are we here, sir?"

"I want to ask you directly, George. Reply truthfully—the answer won't reflect on you. Did your father have any truck with devils?"

George's face remained calm. "Enough people said he was the Devil. I don't know. I've heard it said. But . . ."

"Well, exactly. The low people like to believe that because it holds out the possibility that God will deliver them."

"I was rather going to say that the high people like to believe it too. If the old king was bewitched, then he was not guilty of tyranny but rather the victim of magic. So we do not blame the king, and thereby God who appointed him, but blame the Devil for leading him astray."

"Well, quite." Montagu would have sent a poor man to the stocks for expressing such a view, but he just smiled at George.

The door to the chapel was boarded up and its windows had been sealed with brick. Why? Why not let the place go to ruin if you were going to abandon it?

"Who did this?" said Montagu.

"My mother," said George.

"Why?"

"I don't know. It was a pretty little place. There was an angel here for several years, though I never saw it."

"An angel?"

"Yes. Old Edward drew it out on a visit here and it loved the light so much it remained for a while. That's what my mother said. My father . . ." The young man's voice faltered.

"Yes?" Montagu asked him.

"My father knew she took joy in it and defiled the chapel during one of his rages, so I understand. I was away—my mother liked to keep me from him."

"Very wise. Not much light now," said Montagu, tapping the brick of the window.

"No, my lord."

Montagu wondered why even Despenser would risk displeasing an angel. Smashing churches was a recognized way of denying the enemy the favor of angels. The angels tended to blame those who were charged with protecting the church, rather than those who did the smashing. But this was Despenser's chapel. The angel would blame him. It might even move to defend the chapel—that was not entirely unknown, though the angels tended to simply move on. Very odd behavior, anyway.

"Be as good as to break this in, would you, George?"

"They do say it's cursed, sir."

"They say that of a lot of places they don't want people going into."

The young man grinned nervously. "I'll send for the men-at-arms."

The men-at-arms were sent for, and they sent for the squires, who sent for the pages, who sent for the smith. He had the tools for the job—hammers and chisels to hack away at the nails that secured the planks over the door.

"What are we hoping to find?" said George.

"Just satisfying some curiosity about your father."

"I hope you're not going to bring any more dishonor to our name."

"Don't worry, you're going a long way to repairing the damage your father did." Montagu eyed the young man and fought down a rush of hostility. His father had been Isabella's ruin. Could that stain be erased in a generation? He checked himself. *Wake up, Montagu—you're acting like a squire in his first infatuation.*

The planks came away and the door was opened.

"Get me some sort of light in here!"

A page lit up a rush torch.

"Only the baron and me in here," said Mortimer.

"I'm not a baron," said George. "That was my grandfather's title. Mortimer stripped it from my father."

"We'll see about putting that straight," said Montagu, "might allay some of your fears about your family name." *What are you thinking, Montagu?* His mind was veering between irrational hostility, shame at that hostility, and then irrational generosity. *Grow up, William.*

George smiled and took the torch from the page. "Shall we go in?"

The chapel had, predictably, been stripped of all its gold and precious things. The glass of the windows had been removed. The weather had got at the roof, and the floor was wet and mildewed. Rats scattered to the shadows as the torch came in.

From niches and shelves in the wall, plaster saints looked down. Or rather, didn't. Each one had had its face smashed. All that was left untouched was, high up in a niche, an indistinct, time-worn stone statue of a saint. Its face was hardly distinguishable.

Montagu said, "Dark work went on here, George."

"Yes, sir. My mother would not have sanctioned this; she's a holy woman."

They walked on through the torchlight to the altar. It was no more than a stone table now—no cup or cloth adorned it.

"Hard to believe there was an angel in here once," said George.

"Really?" Montagu recalled that Despenser was descended from the first Norman King Edward, known as Longshanks. It wasn't impossible an angel watched him still. "The old king came here?"

"Yes, and it was said the angel lived here for a while afterward. My mother said she saw it, even after the king was gone. It loved the chapel's light, she said."

"Can't be loving it anymore," said Montagu. "You have noble blood in you, George. It offsets the viciousness of your father."

Behind the altar, steps led down to the crypt. Montagu walked toward it.

He said, "Can you talk to saints, George?"

"Those of my family, yes."

"Which are?"

"St. Offa was the one my father insisted we dedicate to."

"Scourge of the Welsh. Like him."

George said, "Yes."

"Any chance that's Offa up there in the niche?"

"I don't know."

"Can you try for me?"

"It'll take a while. I'll need to keep vigil for a day or two."

"Then do."

He said, "I'll try my best. I'll fetch my armor." George went outside, leaving the torch with Montagu.

Montagu felt alone and vulnerable in the church, scared even. He'd faced enough men in battle to be able to call himself courageous without thinking it a boast, but he hesitated to go into the crypt.

"Stop it, William," he said to himself.

He went down, resisting the ridiculous temptation to draw his sword. If any of his men saw him do that, they'd assume he was terrified of rats.

The crypt had a low ceiling and Montagu had to stoop slightly to get in. There were six obvious graves in there—three of warriors with their ladies alongside them. What had made Eleanor Despenser board up this place and commit the Despenser line to spend the centuries unvisited?

He wondered who was in there. Not the Hugh who was Montagu's squire's father. All that remained of him was a thigh bone that had been returned to his wife. Not his squire's grandfather, either. Mortimer had hanged the grand old man of the Despenser clan in his armor and fed his body to the dogs. Maybe one of the really old Hughs. Montagu wondered why the whole bloody line had been called Hugh. Must have made for dashed difficult storytelling around the family fire.

There were inscriptions in Latin around the bases of the graves. He didn't recognize the names. Local knights, no doubt. One grave, though, had the names chipped away. It had been done recently—the chips were still on the floor. He picked one up. It wasn't stone—it was cement. He rubbed at the joint between the slab and the sarcophagus. It was cemented but poorly. Someone had made a bodge job of it. There was plenty of cement on the join, but plenty down the side of the sarcophagus too. It was shoddy work indeed. He turned to the grave behind him and rubbed at the joint there. The cement on that was darker, dirtier, older than the stuff on the tomb with no name. What to make of that? Probably nothing.

A chink of mail came from upstairs. Montagu walked back up.

"You've told the men what you're doing, George?" he said.

"I've said I'm keeping vigil to see if the saint can provide guidance in a matter of importance to you."

"Good. I like the men to be reminded we have the ear of God. Did you bathe?" For all the good it did. No saintly direction so far over what had happened to the angels. The disappearance at Orwell in front of Isabella's invading army was particularly perplexing. Perhaps George would shed some light on it.

"I had a good wash. No white robes though, so the formal stuff will have to do."

Montagu said, "Very good."

George knelt before the altar. Then he took out his sword and held it between his hands, point down to the floor. Montagu went out into the spring sunshine.

He clicked his fingers to summon a page.

The page said, "Yes, lord."

"Go back to that village down the way—take a couple of men, I don't want to lose you to bandits. Ask for masons—see if you can find one who served Lady Despenser, but if not, any will do. Bring him here."

"He'll ask for what work, sir."

"None. I just want to speak with him. No, second thoughts, have him bring his tools."

Could he justify opening a family grave on nothing more than a hunch? He could do what he liked: he was Marschal of England. But would it be right?

Montagu mulled the idea over for the next night, while a mason was found and George kept his vigil, glad of something other than Isabella to occupy his thoughts. He felt sorry for the young man, kneeling in his full armor throughout the night, but without an actual relic of the saint and not in the presence of an angel, this was the only way to talk to the saint. He had no expectation George would get any more sense than he had achieved himself from St. Anne, but he thought it worth a go.

An hour after dawn the mason came—a squat little man, toothless with a broken nose. Had he worked on the church? Certainly not, he said. Who had? Men who were no longer alive. Men that Hugh the Devil had killed.

Montagu asked, "Why did he kill them?"

The mason just looked at the ground.

"Go on, man," said Montagu. "I'm not a tyrant. When I ask a question it's because I want an honest answer."

"Sir, I . . ."

"Don't worry about displeasing me. I was no friend of Despenser and if Mortimer hadn't had killed him, I would."

"He killed many people," said the mason. "The Despensers didn't need a reason."

"But he killed people who worked here within living memory?"

"Yes. Easier than paying them."

Montagu nodded. "Little short-sighted, though. Good masons are difficult enough to come by without killing them to save yourself a groat."

The mason just looked at the ground again.

A scream came from inside the church, a terrible note of agony cutting through the chill of the autumn morning.

"What in the name of God was that?" said Montagu. He ran toward the church, squinting as his eyes adjusted to the darkness—the sun through the door the only light.

He cried out, "George! George!" But Despenser was lying on the floor, three of his men around him trying to revive him. The knight was fighting for breath, sucking in great rasping gulps of air.

"Get his mail off him—he'll breathe easier without that, and get him into the sun!" said Montagu.

They stripped him down, but Despenser was suddenly awake, more than awake, sitting up with his eyes staring. He grabbed at Montagu.

He said, "It died here, William, it died. He saw it. Offa saw it! It died." "What died?"

"The angel," said Despenser, "the angel!"

"Get outside now!" said Montagu to the men.

That night, while George lay recovering in his tent, Montagu led the mason into the crypt, two horn lanterns their only light. He would have liked to do the job himself, but as a nobleman, he disdained to pick up a chisel or a hammer. Old King Edward had spent enough time mooning about in the countryside digging ditches and thatching roofs that he lost all authority with his nobles.

No one else was allowed in. Montagu had a dreadful feeling of foreboding about what might be in the grave. It had been disturbed, no doubt. He took out his sword and the mason gave him a fearful look. But Montagu just kissed the pommel, saying, "St. Anne, St. Anne!" The blue light in his mind, a feeling of great anticipation. Nothing more. Something had gone on, something very odd.

An angel had died, George had said. He wondered if he was going to find the body of an angel in there—if angels ever took bodies. He knew it was said that they did, but Montagu had never seen any evidence. The body of a devil? He prayed that he would find the remains of a knight.

And he prayed that whatever was in there wasn't so important that he'd have to kill the mason to protect the secret. He hoped not.

Both men put down their lanterns, the soft light just enough to see by.

"Open it." Montagu put his sword back in its scabbard and the mason crossed himself. The earl almost had to laugh—the man had thought the sword was for him. The mason opened his bag and took out a chisel and a hammer.

He said, "You might want to cover your ears, sir."

Montagu did as he was bid as the mason banged into the cement.

"Whoever put this bit of pug together didn't know what they were doing. It crumbles as soon as I tap it," said the mason.

By "pug" Montagu assumed the man meant "cement." So not done by a man who knew what he was doing. By whom then? A noble? Someone in a hurry. He couldn't accept that Eleanor Despenser would allow such a shoddy job.

The mason tapped around the edge of the sarcophagus.

He said, "It'll come away now, sir. Do you want me to send for another common man? I'll never shift it on my own."

But Montagu could stand to wait no longer. No one was watching.

He said, "No, I'll help."

The mason took one end of the great slab, Montagu the other. They slid it aside and, when a crack of a handspan had appeared, Montagu signaled to the man to stop. Nothing could be seen inside in that light—the lanterns were at floor level.

"Step away," he said, "this isn't for the eyes of commoners." The less the man saw, the safer he would be.

"Very good, sir."

The man stepped back. Montagu picked up the lantern and looked within. Nothing. Nothing at all. The sarcophagus was completely empty.

"Come back, it's empty. Help me get the lid off completely."

The mason returned, and, very carefully, the men leaned the top against the base to guide it to the floor. The mason instantly withdrew. Montagu took up the lantern again and peered inside, thinking perhaps that there might be a body beneath and that this was just a decorative plinth—that was not unknown.

But there was something in there. A residue? The merest smear. He licked his fingers and worked them into the stone, then licked the dirt from them. A strange taste—more than a taste. A tingle went through him, a feeling as if someone had walked over his grave. Blood? Very like it. But beneath that residue the floor of the sarcophagus was strangely marked.

"Get outside and fetch me some more lights," said Montagu. The mason left quickly.

He peered closer. Yes, there were indentations of some sort in there, almost melted into the rock of the sarcophagus. It was like a pattern on a rock on a riverbed, lots of little ripples. Why had the idea of a river come to him? Were they scales? Too big. He leaned right in to the sarcophagus and almost leapt back out again. On the far long wall of the container was the unmistakable image of a human hand—long and slim, its fingers clearly defined. It was as if it had been put into wet cement but there was unmistakably a blackened area around it—ash, perhaps.

The mason returned, bringing two more horn lanterns. Montagu took them and set them inside the sarcophagus, along with the two he had already lain there. He traced the pattern on the stone base. Ripples? Scales? He swallowed. No. Feathers—each as big as a goose quill.

He said, "Help me set the lid upside down. I want to have a look at it."

"It's a weight, sir."

"Lift it."

The men struggled to get the lid upright, but eventually it came to the perpendicular, lying on its long side.

Montagu took a lantern and squatted before it. The mason, out of curiosity, leaned over and, as he did so, the lid slipped. He fought against its weight for a second, Montagu tried to stand to help him—but it was no good. The lid crashed to the floor, breaking into five big pieces.

"Sorry, sir, I'm sorry. I have a wife, a boy. They depend on me, sorry. I . . ."

Montagu raised his hand for silence. Outside someone shouted to ask if he was all right.

"Fine, well!" he replied.

He kneeled, the lantern beside him, touching the biggest fragment. Burned into the stone was the face of a man, a face of divine symmetry and perfection. Montagu was convinced he was looking at somewhere that an angel had lain.

Montagu turned to the mason.

"Get out," he said, "and if you ever mention what went on here tonight I shall send Hugh Despenser's son to see you, along with fifty of his men."

7

T wo weeks after Dow obtained the potion, Orsino had to travel to Windsor. Bardi wanted to see him for a progress report and had sent a boy to summon him.

Dow knew this was his chance. In his room in the night, he pried up the floorboard and spoke to the thing in the circle below. Dow had given up thinking of him as either a devil or a demon and now just considered him Osbert, as he called himself. The whore had known him so perhaps he was indeed a man.

"Be ready to distract him when he takes his cup of wine," said Dow.

"I will that," said Osbert.

The next day Dow worked in the cellar, helping the priest as he went through his useless rituals, his calling of higher and lesser demons, his invocations of angels. Sometimes it seemed to Dow that the priest was near to achieving some effect. The light swam, he heard whispers. But was that just the long hours, the repetition, the sheer boredom of the magical endeavor? The air was as thick as a broth and nearly as warm. Dow sweated. The priest sweated. Only Osbert seemed unaffected.

At Vespers, when the priest habitually took his wine, Edwin moved toward the door, wiping sweat from his top lip. Then he looked back at Dow and returned to the table. Dow guessed what had happened. Orsino always fetched him his cup and Orsino was not there, so he didn't trust Dow to either stay with Osbert or to fetch the wine.

"What is your plan, priest?" Dow asked.

He said, "You'll call me master." Dow said nothing more, but Edwin was in the mood to talk. "The same plan I've had for the year or more we've been here. To force it to speak."

"Open Hell again. Give me the key."

"Four men lie dead. Bardi was badly mauled. If we cannot compel this spirit, we cannot hope to compel the so—much—greater fiends that might emerge if we open the gate."

The priest had a dagger at his belt, but Dow knew he could deliver the murder strike to Edwin's throat before he would have a chance to reach it. This was his time to act, for sure, with Orsino away.

The priest wiped his lip again. "I want my wine. You'll come with me to get it. In front of me—where I can see you."

Dow walked in front of the priest up the stairs out of the cellar, toward the kitchen.

"Open my wine."

Dow went over to where three bottles stood in the corner. He pulled out the wooden bung and its oiled hessian plug. Then he poured the drink into the priest's rude goblet. For all his evil, Edwin did not share the addiction to gold and jewels of many of his fellow priests.

He passed Edwin the cup. Dow had been a boy when he left the moor and had never killed a man. Even the Devil's Men tried to avoid death in their robbery. "Lucifer is life. Îthekter is death," Abbadon had said, and Nan had told him the story of God's many murders, from the flood of Noah to the burning of loving Sodom to the killing of his own son. "We don't kill unless it's unavoidable," said Abbadon, "and never our own."

Dow asked him then, "What if a man of Lucifer tries to kill us?"

"That's how you tell a man of Lucifer," said Abbadon.

"How?"

"He won't."

So killing was wrong, but so were a hundred other things that were necessary for survival. Lucifer said that all such things—theft, murder, deceit—should be avoided and, if done, should be only to prevent suffering to others, never to the self. It seemed Dow had no excuse to kill Edwin, however much he wanted to—the priest seemed hardly to meet anyone else, let alone harm them.

"What does Lucifer do to someone who breaks that commandment?" Dow had asked Abbadon.

He had responded, "Nothing. He says what is right and asks us to believe it. If we break his commandment, then we punish ourselves. The sin is its own punishment to the righteous man."

Osbert screamed out from the cellar, "Do not torment me further, do not press me to yield up the truth. I cannot defy you—your words fall on me like the lions God sent to devour the Samarians!"

Edwin froze for an instant, almost like a rabbit hearing the sound of dogs.

"I will tell you where the Drago is, I will tell you!"

Edwin slammed down his cup and ran down the stairs. Dow reached inside his tunic and took out the wrap of powder and emptied it into the wine. He stirred it in with his finger and then stuffed the piece of sacking back into his tunic.

He hurried down the stairs himself. Osbert was standing fully upright in the circle, his arms stretched out like Christ's on the cross.

"You have named the nine thousand, three hundred and forty-five demons of the lower level of Hell," Osbert said. "You have abjured me with the names of six hundred holy angels and one thousand, five hundred and eighty-five saints. The requirements are met."

"Victory!" shouted Edwin. "Where is the Drago? Where is it?"

"Where did you last have it?" said Osbert. "Think back. Retrace your steps. I find that useful when I lose anything."

The priest actually sat down on the floor, his head slumping forward as he let out a heavy sigh. "Hell," he said, "why do you torment me?"

"I'm supposed to be a devil, aren't I? Torment is rather my raison d'être, according to you," said Osbert. "Isn't it a bit like asking why the rain gets you wet?"

"You deserve all the torments that God can devise," said Edwin.

"I'm undergoing one of the torments that, presumably, God has devised," said Osbert. "I'm stuck in this stupid circle and have only an idiot like you for company."

"You test me, as Christ was tested in the desert."

"Except I haven't offered you anything and, in my reading of the Bible, Christ tried to get rid of the devil, not confine him."

"Once again, you confirm your nature with your own lips. You admit you are a devil." He turned to Dow. "There's progress, boy—we'll hook this creature yet. Now get to the kitchen. I want my wine."

Dow went up the stairs. In the kitchen Edwin picked up the goblet and drained it at a go. Then he chewed and spat.

"By God, boy, don't you know how to pour wine? You must do it gently so the lees doesn't enter the pure wine above. This is like drinking grit! Orsino never makes that mistake!"

He banged down the cup on the table and Dow saw that, grit or no grit, he had drained it to the bottom.

"Pour another cup—and properly this time," he said.

Dow picked up the wine bottle and poured. Outside the sun was setting. He looked at the thong around the priest's neck. He would soon have that key.

The hours crawled until midnight. At last the bell tolled. Nearby a drunken voice called out for God's mercy. Some rich man relieved of his money, maybe his life.

Dow would not risk a candle. He felt his way across the room to the door. Then he took up his knife and worked it into the lock. Edwin would be dead to the world and he could risk a little noise. He pried the whole mechanism off, the cheap rivets sheering easily. Then he just smashed in the door.

And if the priest were somehow awake? Dow had taken his last beating. He was a warrior now; Orsino said so. No little monkey of a priest would take a stick to him again. What he couldn't achieve by subtlety, he would gain through force.

Dow felt his way up the stairs to Edwin's room on the top floor. The doorlock was old, and gentle pressure revealed a lot of play in the door.

He put his shoulder to it and gently pushed. Pop! It came open. Moonlight lit a small square at the window, giving just enough light to see by. Dow had never seen the priest's bedroom before. There was the priest in a bed, almost the only furniture in the room. The reeds on the floor were dry, giving off the thick, musty smell of long and slow decay. The old man snored like a pig in a byre.

Dow approached him. The pouch was at Edwin's neck, his dagger underneath his pillow. Dow slid the dagger out, then reached forward and cut the cord. He opened the pouch and took out the little box, squeezing it in his hand. He felt a charge go through him, nothing magical, just the excitement of being so near to what he wanted. To see the Southampton demon again, to thank him for the gift of his branding and ask him more about his purpose.

The priest's keys were on the chair. Dow took them. Then he went to the washstand where there was a candle and the priest's flint and tinder pouch. He took them and felt his way back downstairs to the cellar. There he struck the flint, blew on the tinder, and lit the candle.

The key slid into the lock and he opened the door. Downstairs he found Osbert hopping from foot to foot.

He said, "You're here at last! Set me free."

"In good time. You need to do something for me first."

"I can't do anything. You're as mad as he is. I've been telling you the truth since the moment I arrived here. I'm just a pardoner. Did you go to Greatbelly?"

"Yes."

"And didn't she know me?"

Dow replied, "Yes, she did."

"So do you think she consorts with demons? She only consorts for pay."

"If I thought you were a demon, I'd let you go now."

"What?" Osbert said.

"I am a friend of Hell."

"All right, I'm a demon. There, I confess, now let me go!"

"You are a man, I think. Demons and devils both are unlike you."

"How unlike?"

"You are a beggar," said Dow. "Downtrodden. I think neither a demon nor a devil can remain so pitiable so long."

"That's right. I am a man, and a beggar. So why don't you let me go?"

"I will—when you've done something for me."

Dow took a book and the knife he'd got from the devil into the center of the circle Edwin had drawn on the floor. He made some adjustments to the symbols with his chalk: the sign of Mercury where Edwin had drawn Saturn, and adding Venus—the morning star and the sign of Lucifer, Lord of Light and Love—at the four points of the compass.

"If you are a devil, this will protect me when I let you go. But if you *are* a devil, then I doubt you will come back."

Osbert said, "Come back? From where?"

"Hell."

"Oh, for the love of God. I've been confined here for an eternity. I'm already in Hell, aren't I?"

Dow took out the key. He checked the circle. Hell's gate would be open for a moment, and he wanted something to fall back on should inimical forces break through. He felt more confident facing a devil because of the mark the demon had given him. But Dow wasn't foolish enough to think that it could protect him completely. The demons themselves were afraid of some of the devils. He didn't know if he could ever call the lady again. And besides, the lady was drawn to light and it was very dark in the cellar. So it was a good idea to be cautious.

Dow began his chant, under his breath. He knew what to do. The priest had burned his notes on the devil summoning, but he must have commanded the devil by the name of one that creature deferred to. If he was a devil, Satan; a demon, Lucifer. What if he was an angel? That hadn't occurred to Dow. Could you trap angels in circles? He didn't know.

So Dow took out the key from the pouch. He studied it, marveling at how fine it was, how thin. Even in the anemic candlelight of the cellar he could almost see through it.

"What have you got this time? I'd hurry up if I were you," urged Osbert.

"Don't worry about the priest—he's dead to the world."

"You should have killed the old madman."

Dow said, "I thought of it."

"Why didn't you?"

"Lucifer says it's not right to kill." Even as he said the words, they didn't sound convincing to Dow. He had vowed to kill Orsino and Edwin, felt an almost palpable need to do so. But he hadn't killed Edwin when he got the chance.

"Not even in self-defense?"

"He doesn't make rules like your god. He says it's not right to kill, but he accepts that many necessary things are not right. Yet if we can avoid it, we should. If we can't, there is no penance and no crying over it."

Osbert said, "I know men well enough. I can tell you want to kill both of them, the soldier and the priest. What stopped you?"

"I have a great mission to complete. I may need them to help me."

"What great mission?"

"To find the Drago."

"You as well? You're all as mad as bats."

"I should hurry," said Dow.

How to use the key? What to do? He tried commanding the gate in his own name.

"Open in the name of Dowzabel, I who commanded you to close."

Nothing.

He tried the angels, the demons, and mixing the names of the demons and angels. Nothing.

He burned some incense and expressed his friendship for Lucifer while walking around his circle counterclockwise. Nothing.

"Have you any idea how tedious this gets?" said Osbert.

"How can it open? The key was made by Îthekter, or by Satan. What do they require to open the gate?"

He thought of the priests, he thought of the image of Christ on the cross, of all those martyrs Edwin spoke of in an effort to convert him—as if he too had suffered being broken on the wheel, pierced with arrows, or fed to wild beasts. What did the key want? Dow thought of himself in the circle in Southampton. The priest had wanted to kill him. Perhaps that's what God wanted—blood.

Dow took out the devil's knife with its fine bone handle. Lightly he drew it across his little finger. Then he squeezed down on the key.

"Open," he said, "in the name of Dowzabel."

Little lights began to play at the edge of his vision, as if he had stood up too quickly.

"Open. In the name of Lucifer. Of the two hundred fallen angels who watch for his return."

The lights grew more intense.

"Go to the circle. Go to the circle," said Dow.

The lights began to swim and dance.

"To the circle, in the name of the expelled Grigori who so loved humanity."

He could see the lights move now, little pools with the texture of mother-of-pearl flowing toward Osbert's circle.

"What's this? What's this?" Osbert was shouting. Clearly he too could see the lights as they began to swirl around the circle.

The gate had opened differently last time. Then, in pain and fear, Dow had hardly been able to take in what was happening. Now he saw it all. The lights ran all around the edge of Osbert's circle.

"Are you letting me out, or what?" said Osbert.

The lights went on moving, there was a feeling of pressure in the air. But something was missing, something did not work. He couldn't understand why the gate would not open. And then he remembered—the priest had commanded, not in the name of a demon but of an angel. Dow hated to do that. But a name came into his mind.

"Open in the name of Sariel, lady of the moon and of the light of God. She who is called Suriel, Suriyel, Sahariel, Juriel, Seriel, Sauriel, Esdreel, Surya Saraqael, Sarakiel, Jariel, Suruel, Surufel, and Sourial. She who has fallen."

"What, what? What's happening to my ears? I can't hear anything. No, I can hear something! What's that's noise? What's that scraping?" Osbert sounded near hysterical.

The lights fused together, began to warp and mold the air, a jelly of light hovering there, a glutinous curtain shivering at the limit of the circle.

Dow said, "Open. Open."

"What are you doing? What are you doing?"

"Get me an answer. Tell me how to find what Free Hell wants."

"I'm a pardoner! A pardoner! And I tell you what, mate, I don't pardon you! You should rot in Hell for what you've done to me! Rot! Ro . . . what's that?"

The candle smoke took shape inside the pardoner's circle. It was a wolf's head, then a pig's, then a man's—with great horns.

"Get away from me! Get away!" the pardoner screamed.

At the top of the stairs, the door rattled. "What's going on? What's going on?" It was the priest's voice.

"Get off me, get off me!"

"Can you speak, spirit?" Dow asked.

There was no reply from the floating head.

"I command you, in the name of bright Lucifer, the morning star, to take this man to your realms, let him question your wisest leaders, bring him before them, and answer his questions."

Osbert leapt up. "A way out!" he shouted. Then he ran forward, the veil of light collapsed like an icefall, and the pardoner and the spirit were gone.

8

W hat is this place?" Osbert asked.

The pardoner had stepped out into a cellar, but one unlike that in which he'd been trapped in for a year. This, he thought, was a quality cellar. It was dry and well-made, with a solid stone floor and good arched stone ceiling. It was also full of wine—some in bottles. He went to one and popped out its cork. My God, that smelled nice. He swigged several mouthfuls down. It felt so good after so long. Priority one taken care of—a drink. A shag and shit were still on his "urgent" list. He strode forward, stretching out his legs. The smoke demon he'd seen was nowhere.

"I'm free, I'm free!" Osbert exulted. The relief was overwhelming and he sank to his knees, weeping.

"Thank you, God, for getting me out of there. Thank you, Lord, thank you!"

A thought came into his head, unbidden. *If God got me out of there, might it not be reasonable to ask if He put me in there? And why He didn't bother getting me out earlier?*

Still, these were theological questions. The fact was: he was out. Ish. A set of stone steps led from the cellar. He went up them to a door. Thank God it wasn't locked. He opened it. He was in a broad, timber floor-boarded room with a fine carpet on the floor. A handsome chest stood at one end; a tapestry showing a hunting scene hung on the wall. It was clearly the main room of an affluent merchant's house. There was even a table with some silver goblets on it. Osbert considered stealing them but wanted to make sure of an exit first.

There was no fire, nor any conspicuous chimney vent or louvre. Mind you, it didn't need one. It was hot. Very hot. The cellar he'd been trapped in had been stuffy, but this was something else entirely. Sweat was pouring off him. And the light was uneven, flickering. Was there a fire? He could smell a fire.

He went to a window. It was very dirty, covered in a sort of soot. However, Osbert found he could open it. Immediately a blast of heat hit him, as from the mouth of an oven. The air was smoky too and stung his eyes. He closed the window quickly and took a swig of wine to clear his throat. My God, that was good, he thought, although he almost immediately felt lightheaded—but that could have been the smoke. Osbert wanted to get out of this place. He headed across the room to another door, emerging into a short corridor that appeared to lead to an external door. Good. The pardoner nipped back and stuffed two goblets into his coat. He wanted to take more, but he was limited to what he could easily conceal.

He went out into the corridor, opened the door, and stepped into the street. Finding no street there, he stepped back in, smartish, tumbling on his backside, scarcely able to believe what he had seen. Osbert had been high up—very high up, higher even than when he'd hidden from a disgruntled customer up the spire of St. Paul's. Outside the door had been a vast burning plain. A lake, so bright its image was still imprinted on his eyes, was away in the distance, looking for all the world like the metal that is poured into a smith's mold. But vast, stretching out for miles. A range of mountains had been in the distance, steaming under a brass sun.

He crossed himself and dropped the goblets. They clattered against the wooden floor. There was a sound of scratching inside the house. A rat? A big one if it was.

"Who's here?" The voice was not human—more like the buzzing of a great fly. Osbert suddenly felt very scared. Where was he? Well, that didn't need a whole stack of learning to work out, did it? Lake of fire present, soot and ash present, all it required was a . . . oh dear.

The second door in the vestibule opened and a figure stepped into the corridor. It was like a man but a head taller—and what a head: that of an enormous wasp. It was dressed in a tunic of fine blue velvet and wore matching pantaloons. Its feet, though easily as big as a man's, were those of an insect. Osbert, who had not pissed in more than a year, felt the distinct urge to do so now.

"Ah . . ." said Osbert, glancing down at the cups, "this is not what it seems."

"Where's my whip?" shouted the wasp man. It turned back inside the house, but Osbert was now through the door. He was on an open staircase clinging to the outside of an enormously tall building. Or rather, a conglomeration of buildings. It was as if all the higgledy-piggledy houses of London Bridge had been turned on their side to construct a sort of a hive of wattle and daub houses, all stuck on top of one another. The lake of fire blew a wind of sparks toward the building and a black smoke drifted up from below.

Other people were on the staircase—or rather other things. A young monk raced screaming down the stairs, nearly shoving him off. The monk was pursued by a something that seemed half a man, half a shrub—its legs human but the top of its body a large and thorny bush, its face just visible within.

Osbert rushed up the staircase, past doors and alleys, windows and roads. Every time he thought to duck off the stair something stopped him. On one occasion it was a rattling cart dragging people in cages, pulled by teams of emaciated children. A great fat devil drove the cart, his head that of an enormous ox.

"Thou shalt honor thy father and thy mother. Now pay the price of your cheek and disobedience!" he shouted.

Osbert pressed on. Other people came past him from below, screaming and wailing, cannoning into others running from above him. He was buffeted and jostled as he climbed. A knight in full mail came bundling down the stairs, nearly knocking him off. The man waved his arms and cried out, "Help me! Help me!" Behind him lolloped a devil from a fireside tale—head of a goat, legs of a goat, body of a man. "Here's one who cast lustful eyes on his friend's wife! Here's one who sinned in thought and imagination!"

At points the stairs were crumbling and Osbert had to leap to go on. He heard the crack of a whip.

"A live man in Hell! A live man in Hell!" The wasp was behind him.

Up, up, up on the treacherous stairs, ever steeper, ever narrower. Then the wattle and daub of the walls gave way to stone. He was at the foot of an enormous castle, it appeared. The climb and the heat were taking their toll, the panic too. He was finding it difficult to breathe and he could hear the crack of the wasp's whip behind him.

"Live or dead, you'll pay for your sins! Have you cozened and lied? You look like a cozener!"

Osbert's legs were giving way. He crawled on up the stairs. Sweat and tears streamed down his face; he could taste sulfur and soot.

A hand seized his coat and pulled him from the staircase and into an alleyway.

"No!" He tried to struggle. A man—something like a man, dressed richly like a merchant—had hold of him. His skin was ghastly pale and at the center of his chest was an enormous hole. Osbert said, "Let me go!"

"If you don't want to spend your days swimming in the lake of fire, come with me. Come on, that devil will find you soon!"

Osbert was pulled down the alley as far as a little door. The devil—was it a devil?—shoved him through it and closed and bolted it behind him.

The pardoner lay panting against the door. It felt wonderfully cool. The man—the walking corpse—that had rescued him put his finger to his lips. Outside he could hear the buzzing, humming voice of the wasp devil.

"What sins are yours? Have you taken the Lord's name in vain? Did you cry out 'by God's holy bollocks!' or some such profanity? Is that why you are here? Where are you? I can sniff you, but I can't see you," said the wasp.

There was a scratching at the door. Osbert tried to stop himself from sobbing. It had all been too much for him—so long confined. *What could be worse?* he'd asked himself. Hell could be worse, and before he'd even died too.

The handle turned on the door, but the man who had rescued him had bolted it.

He said, "Don't worry—it can't get in. It's a lesser devil and they're none too bright. Obsessed with minor rules, no flexibility. I mean, I know they're enforcing the word of God, but they haven't factored in that God is a lunatic. The higher fiends are much more amenable to reason."

"It can't get in?" Osbert asked.

"No."

Osbert stood away from the door, made brave by safety.

"You've got some wine?" said the man.

"Yes. Didn't want to let that go." Osbert swigged the last of it before the man asked for any.

"My name is William De La Pole," said the man. "You are . . . ?"

"Osbert—a pardoner."

"You talk like a more educated man."

"I am of a good family. Life treated me harshly." Osbert looked around at the room. It was just a stone entrance hall, tall and arched with steps running down into darkness.

Pole snorted. He said, "Can't blame others. A man's destiny is in his own hands. Take me. I've been condemned to Hell, but I don't bleat about it, crying out for another man's charity to spare me. No, I got out here and I looked for work, made a little money, invested in a little business. The industrious man can make his way in Hell, yes, very nicely thank you."

"So this is Hell?"

"Well, if it's Heaven, then God's a cozener, all his priests and the Bible too. Follow me." Pole went down the stone stairs of the castle. "As a man of rank and proven worth I'm allowed in here and trusted with certain keys."

Osbert said, "Hell is organized according to rank?"

"Of course. You don't think God would make men of worth suffer the same fate as commoners, do you? He sets men in their places on earth and so does he in Hell."

"That's horrible."

"I believe that's the general idea. But only up to a point. It's logical. Those who have suffered more in life need to suffer more in death to make a difference. Otherwise the suffering doesn't increase at all through being dead. I believe I suffer as much from the lack of spiced fruit as a beggar would being thrown into a fiery lake. Now follow me. We're going back down to my house. It's among the lower sort, but it's big enough and away from the outside so not forever burning."

"Burning?" asked Osbert.

"On the lower levels, the wind off the lake of fire blows sparks up against the walls and ignites them. We organize parties of the lower sort of tormented soul to put them out—we draw water up from a central well. I tell you, fire fighting and rebuilding are never-ending tasks here."

The pardoner said nothing, just noted that the walls were mighty dry—like the paper of a wasps' nest.

"I say it's a never-ending task," said Pole, "a joke. Oh well, the amusements of the damned."

"Why aren't you tormented?"

"I was. I expect I will be again. Everyone is, even the devils. Builds up a sort of camaraderie. But I immediately saw that this place lacked organization. Just about managing one alarm or catastrophe before the next came thundering along. I've brought planning here and reduced the devils' workload. I did a similar thing with my wool exports."

He said to Pole, "And the devils listened to you?"

"All my life I've gotten people who don't *want* to talk to me to talk to me. No more difficult persuading a devil than an earthly monarch. Devils can be persuaded, bought, and bribed like anyone else. They have needs and weaknesses. There's a choice here. Be a devil or be a devil's victim. I know what my choice is. Like anything in life, death is all about your connections."

The pardoner marveled at Pole's resourcefulness.

"Where others see difficulties, I see opportunities."

"So why are you helping me?" Osbert asked.

"You're an opportunity," said Pole, "a great opportunity. Believe me, I've been watching you."

"How?"

"Ways and means," said Pole.

They continued down. There was no light.

"I can't see."

"Can't risk a flame in here," said Pole. "Everything's tinder-dry. It's a different case in the middle; we'll soon get there."

The pardoner felt his way on and on. Things brushed past him in the dark.

"Don't worry," said Pole, "you're with me. There's nothing going to do you any harm here."

Down and down and down they went, winding through doors that Pole had to unlock, descending vast staircases where Pole told Osbert to be careful—there was a huge drop either side of the unguarded steps. He could *see* nothing, but his other senses were fully engaged—smells of burning and sulfur, sounds of groans and clanks in the dark, the papery walls crumbling beneath his touch, the acid taste of hunger in his mouth.

He asked Pole, "Is all Hell like this?"

"No, this is the city of Henochia. The demons have quite a nice place in Dis, apparently, for as long as they resist. And some places are much more overcrowded. If you think about it, the Ten Commandments condemn anyone who worships any god other than the God of the Bible. Well, you can imagine with all the old Romans, the Vikings, the Greeks, and then all the strange peoples of the east filling up the place, it's getting pretty crowded."

"Didn't Christ come down to Hell to release all those just souls who had gone before him but had had no chance to come to his Grace?"

Pole said, "He did. And he freed both of them."

"No more?" asked Osbert.

"Have you any idea how difficult it is to keep the Ten Commandments? Thou shalt not covet? Coveting's what makes a lot of people get out of bed in the morning."

Finally Pole opened a door without rushing immediately to the next. Instead, there in the corner of a plush room sat a little devil, horned and tailed like a winged gargoyle, glowing.

"This is Stinger," said Pole, "my attendant devil. Raised to be pestilential, but I'm slowly training him. As you can see, he's quite useful for his light."

Pole sat down on a well-upholstered couch and gestured for the pardoner to pull up a chair.

"Do you have any food, any drink?" Osbert asked.

"I'm sorry if the service in Hell is a little lacking. Mind you, I've eaten at the Bull and Bush in Shoreditch and it's not as bad as that. I'll see if I can get you something to fill a hole. Stinger, food."

The little devil buzzed its wings, fast as dragonfly's, and rose into the air, flying out under a gap in the door. The room returned to blackness.

"You can see Hell does have its inconveniences," said Pole, "but once one has made certain adjustments, life can be very tolerable."

Osbert said, "Why are you helping me?"

"Why does anyone help anyone?" said Pole. "To get something in return."

"What do you want me to do?"

The door opened and the light returned. The little devil flew in with a loaf of bread, delivering it to Osbert, who grabbed it and bit into it hungrily.

"I've got someone I'd like you to meet."

Someone was coming down the stairs into the chamber. A figure took shape in the gloom. It was a man—very richly dressed, but his clothes were torn and tattered, his nose a bloody stub, his face almost skinless. Around his waist he wore a great corset, strapped tight, and his head—his head was secured to his neck only by what looked like laces. It was unmistakable: his head had been cut off and tied back on with what looked like shoelaces.

"This is the fellow you've been tracking?" said the figure. The accent was upper class, heavily tinged with French. Osbert instinctively bowed.

Pole said, "Yes, my lord."

"Will he do our work?"

"I believe he will."

"Who's this?" said the pardoner.

"I am Hugh Le Despenser, Lord of Wales, Royal Chamberlain, favorite of King Edward and of Satan, Lord of Hell. Get on your knees when you address me, and don't speak until you're spoken to."

9

They found Eleanor Despenser, now Eleanor De La Zouche, formerly Eleanor Claire, at Tewkesbury Abbey. The main church—a huge building in pale stone with a handsome square tower dominating the flat land about it—was under heavy reconstruction, workers clambering up wooden scaffolds on the tower and crawling all over the roof.

George Despenser shifted in his saddle and crossed himself at the sight. The young man had recovered slightly from his ordeal on the short journey to the abbey, but Montagu could see he had had a major fright. St. Offa had not spoken to him, only screamed. But George had seen what was in the saint's mind—the smashing of the icons, the presence of the angel and more than the angel. He had seen a vision of great wings, a woman of terrible perfection, her dark hair lustrous in the chapel's dawn light and he had seen blood too, heard the woman screaming, seen the knife, and known that an angel had died there.

Montagu had a tough time hiding this from the men. "A glimpse of his father's offenses against God," he told them. "It was he who smashed all the saints. God hates such men."

But privately he asked George, "Can angels die?"

He replied, "It wasn't an angel—not like I saw as a boy in the presence of the old king. It was a thing of flesh, I'm sure."

"What did it look like?"

"Like an angel from the tapestries, from the windows. A perfect man."

"Wings?"

"Yes. That's what they have, don't they?"

Montagu said, "I was there with the old king when one manifested and that looked like, well, light. Colors."

"So where does the idea of them with wings come from?"

"No idea. Seems we're in the right place to ask."

"My mother will want to know what we were doing at Hanley."

"Let me explain that."

George said, "Very good."

The men rode on through the monastery's miles of fields, orchards, and vegetable gardens. Monks at work gaped as the great procession of riders moved forward.

"They've never seen such a sight. Look at them with their mouths open!" said a little page, trotting beside Montagu on his pony.

"Don't believe it, boy; these monks are more worldly than you know," said Montagu. "They're just wondering how they're going to feed us all."

They'd been directed to the monastery from Eleanor's Tewkesbury manor. She and her new husband had invested mightily in restoring the church. Montagu couldn't help wondering what sins lay on their consciences that they needed to spend quite so much money winning indulgences. Well, he hoped it had worked for them. De La Zouche had died not five weeks before they arrived, it emerged. The amount of work that was going on, you'd think the man had paid enough to buy him entry to three Heavens.

A rider had been sent the day before to alert the monks of the Marschal's arrival and there was a party of the higher-ranking brothers outside the great abbey, waiting to meet them. At their front, alongside a man Montagu took to be the abbot, was a tall eagle of a woman, her bearing and her imposing manner lending elegance to her green dress, otherwise unfashionable and baggy.

The retinue came to a halt and Montagu and Despenser dismounted.

"George!" called the woman with a beaming smile. "How like you to drop in without warning. And what exalted company you keep! Great Montagu, a king in all but name."

"Not so, madam, not so—a glorified servant, no more," said Montagu with a deep bow.

George strode up to his mother and bowed before her. He said, "King Edward's vicar on earth, the rock on which the ship of state rests, the earl of Salisbury, Lord Montagu."

"Is it desirable that ships rest on rocks?" said Eleanor. "Although I'm sure the earl knows what you mean. Welcome, William! I owe you more than I can say. If it hadn't been for your bravery, these monks would not have their new roof, nor benefit from any of the fine work we're doing here."

"Glad it was worth it, ma'am," said Montagu, though the comfort of the Tewkesbury monks wasn't foremost in his mind as he'd dragged the tyrant from his bed. The lady certainly did owe him. She had been imprisoned under the usurper, Mortimer, and, in overthrowing him, Montagu had eventually enabled her to petition the new king to restore her considerable fortunes.

The abbot introduced himself, a swollen little man full of pork and importance, thought Montagu. That was a problem. He wanted to talk to Lady Eleanor privately. He knew the abbot's type—they stuck to influential men like bird shit to a hedge-dried sheet.

"Will you tour the abbey?" said Eleanor. "We're making such marvelous changes."

"Gladly."

Montagu really wanted to sit down a while, take a cup of wine, and prepare himself for the uncomfortable talk with Eleanor Claire yet to come. Why did he still think of her as Eleanor Claire? Because he'd always liked her—a clever, resourceful woman who had needed to stand up to her husband. She'd quickly realized the best way of dealing with her husband Hugh was minimally—that is, she'd seen him when she had to, shared his bed when she had to, encouraged his ambitions at court, and kept herself tucked away in the countryside.

He couldn't bear to think of her married to Despenser. He was convinced any woman of lesser mettle wouldn't have lasted the distance—driven mad by Hugh, maybe even killed.

They walked around the great church while Lady Eleanor explained the works taking place.

"My late husband De La Zouche is buried here," she said. She caught a look in Montagu's eye. "You wonder that I don't mourn his death more visibly. You wonder that I can smile and be happy. I have faith in God, William—real, consuming faith. It is all in His hands and I shall see William one day."

"You shall, ma'am."

Now they came into the church. The Abbey was massive—not quite Westminster but a fair imitation. It too was full of scaffolding, workers swarming around the ceiling, hammering, gilding, painting.

"The lady has been very generous," said the abbot.

"Indeed," said Montagu. Should he bring it up now? Well, why spoil dinner?

The tour continued, through cloister, apiary, living quarters, little chapels, larger chapels.

At last it was time for dinner—not held in the refectory because the order's rules prohibited a woman from eating there. There was a separate, private hall for that, newly built. Montagu thought how lucky for the monks that Despenser had died. Had *he* visited the abbey, he would have left with the silver.

It was a fair meal—well cooked, though not elaborate, give or take a stuffed peacock. The meat complemented the sweet custard and almond darioles perfectly, though Montagu found it hard to concentrate on his food. The room wasn't big enough for the entire retinue and the monks served many of Montagu's men out in the open. The night was mild enough.

Eventually, Eleanor Claire, seated at his side in a fine dress of red taffeta, said, "I'm not a fool, William. I'm still alive because I can read men's moods. What brings you here and what's troubling you? There's already talk between your men and mine. What happened at Hanley? Why did you violate the chapel?"

"Ma'am . . ." Her directness had taken Montagu by surprise. He said, "Your late husband—"

"De La Zouche?"

"The other, the one you would not anticipate meeting in Heaven."

"Yes?"

"He . . ." Montagu struggled for the words. "Did Hugh violate that chapel too? Was something done there that caused you to close it down and board it over?"

The lady went pale but answered without hesitation. "Hugh had one of his tempers. The priest displeased him. He killed him and smashed the church. It was only the refusal of his men to burn it that saved it."

"I see." Montagu was curt. He didn't believe her and clearly she could see he didn't believe her.

"I went into the crypt," he said.

Eleanor tensed. "And?" she said.

"What really went on there? Was it you or was it Hugh who mixed the cement to seal the sarcophagus? It was no expert mason. What had been kept in there?"

Now Montagu saw something he had not expected. Eleanor Claire had tears in her eyes and her lower lip trembled. "Excuse me," said Eleanor, "suddenly I feel very ill. I can't stay here. I will return to my manor."

"Lady, it's dark. The distance is five miles."

"I have done it before. I have three good men with me."

Montagu said, "If you're ill, you can't ride."

"I have some medicine I need at home."

"Then let me afford you some men to escort you. Your son, at least."

Eleanor said, "Yes, my son. I would like my son to come with me."

The whole room was looking at her. Normally she would have stayed in the sumptuous guest house she'd had built for the monks. Traveling home after dark was unheard of.

"George," instructed Montagu, "see your mother reaches her home safely. Take five of my men."

"The road is not dangerous," said Eleanor.

"But will be less dangerous with five men at your side. Our doctor can attend you."

"Really no, it is a familiar malady and I have the cure at my manor. Foolish of me to forget it." The tears were flowing now. What, thought Montagu, could make a woman like her cry?

He had been asleep an hour in the guest house when George came in to wake him. Eleanor had constructed three private guest rooms there—one specifically for entertaining royalty. It was an extravagant gesture that reflected the monastery's ambition.

"Lord, I'm sorry for the hour." The young squire held a candle, dimly lighting the room.

Montagu sat up in bed. "How is your mother?" he asked.

"Not well, I fear. I wouldn't have left her, but she gave me these for you." In his hand was a bundle of letters.

"They are—?"

"I haven't looked; she asked me not to. She said they were to be presented to you tonight."

"Pass me the candle."

George handed it over.

"You may as well go now," said Montagu. "I'll talk to you in the morning."

Montagu arose and went to the little writing table that sat near the window of the room. He put the candle on the desk and studied the letters, scanning them all quickly to pick out the most interesting. Some were legal documents, sent from the Tower of London when Eleanor had been imprisoned, arguing her rights that her husband's property should not be touched, demanding his personal effects for "a loving wife to cherish." A sudden fit of sentimentality, from a woman who was notoriously shy of her husband's company.

There were several other requests for the body of Despenser to be returned, ever more desperate in tone. Why did she want his body? Here was a clue: "Lest forces malign obtain it. It is especially necessary that the Hospitallers and those who give shelter for gain to the old order should have no claim to my husband's body or possessions." What would be the use of the vicious Hugh's bones? He was hardly likely to be made a saint. And who were the old order? The Templars? What would *they* want with a sinner's dead body?

Another clue: correspondence between the Grand Preceptor of the French tongue of Hospitallers—their order was split into eight "tongues"—one "Brother Adam" and Hugh Despenser. The letters—of which only the ones from the Grand Preceptor were present—began with a huge and pompous list of each man's titles.

"Further to our meeting on your proposed creation of relics. We are prepared to deliver what we found, if you provide what you say you will. We will not provide the necessary weapon nor see it moved. You know where it is and how to get it. You are the motivating force in this. What you propose is unholy and without precedent. We work under the eyes of God and St. John, and will not have any part in the sin in any way that makes us answer before God. However, the deal we offered at Paris stands and the banner will be yours, boxed and sealed, on delivery of what you promised. Destroy this letter."

There were more, some with next to no introduction but written in the same hand.

"She will respond to a promise of light. You ask for assurances, but I can give none. This is what our communicants tell us. I now formally beg you in the name of God and St. John to give up this business. You will answer before God. Should you go through with it, our arrangement would stand."

He noted the reuse of "stand," "answer before God," and the appeal to St. John. There was no address on this at all.

Another: "The banner will help you fulfill your wish. Only the strongest kings with the most loyal angels could stand against it. I warn you again to give up this unholy business. Your soul is in peril. As the presence of Mortimer has changed your plans, we would be willing to add a coin payment in addition to the banner. The seal of the Florentine stands surety for the money. Good Jacques will come when you say you are ready."

The seal of the Florentine. Montagu recognized it immediately—he had witnessed half of Edward's loans. It was the chain and key of the Bardi family. Isabella had seemed sure he was behind their entrance to the castle. This was proof of his involvement some four years before.

But perhaps she misunderstood the role bankers played. Perhaps Bardi had just been asked to guarantee a transaction? Such deals weren't unheard of—promises to pay that would be honored by a bank in the case of a noble family or institute reneging on its debts. The money would be set aside and paid by the bank only on the completion of a transaction. What did Bardi know? And what did they mean by "the presence of Mortimer has changed your plans"? What were Despenser's original plans?

Montagu didn't know what to make of the rest of it. The letters were so contradictory—giving advice on some unnamed project, while begging Despenser to give it up.

A phrase stuck in his mind: "creation of relics." He was convinced an angel had died at Hanley. A saint's tooth in the pommel of your sword would protect you in battle, a piece of his robe bring a blessing. What protection would an angel's feather bring? What miracles might be wrought with one of its bones?

"She will respond to a promise of light." Hugh Despenser had put up that chapel at huge expense and, as soon as she was able, his wife had come along and bricked and boarded it up.

The sarcophagus itself was a relic. Why hadn't Lady Eleanor smashed it to cover all evidence? Because she was so holy. It had been touched by an angel—she would not desecrate it, though she couldn't bring herself to use it. So she sealed in its secret. The cement work must have been done by her—she would have had some idea of how to mix it: she'd seen enough building work.

Montagu took out his sword and kissed the pommel, kneeling to pray. Did he receive divine help? Probably not, he thought, but he felt the blue light in his mind and his thoughts were very clear: Hugh Despenser wanted something from the Knights Hospitaller—this banner. For what? To drive off a king's angels. Had he been planning rebellion against old Edward? Montagu would not have put it beyond the man's ambition. But to do so he had to give them something in return. The body of an angel. It was killed, Montagu could not guess how, and then its body kept in the sarcophagus until the knights came to collect it.

Hugh got what he wanted and set off with it, not bothering about any trace he left behind him, because he had no immediate expectations of having to answer to anyone. And besides, it wasn't Despenser's way to worry about such things. He was secure in the king's love and feared no accuser. The whole barony of England had only succeeded in having him exiled, and then only for a few years, after he'd been on that murderous rampage through Wales. He was taken back by Edward after living three years as a pirate in the Channel.

Despenser hadn't taken the sarcophagus, or the angel's blood that lay smeared within it. Why? Because he had something more powerful by far. Whatever this banner was, it must have been a rare prize to warrant risking his immortal soul. Why the contradictory messages from the knights? To cover their backs. They'd take the angel's relics, as they'd take any relics. But they would save their souls by putting all responsibility for the angel's death onto Despenser.

There was a further, final note. It was signed Eleanor De La Zouche.

A note. "As I am not guilty of my apparent sin, they avoid the guilt of theirs. I have sought only to protect him. Let the shame be mine. Exodus 20:5."

Montagu went to the big Bible that lay chained on a plinth and opened it. His Latin had always been poor and neglect had not improved it. He could make no sense of it.

He pulled on his trousers, coat, and boots while calling for George. The squire came into the room.

"Get that fat abbot up here, now," Montagu said. "Tell him to bring one of his learned monks." Twenty minutes later, the abbot was in the room, torn between outrage at being woken and self-importance at being summoned. A thin, bookish monk stood behind him holding a big Bible.

"Exodus 20:5," said Montagu.

"Look it up," directed the abbot.

"No need, sir," said the monk. "It's the Ten Commandments. *'Non adorabis ea neque coles ego sum Dominus Deus tuus . . .'*"

Montagu held up his hand. "In God's French or the Devil's English."

The monk smiled. "Thou shalt not adore them, nor serve them: I am the Lord thy God, mighty, jealous, visiting the iniquity of the fathers upon the children, unto the third and fourth generation of them that hate me."

Montagu picked up the papers and stuffed them into his purse, tying it to his belt. Eleanor feared Montagu knew what had happened at Hanley and the shame would impact on her and her boy. She couldn't bear it and hoped that by appearing culpable herself, she might deflect any suspicion from her son. "My apparent sin." Suicide.

He said, "Get my horse. We're going to your mother's house."

"Why, sir?"

"Just do it, George!"

Lady Eleanor was not there when they arrived, to the surprise of her servants. They found her at ten the next morning, facedown by the bank on that broad reedy stretch where the Severn meets the Avon. Montagu was called from farther upstream, where he had been searching. Her body lay on the bank, her servants silent about her.

George cried out and ran to her.

Montagu dismounted and put his hand on his squire's back.

"My mother killed herself," said George, his voice choking. "She will go to Hell for this."

"No, George," said Montagu, "your mother would not have committed such a sin. This is a considered act. She went into the river and put herself into God's hands. She didn't kill herself—God took her. She is in Heaven. She'll be buried in consecrated ground, next to her William."

"What is behind this?" said George.

"I fear your father's shadow stretches a long way."

It was surely time, Montagu thought, to tell the king what he suspected. Edward could no longer leave his mother in the control of men who had conspired to kill an angel. And it appeared they had either abducted his father or conspired with him to help him disappear. The king needed to know, but first Montagu wanted to find out where the knights had taken old Edward. Montagu had little confidence he would get the explanation he needed.

He was tempted to go back to Castle Rising and put pressure on the Hospitallers until he got some information. But these men were trusted by the king. He must have solid evidence before he moved against them.

So how to get it? Montagu needed a man with contacts. Who? He could kill two birds with one stone here. Bardi, the banker. He had some dealings with the Hospitallers, and there was enough in the letters to deeply discomfit him, hang him even, if they picked the right judges. Wicked thoughts slipped into his mind. Perhaps the Florentine wouldn't even need coercing. He had a great investment in England's regaining its angels.

Montagu was sure that, given the right information, Bardi would undertake the right inquiries, make the correct inferences, and act. So old Edward would die at last, but Montagu's conscience would be clear. He would never issue an instruction to kill the old king, nor even suggest that it might be done. But Montagu knew the Florentine well enough to believe that Bardi would have the guile, resources, and manpower to do what was needful.

No. That was the coward's way. Montagu was no dissembling Hospitaller. He was a true knight of chivalry. He needed to talk to Bardi, but that alone might be enough for Bardi to kill old Edward. If he gave the banker strict instructions Edward was not to be harmed, would that be enough? Enough to save Montagu's soul perhaps, but not to absolve him in his own judgment.

"It is as it is," he murmured. He would arrange to meet the banker.

10

We need gifts for Edward's queen, sir. She is with him and conspicuously pregnant yet again, according to spies." The count of Eu, Constable of France, stood solemnly by Philip's side. King Philip was outside the royal pavilion at Buironfosse, the nobility of France and its allies around him in all the gaudy colors of war. Sometimes he felt like a king among all those surcoats of bears, lions, leopards, and wolves. Other times he felt like their quarry.

A gaggle of nobles around him were theatrically attentive to Philip's every word. Four of them were dressed in fox fur. He knew what that meant—they were accusing Philip's advisers of foxiness in refusing to come to battle with the English for so long. It was tantamount to accusing him of the same, though no man would ever be bold enough to criticize the king. The advisers took the blame, no matter that they were urging war. The count of Foix was actually in full mail. The message could not be clearer.

"My God, she's only just had one. She must get ridden like a messenger's pony. How many children will that be now?" Philip said.

"I've lost count, sir. Do we include girls nowadays? Our spies report the pregnancy may not be going well. Priests attend the queen night and day, laying blessings and charms, and Edward makes particular mention of it when praying before his angel, even beyond what might be expected. I don't understand his concern; he already has two sons."

Philip grunted. "Rattle up a few jewels for him. Distinctive, inscribed personally from me—the sort of thing that's shameful to sell. I don't want to end up paying his troops myself. Better make it costly, though; we want to make a point."

Eu bowed.

It was late October, not far from All Saints' Day. Winter was nearly upon them and finally they had come to battle. Edward's forces were drawn up on good ground not four miles away at La Capelle. The English had a slope in their favor, a forest protecting their west flank, and a good force protecting the road to the east, according to some captured Germans. The angel was with them, but that was as good as it got for Edward. He was outnumbered five to one.

But still, no angels for France. No Oriflamme either. The archangel Michael at St. Denis had refused to release it, or rather not given his blessing. Philip could not take the holy banner without the angel's consent. Fighting without it? Too many possibilities. Too much uncertainty. And the south was in flames too, under attack from English freebooters. That would require his attention soon.

Philip put his hand to his brow to shield his eyes as he gazed to the distance. There on the horizon, beyond the brooding copses, shone something like a sun. The English angel. It sat above a wide area of smoking land. The English were excellent wreckers, and they burned everything for roughly fifteen miles around anywhere their army marched. The people were suffering terribly.

"What of the angel?" said Philip.

"No need to worry about that, Majesty." The constable was at his incredibly expensive sleeve.

"No, Eu?"

"No, lord. We harried the English this morning. It just turns in the air, all eyes and fire, no action. It won't attack France. Our angels may not be convinced out of their shrines, but I feel sure it's because they think we can win this on our own."

Philip said, "Really?"

The chase had been on for more than a year now, Edward stamping about the countryside looting and burning, Philip drawing up plans, redrawing plans, summoning armies, dismissing them. Nothing had gone quite right. The Genoese mercenaries, for instance. Some talk had broken out in Genoa, some strange sect on the rise, worshipers of Lucifer. The ruling families had been overthrown and now the availability of mercenaries had declined sharply, in the short term at least. Who could have predicted that?

All this gave him the distinct and sharp feeling that God was not with him. Philip wanted to see some angels before he would feel safe, but none would come. They talked, they spun in the air, but something had rattled them. An Antichrist. Was it Edward? The angel had said the boy Charles would never be king, so it couldn't be him.

Philip said, "Give me reports of the enemy."

Eu replied, "Dug in, sir, archers deployed behind stakes, men-at-arms dismounted and ready to fight. We outnumber them four to one, though. I'd be confident of winning."

"How're his finances?"

"I don't see what that's got to do with it, sir."

"No, you don't, do you, Eu? Flambard?"

A noble stepped forward, his surcoat displaying a prancing white horse on a blue background.

Philip turned to him. "What are our spies saying about Edward's readiness to face us?" he asked Flambard.

"The new baby is not dressed in the finest of clothes, sir, and his wife keeps fewer ladies around her in her latest pregnancy. The crown and jewels are pawned and Edward is feeding his allies from his own supplies." Philip made Flambard report the situation so that Eu might be reminded of a few realities.

He added, "He has Germans with him, Flemish weavers, the duke of Brabant, Nevers, and a few others. Tell me, Constable, why did William of Hainault come begging to us this year, having deserted the English pirates?"

Eu said, "Lack of pay, largely, sir. And because he is a treacherous dog."

"Indeed. All men are treacherous dogs if you don't pay them. Dig in."

"What, sir? Look at our array of knights. We have ten thousand mounted. We don't need to dig in."

Philip rarely got angry, but he did now. "Dig in," he said. "And let's see if he can afford to fight in France. He'll never dare to attack so many men in a well-fortified position. His only hope is that I charge into the trap he's set—which I won't. My bet is that Edward'll up sticks and be scuttling back to the Low Countries before the first frost."

"Sir, men have mustered from all over France. How will I explain this to them?" Eu asked.

"Pay them," said Philip. "I find that's usually explanation enough. When Edward can raise a force to make our angels stir, then we'll fight him. Until then, if God cannot be bothered to face him, neither can I."

The nobles muttered, a few cursed, but they dispersed to organize digging the defensive works.

Philip went to bed. The next day he sat in a chair watching the English angel again. Just before dusk it reddened like the sun. Then it too dipped below the horizon.

Eu came striding up. He said, "The spies report the Flemings have gone home on report of your refusal to give battle, for want of pay. The Germans and Hainault too. The angel is quite a lowly one. Our churchmen are sure it won't move against an army led by a king on his own land—well, not until the English have bled enough into the soil to make its intervention useless. He is alone in the field, sir. If we attack now, England will have a new king by tomorrow. Edward will be dead."

"And why would I want that, when this one proves so inadequate? Why would I want to relieve Edward of his debts to man and God?" said Philip. "We'll sit here for a few days to make sure he doesn't attack us in retreat, and then disperse when he's gone. Try the local cider; it's wonderful. We should rejoice that we can afford to buy it. Edward can't."

"It's no sort of victory I recognize, sir."

"Well," said Philip, "I suggest you learn to, for you'll be seeing a lot of it in the future. Edward is writhing and in agony. I'm not going to put him out of his misery."

The Constable bowed and Philip drained his cup. When he put it down, he had a large smile on his face. The English king, he thought, would head back to Antwerp, bankrupt—owing his enemies thousands. He wondered if his creditors would let him go home. In the meantime, Philip would work out a way to engage his own angels and take the Oriflamme that would lead them. Then Edward's current sufferings would be as the bite of a fly compared to a swarm of locusts, or some such Biblical analogy.

"More cider," he said. "More cider!"

11

C an you read?" Despenser asked.

Despenser had his back to the pardoner, very much tempting Osbert to make rude signs. However, he didn't want to risk the lord turning around and catching him. Any man who could have his head cut off and restitched with twine was obviously a tough sort.

"Yes, I was educated at . . ."

Despenser turned on his heel. He said, "Concentrate on answering the questions you're asked and no more."

"Yes, sir."

"How did you manage to get down here?"

"I was trapped in a magic circle by a devil who looked like a cardinal. And then a boy cast a spell and suddenly I was here."

"Nergal," said Despenser to Pole. Pole lowered his head, half nod, half bow, as if awed by Despenser's deep sagacity. The merchant was afraid of the noble, then. The word meant nothing to Osbert.

"What's Nergal?" Osbert said to Pole.

"He's a devil Satan sent to do his work," said Pole. "We'd like to send some of our own."

"You get to command devils?"

"I'm a great lord. Do you think my God-given rights cease when I get to Hell?"

"Yes, I'd sort of counted on it. I'd hoped you'd burn. Like a bunch of right bastards." Osbert didn't say this aloud.

"I suffer the most of anyone here," said Despenser, "so close to base men for so long. My food is poor, my clothes no more than a successful merchant would wear. I lack the means to impose my will. When I lived I could send a thousand men to death with a wave of my hand. But, when I arrived here, they were all waiting for me."

Osbert said, "They attacked you?"

"No, they ran away. You give a dog the right kind of beating and it never comes crawling back to your table. So the boy who opened the gate, who was he?"

"Dowzabel. Not a lot of laughs, that one."

Despenser and Pole nodded.

"The abhorred of God," said Despenser. "The Antichrist."

"I don't like him much but I wouldn't go that far," joked Osbert nervously.

"He's the only one who can open the big gates. God doesn't move against him for some reason."

"Then how did your Nergal get to leave Hell?"

"Dowzabel can open the gate to demons and the souls of the damned!" said Despenser. "Devils can get through at postern gates if they have the right passes. Not that the passes are easy to come by, God having set us each in his realm, nor is there a great rush to take them. Angels dislike the presence of devils."

"Though you're on the same side."

"Nobles dislike the presence of low men, though they often fight together."

"So what do you want from me?" Osbert asked.

"Your help," said Pole.

Despenser took on an expression of lofty disgust. "Don't say such things, Pole! My God, you merchants! That a man like me must suffer your company. Base man, you—" He pointed at Osbert. "We demand your service."

Osbert nodded. "Good. How much do you demand it? In terms of pay? Because, my lord, it doesn't look to me like you're in much of a position to be demanding anything." Osbert regretted speaking so freely the moment the words were out of his mouth.

Despenser smiled. Then he walked up to Osbert and struck him hard across the face with his riding whip. Osbert cried out, putting his right hand up to the cut as Despenser hit him again in the same place, this time lacerating his hand. Osbert put his left hand up to cover the right and Despenser hit him a third time.

"Lord Despenser, we need this man!"

"Don't talk to me of practicalities when I'm faced with open contempt! I'd rather lose everything we're struggling toward than tolerate this beggar's sneers!" shouted Despenser. He drove his boot hard into Osbert's groin. The pardoner fell forward and hit the floor like a sack of sand.

Now Despenser kicked Osbert hard in the head and the pardoner raised his hands to shield his face.

"Sir, sir!" cried Pole. "I'm all for whippings, sir, but leave him alive! We need him to go back to do our work. Our future prosperity depends on it!"

"Prosperity, Pole? We're talking about honor here!" He kicked Osbert again. "If I kill him, do you think he'll reappear here so I can kill him again?"

"Sir, sir, he is our way to greater preferment!"

Despenser paused, his boot hovering in midair. He placed it down on the floor again and said, quite calmly, "Discuss terms with him, Pole. I don't trade."

"I can offer you £10," said Pole, "or rather, tell you where to go to get it. And if you do as we ask, you'll get remission from Hell—which means you won't have to spend eternity with Lord Despenser here explaining the error of your ways to you."

The pardoner looked out from behind his bleeding and bruised fingers. "Would it be presumptuous to ask what service you demand?" he said.

"You see, Pole," said Despenser, "politeness itself, when properly chastised."

"We want you to kill the boy Dowzabel," said Pole.

"Well, that should be straightforward." Osbert wasn't sure he wanted to kill anyone, but his hands were agony and he didn't want to antagonize Despenser further. Murder wasn't the pardoner's line; he hadn't the stomach to do it in hot blood, nor the spite to do it coldly. Mind you, if anyone deserved to die it was that idiot priest and his morose little sidekick.

"Not straightforward, lout!" said Despenser, finding a little of his temper again. "Because if it were he'd already be dead!"

"Right."

"A direct attempt on his life by mortals won't work. We're fairly sure of that. He has some powerful protection now. May always have had it."

The pardoner said, "Well, that's a relief. To be honest, I'm not much of a killer. Can I ask why you don't come out yourself and kill him?"

"I am an angel sent to the realm of men, made flesh to steer the hand of a king," said Despenser. "And then I fell again. I would need a bodily form on earth to inhabit and no mortal flesh could hold my soul." He looked almost proud.

"We want you to conspire with devils to lead them to him and then help them rip him to bits," said Pole.

Osbert said, "Right. Er. Very well . . ."

"Satan has made this boy his particular focus and instructed the dukes of Hell to do their best to kill him," said Pole. "We would like to please the Lord of Hell by eliminating the boy ourselves."

"If Satan can only get one devil to earth, how can *you* get more?"

"Satan gets many devils to earth, but he likes to see them compete. He believes it's more efficient than having them cooperate. Also I know more of the earth and, let us say, think more strategically. I'm afraid Satan's reputation for cunning has been lamentably oversold," said Pole. "He relies on dead men like me and the lord here too . . ."

"How dare you?" Despenser lifted his whip, and Pole put his hand up to shield himself. The blow never came.

He said, "He relies on lords such as Hugh Despenser to do his planning for him. While more humble knights like myself are left to the details."

"Better," said Hugh. "If you ever couple your name with mine in the same sentence again, you'll feel the taste of my whip, and don't think I didn't notice that you put yourself first, either."

"Sir." Pole looked at his boots.

The pardoner rose warily to his feet. "So what do I do?" he said.

Hugh said, "One way to have the boy killed would be to put him in front of an angel. But that is no guarantee of success and even may be one of failure."

"How so?"

"It's not entirely clear what God wants to do with him."

"If he's the Antichrist, surely he wants him dead."

"So why isn't he dead? Do you know your Bible?"

Osbert replied, "Those bits that profit me."

"Well, you'd know that anyone who crosses God has a rather limited life expectancy. Remember Noah?"

"Something about an ark," said Osbert.

"Don't be sarcastic with me, you churl. Everyone but Noah displeased God. So God killed everyone. Consider Sodom. If God will blow your city to smithereens for having your squire toss you off so you can fit into your trousers in the morning, what do you think he would do to the Antichrist?"

This was too much for Osbert to take in. The fumes were getting to his head. "Kill him?"

"What a wondrous philosopher you are. Indeed. And he's not dead. So . . ."

"So?" Osbert had that feeling that had overcome him during geometry at Oxford, as if his head had been replaced by an enormous cheese.

"God must have some reason for keeping him alive. Therefore God does not want him dead, therefore angels may not want him dead, therefore he might stay alive in front of an angel. Might."

"Oh. Errrr . . ." stammered Osbert. "So Satan wants him dead. God may or may not. But Satan is God's servant. So why doesn't he want what God wants?"

Despenser laughed at this—for quite some time. It was one of those laughs that make you anticipate the person laughing is going to suddenly stop and cut off your head with a sword.

He said, "Do servants always want what their masters want? Some servants would become masters."

"This is all conjecture," said Pole.

"Indeed it is," agreed Despenser. "The fact is that you please the master you have. Ours is Satan. He wants the boy dead. The boy must die. That requires an angel to distract the thing that protects him."

Ah, finally the conversation had turned to a subject where Osbert had at least half a clue as to what it was about. "The woman? The priest asked me about her. Is she a demon?" he asked.

"A fallen angel," said Despenser. "And the boy's mother, it appears. Sariel."

"Why would she be distracted by an angel? What would happen if she met one?"

Despenser replied, "I had a little business I needed sorting out with an angel, and I discovered through my magicians that Sariel might be of use to me. She enraptures them and calls them to flesh. They descend to couple with her. Quite a sight seeing something condense from the light—darkens the sky for a couple of hours and puts the fear of God into the lower sort, very amusing. When they're in the flesh you can kill them if you have the right weapons and balls of stone. Their big weakness is that they're very easily distracted."

"Who is the child's father?"

"You'll like this," said Pole, "quite an eye-opener."

"My dear old Edward," said Despenser, "appointed by God, handsome as a destrier, with his familial love of the pleasures of the flesh. The fallen angel was with me at Carnarvon for a while and the amour blossomed there."

"So this angel is quite a slut," said the pardoner, "if it's coupling with kings and angels."

"They all are, to an extent," said Despenser. "They hanker after what they've lost. Even if they do give themselves to Lucifer completely it's only because they think he's the quickest way back to the light. Some pester God, some just moon about. They're in love with beauty, and with God. Kings and angels are the nearest things to God on earth, so they love them, when they meet them. They're passionate things. Damned thing wouldn't go anywhere near me." He smiled, as if he regarded that fact as very much to his credit.

"She returned to the king with the baby," said Pole, "but he wouldn't take it. And she wouldn't raise it herself."

"You weren't there!" said Despenser. "Get your own stories."

Pole suddenly found the hole in his chest interesting.

Osbert asked, "Why didn't she want the child?"

"When I killed an angel, Sariel went mad. I would have done for her too, but she fled screaming from the hall. She was a torn and tattered thing when she surprised us on the road near Corfe. I wish I could have killed her too. One day I'll get out of this backwater and come back to earth. If I can work this properly, then my chances are good. I'm not a man to let being dead stop me ruling. Then maybe I will kill her. And take my time about it."

The pardoner struggled to take in what he was hearing. There was something childish about Despenser and the way he reveled in being shocking. No one could kill an angel, could they? That must be a boast. He was doing his best to appall but would be outraged should anyone declare him appalling. Osbert could think of little worse than being under the sway of such a fool for eternity.

He said, "So what do I do?"

"Get the boy to Paris—to the court of King Philip. There Nergal will meet you. We have whispered at the gates of Hell to alert him. You will summon six devils, which he will direct. Do not allow him to see the details of the summoning spell."

"Why not?"

"Because these devils need know only enough to do their job and no more. If devils learn summoning, who knows where it could end."

"Why Paris?"

"Well, there's the thing that makes it worth the £10," said Despenser. "You're going to have to do all this under the nose of the fallen angel. Sariel will be on hand to protect the boy. She needs to have some sort of distraction while the devils kill him. Do you have the art to persuade him to Paris?"

The pardoner let out a long breath. "I have the art to persuade many men of many things. But I think we need to talk about the fee," he said.

PART IV

1340

In the year that John, fourth son of Edward, was born in Gaunt, that the great water battle of Sluys was fought, and that Montagu was captured by the French.

1

On the day the pardoner returned from Hell, Dow sat reading the Bible, annotating it for the priest's benefit. He was marking passages he understood to be true, changing others to fit with what he had been taught on the moor.

Dow was marking the passage concerning Mary Magdalene, from whom the Bible said Jesus cast out seven devils. She had, indeed, been sorely oppressed by devils, but that was because she was a fallen angel, newly escaped from Hell, weakened by her ordeal and pursued by the devils. Lucifer, known then by the humble and conciliatory name of Jesus, meaning "God saves," had slain the devils and taken her as his partner in spreading the message of peace.

Edwin eyed Dow with suspicion. The priest gave him less trouble now. Dow had spent a long time studying, but a long time with Orsino in the garden too. He could jump directly onto the blind horse's back, fight with sword and spear, wrestle and punch. When Dow had come to Edwin, he had been a half a head shorter than the little priest. Now he was half a head taller, and thick of arm and sinew. A tailor so minded might make two Edwins from one Dow. Edwin, a small man, light as a ghost, had to be careful around the boy.

In truth, their relationship had changed from that moment two years before, when Edwin had wept to find his circle empty. He had pulled at his ears and beaten the floor. The devil was gone, only a vague smell of ashes in the air.

"Where have you sent it? What have you done with it?" he said.

"He's gone to get what I want," said Dow.

"What?"

"He's going to find the banner I seek. Or where it is."

"The banner *I* seek. Your job is to help locate it. Your involvement will end when it is found."

Dow said nothing, just gave Edwin a simmering glare.

"You took it on yourself to dismiss him?" said Edwin.

He replied, "Yes."

"How?"

"You want to be careful where you leave your keys." Dow held up the pouch with the key to Hell in it.

The priest snapped into fury. He grabbed Dow by the shirt, forcing him back across the bench.

"Give me that! What do you know that I don't? What have you discovered? I've seen it since the first day I saw you—you would be greater than me, greater by far, with your heresies and your deceits. You have known all along how to control this thing. Teach me, I beg you. Teach me."

The priest had taken Dow by surprise, shoving him back across the bench. Then the youth reacted. He lifted the little man off the floor and carried him backward, tripping him in a wrestling throw Orsino had shown him, but lowering Edwin quite gently, not slamming him as the Florentine advised.

Dow held him by the scruff of his cassock, so the priest dangled just a few inches off the floor. "That priest who came for me before," he said, "we caught and killed him after he put my dear nan in the ground and cut me so bad. I got the taste for priest-killing then. Shall I throw you down the stairs and we can say it was a fall?"

Edwin stared back into his face. He said, "Kill me and you will hang."

"But I, sir, don't fear to die. For I am one of the poor and downtrodden and Hell has no furies I have not faced in this life. Hell is home for the likes of me. Gentlemen like you, I suspect, might have a harder time."

The priest trembled in Dow's hands; the boy was almost surprised by how delicate the old man felt, how fragile. He had wanted him to be tougher, worth breaking.

"I want to know," said Edwin. "I *need* to know what you know. My curiosity is a raging fire and only knowledge will douse it."

Dow thought to kill him, this snatcher, this violent, screaming, obsessed little man who had ordered him torn from his home. But he had also brought to Dow knowledge of Free Hell's intent, educated him, put tools of knowledge and swordsmanship into his hands.

He thought of the moor, all those years ago, the kestrel poised so still in the air, a spirit, a divine thing. And what had it been after the kill? Just a bird with its dinner, flapping home against the evening sky.

"Come to Lucifer," Dow said.

"I will not." Edwin shook his head so violently he nearly fell from Dow's grasp.

"You have the knowledge, priest. I told you all I knew, as you told me what you knew. Only one of us was listening. So now your devil skips to my command. And you are a foolish man who will not hear, in the power of a boy you despise. Remember this day, for this—me, your slave, with you at my mercy—is an image of things to come. Now we need to set a watch, for the devil will return by the by, I guess."

"Your rebellion is against all nature," said Edwin. He lay on the floor, his eyes on the ceiling.

"It's not against my nature, priest," said Dow.

"I think you are a devil. Or a demon, if you prefer."

"No. I am a man. One who disagrees with you and opposes you. That doesn't make me evil or diabolic. But it does make me your enemy. For the moment we have common cause. I want to find this Drago as much as you do."

"You would save England?" The priest could not disguise his contempt.

"Yes," said Dow, "exactly that. But not from the French. From the highborn and the noble, from the clergy who grow fat on the labors of others."

"You are a heretic. You should be punished for such talk."

"I talk in such a way because I have been punished—all the poor are punished by the thieving rich."

"I won't debate the rights and wrongs of God's ordained order of men with anyone. Why are you so sure the creature will return?"

"Because I forced his promise," said Dow, "and besides, he isn't a devil, or a demon either."

"What is he?"

"You need to learn to listen, priest. It's the weakness of your sort. He told you what he was. He's a man. And not the sort to enjoy his stay in Hell, I think."

So two years had passed and Dow had waited by the circle. He never doubted the pardoner would return, not through any thoughtful deduction but because he did not want to doubt it. When he was not at his practice of arms, then he slept in the cellar. More and more he took on the domestic duties of the house too. Orsino was often gone, wandering the city. Dow knew Orsino had been so struck by the beauty of the demon who had saved Dow that the mercenary must search endlessly for her. The Florentine had admitted as much. Good luck in such a teeming city, thought Dow.

It was spring when Dow heard the whispers—creaking and groaning from inside the circle, voices and chants. Fighting too—something was trying to break through, and something else was trying to stop it.

A voice said, "Let me from Hell."

Dow said, "Your form is bound to Hell, Lord Despenser."

"Then find me another."

"Go back to Henochia, my lord."

"Let my servant through. He does not belong here. He is a living man."

The smell of sulfur was in the air, night and day, and of smoke and noxious fumes.

Dow sat stroking the pouch that held the key with his thumb. Edwin had never dared ask for it back. Should he open the gate?

"Let me out! Let me out! In the name of God's blood, let me out." Dow recognized the voice. It was Osbert's.

Dow turned to climb the stairs, but Edwin was coming down. He had heard the noise.

"He is back?" said the priest.

Dow said, "Yes."

"I'll send for my master," said Edwin.

2

M ontagu met Bardi at Windsor—in the chapel of Edward the Confessor. It was one of his favorites: not large, but with a wonderful rose light from the windows, windows that seemed to float in the dark of the interior, rich with the presence of God. Just another place that she was not. *Isabella*. He said her name under his breath as he waited for the Florentine. An angel had dwelt in the chapel once. Not anymore.

A candle burned on the altar and monks sang masses for the souls of the dead. It was Vespers and the evening mass was about to begin. It was well attended. The latest army was ready to sail to join the king in Flanders, and many other men knelt there too—all the best and noblest of England, bowing the knee to their creator, knowing that without his favor they would surely perish before the might of the French. The talk was that old Philip had his angel, and he wouldn't run this time. They all came in to pray: the nervous, the braggarts, the nervous braggarts, the greedy and the plunder hounds, the pious and the chivalrous, raw boys and the grim-eyed men who'd been and fought before.

The squire, young George Despenser, knelt before the altar and said his prayers. George had spent a lot of time in prayer since his mother died.

"Strange place for a meeting," said Bardi, emerging through the throng. His face, thought Montagu, was weatherworn, red at the brow.

He said to him, "What I have to say, I want to say under the eyes of God."

"Aren't we always under the eyes of God?" said Bardi.

"These windows provide his lenses," said Montagu.

Bardi smiled. "As elegant and witty as ever, Montagu—the image of a gentle chivalric knight."

"I do my best. You have the reputation of a problem solver, Bardi."

"You flatter me."

"No, I don't. You're good at it and you're good at it because you lack moral iron in your soul. For that, you are a useful man. Tell me what you know of the death of the old king."

The paternoster was being said. Both men crossed themselves as the warriors murmured, along with the monks.

"Pater noster, qui es in caelis . . ."

"Are we to talk frankly?" Bardi spoke quietly.

"It's the only way I know," said Montagu. "I'm not Edward with his anger and his violence. Our noble king is a great man and cannot bear to hear things he does not wish to—as is right for one in his position. I am a lower man, a man of policy. I will not blame you for telling me what you know so I can make my decisions with all the facts before me."

"I know England has no angels." Montagu was surprised at Bardi's candor, despite what he'd just said.

". . . sanctificetur Nomen Tuum; adveniat Regnum Tuum . . ."

Montagu asked, "How do you know that?"

"I've always found that clergymen are excessively easy to buy," said Bardi, "and were there not clergymen there when Edward ascended the throne, and when he went so many times afterward to kneel at Westminster and beg the angels to appear?"

". . . fiat voluntas Tua, sicut in caelo, et in terra."

"How long have you known?" asked Montagu.

"Not long enough. I saw what happened at Dupplin Moor, how the Scots were routed, and I thought England a safe place for an investment. Subsequently, information came to me, as it often comes to men of wealth. Too late. Edward had spent my money."

"Panem nostrum cotidianum da nobis hodie; et dimitte nobis debita nostra . . ."

"And why has this happened?"

Bardi shrugged. "It is difficult to speculate without speaking treason."

"You're not an English subject; you can't commit treason."

He said, "I could still have my head cut off for saying something the English king would not like to hear."

"Speak freely, Bardi. I need all the information I can get."

"He has displeased God."

"How?" Montagu asked.

Bardi shrugged. "Who knows the mind of God?"

". . . *sicut et nos dimittimus debitoribus nostris; et ne nos inducas in tentationem.*"

The notes of the prayer delivered by the monks were long and sonorous, and the fighters joined in, their voices varied, earnest.

Montagu breathed in. If the necessary were to happen, Bardi would need full understanding.

He said it as a murmur, under his breath: "The old king may still be alive."

Bardi clutched at his purse, as another man might have crossed himself. Montagu shook his head in disgust. What had it come to that he was dealing with men like Bardi?

". . . *sed libera nos a malo.*" The prayer finished and the priests moved among the men, flicking holy water over them, blessing the sites of corruption: the eyes, the chest, the hands, the genitals.

Bardi said, "What makes you say that?"

"I have spoken with certain men. I am convinced the king did not die at Berkeley Castle. Utterly convinced. You know me as a thorough and serious man."

The banker stood for a moment with a mouth as wide as a gargoyle's.

"Do you think the king knows his father lives?" said Bardi. "No, wait, he must. Oh, God's wounds—Mortimer *must* have told him."

"And he would have believed him?"

"He should have. Oh, blood of Christ, it's all so obvious now. I am such a fool. Think about it and you see there was nothing politic in killing the old king. I should think it was an obvious thing to keep him alive—though the obvious sometimes requires a certain genius to see it. Why, if you are to rule as regent, why not put a terribly compromised king upon the throne—one you can at any minute reveal as a usurper; one whose divine power you have neutered? So Edward knows Mortimer has a secret that can damn him as a usurper. Tell me, when you took Mortimer at Nottingham, what were the king's instructions?"

Montagu replied, "That he be bound and gagged."

"And how was he tried?"

"Bound and gagged."

Bardi turned up his palms. "The king must know," he said. "Whether he chooses to believe, or whether he can do anything about it is another question. He is where he is. Funny he chose that, or something like it for his motto, don't you think?" He was shaking his head, almost laughing, like a losing gambler unable to quite accept his luck.

"Do you think the king knows where old Edward is?" said Montagu.

"No. Or the old man would be dead."

"Watch what you say, Bardi. We are Normans, French lords of the English, not scheming Florentines. Edward would not move against his father. Such a thing would be an offense against God."

Bardi stepped back a little way from the warrior, clearly not too sure that Montagu's assurances of his calm nature were worth very much.

He said, "His whole kingship would be an offense."

Montagu said a few words in Latin: *"Sed libera nos a malo."* Deliver us from evil.

"So who has him?" asked Bardi.

"The Hospitallers took him," said Montagu.

"Did they keep him? And, if they did, does the king know that? He may know his father is alive but not know where. Or perhaps he knows he is alive and pays them to keep him isolated. Sweet tits of Mary, what are we to do? I am royally swived, back sarded. I'm . . ." He threw up his hands.

Montagu waited for Bardi to control himself, refraining from comment on Bardi's excellent grasp of whore's English.

"Perhaps the Hospitallers have cozened young Edward. Perhaps he suffers under a lie. Why do the knights isolate Isabella?" Montagu was thinking out loud. It was useful to speak to Bardi—a man of intelligence, at least. And Bardi would be easy to kill if he did betray him. Bankers had many friends in life but few the moment you stuck a sword through them. No one mourns bankers; no one, thought Montagu. No one builds monuments to them, no one sings their name in songs. Why would a man choose that path? He had no idea.

The priest began a reading—the life of St. Stephen the martyr.

"Perhaps he isolates her to stop her talking to anyone? He won't kill his mother, but he will lock her away where she cannot damn him," said Bardi.

"And surround her with charms. There are magic barriers at Castle Rising," said Montagu.

"Well, it might not be a bad idea. Despenser hated her more than anyone alive. If he had magical power, perhaps it still threatens her. Once you trade with demons, it can be hard to put them back in the box, so to speak."

Montagu recalled Isabella, her hands in his, in the candlelight. "This is adultery," he'd said. She'd laughed. "But my husband is dead." The tilt of her head, the slight mischief in her voice. Had she been trying to tell him something? And why tell him? He already knew the truth. Why should Isabella risk raising her son's anger further to point out something Montagu seemed to have already worked out?

"And Stephen performed many signs and wonders, which persuaded certain men to speak against him, saying, 'He has declared that Jesus will destroy the temple,'" intoned the priest in high, nasal Norman French.

"Whatever it was," said Montagu, "he invoked something he could not control, something inimical to angels. The king and his angels wrestled with it, contained it. At what cost I do not know. The king took it with him. It was a banner of some sort—or at least, that was what Despenser thought he was getting when he opened its box."

"And they gnashed their teeth upon him." The priest thumped down on the pulpit.

Bardi said, "The Drago!"

"What?" Montagu asked.

"But they beheld his face and it was the face of an angel." The priest stretched out his hand, almost as if pointing at Montagu.

"The banner of St. George. The Drago. My investigations have revealed that it might be England's savior against the French," said Bardi.

"But that's a holy relic. The king would have no trouble with it."

"But who knows how it reacted to Despenser? He was evil to the core. Half devil, some said. What happened to the banner?"

"The king took it with him."

"So find the Drago, find the king." Bardi actually made a little strangling motion with his hands. Montagu longed to strike him for that. A king, a holy king appointed by God, was just an impediment to Bardi—something that stood between him and his money and therefore needed to be removed. Montagu wanted old Edward dead, but not for profit, not for the money to walk around in fine clothes or buy grand houses. For order, for rightness. And for Isabella. Old Edward had committed many crimes against that lady—he got his children from her without passion, then had spurned her.

God may have appointed old Edward, protected him from Mortimer. God had been wrong to do so. The old king had to die. A hot feeling came over Montagu, shame and pleasure mixed at the thought of the old king's murder.

Montagu mastered himself. "This much is imponderable. He may have the banner, he might not. The Knights Hospitaller—what do you know of them?"

"A successful order. Very rich. They got all the Templar lands. Made themselves a pretty penny there."

"Magicians?" he asked Bardi.

"The Templars had magicians. It was said that was why the French king had them dissolved."

"Not just a land grab?"

"The French king gave their lands away—to the Hospitallers."

Montagu said, "I never heard of the Hospitallers having magic. Wards and prayer, yes, but no magic." Bardi's insouciance was an affront to Montagu. Did he take him for another one of the gulls he lent money to? "Unless they offered shelter to the Templars. Or coerced them in some way. A Templar magician would be a valuable quantity."

"Yes," said Bardi. Still not open, still not frank. Well, let's see how long that lasts.

"Could you contact one?"

Bardi's face was impassive. He asked, "What sort of question is that?"

"What do you know, Bardi?"

The Italian widened his arms. He reminded Montagu of a marketplace pickpocket, caught but his incriminating evidence long gone. The priest's voice rose and fell: "Then the men shouted. They put their fingers in their ears. All together they ran at Stephen. They put him out of the city and threw stones at him. He spoke to God and said, "Oh, Lord Jesus, receive my spirit."'

Montagu noticed Bardi's eyes were on Arondight. The earl was too direct to be much of a politician, but he had been in enough fights to know what a man was thinking by studying his eyes. Bardi was afraid Montagu was going to kill him. Montagu didn't know whether to increase that fear or offer reassurance.

"Then he kneeled down and said in a loud voice, 'Lord, do not punish them for this wrong thing they are doing.' After he said this, he died." The priest made the sign of the cross.

Montagu said nothing. Bardi was pleasantly rattled. Now Montagu did touch the hilt of his sword. Bardi coughed.

He said, "It is of no consequence, lord. I have carried a letter. More than once. Your king owes everything to me."

"Then say what you have to say. If you are an honest man, you have nothing to fear."

"I arranged a meeting between a Templar—a man working with the Hospitallers and your king. That is it. You know all the details now."

"A magician?" Montagu asked.

"Maybe a fraud. Maybe a magician."

"When?"

Bardi said, "In the year that Mortimer died."

Montagu rubbed his hand hard across the pommel of Arondight, hurting himself rather than Bardi. So that was how they'd got into Nottingham Castle—magic. He shivered.

He said, "How did you know of this magician?" Montagu recalled something Eleanor had said: "It was a relief to find we weren't up to our ears in debt to the Florentines. I feared the worst with the company he was keeping."

"I know a lot. I am a man of contacts. He was a contact."

"A contact made when you were working for the king's favorite, Hugh Despenser."

"I do many things for many people. I carried a letter. That's all."

"And you didn't pry it open and replace the seal?"

Bardi replied, "Would you pry into Despenser's letters?"

"I would if I were you."

Bardi shook his head and held up his hands. "Not me, not me! If you think I was going to risk Despenser's wrath, you've got another think coming. A wise gambler quits while he's ahead. I had contacts with old Edward, I had contacts with his favorite. I also had contacts with Despenser's enemies and with the French court and the Hospitallers. I provided safe passage for one of the Hospitallers' men and I was led to believe he had certain uses."

Montagu said, "Magical uses."

"Yes. But I never inquired further until young Edward asked for my help. Why would I risk Despenser's anger by being too ambitious? I took the letters back and forth like a good boy and never cried 'what's here?'"

"I have them here." Montagu gestured to a bag that lay by the foot of a pillar.

Bardi's eyes widened. "So what did they want the magician for? May I see?"

"You may not. Banners. Despenser wanted a banner and in return he was to provide them with some relics. A dead angel, to be precise. You facilitated that, knowingly or not."

He said, "He killed an angel? Have I undermined my own investment? Mother of God!"

"The least of your concerns. You have imperiled your immortal soul."

"I had no idea. I . . ." Bardi had broken into a sweat, as well he might—he'd been part of a plot that had offered the worst kind of insult to God.

"Some people might wonder, if you have killed one angel, have you not killed more? Is that why England is missing its angels, the work of you, a foreign spy?"

"My lord, you cannot mean to hang me."

"When a man like me is told what he cannot do by a man like you, Bardi—that inclines him all the more to do it."

"My lord, my lord Marschal, my . . ." Bardi stammered. "If you kill me, people will say it was to avoid the debt and you will never be able to borrow money again."

"Not when the letters are made public. You underestimate how quickly you will be forgotten, Bardi. Not even bankers mourn bankers. Does the fox mourn the passing of another fox? No, he rejoices—all the more food for him. Yet he weeps for the lion, whose prey's bones he picks clean when the noblest of beasts has eaten his fill."

Bardi extended a hand as if to snatch the letters away from Montagu, but he withdrew it just as quickly. If he didn't know how to bully or buy someone, Bardi was left relying on his charm, all of which was clearly lost on Montagu.

"My lord, the king is in my debt. What preferment do you want?"

"You presume to bribe me?" Montagu spoke too loudly and a murmur went through the church.

"My lord," said Bardi. "I must away; there is business that I . . ."

"You will leave when I dismiss you and not before. Who is Good Jacques?" That was like enough to the name Montagu had seen in Eleanor Claire's papers and Bardi had featured in those.

"A Hospitaller. A Templar. I don't know. A pauper. A magician by repute. I hardly spoke to him! I know him only by reputation. You may have known him as William Eland."

Montagu felt all the breath leave him but rapidly recovered his composure. "You met him?" he asked.

Bardi reduced his voice to a whisper. "The king wanted a magician. Good Jacques had made God knows what bargains with the Hospitallers, or perhaps they held something over him. He was a former Templar magician. The Templars were enemies of God, it was well known. He had helped Despenser, I knew that much and I thought he might be useful to . . ." Bardi indicated with his eyes toward the main keep of the castle. He meant useful to the king. "I bargained with the Hospitallers. They used him. Or they thought they were using him. I don't know what happened. Genuinely, I don't."

So a sorcerer, a demonic sorcerer, had led the way that night at Nottingham. *And Edward sought him out.*

He said, "Where is he now? You aren't a man to give up a contact like that."

"He was expelled from the Hospitallers just after Edward came to the throne. He was useful to them, but his heresies were too much."

"So he is dead?"

"Maybe."

"Maybe?"

"Men like that are survivors."

"If I wanted you to contact him, could you?"

"I don't know where he is. I heard he was at La Grève—the Paris slums outside the walls. Perhaps he's there, perhaps he's gone. He's drawn to the poor like a fly to shit."

"And no king, no prior has moved against this heretic?"

"The people protect him. He is forewarned."

"How? Magic?"

"I don't know. It must be. That or . . ."

"What?"

"You are naïve, lord. Do you imagine that we are loved by our servants? The scullery boys and the maids? Those who dig our shit from our latrines?"

"They respect their betters."

"Some do. And some do not. They might warn Good Jacques."

Incense was lit and the men in the chapel stood.

Montagu said, "I need to speak to him and I want you to find him."

"He won't be found unless he wants to be found."

Montagu wished it was politic to give Bardi a turn on the rack to establish absolutely what he knew. "You have some strange friends, Bardi."

He said, "Not friends. I am a banker. I do deals, I make money, I make *acquaintances*, so I might make money. There is no plot here, Lord Salisbury, none. I was making contacts, doing favors, putting myself in a favorable position to make money. That is all. I concerned myself only with my part and did not ask and was not told anything outside that. It does not do to know too much of the business of kings, remember that."

"You aided an enemy of the king in Despenser. Isabella despises you."

"Not knowingly. The good queen should know I am blameless. Whatever I brought Despenser, it did him no good. You might argue Edward might not be on the throne today had his father's favorite not been encouraged in such a grievous sin that it inflamed God's wrath."

Montagu raised his eyebrows—an expression that conveyed as much as other men do when they bang their fists upon a table and scream. He waited a long moment before he replied. "So your defense is that you are devil, but a useful one."

"I am a man making a living, no more. You have no idea how hard that is. Bankers are hard-pressed nowadays. Kings borrow and do not repay."

"It'll be a long time before you have to take up the begging bowl, Bardi."

Bardi nodded, a little scoop of the head, like a dog creeping back for forgiveness to the owner who had beaten it. He said, "The course is clear. If old Edward can be located."

"I believe him to be with the banner. That is what I have been told."

Bardi bent forward, another little bow. My God, these bankers. A true nobleman would have scorned to have begged and recommended himself to the scaffold. This man had no honor and thought nothing beyond his own comforts, his own profit. A worthless life. The priest snuffed out candles. The mass was ending, the chapel cast in the cold fading light of the windows.

"Then there is hope he could be found. Others have made mention of banners."

"Who?"

"I have a man looking into alternative avenues to angelic help. He has been seeking the Drago, and I have had word today that he may be getting close. Perhaps this new information will allow him to narrow the area of his search."

"He has been working with devils?" Montagu's voice was low.

"Yes. But God works with devils, doesn't he? Have you heard the book of Job? God works with the great devil there, sending him to test his follower. The Drago was mentioned by a demon that my man spoke to. A demon or a devil."

"Aren't they the same thing?"

"The occultists like to make a distinction. The demon is an enemy of God, the devil his friend. I have intelligence from infernal spirits that says the Drago could save England. Perhaps it meant it would lead us to you-know-who. I have word only today that my man expects progress."

"Do you think your man could find him? The Knights Hospitaller will have no more than twenty castles suitable to hold a king. Fewer if he has his angels with him. They'll need a spectacular chapel."

"He could try. And then I could send one of my men to speak to him. If Edward were to die during the conversation . . ." Bardi shrugged, his body hunched, his mouth turned down like a mastiff's.

He had spoken what Montagu had been thinking, but hearing the offense against God said out loud brought the earl into a sweat. "If I thought that was your aim, Bardi, I would have to oppose you." Montagu spoke with more heat than he'd intended. The idea of killing a king was abhorrent to him. Abhorrent.

But Isabella had been marooned at Newcastle by old Edward, left to the Scots. Isabella, scorned in favor of those tyrannous favorites. *Isabella*, no reason, no thought beyond her name, the memory of her in the morning light, the curve of her back, her fine gold hair, her touch. Isabella. Isabella! He hoped she had bewitched him, because if she hadn't, this unholy and forbidden passion came from within himself.

"Then it is not my aim. A conversation, no more. I would ask for the banner," said Bardi. Bardi appeared cowed, and Montagu realized his fury had shown in his face.

He said to him, "Good, we understand each other."

"We should meet again after I have made my inquiries."

"Yes. How long will that take?"

Bardi said, "I don't know. Not too long. Six months?"

"I need to travel to meet the king's army. He's going to force the French to fight in the Agennais. Hurry up or you may not see me again." Montagu spoke of the possibility of his own death as another man might discuss the prospects for rain.

"How shall I contact you?" asked Bardi.

"Send your letter to Antwerp. I'll have a man there."

"Very good. I'll be quick. Do not tell the king, Lord Salisbury. There is no profit in it. Nor any sense either." Bardi made a patting motion with his hands, to illustrate his call for calm.

Montagu tapped his tongue against his teeth. He said, "There are only so many deceptions a man can bear. The king must know what I know."

"But what advantage is that to you?"

"I think not of the advantage to me but of the advantage to him."

Bardi said, "He might kill you."

Montagu shrugged.

"If God wills it."

"Hang on, he could have me killed! I was an unwitting gull in all this, but I know kings. Edward will not see it that way."

"Rest easy. I promise I will petition him that you die quickly, if that is his will. They may even grant that you die by the sword, not the axe."

Bardi was pale. "There are courses of action that the young king's friends might take that he could not sanction. Some friends might think the old king better dead. Young Edward would have to oppose that, no matter what the personal cost to him. But whether he knows already that old Edward might be alive or if he discovers it, he would prefer him dead. In his heart, he will want him dead—I am sure."

At Castle Rising, Montagu had awoken before Isabella and known even then he was lost. Nothing would ever compete with the sight of her sleeping, naked, as the sun rose through the window, the birds sang, and the smell of the wet grass filled the chamber. No point seeking chivalrous old Montagu anymore. He had gone. Now the earl was simply a man doing an impression of his former self.

"I could not sanction the death of the old king. He would have to be brought back here, no matter the chaos that would cause." But he couldn't help himself and had to continue. "You talk of what the king wants in his heart. I want what is in the king's heart. The king's position is my own. I am sure of that. The king's position is my own." *God's hot piss, William, how clumsy can you be? Why not ask the man to choose from a range of daggers?*

The mass was dismissed and the priest uttered his final blessing.

"Of course," said Bardi. His face was frozen in the candlelight, unmoving, a hideous smile of complicity carved into it like a scar into the skin of an apple. Montagu longed to wipe it away. Other men would have scorned Montagu's hypocrisy. Bardi appreciated it. He understood the meaning behind what Montagu had said. Montagu knew it, but he would not retract it—not with the memory of the injustices *she* had suffered.

Montagu felt himself coloring with self-disgust. He reminded himself he was under the eyes of God. A business begun in this church could proceed only with the Lord's blessing. And old Edward could not die if God did not will it. *Don't gild it or lie to yourself. You dog, William, you dog.*

"I will inform my servants. We will search for an elegant solution," said Bardi.

"Do not kill him."

"No. Too simple a solution for Florentine tastes anyway."

Montagu said, "Swear you won't kill him."

"I swear I won't kill him."

Montagu knew well that he was leaving the door wide open for Bardi's servant to kill him. Make him swear he won't even command his death. The earl couldn't get the words out.

Bardi gave a little bow.

"Is that all, my lord?"

It's done, thought Montagu. Best not think of old Edward as the king. Best think of him as her enemy. He looked up at the rose windows. He'd tear God from His throne for her if he had to.

"Yes. Now get out of my sight, you gilded toad," said Montagu. Bardi bowed and was gone like a wisp of incense. Montagu strode to the altar and kneeled to pray—but not for Edward, for Isabella.

3

B ardi was admitted to the dingy hall of the priest's house. It was cleaner than the last time he'd visited, he noted, but comfortless— no rug, no wall hanging, nothing but the bare boards. You could believe no one lived there.

In truth, Bardi was sorely troubled. Firstly, he had received a letter from his father that morning, imploring him to get payment out of Edward—but Bardi knew that wasn't going to be possible. His father spoke of "grave dangers." That, Bardi thought, meant the bank was as good as sunk.

He was not sure of Montagu. The only way to get a return on his investment was an English victory over the French. That meant Edward must have angels. But if Edward knew that his father was alive, and that others suspected it, then he might very well move to protect him. Or he might move to protect the secret—particularly if Montagu was indiscreet. This placed Bardi himself in a mightily vulnerable position, somewhere he did not intend to remain. Montagu had promised him that he would be murdered nicely. That might be a consolation to earls, but it was scant comfort to this merchant.

Bardi considered Montagu an idiot. Going before the king with his great secret, earnest, willing to act. To Edward he might appear as a viper to be crushed beneath his foot. Montagu relied on his friendship with the king to protect him. But kings don't have friends, Bardi well knew. A threat to Edward was more than something personal—it was a threat to his whole line, to the state, to England.

Killing Montagu would leave Edward in a fearfully bad mood and, when kings lose their temper, they look for targets for their wrath. Would he torture Montagu to get the names of the others? Might Montagu reveal those letters, showing where Bardi had first encountered Good Jacques and the service he had done Despenser? Edward couldn't just kill Bardi out of hand to cancel his debts, but if Bardi was convicted of a crime, with letters to prove the truth of the accusation, the king would be free of a huge financial burden.

Consequently, Bardi had spent the morning drafting a letter to Joan of Navarre to ensure Montagu would never reach the king on the continent. The banker reflected on his correspondence with the queen. He had used bank contacts to offer her the Drago. She said she would not be interested and to address all correspondence to her husband. That letter had been signed and officially sealed.

Then, unsigned, and with a standard French court seal, had come another letter in the same handwriting. It mentioned no one by name but said that certain alliances might be possible—that the French crown's aims were not that of all its allies. It called Philip a usurper and said that anything that could be done to hurt him should be done. So she *might* buy the Drago. Joan had money. Enough to save a bank? It would certainly be a big help. Interestingly enough, the letter mentioned the boy Dowzabel and asked for him to be sent to France. How had she heard of him? Bardi had been around long enough to realize that great queens don't request to see vagabonds without great reason.

His man Orsino came back up. The soldier was fatter, Bardi thought— sitting around on his behind, living the easy life at his expense. Well, that was over.

"He's below," said Orsino.

"With the devil?" Bardi asked.

"Not yet. We're waiting for you."

"Wait no more."

Bardi followed Orsino down the stairs.

There was the priest, who at least hadn't been gorging himself on Bardi's money. The boy, though, had grown somewhat taller, and stronger. His hollow face had filled out and he looked healthy. The room was the chaotic mess he remembered—books, potions, and dismembered animals everywhere. Leaning against a table he noticed some disgusting goo too near to his hand. He moved the hand away. There was the magic circle—empty.

Bardi walked up to Dow and pinched the flesh of his cheek. He said, "You've had some fine dinners at my expense, boy."

Dow grabbed the banker's hand and held it with a firm grip. Bardi wasn't going to do anything as undignified as struggle, but he was in pain.

"Orsino, make him let me go, then thrash the boy."

"Dow!" warned Orsino.

The boy released Bardi's hand. Bardi felt like slapping him but thought twice about it. He didn't fancy being slapped back. "Thrash him, as I told you to."

"He's a little beyond thrashing, sir," said Orsino. "If you want that, I suggest you do it yourself."

Bardi looked at Dow. The boy was not tall, but still much taller than the banker. And he was strong-looking, his muscles hard beneath his shirt, visible at the neck. Better dressed, he could be mistaken for a knight's squire. Bardi should ask Joan of Navarre a high price for him. He felt sure she wanted him for purposes of sorcery. Edwin's devil had identified Dow, Bardi's men had found him, and he had delivered at least one summoning to match Edwin's. But Edwin's had taken thirty years of study. This boy had called a spirit of Hell at his first attempt.

Bardi said, "No dinner for him then, for a week."

"We have made breakthroughs, sir." It was the priest.

"What breakthroughs?"

"The devil you saw has been sent back to Hell for answers; we expect his return imminently."

"Do you? Well?" He gestured for Edwin to explain.

"The boy can best tell you."

"Then tell."

Dow said nothing.

"Talk, Dow—the sooner you do, the sooner this man is out of the house," said Orsino.

"I think the devil who was in there ain't in there any longer," said Dow.

"I can see that," said Bardi.

"But he never was. He come after me in the street and he got sent packing. What was in there was a man. And now he's in Hell."

"How do you know?"

Dow said, "Because I sent him there."

"And now?"

"He's coming back."

"You're sure of that?"

"I can hear him calling. I just have to open the gate."

"And why haven't you?" asked Bardi.

He said, "Priest here thinks you should see it. So do I, as it happens. Maybe it'll kill you."

Bardi smiled and tried to look unfazed. "You do know, boy, that when you are no longer useful to me, I will have you flogged, don't you? What do you think this man is going to tell you on his return from Hell?"

"Something about what we want to know, because if he don't, I'm sending him back," said Dow.

Bardi walked around the cellar and looked at the second magic circle Dow had drawn. "Is that the name of Lucifer?" he said, pointing down to some chalk writing.

"Pretty much," said Dow, "though it could just as well be a stone put down there with the idea of Lucifer in your mind. He don't bother much about writing."

Bardi crossed himself. He somehow instinctively trusted the boy to deliver what he said he could.

But Joan wanted the boy, and to kill an angel. Bardi looked up at the ceiling of the cellar, imagining Heaven beyond it. God could not blame him—Bardi would have nothing to do with the death himself. You could not say the man who supplied the sword was responsible for the death of anyone killed by it. Being well away from the killing when it happened would ensure his innocence in the eyes of God.

Three big bangs, metal on metal like a dissonant bell, sounded through the cellar.

Dow took a little pouch off Edwin and took something from it. He put it inside the empty magic circle that had contained the devil. Then he walked calmly to his circle. Edwin, with less assurance, stepped in beside him, and

Bardi, who was nothing if not quick on the uptake, followed suit. Orsino too stepped over the chalk.

"No faith in Lucifer, but faith enough when you're scared," said Dow. "Give me the key, priest."

Edwin spat but handed over the pouch.

Dow began to intone in his lisping voice: horrid names, demonic summonses, commands in the name of Lucifer.

Bardi felt that terrible pressure in his ears again, a mad rush of blood. A smell like sulfur, a taste of ashes. The light was jelly—a heat haze but concentrated only in the circle. Mad voices, skittering like loose rocks on a hillside path: "Here's one who took a pat of butter when his master was not looking. Here's one who thought of his neighbor's pretty wife. Here's a wench who kissed a dolly and said, 'melt my lover's heart.' Sinners sizzling on Hell's hot grill. Sycophants and hierophants paying Hell's hot bill!"

Bardi's head spun and his knees felt as though they might give way. "Will this circle hold, boy?" The banker felt as though he was going to be sick, sicker than he'd ever felt with excess of wine or food. There was a salt taste in his throat, a heat there too.

"Don't know," said the boy, his eyes on the other circle, "but I reckon we're going to see." He held up the key interposing it between him and whatever was coming from Hell.

Now a wind came, hot and gritty. Bardi shielded his eyes. There were figures in the circle, as if concealed in a mist, shadows that leapt and turned. A fat man strode forward. Bardi could just make him out. It was Pole! Now he seemed clearer. He was chained at the throat by a great iron collar. What was that behind him? A huge, shambling, shuffling thing, a giant, a great giant, towering, despite crouching behind Pole, a vast muscular body, holding the chain that secured the merchant. But it had no features, or rather its head had only gestures toward features, like a half-finished clay model that the artist had discarded before he bothered to put finer work into the nose, the eyes, and the mouth.

The jibber-jabber of voices was at an almost unbearable level. "Here's she who gossiped during mass, her tongue quite torn and ripped. Here's he who sold customers short, his fingers turned to stone. Here's one who railed against his lord, his treacherous heart full of coals."

"What is that thing?" Orsino spoke. He was on his knees, crossing himself, clasping his hands in prayer, then crossing himself again.

"A devil, I should say," said Dow, "sent to stop the damned escaping Hell."

"Is Despenser there?" said Bardi. "The one who grabbed me before?"

"You'll be safe, don't you fret," said Dow.

"Pole, is that you?" Bardi could hardly see for the wind. The boy, however, seemed unaffected by it, his hand holding that tiny bone key.

"Come through, pardoner, if that's what you are; come through!" shouted the boy. "Come through, Master Osbert!"

Pole shoved someone forward. Bardi didn't recognize him—a terrified and bloody man, crouching almost, creeping. Bardi had seen enough beaten servants to recognize the gait. The man had received a thrashing.

Other things were coming through now, little scampering creatures. The big featureless devil smashed at them with his fists, jerking Pole this way and that. The man the boy had called the pardoner collapsed into the circle. There was a rush of wings, flapping and screeching. Bats? No—tiny demons, horned and tailed, swarming as if in a funnel around the circle, a whirlpool of beating wings. Faces loomed among the swarm—misshapen, odd things: a baboon with a man's head, a man with a spear through him—but they were being beaten back by the eyeless devil and others who were rushing in to join him. One made the exit. It was a funny, female thing, exaggerated teats like a dog's, stone-gray skin, a wide mouth with peg teeth, plus horns and a stubby pointed tail.

"I am Know-Much," it said in a crackling, spitting voice.

Now another figure loomed in the background. The man with the tied-on head.

"Despenser!" said Bardi. "He is a dangerous one, don't let him in! For God's sake keep him away, he's a lunatic!"

"Who is he?" asked Dow.

"Don't question me, boy, do as I say and close the gate."

He replied, "When you answer me."

"A lord of England. A bad one. The worst man I've ever known and I have known many."

"I'm bad, according to you."

"He was a lord of this land and killed thousands of people like you, and a fair few of greater worth. He is a tyrant, given the chance."

The panic in Bardi's eyes convinced Dow.

"I close the gate!" Again the creaking, again the sound of metal on metal. Pole was jerked back on his chain. The heat haze faded; the pardoner was on the floor, curled up in a ball.

Dow repeated, "I close the gate!" The jellied light collapsed like a falling veil.

The man on the floor whined and gurgled. Creatures swarmed above the circle, as if trapped in a vast invisible bottle.

"Please let me go! Please let me go!" Osbert's face was contorted like a sinner's in a doom painting. He beat the floor and wept.

The boy walked out of his own circle.

"You'll release those demons!" screamed the priest.

The boy ignored him and kicked a gap in the other magic circle, stamping out an area a yard wide. The buzzing, flying things rushed out, as did the pardoner, diving from the circle to land sprawling on the floor of the cellar.

On the boy's shoulder landed something with wings, tall as a blackbird, but it was no bird. Its skin was piebald, shot through with stains of yellow and its wings were like a bat's. Bardi crossed himself. "I am Murmur, an ympe," it hissed.

The other escaped creatures were smaller, some flying up to exit through the gaps in the boards, some swarming up the stairs to crawl out under the door. So many flapping and beating things, pouring forth, desperate for the sky.

"A familiar!" said Edwin. "And I have struggled to gain one for so long!" He tried to snatch at the cloud of flying demons as they passed, but they avoided him easily.

"Do you want one?" said Dow.

"Yes!"

"Then say that you follow the Son of the Morning, not because he commands you or owns you but because you choose to do so and as an equal—as all men are equals."

"So I swear!" said Edwin.

A creature from the circle scuttled toward Edwin and leapt upon his back. It was large, as big as a three-year-old child, and Edwin struggled to bear its weight.

The pardoner cried out, "You will find the banner by asking the angel at the French court. Find the woman who chased away your devil, Dowzabel. She will help you speak to the angel! The old English king has the banner, but the angel will know where to go." He choked, heaved, and spat. "Now get me ale, for my throat is full of coals!" The effort of his pronouncement was too much for the pardoner, and he collapsed in a dead faint to the floor.

"Get him ale," said Dow. Orsino ran up the stairs to fetch it.

"I give the orders around here," reminded Bardi.

"No," said Dow, "I'll consider what you want for as long as you put your hand into your purse and inasmuch as it fits with what I seek to do."

Bardi smiled. "My God, you do deserve a whipping. If the angel can tell us the location of the Drago, then you must go to France. You will travel with Orsino and you will find this woman to go with you. I have contacts at the court. You will ask for the prince of Navarre."

That would definitely smite two birds with one stone. He'd give Orsino a letter for Joan explaining the boy's worth as a sorcerer, whilst requesting she return him to enable a "mission of mutual advantage." Bardi would look generous in sending the boy free of charge and whet her appetite for when he sold her the Drago.

"You must take me," said Edwin. "I need to find the Drago. What other knowledge might be unlocked in the search for it? Think of what I could learn with this spirit's help." The little creature was playing gently with the priest's ear.

"No," said Dow, "your use is at an end, priest. You're fine in front of a book—this requires men of action."

"I could use my art to find where the lady is?" offered Edwin.

"No need for that," said Orsino, who had returned with the drink. "I know where she is. She sits every day in the abbey at Westminster. I've seen her there. I watch over her." He cradled Osbert in his arms, feeding him the beer. The smell of it brought Osbert around and he gulped at the cup.

"Edwin will stay," said Bardi. "You two be ready by the end of the week and make sure you get this woman to come with you."

"If she says no?" said Orsino. He put the cup to the pardoner's lips.

"Then make her say yes," said Bardi. "And you, Orsino, let me speak with you in private. I have a mission for you."

"Killing?" said Orsino.

Bardi laughed. "Well, you're too expensive to employ as a gardener."

He took him up the stairs, out into the garden.

"Yes?" said Orsino.

"I want you to kill a king," said Bardi.

4

D ow did not like the ship. It struck him as unnatural that something
so large should be able to float upon the water and, as it shot clear
of the Thames's mouth at Margate, he felt a lurch in the pit of his
stomach, almost as if he could feel the river become the sea.

They ran quickly on the ebb tide, the wind at their backs. The cog put
only half a sail to the wind for fear of swamping, the sailors nervous to travel
so late in the year.

Orsino came alongside him. He said, "God's granted us a fair wind."

Dow said nothing, just looked out over the gray swell that heaved
beneath the ship.

"I fear for your soul," said Orsino.

"And I for yours."

"Is that thing that came from the circle still with you?"

"The ympe?" Dow said.

"Whatever you call it."

"It is."

"And what blasphemies does it speak?"

"It tells me its fellows are abroad in the world. Whispering to them who
need whispering to, persuading and encouraging."

Orsino crossed himself. "I should cut your throat."

"It would make no difference," said Dow. "Each ympe will claim a soul,
each claimed soul another."

"They're not going to claim mine."

"No," said Dow. "I think that's Sariel's job."

Orsino glanced at the forecastle of the ship. There the lady, clad demurely in the drab cloak and hood he had bought her, stretched up to the morning light, turning her face to it.

Beside her was that wretched man, the pardoner. He moved stiffly but otherwise looked well enough. Bardi had sent him some clothes—a rich yellow doublet, fine brown hose, pointed shoes, and a baggy armless heuke in green velvet, complete with hood. The robe was in good red wool, lined with rabbit's fur. For diversion they had all agreed the pardoner, who had pretty enough manners when he chose, should play the master among them. The pardoner played the role a little too well, dispatching Orsino and Dow to fetch and carry for him, particularly wine.

Orsino had wanted to leave the man behind, but the pardoner had claimed to have a message for the angel only he could deliver, one that would force it to reveal its secret. And he had persuaded the lady to join them.

Orsino said, "How do you think he got her to come with us?"

Dow thought. He remembered the light in the great abbey, the woman kneeling beneath the great windows, tears in her eyes. Her beauty was daunting, like the windows of the abbey, like the spirals of incense caught in the beams of light, like the gold and the silver that stretched out forever in splendor that could have housed a nation of poor if it had been sold. Dow had been afraid to approach her—though he had carried her once before. She was the proof of his faith, its embodiment, and he was awestruck before her. Orsino too hesitated, stumbling over his words, not knowing what to say.

In the end the pardoner had spoken to her and she had agreed to leave. She seemed strange to Dow—not quite mad but distracted. She was a demon, he was convinced, and it filled him with joy and with security to have her along. Orsino said she was a woman like any other and that Dow was just smitten with her. The Florentine watched brooding as the pardoner led her from the cathedral.

The pardoner intrigued Dow. A high man who had fallen. He had never met one of those before.

"You're unhappy with him?" Dow spoke.

"I'm unhappy with everything about this." Orsino took out a piece of cloth and kissed it. Some bit of a saint's codpiece, no doubt. He added, "I'm unhappy Bardi got us letters of passage from the king of France. If we're caught with those, we're dead meat."

"And yet you still come along."

Orsino jabbed a finger toward the pardoner. "I had hoped he would not persuade her. This is a dangerous trip. What are you looking at, boy?"

Dow was staring directly at Orsino. "You would make her your wife?"

Orsino laughed. He said, "And what would she want with a man like me?" He stiffened and straightened. "Yes. I would. But I cannot ask her."

"Why not?"

"I think the lady has suffered a great shock. I've seen it before—after sieges, mainly. We make war on men's bodies, but sometimes on their souls too. There's a madness comes down on people with too much misery. For most it passes and it is not always severe. I think this is what has happened to her and I want to help her."

"Because she is beautiful?"

Orsino looked out to sea, avoiding the boy's gaze. "Yes."

"Better help the ugly. They need it more. What do you think the pardoner said to her?"

"He plied his old trade. He offered her forgiveness."

"For what?" said Dow.

"He didn't say. Why don't you talk to her?"

"She doesn't talk to me. I believe her to be divine. She is a gentle soul, a kind demon. She will speak to me if she wants to. I won't go bothering her."

"I'd call you an idiot if I hadn't seen all these offenses to God with my own eyes. But she is no demon. Beauty like that doesn't come from the Devil." Orsino turned to his pack and rummaged in it for a little while, rearranging its contents. The sun broke from behind a coal-black cloud, streaming its bright banners across the sea. Dow put his hand to the tiny demon inside his coat. It took his finger and squeezed it. "Lucifer is showing us the way," said Dow into his chest.

He turned back to his pack, to sit against the ship's rail. There on the aft-castle was the high man who owned the ship. Earl Montagu of Salisbury. He was everything Dow hated in life, a condescending, hard-looking man—no doubt a beater, a torturer, and a killer of poor men. He looked at the sea as if he owned it, tall and proud, his one good eye scanning the horizon.

The earl wore a fine coat of black fur that must have cost him the price of a good-sized farm, and his lackey—another rich brute—fetched him ale and bread from below the decks. Well, at least they made one another servants too. Dow would have liked to have pitched them both over the sides. Not practical. Thirty fighters sprawled about the deck, or under the aftcastle platform. Dow was a confident youth now, strong and tough.

But he had noted Montagu's unpretentious, undecorated sword and doubted his life would be worth much if he confronted the lord in a fight. The earl wasn't like the banker, a rich popinjay, or like Edwin, a frail and intense madman, or even like Orsino, who bore himself with quiet confidence. Montagu was a man other men feared to meet eye to eye. He stood like a fortress. It had never occurred to this man that the world wasn't his to do with as he wished. And why wouldn't he think that, flying under the royal pennants, his own banners streaming in the rigging and men skipping to his every command?

The boat slowed as the tide dropped, and Dow, lying against the rail, watched the light change. He found himself dozing, the ympe clinging to his shirt beneath his coat. Dow didn't feel strange to have this creature so close to him. It felt as if it had always been by his side. It had said its name was Murmur. When it spoke it was as if it spoke in his head, its voice an echoing whisper, sucking and drawing like the sea on shingle.

It was a demon of Hell, it said—one of a host of smaller demons who could sometimes crawl through gaps in the walls of Hell. It bore messages from the citizens of inner Hell to those on its outer limits. When the gate had opened briefly once again, as Lucifer had thought would happen, it had flown out to earth, along with its fellows. Its mission was to prepare the way for a complete opening of all Hell's gates, allowing all the demons into the realm of the living.

"What's stopping them?" said Dow.

"The devils. Lucifer knows that he can't come here until the angels' power is tamed, nor will he come here while he will bring devils with him—or at least not till he stands a chance of beating them when they arrive."

"What would he need to beat them?"

Murmur replied, "Help from the realm of men."

Night fell and the boat moved on under a big half-moon. The pardoner snored at Dow's side. Orsino sat close to the lady, whispering to comfort her in the darkness. Montagu was back on the aftcastle, gazing back in the direction of England. Murmur stirred and poked a wary eye out of the folds of Dow's coat. All around, the men were asleep, commoners, squires, and knights. All of them except Montagu, who remained where he had stood all day, looking out over the ocean back toward England.

"You're looking at the grand lord?" said Murmur.

"Yes."

"He's troubled."

"How can you tell?" Dow asked it.

"I have been long enough in Hell to know a tormented soul when I see one."

He said, "What troubles him?"

"I do not know."

Osbert asked, "All right, boy?" The pardoner came to sit beside him.

He looked with great distaste at Murmur, the ympe's face just visible in the ghostly light.

Dow said, "I'm well."

"Good. Thank you again for releasing me." He wore a grin like a market day whore, and Dow was surprised at his friendliness.

"I would have done it earlier, but for the priest."

"Yes. Well, you got what you wanted. The devils were very forthcoming."

"So it seems."

The pardoner looked up toward Montagu. "Want a bet I could sell him some indulgences?" he asked.

"What makes you think you could?"

"Look at him. Not sleeping, staring at the moon. There's a man who's got three or four shillings' worth of sin in him, minimum."

"Do you ever use what people tell you against them?" said Dow.

"Well, of course. It's a valuable second stream of income," said the pardoner, "though blackmail isn't the easy art some would have you believe. First, you mustn't get a reputation for it. Second, you need to tickle, not beat your gull, or things can rebound on you. A few dead pardoners are proof of that. But it would be good to know his heart."

"How so?" said Dow.

"You're naïve, aren't you, boy, for all your art. Hanging pardoners is quite a fashion in some parts of the country. Less likely if you could call on the help of the Lord Marschal of England."

"Surely he'd let you hang?"

"Not if you let him know there were certain letters that would be opened if you were to die. Oh, to be so close to powerful men!"

"I could watch him, brother," said Murmur. "I can fly and crawl and creep. Let me go to his cabin, see what he writes to his wife, what he writes for business, what he says in his sleep and mumbles as he wakes. I am a skilled observer."

"Worth it, boy," said the pardoner. "If the creature could steal a compromising letter, it would be best. Not until we're off the ship, mind—we don't want a search, because it's a long way to swim home. We get that, then a couple of missives to him, 'Drop us ten coins, buried beneath the cross at such and such, or your king finds out you're tupping his wife.'"

Dow said, "Say he sends a couple of his fighters to greet you."

"You make it plain in the letter that others know and if anything happens to you, the king gets the evidence anyway."

"There might be no such evidence."

Osbert replied, "Worth a shot, though, if your little man there can sneak about a bit. Nothing ventured, nothing gained."

"Let me, brother Dow—I would be useful." The demon looked up at him, smiling.

He said, "If it pleases you, Murmur."

The creature flapped up into the air, an uncertain, zig zagging flight like a bat, just a fluttering shape across the moon toward the cabin beneath the aftcastle where Montagu had stored his things.

Morning dawned, and night came again before the ympe returned and wept on Dow's shoulder.

"What is it, Murmur? What is it?" he asked.

"I could not go in," he said, "though I spied through a crack in the cabin wall."

"Why are you upset?"

"Friend Dowzabel," it said, "I believe Montagu to be a servant of Satan, the gaoler of Hell. He will send me back to the flames and the darkness, I know!" The little ympe tugged at Dow's tunic for comfort. "He is a sorcerer, friend Dow, a sorcerer! He is in league with devils. I heard them calling in there."

"Well," said Dow, "they haven't bothered us so far and we have a protector with us." He nodded toward Sariel. "Devils have other work in the world beside hunting us."

"They might cast me back down to Hell!"

"Not while I am here, Murmur. Come, take comfort."

The ympe crawled back into Dow's coat and the boy turned over on his pack to get some rest.

5

M ontagu took the letter from Orsino at Bruges. It was a fine spring morning, the sea fresh once you were away from the stinking docks.

He said to Orsino, "Why wasn't I given this sooner?"

"I only obey my master, sir. I don't question what he tells me to do."

Montagu opened and read it. *I have made inquiries about the Welshman. Too dangerous to convey this way. You will meet my man at the church of St. Denis in the countryside by Lille before April 10. They will be looking for you. Failing that, they will seek you in the field. They will furnish you with the latest information.*

The Welshman. He'd forgotten the old king was called that—born at Caernarfon and Prince of Wales.

There was bad news—the king had embarked for England not a day before, leaving his wife, who was recovering from the birth of their son John. He required more money and had been released from effective capture by his creditors to face Parliament to demand it—on the grounds he left his noblemen and family in Antwerp where Emperor Louis in particular could keep them hostage against his absconding. Montagu smiled to see his own name listed among the captives. "Sorry to disappoint, Louis," was his response.

The French were in the field again and this time looked to be spoiling for a fight. Mind you, they'd looked that way before. No angels for them yet, and Philip was notoriously wary of engaging without them. And why bother, when you can have a victory without lifting a sword? This time, though, Montagu was determined to force Philip to battle.

Montagu was to lead his forces in an attack on Tournai, feinting first toward Lille. A coincidence, perhaps, that Bardi wanted to meet him there. Montagu laughed at the thought. Of course the banker had managed to find out the king's plans. If he could, so could the French. But Bardi would not want his investment seriously compromised, so he would not go to the French. Montagu couldn't worry too much about spies and conspiracies.

He looked around him. Fifteen other cogs were docked there—ships that had been ordered from England to assist him. Oxford and Warwick were aboard but had brought scarcely thirty men with them. They were good men-at-arms, but he would have a total army of two hundred men-at-arms and whatever archers had been levied to meet him at Ypres—two thousand according to the information he'd been sent.

He hoped that was a genuine two thousand and not a "knight's two thousand." And levies! My God, he hoped they could shoot straight! The immediate situation looked poor. Still, the princes of Hainault were going to attack from Hainault in the south and the brewer Jacob Van Artevelde was to lead his men of Gaunt from the north. Montagu didn't like that at all. Artevelde had overthrown the count of Flanders in a merchants' revolution. How could he be a godly man?

He still had the letter from Isabella inside his travel bags and was desperate to give it to her son. Montagu smelled the wax of the seal and thought of her.

"George," he said to his squire, "no point hanging around here. We're to meet our archers and the rest of our men at Diksmuide. Let's get our horses out and be on our way."

"Very good, my lord."

It was only a day's ride to Ypres, a walled town where it would have been good to spend the night. It wasn't big enough for the English army, though, and the inhabitants of the town would not open their gates to allow them in—fearful of what two hundred men-at-arms, facing death within the week, might do if its leadership failed to control them.

The town dwellers preferred to send their own men to array before the walls. Montagu was unimpressed by this and immediately had his sergeants try to drill some organization into the rabble. The Flemings had a good reputation as foot soldiers, but this lot were no more than weavers with makeshift weapons. One man only had a bargepole—what would he do against a fully armored knight?

Montagu met the stout Earl of Suffolk in some pretty pastures before the town. The sun was setting behind smoky clouds.

"Is that what I think it is, Suffolk?" Montagu gestured to the sky.

He replied, "The country's burning for miles around. Hainault's got into Aubenton and I think he's taken some plunder there."

"That's a way off from Tournai."

Suffolk shrugged. "We'll have to hope he gets there—eventually."

Montagu asked, "How are our chances, do you think?"

"If the French army can pin us down, very poor," he said, "but they're not full strength yet, so we have a chance to hit and run."

"How long before they reach full strength?"

"My spies say they're planning to achieve full muster by the eighteenth of May."

"Sixty thousand?"

"Nearer ten. Only twice our size."

"And under Philip?" Montagu said.

"Under John."

Montagu laughed. "Well then, send these Flanders mares back to their fields and we'll take on the ten thousand, you and I on our own. The best news I've heard in a while."

His men around him caught the laughter, and the earl's words were soon being passed among the men-at-arms. Montagu knew how to do his bit for morale.

Montagu ate roast pork by a fire outside his tent as night fell. It tasted very sweet and good, seasoned with honey and mint. For the first time in an age, he felt relaxed and happy—or at least that he knew what he was doing. Isabella was still an ache in the pit of his stomach, his wife another. Well, the swords of the enemy were soon about to focus his mind on the present.

All around the men were talking quickly and with passion. Smiths used the last of the light to straighten swords and fix rings in mail. The sergeants were barking instructions at the men of Ypres in their dog's French, telling them they were lucky to be fighting under England's greatest soldier, that Earl Montagu had never been known to lose a battle and wasn't about to start. Not true, thought Montagu—the siege of Dunbar had been abandoned, and Black Agnes left to go back to berating her husband. Not a loss, but not a victory either.

The sergeants were shouting at the tops of their voices: "Stick together, fight together, listen to your captains!" "Trust to the men-at-arms to repel the horsemen. They will repel the horsemen! That way you survive and come home with the English shilling." "Run and die under the hooves of the Valois alliance's knights!" The smoke of the fires smelled wonderful on the cold air, a hum of purpose, nervousness, and excitement filled the camp.

"You're smiling, lord." It was George.

He said, "I'm no wool collector, Baron Despenser. Nights like these are what a man craves."

"And days like tomorrow!"

"Indeed. Time to crack a few Valois heads, boy!"

"Do they outnumber us by many?"

"Thank the Lord, yes," said Montagu. "God save us from easy victories! They'll be singing our names the length and breadth of the country when we pull this one off, George!"

"And the angels?"

Montagu pointed to the smoky horizon. He said, "Not doing them a lot of good at the moment."

In two days' march he would be north of Lille. News of his army's movement was bound to tie up the garrison there and stop it coming to the aid of Tournai. He could stop at the church of St. Denis, though it would involve a risky diversion close to the city walls. He could press on and hope Bardi's men found him, but he wanted to know what had been found out as soon as possible. A quick raid to the church, burn it—to anger the French angels and do a little to weaken their attachment to Philip—and then back and on to Tournai. He grinned at the thought. Thirty men would be enough.

They'd rattle the enemy, grab this man of Bardi's, and be out of there, hooves flying. He looked at his destrier by his pavilion, blinkered to avoid its spying any other stallions to fight. It would be good to take that for the fun of it, in case they met any opposition.

Practicality, though, meant he should take one of his lighter hobelars. No, he would take the destrier. The hobbelar was maybe the better horse for the job, but Montagu was in a reckless mood and knew his knights could get among the enemy in open order in that country. A war-horse could cause some damage. They'd be moving quickly, perhaps facing mercenary crossbowmen. If they could draw a volley, then a charge would be decisive, giving the crossbowmen no time to reload. Montagu actually found he was humming to himself.

He finished the pork.

"George," he said, "convene the men of quality at dawn tomorrow. I have an adventure for them. Now I'll sleep and I suggest you do too. There's going to be some hard riding over the next few days and we all need to be ready for it."

"Yes, my lord."

Montagu watched the young man walk off through the camp. A bit of a scrap was just what he needed to take his mind off his dead mother. There was no better place for George to be than at war in such a time of grief.

The next day went better than Montagu could have imagined. They forded the leafy Lys in a cold pink dawn and fell upon Armentières—a pretty little town on the river. It was defended only by a small number of Genoese crossbowmen and the walls were quickly stormed. Montagu led the attack himself—important to establish early on that he had what it took in battle. There was very little resistance—the day was cold for April, a hint of snow in the air, and his men fought hard for the warmth it brought. He had enough archers to keep the crossbowmen pinned on their walls until he got a ram into the gates. The biggest problem, in fact, was not to get shot by his own bowmen.

He was first through the gates—an old-fashioned shield on his arm, in case there were crossbowmen lurking behind it. He had been disappointed that no one had fired a single quarrel at him. Resistance had crumbled as soon as the gates went through.

They sacked the place and burned the church, but Montagu managed to avoid too large a butchery of the citizens, many of whom had fled to the countryside, anyway. It was ungodly to hack down women and children and, moreover, it undermined the opponent to have so many displaced people scouring the land for food. Better drive them away than kill them.

A scout came to him as he took dinner in the mayor's house.

"Lille is locking down for a siege. They've demolished the suburbs and the people have retreated inside the walls. Men are coming in from Tournai."

Good. The commander there was a civil servant—Godemar du Fay—a lousy bookman but an excellent soldier according to reports. Good to have a man like that run to earth, pulling in resources from the real target at Tournai.

Dawn the next day and they pulled out of the smashed town, riding on to the River Deûle around noon. Montagu made camp there, insisting that the men of Ypres dig trenches. They complained about it but—as Montagu pointed out—they'd complain a whole lot more if Du Fay came through their tents with two hundred knights at the charge.

It was a clear day and the sun was overhead. Did he have time? If he went to the church now, then he could be back with the army before sunset.

He walked over to Suffolk's tent. The stout knight was seeing to his horse—a magnificent brown destrier that looked far too big for the little man to ride.

"Fancy an adventure, Robert?" Montagu asked him.

He said, "What do you have in mind?"

"There's a spy I need to pick up near the church of St. Denis."

"That's close to the walls of Lille, isn't it?"

"Close enough to make it interesting. What says we give Du Fay a bit of a fright?"

Robert said, "Why not? I'm with you."

"No need for you to come yourself, old man. Just thought you might like to lend me a few of your more likely lads."

"If you're going for a crack at the Valois, I'm coming with you, dear boy. I have a French knight who's come to our side, he can show the way."

"Very well. We'll assemble beneath my banners at my tent in short order."

"As soon as my mail is on my back, I'm ready to go. Ten men do you?"

Montagu replied, "Taking twenty of my own, so that'll make a decent enough number. Yes, ten will be very good indeed."

The party was guided by Perceval d'Aubrequin—a renegade French knight who knew the land well. Montagu had his best men with him, his own diamond pennants ruffling in the light breeze, a high, cold sun in the sky, his reins holding back his destrier's fury. It felt good.

Thirty men, among them George Despenser—God, the French must curse to see that family's colors in their lands—Guy of Flanders, with his black lion on his surcoat pawing the air; Sir William Malmsbury with his three robins; Philip Lacy with that huge sword of his; John Bruce all in yellow. Five horse archers were with them too. He'd trust any of these men with his life, which was fortunate because that was exactly what he was about to do.

He had thought to leave the letter in his camp. It seemed treacherous to his wife to carry Isabella's sleeve into battle with him. The letter, though, was a token of hers that would cause no anguish to Catherine should it be found on his body. Montagu put it into a wallet and slid it under his gambeson.

"Ready?" he asked.

"Ready!" said Suffolk.

The camp had turned out to wave them off, and Montagu led them out at the canter. The chapel was in the village of Marquette—essentially a suburb of Lille.

It was an hour and a half's ride away, and d'Aubrequin led the way, across a leafy ford on the Deûle. Here, Montagu could smell the burning. This wasn't the destruction of the English, though—the French had burned their own suburbs to deny the English the use of the houses. He sent George and two bowmen to keep a watch on the ford. He could sense the young man's disappointment, but George had to learn that not all soldiering was glamorous.

"You think this spy of yours will still be there?" said Suffolk, his horse shaking the water from itself alongside Montagu's.

"Only one way to find out," said Montagu.

"If he's not, it'll be good to have a look at the walls," said Suffolk. "If we're lucky, they might see us and attack."

Montagu knew this was bravado. Suffolk loved a fight as much as anyone, but he knew that Du Fay might be able to sortie with up to five hundred men-at-arms. They couldn't win against those numbers. It didn't matter. He could get to the church, do what he had to do, and get away. And if he was caught? Visibility was good, the smoke aside. Montagu didn't anticipate that happening.

He spurred his horse on, toward the smoke, toward the ashes, toward the flames.

6

D ow and his companions had stuck with Montagu as far as Ypres. The earl had a good party of men-at-arms with him, and that made the going much safer. There was an attempt to press the men into the army at Bruges, but Montagu himself intervened.

"You are Bardi's man, Florentine?" he asked Orsino.

"Yes."

"I've seen you at Windsor. I vouch for this man; he can travel beside us unmolested," said the earl to the recruiter. He strode off, calling to his men to be careful unloading his horses.

"Friends in high places?" said the pardoner, who had obtained a pie from a seller at the quayside.

"And in low," said Orsino, his eyes on the dribbling pastry.

"A bonus," said the pardoner, brandishing the pie. "I sold a soldier a part of Christ's robe! By Mary's curly placket, I love a war!" Dow marveled at the pardoner's resilience. He had spent quite a while in Hell and yet here he was, stuffing himself, drinking and cozening people as if nothing had happened.

"Good thing," said Orsino, "because between here and Paris I reckon it's ten days minimum. And we'll be going through one."

Dow tapped his foot on the ground of Flanders. It felt like English soil, though he had half expected it to feel different. The people were certainly odd. They wore wide collars, the women big skirts, the men floppy big hats without plume or badge. Dow found them almost comical to look at.

Their language was strange too, and it conjured up old feelings, those when he first came to London and couldn't understand too much of what was said in that odd accent. He glanced at Orsino. The man was now joking with the English sergeant who had tried to force him into service, saying something about how the English didn't need a Florentine to tell them how to beat the French.

Dow owed Orsino a great deal. In the three years he had been with him the Florentine had turned Dow from a boy into a young man. Dow could fight, he could dress a wound, he could mend and sew, and he could talk English. Orsino was a gentle enough soul underneath, a man who wanted simple things. Dow understood that Orsino had not held any personal malice against him when he had abducted Dow. He had been working for the banker.

Yet that did not excuse him. He should have refused to commit such cruelties on Bardi's behalf. His hypocrisy was expected, for Orsino was a man of Christ. Dow touched the hilt of the old sword Orsino had given him. If Orsino would not convert, he would have to kill him, to save the world from the atrocities Bardi might have him perform. It would be hard now, very hard. But it would be right.

They moved through the flat country toward Ypres and camped with Montagu outside the walls. The pardoner was making a fortune, his trade increased by his fine clothes. Men believed him to be a merchant, not a vagabond. Still, Osbert was generous with his money and even offered to send a whore on to Dow and Orsino once he'd finished with her.

Orsino declined. He was busy fetching and carrying for Sariel and warding off the unwanted advances of the Flemish traders. Dow declined too. The idea of lying with a woman who disliked the act so much she would need to be paid to perform it was distasteful to him. Lucifer was a joyous presence, and his followers believed in spreading joy. There was nothing joyful in the couplings he saw in the camp.

Sariel came and sat beside him, gazing into the firelight. She had covered her hair on the pardoner's advice, to attract less attention from men. Any woman showing her hair in a military camp—and many other places, for that matter—would be assumed to be a prostitute. Orsino sat next to her, alert, eyes on her like a dog by a table, waiting for a morsel to fall. Dow could see he found the woman a mystery. She hardly spoke and when she did, little made sense.

Dow found her presence difficult too. He wanted to question Sariel about so many things, but he would not. She was a fallen angel, he was convinced, and it was for her to decide when she would talk to him. "They don't think like us," Abbadon had told him, when reciting the names of the fallen. Watchers, he'd called them, as they watched for the return of the Son of the Morning. Only Osbert the pardoner seemed to be able to get through to her. Away to his right, the pardoner was regaling some English bowmen with tales of the whores of London, raucous laughter drifting over. He at least was joyful.

"The thought of happiness disturbs you." She spoke to him—in Cornish. Her voice was as he remembered it, soft but strong. It conjured strange feelings in him—a sadness, a longing for home. Dow tried to speak, but his voice was choked, his throat tight. His ympe stirred in his tunic.

Orsino leaned closer to listen to her.

Sariel said, "All your days in resentment. Lucifer is the child of joy."

Orsino crossed himself.

"You can tell my thoughts?" replied Dow.

"No. But I watch you. It is easy to see what you think."

He said, "You rescued me."

"I found myself there. That thing would have killed me."

"*This* called you." He moved his shirt to expose his wound.

Sariel caught a laugh in her hand as the little ympe poked out its head.

"Lady of Light," said the little creature.

"Soul who would be free," she said.

She looked at the scar on Dow's chest. "You are marked for great things," she said. "I saw the light that shone from you."

"How does this call you?"

"It's a tear," Sariel said, "a rip, and sometimes it lets out the light of which you are made. They hurt you, didn't they, God's men?"

"Yes." He felt his eyes filling up.

"Who is it that you think of? Not of downthrown angels."

"Of my nan." Dow rubbed at his eyes, willing his tears back in. "The fire is smoky," he said. The ympe fluttered from his shirt to settle on her hands.

"If someone sees that, we'll all be hanged," said Orsino.

Sariel cupped the little demon in her hands and it gazed up at her.

She continued talking to Dow. "Your nan would have wanted to see you so sad?"

He said, "No."

"Then be joyful. Smile in the morning light; it is the best prayer Lucifer knows."

"I want to see them all downthrown."

Sariel replied, "You are young and strong and able. Take joy in that, then. Take joy in the power you have to shape your destiny and share your joy with the Lord of Light accordingly."

Dow thought of his nan. She had told him he would be a great man. But he didn't feel like a great man; he felt like a miserable boy. He couldn't pray for himself—he had been taught never to do that. "Take joy," Abbadon had said to Dow. "Try to remember all those who would change position with you in an instant." He was fed, he was warm, he had a purpose granted him. He wasn't a beggar or a cripple or a twisted priest. So he prayed to see that, to understand that, though he was hard done by, at least means of redress had been put in his hands—the sword, his education, the ympe that gazed up in wonder at Sariel.

"Pray with me," she said.

A prayer to Lucifer, though, was not like a prayer to the god of the priests; Dow did not ask him to grant things or for blessings.

Sariel said, "Lucifer. I declare to you that from this day forth I shall keep my anger like an arrow in a quiver, untouched until required. I shall see the world as you made it, bright and lovely. I shall be joyful. I make this bond with you in friendship and brotherhood. Call me to account if I fail to honor it." She spoke the words slowly and he said them after.

Orsino sat by the fire, so uncomfortable he looked as if he was being roasted alive. He bowed his head himself and prayed loudly, "Lord, master of this earth, do not judge these your servants in their sin. Come to them, forgive them, set them on a path to obedience and righteousness, Father. Spare their souls."

Dow felt his anger rise. So much for leaving it untouched. He said, "Who is it that sets himself so high he can damn and forgive? What manner of thing demands worship and obeisance?"

"Silence your blasphemy or get us killed!" said Orsino.

Sariel smiled at him. "It doesn't matter what Orsino thinks or says," she said. "It is what you believe. Be strong in yourself, unthreatened and open. Wait for the dawn. You could learn from him." She nodded toward the pardoner.

"How?"

"See how he smiles despite what life throws at him. See how men warm to him. See how cleverly he makes them believe in him. He has a role to play in your struggle, I'm sure."

"Can you see the future?" Dow asked Sariel.

"No, not at all. Who can see that? I have a sense of people—that is all. He feels . . . underused. He is capable of more than he allows himself to do. He could help you."

"Will you not help me?"

"I am looking for the light," she said, "to take it and shape it and bring it flesh."

"Why?"

"To let it know suffering. Angels do not know suffering. So they cannot feel the suffering of the world. They know only beauty, see only beauty, and so worship God. This is why they will lay waste to an army for a king who builds them a fine chapel. They do not understand the pain they cause, only that in glass, gold, and paintings they have made the world more lovely."

Sariel patted him on the leg and said, "My head is clearer when I talk to you. You are a healer, I think."

"Do you need healing?" Dow asked.

"I was deceived," she said, "but in you I take joy."

She let the ympe go and it flew up into the night and was gone, chasing the moon through a tangle of trees.

Dow felt very sleepy. He put his head into her lap. She smelled of peat and of rain on the moors. She sang to him, a song he'd heard before when he was a boy and in his nan's arms.

This is what she sang:

> Heather is your bed,
> The stars are your candles,
> And your blanket is my caress.

She stroked his hair and he fell asleep in her lap. The last thing Dow recalled was Orsino standing and stomping away from the fire.

7

The church had been razed, which pleased Montagu. The French were firing the suburbs to deny the English shelter from the weather or attack. If they were burning their own churches, then God would love them a lot less. Marquette was a collection of about twenty houses to the direct north of Lille—most of them burned to nothing. There was a long strip of woods to the east masking anything that went on behind it. He didn't like that. Nor did he like it that the village was right on the river and that—not two hundred yards away—the water had been diverted around the town to form a large moat. He was in the crook of an elbow of water.

He rode around the village, his horse skittish because of the fire. No one there. Bardi's man would have to come and find him if he could. Montagu was already beginning to think he had been foolish. Why come here? Too long counting wool and worrying about angels, too itchy for a fight.

"You want a closer look at the walls?" said Suffolk. "It'll do 'em good to think we're recceing a siege."

"Why not? Though let's be quick. I don't want them having the chance to get a run on . . ." The words died in his mouth. There was movement in the line of trees and a flash of bright blue. That could only be a knight's surcoat.

"We should get back to the ford," said Montagu.

"Trouble?"

"I should say so."

Too late. From the trees, a column of mounted men began to file across the country, a line of crossbowmen and men-at-arms on foot in front of them. Sixty horsemen, one hundred and forty crossbowmen, one hundred foot soldiers, at a guess. Montagu had only a breath to decide. Could they charge down the crossbows and punch a hole through the enemy? They'd need to connect before the foot soldiers put up spears in front of the cross-bows, before the crossbows could load and fire. Not possible. Too far. At one hundred yards he'd have had a chance. This was more like two hundred and fifty.

"Will George see them?" Suffolk was calm, a soldier practiced at keeping his inner feelings to himself.

"Well, let's hope," said Montagu. "Although there's a good hill between us and them."

"Run east?"

"Seems fair. If that fails, fall back here. There's enough cover that we can make them come and fight us in the houses, which takes the crossbows out of it and means they can't charge. One hundred and sixty of them—those crossbowmen won't want to fight up close. Twenty-five of us. What do you think?"

"I'm not surrendering—they'll hang me," said D'Aubrequin.

"Perceval, we are the English army," said Montagu. "There's no question of surrender to a Frenchman. My God, the very idea. Insupportable. Come on, lads, stick your spurs into your horses and we'll try to ride around the back of those woods behind them."

He kicked his destrier forward and they thundered across the fields toward the woods. Montagu heard the Genoese captain give the order to fire. A rain of crossbow bolts struck the land, thirty yards to his right. The idiot didn't know his range, either that or had been commanded to fire by a Frenchman who thought he knew better about crossbows than the master of crossbows about crossbows.

The bright colors of the horsemen, so vibrant under the steel blue sky, wheeled and charged to cut them off, thumping out a long diagonal toward the bottom of the woods, others going around the top. Montagu realized he wasn't going to make it. He put his horn to his lips and turned his horse around.

His riders followed him and charged again, going the one hundred yards back to the town.

"Archers! Archers!" shouted Montagu.

The bowmen dismounted behind a row of smoldering stumps that had once been houses, and D'Aubrequin marshaled three men to grab their horses and tie them in as much cover as could be obtained from the broken-down buildings. They needed to keep the animals if they were to have a chance of breaking and running.

The bowmen were not the raw levies of Ypres but professional soldiers, not gentlemen—no one could call them that—but tremendously well drilled.

In an instant they had formed their longbows into a platoon and the first dark flight of arrows sang toward the onrushing French. Too long! The second flight, though, was not, ten shafts landing and then another ten as the men-at-arms came forward. Two dead. Then three. The arrows disordered and maddened the advancing troops, who broke line and sprinted toward the houses.

My God, who's commanding this lot, a child? thought Montagu.

Twelve men still mounted, a vast body of foot soldiers rushing toward them in a chaotic mass. No English knight needed telling what to do. Montagu urged his destrier forward while screaming at the French. The bowmen could not shoot now, nor crossbowmen, for fear of hitting their own troops—but twelve horses ate the ground toward the onrushing horde, lances leveled, in as close a formation as they could muster, a charge of no more than forty yards.

Montagu lost his lance through a spearman as soon as he struck, but his war-horse cut a swathe like a ship through a lake among the men-at-arms as it smashed into the enemy's lines. He felt the impact of the collision through the body of the horse. Around him the French panicked, shouted, and died as the turf flew under the pulverizing hooves of the war-horses. Montagu's sword was free and he shouted the name of his protectors, "St. Anne! St. George!"

To his right, Suffolk's horse sent men flying as it turned and kicked. D'Aubrequin had kept his lance and managed to ride straight through the whole enemy line. He turned and charged again.

A circle of the enemy was all around him as Montagu's horse spun and wheeled, kicking at the foot soldiers, sending them stumbling

backward. The animal had cost him half an estate in Norfolk. He'd
got it cheap—it was like riding a dragon. He kept the horse moving; to
stand still was to be swamped. The braver foot soldiers came rushing at
him, but those closer didn't fancy the scrap so much and backed away.
Men tripped over men. One spearman dropped his weapon and ran;
another—a boy no more than fifteen—just sank to his knees, crossing
himself. He was a weak point in the line. Montagu rode him down,
hacking and slashing with his great sword, two spears bouncing off
his horse's thick caparison, one of the spearmen losing half his head to
Montagu for his presumption.

Young Charles de Beaumont was dragged off his horse and went down
fighting, flaying at his attackers with his sword. Roger Mandeville's
horse died underneath him, collapsing onto the man who had killed it.
No time to help them. Montagu remembered his father teaching him:
"Head up. In battle, a leader gets his head up!" He flicked up the visor
on his basinet and looked around him. Two hundred yards away the
French horses were wheeling, forming up. The idiots couldn't charge
their own men? They could! A group of ten French knights broke away
from the main group.

"The village! The village!" shouted Montagu.

The English knights broke—ten of the twelve who had charged
returning. The French foot soldiers took a heartbeat to realize what was
happening, but the horses had put distance between the groups, and a
black swarm of English arrows came hissing down on them from the
village.

It broke Montagu's heart to do so, but he had to abandon his horse. He
tied it as best he could, but he knew that it would very likely be stolen in
hand-to-hand fighting.

The knights picked the narrowest street between the most intact
houses. Here the mass of the French numbers would count for the least.
Montagu stood at one end of the street with Suffolk at the other, both
with their great swords held like spears to thrust with, their shields on
their arms. Those who still had lances or spears went behind. The bowmen
stood in the middle, to fire over their heads. The French would want to
capture them—Montagu had seen the colors of many noble houses among

the knights. They would want the honor—and the ransom—of taking their enemy alive if they could. Montagu's men would be aiming to kill. That at least was an advantage.

The onslaught didn't take long to arrive. The foot soldiers had lost their fear once the English knights had dismounted, and they came charging in. Montagu thrust with his sword, as arrows snicked over his head, far too close for his comfort—but men died in front of him. They died at his side too. Charles Bruce stumbled and fell, a spear clean through him; other men tumbled behind him.

He feared for a moment that the French would try to burn the houses that made up the street that protected them. The walls, though, were good stone—this was clearly a prosperous village. They should be safe from being burned out of the alley at least.

Montagu was quite resigned to dying now. He would not surrender and it would be impossible to defeat these odds. The attacks became more sporadic. Where were the English reinforcements? He stabbed and he kicked, headbutted and kneed. His hands grew tired and blistered on the sword, bodies fell about him, friend and foe. He screamed the name of his saints, of his house, of his wife, and once, when sore pressed, of Isabella. Did George even know what had happened to them? Half the time Montagu used his sword reversed, the cross piece making a fine pick to punch through mail and helmets. Hour after hour went by, the attacks fading back, resting, coming again.

As night fell, the press of men became irresistible. The men in the alley were assailed from the front and the rear, forced to step back on their fallen comrades.

"Surrender, Lord Salisbury I have a hog on the roast and good beer waiting for you!" A voice in French. Du Fay.

Montagu replied, "Not to a commoner like you, Du Fay. It's awfully inconvenient, but I'm afraid you're going to have to kill me."

More men were piling in now, slipping on the bodies at his feet, but their numbers were overwhelming. He stabbed forward with his sword; a knight deflected it with a red-and-gold-quartered shield and leapt upon him. Montagu thrust up with his sword, but another man had grabbed the blade.

Yet another was on him. Montagu's hands were rubbed raw and all feeling had left them; they had no strength to hold the sword, and he dropped it, grabbing for his misericorde.

"Hold on, Will!" Suffolk hacked a man away. Suffolk! My God, the two ends of their defense had met, all other men between fallen.

French knights were scrambling in. Montagu had two men on either arm, another on his foot. He lifted his free leg to kick out, but that leg too was caught, and five knights lifted him bodily off the floor. Suffolk too was overpowered.

He was dragged from the alley, with D'Aubrequin screaming his defiance behind him. Montagu didn't know if he would live or die, though he was so exhausted after fighting so long that he ceased to really care. They were stripping his mail from him, his boots, his gloves. The letter!

"Leave the lord before he's naked!" Du Fay was there. Montagu still had his gambeson on, but he was down to his braies and his hose.

The men stopped stripping him but still held him firmly.

"Glad to make your acquaintance, lord—Godemar du Fay, your servant." A tall knight in a green-and-white-checked surplice spoke.

"Don't you bow when you greet a superior?" said Montagu. "I'm an earl, for God's sake, man."

"Sorry. Forgot the niceties in the heat of battle." The knight bowed.

"More like it," said Montagu. "Form is everything in life, Du Fay—it's what separates us from the savages."

Du Fay said, "That and the love of God."

"Indeed, indeed."

Suffolk and D'Aubrequin were manhandled alongside Montagu. Suffolk bore a huge wound to his cheek and the front of his basinet had been knocked clean off. Montagu got a glimpse of the dead. There must have been fifty bodies on the ground, but it didn't seem to affect Du Fay's mood. Suffolk was clearly thinking the same thing.

He asked Montagu, "How many of you dead?"

"I think forty, another twenty-five so badly injured they are unlikely to live. Forty wounded above that."

"My God, we were slack today, William!" said Suffolk. "That's only three of them for every one of us."

"We have prepared a dinner for you. After that, we'll set you on your way to Paris at dawn," said Du Fay, "where I know Philip intends to execute the traitor here"—he jabbed a finger in D'Aubrequin's direction—"and, I regret to say, may do the same for you."

"You'll give Suffolk and me the head of the table?" Montagu was tired, parched, and thirsty—he had a great sore on his head where his basinet had rubbed after being dented deflecting a sword blow and, he noticed, he was bleeding from a wound on the thigh. The chance to clean and care for his wound, to sit down and take a cup of ale, was very welcome. But rather than sit down-table from a man like Du Fay, he'd spend the night tied to a cart.

"Of course, you are the great men here," said Du Fay.

"Then it might be acceptable," said Montagu. "Send me a tailor too—I can't go about dressed like this. And a barber to stitch Suffolk's wounds."

"Of course. The people might be a little rough on your way in," said Du Fay, "but they have seen your army reduce the countryside to ashes, slaughter their sons, and rape their daughters. I will offer you every protection and we should be fine by the time we reach the Great Hall."

"Lead on, then," said Montagu.

He was marched forward at the point of spear. He was weak, captured, and, very likely, about to be executed. Worse than that, his army would never reach Tournai without his leadership; his king would lack his help. But two things stood in his favor. Bardi was moving against the Welshman—that would not change. In fact it might help Montagu's case with the Almighty. How could he be responsible for the old king's death while he was captured by the French?

But above all, Montagu still had the letter. He would find a way to deliver it, fulfilling the lady's wish. He knew that his desire to please her, to honor the promise he had made, would sustain him. Montagu would be free again and he would bring the letter to the king. "Isabella," he whispered to himself as they shoved him toward the jeers of the town.

8

P assing south, the pardoner began to believe he could be back in
Hell. They traveled with the army as far as Lille, then struck south
for Lens. All around them the land was burned. The English army
had been there; the French had recaptured it.

The fields were black, all buildings charred and smashed, every ditch
containing a body or even a skeleton. The devastation had been so complete that there had been no one to bury the dead. Now, six months at least
after Edward's ravages, the land showed no signs of recovery. At Roeux he
nearly wept. The town was entirely burned, and a grim scaffold outside its
walls showed the English had hanged everyone they had not taken in the
first attack. The bodies of fifty men swung from them—crow-eaten, frost
black. Everywhere itinerant families roamed the land, starving and riddled
with disease.

Osbert awoke each morning and forced his face into a grin. Cheerfulness
was a habit to him, and he feared that if he ever let it slip, he would never
get it back again. He had been shaking inside since his ordeal in Hell, had
seen things there that terrified him, scarred him, and were it not for a good
draft of French wine each night, Osbert would never have slept.

He was convinced of one thing—he did not wish to spend eternity in
the company of Hugh Despenser and Pole. His belly still hurt terribly from
where he had been branded. He needed a magic circle to call the devils
that were to kill the boy and had had some difficulty reproducing it. To

remind him, Despenser had it branded onto his belly by a headless man with flaming fingers.

Osbert remembered the spell in his head: "By the fifteen names of Satan, by Baal and Beelzebub and Asmodeus . . ." and knew that he must complete it under the nose of the angel. He needed to present himself to Charles of Navarre when he got to court. The prince would be expecting him. All good.

So he needed to redeem himself, desperately. His understanding was that the devils were on the same side as the angels. This had come as some surprise to Osbert, but it tallied with what the boy had said and the lady too—when he could understand her rather obscure comments.

Was she an angel? Well, Despenser had described her as such, as a *fallen* angel, and she was certainly an unearthly beauty.

The pardoner would dearly have wished to give Sariel a tumble, but long experience had taught him when a woman was out of his reach. No point thinking about her. Well, every point in thinking about her—but none in letting it trouble him. He might as well wish to become pope.

Besides, she had a strange effect on him. The past came flooding in on Osbert when he spoke to her, and he remembered how far he had fallen. His father had been a yeoman, a villein who had worked his land and done his deals well enough to become wealthier than the local knights, and he had bought his freedom. He'd been proud to send his son to Oxford. Osbert had drunk and whored his way through university, securing his degree only by dint of his father's bribe. Osbert had no desire to work when he left and eventually he had quarreled with his father and his allowance had been ended. It was then he'd been forced into holy orders as an alternative to starving.

Faced by Sariel, Osbert remembered all this and, for the first time, felt it from his father's point of view. Of course he could understand why the old man had been angry. With Sariel beside him, he wanted to go back to his father, apologize, and promise to be a good son.

The Florentine seemed to accept Sariel's unearthly nature and had taken on himself the role of her guardian. Orsino shot him dark looks whenever Osbert spoke to Sariel. Clearly sweet on her, clearly jealous. He'd even bought her a horse at Ypres so she wouldn't have to walk.

Osbert looked at the boy. Dow was sixteen years old and of a good strong form—not tall for his age, but tough and wiry. He carried a sword and knew how to use it. The pardoner had mixed feelings toward Dow. The boy had released him from the circle, but only to send him to Hell. Dow had clearly been under the sway of that mad priest, a man as wedded to unreason as any he'd ever met. That wouldn't stop Osbert doing what needed to be done, though. The boy was a heretic, an enemy of God. Heaven awaited his killer or, at least, not Hell.

But was Osbert up to being an assassin? Should he go through with it? Was he doing God's work? Yes. Anything to avoid returning to Hell. He'd seen that boy's tongue, seen the little ympe that clung to him. A demon, no doubt, who would also have to die.

It was in a black and burned land that the army swept over them—Flemings of Gaunt commanded by the merchant Van Artevelde under their strutting white lion. There was little strutting from the men. The pardoner discovered that the siege of Tournai had failed. Earl Montagu of Salisbury had been captured; William of Hainault was nowhere to be seen.

Two thousand men passed by, their steps hurried, their carts abandoned in the rush to get back home. The bulk of the men were on the road, and Orsino directed his group out into the wasted and overgrown fields to let them pass. The men saw them, and Osbert knew he and his companions were easy targets for robbery, but the army hardly broke stride. They were running north, in fear of their lives.

"We're going toward what they're running from?" said Osbert.

"Paris is south unless they've moved it," said Orsino.

"The army is a big one," said Osbert. "I wonder what's pursuing them."

"I think we'll discover that in about a day," said Orsino. "The French army, I should guess."

"What are we going to do when we encounter it?"

"I have my letters," said Orsino. "Let's hope we can survive for long enough to present them."

"*Bonjour, mes amis, j'ai les lettres par Charles of Navarre.* Or is it 'de Charles of Navarre?' Oh, God."

"How well can you speak French?" said Orsino.

"I get a lot better when under threat. Or drunk," said the pardoner. He took a bottle of wine from his pack, opened it, and guzzled at it.

"You won't need that," said Orsino, "because I'll beat your brains out if you make a mistake. Is that threat enough for you? We must try to surrender to a nobleman. The letters will be no good if the people we meet can't read."

"Il y a beaucoup d'argent pour l'homme qui m'encontre le Prince Charles of Navarre. Il me voudrais!" shouted the pardoner.

"What's that?" said Dow.

"An offer of money," said the pardoner, "works a lot quicker than appealing to men's better natures, I can tell you."

"Well," said Orsino, "you're going to get the chance to test that theory."

He nodded ahead. In the charred distance on the wide ridge of the hill that determined the horizon, the pardoner saw what he at first thought were trees, shadows against the smoky sun. But shadows did not move like that.

Horses, lines and lines of horses, came sweeping down the hill, bursting into color as they out of the silhouetting sunset like things grown from fire.

There was fire too. Osbert could smell it on the air. The French army had been burning as they came forward and he felt sorry for the poor. The knights and the nobles who fell to the invaders would be well treated. The ordinary people would fall to the sword.

At the front of the column rode a splendid tall knight on a black destrier, with a boy trotting along at his side on a white pony. There must have been ten thousand men behind them, pouring down the hill, their banners waving overhead.

"I think," said Orsino, "we are about to meet some nobility, at least."

9

If the mob at Lille had been intimidating, the one at Paris was murderous.

Montagu and Suffolk were taken in on an open cart flanked by thirty men-at-arms, but still the press of hate-filled people threatened to overwhelm them. All manner of rubbish, shit, and stones were hurled at them, so much so that at one point the horse panicked and made a bolt for it.

By the time the cart driver had it back under control, the cart had broken a wheel and the men-at-arms had to drive the mob back with the butts of their spears and form a phalanx around the two nobles and run them into the city. Montagu was glad of it. It was much harder for the crowd to get a clear shot at him that way and, if he ducked, it wasn't conspicuous because he was running.

And after all, he and Suffolk fared better than D'Aubrequin. The Frenchman hadn't even made it to Paris—he'd been butchered by their guards on the road. The trouble had begun in the suburbs, and he suspected one of their guards' camp followers had run ahead to drum up a hot reception in the city. By the time they got to the walls, a mob was straining at the gates and the captain of the guard had to assemble five crossbowmen at the front of his column and indicate they would fire before any sort of headway could be made.

The party entered from the north down a wide road, the tall, narrow houses leaning in on each side as if to get a better view of the captives. So numerous, so densely packed were the houses in the center that they made London look like a suburb. Alleys jutted off in all directions and the clamor of the streets was immense, even above the boos and jeers. Smiths hammered, builders sawed, and they were briefly impeded by a whole herd of cattle that was being driven up the street.

A man lunged toward him, and at first Montagu thought he was under attack. But the man just flourished a piece of purple cloth—he was trying to sell him something. Having realized aristocrats were being brought into the city, he was seizing a possibility to trade. Montagu admired his enterprise.

Above him now loomed the great towers of Notre Dame, and beneath his feet was water. The river had flooded a little and they splashed forward, wet to the ankles.

The water and the more expensive area meant reduced crowds. Few people came out into the streets, but plenty hung from windows, balconies, and roofs. Many of the citizens here had donned their best clothes to see him. Some even cheered and inquired loudly after his health, implying that they knew him, that they were his equals. My God, a merchant leering from a window even asked to be remembered to his lady wife. Better the man had flung dung in his face than imply he was on familiar terms.

He was glad he'd insisted on having decent clothes fitted at Lille at Du Fay's expense—his scarlet velvet tunic and blue hose at least marked him out as a lord. His beaverskin hat had, regrettably, been lost when the cart smashed its wheel. The men slowed to a walk and Montagu was pleased to see some of the men-at-arms were showing signs of fatigue, groaning with relief as they stopped running.

Montagu said, "An Englishman would run ten times as far in his full mail, right, Suffolk?"

"And fight a day's battle at the end, Salisbury!"

"Are you all right, Robert?" Suffolk, it had to be admitted, was breathing heavily. A fine horseman but no foot soldier.

Robert replied, "Well enough. He'll kill us, you know."

"Not if he's got any sense. His nobles won't let him. They won't fight for him if they believe Edward would hang them in reprisal, rather than ransom them."

"He hasn't got any sense. Or rather he's not the kind of man to be concerned about losing any nobles. God's on his side, remember."

"He might be right," said Montagu as they looked across the water toward the Île de la Cité. They were opposite the chapel of the Great Hall, the light of its vast windows answering the light of those of Notre Dame at the other end of the island. No wonder the angels loved France when its kings built them such monuments.

Montagu had expected to be taken across the bridge to the palace, but instead he found himself corralled into a large, round crenulated structure—a little castle. He had been on enough diplomatic missions to Paris to know what it was—Le Grand Châtelet.

"My God," said Montagu, "this is a court!"

"And a prison," said Suffolk.

"Well, looks like we won't have to worry about having fine clothes for royal dinners," said Montagu.

"I tell you, we won't see morning," said Suffolk, "and if we do, I'll bet we don't see noon."

They were run up a flight of stone steps under a vaulted ceiling and into a dingy old room. It was circular and dark with a floor of beaten earth, lit only by a couple of slit windows and some reed torches. Clearly part of the old keep.

At the center of the room, crown on head and scepter in his hand, sat Philip in full royal regalia trimmed with ermine. At his side sat his wife and, standing behind them, the court. For a second Montagu's heart skipped. He thought he saw Isabella in the throng. But it wasn't Isabella—it was her niece Joan. She looked scarcely younger than her aunt, though she was—by seventeen years. Another beautiful woman, as the Capetians tended to be.

Perhaps he could give Joan the letter before he died. She would see it got to Edward. Next to her stood blind King John of Bohemia, the white and red lions of his house embroidered on a rich blue surcoat. Montagu almost smiled to see him. An honest and decent soldier, certainly brave as a lion, Montagu had met him before he lost his sight crusading in Lithuania.

Montagu was pushed forward.

"Salisbury," said Philip, "as grim a dog as ever bit."

"The same, Your Majesty," Montagu bowed.

"And Suffolk. Doesn't even pretend to be a Frenchman. Ufford. What an ugly, English name."

Suffolk—Robert Ufford—bowed.

Philip stood up. He said, "The Agenais in flames, the land burned and ravaged, the count of Flanders put out of his lands by merchants backed by your king in a manner that can only be offensive to God, our ships attacked and stolen, Robert Morley the pirate given license to burn and pillage where he will on our coasts, Mortagne in flames, the Cambrésis devastated, your forces refusing to come to honest battle."

"Well, that's one reading of it," said Montagu. "I must say it seems to me that it was you who invaded Aquitaine to start this whole mess, burned the Channel ports, went storming about our lands in Guyenne and Gascony. You had to expect a scrap, my lord."

Now the king began to rage. "Endless musters of troops, endless expense! Have you any idea what you've cost me, Lord Salisbury?"

"I flatter myself it's a tidy sum, sir." Montagu's heart was pounding, but he was determined to be light. With execution inevitable he refused to go cowed and begging. He nodded to Joan of Navarre. He said, "Your aunt sends her regards, ma'am. I found her in robust health when I last saw her."

"I am grateful for the news." Joan bowed a little.

"We're not here to exchange Capetian tittle-tattle!" shouted Philip. "You've heard the list of charges—how do you plead?"

Montagu turned to Suffolk. The other earl was as pale as Montagu felt. "I don't know, Suffolk, what do you think?" Montagu looked back to the king. "I find it difficult to plead anything. It's war!"

"Then you are a true warrior and not afraid to die."

"Not a bit." Montagu stood tall. "To be honest, I could do with a lie down."

"I scorn fear." Suffolk did his best to look down on Philip—a man a good handspan and a half taller. Montagu could see his fellow earl was trembling, though he put on a good act of being indifferent to his fate.

The king said, "Then you'll be executed at dawn."

"I disdain to point out the folly of that," said Montagu.

"England will be invaded by the end of the year," said Philip. "There will be no king left alive, no nobles either, so no considerations of exchange. Even now our fleet is moving, the angel Jegudiel sparkling on the waters before it."

Joan of Navarre whispered into Blind John's ear. He in turn whispered to Philip. The king erupted.

"Not politic! Not politic! I'll tell you what's not politic—half the country in flames between here and Flanders, that ridiculous upstart Edward proclaiming himself king of France when he should be here on his knees doing homage. Not politic! Well, let me tell you, Blind John, God is behind my every action. The angel is stirring. It has appeared with our men and it assures me it will stay longer come our hour of need. Christ blesses our swords and multiplies our victories like so many loaves and fishes. Not politic! Lock them up and tomorrow we'll hang them in the courtyard right here."

"That is barbaric," said Montagu. "We are noblemen. You will kill us by the sword!"

"Get him out, get him out!" shouted Philip. "Tomorrow on the scaffold, like the thief and murderer he is!"

Montagu and Suffolk were hustled up a winding set of stairs and left in a large comfortable cell with two beds, a writing table—complete with pen, penknife, and ink for the purposes of writing last letters—and an ordinary table appropriate to their status. The door was locked behind them and the two nobles stood facing each other. Suffolk crossed himself.

"Indeed," said Montagu, doing the same, "I think tonight may be an occasion for prayer."

"And wine," said Suffolk, "my God, they'll bring wine won't they, William?"

"Of course," said Montagu. "There are depths of depravity to which even Philip cannot sink."

They received their wine and food quite soon and, with it, a note: *I will speak to you before the morning.* It bore the seal of the house of Navarre.

"Well," said Montagu. "That should prove diverting at least." Suffolk wasn't really paying attention.

"Sorry, old man," he said. "But I propose to violate the law of Leviticus tonight."

Montagu raised his eyebrows.

"Get pissed as a polecat, I mean," he said, raising his cup.

"Thank God for that," said Montagu. "You're not as pretty as my wife."

"You're fair competition for mine," said Suffolk.

Both men laughed, dreading the dawn.

10

D ow watched the huge force advancing toward them across the land. Murmur, who had returned with the morning, now flew forth again, rising up into the cold blue air until he appeared nothing more than a dot in the sky.

Osbert asked, "How are we going to stay alive here?" The pardoner crossed himself repeatedly.

"We should manage it," said Orsino. "Make no attempt to run. They'll want to quiz us as spies. Dow, time to play the mute."

The army had seen them now and two outriders—knights, armed and pennanted—came galloping toward them.

Orsino immediately sank to one knee, as did the pardoner. Dow remained upright.

"Dow, get down if you want to have any chance at all of getting to see the angel," said Orsino.

Dow bent his knee. Sariel remained on the horse.

The riders drew to a halt. They were very young—no more than sixteen; squires flying their lords' colors—their horses caparisoned in blue decorated with fleurs-de-lys. One had his sword free. He jabbed it toward Dow. "Who are you?" he asked him.

Osbert said, "We is folk who wishes it being to observe fat men of your nobility." The pardoner's French was appalling.

"English!"

"No," said Sariel, "I am a lady of Navarre, caught by the English and rescued by these good men." Her French was perfect.

The young man colored when he looked at Sariel. He replied, "Of course, my lady, we have men of your country here, and your prince Charles rides with us. We'll convey you to him immediately."

He brought his horse about and took her reins to lead them toward the great throng. The others scrabbled along on foot behind.

"She kept that well hid," said the pardoner.

"She is holy," said Dow.

"She keeps on like this and I'll start believing it, kid."

It was dusk, and the army set down to camp in the black fields. Foremen directed carts into lines, tents in every color sprang up, wood was unloaded, and fires soon started.

"Our prince won't be far away," said Orsino.

Closer up, the size of the force took Dow's breath. The English army had been quite the biggest gathering of men he had ever seen, but this was on another scale entirely. It was a moving city—a giant marketplace in carts, trundling behind the riders and infantry. Everything was there, everything. He even saw a barber's pole on one cart. Shoemakers, glovers, hatmakers, cutlers, tailors, and smiths were unloading their wares, and swarms of children ran among them to help or to hinder, depending on their age. There were scores of strange carts, full of smoky-faced men with odd equipment—chains and hooks, barrels that leaked tar. They bore axes too, of the sort more suited to cutting wood than felling enemies.

"Wreckers," said Orsino, "men skilled in the arts of demolition and ruin. They burn the land and deny the enemy its use. This number—there won't be a farmstead standing for twenty miles about."

"Why do they burn their own land?" said Dow.

"This isn't their land. We're still in Flanders. France is a way down yet."

So many flags and pennants—deep blue, sporting wide-armed golden birds, vaunting red lions, yellow castles, stars and crosses, diamonds and rearing horses—a forest of strange trees sprouting out of the black soil and at the center of them all, the fleurs-de-lys.

"The king," said Orsino.

The pardoner crossed himself and Dow looked heavenward, trying to see Murmur up in the sky.

"I see what you're thinking, but don't," said Orsino.

"What?" Dow asked.

"High men. This is the highest you'll ever have met. Believe me, you'll be throwing away all our lives if you lift a finger against him."

Dow smiled. "I have greater purposes in mind."

The camp was deploying at an amazing speed, and Dow soon found himself outside a huge deep blue tent decorated with fleurs-de-lys. A magnificent white warhorse stood outside it and everywhere liveried servants and squires were rushing around carrying wineskins, food, and weapons. There was another flag outside the tent too—the fleurs-de-lys of the French king quartered with a web of golden chains on a red background.

The young squire who had led them there ducked inside the tent.

In a few moments he emerged. "Put your weapons in a pile at the door," he said.

"Won't be necessary!" came a child's voice from inside. "These people are expected!"

The pardoner glanced at Dow, as if he might read some explanation in his face. There was nothing to read.

They entered the pavilion. Dow had never been in such a luxurious place. The black ground was invisible, covered by rich carpets in red and blue, three couches sat around the room beautifully decorated with hunting scenes, and two gorgeous tapestries featuring prancing unicorns were hung from stands to the left and right of the entrance. A minstrel on one of the couches was strumming, and two servants were setting up a book on a reading stand.

In the middle of the room, being disrobed by three servants, stood a tall man of around twenty-one. He wore a dusty riding coat and fine boots, which one of his men struggled to pull off. Next to him, equipped almost identically down to a sword at his side, was a boy of around eight. His surcoat bore the quartered arms they'd seen outside the tent.

"These are your countrymen, cousin?" The older man spoke.

The boy smiled. He said, "They are indeed. Welcome, lady, welcome friends. You are very welcome!"

He smiled and walked forward to Orsino. The boy said, "The protector." He walked on to Dow. "The one we've been very keen to meet." The boy walked up to the lady. "No doubt who you are." Then, to the pardoner the boy said, "What do *you* do?" The question was suddenly sharp.

"Help," said the pardoner, a word that could have been mistaken for a request to God rather than a statement to the boy.

He repeated, "Help."

"Yes, help."

"Help!" The boy suddenly screamed in the pardoner's face and Osbert leapt backward. The boy burst into laughter, as did the tall noble and the servants. Even Orsino conspicuously smiled.

"Help," said the boy, calm again. "Well, I should say you're certainly going to do that."

"Who are they, cousin?" asked the young man.

The boy turned to him. "The lady is a relative of my mother, Uncle John," said the boy, "and I'm dying to get back to Paris to introduce her."

"Oh, Charlie, we have a little warring to do before that. Will you not stay at least until Valenciennes? It's a pretty little town and will look so lovely afire."

"My mother wishes to see this lady. She is a relative after all and my mama was concerned for her, knowing she was in this part of the country."

Dow swallowed. This was the prince who might lead them to the angel?

"What's her name?" said John. "She looks rather dark for your mother's line, Charlie lad. A rare beauty, though."

"Oh, we don't worry about that sort of thing in our family," said the boy. "It only gets confusing."

"Very wise," said John, "impossible to keep track of all one's relatives so best not even to try. Everyone's called Joan or Philip, if in doubt I just go with that. Or set a man to remember it for one—I recommend that, Charlie. You know how people stand on such things."

Sariel stared at the little boy like a cat at a sunbeam, trying to work out what it was.

"I'd love this lady to see the angel," said Charles.

"We can't have half of Navarre making a beeline in there," said John, "although she is very pleasing on the eye. Will you dine with us tonight, lady?"

Sariel turned her eyes to John.

"I would regard it as an honor to speak to princes," she said, "for you will one day be kings and speak to God."

"That's settled then," said Charles. "And the rest of you, once you've tidied yourselves up, can eat with the servants, which—let's face it—is what you are." He looked directly at Dow. "A rare sort of servant but a servant nevertheless."

He clicked his fingers at a nobleman who stood close by. "Arnaud, see these men get a space in a tent appropriate to their station. Stick them in with some of the crossbowmen, failing that a smith. Some sort of useful lower man. Lady, I'll have a knight vacate his tent for you. I'm afraid we have no higher quarters, but I'll make sure you are very well attended."

"Thank you," said Sariel. Dow had never seen her like this. She seemed almost entranced by the princes. But then he remembered—she was a fallen angel and royalty was appointed directly by the spiteful Îthekter. Was she seeking a way back to Heaven? He saw the little boy staring at her, his perfect, pampered face like a grinning moon. At Dow's belt was the devil's knife. For the moment, he kept his hand away from the handle.

11

E dward knelt before the statue of Mary at Ipswich, gazing up at the image of Christ's mother, her infant on her knee. He was about to set sail again, bringing reinforcements but nowhere near as many as he wanted.

He tried to summon her presence, the cool blue light he'd known as a child, the sense of peace. Nothing.

"Holy Mother, grant us now our deliverance in our hour of need."

A year and a half before the demons would take another of his children. Was it enough time to carve out a piece of France to give to Free Hell? It had to be. What Edward would do for Montagu. Taken by the French! God's judgment on him for disregarding the order to stay away from his mother. When he thought of Montagu's disobedience, his mouth became dry with anger. At least, according to reports, the earl had come away his own man. Edward was thankful for that and reminded himself of Montagu's great service to him.

Doubtless he had gone to his mother in a misguided attempt to further Edward's cause. He could forgive him for that, and Montagu's current perilous situation caused him anguish. He had heard nothing from the French concerning a ransom. Thank God, as he couldn't afford it and needn't suffer the embarrassment of saying so. Montagu's visit to Castle Rising provided the ideal justification for telling the French to keep him. But could Edward do that to his friend? And yet his debts. God, what confusion, in the state and in his heart.

There was a murmur behind him, the sound of the guards admitting someone. He kept praying. The footsteps came closer.

"Do you need to make confession, lord?" It was the voice of the Archbishop of Canterbury, John de Stratford. Edward didn't bother with the "De." The French were his enemies now, and it was good to mark the difference between them. The king himself had given up speaking French earlier in the year—roughly when he'd declared himself king of France. The English were afraid that, should Edward make good his claim, they would become a vassal state of France. Edward had never been so English as in the months following his announcement.

The king kept his eyes on the statue. He did, desperately, need to confess. But he couldn't. That would put him too much into the power of the priesthood. And what penance could he do that would shrive him of his sin? A usurper, exactly as Mortimer had said. A usurper.

Edward stood and faced Stratford. The archbishop was an athletic-looking man in his late forties, soberly dressed for a churchman of his rank, in a plain green surcoat decorated with a simple diamond brooch in the shape of the cross. He spoke his mind and had been greatly disliked for it by the king's father—the exact reason the young Edward favored him.

"God hears me directly, Stratford. I have no need of priests."

He said, "I have need of you, sir. You have imprisoned my brother."

Edward replied, "The chancellor was responsible for raising taxes for the war effort. The taxes have not been raised, whether through sloth, indolence, or incompetence, I cannot tell."

"Do not blame him, sir. Or at least hear his plea. Let him be judged by a court of his peers."

"You say that I, who stands in the place of God who judges us all, am not capable of judging him?"

"Yes, I am. You weren't here. You do not know the difficulties he faced."

"Is this why you traveled to see me?"

"No, I have received a letter from the duke of Guelders. Your collection for the war effort is in vain, anyway. I have news that the French have blockaded the Zwin at Sluys. Between two and three hundred ships. Nineteen thousand men. The angel Jegudiel was seen over the skies behind them, blowing their sails full. God has declared his hand. The mission must be abandoned."

"Get out!" Edward bawled at the guards at the doorway. The men instantly withdrew from the chapel, closing the doors behind them.

"We have forty ships out there," said Edward, "Forty! This is the result of your lazy brother's efforts! Forty to take on two hundred!"

The king tried to clear his thoughts. A blinding white light seemed to descend on him, and it was all he could do to stop himself cutting down Stratford on the floor of the chapel.

"If the French try to invade it will be costly for them," said Stratford, undaunted. "We fight them here, on our soil, well supplied, well defended. Their angels may not travel. Ours are certain to come to our aid."

"You know our angels retreat inside their shrines, Stratford. They haven't spoken for years. We are lucky to have the one. We cannot wait until the French muster all theirs."

The archbishop glanced at the statue of Mary before continuing. "Our angels are absent at the moment. But the threat to their shrines, to their dwelling places, is all it will take for them to rise again. We have an Ophanim at Canterbury, Uriel in the light of Westminster Abbey, Seraphiel dwells not sixty miles hence at Walsingham. They will come when threatened, believe me."

Edward threw back his head, as if indeed asking for help from the Almighty.

They would not come, he knew. His one course of action, his only way forward, was to smash his way into France, show his faith in God before almost certain death. The longer he left it, the more angels Philip would raise. To allow the French to come, to risk more burned churches, more ruined and smashed monasteries, was to invite disaster. He knew one way only, the way he'd known all his life. Attack.

"The fleet will sail," he said.

"You have forty ships!"

"And whose fault is that?" Edward was an inch from the priest's face, though he shouted loudly.

"It cannot be done. It will not be done," said Stratford. "I will not stand by and watch my countrymen go to slaughter."

Edward shoved Stratford in the center of the chest, sending him staggering backward.

"Those who are afraid can stay at home. I am a lion! An English lion and I will devour these French lambs!" Again, the white light, the pulsing in his head, all reason burned away.

"You cannot fight an angel! I speak on behalf of all my advisers."

"So you have crawled behind my back! I have faith in God," said Edward. "It is a pity that you, as archbishop, can't have the same. Where was the French angel when we ran his army so close at Tournai? He refused to come to the fight, despite an official invitation to battle. Were Philip so confident he would have leapt upon us."

"He had no need to disturb his angels. He knew that he only had to prance around for a month or two to bankrupt you."

"Which brings me back to your brother's inadequacies," said Edward.

"You cannot milk a stone," said Stratford. "The country is bled dry."

"Which is why we will restore it with the plunder of France. Now get out of my sight and send Morley and Crabbe in here."

"I would have my brother tried by his peers."

Edward felt his anger cooling as quick as it had come. Stratford had been his close ally, provided good and honest counsel for years. He probably spoke sense of some sort. He just didn't see that God required an act of faith from kings. Faith, faith. Then God would reward him with his father's death and the angels would attend him, freeing him from all bargains with Hell, and save his sons.

"Give your brother his trial. I haven't time to oversee it."

Stratford nodded and strode from the hall. Ten minutes later, Crabbe and Morley came into the church, each grimy and wet with sweat from overseeing the preparations for departure.

The men bowed.

"Hear this," said Edward, "and mark it well. Your days of idleness are over. Dispatch your officers, gentlemen. I want every ship over forty tons to assemble ready for my attack. From the Downs to the Cinque ports they will assemble in the Pool of Orwell. The ships of the western Admiralty too—our troops are ready to depart."

"That will strip the land of all defense, sir and cause great hardship to the merchants," said Crabbe.

"I am king of England and of France. I am not interested in the hardships of ordinary men."

"The men of Yarmouth will refuse flat, sir," said Morley. "They value their ships highly and do not easily submit to the will of kings."

"We'll see," said Edward. "Summon my horses. I'll pay a visit to Yarmouth and test the resolve of these jumped-up mariners face-to-face. In the meantime, a week, no more to assemble all ships. How many will that be?"

"One hundred and twenty, at the most, sir."

"Three times better than forty. Good. Well, don't just stand there; go and do what I tell you."

The men left the hall and he kneeled again before the statue of Mary.

"Well, God," he said. "Abraham offered you his first son as a sacrifice. I offer you an army. Let not their deaths be in vain." He crossed himself and strode from the chapel, calling for his horse. This time, there would be no running from him. There would be war if Edward had to fight Philip alone.

12

Suffolk was quite drunk and lay sleeping on his bed, but Montagu had drunk no more than a cup of wine and could not sleep.

The room was well-appointed and they had a good fire, but still Montagu shivered. He was thinking of Isabella. Had she had robbed him of his courage? He had always disdained to value his life too much. He had loved his wife greatly, his children equally. The service of Edward had given him purpose and his wars had brought danger and fame. Montagu had lived so boldly, so vibrantly.

And yet, and yet, there was always a distance between him and the world. His closest friends saw it. Everything to Montagu was a joke or an adventure or something between the two. No matter how hard pressed he was, how concerned about the fate of England and Edward, it was always as if he was acting the role of himself in some old court play. When he thought of Isabella, there was no distance, no pretense. He was utterly himself, knowing himself completely. There, in that prison, he was not Montagu nor Salisbury nor the Marschal of England. He was a man desperate to see Isabella again. No more.

Montagu thought to destroy her letter to Edward. It should not fall into the wrong hands. He had no idea what was in it, but it might prove a peril to Edward if the French king found it. But he could not destroy it. Mortimer, the traitor, had broken walls thicker than these for the love of that woman and Montagu could not esteem himself less than that man. He would live, if only to deliver the letter, if only to please her and be by her side again.

Walls, castles, oceans, and wild places seemed insubstantial when compared to his passion.

Suffolk snored like a prize pig on the eve of market. The Nocturnes bell sounded. Montagu looked out of the window. The moon was full and fat, the stars wide and deep. Everything was so vivid.

"I want her," he said under his breath. The stupidity of that thought struck him. *Be concerned for yourself, William. Think of Catherine, of your children; think of Edward fretting in Ipswich hearing that his best commander has got himself captured like a stupid young squire.*

A man is allowed some indulgences when he awaits his last dawn, and the thoughts Montagu demanded of himself were no more than shooting stars, there and gone in a moment. He thought of Isabella, of the way she looked through him to understand him absolutely, to challenge him more fundamentally than any opponent ever had. Montagu was under no illusions, either, that she was his friend. Had she forgiven him for taking Mortimer? When he'd lain with her in Castle Rising it almost felt better thinking she hadn't, because that meant her passion for him knew no reason either. He'd loved women and he'd loved conflict. Isabella offered him both at the same time.

The bolt on the door drew back and Montagu looked toward the candlestick holder—a good heavy thing in pewter. If it wasn't Joan or one of her representatives at the door, it would be an assassin. Despite Philip's statements, he was well aware that his court wouldn't want the Marschal of England publicly hanged—not least because there was a possibility they would one day find themselves depending on King Edward's mercy, should they be captured in battle.

The door opened, and for a second Montagu thought it was her—Isabella. Her niece was so like her, so fine and blond and beautiful, as the Capetians tended to be. In the presence of Isabella, though, he felt as if he was standing on the edge of a high cliff, resisting the mad impulse to throw himself down. He admired Joan as he might a painting. She was beautiful, but the world was full of beautiful women.

Joan wore a trailing coat of dark blue velvet and a deep red hood. She came into the room and the door locked behind her.

She said, "Lord Marschal."

"Queen." Montagu bowed as Suffolk grunted like a boar breaking cover.

"Shall I wake the earl?" said Montagu.

"No need. I understand Suffolk is a soldier, not a politician."

"He is currently at his most diplomatic," said Montagu, gesturing to the sleeping lord.

"Quite. You are to die tomorrow, sir."

"If it is God's will, lady."

"It seems it is, for God makes his will known through his kings, does he not?"

Montagu did not reply. She continued.

"It seems unfortunate that so valuable a soldier of our cousin should be taken from the field."

Montagu found this puzzling. Why would Joan want the English king to have good generals?

"Navarre allies with Philip, does it not?" he asked her.

"Because it is in its current interests to do so."

Montagu tried to work out what she was driving at.

She clarified it for him. "Look out of the window, William. What do you see?"

Montagu regarded this as slightly theatrical, but he was used to indulging monarchs' fancies. He went to the window and gazed out. "Stars. Darkness over the Îsle. The Great Hall under the moon."

"You see my property," said Joan.

"You have sworn it away, lady."

"And so I have. Yet my treaty is with Philip, not Edward."

Montagu tried to keep the surprise from his face. Queen Joan had just offered him, as straightforwardly as she could, an alliance. Well, *that* would be worth bringing to Edward.

"Your husband is well?" Montagu needed to establish if she moved with the authority of the king of Navarre. He was a loyal ally of Philip, and the earl could not believe he would contemplate fighting for Edward. He'd been burning Edward's lands and sacking his castles in the north in league with the Scots for long enough.

"My husband is a soldier and so far has resisted a soldier's death," said Joan. "He is a bold man but so are you, Marschal, and we see where boldness can lead. The gallows or the field of slaughter."

So kill Navarre, and Joan would back Edward. Such a strategy wasn't impossible. The woman was morally disgusting but no less useful for it.

Montagu asked, "Where is he now?"

"Fighting your armies in the Cambrai. Although I believe he is also planning to make war to the south of Iberia. He regards freeing the land from the Moors as his Christian duty."

"Let us hope news of his intentions doesn't reach the Moors," said Montagu. "They are formidable fighters and, forewarned, would be a match for any army."

"Indeed," said Joan, "so God spare him from becoming the particular target of any of your soldiers. And God spare him from the Moors."

Montagu thought it best to come to his point directly. He said, "You could make these representations to the king through a messenger."

She said, "And trouble myself with secret codes, put myself at the mercy of unreliable servants, untrusted intermediaries?"

"You've had dealings with Bardi."

"He came to Flanders when I was there. He is useful, but I would not put anything of value into the hands of that snake."

"He has a heavy investment in England. He would want to see us succeed."

"Bardi is a banker and thinks of nothing of worth, just profit. He will play all sides in the quest for money. Why not sell me but use my son? Why not do a hundred unguessable treacherous things that bubble in the cauldrons of these bankers' minds? I cannot understand a man who is motivated only by profit—it is against all human nature. Better to deal direct with a man of honor, no?"

"You brought me here?"

"I am not a sorceress."

That wasn't a "no." Had Joan arranged for Montagu to be tricked by Bardi? Perhaps. He guessed the banker wouldn't have sold him just to Joan, though, not while he could get a price from Philip too. The next time Montagu saw the Florentine, perhaps he'd cut his throat and tell him off. If there was a next time.

He said, "It's a poor messenger who never returns with his message."

Joan replied, "We must address this. I confess I did not see it coming. I have bought you a stay of execution, anyway."

"Thank you for mentioning it." Relief swept over Montagu, and he cursed himself for it. It was the behavior of a merchant. A nobleman should be indifferent to whether he lived or died.

Joan smiled. "I wanted to get the niceties out of the way first."

Montagu sat a while, feigning indifference. Both he and Joan were smiling by the time he spoke. She knew he wanted to ask how she'd put off the execution, but found it crass to do so. Montagu knew she knew and they were playing a game. In the end they both started to speak simultaneously and both laughed.

"I asked for my son to see you hang," she said.

"Is that one of the boy's interests?"

"All boys love a show. But no. He is particularly beloved of Prince John. We will arrange a meeting. You will amuse my son in some way that he will prevail upon John to prevail upon his mother to prevail upon his father to spare you."

"What could possibly go wrong with that?" Montagu said.

Joan laughed again. "Men could learn a lot from you, William. You approach life in the right way—you are not afraid to lose it."

"It is only an appearance. I fear as much as the next man, but I have schooled myself not to show it."

Her fine features, her light manner, not Isabella, but enough like her to put a hunger into him. He wanted to tell her, desperately wanted to tell her, how he loved her aunt—to share the joy, the confusion, the shame he felt.

Joan, though, would make a bad confessor.

"Something troubles you?" she asked him.

Montagu said, "My capture and imprisonment have hardly put me in the mood for dancing."

"Something more?"

Perhaps he could turn this to his advantage. He said, "An interest, that's all, something that has piqued my curiosity. Do you know of a fellow called Good Jacques?"

"Not at all."

"A friend of the Hospitallers. An old Templar, perhaps of Paris."

"I could try to find him."

"I would advise discretion."

"Do you enjoy the company of monks, William?" Joan asked.

"Hardly, but I believe he may have something interesting to tell us. Something that could be of use to us in our dealings with Bardi." Despite Bardi's assurances he could find the old king, Montagu thought it best to inquire independently where he could.

She nodded slowly. "Good to have a few of that snake's secrets for sure. I'll ask. Discreetly."

If Good Jacques had helped in the raid against Mortimer, then he was a man the Hospitallers turned to for secret work. So why not to hide a king?

Joan patted Montagu on the knee. "See that you please my son."

He said, "I am not a child's fool, lady."

"I'm not asking you to be. Amuse him with swordplay, show him a trick or two. You can do that, can't you?"

"If you consider splitting a man's skull a trick."

"No better one for a boy to learn. Tell me, lord, have you ever been bested in the lists?"

Montagu replied, "On horse, madam, yes. I have been lucky in the foot mêlée. Good men around me and the blessing of Heaven."

"Then that is our way forward. We'll put you in a tournament. You knock over a few French knights, and then it becomes impossible for Philip to hang you without looking like a bad loser. Once you are under my son's patronage here, life will be easier for you."

"I have no arms or armor."

Joan said, "Prince John and his father do not see eye to eye. I'm sure you could go in as his champion."

"A better end than swinging from a rope," said Montagu, "if you can manage to secure it."

"It won't be your end. It will be your beginning. I will ask Prince John that you might enter my son's service for as long as you are here."

"And he will agree to that?"

"He grants my son anything," said Joan.

"He sounds like a remarkable boy," said Montagu.

"He is that," said Joan, "and you are a remarkable man who will be much use to him in all that he plans to do." She smiled softly. "You want to live, William. No shame in admitting it."

Montagu snorted, then frowned. "I made a promise to your aunt. I would honor it."

"What promise?"

"I have a letter I need to deliver to King Edward, her son. I made a solemn vow to put it into his hand myself and I would not break it."

Joan said, "May I see it? It would comfort me to see her hand again. She was always such an accomplished writer—as good as any monk, my father said."

"Of course." He took the letter from his tunic and passed it to her. She studied it.

"Her seal is unusual."

"Yes. Her own seal was denied her by Edward, I think. She scarcely has use for a seal—none of her letters ever get through."

Joan ran her long fingers over the wax. Montagu guessed she wondered what was in the letter but knew she would never stoop to ask.

"You should keep it away from your person, William. It's not good to keep it next to your skin with all that fighting you do. It'll be soaked with sweat and stained beyond recognition. I believe the seal is cracking already."

He said, "I'll take the advice, ma'am."

"Good." She touched him briefly. "It's been good to see you, William. You won't die here; I have a feeling help is on its way."

"I'd prefer an assurance." Sipping at his wine, he smiled at her.

"Though not easy in these times, have faith, William. And in the name of God, look after that letter properly. I know you chivalric knights. If it ends up illegible, you'll never forgive yourself."

"And neither will your aunt, which I would account more important."

Joan said, "Adieu."

Suffolk grunted like a man inhaling a goat.

She added, "Do you want me to buy you a separate cell? It must be like sleeping next to a pigsty."

He replied, "I'm fine here. I've been twenty years on campaign, ma'am. Men's manners can scarcely surprise or offend me anymore."

"As you wish. You have an ally in me, be sure of that."

"I am grateful for it."

She stood and rapped at the door. The bolt slid back; Montagu stood to bow. He did not look up again until she was gone.

13

Only the flag of Navarre flew outside the Great Hall as Charles's party approached through the streets of the Île de la Cité. The king was away fighting in the north, and his standards had gone with him. The townsmen thronged the pavement, shouting for news of the battle in the north. The troops reported it was going well. Hainault was in flames, thirty-two towns burned, the count of Hainault betrayed by one of his own commanders enabling the capture of Escaudoeuvres. The armies of England, Hainault, and the Germans were in the field but had yet to force a battle and were finding food scarcer every day.

And most promising of all, said the returning men-at-arms, from Normandy at Harfleur, the great army of the sea had sailed, picking up more ships along the Picardy coast. Two hundred ships had burned Cadzand and now lay at anchor in the Zwin estuary, completely blockading the harbor at Sluys. All provisions and reinforcements from England for the enemy army were now cut off and the angel had flown with the French, sparkling above their masts, blowing them a fair wind, the men rejoicing in its presence.

It was a mighty army and, noted some of the commanders, a cheap one. The angel meant Philip could cut back on the number of fighters on the ships. Sailors came cheaper than men-at-arms, and there was no point in the king investing in squadrons of fully equipped soldiers when the angel was going to blow Edward's ships to the bottom, anyway.

Charles led the procession—three hundred men under his own banners. He was just a boy, but with a full-blooded white destrier beneath him, though that was led by a knight. He was mailed and helmeted, cloaked in red, riders on black horses flanking him. Charles attempted an extravagant leap from the horse and was lucky the man-at-arms leading it was alert enough to catch him.

Joan hugged her boy. She was pleased to see her son safe—even though she'd known he'd gone at the center of the world's biggest army under the best generals imaginable, not the idiot John, but Miles de Noyers and the counts of Alençon and Foix.

"Philip is gone," she said.

Charles said, "I know. We met him on their way to join John. The men say the angel has gone to Sluys. Will our plan work if it's not here?"

"I don't know. Nergal seems to think it will come to the chapel if the woman is presented there. Did you bring the woman?"

"Then it will come to the chapel, Mother. I am blessed. Please, there is someone I should like you to meet."

He took his mother down the line of men to a gilded carriage painted in the green-and-white-striped arms of the city of Escaudoeuvres.

"The plunder of war, Mother!" said Charles.

"I hope you haven't brought me all the way down this street to view a merchant's coach, Charles."

"No, Mother, I have not. This coach is comfortable, but I do not think it worthy of a queen's attention. What is behind it is what might please you. May I draw your attention to that cart?"

At the rear of the carriage, drawn by two good strong horses was a cart full of packed tents. On top of them sat a collection of disreputable-looking individuals—a strange dark boy, a fighting man, a gaudy merchant, and another figure with its back to the queen, cloaked and hooded in blue.

"Can fine things come in such poor packages?" Joan asked.

"Oh, they can. Princes enter the world in blood and to the sounds of shrieks. So beautiful gems may be set in a base foil. Sariel!"

The figure in the cloak turned to face her. Sariel. She was the most beautiful woman Joan had ever seen. She was both dark and pale and, when she threw back her hood, her uncovered hair shone like a black pard's back in the morning sun.

"She is bold to appear so licentiously before us," said Joan.

"Oh, Mama," said Charles, "don't let's talk so. We are royalty, not country prigs. Meet her. She is just the lady for our task; Bardi has delivered as he said he would."

Joan felt her heart skip. She had become used to the presence of the cardinal, as she called Charles's devil and, in truth, was a little contemptuous of him. He was a violent and scheming creature, but he lacked subtlety of thought or refinement of manners. He smelled vile and he was ugly—ugly as had been the cardinal she had given him so that he might take his face, but with a crudity to his features the cardinal had lacked. Villeins looked like that in those little villages where cousin married cousin for generation upon generation. Low, lumpen.

The woman, though, was beautiful and, as a beautiful daughter of a beautiful family, Joan could not but equate that with virtue.

"We have Montagu," said Joan. "Have you heard?" She spoke to her son, but her eyes were on the lady.

"Philip's men said so. We ran into him on his way to join Prince John. I didn't speak to the dry old stick himself." Charles drew his mother close. "With Old Lofty out of the way we could just let Montagu go. He's a fair killer, so they say and could cause our Valois cousins a bit of bother. Errrgghh!" He mimed sticking someone with a sword.

"Let's move more carefully," said Joan. "We may yet find some other use for the good earl."

"Like what?"

"Like being blamed if an angel goes missing?" she whispered.

"Very good," said Charles. "These are Englishmen I have in tow here. Well, one Florentine besides them and the lady. Curious, isn't she?"

"Very—so let's get her out of sight before she excites comment. Couldn't you have put her in the carriage to keep her from men's gaze?"

"She wouldn't go, Mama. She needs to be in the light; that's very important to her," said Charles in a way that seemed to indicate he was becoming an authority on fallen angels.

Joan clicked her fingers and Chevalier D'Évreux came forward to take the lady's hand and help her down from the cart.

"You are very welcome, lady," said Queen Joan. "We have prepared a room for you and we would very much like you to take mass with us this evening. The light in the Haute Chappelle is wonderful at that time of night."

"I would like that very much," said Sariel. "There is beauty here, so much beauty. I would like to see the great cathedral too. Does it have an angel?"

"Notre Dame does not at the moment, lady, but it seems certain one will come to inhabit it when the works are completed."

Sariel gazed around her in wonder at the bright summer street, the crowds and the color.

She said, "An angel must want to live there."

"Sainte-Chapelle is where ours dwells," said Joan.

"Is absolution there?" said Sariel.

"I very much expect so, my dear."

D'Évreux, who held the lady's hand, seemed enchanted by her. "To the chapel, without delay," said Joan.

The Florentine mercenary jumped down beside the lady, and the chevalier's hand went to his sword.

"I have guarded the lady from London," said the Florentine. "I see no reason to stop now."

"Your service is noted, soldier," said Charles, "and you are dismissed."

The Florentine stood uncertainly before the lady. Joan knew enough of fighting men to realize this might end badly. The soldier's hand was not on his sword but it rested next to it, on the buckle of his belt, his fingers drumming, and one foot was behind the other—a fighting stance if ever she saw one. The queen didn't want some suicidal lovestruck mercenary hacking into her men. He could be removed later.

Joan put up her hand. She remembered Bardi had mentioned this man and praised his usefulness—even hinted he might be on a mission that would help their cause.

"Son," said Joan, "let the lady have her servants. It is only meet. As I have the seigneurs, she has this fellow to look out for her."

"You are Queen Joan?" said the mercenary.

"I am."

He took a letter from his tunic and passed it to her. A lady-in-waiting came to take it, showing it to Joan. It bore Bardi's seal.

Joan nodded, hardly acknowledging it. "Proceed," she said.

"Very well," said Charles, and the lady was led away, the dark figure of the mercenary behind her.

The merchant, the low fellow, was waving to her. She ignored him, but he got down from the cart. For an unpleasant moment, Joan found herself unattended by nobles, only three men-at-arms with her.

"Queen Joan," said the pardoner in appalling French, "I message to give you."

"Soldiers!" called her guard.

"From Hell," said the pardoner. "I must to meet cardinal—man fire breathes, is your friend."

Joan said, "In the name of God, not in the street, man. Men of Navarre, commit this fool to Le Châtelet immediately."

"Madam!" he said.

"And if he won't be silent, take out his tongue!"

The pardoner had enough French to understand that and immediately went quiet as he was marched away by two of the men-at-arms.

"Bring the English boy," said Joan to the remaining man. "I would speak with him. And use my son's guard to seal off the entrance to the palace. I want no one on this road or approaching for the rest of the afternoon."

Perhaps the youth could work out a way to bring the angel to the chapel, thought Joan. And besides, she was interested to meet him. It's not every day, she thought, that you get to meet the Antichrist.

14

M ontagu kissed Isabella's letter before he went to sleep. Improper and wrong, but he could not stop himself. He wanted it with him in the bed, but Joan was right: he needed to take better care of it. But if Montagu left it next to the bed and they came for him suddenly, he would be parted from the letter. Should an opportunity to escape arise, he would be forced to leave Paris without it.

In the end he pushed it inside one of his boots—they might hang him like a criminal, but they wouldn't send him to the gallows without his boots and decent clothes. That would be a barbarity too far.

Sleep didn't come easily, though Montagu was very tired—his mind as much as his body. The night sounds only gradually soothed him—the hour bells and the distant prayers of monks, the guards hailing one another with every change of sentry; even some shouted insults from far off, telling Montagu he would be dead by the morning. The people of Paris knew he was in Le Châtelet, and some thought it proper to pour their scorn on him. Good. If the French hated him, he was doing something right.

His mind drifted, and Montagu thought he had fallen to dreaming. The cell was full of smoke, it seemed. He lay on his bed, unable to command his limbs, to make himself get up and see where it was coming from.

Shouts came from farther up the corridor.

"William! William!"

It was Suffolk, shaking him awake.

"What?" Montagu asked.

"Wake up, I think the place is on fire!"

Montagu got out of bed and immediately removed the letter from his boot. He put on his tunic and carefully placed it inside, pulling it tight about him.

"Which way's England?" The voice was a low rumble, an animal growl that set his bones trembling.

I want to live. Dying in a prison fire is not a noble death. Montagu put the cowardly thought out of his mind. The smoke was coalescing and condensing, plaiting almost, funneling in to one point, taking shape as something like a man.

"In the name of God!" said Suffolk, crossing himself again and again.

"Yes, in the name of God and of Satan who does his good works," said the voice.

A wind sprang up in the cell, cold and strong. Montagu couldn't tell where it was coming from—it seemed to swirl and twist. As the smoke cleared, he saw the shape more clearly—a huge lion, ash-black with a stiff mane of metal spikes, standing on its hind legs. It was dressed quite splendidly in fashionable, tight-clinging hose and a black silk doublet picked out in stars of silver thread. In its hand, it carried a great axe of the sort Montagu associated with the Scots.

Like him, it bore an eye patch on its right eye and its fur steamed like something newly cast. The creature watched as its left paw formed from the smoke, great talons taking shape. Montagu almost had to applaud. He saw it perfectly—Philip or that witch of a wife of his had called up this fiend to kill him. Then his mauled corpse would be displayed, the locked door examined, and it declared that Montagu had tried to escape as Mortimer before him had escaped—by summoning a devil.

But instead Montagu had been devoured. That way Montagu suffered an ignoble death and Philip didn't have to explain to his own nobles why he was endangering their lives by slaughtering one of the most powerful lords of England. Edward would want no revenge for a sorcerer, close friend and ally or not.

Montagu saw all this in the space of breath. Then he looked around for something to fight the creature with. The cell afforded nothing of use. He picked up the penknife and then threw it down again—the blade was no bigger than his thumbnail, good only for sharpening a quill. He laughed ruefully: if he'd had his sword and his shield, he would have delighted to have fought this creature—it wasn't quite St. George's dragon, but it wasn't far off. They'd make Montagu a saint. He made a fist. *Here goes!*

"Don't just stand there like you've been slapped—which way's England?" said the lion. It sniffed the air. "There are others here, for sure. I heard them scratching; that's how I found the gate. Have you summoned them?"

Suffolk was on his knees.

"We've summoned nothing!" said Montagu. "You are an abomination, abhorred of God!" Montagu took a pace back. His entire upbringing taught him to shout defiance in the fiend's face, but inside he trembled like a greyhound in the rain.

"God likes me well enough," said the lion. "Now—for the last time—which way is England?"

Montagu's thoughts cleared enough for him to realize the creature wasn't about to attack him. "Through that door, for certain," said Montagu.

"What's going on?" The gaoler's voice was at the door. "Stop this commotion or me and a few of my boys will come in and stop it!"

"You base dog!" said Montagu. "Bring thirty of your men and I'll chastise them with my bare fists!" The unexpected presence of a devil in his cell was not enough to make Montagu stand for insults from the lower sort.

"Right, I will!"

"Through that door?" said the lion.

Montagu said, "Yes."

It threw back its head, sucking in a huge gulp of air with a noise like the wind in a chimney and then snapped its head forward and roared hard at the door. The wood splintered as if hit by a battering ram, and a great hole appeared in it near its bottom. On the other side, Montagu saw the flash of a gaoler's heel as he made a run for it.

"North?" said the lion.

"Yes."

"Have no fear, Lord Montagu," said the lion. "Great forces are coming to England's aid. You have friends in Hell!"

It ducked through the shattered door into the corridor. A terrible stink drifted into the room—brimstone, burning, along with a menagerie noise, cluckings and brayings.

"Hail, friends," the lion said.

"Lord Sloth, we offer you our obedience."

Montagu poked his head through the door and withdrew it pretty quickly. In the corridor an upright gray mule with a huge steel gray peacock fan sprouting from its rump bent one knee.

"Why are you here?" The lion's rumbling voice spoke again.

"Free Hell has a standard-bearer on earth. We are going to kill him."

The lion replied, "A noble task. Join me in England when it's done."

"Yes, my lord. How shall we get there? We are in France."

"Well, swim, you fools," said the lion.

Montagu watched as a procession of the legs of strange creatures ran past the door—the legs of an impossibly spindly man, the legs of a horse, those of a devil such as you might see carved in a church, the legs of a giant bird bounding by.

He needed to escape, but he felt compelled to follow. Devils appearing on the streets of Paris was something Edward ought to know about.

Montagu heard a voice from outside.

It said, "Wait for me. I summoned you; now I command you!"

"Who's there?" demanded Montagu.

A head popped through the hole in the door. It was the merchant he'd seen on his ship, that weasely one with few airs and no graces.

"Osbert of London, a pardoner, at your service, my lords," he said. "My devils have freed you."

15

The pardoner's escape from prison had been remarkable. He'd sat moping in a dingy cell in Le Châtelet. It was hardly big enough to lie down in, bare and damp with piss, though it had the small convenience of a tiny slit window that, though it admitted a draft, also let in some light.

Osbert had had his fill of confinement in London and was determined to be speedily free of this terrible place. Consequently, he studied the scars on his belly with great attention. Only representations of the names of God and those of the devils he required were there, but Despenser had beaten their names into memory. Caym, Abigor, Adramelech, Alastor, Amduscias, and Eurynome. Nothing ensures instant recall like a boot on the throat, Despenser had said, and in that, he was proved right. The magic circle was constructed around Osbert's belly button and he did wonder if, when he drew it up, he should include a representation of a belly button. He decided he should not. Osbert needed, however, to get some chalk if he was to begin.

"Hey! Hey!" he shouted down the corridor to the guard. "I am licensed to remit sins. For a piece of chalk I can gain you forgiveness for anything up to murder. Two pieces and I'll throw in fornication and taking the Lord's name in vain too."

No one responded. Oh, when would he be fed? He guessed never. He had no means to pay for his food because all his money had been stolen the second he arrived by the brute of a guard who had rummaged inside his trousers to find it.

How to conjure a devil? Hmm. From his time in the cellar he'd seen enough attempts at conjuring by Edwin and at least one successful opening of the gate of Hell by the boy. But this was something different. There were devils on the earth, Despenser had said, who whispered through the gates of Hell, receiving instructions from their brothers, reporting on the world. It was these earthly devils that Osbert sought to call.

But how?

There was movement in the corridor that led to the cell. A voice shouted, "A pardon for all! The king has had a great victory and all the prisoners are to be let go!"

Osbert leapt to his feet. *Yes!*

"Just my little joke," said the voice. "He's still in the field and you're all still in here. Oh, I'm a funny man!"

A scrape and sliding. Someone was opening his cell!

Osbert primed himself to make a run for it. He felt sure he was going to receive a beating whatever he did, so he might as well try to rush the guards and break out of the place.

"Important visitor!" shouted the guard.

The door opened and the pardoner gave a shriek. There, in front of him, was the cardinal he'd seen in the priest's house. Or rather, not the cardinal. The face was subtly different but the clothes were the same, as was the lantern he bore with him.

Osbert cowered at the back of the cell.

"Leave us," said the cardinal, dismissing the gaoler.

The man just stood there whistling. The cardinal put his hand into his pocket and withdrew a coin, dropping it into the gaoler's hand.

Now it was the gaoler's turn to shriek. "That's red-hot!" He dropped the coin to the flagstones.

"I'm a funny man," said the cardinal.

The gaoler gave him an odd look, stood on the coin, and went off down the corridor, dragging the coin under his foot.

"Not you!" said Osbert. "I'm not going back in any magic circle!"

"That's rather for me to decide, isn't it?" said the cardinal.

"I'd rather die."

"You've seen where you'll end up if you do."

"I can't think dealing with you is likely to get me out of Hell."

"No, but it might get you a more comfortable time there. Less severely uncomfortable, anyway."

Osbert said, "Why did you lock me in that circle?"

"The priest had annoyed me. I thought to kill him, but I decided his quest for knowledge might go a little more frustratingly if it was you, rather than me, in there. Intellectual frustration to him was more annoying than death. You are the embodiment of intellectual frustration."

"You had helped him before I got there."

"I came to answer his call, to get him to move against the boy. But he trapped me there and compelled me to answer endless questions on subjects unknown to me. I saw he was as trapped as I was in that cellar, so I used you to keep him there."

The pardoner had a strong urge to plant his fist on the end of the cardinal's nose, but he sensed that such action was unlikely to end well for him. The cell was already uncomfortably hot in the devil's presence, and Osbert wondered if he'd burn himself if he touched him.

"I have messages from Hell," said the pardoner.

"I know," said the devil. "I have been told to expect you. You have a summoning circle for me to study. We must be quick. Already they have taken the fallen angel to the Sainte-Chapelle."

The pardoner pulled up his tunic.

"Fascinating," said the devil, bending forward to look at it. "Well, let's not delay—the boy is here and we must set upon him as soon as we can. He is due to confront the angel, but we must be ready for him as soon as he kills it."

Osbert said, "He's going to kill an angel? What makes you think your devils can take him?"

"The angel will be distracted. Both angels will be distracted."

"The second being Sariel?"

"The one who traveled with you. I saw her from my window."

Osbert said, "Sariel."

"Then Sariel."

"Is he to kill her too?"

"No," said the devil, "but she will very likely go mad with grief—that was what happened before. Frankly, I'm surprised she's recovered her wits."

"I'm not sure I would want that; she's a nice girl."

"Well, if you don't, I can always rip you to bits and eat you."

"It's more of a theoretical disagreement than anything that will cause us any problems. I'm a compassionate man, but only as far as it doesn't cause me the slightest inconvenience. Well. Hmm. Shall we get on with it? I want to pay my debts and be gone. Did you bring chalk?"

"What for?" the devil asked.

"To draw the circle."

"I can't draw this circle and neither can you. It is a circle of higher summoning and thus its construction is forbidden to devils and impossible for fools."

"You trapped me in a circle."

"I simply completed a binding circle that was already drawn, and a simple affair it was. This will summon creatures stronger than me."

"So why can't I summon them, then?"

"You have not the knowledge nor the art."

"Then what are we going to do?"

"The circle is already drawn," said the devil, extending a long finger toward the pardoner's belly. "Lie down and we can begin."

"It's too small, you can't. I . . ." For once, Osbert was at a loss for words.

"I can always tear the skin off your belly and complete the summoning somewhere else," suggested the devil.

Osbert looked at the creature's nails. They were a dirty gray, long and strong, like the claws of a gigantic rat. They looked suitable for the task suggested, and the cardinal didn't look used to issuing idle threats.

"Here, on the floor?" he asked.

"That will suffice. Expose your belly and say the words you have been taught."

The pardoner began mumbling out the names of the devils.

The devil put something into the pardoner's hand. It was a vial of some sort, stoppered with a wooden bung.

"Open it."

The pardoner did so. It was blood.

"Describe the outline of the circle with the blood."

Osbert asked, "What blood is this?"

"Angel's blood, fresh from the Despenser cache. Use it well. I had to swim to get it and I hate to swim."

"I will not touch it."

"Suddenly so sensitive about the use of relics?"

"It's . . ." Osbert wanted to say "sacrilegious" but somehow the words "potentially dangerous to me" emerged.

The face of the cardinal loomed above Osbert. He opened his mouth—it was a little furnace, burning with flame.

"I repeat, I can cook you and cut you and still have my summoning. There are a hundred men of the town whom I can command to daub on that blood."

"All right, all right! Why don't you do it?"

The devil said, "It'll burn my fingers."

Osbert thought to fling the angel's blood at the devil but feared it might not permanently disable it. Even if it did, it would not pay his debt to Despenser, who would be waiting for him in Hell. More immediately, it wouldn't get him out of the prison.

He dipped his finger in the blood. A delicious tingle shot through him—the feeling of a stepping into a crystal-cold morning, having spent the night in a muggy inn full of farts and fleas—and traced the circle and markings with it. Then Osbert waited, restoppering and pocketing the vial in case he should ever have a future need to sell it to get drunk and forget this entire episode.

He said, "Nothing's happening."

"Look!" said Nergal.

"Oh, God's collions!"

The scars were transforming, each mark, each circle, each name, replaced by burning white light. The light shone up from his belly and, as it did so, it seemed to turn like a whirlpool in a river, swirling up from his stomach to the ceiling of the room. And, like a whirlpool, it was pulling things in.

Shapes appeared in the whirling light above his belly—smoke monsters at first, huge mouths, great claws. A high bell sounded and there was a noise like a dog worrying at a bone. Someone was drumming, a skittle-skattle beat like the running of a rat in the rafters; the smell of shit and incense was in his nostrils, and his thoughts were slow and heavy as if waking from a drunken sleep.

The devils spoke their names. "Caym, Abigor, Adramelech, Alastor, Amduscias, and Eurynome." They were like whispers on the wind at first, like the rustle of leaves in an autumn forest, but quickly the names grew in strength to a shrieking chorus. Above him in the tiny cell, figures were taking shape in the mist: a giant blackbird, a sword belt around its waist and a big thick knife in the clawed hands that extended from the end of its wings; a hook-nosed devil carrying a lance and riding on a bat-winged horse; a vastly muscled donkey-headed man with a plume of smoky gray peacock's feathers at his tail; a skinny, spindly man with a rotting dog's head skull, who grasped cruel barbed daggers in his fists; a man with the head of a demented unicorn—its eyes bulging as if they were boils about to burst, its horn monstrously large; a twisted devil with a gargoyle's face. Osbert heard a cracked chant issuing from somewhere very close by.

These are the devils of death,
The takers of heartbeats, the robbers of breath.
These are the devils of death.

Osbert felt terribly sick. The smoke that spewed from his navel was like a rope wound around his intestines . . .

"Say the words! Say the words Despenser told you!" commanded the cardinal.

"Devils and servants of Satan, know that it is the command of the great gaoler and his favorite, the kingly Despenser, that you accompany this wretched pardoner to assassinate and thereby remove the boy called Dowzabel. This is the requirement of your release, otherwise, should you fail to respect his servant Satan's command, you will be ever bound here in this circle, to await the judgment of God on the final day. Will you swear?"

A cacophony from within the swirling smoke. Osbert felt a terrible weight on his belly.

"We swear!" The voices were those of men, of birds, of dogs, and of horses.

"Open the circle!" said the cardinal.

"How?" he asked.

Osbert felt a knife pressed into his hand. "Cut!" instructed the demon.

The pardoner had no choice—the weight on his belly was so great, his terror of the beasts that spiraled above him so overwhelming that he must end it. He sliced a small nick into his flesh where the light poured out. Immediately a tiny sliver of darkness appeared in the wall of light, and the devils seeped forth in a hiss of noxious smoke, the smell of burning hair filling up the cell. The room could not accommodate all the devils and the door burst from its hinges, spilling them out into the corridor.

"What's going on in there?" The chief gaoler's voice came loud and strong from outside and then said, "Sweet Mother of God!" perhaps louder, but nowhere near as strong.

The skinny, spindly devil with the rotting dog's head on his shoulders was in the corridor. "My name is Alastor, and that means death!" he shrilled, springing forward down the passage, his daggers slashing at the air.

"Get to the Sainte-Chapelle!" shouted the cardinal, to the devils. "The boy you seek is going there!" Osbert looked at his belly. The magic circle of scars was still there, but no light—only a small cut just below the navel.

The blackbird demon stepped over the pardoner, as did the mad unicorn man and the gargoyle devil, joining others already running out of the prison.

Osbert got to his feet and pursued them, hoping that this day would be his last in the company of such abominations.

He was checked by words in English, clear in the babble.

"Who's there?"

Osbert stopped by a cell door with a big hole in the bottom. He had recognized the voice. He poked his head through. "Osbert of London, a pardoner, at your service, my lords. My devils have freed you."

"William Montagu, Earl of Salisbury and Marschal of England, and Robert Ufford, Earl of Suffolk! You are clearly an Englishman. It's your duty to give your life to help us escape!"

Osbert wanted to respond that he couldn't think of what the punishment would be that would be worse than the death that would be his due for performing his duty. But he had care of his immortal soul and was in no hurry to return to Hell. Marschals knew kings, and kings knew God. Could

Montagu get him absolution? In addition, whatever the immortal torments awaiting him, the habits of a lifetime meant Osbert could not turn down the chance of earning a few coins.

"The way is clear!" said Osbert.

Montagu was through the door in a breath, stripping the sword from the gaoler's side. "Arondight!" he said. "The sword returns to its rightful owner!" He held up the blade.

Osbert could not help but be impressed—it was slender as a wand, brilliant silver, so bright it was almost difficult to look at. If that was his sword, how much was this man worth?

"My lords," said Osbert, "it is a pleasure to offer you this service and—"

"We need a disguise," said Montagu to Suffolk.

"Take these low men's clothes," Suffolk replied.

"I have, by my service, freed you," said Osbert, "and would ask—"

"Yes, yes," said Montagu, who was already changing out of his noble's clothes. "I have seen you before. Do you know a safe place in this city?"

"Of course," said Osbert, who did not. As the men discarded their clothes, he changed out of his to take Montagu's fine tunic and soft woolen hose. The nobles were too preoccupied to castigate him.

"Then lead. And how did you make a devil appear in our cell?"

"Oh, er, when I summon them they appear pretty much where they like."

"You should be hanged for consorting with fiends," said Montagu.

"I'll take that as a 'thank you,'" said the pardoner.

The men had the gaolers' clothes on very quickly and ran outside into the street, following Osbert.

"What is *that*?" said Suffolk.

The hook-nosed devil's bat-wing horse was stamping the street, surrounded by men-at-arms. Its rider bore a great sword in its hand and cut down at its attackers, the horse scattering them in stuttering charges, only for them to reform and attack again.

"I believe it's a devil, sent to kill a boy of this town and possibly also the angel of Sainte-Chapelle," said the pardoner, "but I do feel we should now make our way—'

The press of men around the horse suddenly broke as a twisted, galumphing devil carrying a thick stick set about them from the rear, smacking five or six at a time to the street. This devil jumped to join its fellow on the horse's back, and the horse charged up the steps toward the Great Hall and Sainte-Chapelle.

"We should find out more before I go to Edward," said Montagu.

"Then let's chase them!" said Suffolk.

"My lords," said Osbert, "God forgive that a humble man may presume so to counsel his betters, but that would be a bollocking bad decision."

The two nobles ran off toward the Great Hall and the pardoner felt he had no option but to follow them. They could save his immortal soul by interceding with the king, and, in addition, they owed him a decent sum for pulling devils out of his belly to tackle the gaolers. He hared after them, toward the sound of battle.

16

T he cog *Thomas* labored in a big sea, the sails of the invasion force plunging to vanish and then rising alongside it on the swell.

Edward hated to travel by sea. One advantage, if he ever became true king of France, would be that he could fight his wars without ever tasting salt on the wind.

He looked up into the swirling gray clouds. Enemy angelic intervention? No, just a lousy day in an English summer—nothing unusual there. Fortunately, the wind was at their backs. If an enemy angel were present that would not be the case. And where was his angel? It had sparkled above the fleet at Ipswich but hadn't been seen since. Edward knew from what his father had told him that angels might wait for the men to show their valor and engage before intervening. God, let it be so here!

He had moved among the men, telling them the wind was a sign God was with them and had made his way back to the aftcastle to give what little reassurance he could to the ladies of his wife's household. His wife was surviving in Gaunt with a staff of less than ten. She needed her ladies and so they had to travel. He had told them they would be in little danger but given strict instructions they were to remain under the platform of the aftcastle "should we engage the enemy." There was no "should" about it. Edward was taking his ship into the press of the enemy, looking to grapple and board their ships.

He picked his way back down the ship, using the rail and rigging for support. The men were still on the deck, packed tight, swaddled sailors huddled against the wind for warmth, a hundred of his best men-at-arms and eighty archers. Thomas Holland was there, with twenty of his men-at-arms, their silver lion rampant on their surcoats. Edward had asked for the baron on his ship because there was no fiercer fighter in Christendom. The sight of that lion was enough to terrify most of the French nobility.

They had the guns too: the pot-de-fer, tied to the rail, their stacks of huge quarrels lashed in beside them and a couple of giant crossbows—the springalds—mounted to the forecastle.

Sir Reginald Cobham sat up beside one, a long metal tube on a stick at his side. This, Edward knew, was his handgun. By the time you'd loaded and fired the thing your enemy could have run you through a hundred times, but the noise it made was terrific and it did the job of spreading panic. It would be useful in the first boarding, thought Edward, because it fired a mighty stone and would be effective against a press of men.

Cobham was a slight and short man and had been picked to lead a scouting party once they found a place he could be put down. It would be a hazardous trip through enemy-held territory but Cobham, Edward thought, was up to the job. And at least, with that ridiculous gun at his side, they'd hear if he came into contact with the French.

The swell dropped as they approached the Flemish coast. They put ashore Cobham and two knights in darkness, the men slipping away by rowing boat. By dawn they had returned with bad news. The French had completely blockaded the harbor from the island of Cadzand on the northeast to the long dyke that marked Flemish territory on the west. They held conference on the forecastle of the *Thomas*. The king was already armored, in his heavy mail and surcoat, his basinet helmet with its visor raised, with his great sword at his side. He felt secure in his armor, even pleased that, if he fell from the ship, there would be no lingering death for him. No one could swim with that weight of mail.

A knight said, "They're like a row of castles, lord—three lines all roped to one another side to side to defend against boarding."

"The state of their ships?" asked Edward.

"Huge ones to the front, sir, near twenty of them."

"Including our *Christopher*."

"She towers above them, sir."

Edward breathed in. The *Christopher* alone could hold two hundred men.

"The French angel?" he asked him.

"We saw the fleet at night but it's like day over the harbor. The cloud above the estuary is on fire. It's there."

The king asked, "Did it see you?"

"Who knows?"

"Where the bloody Hell is ours? We'll attack with or without it."

Crabbe and Morley were alongside him, come over from their ships for conference. A dozen other important captains were there too.

Crabbe, a weather-beaten elderly man of around forty-five, shook his head. He said, "We can't take them in the harbor. We must lure them out to sea."

"Agreed," Morley said. "No room to maneuver in there."

"Will our angel come to our aid?" Cobham, of all people, a nerveless spy, looked worried.

"It will come," said Edward, "I have its assurance. The wind is with us and we will attack the French directly."

"That is suicide, sir," offered Morley.

"I didn't ask for your opinion, Morley. I simply demand your obedience. You are here to receive orders, not to indulge in a debate."

But even as his anger flared, he reminded himself of Morley's many services to him. Edward added, "Have faith, Morley. Direct attack. You may have the honor of taking back the *Christopher*. Three lines, as is customary. I'll lead the way myself." Four of the assembled captains crossed themselves. The rest just looked at their feet—only Crabbe, the old pirate, met his eye.

"Don't look so pale, men!" said Edward. "If the French have been chained together since Cobham saw them, then they'll be in a sorry state. You can't hold a line like that for long in an estuary before the tide'll have you to one side or another and you, as men of the sea should know that!"

"You should speak to the men, sir, so we might relay your words to our own."

"Yes, of course."

The king turned to the rail of the forecastle to look down on his ship. A trumpeter beside him sounded a flourish and the men fell silent. In their war array they looked truly fierce—lions, dragons, and bears looking out from surcoats of every color, polearms sparkling in the sun, the goose feathers on the quills in the quivers white and bright, though the archers themselves looked drab in their poor men's tunics. Already a couple of the more eager hands had taken to the crow's nest, their bows on their backs. The great leopard pennants streamed from the mast tops, snapping gold and red in the breeze.

Edward prayed, "God, this is my sacrifice. God, restore my angels. I am the rightful king. Return my angels to me for this offering of blood I bring you." He crossed himself. What it was to go into battle hoping God would see your sacrifice and kill your father but unable to state your wish directly, even to Him.

He spoke to the men, these instruments of his will. He couldn't bring himself to lie to them.

Edward said, "I stand here before you as your king, appointed by God, God's anger in my soul and God's words in my mouth. The French lie at anchor not an hour away. You may die today—if so, be happy. You die in a just cause, supporting the undoubted will of almighty God, in His service, offering your blood to protect the right of His servant on earth. We are English, blessed by God, and can know no fear. Your Heavenly reward is assured and the day can only end well for you. You will be masters of France or seated at the right hand of God in Heaven. The French will be shaking in their ships for they know that, should they perish, eternal damnation follows.

"I am the rightful king of France; that is my firm belief. God will stand by us. God will not let us fail. When Jesus found the moneychangers and the harlots in the temple of His father, He took a whip to drive them out. By my birth, by God, and by my right, I stand in the place of Jesus on earth. You are my whip. And what a scourge you are. One of us is worth ten Frenchmen, wise men say throughout Christendom. Today, fight well enough to make those wise men rethink their timorous odds. We are worth twenty, thirty of these murdering, burning, plundering fools and we will wash away their sins in their own blood! Forward, for England, for Edward, for the right God gave me and the obedience that you owe me!"

The men cheered and many called "God bless the king." The cry went from ship to ship. "God bless the king! God bless the king!"

The captains returned to their ships and, as soon as the sun had moved above them and was no longer in their eyes, the fleet hauled up the anchors and set the sails, a good breeze still behind them. The harbor was familiar to them, and they swung wide as they approached to attack head on into the estuary, the wind at their backs.

The *Thomas* broke past the headland under full sail and Edward could finally see what he was facing. It really was like a row of castles, or rather a deep and impenetrable mountain range. The enemy ships were no longer roped together as Cobham had reported. They had separated and were clearly maneuvering to regain battle order, having drifted due to the tide.

A great sigh went up from the French ships as the English came into view, men venting their fears as one, and, *yes*! the air above the *Thomas* ignited and a great flaming circle of eyes appeared, facing the French. From above the French ships the light shifted and swam, flowing up off the water to form the image of a gigantic man.

"Sir?" His captain was in front of him, his eyes full of terror.

The king said, "Onward! We can't worry about what they decide, and our actions may influence the outcome."

The English ships ran forward, the longbowmen crowding the forecastle ready to engage.

The sky was yellow and the sky was red and then green. Great clouds raced across it, though the wind did not alter. A voice like a great cymbal sounded across the waters. "Yes?" That was no voice Edward had ever heard. The French angel!

Another—like the roar of a fire—replied, "Yes."

The burning wheel above Edward's ship vanished and only the figure above the French line remained, blazing with light.

Edward fell to his knees on the deck. His men were looking to him to protect them, to use his favor with God to intercede on their behalf.

He said, "Mighty God, I am your servant, your abject servant. I worship you and honor you. Stay the hand of the French angel, stay its hand."

Light flashed across the heavens—tongues of fire. Now it was the English force's turn to gasp, many crossing themselves or shouting out prayers for forgiveness.

A word shuddered through the air: "Jegudiel." It was as if a second sun was in the sky above the French ships. Edward shielded his eyes against the intense light.

"Angel of kings," he shouted. "Angel of authority, of judges and those in authority who labor to God's glory! See how abject I am, how dependent on God's mercy! I have come here ready to die, to send all my men to slaughter! Recognize my faith. Reward my faith!"

The light dimmed and Edward could just make out the figure of a man, as if suspended in a cloud of light, holding forth a radiant crimson heart.

"Forgive me!" said Edward.

"You are not forgiven. You are damned and all your countrymen with you!"

"Listen to our angel! It will represent us!" Edward cast his eyes about— no wheel of burning eyes, nothing.

Jegudiel said, "Your angel defers to my opinion."

Around him ships were foundering, water churning up, sailors unable to see what they were doing in the intense and blinding light.

"Forgive me!"

"You are not forgiven. You have an appointment in Hell, Edward. You have beauty beyond compare. What would it be like to touch you, Sariel? Is it sweet to fall?" The angel had stopped making any sense, though the water still rose and fell as if in a storm—but a storm of smashing, pulverizing light. Edward's ship was thrown sideways, the burning light robbing him of any vision. The French had no need to attack; they could just watch as the English fleet struggled in the furious waters. A sigh of three thousand voices. Screams and curses in French.

The light went out and the sea was still. Edward prised himself off the soaking deck. The French line was still in disarray, ships at all angles to one another, but the angel was gone. *My God, the enemy angel was gone!*

"God favors us! God favors us! Attack! Attack!" screamed Edward. The bowmen around him on the forecastle regained their feet, the sail filled, and as the *Thomas* sped toward the French line, a great cry went up from Edward's men.

"God is with us! The angel has gone! God is with us."

Edward freed his sword as the *Thomas* closed on the French in a hiss of longbow arrows, volley after volley after volley, as they raced forward—with the wind, with the tide.

Holland was at his side. He said, "Are you feeling what I'm feeling, sir?" The knight was grinning wildly.

"A good day to be English!" said Edward. The cog smashed into a big French galley, its sides shearing the oars. Crossbow fire pattered into the deck and men around him died, but Edward's archers' response was devastating. Twenty longbows on the aftcastle, twenty on the forecastle, sent showers of death onto the decks of the galley. A French cog came slamming into the *Thomas*'s side, grappling irons clawing into the wood. Edward was close enough to touch the crossbowmen on the forecastle, and touch them he did, leaping over to be among them, cutting and hacking.

They screamed and fell back in front of him, cowed that the God-appointed king of England was among them like a fox among the hens. Two were battered down by his shield, but three discharged their weapons at close range. A bolt went through his gambeson and into his thigh, another missed completely, and a third wayward shot hit a fellow crossbowman.

Two men leapt from the forecastle in panic onto the deck below. The *Thomas* discharged its pot-de-fers, shivering the French ship. There was another enormous bang from the deck below. Cobham had fired his handgun. Well, thought Edward, a man of noble birth is allowed a little fun in war. He certainly intended to have some himself.

"One of us is worth a score of you!" screamed Edward.

"England! England! England! The Boar is among you!" Holland was alongside him, screaming out Edward's nom de guerre.

A crossbowman went down to Edward's sword, then another and another. A man fired not three paces from him, but Edward's shield slowed the bolt as it flew and, though it penetrated his mail, it hung harmlessly from his gambeson. He cut the man from shoulder to chest.

All around the battle raged to the accompaniment of a tight drum roll of longbow arrows that were fired at ludicrously short range. The French were losing, their sailors easy prey to the men-at-arms who ran rampant over their ships. Edward's men had overrun the two French ships they'd initially attacked, and he jumped back on to the *Thomas*. The captain brought the ship about, looking for more prey, and, just visible in the western sun, Edward saw a magnificent sight. Eight oared galleys of

Genoese mercenaries were making a break for the sea. They wouldn't do that unless they were convinced the battle was lost.

Another loud bang. Cobham had reloaded and discharged his handgun. That alone told Edward his men were enjoying some success in the battle. Cobham couldn't have done that if hard-pressed.

"We're going to win," Edward said to himself, "we're going to win! Praise God! He is with me! He is with me!"

A large French cog was alongside and Edward's pots-de-fer fired, slamming their bolts into its ranks of crossbowmen. As his ship lurched with the recoil Edward saw something in the muzzle's breath. A shape, like that of a man, but a man of coals and fire. The creature who had visited him at Antwerp.

"Remember!" it seemed to say.

"I remember!" he shouted. "I remember, but soon I will have no need of you for God favors me now!"

Edward was hardly conscious of his bloody thigh, desperate to reach more French.

Above him the huge wheel materialized in the sky—a wheel of fire full of eyes. The English angel had come back.

"Burn them! Burn them!" Edward exhorted.

"The French cannot protect the angels of God," said Edward's angel. "I will burn them."

The eyes poured forth fire, streaking out in great blasts toward the French. The skies blazed; God's judgment streamed down on the French, and even on the *Thomas*, the heat was as intense as a furnace. The French ships were no more than floating bonfires all along the line, men turned to fiery devils as they leapt aflame into the water. Edward sank to his knees to give thanks. God loved him; against all the odds, mysteriously, inexplicably, brilliantly, and despite what the French angel had said, the battle was won.

17

Revulsion burned in Dow's chest as he was led into the palace. The beauty of the place was overwhelming—everything gilded, painted, embossed, or jeweled. One of the marvelous pillars in the entrance hall alone would have bought shelter for the poor of a town, he thought. How could men live like this while their fellows starved? What sort of devil enjoyed this display knowing that, not a bowshot away, children died for want of food and clothing? The spectacle was entrancing, he conceded, truly wonderful. Each step invited him to stop and wonder. But at what cost?—the denial of decent treatment of the poor. Dow walked on with unflinching purpose.

The little one who led them in was so cocksure, so lordly. What gave him the right to think himself so superior? Dow thought of his nan, dead on the moor. Who had been better than her? She had never swaggered or sneered, but been kind and gentle. Well, the time for kindness was over; gentleness had had its day.

Sariel would force the answer from this angel, and then they'd be on their way east to take the banner that would rally the poor and smash these palaces to pieces, using their gold to provide bread.

Sariel, though, looked around her, enraptured. "The light in here is wonderful," she said. "See how deep the gold shines, like a summer lake and the rubies, little sunsets each."

They hurried on, the little boy talking all the time. "We'll proceed directly to the chapel," he said. "There's nothing to be gained by delay." He ushered the group past him and waited until he came level with Dow.

"Now I know you," he said, "and I know what you are."

"What am I?" replied Dow in the same language.

"My God, is that supposed to be French? You sound as though you have a mouthful of stones, man. Talk clearly!"

Dow had a strong urge to strangle the child, who didn't wait for Dow to speak again.

"You are no friend of angels or priests, I think."

Dow replied, "No."

The boy said, "Neither am I. The one we're about to see is particularly troublesome to me. I think you have something about you that could prove useful. A knife? Obtained from a fellow who breathes fire?"

"What of it?"

"Well, if you could stick it in the angel if you get the chance, then I'd be awfully grateful."

Dow said, "I am here to ask it a question."

"Wouldn't your lord, Lucifer, favor you if you killed one of his enemy's servants?"

"I am not looking for favor with Lucifer. Only to serve his cause."

The boy craned his head, as if not quite understanding Dow. He said, "Amounts to the same thing, I think you'll find. Look, let me put it another way. You kill the angel when it appears, or I'll have you and your companions killed in the most brutal way imaginable. Take my word for it, I have a rich imagination and have spent some time pondering how to best inflict pain on my enemies. The captain over there, the one who attends the lady, should I start with him?"

Dow shoved the boy hard on the shoulder and grabbed him by the hair as he staggered backward. "Best start with me," he said in Cornish, though he could see the little prince took his meaning well enough.

Immediately three polearms were on Dow, one jabbing into his side hard enough for him to take a pace back. The Navarrese men-at-arms had responded instantly to a threat to their lord.

The queen cried out, but the boy held up his hand and spoke in a language Dow didn't understand. The men lowered their polearms and Dow released the boy's hair.

"Have you gone mad, Dow?" Orsino asked him in English.

"He threatened me," said Dow. "He threatened you too."

"Do you want him to make good on that threat?" said Orsino. "This must be a tolerant prince, because any I've ever met would have had you dead on these flagstones by now."

Of all the people on the stairs, the little boy seemed the least concerned. "High-spirited foreigners," he said. "A misunderstanding, that's all. Let's proceed to the chapel."

They headed up the stairs to the great doors in front of them. Queen Joan told the two guards barring their way to step aside, and they instantly obeyed. Philip had seen no need to protect access to the angel since receiving the good news that Charles would never be king.

The doors were opened and Dow felt all breath leave his body. The glorious sun of the Parisian June was split into a hundred colors here, leaving its memory dull by comparison, as ore is dull compared to the tin the fire pulls from it.

The windows were immense, the gold deeper, the gems brighter than anything he had seen in the palace so far. Light, light—everything wrought from light.

Sariel stepped into the chapel, gazing around her. She seemed transformed by the light, her appearance beyond mere beauty, more akin to a star or the moon, a dawn over the hills.

She went farther in. At one end of the chapel something seemed to shine—itself a small dawn. Dow walked in, his head giddy. On a plinth was a twisted garland of thorns, shining even in the brilliance of that room. Behind it was a cloth imprinted with a man's face, it too leaking light. Dow knew instinctively that this was the crown of thorns with which the horror, Îthekter, had tormented Lucifer; the image was the face of the Lord of Light.

"Can you not see?" said Sariel.

"See what?" said the little boy.

"How it shines, how the crown shines."

"I see nothing but a bit of dusty bush," said the boy, "sold in generations past by charlatans to credulous kings."

"It shines!" said Sariel. "It shines!"

All along the walls of the chapel stood statues of the twelve apostles that now began to babble. Dow didn't understand their language, but somehow he knew what they meant. *A king has come. A mighty king. Half human, half divine. He is the enemy of the true king of Heaven.*

There was a disturbance from behind them, men crying out in panic.

"Call the angel," said Charles.

"Angels can't be called," said Sariel, "or not by any earthly power. They choose to come or they choose not to come, to allow the part of themselves that is here to come to the light or to remain in darkness."

"What's that noise?" said the little boy.

"Enemies!" shouted Queen Joan.

"I was told angels could be called by her!" said Charles. "I've been lied to!"

The commotion grew louder—the sound of battle, steel on steel. A smell drifted up the stairs—brimstone, smoke, and sal ammoniac.

First around the corner came the monstrous blackbird, tall as a man and gripping a sword in the talons that sprouted under its wings.

"Devils!" shouted Dow, but Sariel wasn't listening—she was lost to the light.

Orsino drew his sword and kissed the cloth of St. John, while Charles and his mother ran to the end of the chapel farthest from the door. All their men-at-arms drew steel to face the devils.

The boy desperately tugged at a lance that was mounted on the altar. Dow saw that it too glowed. The lance that had pierced Christ's side. All these relics, all these things endowed with Îthekter's power, were things used to harm Lucifer—whom they called Christ. These were the enemy's implements, the enemy that had fooled the angels, fooled the saints.

Dow drew his knife.

"We come for Dowzabel," chirped the blackbird. "No other man need fear us."

"Ask not who need fear you but whom you need to fear," said Orsino.

"Give him the youth!" shrieked Joan.

A man-at-arms grabbed Dow by the shoulder, but little Charles cried out, "Give it a moment, men. I want to see if the angel appears."

Dow felt giddy. It was as if his eyes not only drank in the light of the chapel but radiated it too. The mark on his chest flared, burning white light in the shape of the fork through his tunic. But what was happening to Sariel?

She was dancing in the chapel, her arms loose, her dark hair like a living thing as it swung about her, fell forward and was tossed back behind her; she moaned and called out in a voice that had all the beauty of the bird-bright dawn, of a clear river singing at a weir.

The bird-devil leapt up the stairs, cleaving a man-at-arms, shearing through the sword he put up to block and hacking into his side. Orsino got a good blow at the creature, but its head retracted into its neck just before his sword struck. The blade bit the doorframe and the bird backhanded Orsino down the stairs. Other frightful figures were emerging—a man with the face of a decomposing dog, a mule with a steel peacock fan tail.

With all the devils up the stairs, the men-at-arms fell like barley in the harvest.

The blackbird hopped forward at Dow, knocking him down. It turned its head this way and that trying to avoid being blinded by the light that poured from the fork on Dow's chest, but still it slashed with its sword. Its strength was enormous, its body heavy and solid, and Dow had to writhe and dodge to avoid its blows. He stabbed at the creature, but it just brushed his arm away, sending the dagger sliding across the floor. Then it had him by the neck and lifted its sword to strike.

Hot blood pulsed over Dow's chest; the creature dropped its sword.

The boy prince had run the length of the chapel with the holy lance to spear the bird through the heart.

"Not until the angel is here. He's going to kill it, isn't he? And drive his guardian mad? It's your blasted plan!"

Something odd was happening to the light in the chapel: its beautiful colors were splitting into shining rays, each one itself a rainbow.

The cardinal was at the door. "Back! Back!" he shouted to his devils. "Let the boy do his work and then we'll be on him."

A sound was in the air, a beautiful song, high and clear. Sariel joined it in counterpoint and Dow felt it doing something very strange to him. He was light, not flesh, a thing born of the light.

The light in the chamber was full of memories. It was the light in the wine they'd stolen from a merchant's house, the light breaking from behind a cloud over the moor, the shimmer on an eel's back, the flash on a king-fisher's wing.

Dow found the sensation overwhelming. He heard a voice like the boom of the sea.

"Jegudiel."

The devils outside began to twitter and squawk, two running back out of the palace, the cardinal diving to the side of the door to be out of the burning light.

Dow felt the light pouring out of him, from his mouth, from his eyes, from the mark on his chest—and he knew the angel was there, stripping away all pretense and illusion. He was light. Everything was light, the chapel a shattered gem spawning rainbows, the windows shimmering veils of blue.

A voice said, "Jegudiel. Such beauty."

"None such beauty as you, radiant and shining one." Sariel stretched out her hands to the light.

"Who are these?"

Dow could see a figure in the light—a perfect man, winged and haloed, a dancing aura of violet and green around his head.

He had to ask it. "Where do we find the king in the east?"

No reply.

Sariel was calling to the creature, "Take me to the light, give me forgiveness."

More shouting down the stairs as the devils engaged more men-at-arms. There was a roar and a flash, screams and shouting.

"You have beauty beyond compare. What would it be like to touch you? Sariel, is it sweet to fall? What it would be to dwell in the world of flesh. I am lonely sometimes in the light."

She repeated, "Take me to the light."

"You are a perfection. No glass, no gold, holds the luster of your skin. Your eyes make the jewels of this place seem dull indeed."

"Take me to the light!"

"Is it sweet to fall? What sour pleasures you must feel, embodied and vulnerable. What it must be to scrape a knee, to feel hot porridge burn the mouth, to lie with one such as you in sweat and secretion."

"I will join you! I will join you in the light."

The man, the perfect man who had only been a multitude of glistening crystal sparkles, now started to take shape. His hair was like wrought gold, his skin like ivory, his eyes blue sapphires, yet it was a man who took shape in front of Dow, not a statue—impossibly tall, with enormous wings of shining white feathers, plated armor like a mirror, a sword at his side, a shield on his arm that bore a flaming heart. He sat down on the altar as if it were a chair.

"Kill him!" shouted the little boy. "That's your job, isn't it, Antichrist? Kill him!"

But Dow could not move. The light still poured from him.

Sariel ran to the angel and it gathered her into its arms as she sobbed, "You fell, you fell! You were not meant to fall. I wanted to come back to the light!"

"There is light enough," said the angel, cradling her to it.

It held up its hand and the colors in Dow stopped their flow. The little boy pressed something into Dow's hand. The devil's knife.

Dow gripped it, but the angel stretched its hand toward Dow.

"Brother," it said, and Dow knew that it spoke the truth. He had been born of light and born of woman.

"Mother?" he said to Sariel. In the presence of the French angel, he knew now who she was—he felt it in his heart.

The devils came whooping and clattering into the hall. A dog-headed man on a great horse charged for Dow, who gripped the knife and swung it, but to no avail. The horse charged him down, battering him to the floor.

"Never mind the angel. Take the boy!" The horrid cardinal took a candle from a votary and put it into his mouth. The dog-headed man jumped down from his horse, stabbing at Dow with his spear. But the cardinal never got to breathe. Orsino had picked up the blackbird's sword—a big, heavy-bladed falchion—and struck the cardinal hard across the back of the neck. His head came clean off at the shoulders and a pillar of flame burst up to the ceiling.

The trident on Dow's chest shone as he rolled aside from the dog man's spear. The dog thing stabbed and stabbed again, but Dow ducked and rolled as Orsino had told him to do. The ceiling of the chapel was now on fire, thanks to the exploding cardinal.

"Fetch more guards! More guards!" shouted Joan of Navarre. She tried to pull little Charles with her, but the boy would not go.

"Fetch the guards if you must," he said. "This is the moment of our victory and I want to see it."

She said, "You will die."

"No."

"Come, son! The place is burning."

"I'll wait a while yet, Mother. I fancy the angel will not let the fire consume such beauty. Fetch the guards."

Joan pulled at her son hard but found she could not move him. She crossed herself twice and ran from the chapel.

Jegudiel was rapt, staring into Sariel's eyes. "Your beauty is enchanting. On the river Swin, in the setting sun, ships are burning as men fight for the honor of the Lord. It is a wonderful sight, and yet nothing compared to the glory of your eyes," said Jegudiel. His voice was all beauty, like the sucking and drawing of the tides, like the wind in a forest.

The horse creature with the peacock fan had taken up the holy lance and now rounded on Orsino, shrieking. The mercenary was quick, though, twisting and turning, not bothering to parry, cutting at the devil's head so it had to look to defense rather than attack. It goaded him as they fought. "Here's one who cursed the lord's name when he should have prayed in grief. Here's a killer and a thief!"

The flames above filled the chapel with a noxious smoke, hazing the light of the windows. For the first time, Jegudiel looked up. He held out his hand and the flames just weren't there anymore. The unicorn devil leapt at him, his daggers whirling, but Jegudiel simply turned his hand to the devil. A flash of unbearable intensity and the devil had vanished.

Again, the dog-faced man came for Dow, but the flash had given Dow time to recover his feet. He knocked the spear aside, just enough to make it miss, and then he was on the devil, the dagger stabbing down into its chest and shoulders.

A clinging black ichor burst from its wounds, covering Dow's face, but the dog man seemed unaffected, punching and kicking at Dow so hard the boy retched. It seized him by the throat, driving him back onto the floor.

Dow felt something humming inside him; his head was a blister ready to pop. The devil couldn't focus on Dow, the burning light from the fork on his chest blinding its eyes and forcing it to turn its head. Dow's hand went to the fork and, without thinking what he was doing, he lifted it from his chest. In his hand was a trident of searing light and he thrust it into the dog creature. It screamed and shriveled in on itself like parchment in a fire, reducing to nothing.

The angel was watching him now, though Sariel just gazed up at Jegudiel in bliss.

The peacock creature leapt back from Orsino's flashing sword. Then it threw the holy lance. Orsino tried to swat it aside but it was thrown too hard, too quickly, and took him straight through the chest.

The mercenary fell back, grasping the shaft of the spear, trying to pull it out, but it was no good, the lance had gone through him to protrude a foot behind him. He fell heavily, gasping.

Dow ran at the peacock devil, which, unarmed, turned to face him, claws raised. It cried out in alarm as it saw the fork of light and put out its hands to grasp it. The fork struck the creature, which collapsed in on itself and disappeared.

All the devils were now gone and Dow dropped to his knees, the trident blinking and fading in his hand.

The angels still sat on the altar, holding hands, their eyes locked. Jegudiel lifted Sariel's hand and kissed it.

Montagu came running into the hall.

"An angel!" he cried. "As Lord Marschal of England, appointed by Edward, appointed by God, standing in his place as Edward stands in the place of God, I charge you to tell me, does the old King Edward live? If alive, where is he?"

Jegudiel looked up from his rapture. "Kings," said the angel, its voice like the crash of many cymbals.

Montagu said, "Where are the angels? Where is Barachiel, who dwelled in the abbey? Where is the seraph who lived at Walsingham? Where are the Elohim who lived in the light at Canterbury?"

"Where they always are."

"Where is that?"

"Where God wants them to be. With the king."

"Does old Edward live?"

Jegudiel said, "His angels attend him. God still waits for him."

So that was all the proof Montagu needed. Finally, from a divine being, confirmation the king lived! Any lingering doubts were now gone.

"Where is the king? Where is old Edward?" he said.

"I cannot tell. The snake eats the man. There he lies."

"Where is old Edward?" begged Montagu, but the angel said nothing, just returned to gazing at Sariel. He held her and kissed her and she was rapt.

Dow got to his feet and went to Orsino. The mercenary had heaved the lance from his chest, but his breath was rasping, and his mouth bubbled with blood.

"Sariel, help him!" begged Dow, but she was lost to the angel's beauty.

Orsino got to his feet, the lance in his hand. He staggered forward in a weaving line, up toward the altar where the angels sat. He spoke directly to Sariel. "You are the light and I love you," he said.

Neither of the angels replied; both just sat as if entranced, staring into each other's eyes, Jegudiel's arm on Sariel's shoulder.

Dow ran to support Orsino, knowing he might fall. Orsino coughed and hacked, blood on his lips. "Darkness, then," he said. He stabbed the holy lance up into Jegudiel's armpit, where the mail did not protect him, and collapsed against him.

The angel looked down at the lance. Then its beautiful eyes settled on Dow.

"You," it said. It reached out its hand to touch him but Dow struck him at the neck with the dagger and the angel collapsed.

18

E dwin sweated, giddy at the edge of his bed, holding back from a lifetime's habit of morning prayer.

"You must break this practice. You have chosen now." Know-Much sat at the corner of the room, his little legs poking out from his fat belly, his arms resting on top of it.

The priest almost felt like crying when he looked at the little demon. In one moment he felt elation—he could learn so much about the inner workings of Heaven and Hell. In another, despair—as he felt certain he was destined for the latter as soon as he died.

"Are angels individuals, Know-Much? Have they material form or are they, as Aquinas tells us, pure forms, immaterial minds?"

"Angels are light."

"And so is one separate from another?"

"Better to ask if one person is separate from another."

"I have form and substance and so do you. Therefore we are separate."

"So are angels, who have no form, separate even from us. We are light." The demon spoke in a slow croak.

"We are clay, and to clay we return," said Edwin.

"In the beginning was the void and then there was light. Light is everything. Everything is light."

"Even you, Know-Much? For to me you seem a creature of darkness."

"And yet you look to me for enlightenment. How dark a creature must you be?"

The priest had tears coming down his face. "I need to pray."

"Then pray," said Know-Much, "for Lucifer would not wish to see you distressed. If you are happy as a servant, then be a servant."

"It is right that I serve the king of Creation."

"Creation has no king. How can a tree have a king? Could your Edward bid it walk?"

Edwin put his head into his hands. "I know no purpose, for I have no master to follow."

"But you have a friend to help, and to help you."

"Who is that friend?"

"Lucifer."

"I am damned."

"You were damned before you rejected your God. He damned you for raising spirits. He damned you for impure thoughts. He damned you for coveting knowledge, though it was your nature, the nature he claims to have given you. If he really was the creator, what a funny fellow he must be to make such a flawed creature and then blame it for its imperfections. Bring me a fish, good Edwin, for I am hungry."

The priest got up off the bed and went downstairs. There was a knock at the door, which, as usual, he ignored. Beggars often came for alms to the house, but they should have known to apply at the church.

He went into the kitchen. Since the demon had arrived he had been forced to take better care of his domestic arrangements because it had a prodigious appetite for salted fish. He took a herring from the cool slab and walked along the corridor back to the stairs.

There was a click and Edwin realized with a shock that someone had picked the lock in the front door. His instinct was to run off and raise a hue and cry, but he couldn't do that with the demon in the house. So he remained transfixed for a heartbeat too long.

Suddenly, in the doorway, stood one of the most remarkable figures he had ever seen—a giant of a man with a shaggy red beard and long red hair, a pauper by his dress, lean but muscular. He strode toward Edwin and lifted the priest up by his throat, pinning him against the wall.

"Where he?"

Edwin could hardly speak. Around the stranger's head, rising and falling with the bouncing flight of bats, two little demons chattered and pointed, tiny men with horns on their heads and pitchforks in their hands, wings beating the air. One was a mottled blue, the other a patchy black and red, and both seemed in a state of high excitement.

"Where's who?" Even in his predicament, Edwin was fascinated by the demons—wanted to question them, to measure and draw them.

"Dowzabel. Where Dowzabel?

Four other men were in the house, running up the stairs, down into the cellar. Edwin's mind was shot with panic and he feared they were magistrates looking for evidence of his magical investigations. Bardi and the influence he bought had long protected him, but now Bardi's money was withdrawn and, with it, his protection.

"We're looking for the boy." It was a female voice. The pressure on his throat lessened slightly and he managed to turn his head to see a great fat woman in a ragged red velvet gown beside him.

"He's not here," said Edwin.

"Where he? Where he?"

"Gone to France to seek an angel."

The big man clearly didn't understand what Edwin was saying.

The woman took Edwin by the arm in a meaty grip. "He must come to Southwark with me. He cured my girl and there are plenty more who need his touch."

There was a shout from upstairs and the big man bundled the priest down the corridor and pushed him up the stairs. The men had found Know-Much.

Edwin went into his bedroom to discover the demon sitting in a corner and the men surrounding it. The demon spoke in a strange language and the men answered it in the same tongue. Edwin recognized it as the Cornish the boy had spoken when he first arrived.

One word emerged again and again: "Cuthman."

"What are they saying, Know-Much?"

"They call me cuthman, which means friend," said the demon, "and are asking if you are lying about the boy."

Edwin asked, "What did you say?"

"I said not. I said you were one of them. It's time to move, Edwin. Lucifer is coming back to the world and has sent his Antichrist ahead of him. The world needs to know. Will you announce it? Will you be John the Baptist?"

"Why me?"

"People will believe a priest. You can persuade your fellows."

"That way lies death. The church would burn me."

"They'd have to find you and take you first." It was the woman's voice. Edwin thought it shameful that she was coming into his bedroom, but he tried to heed the demon, who had said there was no shame in the intermingling of the sexes, even in nakedness.

"What do you mean?" he asked her.

"These men of Cornwall are twenty strong, fierce robbers, led by an ympe to seek Dowzabel. In Southwark, people are more loyal to the whores than they are to the king. You preach there, you go to the woods in Peckham and beyond and come in and out of town. They'll try to take you, but you'll spread your message."

Edwin bowed his head. "I have not the strength. I have rejected God, but I cannot yet embrace Lucifer."

Greatbelly laughed. "You seem to have done a good job of embracing him here. Listen, priest, I was as godly a whore as ever lay with a man, but I saw what the boy did for my girl."

"That is not proof."

"It was proof enough for Elijah's housewife," said Know-Much.

Edwin remembered the passage from Kings. Elijah had cured a woman's sick son. The woman said: *Now by this I know, that thou art a man of God, and that the word of the Lord from thy mouth is truth.* Dow had affected a miraculous cure, he had commanded demons back to Hell, sent a man to Hell. Edwin could only believe the words of the demon to be true. Why quest after knowledge, why go to such lengths, if you did not believe what you discovered? And then, if you did believe it, if you were sickened by seeing the bishops and the cardinals preaching a creed of poverty while drinking from jewelled cups, how could you not act?

"I've seen your sort before," said Greatbelly, "loitering at the knocking shop door: the first time, coming on a Monday, not making it in; coming on the Tuesday, turning back on the step. By Saturday, drunk, full of piss and wind, you finally make it in and up the stairs. After that we're seeing you nightly for the rest of your life. You can't admit what you know you want for shame of what others might think."

The big man pointed at the demon, spoke, and then pointed back at Edwin.

The demon translated. "He says that if Hell has granted you a familiar then your destiny is set. Lucifer has put his trust in you."

A little demon settled on Greatbelly's shoulder and another on the shaggy-haired giant's. The giant spoke again, using that word "Cuthman," and his demon translated for him, its voice like the buzz of a wasp. "Already the Welsh bowmen the English king invited here have called Lucifer 'friend.' My brothers and sisters fly to the country too."

"You will be crushed if you try to revolt," said Edwin.

"Now we will," said Greatbelly, "yes, we will. But in five years' time, when the demon's whispers have echoed to a roar, when your voice has stirred up the poor, what then? I have listened to these demons spreading the word of these honest men of Cornwall and, like you I know there is naught as strong as truth."

"We rise in secret," said the wasp-voiced demon, "and when we are legion, then it will be too late for the armies of the Usurper God, of the Horror, to overthrow us."

"Imagine," said Know-Much, "you can create a paradise on earth."

"And have a roll in the hay without feeling guilty," said Greatbelly, "though I am not yet decided if that will increase or decrease the need for whores."

Edwin looked around him, the bare boards, the moldering walls. He had ignored the world even as he had sought knowledge of it. He had discovered what he had set out to discover, achieved enlightenment. Now was the time to put his theories into practice. And would he not be an important man?

The giant put one hand on Edwin's shoulder and with the other he made the sign the boy Dow had made—two fingers and a thumb, palm toward his face, the three tines of the pitchfork.

"Pestrior," he said.

"He calls you 'wizard,'" said Know-Much.

"Got a better ring to it than 'priest,'" said Greatbelly. "Return his sign, answer that you are his friend with the trifork."

"What's that?"

"His hand sign," explained Greatbelly. "Lucifer's pitchfork, sign of the cruelties of the devils, sign of cruelty turned against itself in revolution."

Edwin extended his hand to mirror the giant's. "Cuthman," he said. "Now come on, because we have work to do."

19

J egudiel hit the floor with a sound like the boom of the sea; Sariel screamed and in her scream were all the hateful noises Montagu had ever heard—the death of horses, the anguish of men burned by oil or crushed by rocks, the cries of the women in looted and smashed towns. There was a flash of white light, so intense that Montagu lost his vision for a moment and when it returned the woman lay still on the floor. The mercenary, the youth, and the angel all lay in a heap nearby. The light from the windows was dim now, as if dusk had come down. Only the votive candles gave any light to see by.

Montagu shivered. A couple of years ago he would never have thought such an act of sacrilege possible. Now he saw it with his own eyes. He immediately realized he could not allow the angel's body to fall into the hands of the French. Too many potential relics.

Osbert crouched with his hands over his ears. Then he began trying to pluck the angel like a goose, not minding that it had a dead soldier and a fallen boy slumped on top of it.

Montagu had never seen such sacrilege—that a low man should presume to act so. He leapt forward and kicked him away, ignoring his indignant cries.

There were voices outside the chapel. The little boy Charles ran to the doors to shut them, shouting to those still alive among the guards outside that he had vanquished the devils and they had better guard the doors better this time.

He then turned to Montagu. "Who are you that kicks his superiors as if he were a king?" asked Charles.

"Montagu, Lord Marschal of England, who bows only to kings," said Montagu.

"Montagu—in those rags?" said the puzzled young boy. Charles had seen six devils and an angel die in front of him, but he seemed to find it more remarkable a nobleman should dress in a pauper's clothing.

"Yes," said Montagu. He bent to the angel, pulling the soldier and the youth off its body. The lance was right through it and the angel showed no signs of life. Montagu checked the soldier's breathing. None. The youth seemed dead too. Long habit made Montagu ignore the common men's misfortune. Nobles received care after battle; everyone else was left to the mercy of God.

"This is too valuable to your Valois enemies," said Montagu. "Its relics could turn the war in their favor. You need to remove it."

"Which was sort of my point in pulling out its feathers," said the pardoner. If the man hadn't helped him escape prison, Montagu would have cut him down where he stood.

"Get a cart of some sort," ordered Montagu. "We'll get its body onto that and remove it from here."

"As a prince, I'm not sure I like taking orders from earls," said Charles.

"Then watch the Valois prosper," said Montagu.

"I can't order a cart," said Charles. "A man of my station cannot be associated with farm transport. That may do for you English nobility, but we of the higher courts of France cannot speak of such things. We're not"—he pondered, searching for a word—"rural."

"I'll get the cart," said the pardoner, "if you tell me who is ordering."

"Go outside and tell them the prince of Navarre commands it," said Charles.

"And a big cloth, a tapestry, a sheet, anything to cover the body—but a big one," said Montagu.

The pardoner sidled through the door.

"We'll need a few men to move the angel," said Charles, "and that knave who killed it too."

"Why him?" said Montagu.

"He is a useful servant," said Charles, "alive or dead."

"What do you mean?"

"He may be holy or unholy. It's worth slicing him up for relics just in case."

But Montagu knew time was short. "We need to focus on moving the angel," he said.

"Agreed," said Charles. "It might suit my enemies at court very well to blame me for this crime, and the longer we stay here the more chance we have of being discovered."

"How old are you?" said Montagu.

"Eight, by my count."

"God help us when you're twenty," said Montagu. The boy spoke like a seasoned courtier of thirty.

"My God, it would be good to take the woman, also, if we could!" said Charles.

"Why?" Montagu was casting around for something that he could wrap the angel in. He could hardly drag a nine-foot-tall winged man out into the streets of Paris and hope to escape notice.

"I find your questions impertinent, Montagu," said Charles. "This woman brought about the situation where this murder was possible." He nodded to the body of the angel. "That is all you need to know and all I will tell you."

Montagu snorted. He inspected the body of the angel, crossing himself. He was somewhere between panic and glee. They had dealt a blow to the French from which it would be difficult to recover. Perhaps Charles was right. They'd accounted for a French angel at no peril at all to their immortal souls. The French had six other angels, but this, Jegudiel, which some said was an archangel, was the one that had regular contact with the French king, the one on whom had been lavished the greatest splendor, the most wonderful architecture.

He thought of old Edward, still alive in the east, surrounded by his angels. Montagu felt again for a pulse on Dow. This boy, an angel assassin, could be useful, if he could repeat the trick. The best thing about him was that he identified with Lucifer, so he needed no prompting to do this work. Montagu took the blackbird demon's sword and stuffed it under his arm. He might need to arm one of his companions yet.

He smiled to himself. Perhaps Edward had been right to be confident. The English army was well-trained and drilled, though small. They could face the French and win without divine help. That was cause for celebration. Though the death of one of God's holy angels was not.

As they waited for the pardoner, Montagu noticed the head of the cardinal on the floor. It was blinking at him. Montagu crossed himself and the head moved its lips. It was trying to speak. A devil, no doubt. No time to worry about that now.

The pardoner returned. "I have six good men to help, and transport is at the ready," he said.

"No, no, no, that won't do at all," said Charles. He slid through the doors himself and Montagu heard him ordering the hall cleared. There was a dragging noise and the pardoner backed in to the chapel, pulling an enormous tapestry.

"Well, help me then!" he said.

"Princes do not toil," said Charles.

Under the circumstances, Montagu opted to forego his pride and pull the tapestry into the room.

They removed the lance from the angel's chest and covered the body with the tapestry, spreading it carefully over the wings.

"Come on," said the pardoner, "this beats a shawl of St. Anne knocked up behind Spitalfields market! Even the tapestry will be valuable once it's bled out a bit onto it! You've earned damnation but will gain coins."

"Shut up," said Montagu.

They tried to lift the angel but, though it was much lighter than a man of its size would have been, its wings rendered it cumbersome.

Twice they dropped it. When finally they dragged it from the other bodies, the Florentine sat up, blinking. There was a hole in his tunic, but he bled no more.

"Sariel! Dow!" Orsino stood, then knelt to check Dow. "The boy's breathing," he said. He put his hand to the girl's neck and then to her mouth.

"Dead," he said, and crossed himself. He made the sign of the cross over her. "She needs blessing. She needs a priest. She . . ." His voice faltered and he cast his arm around her, sobbing.

"Pull yourself together, Florentine!" Montagu shouted. "The royalty here can protect us for only so long. If you want to live we need to leave now!"

"The French will honor her?"

"She'll have a Christian burial, I'll see to it," said Charles. "Now hurry."

"You see to it," said Orsino. "I should stay here and die. I have gone beyond sin; there is no way forward."

"Only *do* then," said Montagu. "Follow orders, low man, and weep when there is time for weeping. For now, assist me."

Orsino was a soldier to his boots, and the command snapped him from his reverie. He approached the bundled angel, taking the end the pardoner had been holding, and, with Montagu, on his command, they lifted it.

Orsino grunted. His eyes were vacant; he was still recovering from what would have been his mortal blow were it not for the angel's blood.

Four thumps hammered on the door. "It's me, Joan!"

"With guards?" shouted Charles.

"Yes."

"Put them to clearing the street!" said Charles. "We're coming out soon!"

"There's no need to clear it. It's dark out here," said Joan. "Like night! The commoners are running for their burrows like rabbits from a hawk."

"Just clear people from the street, Mother. No one must see us come out. Tell the guards to kill any who do!"

"Yes, son!"

"Glad to see you alive, Orsino," said the pardoner. He had the crown of thorns down from the altar and was trying to look for somewhere to stuff it that wouldn't prick him.

"Thank you, pardoner." The soldier glanced to the tear in his tunic.

"Angel's blood," said the pardoner, taking off his borrowed surcoat to wrap the crown. "It's a great healer. I know; I sell it for tuppence a bottle. Can heal the body but not the soul, eh, Florentine?"

"Why isn't the angel healed, then?" said Charles. Osbert saw the boy's eyes flick to the crown of thorns, but the child said nothing. Perhaps he would let him have it as a reward. Or perhaps he would just let him carry it and take it off him later. The pardoner knew which outcome he'd put his money on.

"The lance killed Christ," said the pardoner. "It is a bane to holy things. Probably why it didn't do you much harm, eh, Orsino? An angel killer, imagine that! And I thought I had some sins to answer for!"

Orsino's stare was empty. Montagu had seen that look before—siege madness, when men had been under assault for too long. They were there in body but not in mind. You never really recovered from it, in his experience.

Orsino and Montagu carried the angel out into the street. The guards had done a reasonable job of clearing the area, aided by a suddenly dark sky. It was as if twilight had come at noon—the sky was cloudless but the sun unaccountably dim, no more than a silver disk, the morning star visible beside it. Men had made themselves scarce.

"There's no cart!" said Charles.

"I found a boat," said the pardoner. "Harder for people to poke their noses under our blanket that way and more private."

"Very well," said Charles, "we'll head for my cog *Esperanza* and ship this off to Navarre where it belongs. And you can rejoin your army, Montagu—if they'll have you in those rags."

"Indeed," said Montagu.

He thought of the letter that he so wished to give to King Edward. But France had suffered a blow in the Sainte-Chapelle. If England could recoup all its angels, it might deliver a decisive blow. He had to find Good Jacques, to discover where the old king had gone.

They carried the angel down to the boat—just a small river barge. It had one man on board, on old countryman who repeatedly crossed himself as he looked up at the dark sky. Chevalier D'Évreux and Count Ramon came running to Charles's side as Orsino went back to fetch Dow's body.

"We must go with you, lord."

Charles said, "I will be perfectly well on my own. We have an excuse. Say these men kidnapped me."

"Are you sure, son?" Queen Joan was behind her nobles.

"Perfectly sure, Mother," said the boy. "You just stay here and concentrate on explaining all this to our Valois cousins. Uncle John and Uncle Philip will need some sort of letter explaining this lamentable Satanic attack upon their angel, and before any other interpretations can reach them."

Montagu stared in wonder at the precocious child. He turned his eyes to Joan. He knew what was said of the Capetian queens. Had she bought blessings on her son through sorcery?

"Montagu, I want your word you will protect my son," said Joan.

"You have it, madam," he said.

"Good," said Joan. She reached into the folds of her dress, took out a small purse, and threw it to the earl. "Recompense for whatever they took from you when they put you in the prison," she said, "and funds for our ally."

Montagu was too practical a man to object. He simply bowed and said, "I shall return the favor at my earliest convenience."

Joan waved in dismissal. "Think nothing of it, William. It's good to have dealings with men of true breeding after so long in the company of these merchant-mannered Valois."

Again, Montagu bowed. He glanced toward Orsino, toward Dow. Charles ordered the boat pushed off and it slipped into the main course of the river.

20

They bled the angel in the barn, like a pig. The farmer left the buckets at the door, forbidden from entering by the men of the *Esperanza* who were, in turn, forbidden from entering by Charles. Every bottle in the Navarrese fleet had been requisitioned for the angel's blood. Montagu had guarded the angel every inch of the way down the river but, as the pardoner helped carry the angel into the barn, he put his finger into the wound at its throat. Then he went to the youth and rubbed the blood onto his lips.

The first thing Dow knew was a cold, prickling sensation. He opened his eyes to see the great body stretched out before him, its wings spread. In the dark of the barn it glowed faintly like a hoard of treasure in a fireside tale, its symmetry, its perfection, even more striking in death. Dow felt sorry for it. It was a thing of great beauty, but it had been rotten. Why could it not rejoice in its own perfection without scorning others less lucky than itself?

"I did that?" he asked.

"I did," said Orsino. He crossed himself.

"Sariel?"

"Dead."

Orsino took Dow's hand and the boy let him. For the first time since Orsino had known him, he saw tears in the young man's eyes.

"She will go to Heaven," said Orsino.

"Or to eternal torment," said Dow. "For that is where God will send her."

Orsino let go of Dow's hand. He said, "You are cruel."

"God is cruel, Orsino. Read your Bible." Dow thought of the dead angel. Others would need to die if Free Hell was to come to earth. The banner, the banner could answer all those problems. But would he have the strength to carry on if he let go of his hate? Sariel had asked him to do so. In honor of her, he must try.

"Help me open the gates of Hell and you may see her again," he said.

"You think she will live again?"

"When Hell is opened there will be a resurrection, but it will be God who is judged, not he who does the judging."

"We should atone."

"There is no atonement for what we have done," said Dow. "Our hope lies in Lucifer."

Montagu looked up from examining the angel. "You follow Lucifer?" he asked him.

"I've nothing to say to you, high man."

"I should kill you," said Montagu.

"Then you'll need to kill me first," said Orsino.

"Thank you. I'll remember that," said Montagu.

Outside the light was growing. Osbert put his eye to a crack in the boards. "Day's coming back," he said, "just in time for dusk. Story of my life. What caused that darkness, do you reckon?"

"The angel's death," said Montagu. "I've heard of such a thing happening before." He bent over the body.

The pardoner nodded, seemingly impressed by Montagu's wisdom.

Montagu ran his fingers over the creature's feathers, while the pardoner hunted through the barn.

"What are you looking for?" said Montagu.

Osbert replied, "A sack."

"For what?"

"The crown of thorns."

"Good. Find one, then give the crown to me."

"Er, it's mine. I took it."

Montagu tapped the sword at his side. He said, "And this is mine."

"I'll get you a sack," said Osbert hurriedly.

"I am the prince here," said Charles. "Rightfully, that is mine."

"I am the Englishman," said Montagu. "And as such, the pinnacle of God's creation."

The boy gave Montagu an evaluating look, a cattish, sideways movement of the head, but he said nothing.

Orsino sat with his head in his hands. "Sariel was so like my wife," said Orsino. "I was always a fool for jealousy. I must atone."

"I could probably help with that," said Osbert, from the back of the barn. "Anything can be forgiven for the right price. I mean anything. St. Julian the Hospitaller stabbed his parents to death, gave the church a load of coin to build hospitals, and, before you know it, his face is turning up on pilgrims' medals. That shows how forgiving the Lord is to those who have the coin to pay. Absolution's my game. I'd be prepared to try to arrange a donation, for a reasonable cut of course."

"I killed an angel."

"You could kill him," said the pardoner, nodding to Dow. "He's a morally repulsive heretic. That's got to be worth a few years off eternal torment."

Orsino stared at the angel. "There's been enough killing," he said.

"How many have the angels killed?" said Dow. "How many will they kill according to your holy book? You acted as God acts, that is all."

The Florentine said, "And that in itself will see me in Hell."

Dow put his hand on Orsino's shoulder. "I killed it," he said. "I struck the last blow."

"But I struck at it. I am damned."

"Oh, don't be so glum," said the pardoner. "Absolution's an easy thing! Gold here, deeds there. Gold and deeds, that's what God likes. Try bringing Dow back to God's purpose if you're not going to kill him. Convert one such as he and surely God would love you."

"There is no way back for me," said Orsino.

"Is your God so unforgiving?" asked Dow.

"Yes," said Orsino.

"No!" said the pardoner. "Raising your hand against an angel and surviving shows God must be on your side. He might not have liked that angel. It probably had a sarcastic tone when it was praising him or something."

"Oh my word, this is tiresome," said Charles. "Men, this is all very well, but we have a task here. If it is to be hid it will need to be cut up."

Dow looked down at the glowing corpse.

"Who will do the work?" said Charles. "A good purse for any who say yes."

"I'll do it," said Dow. Money would be useful for wherever he went next, and it pleased him to see such a being bled, plucked, and skinned. Great men had built palaces in its name, using wealth that could have fed a nation. Now the poor would reap some return on the investment—he would make sure of that.

"This is sacrilege," said Orsino.

"They hack to bits every saint they ever find. How's this any different?" said the pardoner.

"Can it be cut by normal knives?" said Charles.

"This isn't a normal knife," said Dow, producing the long, thin boning blade he had taken from the cardinal devil.

"How far shall we render it?" said Charles. "Do we just bleed it or pluck it or chop it up? We could put a tooth in the pommel of all our best knights' swords. Chop, chop, chop, so goes the sound of the cutting block!"

"Just make sure people can't know what it is. If your men found out they were transporting the body of a murdered angel, God knows what effect it would have on their morale," said Montagu.

"Send for barrels," said Charles to the pardoner.

"Do you not have a coffin?" Osbert asked.

"They don't need them at sea," said Charles, "and besides, where would we get one big enough? Cut it up for transport and drain the blood if we can—that is full of holy power, as we saw by what happened to these low men." He nodded to Dow and Orsino.

"Don't be stupid," said Montagu. "Wrap it in cerecloth as if it were embalmed. Then we can carry it to the boat ourselves and have it hidden in the hold. You can't chop it up like a bit of mutton."

"Although you can pluck it like a goose," said Osbert, pulling another feather from the angel's wings.

"Don't you defile it, common man," said Charles. "Go and communicate our message to our men. Bring cerecloth."

Osbert stuck his head around the barn door and spent some time trying to get his point across to the Navarrese. Eventually, the cloth was brought.

First they took the angel's armor. The mail was marvelously light, more like tightly woven wool than metal. Like the angel's corpse, it too faintly glowed in the barn's dark. Montagu put it on. It was too long by far for him, more like a gown than a hauberk, but it was so light that it didn't matter. It was no encumbrance at all. The breastplate was enormous, covering all the angel's chest. Dow went to take the great sword, but Montagu got there first.

"This isn't a knave's weapon," said Montagu. "Angels are the nobility of Heaven and their artifacts by right belong to the nobility of earth."

If Dow hadn't been hoping that Montagu had information about the king, he would have stabbed him there and then. Instead, he let the noble take the sword.

"It's as light as a reed in the hand," said Montagu. He tried it against a log in a woodpile. A lazy swing was all it took to split it.

"Those things are rightfully mine," said Charles.

"You cannot use them," said Montagu, "and if France is your enemy, it is best that they go to a man who will split French skulls with them." He picked up the shield.

"Recognize my royalty and pass it to me," said Charles.

"I recognize you're a little boy, though a precocious and forward one," said Montagu.

Charles stood up tall. "You have no right to snatch it for yourself. Does rank and propriety mean nothing to you, Montagu?"

"They mean everything," said Montagu. "But I am a practical man. And it's not even for me. You—Florentine."

Orsino lifted his eyes from his boots.

"I know your master. I know your purpose. Take the sword and the armor. You'll need to buy horses for where you're going. The knights won't take you seriously without one."

He passed Orsino the sword and shield. "Take the mail, too," said Montagu, taking it off.

"Why not give him the holy lance of Christ while you're at it?" said Charles.

"I'll take that myself."

Charles was too well bred to make any great demonstration of disapproval. "Am I to have nothing?" he said.

"You get the body," said Montagu. "Care for it well."

This brought a smile to the boy's lips.

"How about me?" said the pardoner. "Without me you wouldn't have escaped."

"You," said Montagu, "were consorting with devils. You are lucky not to be killed where you stand."

"That's interesting," said Charles. "Did you know devils serve God, Montagu?"

"Heresy," said Montagu.

"The truth," said Charles.

"Devils have whispered in your ear, and I won't listen to their lies."

"But you will strip and gut an angel?" gibed Charles.

"These artifacts will still do God's work," insisted Montagu.

"They certainly will," said Charles, "as interpreted by his devils."

When the angel was naked, Dow threw a rope over the rafters and hoisted it up by its feet. Orsino just sat in the corner of the barn, rocking back and forth, crossing himself and muttering prayers.

"Will the blood flow now?" said the pardoner. "This wouldn't work with a pig—it would be clotted."

"It may surprise you," said Montagu, "but I have no experience of bleeding an angel."

The angel's wings were spread wide and Dow was struck by its fearful beauty, the pale bright skin, the long limbs, and the hair of gold. He moved his knife across its throat. A bright stream of crimson splashed into the bucket.

"They bleed better than a pig," said the pardoner.

"The low man's view of the most wondrous of God's creations," said Montagu. "'It bleeds better than a pig.'"

The pardoner reached around the back of the angel to squeeze and push at its chest, trying to press the last of the blood from it. "More valuable than gold!" he said.

Dow filled the bottles as best he could. Dow knew that angel's blood was an ingredient in the most ambitious summoning spells, and he also knew that high men would not allow him as much as a hair from the angel's head, so he was careful to use a number of small bottles to collect the blood, to make it easier to steal one. As it splashed on his hands it tingled on his skin.

"Pluck it," said Charles, when the angel was drained, and Dow did. As he plucked Dow was amazed to find no structure beneath the feathers. All there was were feathers, layer upon layer of them. By the time he'd finished he'd filled six sacks with them and secreted one feather for himself.

When that was done they took it down and wrapped the body in the waxy cerecloth. Dow was covered in the blood by the time he'd finished, his whole body tingling.

Montagu took a bottle of blood and passed it to Orsino.

"He's having those as well, is he?" said Charles.

"You have the bulk of the body and the feathers," said Montagu. "There lie the most powerful relics in Christendom. Be grateful for them."

"Gratitude is not for princes. I'm not sure I like your tone," said Charles. "And you still have the crown of thorns."

"Yes," said Montagu, picking up the sack from where the pardoner had kicked it behind a pile of straw.

"I took it, I should have it," said the pardoner.

It was as if he didn't exist. No one even acknowledged that he had spoken.

"I'm not expecting you to like it," continued Montagu. "I defer to you as a prince, but you must defer to me as an elder."

Charles snorted. "I want that crown," he said.

"Not possible," said Montagu. "Now, Florentine, you are commissioned by Bardi?"

Orsino replied, "I am."

"To the purpose of murder?"

"That is my trade."

"This angel spoke before it died. It said the one you seek is where the snake eats the man. Do you know the place meant? Answer me, man. You've sinned and now you must seek redemption, do what you have to and King Edward himself will intercede for you, I guarantee it."

Orsino shrugged. "Sounds like Milan," he said. His voice was weak and he did not look at Montagu directly.

"Why so?" Montagu asked him.

"It is the city's sign."

"Then go there. Though why it's beyond these creatures to speak plainly, I don't know."

"How shall we know the man we're looking for?" said Dow.

"You know who he is?" said Montagu.

"Yes."

"The Hospitallers have him, I believe. You can find a way. I have questions to ask here and when I get the answers, I'll send word to you. Is there an inn you know that could receive a letter?"

Dow whistled and down from the rafters fluttered Murmur to perch on his shoulder.

"Good God!" said Montagu. He drew Arondight.

"I don't like that thing," said Charles. He drew his little sword.

"This is Murmur," said Dow. "Call his name."

"And he'll hear me across a continent?"

"Say it to the skies," said the ympe. "Free Hell will hear you."

"What it is to trade with demons," said Montagu. Montagu gestured to where he had put the blackbird demon's sword, the falchion, big and heavy. "There," he said to Dow. "Take that. You are an enemy of God and so more useful than you think. You can't damn the damned, eh, Florentine? Take the youth. Let him do what needs to be done. Edward will absolve you of all sin as is his right to do."

"Can he really do that?" said Orsino.

"He can. Forgiveness is there for you. God's, if not your own."

"Returning to more immediate concerns," said Osbert, rubbing his hands. "What's my share of the loot?"

Once again he was ignored.

Montagu turned to Charles. "Now, Charles, clear all your men but those you trust the most. We'll convey the angel to the ship. After that, you indicate you've been abducted by us and threatened, and want a rowing boat. We'll drop the mercenary and the boy as soon as we can and then I'm afraid you're going to have to walk back into Paris. Are you ready?"

"Yes," said Charles. "With these relics we'll lead old Philip a merry dance."

"So I get nothing, do I?" said the pardoner. "The sum total of my reward. Sod all. A bucket full of nowt. Not even crap in my hat."

Montagu took a handful of feathers and a bottle of angel's blood and stuffed them inside his tunic. Then he pulled back the door of the barn and Charles called for his men.

21

T he *Thomas* lay at anchor in the broad estuary of the Swin. Around it in the pale dawn lay the spoils of the battle—nearly two hundred ships captured, among them the *Christopher* and the *Edward*, both back in English hands where they belonged. Many were beyond claiming, though, burned hulks clinging to the shore, black and wet as mussels, stranded where their captains had beached them in a bid to make the land before the angel's fire consumed them.

Edward looked over the scene with satisfaction, a rosary in his fingers. God had made it clear whose side He was on. The angel turned and sparkled above Edward's mast, a huge circle twenty yards around. Beneath it Béhuchet, that Channel pirate, swung by his neck from the yard of the *Christopher*. It had been more than a week since the battle, but Edward would leave him there until he rotted away. Still the water around him bobbed with corpses like so many lilies in a bloody pond.

"The figures are in, sir. Eighteen thousand dead French, at my estimate."

Sir Robert Morley, the admiral, was alongside him, in a fine green coat embroidered with a golden ship. He'd been wearing it daily since the battle. He must have been confident of a victory, thought Edward. No point splashing out on something like that if you were going to get caught or killed. Then again, if you were going to drown, you might as well do so looking good.

"Only God could have given us such a victory," said Edward.

"Him, his angel, and some tough English bastards," said Morley.

Edward laughed. Morley was a pretentious sort of admiral who had always affected to speak French and know little of the language of the common man. He'd become a whole lot more English after the battle and now spoke like a London merchant.

Edward had several plans forming in his head. He had two thousand men with him—around thirteen hundred archers. They'd need horses—there simply hadn't been enough space to bring them, so he had to wait until they could be brought from England, hence his delay in Sluys. These men were his core. He could rely on his Flemish allies for thousands and thousands more men—one hundred and fifty thousand, his negotiators were saying, though that struck Edward as highly optimistic. Even if it were true, most of them were more at home pulling the shuttle on a loom than a longbow string. Still, the situation was promising.

The French were in Artois, so Edward's force would divide, some marching under Robert of Artois to stop a counterattack on Flanders. *He* should cause Philip problems as the locals rallied to his flag. Philip had disinherited him from his ancestral lands, which was why he had come to the English flag. With luck the French might face a battle against both external and internal foes.

Edward would go south to the rich town of Tournai, the strategic key to the whole North. That taken, and the valuable weaving town secure, they could strike into France proper and take Lille. There he would await the demons, hand over the town to them and be done. Lille was too strategically important to the French for the town to be allowed to stay in enemy hands and, Edward's bargain fulfilled, it would bound to be retaken, with luck at great cost to both the French and the demons. That didn't matter—his part in the whole business would be done and his children safe.

A small cog cut a broad arc into the bay, flying the cross of St. George from its mast. At the side of the *Thomas*, rowing boats were docking. Edward's commanders were coming aboard. Doubters, the lot of them, dogs come to feast on the lion's kill. Well, he'd let them. At least Robert of Artois was among them. There was a warlike man, even if he was French.

Edward looked out at the scavengers looting the bodies on the shore. Flemings—they'd stood half the battle on the shore waiting to see who was winning and come to the aid of the English as soon as it was obvious the battle was going their way. That, he thought, was a taste of things to come. Victory breeds allies. A party of his longbowmen moved among them. One of them was talking loudly, gesturing and pointing up at the angel. There was some sort of disagreement going on between them because some men applauded what he said, while others tried to shout him down.

He turned to Morley. Edward said, "You'd think we could have unity after a battle like this."

Morley replied, "That's what happens when you stick the Cornish in units alongside anyone else. There's a reason God put them so far away."

"Trouble?"

"Talk. We should hang a couple of the dissenters."

"Dissent?"

"Religious. A cult. They put Lucifer above God," said Morley.

Edward crossed himself.

"We've let it go so far because they're bowmen. We can't start hanging them and doing the enemy's work for them."

"What dissent?" Edward asked him.

"Oh, don't ask me. I can hardly understand a word they say. I had a man flogged for it a month back. He said the fighting poor have more common cause with the fighting poor of the enemy than they do with any high men."

"That's unnatural talk."

Morley said, "Quite. I've heard less of it since the angel appeared."

Edward watched the men a while longer. Eventually the man who had been talking the loudest was left alone, even by those who appeared to agree with him. He pointed up at the angel and began to shout, "Drogoberer! Turant!"

"What is he talking about?"

"Cornish gibberish."

"Have him brought here," said Edward. "I want to talk to him and, if he can't speak English or French, get someone who can translate."

"Very good, sir."

The little cog was nearing the ship now, and he could look down to see two of his paymasters, Sir Peter Henry and Sir Robert Jollibois, on its deck. Messengers from England. He hoped they had more money for him. They wore big smiles and waved as grappling ropes were thrown up onto the *Thomas*. Shortly a sailor secured a rope ladder and they boarded.

"God blesses you, Edward!" Henry threw his arms around the king.

"I never doubted it. I am England. What else could He do?"

Jollibois gazed up at the angel. He said, "All doubt ends when you look at that. Have you ever seen anything as terrible? Did it smite the French?"

"It caused a good deal of panic and set fire to some of their boats," said Edward, "but most usefully it persuaded their angel to go away."

"Praise to God," said Jollibois. "And thanks for talking to him, Your Holiness. Consider my mother, sick at Hythe." He bowed to the angel.

The king said, "There is no question: God weighed my right against Philip's and decided for me."

"Marvelous," said Henry.

"Do you have good news for me?" said Edward.

"Parliament has sent us to confirm the news of the battle," said Jollibois.

"They think I would lie?"

"Surely not sir," said Jollibois. "It's just that . . ."

"They think I lie."

Jollibois smiled. He said, "You do not lie, my lord; we see the evidence here. We'll sail back on the next tide and then the news will be good indeed. I'm sure of it. They have to back you, Edward!"

On the shore the Cornishman who had been shouting at the angel ran as he realized the little rowing boat released from the *Thomas* was coming for him. He wouldn't run for long. The men-at-arms on the boat had a big alaunt with them and already it was straining to jump from the boat to chase the man. Edward regretted that. It wasn't good for his men to see their masters treating their fellows that way. Although, if the man was a troublemaker, they'd have to make an example of him. It was the only politic thing to do.

"A criminal?" ventured Jollibois.

He said, "A troublemaker. A heretic, by all accounts."

The two nobles exchanged glances.

"The *Thomas* has a cabin?" said Henry.

Edward said, "Yes."

Henry said, "Can we go within?"

"It's mighty small."

"We have something that is not for all men's eyes."

"As you wish."

The men walked back to the cabin. It was indeed small—room for a bedroll, a chest, and not much else. Edward kicked the mattress onto its side to give the men more room to stand. Still, they had to crouch.

Henry spoke first. "The wool levy at home is not going well."

"Montagu turns his back for a second and I hear this. Not well, meaning badly? How badly?" Edward asked.

"Very badly. The expected money will not arrive. We have enough to pay *some* of the bankers." Henry swallowed. He added, "At present we don't have enough money to cover even the daily expenses of your household. But there is hope. Parliament must offer to raise taxes after this success."

"What's the excuse?"

"The normal ones. And the pirate Robert Houdetot has raised a squadron of ships under Philip's flag and captured thirty wool ships on their way here. They have also burned towns on the Isle of Wight, on Portland, Teignmouth, and made damage at Plymouth. Sark has fallen."

"This," said Edward, pointing to the captured ships of Sluys, "was supposed to have ended French sea power for a generation! You're telling me they're back up and running in just ten days? Send the ships of the northern Admiralty to the Channel Islands and make sure all ships leaving are in convoy. Morley, raise a fleet and attack Brest—there are plenty of merchants sheltered there. We'll pick up their cargoes."

"Brittany has not declared herself in this war. Brest is a neutral port, lord," reminded Morley.

"Not anymore," said Edward. "And speed up the wool collection."

No one could meet the king's eyes.

"What?" said Edward.

"The wool collection itself is failing. It's not a matter of efficiency. We're meeting resistance."

"What resistance?"

Neither of the nobles wanted to speak.

"You, Jollibois, tell me."

He said, "There is real fear the wool levy will spark a civil war."

"How so?" asked Edward.

"Men are openly defiant, and the poorer sort are preaching a new heresy. Revolution. The upending of God's order. They would make kings paupers and paupers kings."

"Society could not exist that way. They depend on us for each breath they take. The poor owe us everything. Who owns the lands they till? Who protects them in war and prays for them in peace? This is ingratitude."

"It's worse." Henry had a shoulder bag. He opened it and shook its contents onto the chest. Edward sank to his knees to examine them more clearly. On the top of the chest lay the body of a demon—a mottled green and black, no bigger than a rat, but with folded wings and a horned head. It had a big wound in its belly, going through to its back.

"What is this?" said Edward.

"The people call them whisperers," said Henry. "It's a whispering demon."

"Explain yourself."

"These are behind the sedition—well, them and few mad marketplace yammerers. They've been turning up all over the place. We've reports of many in London. They creep to the beds of the poor at night and whisper lies in their ears. There was a swarm of them over Shoreditch."

The king said, "Are they believed?"

"To some degree. Yes."

"What do they say?"

"That Lucifer is Lord of Creation, God the usurper. Christ was Lucifer come to earth—his memory tarnished and stolen by God."

Edward crossed himself. He said, "Ridiculous."

"But stopping our supply of funds. The poor have little wool and need no incentive to hold on to it. But this doctrine has sympathy among some of the lower merchants, and the disobedience of low men emboldens those above them."

"How was this killed?" He went to prod the creature but drew back his finger, unsure if it was safe to touch.

"It came to the servant of Sir Geoffrey Cheynes while she was bathing in the river at evening. Sir Geoffrey was watching the girl from a vantage point—as any noble man has the right to check on his vassals."

"Quite," said Jollibois.

"He went away and got his bow, dipped the arrow in oil from the tomb of St. Olaf, came back, and shot it."

"How did he get so good at using a villein's weapon?" asked Edward.

"Sir Geoffrey has always enjoyed his . . . associations with the families of his tenants. Particularly their daughters. As a young man I believe he spent a lot of time, er, in congress with the poor."

"Did the girl reveal what it was saying?"

"As I said, that Lucifer made the world, God is an imposter. That they must oppose their lords."

"She couldn't believe a foul creature like this."

"Perhaps not. But many do. When the Genoese mariners rebelled at Boulogne last year, this is what was behind it. Their leader Boccanegra may not believe this cant, but he knows how to exploit it. He now rules Genoa, and its ancient families are dispossessed of their time-honored right to power."

"Why was I not told?"

"People feared to tell you, sir. I only just discovered this myself," said Jollibois.

"Liar," said Edward.

Jollibois, already crouching because of the height of the cabin, stooped a little farther.

Edward thought of the angel. He had promised France to Free Hell. Other deals must have been made with other kings, he knew full well. Were the demons calling in their debts, moving into *his* country? That wouldn't happen without a fight. Edward almost found the body of the little demon reassuring. They could be opposed and killed. With the angel beside him he was in a very different bargaining position. He'd made an oath, but it had been established by the edict of many popes on many crusades that an oath to an unbeliever meant nothing. How much less an oath to an actual demon?

He could take France, or as much of it as he could, and he could defeat Free Hell when it came to collect its debt. His deal with the demons had been struck only for lack of angels. With the Ophanim turning its great wheels above his mast, things were different.

"One more day at Sluys," he said, "and then we march to Ghent to rally the German princes and the Flemish commoners. Then it's down the Scheldt to Tournai. Let's see if Philip will find his angels, or his balls."

"We've no money to pay the men, sir."

Edward replied, "Pay them in promises."

He pointed at the little body of the demon. "Throw that over the side," he said. "Now let's go to war."

22

C harles said, "You are a rare seamstress, Mother."

"I always had a hand for it, my darling. Of all my sisters I handle a needle the best."

Joan sat opposite her son in the solar at the top of the Great Hall. The boy looked out of the window over the great city as his mother sewed Nergal's head back onto his shoulders. As she worked, the devil ate. He had a great number of candles in a box at his feet, one burning on a table to his side. He lit a fresh candle from the box, bit off its flaming tip, lit it again, bit again until he had eaten it entirely. Then Joan paused in her sewing and he bent stiffly to the box and took out another to begin the process again.

"I am so cold," Nergal said. "And my head is still floppy on my shoulders."

"Be thankful I managed anything at all," said Joan. "If you avoid sudden movements, you should not come to harm." She finished sewing and tied off the thread. "And here, I sent for this. It's adjustable to your size."

She took an iron collar out of a bag. It had a key on the side to tighten it.

"It's really an instrument of torture," said Joan, "but it should keep your head from waggling too much."

She put the collar on the demon's neck and snapped it shut.

"I'll leave you to tighten it," said Joan. "I'm afraid the service doesn't extend that far."

The devil gave a glum nod and tentatively turned the screw on the collar.

"I'll be interested to see old Philip's face when he sees the state of his Sainte-Chapelle," said Charles. "They won't be calling any more angels in there for a while."

"All the heat went out of me," said Nergal, chewing on a candle. "I wonder if my fire will ever rekindle. You'll be lucky if King Philip doesn't blame you. I'm in no state to protect you."

"I don't need your protection, Nergal," said Charles, "and I am beginning to think you do not have such an elevated position in Hell as you have claimed. Ambassador? Perhaps. Servant more like. Those other devils showed you no respect."

"I am among the foremost devils of Hell's first gate!" said Nergal.

"'Among,'" said Charles as if holding the word at arm's length like a rancid kipper. "Well, I am the only prince of Navarre, doubly royal, wrongly denied!"

"It won't do you any good if Philip decides you're responsible for the death of the angel," said Nergal.

"I've written him a letter explaining the lamentable events," said Joan. "Montagu was a sorcerer. Who would have thought it? A spy sent to murder our dear brother king's main angel. Those Flemings who brought him here should be punished."

"Will the lie work?" said Charles. "He is certain to go to his other angels now. Do you think they will reveal anything to him?"

"I don't know. They are not all-knowing and cannot read minds as far as I've ever been able to tell. The angel did not foresee its own death."

"And yet it said I would never be king of France."

"Perhaps it was expressing a wish, rather than making a prophecy," said Nergal. "They see a lot, but only God sees everything. Or perhaps it was lying. By telling you you'll never be king of France, then it might have hoped you would give up all ambition." His face was deathly pale.

"Perhaps!" said Charles. The thought evidently cheered him greatly, because he sprang up from his chair with a clap of hands to pour himself a cup of watered wine.

"If the angels are our enemies, then we need more devils," said Charles. "They're better than angels anyway. At least they talk sense most of the time. Imagine an army of the things breathing fire, spearing, and stabbing. Men would run like rabbits from a dog."

Joan asked, "Can we negotiate with Hell still?"

"We need to open a postern gate, but the only one I know about is on that pardoner's belly," said Nergal, in the manner of a sick aunt calling for a tonic. "Still, there is another, I'm sure."

"How are you sure?" said Charles.

"I saw an ambassador of the second gate at Le Châtelet."

"What ambassador?"

"Lord Sloth," said Nergal. "He has the ear of Satan himself."

"Sloth? We don't want a lazy devil," said Charles.

"He is very energetic," said Nergal. "He made a specialty of punishing Sloth in Hell and, through hard work and diligence, he was given responsibility for many more sins. He is well trusted in Hell."

A look of great pain descended onto the boy's face. "Mama, there are greater devils than this one in the world. I should be treating with them, not this wretch."

She said, "Of course you should, Charles. Devil, reveal this other ambassador's whereabouts."

"He's gone to England," said Nergal. "He may even be there by now."

"For what?"

"I don't know. You would have thought I was ambassador enough. Have I not proved myself? I should be sent to the king." Nergal adjusted the screw on his collar and winced.

"Do you mean to say he'll be dealing with Edward?"

"Very possibly. He's your ally, isn't he?"

"Yes, but as such we want him weaker than us," said Joan, "not recruiting his own army of devils."

The devil looked about him, indicating that he couldn't see an army.

"Well, you have to start somewhere," said Joan, "no matter how unpromising that beginning may seem. How might we strike a bargain with Hell?"

"You'd need to open a gate. And then you'd need to bargain. Hell would be more favorably disposed to you if you had killed the boy. Why did you not?"

"Six devils couldn't do it," said Charles. "What makes you think I could have?"

"You could have ordered him detained until a way to kill him could be found."

"I could have. But then you devils would know where he was and wouldn't have to bargain with me to find out. It's easier to deal with you when I have something you want. I know where he's going."

"Where?" said the devil.

"Never you mind." Charles tapped his nose. He said, "You come up with more devils to serve us, then we'll talk about killing your boy. Can't see why he frightens you so myself."

"He killed three devils!" said Nergal.

Charles shrugged. "He didn't do me any harm."

"But how shall we summon more devils?" said Joan.

Charles said, "Did not Aunt Isabella have something of that art?"

Joan crossed herself. "Who told you that?" she asked.

"You did. In as many words. You said that when the king of France denied her angels she found help elsewhere."

"So I did. I don't know what she did, but it would be worth talking to her. The English obviously fear her or he wouldn't lock her away so. Whatever she did is no use to us. We can't get a message in or out of there."

"Use the angel feathers," said Nergal.

"How?" said Charles.

"Sew them into a cloak. I know it can be done; I've heard tell of it before."

"What good will that do?" said Joan.

"You will fly as an angel flies," said Nergal. "You would simply think of her and arrive at her side."

"Just her?" said Charles.

"Anyone," said Nergal.

"So I could arrive in the bedroom of a sleeping king at midnight, cut his throat, and fly away?" said Charles.

"Yes," said Nergal.

"Oh, Mama," said Charles, "do send for more thread."

23

The pardoner had drunk a good bellyful of wine obtained from a farmer and had to rise to piss. Osbert had no idea where he was—east somewhere with the boy and the foreigner. He had contemplated cutting and running at Paris, but the boy was not yet dead. What would that mean for him, should he find himself in Hell again? Devils had failed to kill the child, but then the best place for a Satanic attack was not under the nose of an archangel.

Would Despenser blame him for that? Of course, but then Despenser wasn't the sort who depended on blaming someone to torment them. Osbert was sure the lord was just as capable of torturing people he knew to be wholly innocent as those guilty as Judas himself.

He pulled the bloody tapestry about him, for warmth as much as the protection the angel blood would bring. Montagu had been clever making off with the holy lance and sword, but not clever enough to grab the blood-soaked tapestry.

Vague spiritual thoughts troubled the pardoner's mind as he relieved himself in the wood near their little camp. This good hard piss was the first chance for reflection he'd had since he'd been to Hell and, despite the drink, Osbert was thinking about the afterlife.

Everything he'd heard from Despenser had tallied with everything he had heard from the boy Dow. Free cities in Hell, Satan a different being from Lucifer, devils as prison guards, demons as prisoners. Well, did that mean the boy was right? Not necessarily. Not about who was going to win, anyway. If God had usurped Lucifer, if devils did torment demons and lost souls, surely it was better to be on the side of God? The pardoner did not see the world in terms of right and wrong as much as profit and loss. Largely loss in his business career.

This left him with the severe problem of pleasing God—or at least his appointed servants, such as Despenser. Was a bid for Heaven impossible? Osbert reached inside his tunic and squeezed the little bottle he'd stolen in the barn. He'd deserved that for all the work he'd done. Damned or saved, he might turn a few coins out of that.

In another life he might be happy here. It was a mild summer dawn; the promise of heat stirring the trees; the smell of the embers of the camp fire drifting across; blackbirds singing up the sun. The horses the mercenary had obtained for himself and the boy—though notably not for Osbert—were breathing and blowing. If only he weren't a mandated assassin of Hell, life would be bearable.

A tap on his shoulder and he turned around, a bright arc of piss spraying into the moonlight.

"Hey! Careful!" The voice was an urgent whisper.

In front of the pardoner was a long thin devil, its body like that of an emaciated man, its head stretched and thin and sporting a pair of great donkey ears. Its lips were pursed as if it had just swallowed a draft of vinegar.

"Sorry." The pardoner holstered his cock, then crossed himself.

"Which way's England?"

Osbert said, "Er, I don't know. Are you from Despenser?"

"Do I have scars on my back?"

"Yes."

The creature did—and big ones.

"All right, but only on my back. If I was Despenser's, I'd be one living scar. I am called by another."

"Are you here to kill the boy Dowzabel?" asked Osbert.

"Is he here?"

"I think so."

"Ooh, dear! Which way did you say England was? I thought you were going there—that's why I followed you."

"That way," said the pardoner, pointing back down the road to Paris.

"Good, must get going. Can't be seen on the road by day or they'll have a stack of priests down after me. It's no good telling them we're on the same side. Good luck with the Antichrist, I don't expect you and I will meet again this side of the lake of fire. Mind you, if you're trying to kill the Antichrist; Hell can't hold any fear for you. Hang yourself and cut out the middle man; the punishments for suicides are less than they are for arrogance and folly. Just a word of advice. Ta ta!"

The creature looked about and shot off through the woods.

The pardoner crossed himself again. What was the devil on about?

"Hssst!"

Another voice from the woods.

Osbert put his hand to his knife and looked farther in.

"Hssst!"

"Who's there?" he asked.

"Be quiet or you'll wake them! Come here."

"Show yourself. I'm not marching into the woods if I don't know what I'm marching into!"

A big set of teeth flashed from the dark—like a rat's, but bigger.

"I'm afraid that's not very reassuring," said the pardoner.

"I hopped out of your belly. I'm on Despenser's mission. I won't harm you!"

"Is that where that other fellow came from? The long thing."

"I don't think so."

"So where did he come from?"

"I don't know. There must be another gate to Hell around here. Have you been summoning?"

"No, I'm more interested in banishing."

The pardoner ventured a careful step forward and then another. Presently he began to make out the shape of what appeared to be a rat, or rather it had the head of a rat, albeit monstrously large. Its body was something else entirely—resembling that of a bear. The creature itself was no bigger than a dog, a terrier, perhaps, though just too big for rabbiting.

"We need to talk," it said. Its voice was surprisingly deep, like that of a London soldier who had been paid to keep the order in the Crown stew.

"Are you here to kill me?" said the pardoner.

"Don't be a fool. I can't kill anyone bigger than a farmyard hen—look at the size of me. That's why I didn't join your little scrap at the chapel."

He asked it, "You're from Despenser?"

"Yes. I'm the contingency plan."

"How so?"

"Well, if the devils failed to kill the boy, I was to present our fallback position to you."

"Which is?" asked Osbert.

"Kill him yourself or Hugh Despenser will make you the particular target of his personal wrath when you descend to Hell."

"*If* I descend to Hell."

The devil let out a deep chuckle.

"What?" said the pardoner.

"By Satan's smoking ball sack, you weren't serious, were you? 'If I go to Hell'! Very good!"

"Fine. How shall I kill him?" Osbert asked.

"Lord Despenser doesn't tend to concern himself with detail. It's for you to work out that bit."

"Great." The pardoner sat down on a log. "What do you propose? Hibernate for winter? Store some nuts in a cheek pouch?"

"No need to be like that," said the creature, "and I have a name, by the way."

"What's your name?"

"Entirelybloodyuseless."

"Seriously?"

"That's the name Despenser gave me and the one he insists I use. My real name is Gressil."

Osbert said, "So he's sent me an idiot."

"He's killed all the morons, and all the dolts are busy doing other things."

"Wonderful. Have you any ideas?"

"You saw the angel done for by a holy weapon. If it can do for an angel, it can do for him."

He said, "So I need a holy weapon? That Orsino's got the lance of Christ hidden up his arse somewhere."

"That should do it."

"Should? You just said it would do for him! Would is different than should when it comes to risking getting killed."

"He's the Antichrist," said the demon, with a shrug.

"Which means what? That's not exactly helpful."

"The Antichrist," said Gressil.

"I thought his lot say Christ was Lucifer."

"They do, we don't. Christ was the son of God. They say that he was Lucifer and we renamed him Christ. That's why they still call their man the Antichrist. They're not anti the man but anti what they say we made him stand for. You're too thick to take this in, aren't you?"

"Er, yes," said the pardoner.

"He's the Man of Sin. As in Thessalonians—he who will overthrow the law and set himself up in the temple of God, deceiving with signs and wonders. Sound like anyone you know?"

"Terrific. I just have to kill someone who is powerful enough to spite God. Presumably God's been trying to kill him and failing? While I find your confidence in my abilities flattering, I have to disappoint you and report they fall some way short of the divine."

"You'll have to improvise, won't you?"

"Right, right," said the pardoner.

"Look on the bright side," said the devil. "You kill him, and entry to Heaven's virtually guaranteed. Even the attempt bumps you up the holy ladder into the sky. No Despenser, no floggings and beatings and living in a house that's always on fire. Warmth, shelter, and plenty in the land of milk and honey. I wish I had a chance like that. I'd jump at it."

It gave a little hop by way of illustration.

"But how can I? You said that the holy lance might not work?"

"That was deadly to holy things. You need something that's deadly to unholy things."

Osbert said, "Like what?"

"A devil's knife—that might work, although the fact the kid's got one tells you how successful the last attempt to kill him with it was. The angel's sword in the mercenary's pack might be a start."

"Marvelous," said the pardoner, "all I have to do is steal the sword from a professional killer and then eliminate Lucifer's favorite son."

"At least you have seen the goals," said Gressil. "Now you can go about achieving them."

"Anything else I might try at the same time? Sweep the forest clean of leaves? Pull a piece of sky down for you?"

Gressil shrugged. "Killing him's enough to start with."

The pardoner glanced behind him. So deep in the woods, the group had not set a watch, relying instead on avoiding a fire and not being found.

He crept forward to where Orsino lay. The sword was practically underneath him. It would be impossible to remove it without risking waking him. But if Osbert cut Orsino's throat first—how much noise would that make? Not too much. He took out his little knife.

He would not even risk touching Orsino, just drive the knife into his neck and then hold his hand over his mouth. Then for Dowzabel. But the knife felt cumbersome in his hand. What was the best way to do this? *Come on, just like a sheep at the mumbles.* Osbert stabbed down, there was a great clang and Orsino woke up with a shout. The pardoner had his knife back in his trousers in a blink. What had happened? The Sacred Heart shield had flown up from where it lay to briefly interpose itself between Orsino and the blade.

The Florentine cursed in his own language as he seized the pardoner by the mantle, wrapping the lapel over Osbert's head to make an impromptu noose. Lights flashed at the side of the pardoner's vision. And then went out. When Osbert came to, the mercenary was standing over him with a boot in the center of his chest. So little threat did he consider Osbert that Orsino hadn't even bothered to draw a weapon.

He said, "What were you doing?"

"You were snoring, lord. I was simply trying to turn you."

"I'm not a lord. You were trying to rob me, more like. You tried to take the shield!"

"I swear no, sir, I swear no!"

Dow was on his feet. He said, "It was beside me on my left as I slept. Now it's two paces away to my right!"

"Sir! Soft Dowzabel, will you not intercede for me here?" said the pardoner.

"You deserve to die," said Orsino.

"Dowzabel, dear Dow, you released me. Come, let me confess to you. A messenger from Hell came to me, whispering things in my ear, telling me where this banner lies. The one the old king took. I was afraid of it and tried to take the shield to defend myself."

Orsino drove his foot harder into Osbert's chest. "What king?" he said.

"The old king! He still lives. So this devil told me. Gressil, dear Gressil, come and confess what you said."

"You knew this in the cellar at St. Margaret's!"

There was a rustling from the bush and the little rat thing popped out its head.

"There! There!" cried Osbert.

Orsino drew his sword.

"I like not this company!" said Gressil, and ran back to the bushes.

Orsino said, "Where did that come from?"

"I don't know. Out of my belly, I suppose."

"What?"

Osbert replied, "When Dow sent me to Hell, they marked me. Look!" He pulled up his tunic to reveal the circle on his stomach.

"In the name of God!" said Orsino. "We need to break that circle." He drew his knife.

"Don't kill him!" said Dow.

He said, "Why not?"

"He's not our enemy. Save your sword for the high men," said Dow.

"He's a thief and devil summoner," said Orsino.

"And what am I?" said Dow.

"We need to break that circle," said Orsino.

"It's already broken!" said Osbert.

"Better be safe than sorry!"

Orsino fell on the pardoner, grabbed his arm, and bent it, as if to make a four of their entwined arms. Osbert tried to struggle, but Orsino had him in an armlock, and the more he tried to break free the more painful it was.

"I would keep still if I were you," said Orsino.

He pushed the tip of the knife into Osbert's belly and drew it down in a swift nick. Osbert shouted out, but Orsino ignored him, pleased with his handiwork.

"That should have broken it," said Orsino.

"He stabbed me! He stabbed me!" shouted Osbert.

"Rather suggests you've never been stabbed," Orsino said. "I've seen men take the knife up to the hilt and complain less than you."

He released Osbert, and the pardoner sat up holding his belly, blood seeping over his fingers.

"What did that creature tell you?" said Orsino.

"Not much!" said the pardoner. "Just some stuff about salvation."

"We need to question it," said Orsino.

"It'll be long gone," said Dow.

Orsino wiped his knife on the pardoner's tunic. "This one can't fight, isn't clever, he doesn't sew or mend, and he brings trouble on our backs. We should leave him here."

"How will he fend for himself?" Dow said.

"Somehow," Orsino said, "I think he'll manage. Now let's load the horses and be gone."

Osbert said, "You're not going to leave me here are you, dear Dow, prey to wild men and bandits?"

Orsino came very close to him. The man had a dislikable presence, thought Osbert, solid, spiky, as if you could hurt yourself just rubbing up against him.

"I think you'll find a way to survive," said Orsino. He jumped up on the horse and rode it out of the camp, Dow following behind on the donkey.

24

Montagu made his way north around the edge of the city to the place they called either the Temple or Le Grève. It was near to the old Templars' monastery and provided for the men who waited daily for what work they could get at the square of Le Grève inside the city walls. The day was hot, the June sun burning his neck, and there was no wind to drive away the stink of the camp.

The ground here was swampy and everywhere rough little huts sprouted like so many animal shelters from the watery earth. These were not animal pens, though; they were places where people lived. The smell was overpowering—the ground ran with waste of every description; scurf-ridden dogs, lean as skeletons, ran among the rot, searching for any scrap they could get, while bare-footed children chased after them. One boy collided with Montagu, who looked down at him. The child had the face of an old man, so thin that the shape of the skull was visible around the eye sockets.

A pity, Montagu thought briefly, that children should have to live so. But God had set them there, their station in life was clearly described in the Bible. If He deemed things must be so then there was a purpose to it. And besides, it was well known these people knew nothing else and so didn't suffer. Still, Montagu couldn't help thinking of the farm boys on his own estates in the West Country. They lived like kings by comparison—they might know a hungry July one year in five, but the rest of the time they were well-fed on good rye bread and soup. They even ate meat on occasion, and his father had made a great show of cooking a hog for the poor at Christmas.

Not much cooking here. The very few fires Montagu could see were lit for warmth in the cooling evening rather than to prepare food. This was what became of the masterless poor. Without the clergy to guide them and the nobility to look after them, they were like children who fell to ruin. If he'd been given care of the area he would have drained the swamp in no time, had the men build proper shelters, and put them to good work in a healthy state, not blighted by disease.

Of course Montagu had ridden through these tumbledown towns of straw and wood before on his way in and out of great cities. He had never had need to talk to the people who lived there, though, and never lingered. Montagu knew he stood out. He had been born to wealth, well-fed from his earliest years, meat every other day and usually fish on the days when God banned the eating of flesh.

Montagu was a head taller than most of the people here. He was armed with a good sword and, though he wore his prison rags, he knew his bearing would give him away. He had learned by his father's example and from that of the men of the court in his youth to dominate the space around him, head high, gaze meeting the eye, standing tall. That stance would draw notice here, unless it was mistaken for a brawler's bravado.

It didn't matter that they thought Montagu a foreigner—Paris was full of foreigners. It mattered if they thought him a lord, worth robbing or ransoming. He still had the sack and, in it, the crown of thorns. He really couldn't afford to lose that. Still, better that than stooping like a servile man. Breeding couldn't just be abandoned at the first sniff of danger.

The pauper's clothes itched him—full of lice, he guessed—and Montagu was aware he smelled. More than that, it was deeply unsettling to him to disguise his identity. A nobleman did not sneak and hide—he went in with his banners flying, his retinue around him, unless absolutely unavoidable. In his youth Montagu had considered himself ill served if he traveled with one tailor rather than two.

A man, his father had said, is like the peacock. All very well for women to dress more demurely but a man—and especially a lord—should be spending double his wife's clothes' budget, if not triple. A warrior, a man's man, showed it in his fine taffeta, his velvets, his rings of gold—his pearls, diamonds, rubies, and emeralds. In the prison guard's rough braies and mantle he felt less powerful, less masculine, not himself.

The slum went on for miles—rough houses, some no more than lean-tos constructed from draped cloth, from broken carts, from turf, and, occasionally, from rough piled stones. Montagu didn't understand why more of the inhabitants didn't build in stone. To live in such temporary accommodation year after year could only suggest they had hope of advancement, contrary to the will of the Lord. Could a knight live here as Bardi had suggested? Hardly.

Montagu was bone-tired and needed to find somewhere to sleep for the night. He thought to walk back into the city and find an inn. But at this hour that would require him to talk to the city watch, and it was certain the French queen had been alerted—even if she was out at one of the hunting lodges in the countryside. She would have her men searching for him now. The death of one of the French angels was a serious matter. An inn would be an obvious place to search, and he, with his one eye, would not be difficult to find.

His problem was that he had no money he could actually spend. Joan had given him twenty gold écus in her purse—enough to feed the whole slum for a year. Montagu needed smaller, less ostentatious coins. He kept walking, not quite knowing what he was looking for. Did he really expect the Templars' flag was going to be flying above one of the rough shacks?

He had been walking an hour in the slum and had descended into a little hollow before he realized he was surrounded. Eight men with ravenous eyes converged on him from the deepening gloom. Two of them bore knives; the others were just armed with stones. Montagu drew the sword from his belt.

"I'm looking for Jacques the Good," he said. "I will pay well to be taken to him."

"Who are you?" The accent was so thick Montagu could scarcely understand it. He guessed, more than knew, what the man said.

"A friend of the Templars."

"None we've seen. You're a foreigner by your voice and of a good family. They'll pay well to get you back."

"I'll pay you myself if you like," said Montagu. He took up his guard with his sword, a fancy, low stance—not really much good for combat but one that showed he was a master of arms. He'd change into a position more useful for fighting as soon as the men took a step forward.

A knifeman came on, his step halting, his eyes uncertain.

"You really want to make up your mind if you intend to kill me or take me prisoner," said Montagu. "If you cut my throat, I'm going to be of value to no one."

The man glanced at his fellow, and, in the instant he had taken his eyes off Montagu, the earl had closed the distance between them to deliver a hard strike to the collarbone with the pommel of the sword. He didn't want to kill the man and antagonize the whole camp. The blow sat the robber straight on his backside in the mud and Montagu kicked his face to encourage him to stay down.

He wheeled around as the next men came in—three of them running at him, trying to attack him from behind but, faced by the point of his sword, all three lost their footing on the mud as they tried to stop on the wet ground.

Montagu's pride wouldn't let him take advantage of their floundering to run. Eight starving paupers weren't going to put him down—he'd felled three Scots clansmen at the siege of Berwick, any one of whom would have eaten a dozen French alive. He was Montagu, scourge of the Scots, the man who had lost an eye and won the Isle of Man when he killed Archibald Douglas, Guardian of the realm of Scotland at Halidon Hill. Retreat was not in his nature.

He attacked, running screaming into the dusk. The men scattered, fleeing before his sword, which Montagu kept raised en garde, not wasting energy on showy swipes. He turned back to the three who had slipped. They were getting up. They were scared and beaten, and he should have let them go. But his blood was up and Montagu charged toward them, launching a good kick into the face of the nearest. The ground, though, was slick and he missed his own footing in the dark; his standing leg went from under him and he fell heavily.

Immediately he parried to block anyone swiping for his head, but too late. They were on him, all over him, dragging him down, pulling at his sword arm. One had his purse, but Montagu would not release Arondight no matter how they beat at him. There was a cry, a scream like that of a monstrous gull, and the men scattered. A little hopping devil sat up on Montagu's chest—a head supported only by spider legs. It blinked at him for a second and then scuttled away.

The hollow was now empty. Montagu ran to the top of the rise, still breathless from the fight. It had escaped his attention, but the fight must have drawn a crowd because a mass of people was fleeing, like rats down a riverbank. As the head scuttled over a ridge and disappeared, people were still screaming and running from it. Well, if the sorcerer Jacques was in the slum, he would know Montagu was there now. Perhaps he could explain where the devil had come from. And perhaps not. Nothing to do but sit and wait.

25

The land around Tournai was already burning when Edward's army marched in. The French had fired their fields—only a month from harvest—and burned their suburbs too, to deny the invading army food and shelter.

Edward had swept wider, first pillaging and then burning, trying to make more land useless to the French. Edward, as any invader would, looked for the dual benefit of feeding his army and denying his enemy revenue. The angel had been useful there—tongues of fire flashing from its great sparkling wheel body incinerated the farms. The people who lived there built no chapels, offered no great donations or sacrifices, some even went to church with heavy hearts, said the angel. They deserved to burn.

It was now August, and Edward sat through the long evening watching his siege engines fire at the walls. He felt inclined to tell them to stop. Every time they got a big rock into the town, it came back at them within the hour and to worse effect. His troops were stationed in tents, the townsmen of Tournai in buildings. Already his chief engineer—the man supposed to advise on winning the siege—had been decapitated almost in front of Edward when a stone from a French trebuchet had struck the man at a supposedly safe distance of nearly two hundred and fifty yards.

There was a bang and a satisfying puff of dust as a stone landed in the town. The dust was scarcely in the sky before five or six crossbow quarrels slammed into the carts that had been put in front of the siege engine as a barricade.

The angel, manifesting as that great wheel again, turned and sparkled above the field, its many eyes looking out on the town. It was a frightening sight, but so far it had done nothing to help the siege.

Edward looked up at it. "Why do you not help us? Why do you not lift this siege?" he asked.

The voice when it came was like a whisper on the wind. "They are holy people within. They follow God's will. Even under your assaults and bombardment they keep God's holy law."

"We keep God's holy law."

"You build no chapels for me, no great church."

Edward said, "How can I do that out in the field?"

"I tell you not how to serve God. I only ask that you serve Him."

"You will have a chapel, when we take this town."

"Tournai built a great church that was finished only last year. Its townsmen invite me to enter it."

"You are an angel of the Holy Roman Empire. I am its Vicar and you will obey me."

"I will weigh what I owe you against what I am asked and what is required of me by God."

Edward gave up. It wouldn't do for his men to see him arguing with the thing. He'd said the blame for the angel's inaction was down to his men who had not thanked God enough in their hearts for their victory at Sluys. The bowmen, in particular, had not worshiped as they should have. He had to be careful there. He couldn't risk alienating the archers.

And yet more and more Edward saw them make that gesture—the one where they held up the three fingers. Lucifer's pitchfork. They'd fight for him while he paid them—because the alternative was to starve. But there was something in their eyes he didn't like, something that said that but for pence a day they'd be directing their arrows not at the French, but him.

And where was that coin going to come from? Even after Sluys the collection of taxes was meeting terrible resistance all over the country. There was talk that even merchants were turning to this Luciferian cult—because Lucifer let them keep their money, whereas God told them to give it to the king. Render unto Caesar what is Caesar's! Had these people never heard the word of God? Edward had told his bishops to tell their priests that Matthew 22:21 was to be the basis for their sermons for the foreseeable future.

There was further troubling news from London—a riot on Seething Lane. The priest of St. Olave's had sold the church's silver and given the money to the poor. He had tried to hold a Luciferian service there, but his curate had called the city watch. In the standoff a constable had been thrown into the river and two of the mob arrested. Even their hanging seemed not to have dampened the revolt.

A voice said, "Majesty." A squire was at the entrance to his pavilion.

Edward replied, "Yes."

"The banker Bardi is here to see you."

Edward breathed out. At least there was some relief. He could touch Bardi for a loan, even if he would have to pay the Florentine's usurious rate of interest.

Bardi came into the tent, dressed in a cloak edged with ermine. He'd obviously put it on as an honor to the king, but Edward found it irritating. He wouldn't be affording any ermine cloaks any time soon.

"Great king!" Bardi bowed extravagantly.

"Bardi. What brings you to France? Hoping to press sixty instead of fifty percent out of me this time?"

"No, lord."

Edward didn't bother to tell the banker to sit. At his rates he could provide his own chair. "So what rate are you proposing?" he asked.

"None, lord." The banker looked even more shifty than usual.

"I'll take a loan at that price, Bardi."

Edward noticed something extraordinary. The banker had tears in his eyes.

"Are you ill?" said the king.

"Great king," said Bardi, "I regret to inform you that our bank has its own creditors and they want their debts repaid. I need—" He almost couldn't continue. "I need you to pay back what you owe."

"£300,000?" Edward felt the blood draining from his face. This man's impertinence—to come to him whining about personal difficulties when the fate of nations hung in the balance.

"Plus interest, lord. The true sum is £425,987, as of today."

Edward stood, fast enough to make the banker take a step backward. He went to a chest at the rear of the pavilion and opened it. In it was a purse. He took it out and threw it to Bardi.

He said, "Open it."

Bardi did as he was bid.

"Count it!"

Bardi said, "There are three pounds here, lord."

"Well, there you have it then: the sum total of my wealth."

"You have your crown."

"My crown is pawned."

"Your wife's marriage jewels."

Edward said, "Pawned."

"The castle at Windsor could be sold. The . . ."

Edward felt as if his head was a boiling cauldron. He said, "I should live like a common man in the street so you can live like a king? I should take any shame so you can save face? You loaned the money, Bardi, remember that. You loaned it. Don't go changing clauses or putting in special provisos now your own incompetence has cost you."

"My lord, our contract makes plain we are entitled to ask for the money whenever we want. That is what you signed."

"The devil take what I signed! You swore as a gentleman to support our war and now you cut the ground from beneath my feet!"

"My lord, I am desperate! Our family firm is of great antiquity, but the bank could collapse within the week. I have bent myself to England's cause. Even now my agents are working to secure something that could restore all our fortunes. They are closing in on the holy banner of St. George—the Drago. Closing in on more."

"On *what* more?" Edward asked him.

Bardi's lip trembled. He had terror in his eyes.

"You fear to tell me."

"Yes."

"Then keep your counsel and leave. We will pay what we owe to your bank when we have it and, if your bank no longer exists, that is the will of God, and we will keep our money."

"You will regret this course," said Bardi.

"Regret is for common men. The angel above is a gift from God. Your bankruptcy might be seen in the same light. Go, now, before I charge you for stabling for your horse."

Bardi said, "I travel alone. I cannot pay my men."

"Then you know what it is to be a king. Get out of my sight."

Edward could already envisage what it would be like to smash his sword into the side of Bardi's head, to trample him in the mud as the banker had often trampled him, forcing him to beg, forcing him to drive his country to ruin to pay his interest. Bardi saw murder in the king's eyes and withdrew speedily.

◆—◆

The evenings shortened. August became September and Edward's army was more restive. The war was such a grinding, miserable affair. Such a mess. Robert of Artois and his men of Ypres and Bruges had not received the ecstatic welcome he had anticipated and had fought a near-ridiculous battle at the town of St. Omer. No one on either side had followed orders, and a crazed charge from one side turned into retreat to be met with a crazed charge from the other.

The upshot of it was that Artois had lost badly and had gone scuttling back to Cassel and Ypres. But it was not all bad news. Philip had advanced to the edge of Flemish territory and was now threatening to attack Edward at Tournai. Let him! The sooner the better!

Men were leaching from his army—useless men of Ghent and Flanders mainly, conscripts. Cowards, every one. It was their homes that Philip would soon be threatening. The archers remained, waiting for their pay, his men-at-arms and nobles still kept in good spirits, but the town showed no signs of falling. It had to fall, a demonstration to Philip of his power. Or Philip had to come to battle. Edward had an angel on his side, and it was rumored that Philip's angel was dead, with others sulking in their shrines, angry that Philip had not protected their brother—victory could still be had. His archers were the masters of the French horse if only they got the chance to face them.

Edward sat watching an attack on the city with Van Artevelde, the Flemish leader. Brushwood had been piled against the city gates and fired, and a battering ram was banging away under a hail of stones. He couldn't even bring himself to speak to Van Artevelde. He was a valuable ally but a jumped-up merchant, elected, *elected* by other merchants of the Flemish towns—an offense to God if ever Edward heard one. Christ's dick, he wished Montagu was there with him. William was a proper fighting noble and would have found a way in, he was sure.

A crude model of Tournai lay on the floor in front of the king, made from packed mud and sticks to indicate the walls, the water sources, likely routes of relief. Edward felt like smashing his foot into it in the hope that, like some spell by a village witch, it would cause a similar breach in the town itself.

A squat captain waddled past in his mail. A professional soldier, not a knight. Now that was the sort of function low men were intended for, not sitting at the ear of kings, crunching away in that horrible language.

"How long for us to take it now, captain?" called the king.

"We have another month."

"Before they crumble?"

The captain replied, "Before we do. There's dysentery in the camp now, sire, and the men do want paying."

"We've given them the run of the land. They've looted a swathe of countryside from here to the Flanders coast."

"They're of the opinion that represents a bonus on top of their pay, sire."

"God's nuts, we have to contend with the opinions of common men. What is the world coming to? I ask you, Captain, did my grandfather have to contend with the opinions of knaves?"

"I didn't know the great Edward, sire."

The king said, "No, but I tell you he'd have strung up every fifth one of them and told them to offer their opinions to the crows. We're too soft today, Captain, too soft by far. Everyone says so." But his grandfather had won battles with the prowess of his knights, not relying on commoners—the bowman and the pikeman. A golden age.

"Can't our engines make any impression at all on these walls?" said Edward.

"It would seem not, sir."

Edward stood. Now he did drive his foot into the mud model. He said, "Then the time for dallying is over. We'll scale the walls and accept the casualties. I'll lead the charge myself."

"The defenses are very strong, sire."

"And they will be well-attacked. Get those archers to lay down fire on the walls over our heads; that should keep the crossbowmen honest and discourage anyone trying to throw rocks down at us."

The captain said, "It's suicide, sire."

"I've heard that all my life," said Edward, "and I'm still here and in fine health, thank you very much. Prepare the ladders! That angel had better decide if it wants to side with a king or these commoners."

"We've been thrown back three times."

"Well, let's make it four. I'd rather die by a French bolt than by sitting here shitting myself to death. Get to it!"

At that moment a ragged man ran toward his tent, flanked by men-at-arms. "My lord! My lord!" he cried.

"A scout, sire."

The man ran up to Edward and sank to his knees. He was breathless and could hardly get his words out. "The French, sir. Philip. In battle array. He's got twenty thousand in the field at Bouvines, not ten miles from here."

Edward leapt to his feet and shouted, as loud as he could, "And we've got an angel, which he hasn't. Captains! Captains! Tell your men! The cowardly cockerel of France is come to battle at last! We have dragged him to do what he fears the most, to face the English leopard in the field. We'll have our battle, lads, we'll have our plunder and you will go home!"

A cheer went up around him, followed by more shouting and cheers throughout the camp as the message was relayed on.

"God is with us!" shouted Edward. "God is with us!"

Above him the angel wheeled and sparkled. Its voice was like the wind in the rushes. "Vicar no more." The light flared, like the sun breaking from behind a crowd—but when it died again, the angel wasn't there.

Edward crossed himself. Vicar no more! The Holy Roman emperor had withdrawn his office! French double-dealing, no doubt about that!

Men screamed and shouted. Some fled at once while others, the worst kind of coward, calculating dogs, actually started stuffing things into sacks, collecting what booty they could to prepare for a retreat.

"He has us, sire, Philip has us," said Sir Stephen Mortlake, a rather excitable young knight.

"I'm aware of the realities of the situation, Sir Stephen! This may be temporary, the angel disappeared at Sluys, didn't it? And then came back."

"What's that?" The scout was indicating a commotion in the camp. Trumpets sounded and men were shouting.

Ten riders—knights in the full livery of Philip VI—in blue surcoats with gold fleurs-de-lys, trailing matching banners that blazed in the dusk.

"The ambassador of the French king," said Sir Stephen. "The angel must have deferred to Philip's royalty and withdrawn from the battle."

Mortlake was about as good for morale as dysentery.

"No!" said Van Artvelde. "It's Jeanne de Valois, Philip's sister!"

And there she was, the old lady herself, trotting in on a white horse, beside her royal pennants. This meant one thing. Jeanne was well known to hate the idea that her family should make war on itself. She was known as "the peacemaker."

"My God, don't tell me he's going to sue for a truce," said Edward.

"Then we're saved!" shouted Sir Stephen, who wasn't really doing any more damage to his hopes of preferment with the king—those had ended entirely not moments before.

Saved—up to a point, thought Edward. He could see Philip's plan. Without a battle, Philip kept his men alive and left Edward with a problem. If there was a battle and Edward escaped the field, he might live to fight another day. Yes, there would be ransoms to pay for his top men, but those could take a while to be answered. Dead wood would be cut away, perhaps even some of his creditors killed. The lower sort would certainly die. Seven thousand bowmen, so many ordinary foot soldiers, however many sponging weakling Flemings. A battle would be a disaster, but a disaster that would save him a fortune.

Edward had to accept a truce—he could not be seen to be a losing king: it would shake the confidence of future allies. But how much would it cost him to walk away from this place with his starving, unpaid army intact? It would be ruinous.

"Tell the heralds we shall be pleased to receive them," said Edward. "Arrange for me to go to Philip's camp. It's about time I sat down and talked to my brother king."

A rush of wings above him—starlings? He hoped so, not a flight of those tiny devils looking down on him and ready to report who knows what to who knows who. Edward hadn't seen any yet, but the reports from London said they were becoming a common sight.

He kicked at the mud with his toe and looked at his son, Prince Edward, running to meet him in his child's mail. His son was well-protected against demonic assault, as were the other children. But Free Hell had found a way to kill a child before. Without the gift of a state to call their own, the demons would strike at Edward again. He had one more summer to get them what they wanted.

26

Y ou saw how he came crawling, Father! Did you see him? Cowed,
like a dog who's stolen a pie!" John was ecstatic, his sword drawn
now the enemy had retreated.

Philip did not smile. He said, "We were lucky. We're responsible for
the death of an angel and it's a mark of the Lord's infinite compassion that
He removed that angel of Edward's. If He had not, just think, John, what
would have happened while our angels cower in their shrines! We lost the
crown of thorns and the holy lance. Can God favor us now?"

The angel, the angel. Would God ever forgive him for exposing it to His
enemies? Montagu in league with demons! Kidnapping the boy Navarre!
My God, to nearly lose a prince in your care was bad enough. But an angel!
An angel! Well, now God would see the English for what they were. Hot
waves of guilt swept over Philip. When they'd first told him the news, he'd
fainted where he'd stood and had to take to bed for a week.

The king crossed himself and a priest brought holy water for Philip to
wash his hands. It had become the king's habit to take mass three times a
day and anoint himself as often as possible since the relics had gone.

"They must emerge after this victory. England would be ours for the
taking if they did," said John.

He replied, "We have nine months of truce. We need to pour all our
money into building. We need the best cathedrals in Christendom; I want a
building sculpted in light! We have a long way to go to get back into God's

favor. We're winning by the width of a pig's bristle here, boy, I tell you that."
Philip was wet at the neck. Sweat. He dabbed the holy water on his face. A
dead angel. A dead angel! In his chapel.

"The finances are not . . ." The count of Eu—Constable of France—
spoke. He was a sallow man with little in the way of a nose, thanks to a
tournament injury.

"Let's not think on that," said Philip. "This concerns our immortal soul."
Hell gapes. Hell yawns, for you, Philip, for you. A dead angel!

"Be thankful for the victory. That alone shows God's forgiveness. He
saved little Charles and his mother from that English sorcerer," said John.

"That Montagu is a powerful wizard," said Philip. "We have nothing
to counter him, nothing!"

"Take heart, my lord," said the constable. "Let the men see you merry
at least."

The priest splashed holy water onto the king's sites of corruption.

"Reward the poor, show largesse. It's a victory!" said John.

Philip said, "And one that will cost me the trust of my nobles! Foix's out
there gnashing for blood! If I had angels I should come to battle."

"Show bravery and the angels will come," said John.

"It's not a matter of that!" The king raised his hand in dismissal,
knocking the priest's bowl of holy water to the floor. Philip crossed himself.
Upsetting the blessing! What was that, if not a sign!

"The angels should be in the sky," he said. "They need to be here to see
our courage."

"They'd need to look hard," said John. "We've not loosed an arrow yet!"

There was a disturbance outside the king's tent.

"What now?" said the king.

The constable looked out and spoke to the knight guarding the entrance.
"A beggar, my lord."

Philip shrugged. "Only one? What happened to the rest?"

"We have the camp sealed, sire. Must have slipped through."

"Go out and show some cheer, Father," said John.

The king stepped outside his tent. His army was immense and he felt
great care for them. The standards and tents stretched out like a vast meadow
of gaudy flowers. There was Alençon, there Foix, there the count of Nevers,

his splendid black lion on his yellow surcoat unbloodied. All still alive. All intact of limb, bodies whole and youthful. All, in some way, unfulfilled. Alençon and Foix had marched north for plunder; Louis of Nevers was hoping to get his lands back from the weavers. Well, they'd have to wait. No more French bloodshed. They'd given enough at Sluys.

Sluys had wounded Philip. So many villages in Normandy stripped of their men, the people impoverished and brought low by grief. Well, he'd avoided that this time. It might have been an idea to chase the English when their angel vanished. But for what gain? Why give Edward the chance to turn a humiliating and expensive climbdown into a victory, no matter how unlikely.

Even worse, why kill him? Philip knew Edward wasn't the sort to get captured—that would only write off all England's debts, leaving his son to start the trouble all over again. No, much better to fight with the new weapons—money, resources, time. Forbear and he will collapse, his wife had told him. Well, Philip had forborne and now he was reaping the rewards.

There were no cheers, of course there were no cheers. His people, even the nobles—especially the nobles—didn't understand how wars were fought. Words such as "revenge" were bandied about. Well, what could be a better revenge than leaving Edward bankrupt, shamed, and discredited? The English king would wish himself dead. The count of Foix greeted him, a big, muscular man who handled his longsword as easily as most men an eating knife. He had brought Philip five hundred men.

"A fine day, Robert," said the king.

"For expense and no plunder to offset it," said Foix. "I've dragged my arse from one end of the country to another to fight for you, Philip, not to sit by a fireside and talk shit."

"You're plainspoken, sir," said the king.

"I am that," said the knight and moved on.

The sun was still in the sky, Philip's army still about him. Since the angel had died, he had woken some days expecting the sun to be in the ground and the earth above him, so far had the world seemed turned upside down.

"Where is this beggar? I am in the mood to display largesse," said Philip.

"This way, my lord. I hope the men haven't killed him yet. Their blood was up and is seeking a way to come down."

Philip was led to a group of jeering knights. In the center stood an extraordinary figure—a merchant by his dress and a rich one. But his clothes were torn, his face bruised, and he was bootless and hatless.

"Great king!" said the man in appalling French. "Great king, I have help for you!"

"You mean you want help from me?" said Philip. "What is your nationality, fellow? If you are an Englishman, you can pay for the damage you've caused in this country or hang."

"I am a Scot, a good Scot; the Scots are your allies and friends," said the man.

Philip had met several Scots, but he couldn't tell the difference between them and the English by their speech. The man's accent sounded gravelly. Scots *were* gravelly, he'd noted.

"He's a liar," said a young knight. "He's a usurious merchant who's fallen on hard times and now wants us, the very people he exploits, to fish him out of the condition into which God has so justly decided to plunge him."

"What is your town, man?" said Philip.

"I am of Edinburgh, lord. I am Osbert the Scottish Scot of Edinburgh, Scottish Scotland, I am known. Do you have a haggis, sir? I long for a haggis, having not eaten one in the three years I have spent serving you."

"And how do you serve me? I don't remember engaging you?"

"I further your cause, sir. I was here spying on the English. Lord Dunbar of Dunbar, Scotland, charged me with this mission. They have a boy, a very dangerous boy, who is seeking to gain for England a mighty banner—the Drago. And to release England's angels. You must know the English king has no angels."

"We just saw one," said Philip, "though I understand it was rented. He may have others."

"No. I swear. I traveled with Montagu over here. I know what his men are planning. May I speak privately?"

"Approach," said the king, waving his men away.

Osbert whispered, "The old king Edward still lives. I heard Montagu say it to the angel. They're going to kill him and then England will have her angels back and the mess they've made this time will seem a blessing by comparison."

"Rubbish, I saw him buried myself at Gloucester. What rot. I won't listen to this a moment longer." He clicked his fingers at a knight. Philip said, "Hubert, kick him up the arse and send him on his way."

"We could hang him, sir. It'd provide a diversion for the men," shouted Hubert from twenty paces away.

"No, no, let him go. The English have cowered before us and gone home. Let's offer some compassion for that, even to liars. Here."

He flicked a silver gros tournois toward Osbert, which he caught as easily as a fish takes a fly.

"Thank you, King," he said, "thank you."

"You've forgotten the kick up the arse," said Philip to the knight.

"Sorry, sire." The knight ran up and planted a hefty boot into Osbert's seat and the man was off, running through the camp.

"Let's move on to Tournai," said Philip. "We have our people to thank for their defiance in the siege."

That night, it took many hours before Philip finally got to sleep inside the commander's house at Tournai—the stink of a long siege did not fade in a day and had kept him awake into the small hours, that and the image of the flagstones of Sainte-Chapelle, stained with the blood of an angel. It had made the shape of the cross and Philip did not dare to have it cleaned away.

He dreamed he saw a light floating toward him, like a candle in strength but much whiter and purer, unwavering. Philip smelled something else too—a sweet, sticky smell. Wine—not the tart appetizing note of a newly opened bottle but the sour stab of drink on the breath, and on a man's breath at that.

"Forgive me." A voice was at his ear. The accent was vaguely familiar.

Someone was lifting his hand, looking at the ring on his finger. In his dream mind this just seemed odd rather than alarming.

"That ring! My God, how even to price that?"

"Who are you?"

"A friend. I could find no other way to convince you what I said is true."

Philip sat up, as awake as if someone had thrown a bucket of cold water over him. In front of him was the man he'd seen in the camp earlier that day: Osbert.

Osbert gestured to the ragged remains of his fine clothing. "I have seen what it is to walk in finery," said Osbert, "and I have known poverty as well. Of the two, I know which I prefer."

Something was glowing inside the pardoner's tunic.

"What's that?" said the king, pointing.

"Magic," said the pardoner. "I am a rare magician."

"You have no power over me; I have turned back to God."

"You have," said Osbert, "but you have been looking for God up there." He pointed to the heavens. "You've overlooked his many able servants who stand ready to help you from below." He pointed down. "What I told you before is true. I was there when the boy killed your angel."

"What boy?" asked Philip.

"The Antichrist. A commoner. Now he's on his way to unleash the power of Free Hell, set it against you. Send for some wine, if it so please, Your Majesty!"

"You are a demon."

"No. I am a man. But I've been to Hell and come back by my magic art. And there are those there who would be your friends."

"Such as who?"

"The late Hugh Despenser," said Osbert. "I met him in Hell. You should talk to him—and I think I know how."

"I was responsible for his death. Indirectly, but nevertheless."

"I think it's the Templars he's after," said Osbert. "They were the ones who tricked him, after all. In my short time with Lord Hugh I notice he has a hierarchy of hates. King, or rather queen, of those hatreds is Isabella. You helped Edward depose her. I should think Despenser regards you as a friend."

Philip said, "How do you know all this?"

"I'm a powerful sorcerer," said Osbert. "I learned my art from Bardi's man, Edwin. I have walked through walls. I have been to Hell. I have turned lead into gold, though I've rather lost the knack."

"Bardi?" The king propped himself up on his hands. "He *does* know some interesting people."

"None more interesting than me. I have harrowed Hell, which is a tough place to harrow, believe me."

The king eyed the glowing thing in Osbert's tunic. He could see it was a feather.

"What good would Despenser do me?" he asked.

"He may have a solution to the problem of the boy. The boy is a killer of holy things. He will kill the true English king—old Edward—and his angels will fly to his son."

"You still say he's alive? There was a whisper from our spies at Avignon, but I never trusted it. Mortimer was full of tricks."

"No. It is true. The Antichrist is on earth and searching for the old king."

"The angel did mention a boy. I thought it would be someone of my rank. Why are you so keen to see Despenser return from Hell?"

Osbert said, "Well, he set me the task of killing the boy. That has proved a little beyond me. At the moment it seems to be beyond all the devils of Hell. However, I think it won't be beyond Lord Hugh if he arrives here. He is a fine man for killing, I believe."

Philip asked, "Why should I trust you?"

"Well, I know where the body of your angel is," said Osbert, "and as a gesture of good faith, I'm willing to tell you, if you swear not to harm me. The boy can be found, England pacified, at least until the old king dies a natural death."

"What's stopping me just invading England now? Our angels may be cowering in their shrines, but if Edward has none then we could overrun him."

"What *is* stopping you? I don't know."

"The concern that God may favor him and not me. That and money. Our nobles have fallen in on their own concerns. They will not follow me unless they can hear the rattle of Edward's armor at the bottom of their lanes."

"So cripple the English king! Keep him from his angels, kill this Antichrist, this boy, this angel killer. Restore faith with God. You killed kings to take your throne. Save one, please God, and prosper."

Philip thought for a moment, his long finger touching his lips. He said, "With the body of an angel the Templars cast a spell and brought down the Capetian kings appointed by God. What might be done with the body of another?"

"Bring down one more?" said the pardoner.

"Can you summon Despenser, at least to speak to him?"

"I can try," said Osbert, "for I have the secret." Here he lifted his tunic to show the circle scarred into his belly, two puffy red wounds disfiguring it. "And if you find the angel's body, I will have some of the ingredients."

Philip said, "Old Edward alive? Well, it could make sense. I had heard the rumor from Avignon but never believed it. And I won't believe it until I hear it from the horse's mouth. Can you summon this Despenser?"

"I am a sorcerer supreme!"

The king took up a little bell. "I'll send for your wine," he said.

27

B ardi's mule was not of the first order of mules. Nor was it of the second or third order. It may once have belonged to the fourth degree of that put-upon breed but, since it had gone a little lame in its hind leg, it could now only lay claim to be considered in the fifth rank of muledom. The sixth rank is generally dead, cut up and fed to dogs—or the villeins, if the dogs were feeling fussy. Bardi distracted himself with such thoughts as he made his way back to Florence.

He'd used nearly the last of his coin getting an English ship to Genoa, but the weather had been terrible, the captain an idiot, and the ship had cracked its mast. They'd limped into Rochefort, still under control of the English, where his traveling companions—as foul a company of ruffians as had ever set sail from England—robbed him as he looked for an inn. He'd been lucky to escape in the clothes he stood up in, with the few coins he'd sewn into his underwear.

He'd made his way across the burning landscape of Aquitaine in the company of a bunch of English freebooters come over from Harwich to see what they could plunder. The answer: not much—everything was ruined, everything burned and smashed. It was as if one of the plagues of Egypt had come down upon the land. The freebooters had headed north and, though Bardi felt terribly vulnerable without them, he had felt scarcely more secure when he was with them.

Now Bardi traveled always by night—skirting any town or settlement, living as an itinerant. There were few towns or villages intact. Armies had been at war here and the people had paid dearly. The smell of ashes clung to him: the taste always in his mouth, the black soot on his fingers, sucking out all the moisture from his skin.

There was no money in a war now, none at all. It should have come sooner and harder, Edward should have plundered this land down to every last villein's penny to repay his debts. If only the Drago had been found, if only the king's angels had been with Edward. Then the French would know destruction, not this awful looting that seemed to do nothing but enrich the basest knaves.

He'd found the mule wandering by a river—an animal of such little value that it had managed to avoid being looted. He'd thought to ride it to save his feet, but that was impossible. Though Bardi had no property to carry, he thought he might trade the mule for a meal if need be, or even eat it. It also represented hope. Bardi was a man who judged his worth by his possessions. A mule was a possession, if the poorest sort.

He had no money for the first time in his life and did not like it. He was not used to living on the land and longed for Orsino, a practical man who could catch rabbits and fish, build a fire, and protect him. Often Bardi cried as he traveled and told the mule that it ate better than he. It did, too. There was no shortage of grass and thistles on their journey. Bardi had tried eating berries but, having no idea which ones were edible, had wasted two days at the side of the road leaking from both significant orifices.

His clothes wore through, and his traveling boots, bought from an excellent cobbler in Florence, turned out to be fine for the gentleman who spends much of his time on horseback, less so for the footslogger. A tear in one seam gaped like a crocodile's mouth. Always a fastidious man, Bardi began to spend more and more time close to the mule as they traveled, preferring its animal smell to his own.

The land was unyielding—no farm, no village remained unburned. The volcano of war had erupted here and burned everything to ashes. He began to starve. One night, when the moon was full, he saw thousands of little bats swarming in the sky—no, not bats, but little men and women with wings fluttering across the moon.

Famished and delirious, he appealed to them to save him, to take pity. Something tumbled from the sky in an irregular, halting flight of fits and starts. Bardi stretched out his hand.

"You are a poor man." It was the voice of a woman, or maybe a girl.

He looked around him. Flitting just above him, silhouetted against the moon, was a tiny figure, a winged woman, her skin white as ivory. In her hand she had a spear, on her arm a little shield.

"Are you a devil come to tempt me?" Bardi asked.

"I am a demon come to rescue you. We are friends of the poor."

Bardi nearly spat that he was not poor—simply inconvenienced—but he knew that was not true. The bank had collapsed, its property seized by creditors. Bardi had nothing now but the hope of charity from his friends in Florence. Yet what friends would a fallen banker have? Many fewer than a rich one, for sure. As the little woman hovered in front of him, Bardi's tears returned.

She asked, "Do your masters oppress you?"

"They have cast me out, as I am no longer useful to them," lamented Bardi. "I have nothing in the world, nothing!"

"And they have everything."

"My fall is a delight to them. They owe me money, but they will never pay."

"Then take heart. Across the world, the poor are rising. The man of perdition is here and seeks to open the gates of Hell. A new paradise will come to earth when all men will be equal."

The idea of equality had never much appealed to Bardi before. It had seemed something unnatural, advocated by the heretic poor. It wasn't so much sinful as unrealistic: men would always strive to outdo one another. Equality, Bardi reflected, would have definitely decreased his riches substantially. Now, however, it might represent a mild upturn.

"Will there be bread for all?" said Bardi.

"Yes, bread for all. And meat and shelter and warmth. We would throw down the high men."

"I am starving," said Bardi.

"Wait."

The little creature flew off into the night. When it returned it flew low, a lurching, bouncing flight. It was hanging on to a dead rabbit. Bardi had to stop himself from rending it apart and eating it at the roadside there and then. He kindled a fire, the ympe striking sparks from a stone with her spear, and was soon tearing into the delicious flesh.

Bardi thought hard. Could he ever regain his former position? No. All trust was broken, all credit withdrawn. He could never regain those exalted heights, unless . . . Edwin had spoken of this Drago. Find that and he could sell it to the highest bidder: France, England, Navarre—they would come queuing.

Or perhaps, if Bardi found where old Edward was being held, he could work to free the old king, to restore him to his former glory. There might be a way back to riches that way. The Hospitallers were holding him, it was said. Well, there was a real opportunity. He could serve them—they were bankers and would welcome a man of his skills. And once you see the accounts, once you see where the money flows, you can see where a king lives. The keep of a royal does not come cheap. But Bardi would need help. His man Orsino.

He said, "Tell me, do you know a boy called Dowzabel?"

"Every ympe of the air knows him."

"Do you know where he is?"

"I will ask the clouds."

Bardi said, "The clouds?"

"Many of us have been released, and I am the largest. We swarm in the upper airs, carrying whispers from fellow to fellow across mountain and sea. I can find Murmur, his ympe."

"I would overthrow the masters," Bardi said, nibbling the last of the meat off a leg bone. "I would see all men equal. But first I would find Dowzabel and those with him. I will not survive without help."

"I will help you," said the demon. "My name is Catspaw."

"And I am Bardi."

The little figure flew away from him, spiraling up like a leaf caught in a whirlwind. Bardi saw a great mass of black in the sky, like so many starlings, whirling and turning on the wing. As he lost sight of the tiny woman against the wheeling cloud, he heard a murmur. It was as if a wave had shot across the sky like a ripples caused by a stone.

Bardi realized the whole sky was thick with tiny demons, long trails of them streaming like clouds across the sunset. He watched them disappear in the night, and return the next evening, a great smudge against the sky. Something fell from the horde. Catspaw.

She alighted on his arm.

"Milan," she said. "I will lead you there, so you may find the man of perdition and help him spread the word."

Bardi smiled. He would go to the Hospitallers in Milan. He could bring expertise with finance. He could bring warning of demons. He could connect with his servants. The Hospitallers would have him, he would have his banner and be back on his way to influence and money.

"Lead on," he said.

28

T he France that Dow and Orsino were not traveling almost seemed a different country. There were no burning fields here, no corpses in the ditches or hollow-eyed children staring out from the ruins of their homes. To Dow it seemed a paradise, the harvest coming in, every village, every town overflowing with things to eat.

The way was easy and direct. They took the road to Troyes and there Orsino offered his services to a group of pilgrims heading for Rome. There were eighty of them and they had already hired three guards, but Orsino with his fine shield and sword was welcomed to join them—his pay: food and wine for him and Dow for the duration of the trip.

The pilgrims headed east on rough sun-baked tracks until they met the Via Agrippa going south. Progress was even quicker then, dropping down to Besançon—a jumblous collection of red-roofed houses tied in a bag of land made by a looping river.

There was a trade-off to using the Roman road—the going was quicker but the roads had been built to connect cities, not the modern abbeys. So the pilgrims often slept out in the open country, rather than taking guest rooms at a monastery. It should have been no hardship to Dow. The nights were warmer than those he had known on the moor. But the night was a black nest, full of hungry eyes. Devils, he sensed it.

"I fear to sleep," he told Orsino as they rested at the foot of the Grand St. Bernard pass, the summer moon a clipped penny in the cold blue mountain sky. They were in light woods, and the track stretched on along the side of a steep hill, though it climbed only gently.

"Some of those things still follow us," said Orsino. "I can see their eyes in the darkness. They shine like those of dogs—but dogs don't climb trees." He carved at some wood with his knife. Since Paris, he had not met Dow's eye. He had talked only of his guilt in leaving Sariel's body and how he should have ensured she received a Christian burial. Now, the threat of violence brought him out of his reverie.

"What can we do?" said Dow.

"We must keep watch and trust to our fellows."

"Do they see them too?"

"They must."

Dow sat by the fire, his hand on his knife. Murmur snuggled at his chest beneath his tunic.

"Will you fly to see them?" Dow asked the demon.

"I will fly."

The demon flitted across the firelight, rising like a cinder blown up by the flames.

A young woman came to Dow, smiled, and offered him a sweetened nut from a pouch. He returned her smile and took it.

"*Je m'appelle Marie*," she said, touching her hand to her neck.

"Dow," he said, "pleased to meet you, Marie." She was pretty, he thought.

He was surprised by the generosity of the ordinary pilgrims. He had thought of these people as servants of Îthekter, always putting themselves above other men. But they were not like that. He knew enough French from Edwin to understand a little of what they said. They referred to themselves as sheep and their God, Christ, as the shepherd. Dow remembered the priests of the West Country, their anger and their bile. More dragons than sheep, he thought.

There was an undeniable gentleness to some of these people. They didn't seem cast down by their groveling prayers but lifted up by them.

Marie said something quickly and gestured to her eyes. Dow couldn't understand a word. There were all sorts of nationalities on the pilgrimage, and he had only poor French, bad Latin, good English, and what remained of his Cornish to communicate in.

She swept her arm up into the hillside, pointed to her eyes. She was saying she had seen eyes there.

"They won't harm you while I'm here," he said.

She said something again. Dow heard the French word for "what?"

"I don't know," he said. He shrugged to demonstrate. "But . . ." He tapped his dagger and then pointed to Orsino. "Safe," he said. "Safe."

Orsino came back to him. "I will take the first watch," he said. "You should get some sleep." He made his way to the edge of the camp, looking out into the falling dusk.

The girl Marie watched him, then smiled at Dow. "*Votre papa?*" she said.

"No," he said, "enemy."

The girl pursed her lips. "*N'entendu pas,*" she said.

"I didn't intend it," said Dow, mistaking what she said. "Friend. I don't know. He needs to change and welcome Lucifer as a friend. Lucifer forgives."

Dow wished he could ask Marie to lie with him, but he knew her people would never allow it. He felt everything a young man of his age feels toward a good-looking girl, and he feared his desire would show on his face and scare her away. But it was more than the prospect of sex that enticed him. It had been a long time since he had been snug in anyone's arms.

Dow slept, and it seemed to him that he dreamed. He was back on the moor again, lying in the peaty smell of his nan's dress. Then his nan was gone and he wondered where. He got up to look for her.

"Dow." The girl Marie was at his shoulder.

He said nothing, just looked into her face. The moon was a sliver and the night was dark, but Marie almost seemed to glow, her face beautiful in the silver light.

She took his hand and led him into the trees. Dow looked into the darkness of the woods. No eyes, no teeth. He had his knife and the heedless desire of a man dragged on by a stiff cock. They made their way through the fragrant wood, up a slope, and to a grassy bank. Dow desperately wanted to kiss her, to touch her; she seemed a glorious thing to him, a gift of the moonlit night.

Marie turned to him and he took both her hands. He went to kiss her, but she drew back. He kissed her anyway, just a peck on the lips. She stiffened and parted her lips, gave a little cough. Dow looked down at her hands.

They were blackened, like some root dug from the earth. Marie coughed again and her head burst open like a puffball mushroom. She did not fall but stood with her arms stiff in his. They were wood, and her ruptured skull showed not blood or brain but a pale and fungoid flesh, a mist of spores floating away from it.

Dow staggered backward, looking up around him. In the trees was a monstrous spider, legs as thin as wires, with a translucent body as big as a mastiff's.

He heard voices around him. "He who would defy God."

"A spirit unconfined."

"What tortures await him?"

"What punishment could ever fit the crime?"

Everywhere were eyes and teeth—in one tree a great grinning cat-headed man looked down; an enormous toad carrying a spear dropped to the floor from another.

Dow coughed out the spores, wiped his mouth.

The toad threw the spear and Dow watched it with a frozen fascination as it flew toward him. A clang and a cry, a scream. Orsino was there: he'd leapt in front of the spear with his shield, knocking it aside, and, in the same movement, advanced on the toad.

The creature leapt to one side and the spider-thing and the cat-man dropped from the trees. Orsino's angelic sword was free, burning with the light of sun on water. The spider wrapped its threadlike limbs around him and drove its teeth into his body, but Orsino's sword slashed through the spider's legs like a scythe through barley.

The cat-man ran toward Dow—he had a large spiked mace in his hand. Dow jumped behind a tree to avoid its swipe. He had his knife free. The cat-man swung again, his whiskered face leering at Dow through the gloom. Dow stepped back, his instinct honed by long training in the garden of the rectory of St. Olave's. Once the forehand swipe of the mace had missed him, he stepped in, deflecting the cat-man's backhand with his left hand to stop him striking again and stabbing down into the side of his neck with the devil's knife.

With a cry the cat-man died, but Dow was driven to the floor by the charge of the onrushing toad.

A "hey!" and Orsino was there, the angel sword flashing.

The toad jumped back into the wood, gave an enormous croak, kicked up its legs, and was gone.

Orsino examined Dow. He was covered in white powder.

"Go to the river and get washed," he said. "I'll come with you. Whatever that thing has put on you, you want it off as soon as you can." For the first time since the death of the angel, Orsino was something like his old self, energized by the battle. The pilgrims from the camp came running, the two guards with spears before them.

There was a squabble and shouting mainly in French. Orsino said something and an old man, the pilgrims' leader, spat. Dow saw Marie peering anxiously from behind her father. Bolder souls went to investigate the bodies of the cat-man and the spider.

Orsino shooed them away from the broken figure of the fungus-headed girl, saying over and over again, "*Dangereux*." Whether they all understood or not, they didn't go near the thing.

Dow went to the river and waded in. It was cold, though the current was not too strong. He submerged himself and stood up again, shivering. He did it again, wanting to clean off whatever that thing had put on him. What had it been? A devil, or a device of devils?

He went back to the bank, coughed, and a taste of blood came into his mouth. The Florentine came to him. "You look well enough," said Orsino.

"There will be more of them," said Dow.

"The fact they try to oppose us shows we are doing God's work."

"They are God's servants."

"That is not so. God's servants are beautiful."

Dow recalled what Sariel had said to him, to understand this man.

He said, "Beautiful or ugly, you kill them both."

"I will atone," said Orsino. "The pardoner was right. There is a way back to God."

"What atonement can there be for what we, *you*, did?" Dow realized he had echoed what the devils had whispered to him in the trees.

"I can claim your soul for Christ," said Orsino. "When you accept His light in your heart, perhaps I will have given God what He asks for. You are the Antichrist, they say. I don't believe that. But if you are, what better way for me back to God than to achieve your redemption."

"Orsino," said Dow.

"Yes."

"You are saved."

"How so?"

"You are a good man. You think more of your friends than you do your-self. Lucifer will see that."

Orsino smiled. He said, "You'll excuse me if I don't find that comforting. You'll take the second watch, and stay in the camp this time. You were saved because I wanted a piss."

"Thank you for saving me," said Dow.

"Atone. Atone. If I can bring you to Christ, I might be saved too." He ruffled the boy's hair.

Dow said nothing, let the Florentine take what comfort he could from such a wasted hope. He walked back to the camp, catching the girl's eye. This time she did not come near.

29

In the darkness of the hold of the ship, the pardoner could pick out a
faint luminescence, a moonglow behind the barrels and the chests.
The place stank, as all ships' holds did after their first spell in bad
weather. Anything that a storm could shake out of a human or animal had
been shaken out down there and scant attention paid to cleaning it up.

Fifty French men-at-arms stood on the riverbank beside the ship, another
fifty on its deck and three came with the pardoner below.

"That's it, boys, in there. There's your angel," said Osbert. "Best let me
go to him first and see what's what."

It had not escaped his thoughts that a good quantity of further relics
might be harvested from the angel. He had brought a hammer, a chisel, and
a sharp knife for that very purpose.

The men were wary. The three knights, with the sort of scars that said
they knew what it was to fight, seemed like scared little boys, whispering
at the foot of the ladder, not daring to come forward.

The pardoner advanced. "You can send your boys to arrest the queen of
Navarre now, I'd say," said Osbert. "Teach her and that bastard son of hers
to look down their noses at me."

"You watch who you're accusing. Kings think carefully before they throw
away their allies," said one of the knights.

The angel was laid out on a pallet. Osbert went to the body and drew
back the cerecloth. He gave a little cry. All of the hair had been cut off and

every tooth in its head removed. The beauty of its face still remained, but its mouth was a bloody ruin and its head was shaved tight to the skin.

"Search the crew for teeth and hair!" said the pardoner. "Hurry! God, there's been dark work here!"

He checked the rest of the body quickly. Fingernails and toenails were still there. At least something was sacred. He took out his knife to try to prise one away. It made no impression.

He drew the knife he had taken from the dog-headed man. Osbert put it against the toe joint and bore down with both hands, severing the big toe. It clacked heavily on the wood of the pallet.

"Just dealing with a rat!" said the pardoner. He stuffed the toe into his neck pouch.

"Quite safe now, gentlemen," he said, waving the men-at-arms forward.

"Thank God," said the knight.

All the men crossed themselves and approached the angel. They lifted the great body to the hatch, expressing surprise at how light it was. There a rope was tied around its arms and it was lifted up onto the deck. Only the light of the pardoner's lantern remained.

Osbert accompanied the body on the barge back down the river, along with the men-at-arms. He'd tried to avoid taking the warriors in order to have more time to remove relics from the body, but they had been insistent. There was a good fog on the water, which suited his purposes. His proximity to a dead angel could raise fear and suspicion among the common people. He knew where that led.

The boat floated on alongside the grand buildings of the Île de la Cité, drawing up on the north bank opposite the Hospital of the House of God, its towers floating upon the fog. A lantern guided them in. Osbert peered through the murk to see eight plainly dressed monks waiting for him with a two-horse cart. Hospitallers. He had not wanted to involve them and they had not wanted to be involved, until the king told them Osbert could find the angel's body.

Now they welcomed them in. The monks took the angel's body from the barge and placed it in the cart. It set off north up the Rue De La Temple. Only a light carried by one of the following monks and the sound of the horse's hooves gave Osbert any sense of direction at all.

After ten minutes' walk they drew level with the temple, a tall, boxy castle with a spindly tower at each corner. A curtain wall ran close by the tower, disappearing into the fog. The cart went in through a gate in the wall and Osbert followed. The grounds were large. A bulky building darkened the fog in front of him, another beside it rising higher, though scarcely visible. This was the temple of the Templars, or had been, where they had done all the foul magic that had wrought their destruction. The monks slid the body off the cart and carried it over toward the smudged outline of the chapel.

"This way, magician." A tall monk spoke to Osbert.

He said, "I'm no more a magician than you are."

"I hope you are," said the monk, "because if you're not, then you've wasted the king's time and that of the Hospitallers. That would go hard on you."

"Oh, *magician*," said the pardoner. "I thought you said *bagician*. It's another word for a barber in our country."

The feeble attempt at a joke was lost on the monk. He went across the courtyard and Osbert trailed behind, now only the luminescence of the angel's body to guide him.

The chapel door was open when they arrived. Inside, the monks were already arranging the body of the angel on a bier. On a seat by the altar sat King Philip, two fully mailed knights at his side. The king was clearly anticipating there might be problems.

Osbert paused in the doorway. Laid out on a bier behind the altar was the figure of Sariel. He crossed himself. She had not rotted and lay, pale and perfect, beneath the flickering candles. So the Hospitallers had got her body. He wondered what had happened to her. He tried not to stare at her. This was his big chance. He just had to wing it.

The inside of the chapel was austerely decorated with many carvings of gargoyles and demonic faces on its pillars and ceiling. A big black banner hung behind the altar bearing the white cross of the Hospitallers—its distinctive inverted arrowheads on the end of each arm. Eight points. Osbert knew each point was meant to stand for something and was sure one of those things was contempt for death. He wondered what his cross would look like, if it represented a deep and abiding fear of death combined with a strong aversion to any sort of physical pain whatsoever.

His thoughts returned to Sariel. He was very sorry for what had happened to her and the part he had played in persuading her to come to France.

He said, "Considering we're hooking a fellow out of Hell here, sir, might God's Holy House not be the very best place for that purpose?" *Get your excuses in first, Osbert.*

"An angel sometimes dwells in this chapel," said the king. "If this is, as you say, God's work; if these devils do truly serve him, then they have nothing to fear from it. If they are God's enemies, the angel will come forward to smite them and we may have conversation with it."

"Angels and devils are not great mixers, lord."

Philip leaned forward in his seat. He said, "This is the security I require. Live with this decision or hang."

"I guess I'll be living with it, then," said Osbert.

"How are you to proceed?" said Philip.

"Something my, er, magical instructor mentioned but never acted on. The angel's body is divine. It has a life spirit that cannot quite be quenched. A devil can be invited to possess it."

"A devil can't even stand the touch of angel's blood," said Philip.

"No, well, quite. But technically it's not a devil we're getting out here. It's a *fallen* angel. Its original being is not unlike the creature's here. I believe it may even be possible to place a devil into a fallen angel's flesh."

"What makes you say that?" asked the king.

Osbert said, "Devils can possess things. The realms of soul and flesh are separate and do not mix. Therefore the devil wouldn't have to touch the angel to control it, providing its spirit was missing. However, you never know with angels; there's a chance it wouldn't be good for the devil."

"You are a learned man."

"I did nothing but study for many years. Not even eat or drink. Can I call my servant?"

"What servant?"

Osbert whistled and the scurrying form of Gressil came into the church. The devil paused at the door, sniffed about, and then scuttled over the flagstones toward Osbert. One of the knights stood and drew his sword. The king waved the weapon away.

"It's hard to believe," said the king, "but this is one of God's servants too."

"You believe what I have told you about these godly devils?"

"I saw with my own eyes what the Templars could do and how they explained it. I would not be here now if I didn't think there was at least some truth in it." He touched that plain little ring on his finger nervously.

Osbert said, "Good. We'll commence."

Osbert took out his chalk. He had made a study of the circle on his belly and was now confident he could reproduce it, despite the knife wounds that disfigured it. Still, he unbuttoned his tunic and referred to the scars for guidance. He had watched Edwin work for so long that the prayers, the incantations, the order of the drawing of the circle and the writing of names came easily to him. One small circle for him to stand in. Another large one around the bier with the angel upon it.

The little devil sat watching until, after an hour or so, the work was complete. Osbert took out the little bottle of angel blood Nergal had given him and placed a drop of blood on the houses of the east, west, north, and south marked around the circle, as he had seen Edwin do with so much holy oil, holy water, holy dust, and holy whatever else he could get his hands on.

"Test it," said Osbert to Gressil. The devil walked forward to the edge of the circle and stopped.

"The circle is sound," it said in its little squeaky voice. "I cannot cross it."

"Good," said Osbert, "so let's begin."

30

Montagu waited for the Templar for a week. The skies were black and the air full of the threat of rain, although no fog came. He woke at dawn wet with dew, drinking the puddles that formed in the rain, eating nothing.

Memories came and went. Isabella, chiefly, sometimes his children, sometimes, bizarrely, of his first sword tutor, Sir Robert Parr. "A man who kicks on the battlefield is one who wants to fall over," he'd said. "Only ever use it in the street, on good cobbles, and then only to finish a fight. God gave you two feet to stand on. Don't mock him by making it one." After all he'd been through, was Montagu childish enough that he was embarrassed to be bested, however fleetingly, by low men? It seemed he was.

No one came near him in the hollow, though curious children watched Montagu from a distance before their mothers called them back.

His sword was by his side, Isabella's letter with him and the crown of thorns. For all his riches in England, they were three things Montagu would not part with. The sky was gray—a storm was trying to come in from the east, where a weak dawn labored under the clouds. He sat up. Still in that little hollow. Had it been seven days or eight? Good Jacques would come, Montagu thought—he had to come.

Finally, as he dozed in a rare interval of sunshine, there was the sound of a man approaching. Montagu didn't draw his sword—he didn't want to antagonize anyone needlessly.

A man appeared above him. He was meanly dressed in just a plowman's rough tunic and braies, no shoes on his feet. At his side, though, he carried a good sword. He was old—around fifty, gray-bearded and tall and lean, with the air of someone accustomed to being taken seriously. Montagu crossed himself. It was the man who had guided them at Nottingham. William Eland. Good Jacques, as Bardi had called him.

"You look hungry," commented Good Jacques. His voice was common, like a market trader's.

Montagu replied, "Yes."

Good Jacques nodded. "Here, catch." He threw Montagu's purse at him. "All monies present," he said.

"I can't eat this," said Montagu.

"A lesson there, I'd say."

"How did you get it back?"

"The people lost their taste for robbing you when your devils appeared."

Montagu said, "What devils? I saw only one."

"One at first, then three big ones: two on the first night and one last night—a monstrous eye, a half-headed man, and, to top it off, a woman eaten by plague. Doubtless if I kept watching you there'd be more, but I think even you need to eat. Here."

Good Jacques opened his bag and took out a loaf of bread.

Montagu took it, counted to ten mentally, and then ripped off a piece as casually as he could. Without form a man is nothing.

"What're the names of these devils?" asked Good Jacques.

"I know no devils."

"They knew you, Lord Montagu. You've cleared half the slum."

Montagu didn't know what to make of this information, so he said nothing. The devils, he felt sure, were something to do with that pardoner— a low and disreputable sorcerer if ever he saw one.

"Who are you?" he asked him.

"Your sworn enemy," Good Jacques replied.

"How do you know my name? And why are you my enemy?"

"You imagine that the rulers of the Great Hall are Philip and his wife? No, the rulers are the kitchen boys and the servants, those that throw out the rubbish and the shit. They are people you notice less than the walls or the buttresses. Yet they are walls and buttresses to that palace. They know all its secrets and without them it falls. I knew you were here within hours of you arriving at Le Châtelet. I have been watching you—or rather have had you watched."

"Why?" asked Montagu.

"Because I think you may help me."

"Yet you call me your enemy."

"I am someone who hates you more completely than any of your royal foes, more than Philip, more even than that prince you ran from the palace with. You look surprised. Has he told you he's your ally? He's a hater, that one, to his core. If it wasn't for the damage he's going to cause, I'd cut his throat now just to take a little bit of ugliness out of creation."

"Nothing wrong with plain speech," said Montagu. "Do you have a name, enemy?"

"I'm Good Jacques," he said. "Or Jack, depending on how you like it. Jack Lebonne to some."

He said, "You're the Templar?"

"Was a Templar. There's no temple anymore, have you noticed?"

"Then we are on the same side. I am an enemy of the Valois too."

Good Jacques replied, "Yet that does not make us allies. My allies are here, the poor and the starving. My enemies are high men like you. Not just the Valois—it was House Capet that overthrew my order."

Montagu knew why too—for the worship of demons, for allying with Hell, free or not. He said, "Those men who attacked me were working for you? Were they Templars?"

"Hardly. They just called me when the rumpus started with those things that were attending you."

"Nothing was attending me."

"I think in the short time you have known me you must have come to the opinion that I am not a liar."

Montagu said, "Did the demons defend me?"

"They were not demons, far from it. They were devils, gaolers from Hell. Soldiers of Hell now. You know you killed an angel?"

Montagu felt very cold, suddenly aware that he was soaking wet. He said, "I killed nothing."

"That's not how Hell sees it. They are pouring as many devils into the world as they can, using whatever gates are open to them. There must be one near here, I should say. How were the devils summoned that freed you from the prison?"

"I don't know. A low man. A pardoner."

"Did he destroy the circle when he had done with his summoning?"

"I don't know."

Good Jacques said, "Likely he didn't. It is much easier to summon a devil than a demon—you only have to open a postern gate and you might persuade one of the guards to do that if you know its name. To get demons out you'd either have to be very lucky or possesses a key to the main gates."

"It's easy to summon devils?" asked Montagu.

"Easier, but still very hard. I have seen one devil in my life before today. Around you there were three."

"I have not traded with devils."

"They are trading with you."

Montagu thought of the lion in Le Châtelet. It seemed to know him, to think it was on the same side. "What are they here for?" he asked Good Jacques.

"One of them asked which way was England."

England. Home. Apples in the orchards, the heavy bees bending the stems of the wildflowers, the dogs crazy to see him. He had always thought of himself as a Norman, not an Englishman. But in this stinking French swamp, far from home and help, he felt English indeed.

"Why would they want to go to England?" Montagu said.

Good Jacques replied, "Ask your king. He trades with Hell."

"Edward?"

"Yes. He does."

"That is a French lie."

"How did you get into Nottingham Castle, my lord? I'll tell you—a demon revealed to Edward what to do."

Montagu said, "I saw no demon."

"Because it wasn't there. I summoned it. One of the excluded, shut out of Hell at the Fall, living eternally in the upper airs. Of course, the demon couldn't open the way itself. It needed an ingredient. On its advice I used an angel's feather to open the way—it revealed that it has that power if you know how to use it. The demon told me little I did not know, but it was important for your king to make his vow face-to-face with the infernal powers. The Hospitallers thought so too. They wanted to tell Philip they had compromised Edward without revealing that they had his old father."

"How did you obtain the feather? That was Despenser's booty."

Good Jacques said, "The Knights Hospitaller had it."

"Why did they pass it over? They were of Mortimer's party."

"They had sided with no one. They had agreed to help Mortimer but for their own purposes. They dealt with Despenser too, but played him false. He gave them the angel's body, they gave them the Evertere knowing he could not control it. At Orwell it drove off the angels and condemned Despenser."

"What is the Evertere? Is that Latin?"

"Yes, not very good Latin but Latin. The downthrower—Lucifer's banner. The one he used in his fight with God. Despenser got hold of it."

Montagu crossed himself. He said, "That was the Drago."

"Not so. A different banner. Mortimer and Isabella had the Drago—lent to them in lieu of angels. You can hardly use angels to help in a rebellion."

"How in the name of God did Despenser come by something so unholy?"

"I gave it to him," said Good Jacques. "We Templars had charge of it."

Montagu could not understand this. "You are a declared enemy of the rich."

"As were all the Templars, secretly. Well, not so secretly. What is our crest, after all? Two knights, one horse: we were the declared champions of the poor."

"And yet you give a weapon like that to Despenser, the living embodiment of everything you despise."

"Yes. Despenser was very useful to us."

"How so?" Montagu asked.

Good Jacques replied, "Think how strong God is. He threw down Lucifer, Lord of Creation. To go against him requires powerful magic, powerful ingredients, almost unobtainable ingredients. An angel's heart, for instance. The final ingredient we needed was the blood of the worst. The blood of an angel killer. Every time you kill a king, you need more difficult ingredients. There have been many angels. How few angel killers?

To kill the last Capetian, to curse his line, we needed the blood of such a man. Despenser did not just provide us with ingredients in our spell. He became an ingredient."

Montagu crossed himself. "You used magic to kill the Capetian kings?"

Good Jacques said, "Yes."

"That is sacrilege, against all holy law."

"Half right. Sacrilege, as I understand it, involves the violation of the sacred. Well, the line of kings is not sacred to me. Unholy? While God is in Lucifer's Heaven telling us what is unholy then I concede, 'unholy.' But unholy to me is good."

Montagu felt like blocking his ears. The Templar's views were filth to him, twisted things, hiding falsehood within truth. He said, "You spited God."

"Yes. Because of me, God's intention, that the weak Philip should be enthroned, was effected. I cast the spell that killed the Capetian kings. God did not interfere, so presumably He was happy to see them go."

Montagu said, "So you admit God appoints kings."

"Of course. We only challenge His right to do so."

A big crow flapped onto the roof of a little lean-to and picked through the piled straw for insects.

"But the Knights Hospitaller took the Hanley angel's body."

Good Jacques said, "They did. There were only four Templars left from the inner circle. Two were captured. I escaped—the other is still in their sway."

"How can they make you do something like this unwillingly?"

"Good rivers must sometimes mingle with foul waters if they want to reach the sea. You don't understand our purpose, do you?"

He said, "Not at all."

"Chaos. The high men at one another's throats, England without angels, France compromised, the flower of chivalry stained with blood. A new day is coming. A man is coming who can lift and control the Evertere and so oppose the high men. With angels dead or gone, with so many brave knights slain, his task will be easier. The man of perdition is coming, lifting up the poor, downthrowing the rich, downthrowing you, my Lord Marschal, who carries enough in his purse to free ten thousand from hunger but prefers to spend it on finery and horses."

"That is my God-given right; you are a heretic."

Good Jacques said, "I cannot argue with you. Your right is given by God, as that of the poor is denied. But the right of the poor will be asserted nevertheless. Given by Lucifer, or his friend here on earth."

"Why am I not dead? Why have you not robbed me and killed me?"

"Because, Lord Montagu, devils attend you. Because you are an able man. Because it is in your interest to prove what I say and present it to the king of England, so he may use it to shake the faith of Philip's people, make them see that their king is a murderer and a usurper. So you may open the way for Lucifer, whom you call Devil and we call friend."

"Who called you to help Edward?" Montagu asked him.

"The banker Bardi. Indirectly—he asked for aid from the Hospitallers, they asked the French king, and he gave the mission his blessing."

"Why?"

"So that Edward might be damned."

"Then Bardi is a snake."

Good Jacques said, "No. The snake has only one kind of poison."

"I don't believe you."

Montagu didn't know what to say. He stood in the cool gray night trying to absorb the information, trying to think where it left him, his loyalties, his plans. Exactly where they were before. Loyalty is not loyalty that is never tested. He was Edward's vowed servant. Montagu had risen with him and, if need be, he would fall with him. But fall to Hell?

Good Jacques continued. "There is a correspondence. A magical record. Philip will not have disposed of it: it contains the keys to the control and summoning of demons. He is afraid of them and fears that he did not honor his bargain, as your king is not honoring his. It's not above your wit to edit it to your purposes, is it, my lord? Half your people consider your king a usurper anyway for overthrowing his father and killing him, as they believe, though they were glad enough to welcome him when he threw off the old man's tyranny. And there is a limit to his offenses against God, isn't there? He won't kill his father."

"Where is his father?" Montagu asked.

"Does Philip know old Edward lives?"

"No. There was no profit to the Hospitallers in telling him. They have great sway in England. No point spoiling that."

They said nothing for a while. Jacques built a fire and toasted some dry bread on it. He offered Montagu a piece. He took it.

Montagu asked, "Why have you not used this information yourself? You have enough to cause all the chaos you want."

"Who would believe a poor knight? And the evidence is hard to come by. Edward has guarded it well."

"Where?"

Good Jacques said, "In the Temple. In Caesar's Tower or in the keep. All the Hospitallers' secrets are there. They are both impregnable on the upper floors. There are no doors. If you want to get in you have to take a stonemason with you—which would tend to attract attention."

Good Jacques studied Montagu's face. He added, "If they have written down the whereabouts of your old king, which they must to pass on if the present prior dies, then it will be there."

"Well," said Montagu. "I'll have to find a way to get it."

"Why not leave it alone? Go back to your war without angels?"

"Because it is not right nor proper that a God-appointed English king does not sit on the English throne."

Good Jacques smiled. He said, "Which he would if the old man died."

"I'll do my duty and find him," said Montagu. "Beyond that . . ."

"You'll leave it to others to do the dirty work."

"I . . ." For the first time in his life, Montagu felt cowed. It was as if this man could see his rotten soul.

"Well," said Good Jacques. "If you want to get into that tower, it's a bit of grubbing you're going to have to do yourself."

"You've never tried to get in?" Montagu asked him.

"No."

"Why not? You had an angel's feather."

"That was only loaned to me. My life as a fugitive here would have been much harder if I'd taken treasures with me."

Montagu took out an angel's feather. It glowed faintly in the dark night. "Can you use this?" he said.

Good Jacques leaned forward, extending his hand. Montagu withdrew the feather. "Well, well, my lord, you are full of surprises. It will help greatly," he said, "though we will need all our courage."

"Why?"

"Because the Hospitallers are no fools, and if they discover us, they will work out why I, who am their enemy, and you, who has asked so many questions in England—yes, lord, I know about that too—are at the tower. They will protect their secrets, and that means no ransom, only death."

"I cannot die," said Montagu.

"No? Is God on your side like all the others?"

"I think he is," said Montagu. "But more than that, I have made a promise to a lady and I will honor that, if I have to kill my way from here to Dover."

Good Jacques smirked in response. "Yes," he said, "I was right to wait for you, lord. You are a killer true, all of Hell whispers it."

"Then I am pleased," said Montagu. "For there's no truer compliment than an enemy's curse. Let's go." He picked up the sack containing the holy lance and the crown of thorns.

The Templar shook his head. "We wait," he said.

"For what?"

"For the night," said Good Jacques. "And for the fog."

31

M other, you exceed yourself," said Charles.

She replied, "I aim to please, my boy."

In the midnight solar the moon shone through the window, the shadows of the lead in the glass making a web of silver and black upon the floor.

Joan worked without candle or lamp. She needed none. The feathers themselves glowed with a moonish light, shining like a horde of silver in a miser's dream. She was securing the feathers to one another with a fine thread, building them up layer upon layer.

"These feathers are wonders," she said. "So fine and yet firm. It's right they should be used to serve our cause, as the crown of thorns that tormented Jesus was used by the Valois to bolster themselves and draw down angels. It's not wrong to profit from the suffering of holy things. There, finished."

The cloak was long, and it covered Charles from his shoulders to his feet. He pulled it about him, resembling some legendary creature of spikes and thorns, the feathers like a white bush on his back.

"Will they really let me fly?" he asked.

"I believe so," said Nergal. He was shivering, despite having spent the day sneaking from place to place sucking at braziers, smithies, and fires across the town.

"If they do, then there are a few people due for the chop," said Charles. He had his little dagger out and slashed the air with it.

Joan said, "It's not for you to use, Charles, not yet; you're too young."

"I could try it, though, Mama. It wouldn't hurt just to try."

"One of the men should try it."

"Can we put such a gift into the hands of a knave? Who knows what resentments our servants bear us? We could be putting a dangerous weapon into our enemies' hands. What's to stop someone flying to Philip or Edward or any king and selling this to them? Imagine what the Bardis would pay to have a means of disposing of their enemies."

The boy swooshed the cloak about him.

"Take it off now, Charles; that is my final word."

Charles jumped into the air. "I don't feel any lighter," he said.

"Take it off!" said Joan.

"Mama, am I not a clever boy?"

"You are that."

"Then why not trust me to be sensible? It doesn't work anyway. Old Loose Top here lied."

"It will work," said Nergal. "It just needs the light. Let the stars or the moon shine on it."

"Please, Mama, open the window."

"Very well," said Joan, "but I am trusting you, Charles. You are not to do anything rash."

Charles said, "I will be careful."

"How does it work, Nergal?" he asked.

"It should lift you with the light. You will be light."

"Have you seen this done before?"

"No, but I have heard tell of it in Hell. There are great men of theory there, for it was their theories that sent them to the pit."

Joan opened the window to a big crescent moon that sat like a sideways smile in the sky. The summer night was clear and bright with stars.

Charles went to the window and looked out. The feathers caught the moonlight and shone bright and silver as fish in a sunny pool.

"Fly," said Charles. Nothing happened. He hopped up and down on the spot. "You *did* lie, Nergal!" he pouted. He stared out of the window. "Fly, fly, fly!"

"Perhaps it's for the best," said Joan.

"Is that a fire on the horizon?" said Charles.

"A fire?" said Nergal. "Is a house ablaze? Some chance to drink a heavy draft of flame?"

"I see nothing," said Joan.

"There is a pillar of flame. It touches the sky. I . . ."

Charles would later try to recall what had happened to him—but it seemed that one moment he was standing in the solar, gazing out of the window, the next he was far above the earth, looking down. France stretched out beneath him but he could see the great sleeve of sea separating it from England too, the hills of the south rolling on toward the tiny flickering lights of London. The pillar of flame, though, rose up from the east. Was it flame? A red light, shining up into the dark.

He thought he would like to see it closer and willed himself forward. The speed of his flight left him breathless. One moment Charles was streaking through the clear skies of France, the next floating above a thunderhead in England, the pillar of red light stretching up through it, as if the mass of heavy cloud was a stopper and the light the bottle. He fell through the clouds with delight, reveling as he tumbled. He fell from moonlight to rain and stretched his hand to the cloud to shoot back into it, fast as a comet.

Elation filled him as Charles saw the spuming clouds below lit up by the moon—but more than the moon. The light was intense. It was him, he realized—light shone out of him, out of the cloak of feathers. He held up his hand. It shone, almost unbearable to look at.

He laughed to think that he was an angel himself. Charles tasted iron in his mouth and a sourness came into his stomach. This was not right. His head pounded and a horrid tickle came into his throat. He dropped back down into the cloud, sucking in its cool vapors to try to calm the dirty itch that prickled his tongue. He wanted to be sick but he couldn't make himself retch. The light hurt his eyes and his ears rang like he'd stood too close to a pot-de-fer. *Get down, get down.* Charles plunged back down through the brumous air, the world swirling to gray as he dropped out of the cloud, rain spattering his face, soaking his skin. He felt very cold now, and a deep, racking shiver took him as he fell.

Everything became red, the clouds outside racing like blooms of blood in water. He had fallen into that strange pillar of light and hurtled down through it as if through a twisting banner of blood. This was not light, Charles realized, but cloth—cloth such as he had never known, finer than silk, stronger than chains, billowing folds of something that was not of the earth, twists of scarlet reaching up to ensnare him and pull him in. The cloth was all around him as he fell, wrapping up the angel cloak, blocking out the light, muffling the light that Charles himself had become. He was human as he plummeted, solid and whole—breakable.

He landed in a tumble of cloth and feathers, thumping down heavily, though much less heavily than he had feared.

He tried to stand but he was entwined. Charles was in a room all paneled in dark wood and gold, behind him a window, its shutters open, its parchment taken down, just big enough for him to have come through. Above him a woman was winding in the cloth, pulling him toward her. She was very richly dressed and she looked very like his mother—slightly older, perhaps.

"Well it's taken me long enough to catch you," said the woman in beautiful French. "Name yourself, spirit. Are you of God, of Satan, or of Lucifer?"

"I am of Navarre," said Charles. He stood and staggered to the window, where he was heavily sick.

"Come in," she said. "I don't want my guards seeing you."

Charles sat down. A tendril of cloth was still wrapped around his leg; he tried to remove it and looked for his knife, but he hadn't the strength to grab it.

"Who are you?" There was some curiosity but also hauteur in her question, intimating that Charles was pushing the limits of civility by arriving in her chamber without an introduction. Charles instantly recognized her great breeding and refinement and guessed who she was.

"Aunt Isabella?" he said. He tried to stand, but his legs would not support him.

"Aunt?"

"I am Charles, prince of Navarre, royal on both sides." He felt so weak, so ill. Tears came into his eyes and he wiped them away, not wishing to appear weak in front of this woman.

"How do I know you're not some sprite of the air?" she demanded. "This banner doesn't work on ordinary men, as it exists half in this world and half in Heaven. It catches devils and demons. Which are you?"

"I swear I am neither. My mother Joan sends greetings and wishes you good health. I did have gifts for you, but they fell from my grasp as I traveled." A lie, of course, but he couldn't bear to be thought remiss in courtesy.

Isabella bent to the boy and pinched his arm.

She said, "You should have been more careful. It's important to bring gifts when approaching a queen, and an excuse is no replacement for a diamond. Hmm, you look like a true Capetian, but looks are nothing. Will you be enchanted? Will you sit in a magic circle so I might test your claim to be human?"

"Gladly, Aunt, but I am weak. Has that banner sapped my strength?"

"No, it ensnares, that is all," said Isabella, "and it ensnares devils. Let me make you a circle so I might question you more."

"Gladly, but you will need to carry me."

"I can draw it around you."

"As you wish."

Isabella pursed her lips as she looked at the little boy. "No demon or devil would allow that," she said, "so perhaps you are not lying after all."

Charles could hardly keep his eyes open.

He said, "I am so sleepy. Let me sleep, while you draw your circle, and we can talk after I have rested."

Isabella wound up the banner. Charles was surprised to see that, as she wound, it got smaller and smaller until it was no more than a strip of white cloth with a single red cross on it.

"What is that?" he asked.

"The Drago," she said. "St. George carried it. It is an anathema and a snare to infernal creatures, which is why I am suspicious of you."

Charles lay back on a cushion his aunt set down for him, so comfortable . . . In moments, the little boy was asleep and his aunt drew a circle around him.

When he awoke she stood before him. "Cross the chalk line," she instructed.

He rose and took a step forward, but a great uncertainty gripped him. It was as if he stood on a very high and precarious place and that any movement might see him dashed to the rocks.

"I cannot. But I am not a devil. I am Charles, your sister's son, truly."

Isabella smiled. "I think you are telling the truth," she said, "for no devil would have allowed himself to have been trapped in there so easily. And yet a devil you are, or you would be able to leave. I think you have some questions to ask your mother."

32

Nothing happened. The pardoner was sweating like a cheese. He had made his circles in exact imitation of the one on his belly, dotted the angel's blood where it should be dotted, mixed the names of demons and angels, shouted his commands—twice—and spoken to the spirits of the east, west, north, and south winds. He invoked Despenser by name as a well-known and notorious consorter with devils, a fallen angel who fell again, more devilish than the devils, favorite of Satan, despised of Lucifer, servant of God.

King Philip sat in his chair, his eyes never leaving Osbert. The gold of the altar shone in the candlelight, the carved faces of gargoyles and devils looked down on the pardoner, the smell of a fish oil lamp brought a faint tickle of nausea to his throat. The angel's body lay on the altar inside a magic circle, perfect in repose, give or take a toe, some wings, all its hair, and its teeth. Its body caught the colors of the chapel and glowed with a golden light.

Osbert had a strong urge just to run for it—but where to? The markets, selling penny indulgences again? Osbert stroked the velvet of the fraying remains of Montagu's tunic, ran his fingers over the shining gold thread that picked out shapes of finches and sparrows. It would be a great thing to return to his father—who had insisted on the monastery—dressed like a gentleman, riding a fine horse, money in his purse and under the patronage of a king. Even a French king. He wouldn't have to go into too many details. But what to do?

"Right," said Osbert, "this particular ceremony sometimes takes slightly longer than we would ideally like."

"How much longer?" asked the king.

"A day. A week. Hell is difficult to predict. The gates between this world and that are, well, rusty at best. And remember, we're only using a tiny postern gate—massively well-guarded, easy to defend and with devilish bureaucracy to contend with. Heh, heh. They're rusty too—they need a little back and forth to open them so to speak. I should say they . . ."

The Hospitaller with the golden clasp at his cloak said, "The Caesar's Tower manuscripts say you need to invite the devil to inhabit the body of a homunculus. That's what you're doing, isn't it? Waking the dead, or bringing life to dead flesh. If an angel can said to be dead."

The man had the frame of a woodcutter, muscular, great hands, great log-splitting beefy hands, great pardoner-splitting hands. Those knights could whump a man like him, wivel him, squamp and skwek him. In his panic Osbert was inventing new words for the historically unique beating he was anticipating, should the spell fail.

"Isn't it dead?" said Osbert.

"Depends what you mean by 'dead,'" said the Hospitaller.

"You've lost me," said the pardoner. "Philosophy isn't my strong suit."

"It could be alive still, just healing while it recovers from being stabbed. Or incorporeal. Angels don't just exist in the physical state. Who is to say the holy lance killed its Heavenly self too? I'd say the threat of devils turning up might reawaken it."

"Good God!" said Osbert, putting his hand to the toe in his neck pouch. He had a fair idea angels were quicker than he was, even at a hobble. He'd known it would contain an irreducible spark of life, but not that it might wake up and start ripping bits off him.

"It's entirely possible that even the body of the angel is putting off the spirits who are trying to come through."

"Since when are you an expert on magic?" said Osbert.

"Since when are you? This looks like no magic at all to me," said Philip.

"Maybe more angel's blood," said Osbert.

"Maybe more liar's blood," said the Hospitaller. He put his hand to the hilt of his sword.

"I'm doing my best," said Osbert.

"We're looking for results, not effort," said the Hospitaller.

Osbert walked across the floor and into the circle with the angel. No voices, no smell of sulfur, no nothing. The ceremony had failed.

"My lords. I . . ."

A tightness at his chest and Osbert flew up into the air. The chapel was below him, Philip, the Hospitallers, the men-at-arms all staring up, though not at him. He saw as he began to fall that the angel had stood up. It had risen, quick as a stoat, and flung him up to the vault of the church.

"Catch me!" was all he could shout as he tumbled. The angel did, one of its hands grabbing Osbert's arm, all but wrenching it from the socket.

"Right, you bastard, now we'll have some bargaining! Let me go or I kill this idiot," said the angel. Osbert couldn't help feeling that the angel could do with a lesson in bargaining. "Indispensible sorcerer" would be a better description than idiot.

The angel shook Osbert as if it thought he might shower coins from his pocket if given a good enough ragging, and the pardoner moaned and shrieked.

The king said, "My God!" Philip upset his chair as he stood. He stepped backward and fell over it, landing on his arse on the cobbles. His knights both drew swords and the Hospitaller put forward a cross.

The angel's face was worse than ugly; it was beauty defiled, the remnants of what it *had been* making what it *had become* so much more hideous by comparison. Still the blue eyes remained, still the fine features, but there were no teeth, the hair was in patches, and the angel's distant smile had been replaced by a gummy snarl.

Osbert bucked and kicked, but the angel gave him a backhanded swipe that made him think better of doing that again.

"Name yourself, spirit!" shouted the Templar.

"I'm an English baron and favorite of the king!" said the angel. "And I'll not answer questions from French knaves."

"I am Philip, king of France; name yourself."

The angel nodded and dropped the pardoner heavily to the floor. He said, "At last, a man on my level. I'm Hugh Despenser, lately of the Welsh borders, now of Hell. And I've got your magician here who called me and is the only one who can send me back, so unless you want me stuck in your chapel for the foreseeable future, I'd start driving some bargains."

Philip said, "What sort of bargains?"

"Release me, and then make me king of England!"

Philip put his finger to his lip in thought as Osbert scrambled to get out of the circle. The angel trod on his leg, pinning him where he was.

"You're going nowhere," he said, "until I get out of here and . . . my God, that's actually quite painful, now I think about it. Where are my teeth? Where my wings? And which bastard chopped off my toe?"

33

M ontagu sat by the Templar's little fire in the squalid camp. A fog had come down on the river at last and it was as if they sat in a cocoon of light.

"God has given us this night to do our work," said Montagu.

"Perhaps," said Good Jacques, the Templar. "Though I would be wary of imparting any intention or human thought to God. How strange His angels. How more strange He?"

"Spare me the philosophy. Are you ready to go?"

"Leave it a little longer. I would hear the Compline bell first."

That was a reasonable idea. It would be full dark then, which allied with the fog would keep them concealed as they approached the tower.

"We do God's work tonight," said Montagu.

Good Jacques looked around him, as if expecting to see God hovering behind his shoulder in the murky air. "Perhaps," he said. "But do not confuse it with good."

"We only know good through God."

"How easily you surrender your moral responsibilities," said the Templar.

"God tells us our moral responsibilities. I don't surrender those."

"But what happens if you disagree with him? What of the moral responsibility to challenge groundless authority? What of the responsibility to recognize the good in you? Was Abraham moral when he went to sacrifice his innocent son on the word of God? No, because he gave up what he knew to be right for what he was told was right."

"You twist words and dissemble. We only know right through God. Besides, God spared the boy," said Montagu.

"Was it right to even ask for the sacrifice? I read God's words as they are written. God will burn you eternally for a lie, for cheating at cards. God will burn the youth for fumbling in his braies, no matter that God gave him both the cock to fumble with and the desire." His voice was flat in the fog.

Montagu drew closer to the fire. He said, "God is just. The correct man need fear nothing."

"So what must you fear, lord?"

"Plenty," said Montagu.

The people still had not returned, though Montagu had seen no more signs of any devils. He had had enough of talking theology with this idiot and itched to get to the tower and get out. "You know how to use the angel's feather?"

"I do," said the Templar, "although it is not a matter of knowing how, more just a way of wanting."

"I don't take your meaning."

"The feather will permit you access to places you want to go. You need to express that wish confidently and sincerely. But I warn you, my lord, it will not make you invisible or invulnerable. If you use it to make a passage through the curtain wall of the Temple, you will emerge in the grounds. The Hospitallers will see you there as if you had walked through the gate."

"Then this fog will hide us."

Good Jacques said, "It might, but best perhaps to make your entrance through the west curtain. There are woods there they keep for contemplation and prayer on hot days and the monks are not allowed to chop them for firewood. That was the way when we had possession of the Temple and I have no reason to think it will be otherwise today."

"Would it be wise to test the feather?" said Montagu.

"There is no need. It will work."

"Where will the letters be kept?"

"I don't know. In the keep or in Caesar's Tower. They are the securest parts."

Montagu asked, "Why does Philip not either keep the letters with him or destroy them? Why entrust them to a group of monks, no matter how dependable he believes them to be?"

"The monks have no designs on his throne. The king has allowed them to keep the riches granted them by his predecessor. And the documents. Philip may need to use them again, he fears. He is a careful and considerate man. They offer him great power, at a cost. He will not destroy them, but he will not have them in easy reach. Besides, they offer his explanation to history. You know how you nobles are concerned with your legacies."

"A man's name is all he has," said Montagu. "He would cast away his life rather than stain it."

"Not all great men feel that way," said Good Jacques.

"All great men do," said Montagu, "though plenty of little men wear crowns and ermine. Our integrity, our generosity and goodwill, are all that stand between man and the devil. I have seen philosophers draw the world as a house, with the many base men as its foundations, we nobles as the roof and gables. Not so. We are the foundation of all that is right and pleasing to God, and He places great trust in us. If we abuse it, then what? The common man rebels and turns to the lies of Lucifer."

"Why should a man toil in your fields for so little to provide your riches?"

Montagu was genuinely perplexed by this line of thinking. He said, "Because they are my fields."

"How yours?"

"By right. By God's right!"

"Because your ancestors came to those lands with fire and with the sword. Because they took them by force. Tell me, lord, why should the base man not follow your example and take your fields from you as your forefathers took them from others?"

"Because God is on my side," said Montagu, "and knows the importance of order."

Good Jacques let Montagu's words hang in the air, poking at the fire with a stick. "We were to have a state," said the Templar. "Philip promised us our own country. And for a while I thought he meant to give it to us. Gascony. Aquitaine, one of the English king's possessions in the realm of

France. But Philip is a waverer, a vacillator, and when he did not win those lands immediately, he took it as a sign of God's displeasure and thought it safer to oppose the tattered remains of the Templars rather than God."

"What would you have done with this state?"

"Returned men to the equality they had in Eden. Before God whispered that some men might set themselves above others."

"Men are not equal because they were not made so. As the lion is not the equal of the ant. As the eagle is not the equal of the sparrow. In nature, everywhere we look, we see how God has set his immutable hierarchies. You have failed because you have opposed the divine will."

"That is why we have failed, but it does not follow that what God wants is right or desirable," said the Templar.

"This is heresy," said Montagu, "and it is unachievable. You cannot oppose the will of God."

"There are a few men who can."

"Who?"

"You, Lord Montagu. You oppose his will and I foresee you have a great part to play in the death of kings."

"I'm not going to kill Philip. Nor any king."

Good Jacques said, "You will kill a king. I see your future."

"In dice, bones, and fire prophecy." Montagu spat.

"No, in your face. When you call the lady's name in your sleep. No need for Chiromancy, Lithomancy, Haruspicy or to pick patterns in the drips of a candle with you, lord. I know whose name you cry and I know you are her champion, whether you like it or not. You're on your way to damnation, but you do not fight it. You hurry down the path to Hell."

"I'm seeking to kill no one. I just want to do my duty and go home."

"Where is home now? Castle Rising?"

"I do the will of God."

"No, lord. You are a creature of the morning light. I see it. I give you a new name. I call you Gallus—cockerel. Herald of the Dawn."

Montagu stood. "I'll hear no more. Where is the tower?" he asked.

"In the inner court."

"Good. You will come with me. Then, if you are playing me false, I will get to cut your throat at least before I'm taken."

"It would please me to come," said the Templar, "though if I am discovered there I will thank you to kill me quickly, lest the Hospitallers catch me and try to bend me to their will again."

The men made their way down the hill, stumbling over ditches—treacherous and invisible in the close fog, the sack with the crown of thorns and holy lance in it bouncing on Montagu's back. The Temple was outside the city walls, but the streets where it was situated were of much better quality than those of the slum—the swamp here had been drained and the ground was firm underfoot. A mean sort of higgledy-piggledy house sprouted here and there, like pale mushrooms burst from the filthy earth.

"There is no real curfew outside the walls," said the Templar, "but it's best to watch yourself. You may be asked to explain what you are doing."

"Damned impertinence," said Montagu, before remembering what he looked like in his gaoler's rags.

The fog cloaked them and they saw little in the way of lights. Montagu wouldn't have had a clue where he was going if it were not for Good Jacques. He seemed quite sure. Presently, a light in the sky. A tower, its bulk just a shadow on the fog.

"Some of the masters keep late hours on the upper floors," said the Templar.

"Whoring, if I know monks," said Montagu.

"Perhaps," said Good Jacques, "but these are severe and holy men. Not all monks are dissolute."

"So you admit that godly men are virtuous men."

"Godliness and virtue can sit side by side," he said, "an abject, cringing sort of virtue but virtue nonetheless. We come to the wall."

A tall stone curtain wall was in front of them, its big blocks stretching up five man heights above them, a parapet at the top, no chance of climbing it.

"The feather?" said Montagu.

"The feather."

Montagu took it out of his tunic, the letter brushing his fingers as he did so. *Isabella.* He could never be with her again, but he could honor her, honor his feelings for her, and deliver the letter. He was close to that. Once this was over, he would buy or steal a horse and ride hard for Antwerp. The king might even be there and, if he wasn't, Montagu would find news of him.

"What do I do with this?" The feather glowed faintly in the fog.

"Tap it to the wall."

Montagu tapped the feather to the wall. Nothing. He turned to Good Jacques. "It doesn't work."

"Do it again but with intention. Think clearly of going through the wall."

Montagu did as he was bid.

A shimmer, and the wall took on a sheen like the sun on a lake where only stone had been, a small patch, a handbreadth around where the feather had struck. Montagu tapped again, with the same result. Then he moved the feather down the wall, describing as narrow a doorway as he thought was possible for him to slide through. The shimmering spread to fill the outline of the shape of the door.

"Walk through?" Montagu's voice was low.

"Walk through."

Montagu stepped into the doorway. There was a ripple, a distortion, like the ordinary world seen from the bottom of a clear stream on a summer's day. He was through, in the woods next to the castle. There were two lights shining—one on the upper floor of the tower and the other in the great, squat chapel.

The Templar was beside him. Behind him, the hole remained for an instant. It stopped shimmering and just looked like someone had chipped an arch out of the wall. Then it was gone. Was that really how they had got in to Nottingham all those years ago? It seemed likely. Montagu tucked the angel feather into his tunic. He dearly wished he'd had one of those at Dunbar. That would have given Black Agnes a shock. On the other hand, he was surprised half the nobles of England were still alive if Despenser had access to such powerful magic. He thanked God the vicious lord had been given very little time to use his angelic relics.

A rumpus away to his right, men running. Nine or ten men-at-arms, unmailed but with swords drawn, were running toward the chapel from the castle. Montagu had the urge to draw his own weapon but resisted it.

There were two towers within the grounds—one the great round keep, the other a tall, slim tower.

"Which one?" said Montagu.

"The tall one is Caesar's Tower. The bigger one is the keep. I don't know. Either might contain the letters. In my day they would have been stored in the keep."

"The keep, then," said Montagu.

More men came running from the castle—these were better armored than the first group, two of them pulling on sword belts as they ran. Montagu, with his soldier's eye, automatically counted them—twenty. Other monks—unarmed and wearing only their habits—ran from the keep and from Caesar's Tower.

"How many fighting monks live here?" said Montagu.

"A good number—maybe fifty," said the Templar. "Some of the healing brothers have training with a sword."

"Too many," said Montagu.

"You'd think to fight them?"

"We might have to if they discover us. With only nine or ten fighting men we might get away. With fifty it will be difficult to avoid being captured."

Shouts and screams emerged from the chapel, the last of the monks pressing inside.

The courtyard was silent. Montagu walked out of the trees, Good Jacques following. The courtyard seemed immense, though it was no bigger than at any other castle and a good deal smaller than some. Still, he felt vulnerable and exposed as he made his way across it. Good Jacques followed.

They were unchallenged as they made the door of the keep. They exchanged glances. Then Montagu went within. He was in a small entrance room with an open door to its far side. The room was well furnished—a long couch at one wall, two crossbows mounted above them, a fluted fireplace below a chimney built into the outside wall. A little fire was in it and Montagu realized how cold he had been.

Time to draw the sword? No. Anyone still guarding the castle would be puzzled by his presence. Why remove that uncertainty from their mind? He could use the confusion to attack with his knife or even go in with his fists.

Through the door. A large reception area—a biggish hall draped with painted cloths showing the arrowed cross of the Hospitallers. This was not a regular dormitory area, Montagu guessed, but where many monks would sleep in case of siege. The reeds on the floor were fresh and fragrant. Buildings like this were rarely greatly occupied in times of peace but provided strongholds, should the enemy breach the outer walls. A single reed torch wavered in a recess in the wall. At the end of the hall was another door—also open—that revealed a spiral staircase going up and down.

"Up or down?"

The Templar shrugged. "The chest room was in the grand solar in my day, but who knows?"

"That will do," said Montagu.

They made the door and went up the stairs, up one level, where Montagu guessed there would be another hall to house defenders, and bedrooms for the Hospitaller grand master when he visited, up another to where—in a conventional keep—the bedrooms of the permanent staff would be.

He opened the door that led off the spiral stair. A small antechamber with four doors off it. One was open, and through it came an old man's voice.

"Is that you, Henri?"

"It's me, William," said Montagu in his best court French.

"What is it in the chapel, boy?"

Montagu opened the door. An old man was in bed in a sumptuous room. He had a long white beard and pale, thin skin, the mottles of age all over his brow.

"It's De Greville," whispered Good Jacques. "That serpent! He's the old grand master of the order."

Montagu wondered how they ever got the old man up and down the stairs, or if they ever did.

He saw no point in pretense now. "I am William Montagu, Lord Marschal of England, loyal servant of Edward, third of his name since the great conquest. We are friends of the Hospitallers, and I mean you no harm and will offer you none if you cooperate. Where do you keep what King Philip has entrusted to you?"

"Alarm!" the old man cried out in a surprisingly strong voice.

A noise behind him. Now Arondight was free in his hand; the voices of St. Anne and attendant saints sang in his head—high, clear plainsong.

"There was no need for that, old man. Blood will spill where none needed to!"

The Templar leapt at the old man. He said, "You betrayed my order, stole our lands, gave succor and aid to high men!" He drove down his sword in three quick stabs.

"Do him no harm, Jacques!" shouted Montagu belatedly, but he couldn't worry about that. He had to get back into the antechamber, to stop anyone going down the stairs to rally defenders.

He jumped out of the room to see three Hospitallers, knives in their hands, hesitating at the doorway. No swords with them, not military brothers, good. One was no older than thirteen.

Montagu gestured to his vacant eye. "You know me, boys—the English king's one-eyed griffin. Put down your arms; there's no need for you to die today." The sword's song was loud in his ears. It was telling him that his enemies were of serious intent—battle was imminent.

A monk slashed down at the top of his head with a dagger—the attack of an unschooled man. Montagu deflected the blade with his hand and turned sharply, using the monk's own momentum to slam his head into the wall, dropping him to the floor like a sack of grain, the knife clattering to the stones.

"You?" said Montagu, leveling Arondight at the oldest monk's throat.

The man dropped the knife. The boy still held his.

"Tell the child to see sense," said Montagu.

"Gervais, let go of the weapon," said the other monk. "This is a great warrior and you are too young to be a martyr." The boy dropped it.

"Are there any more of you?" he asked them.

The elder monk shook his head.

"Do as you are told and you will live," said Montagu. "I am not a butcher, no matter what you may hear of us English."

"We hear you are butchers," said the monk.

"Then be careful not to make me one," said Montagu.

Good Jacques emerged from the bedroom. The monks gasped: he was covered in blood.

"Kill them; they are the lapdogs of tyrants," said Good Jacques.

"Or the servants of God's appointed king," said Montagu. "You have treasures, things the king entrusted to you."

"Not here," said the monk.

"We will look, and if you are lying, you will die," said Montagu. He would let the boy live, he thought. It was necessary to make good on his threats—as a parent must make good on his threats to a child. If he warned the man and then let him go, his reputation would count for nothing with the French.

"You will find nothing," said the man, "and I will not help murderers. Are you from Hell?"

"England, as I said," said Montagu. Then a thought struck him. "What is the disturbance in the chapel?"

"A devil has broken through," said the monk, "and the men are struggling to contain it."

"Watch them," said Montagu to the Templar. Good Jacques, looking down at his bloody hands, seemed surprisingly unnerved and said nothing.

Montagu quickly ransacked the rooms—there was nothing there of any real value at all. Some of the fine cups, plates, and wall hangings would have interested a common thief, but not him. Good Jacques had made a mess of the grand master. Well, at least the old man was in Heaven now. Montagu looked at the body and wondered about the company he was forced to keep to do the king's work.

At the back of the room, new bricks were at the bottom of the wall. Montagu waved the feather. The wall disappeared to reveal a small storeroom.

There was nothing in it.

"Is this where it would have been?" he shouted to Good Jacques.

The Templar poked his head around the door. He said, "I think so. There's nowhere else looks likely."

Montagu left the room. "Lock these two in there and we'll head to Caesar's Tower," he said.

"There are no locks." Good Jacques had grabbed the older monk, a knife in his hand.

"No," said Montagu, "we are not killers. These are holy men and I'll not spill their blood without reason."

"You are not in command here, lord," said Good Jacques.

"With this in my hand, I am," said Montagu, nodding toward Arondight.

The Templar looked at the fine steel, the blade aflame in the light of the torches, and he let the monks go.

"Tie them then," said Montagu. He pointed with the sword to the ropes that secured the monks' robes.

Voices on the stairs. Men coming up.

"Robbers!" shouted the boy monk.

Montagu caught the child a backhanded blow, sending him unconscious to the floor. He was, as always, a practical man, a man who had formed his battle tactics under the arch-pragmatist Edward. The boy couldn't be left to give away their positions, so he had to be silenced. "I won't be so kind to you," he informed the older monk.

"What? Who's up there?" The voices from the stairs again.

Montagu sheathed Arondight and approached the monk, pulling off the man's belt cord. In an instant he had him tied, long practiced at such maneuvers in tournament mêlée and battle.

"You should strike a bargain," said the monk, "your friend in the chapel may prove difficult to contain. It wouldn't be impossible for you to walk out of here."

"It's not impossible for me to walk out of here now," said Montagu. He turned to the Templar.

"Our mission is still on. We'll make Caesar's Tower."

"You can't fight all of them," said Good Jacques.

"I don't intend to. Come on."

The spiral staircase still had one level to ascend. Montagu opened the door to it to see a hare-eyed monk staring back at him—he wore only a plain habit, no mail, and he carried no sword. Montagu put his boot into the center of the man's chest, sending him sprawling up the stairs, his head striking a step with a crack. Montagu hoped he hadn't killed him. He sprang up toward a door at the top. It opened onto the crenellated roof of the keep and he ran out onto it. He was above the fog, and a half moon looked down on him. Below him, lights swirled like strange fish in a soupy sea—torches. Well, the alarm was up, men were pouring into the building.

The Templar joined him on the roof. "Now what?" he asked.

"We make some corpses," said Montagu.

He closed the door to the roof and drew Arondight. Soon men would be pouring up those stairs, coming through that door, and he wanted them coming through blind. He could hold that door forever if he had to. Once as many men as possible had been drawn to the tower, he would cut a hole in the tower roof using the feather, hope to get in unnoticed. If not, Montagu would have the advantage of surprise. He put his hand to his tunic, felt the letter. The feather! It wasn't there. He unbuckled the tunic. Nowhere. He must have dropped it in all the running.

Then he saw the Templar with the feather in his hand.

"I cannot be caught by these people," Good Jacques said. "You will provide a distraction while I find the letters."

"What?"

The Templar held up the angel's feather. He also had the sack containing the holy lance, the crown of thorns. Montagu had only put it down for a breath. Instinctively he felt inside his tunic. Yes, the bottle of angel's blood was still there.

"I was a pickpocket before I ever was a monk," Good Jacques said. He stood on the edge of the battlements and Montagu could see it was hopeless—he could not grab him before he jumped.

Montagu said, "All England's angels are not gone. Some were left. If the Evertere eats angels, how did an angel get it back in its chest?"

Good Jacques replied, "That was not an angel."

"Then what was it?"

Good Jacques shook his head and stepped off the roof, floating down into the fog, just a faint glow against the gray.

Montagu looked to the heavens. Then he smiled. "It is as it is," he said. He put his tunic back on and secured the letter. He kissed the hilt of the sword. "St. Anne," he said, "and Isabella." The saint sang, filling his mind with beautiful music, but the shouts of his foes dinned in his ears.

34

The pilgrims ditched them a day's walk from Milan—the old man whom they called their leader telling Orsino that he considered him and his boy bad luck.

They were then cast into the rather ludicrous position of walking side by side with the pilgrims along the Roman road for much of the journey, separated by two hundred yards and a hard silence.

Orsino got easy access to the city, a coin—and a word that he was attending on a merchant of Florence—all he needed to get him in. His fine armor, good horse, and squire showed him to be a man of quality.

Milan staggered Dow. He had thought London rich, but this place shone as if its streets really were paved with gold.

Dow thought of Sariel—his mother. Was she even his mother? Everything had turned out to be false, everything. He wanted so much to be ordinary, to return to the moor, to give up his cause, to find a woman he could trust, neither devil or demon; to live even as the people of the villages lived, in simplicity. Was it better to bow to a priest, to take the blood and the flesh at the altar and be secure, than to live always in this life of unrewarded struggle?

He felt dizzy and sick, and Dow could still taste that strange dust that had issued from the devil-girl. The city made his head spin. Everything could be bought here—the whole city was a market bursting with produce from all over the world. The main street was less a market than a brawl conducted with lengths of bright cloth, plus loaves, pans, fish, armor, pots, livestock. Everyone shoved and bustled, everyone called out and cried. Here a man shouldered through the crowd carrying a squealing piglet above his head. Toward a stall selling saddles a fight broke out, a man screaming that he had been pickpocketed.

They were looking for the house of the Hospitallers, who kept a small priory in the city. He passed through an arch—above it a carved stone shield featuring the slithering snake of the ruling Visconti family's arms—the Biscone. The snake had a man clasped in its jaws, his wide arms indicating his anguish. Orsino saw Dow looking up at it.

"Like the angel said," said Orsino. He yawned. "We need to find lodgings and stabling for the horses. I have a feeling it won't be cheap."

Dow coughed. The taste of that dust was still with him.

"Are you feeling well?" Orsino asked him.

"Right fine," said Dow.

"Here." Orsino passed a wineskin over to the boy and smiled at him.

Dow took a swig to clear his mouth. "Thank you," he said.

Orsino laughed in surprise. "Would you unhorse me?"

"I don't understand."

"That's the first time you've said 'thank you' in all the years I've known you."

Dow flushed and feared tears might come into his eyes.

Orsino took the wineskin and put his hand on Dow's arm. He said, "I would be a friend to you, if you let me. You have been badly treated, no question, and it was me who took you from your home. But God offers absolution, so you can too. You are dear to me, Dowzabel—my apprentice."

"You are not my father."

"No. And you are not my son. But God has put us together for whatever reason. My son is gone. My daughter and my wife too, and it was God's punishment on me that they went, my sins that they paid for. Through you I would atone."

Dow said, "I am not your way to salvation."

"Perhaps not. I don't seek to make you my son. I seek only to treat you kindly and to behave as a true Christian toward you. I will gain atonement through my mission here."

"You would find your Drago and make powerful men more powerful."

Orsino said, "If it pleases you, I will tell you my mission truly. It is one of which you will approve. Get down from your horse."

Both men dismounted and Orsino drew the horses on through the bustle to a quieter part of town.

In a burning square of pale stone they watered the horses at a fountain. Orsino sat down on the lip of its pool and gestured for the boy to join him. No one was in earshot, but Orsino spoke in English just in case.

"My mission is more than capturing the Drago. I am here to kill a king," he said.

Dow felt a tightness in his throat. He asked, "Which king?"

"The old king of England," Orsino said. "He is still alive and here, somewhere, and he has the Drago with him."

"How will you find him?"

"The Hospitallers are sheltering him. I think the easiest way is to join them."

"That is the shortest course?"

He replied, "These things aren't achieved overnight. If God has kept old Edward alive, then it is for a reason. Unpicking the work of God is not easy."

"You will be damned, according to your religion, you will be damned!" The intensity of Dow's feeling took him by surprise. His mouth was dry and his hands balled into fists.

"I am already damned for what I did in Sainte-Chapelle and for a hundred other things. Our religion offers salvation. I have promises from Montagu. I will receive a pardon from the king of England. It will be the end of my struggles, Dow. I will be well rewarded. You too. An end to arms, to fighting. A quiet place with some land and some animals and my soul at rest. I could not want for more. You will be free to go, Dow—back to your gray country at the edge of the world if you choose."

"Why not let me go now?"

Orsino said, "You have an art that surpasses Edwin's, that surpasses anyone's as far as I know. You will be useful, yet, I am sure. And besides, you don't want to go. I sense you have your own purposes."

"And if I choose not to be useful?" Dow said.

"Then go. Go now. I will find this king and kill him without you if I have to. But if we join the Hospitallers, even as lay brothers, we will have to take their oath. You will have to swear to your faith in God and His son, Jesus Christ."

"*You* swear," said Dow, "and let me be your servant. The order would never have me, they are too fussy."

"They may be too fussy for me," said Orsino. "Can you disguise your beliefs?"

"Yes."

"And even lie about your faith?"

Dow replied, "Nothing is wrong if it serves the greater good."

The square was searingly hot, the waters of the fountain dazzling. Dow found it hard to marshal his thoughts.

Dow could not understand this religion that could commit such barbarities and then, on the word of a king or a priest, have all guilt wiped away. Orsino was going to kill a man, albeit a king. The vast poor would benefit when he lifted the banner. To take a life, though, was such a big step. How could Orsino do it just to gain the favor of his God? A god who loves blood was no god worth having.

"So is it the Hospitallers or the road?" said Orsino.

"Let's find your Hospitallers," said Dow. If he had to, he would swear, and then he would break his oath because it pleased him to defy the God of the priests and the monks.

They pressed on to an inn in a run-down quarter of the town. Orsino was unimpressed with the lodgings but noted that the stables were well kept—more important than his own comfort. In the end the price was too great anyway and they negotiated a stay in the hayloft, along with three cats and a quantity of scurrying rats. It was late and dark when Dow felt Murmur crawl to his side.

"There are many demons here," Murmur said. "All Free Hell who could squeeze through has squeezed through. We cover the land."

"And do you whisper to the people?" Dow asked.

"Yes. In England we are not far from an uprising."

"How do you know?"

"We swarm in the upper airs. Fellow whispers to fellow and the moon is dark with demons' wings."

"And do you meet resistance?"

Murmur said, "The old queen casts a net to catch us. Devils have swum from France. In the Temple of Paris a great evil is coming to earth. Hell is moving against Free Hell."

"Why can they come through?"

"The angels of France are still in their shrines. They do not trust Philip after the death of Jegudiel. The devils are not as afraid of them as they were."

"Then we must move as fast as we can," said Dow.

He had to find that banner, as he had been charged to do by Free Hell. But, though he was nearer to finding it than he had ever been, Dow sensed he still had a long way to go. As fast as he could might not prove fast enough.

35

T hree were dead at the door before they stopped coming. Arondight was as true as ever, the mail of the first monk giving no resistance to its blade. The second who tried to clamber past his fallen companion was dispatched with a flick of the wrist, the big sword as light as a wand in the hand, heavy as a hammer on the side of the head.

Some idiot from the rear tried to shoot Montagu with a crossbow and damn near succeeded, albeit that the quarrel passed through a monk before it shaved Montagu's whiskers. The quarrel-shot monk kept advancing for a few paces before a look of surprise overtook him, and he collapsed. Montagu doubted he even knew he'd been hit.

After that, Montagu got the door shut again. It was a disadvantage that he couldn't see anyone coming, but he could hear them and the singing of Arondight would alert him when danger was close, the saints' songs rising to a tumult in his mind. Two more crossbow bolts came through the door, splintering the wood.

People were shouting at the bottom of the tower, telling him to give himself up. Montagu almost laughed. He'd been involved in many sieges himself, but never one as tricky as this. The obvious tactic would have been to leave him up there to die of hunger or thirst. An intelligent commander would just seal the door and leave Montagu to amuse himself on the roof for a couple of weeks. Of course, there would always be the threat they would take him while he slept. His prospects were not good.

It was quiet on the stairs, and he risked looking out over the parapet. A man went scurrying into the chapel. He was carrying a bundle of papers under his arm, two big quills tucked behind his ear, making him look like he was dressed up for a May festival.

Montagu waited a while.

"Come down. You cannot stay there forever." A voice from up the stairs. He didn't bother to reply.

The voice continued. "We know you are only two. How long do you think you can hold out up there?"

Again Montagu said nothing. He looked over the parapet. The wall had cracks in it, but he was never going to be able to climb down it. Even if he didn't fall—which he would—he'd be spotted and there'd be a reception committee at the bottom, if they didn't bother to pick Montagu off with crossbows first.

The fog swirled about him. Was it fog? It seemed thicker, like smoke. Were they trying to burn him out? No, this wasn't smoke, it was something fouler by far. Montagu coughed, an acid taste in his throat.

The smoke pooled at his feet. Sorcery. More devils? He grasped Arondight in both hands, ready to strike.

"Stay your hand."

The voice was like the rending of metal.

Curling around his feet was an extraordinary creature—a gray snake, its body as thick as a man's. Taking shape on its back were a pair of enormous diaphanous wings. The smoke was still thick about him and he beat it away.

"What are you?" Montagu asked it.

"A devil, come to offer you a ride away, lord."

"I don't deal with devils."

The creature reared up now, its great mouth level with Montagu's face. It said, "I am going to England."

He said, "Get away from me!"

The creature gave a great hiss and shot up into the air, its tail swirling behind it like a rope from the rigging.

"Who's up there?" The voice came from the courtyard below, so loud it was almost like a blow.

Montagu looked over the side and crossed himself. Below him was a gigantic figure—a man with his hair cropped close to his skull, a toothless mouth shouting up at him.

The giant said, "I see you, little Montagu. Don't you know me?"

Montagu took a pace back.

"I am Hugh Despenser, who should have been your lord, come back from Hell to claim what is his and reign forever on earth under the patronage of great Satan!"

Despenser! Back from Hell. Well, if anyone could make himself unpopular enough to be thrown out of the infernal pit, it was Despenser.

Without thinking what he was doing, Montagu ran to the other side of the roof. At the back of Caesar's Tower there was a faint glow. The Templar, or someone, had decided to ignore the exit and come through the wall using the angel's feather.

A thump at the side of the tower and a cry. Montagu ran back to that side of the wall and looked down. The giant figure was near to the wall, holding its foot. It cursed when it saw him and jumped at the wall. Its fingers dug into the stone; it was clearly wounded, as it howled every time it drove its right foot into a crack.

Montagu looked above him. The snake was still up there, its coils winding like part of the fog.

It said, "Come away to England."

Not with a devil, and not without the letters incriminating Philip.

Despenser hammered at the wall. He was halfway up. The fall to the ground would kill Montagu if he tried to jump but not if . . . He had no other plan. He inverted Arondight in his hands, holding it like a knight holds a sword on a tomb and jumped toward Despenser's shoulders.

The giant swatted at him as he fell, but Montagu was on him, landing squarely on his chest and driving him from the wall. Then everything seemed both fast and slow at the same time. Despenser fell backward, Montagu stabbed down with the sword, but Despenser caught both Montagu's hands in his giant fist and they fell together.

The fall was unreal: the two seemed to float down as slow as a feather, Montagu dodging a huge swipe aimed at his head. The unequal combatants rolled as they fell. Montagu saw the ground looming and feared he would be trapped under the giant. A final twist and Despenser finished underneath him, Arondight stabbing down through his arm to pin him to the ground. The giant twisted and screamed, trying to extricate the sword, but the holy blade was an anathema to him and he could not touch it.

Montagu didn't hesitate; he ran. It was too dangerous to pull the sword out and stab the giant again, even if it meant leaving so valuable a weapon. Holy swords came to those who deserved them. The blade had been lost and had found its way back to him before. If God wished him to have it, it would return to Montagu again.

Two steps and his foot jerked back. Despite its injury, the giant had grabbed his leg with the hand that was not pinned. Montagu stamped down on its fingers, but its grip was unrelenting.

Despenser said, "Now you die, Montagu!"

Montagu had no choice but to reach for his sword and yank it free. The giant groaned and immediately sat up, dashing him onto the soft earth, which, luckily for Montagu, left him little more than winded. Arondight sang through the air, severing the giant's right hand. The monster howled and swung for him with its left, but Montagu rolled away. A harsh white light dazzled his eyes, a sound like a crack and the giant standing above him went blurry.

As he lost consciousness Montagu heard a voice he recognized.

"I hope you will remember this service, my lord."

Above Montagu stood someone he knew—a man who had journeyed with him on the cog from England. The companion of the mercenary. Yes, a merchant of the more common sort who had been there when the angel was stripped. A name came into his head: "Osbert." And then Montagu knew no more.

36

The warrior monks stood in the fine mizzle shoulder to shoulder around the perimeter of Castle Rising's earthworks. Each one had a shield marked with the fluted cross of the Hospitallers, and each had a sword, a mace, or a polearm. In front of them, treading carefully on a slabbed path, a priest walked the circumference of the defenses swinging a censer, chanting a prayer. All the time he looked at his feet, careful not to disturb a single mark that had been daubed onto the stone of the slabs. It was a magic circle—dust of the tomb of St. Mark mixed with blood of the Hanley angel—and all that stood between them and the hordes of Hell.

A boy monk crossed himself, looking up to Brother Robert, the huge monk like a castle tower himself, seemingly unperturbed by the siege.

"A message must have reached the king by now," said the boy.

"The king is on the continent with all his best men. We might *hope* for relief, but we cannot expect it. Better to pray to Christ than call for men to aid us."

The boy crossed himself again. There were fires out there in the dark, torches moving, voices calling.

"They will not cross the perimeter," said the big monk, "they cannot. They are Satan's and our circle invokes the name of God."

"So why are we here?"

"They might use men to try to break it."

Something screeched through the darkness, a baggy, flapping thing, big as a dog flying low along the perimeter.

"What was that?" asked the boy.

Brother Robert said, "A thing of Hell."

"It's her doing—the one up there," said the boy. He gestured back to the castle. "Why don't we kill her?"

"She is a queen. That would be against God's law."

"She is to blame for this, surely?"

"How? She's locked inside two magic circles. Nothing that is not of God can cross them."

Something came lumbering forward through the night—a giant of a thing twice as tall as an ordinary man. But it was a man, pale, dressed as richly as any merchant. Its hands were long talons, its teeth a row of shining spikes, and its feet those of a rooster.

"We would have parlay," declared the creature.

"Who are you?" called out Robert.

"Lord Greed of Hell's Cinderlands. You are under siege, and none will come to lift it. I have almost the entire 12th Legion of the Burning Plains of Antenora here. It will be a brave earthly army that stands against it."

In the dark, more devils were assembling, squat figures, gigantic heads perched on bowed legs, no bodies, just cavernous mouths of innumerable teeth grinning from drooping jowls, big eyes flashing red in the torchlight. There were hundreds of them, all bearing spears and axes, many torches too.

Robert said, "We can wait it out."

"Can you? How much food do you have? We have poisoned your water."

"We have a queen in here. God will not let her die."

Lord Greed said, "Not her, perhaps. But you, I think, yes." The stink of the devil—smoke and sulfur—was powerful even at twenty paces.

"Then bring your worst," said Robert. "I will die fighting for right. God does not want you out of Hell, does he, devil?"

"God knows what he wants when he sees it, in my experience," said the devil. "He is first concerned that the sinner is punished. If that is achieved, I think He will be flexible on the rest."

"This is the realm of men and angels," said Robert, "and you offend it by your presence. England is not given to devils."

"Thrones are not always given to kings, but still they take them. We will see. We're needed here. God's order is under threat. We only move to defend it. Let us in—we could be your allies." The creature returned to the darkness. Beneath the torches, the 12th Legion gnashed and gurgled.

"Think nothing of it," said Robert. "We hold the line and they will not harm us."

"Kill the queen and we are safe," said the boy.

"Our bodies, but not our souls. God will deliver us, one way or another."

From a high window, Isabella looked down. A ring of torches out there, movements in the dark, as in dreams—a wing against a flame, great jaws emerging from the murk into firelight, only for the dark to swallow them again.

"How long do you think they'll hold out?" said little Charles, who stood in front of her. The boy was still trembling from the effects of his journey by the angel feather cloak.

"They will die rather than admit the devils," she said.

"So what is the point of the siege?"

"To show we can stage a siege. To show we are a force. When the Hospitallers are dead, I can just walk out of here. And my forces will keep increasing—there is no sign the devils will stop coming."

He asked, "Where are they coming from?"

"What an inquisitive child you are. You don't need to trouble yourself with that. Suffice it to know that they are coming. Once I am outside these holy circles *I* can begin summoning. We can have more impressive devils than these on our side."

"You have used them before?"

Isabella replied, "Yes. In a limited way. My husband had allowed Despenser to ruin the country by that stage. Once my husband's angels had gone, we didn't need any devils. I could have taken the country riding alone on my palfrey. The armies couldn't wait to welcome us in. Still, the devils helped us take the throne. But after that we didn't want them. They'd set themselves up as our masters if they got the chance. There's a never-ending need to control them, to fight with ritual and ceremony to stop them over-throwing you. Better to banish them when they've served their purpose."

"How did you banish them?" Charles asked her.

"As one banishes anything. By making a deal."

She went to the table and took up a looking glass. Isabella turned down the corners of her mouth, dissatisfied with what she saw. From a bag she took out a small vial and unstoppered it. She carefully dripped a tiny drop onto her finger and licked at it. Then she replaced the cork.

"Did you have any angel's blood left over from your little escapade?"

Charles admitted, "I have several vials."

"Bring me one next time you visit, there's a good boy. It does wonders for the complexion. Despenser had some about him when we finally took him and I've found it most useful ever since."

"I will." Charles thought for a moment. He was still gazing out of the window. He said, "Will you banish these devils too? It seems a pity. I could use them in France. I bet they're stripping the land for miles around."

"I don't know. It's time you went. I have a task I need you to perform. If you want to deal France a blow it will be worth your while."

"What?"

"These Hospitallers who contain me have several documents relating to the attack of the Templars on our House of Capet. They contain much that is of interest to me, much that would enable me to persuade and control my son. They lock them in their Caesar's Tower in the Temple in Paris. You could get them."

"The travel makes me sick."

Isabella said, "But it has not killed you. The documents, my spies say, are walled in on the topmost floor. But the tower is impregnable. No door. Anyone wanting them would need to dig them out, something that could take weeks and hardly go unnoticed. You could fly in there, recover them at your leisure, and fly out again. You're a big enough boy to cope with sleeping sick in the dark for a few days, aren't you?"

"My cloak gives light enough," said Charles, "but tell me, Auntie, what do the documents say?"

"They discuss the summoning of certain creatures of the air—those cast down by God when he expelled Lucifer from Heaven, those who were not thrown into Hell before the gates closed. And other mysteries too. Beyond this, I believe a key is there. The first gate has been opened once. When it opens again, someone might step through who can open the second. That would give us more powerful allies. I would reward you for this service with some devils of your own."

"Bound to *my* service?" he asked.

"What a clever boy you are! Yes, bound to your service."

"Then I will bear the sickness for you, Auntie. How shall I find it?"

"It is north of the Great Hall, a huge square castle—you can hardly miss it. Caesar's Tower is the smaller of the two that stand within the grounds."

Charles said, "Then let me do your bidding. I could carry a summoning circle out for you if you like."

"No, we will limit the number of those—it makes my bargaining position stronger."

"With whom?"

Isabella said, "With my son." She tousled his hair. "Ooh, look," she said, "the devils have got a country lad to try to break the circle. Oh no, the monks have a quarrel in him. Two quarrels. Marvelous shots in this torchlight, you have to give them that."

"You have spies here. Can't they break it?" he asked.

"I am never let near the men who tend the circle. My spies are few and good for relaying me news from the few friends I still have outside. The Hospitallers would kill them if they tried to touch the circle."

"Mama says you have a way of getting men to die for you."

Isabella laughed. "Not these men. They are wise to most of my tricks. But you are clever, little Charles. The monks never face me. Though with you here that might change. I have another idea how you might serve me."

A few moments later, Charles stepped out of the window in the angel feather cloak, floating to earth as if a feather himself. The monks did not see him at first and, such was the jabbering of the devils in the dark, he had difficulty making himself heard.

Then someone turned from the line and screamed, pointing at Charles and his glowing cloak.

They ran to him with swords, but he shouted for them to put up their arms, for he was of God. Monks grabbed him.

"A devil!" said one.

"Nothing unholy can break the circle," said another.

"I am of God!" said Charles. "My name is the Doobaloobaloo, a cherub of the throne of God. I have killed the vicious queen to release you."

"What?"

"She is dead, as God intended," said Charles. His cloak glowed and burned with a white fire.

"How did you kill her? How?" But the monks were now grasping only air. The boy in the cloak was shooting up into the heavens.

The monks shot up the stairs to the queen's solar. Her lady-in-waiting lay dead on the floor, her throat cut.

"It's true!" said Robert.

He ran inside, pounding up the stairs to the bed. The queen too was covered in blood, all over her hands, her dress. The monk shook her gently, instinctively asking her forgiveness for presuming to touch her. Only then did the monk realize—she had no wound at all about her.

Isabella opened her eyes.

"Oh, Robert," she said. "You look at me, at last."

37

The pardoner lay in a bed in the guest room of the great keep. Osbert had his wine by his side, a fine lantern, good sheets, and, very important, Montagu's weighty purse. He counted the money again and again. Forty livres. It was more profitable working for the French than the English, that was for sure.

On a table next to the lantern lay the letter Osbert had taken from Montagu's tunic after he had slugged him unconscious. It bore a fine seal that he dearly wanted to break so he could find out if its contents were worth selling. However, he hadn't yet decided if the letter would be more valuable intact.

Gressil, the little devil at his feet, had told him that opening it *would* reduce its worth. And there were some secrets it might be dangerous to know.

As far as the pardoner could see, little could be going better. Hugh Despenser, missing an arm and a toe—and with a bad wound in his shoulder—lay in the chapel, hoping the dawn light might restore his angelic body. The Hospitallers were going to try to sew the arm back on in the morning, Despenser assuring them that it was perfectly possible to mend a devil with patches, like an old cloak.

Philip had been well pleased with the summoning, the capture of Montagu, and the signing of the pact with Despenser. Despenser would get Gascony for his aid in tracking down the prophesied Antichrist. That would certainly awake the French angels. The Gascons were used to harsh masters, and the addition of a few devils wouldn't hurt them.

Montagu was in the dungeons, lashed to a wall. As soon as he recovered, he would be interrogated by rack on his role in the death of the angel and after that he would be killed. Osbert smiled to himself as he lay in his bed. His angel feather was around his neck. He wondered what use that might be. Could it heal Despenser? Even if it could, he wasn't going to try. He preferred devil Hugh injured and cowed. The longer he remained so, the better.

Presently, the wine made him drowsy and Osbert dozed. He snuffed the wick with an automatic gesture and felt the exertions of the day seeping out of him in the luxurious bed. Things were going great. It was only as he fell to sleep, he remembered how often in his life the thought "thank God, I've had my last ever kick in the balls" had been followed by an enormous kick in the balls. His contentment worried him.

It was as if he dreamed. Smoke was in the room, lots of smoke. And then the smoke took shape, grew a voice.

"Form up," said the smoke. Its voice was a scraping squeak, like the rending of metal.

"I am doing. It's not easy, you know."

Osbert opened his eyes, or at least he thought he opened his eyes. In front of him were two extraordinary creatures. They were like dwarfish men—no higher than his elbow when standing, but they had monstrous boar's heads out of all proportion to the size of their bodies. Gressil was on the end of his bed, cleaning his paws.

Osbert asked, "Who are you?"

"Color Sergeant Bale of the 15th Legion of Dis," said one of the men. "This is Sergeant Slurp, of the same."

"You're from Hell?"

"Got that right," said Bale.

"What are you doing here?" Osbert said.

"Clearing up your mess, son. Agent Gressil of the Sneak here managed to get a message to us through a chink in the wall of Hell."

"The Sneak?"

"Satan's spies," said Gressil. "We're active in Hell but most of us are here on earth."

"I thought Hell was sealed."

"You spoke of the postern gates," said Gressil.

"I was making that up."

"It happens to be true," said Bale. "Though there are also cracks in the walls where certain of us may get out—those with the gift of smoke, though we are few."

"You can turn yourself into smoke?" said the pardoner.

"Anyone can turn themselves into smoke, that's a piece of piss," said Bale. "All that takes is a torch and a bucket of pitch. We can turn ourselves back again. That's a lot harder and it takes it out of you but, in extremis, it can be done. Anyway, Gressil here had you down as a likely agent of Hell. But you've been making a mess of things, son."

"How so?" Osbert asked.

"Our allies on earth want the boy dead. But we also need Montagu to get back to his king."

"Why?"

"You ask a lot of questions," said Slurp. "In Hell we don't ask questions because if we do, we find we get answers, some of which we may not like. Know what I mean?" He cracked his knuckles, which Osbert saw were ordinary human hands.

"Where did you come from?"

"There he goes again," said Slurp. "Shall I give him an answer, Captain?"

"Give him two," said Bale.

Slurp drew a sword from his belt and in a quick movement struck Osbert twice on the head with the flat of the blade.

"Arrghh!" said Osbert, holding his head.

"Any more questions?" said Bale.

"I've got a holy sword there!" said Osbert. "Which I don't mind using!" He nodded toward where Arondight lay.

"He's useless in a fight," said Gressil. "Don't worry about that. He's no Montagu!"

"I thought you were my familiar!" said Osbert to Gressil.

"No, you're *my* familiar," said Gressil.

"Rubbish, you didn't help at all in that summoning."

"Yeah, as you might have expected a familiar to. You, however, brought Despenser through just nicely on my behalf. Thanks. Now let's get Montagu out of that dungeon. Move."

Osbert said, "We can't do that. There are gaolers, he's in the middle of the Hospitaller's castle, I'm blind pissed." That was something of an exaggeration, though not much. The room swayed under the influence of the wine.

"He's got an angel's feather," said Gressil.

"Bang on," squeaked Bale.

"What will that do?" asked Osbert.

"It opens passageways," said Gressil. "We'll be able to go straight into the dungeon. I know which one he's in, boys."

"Will you bring it back when you're finished?"

The boars exchanged glances. "We're devils," one said. "If I tried to pick up or use that feather, I'd be dead meat."

"Fried pork," said the other boar, with something of a sizzle to his voice.

"This is why we need you, you moron. Now bring it."

"I can hardly walk. I'm lashed."

"Get up before I get you up," said Bale.

The pardoner slid out of bed. He hadn't bothered taking off his clothes, so he only had to strap on his boots. Osbert swayed as he stood. He really was phenomenally drunk. Situation normal for that time of night; he'd get by. There was no way he was going to join in this mad escapade. He'd decided that France was offering him far more than England ever had and that he wasn't about to turn his back on that. He'd raise the alarm and have the Hospitallers deal with these devils. Osbert dived for the door. Unfortunately the door didn't appear to be quite where he'd left it when he came into the chamber, and he ran straight into the wall. He sat down with a great thump.

"Was that an escape attempt?" asked Gressil.

"Do that again and I'll open up your entrails and chew on them," said Bale. "Slowly, and with malice."

"Right." Then the pardoner was sick.

"Get him some water," said Gressil.

Slurp poured a draft into a cup and gave it to Osbert. He drank it down.

"Look," he said, "can we not rethink this? Life has just picked up in a major way for me. I could be court wizard to King Philip. Imagine that. Fine clothes, women, drink. A bit of light summoning. I could try to find your mates, bring through more devils, I really could."

"Cut out the chat!" Slurp's voice was like the squeal of a greased piglet at a May fair.

Osbert protested, "We'll be seen leaving the tower!"

Slurp said, "Not at this time. Come on, and bring that feather. And the sword and the letter."

They slipped down out of the tower, where, as predicted by Osbert, there was a double guard on the front door—two men. He said "hello" and explained he wanted to nip outside for a piss, on account of being unable to piss in strange surroundings. The guard was about to let him go when a long knife emerged through his stomach and he fell silently to the floor. Osbert saw the boars had used the distraction—of him talking to the guards—to kill them both.

"That's stealthy, isn't it?" said Osbert. "That'll cause no alarm."

"They've only just started their watch," said Gressil. "They won't be missed for a while."

Osbert crossed himself. The forecourt was deserted, but Despenser's moans could be heard from the chapel.

"Godforsaken bleating little girl," said Osbert. "Montagu's in the dungeon under the castle."

"Which side?"

"Other side," said the pardoner. The cool night air was beginning to sober him up.

They skirted the castle. Osbert still had to think of a way to ditch these creatures. Shouting out might do it, but Slurp carried a cruel barbed spear and Osbert knew very well that Bale would happily follow up on his threat of entrail chewing.

"Please don't let me be blamed for this, God," said the pardoner. "Please. I am opposing your enemies, I am working with your devils. Do not let me suffer for doing your will." Osbert considered others who had done God's will

down the centuries. Martyrs, mainly. God hadn't seemed all that bothered
about them suffering for doing His will. In fact, He'd rather seemed to relish it.

No monk was around when they came to a point where Osbert guessed
the dungeons might be. Osbert pissed against the side of the building.
What it would be to empty himself properly, to piss out all the bad luck,
stupid decisions, losing bets, and wrong turns he'd made. He'd have to piss
forever to do that. He'd never expected anything from life, but he'd allowed
himself to hope: that was the problem. When Osbert had no hope in his
life he was happy—he knew where he was. The devils were right, that idiot
boy so wrong.

In the Leadenhall market, selling his bits and bobs among the poultry
and the meat, he'd known where he stood, or rather groveled. Here, in his
merchant's finery, albeit bedraggled finery, he had come to think of nights
in soft beds, women, enough wine to drown him. But, as Osbert looked at
the wall, he thought of himself as one of the foundation stones that wished
to have the weight of the building removed from it and sit on top of the roof.
All that happened when you got up there, though, was that you got rained
on, snowed on, and shat on by birds.

"Are you going to piss forever?" said Gressil.

"I have a feeling it's going to be one of the evening's highlights, so I'm
dragging it out while I can," said the pardoner. He shook and miserably
holstered his cock.

"Use the feather," said Bale.

The pardoner took out the feather. It did occur to Osbert to hit the devils
with it, but he was sure that while he was frying one of them, the other would
be spitting him with his spear.

"What do I do?" he asked them.

"Wave it at the wall," said Gressil, "and want to go through. Really *want*
to go through."

"I don't really want to go through."

Slurp jabbed him with his spear. "Want to go through now?" he said.

"A lot more than I did," said Osbert.

The pardoner waved the feather. For all the trinkets he'd ever sold, all
the saints' bones and teeth, the magic symbols and amulets, he had never
possessed anything with any real power. This was different. The stone began

to shimmer as he traced the outline of a door, to blur like water seen from underneath and finally to open. He was fascinated by it. Despite his fear, he had even been fascinated that time in the chapel, when Despenser had possessed Sariel's body. Osbert thrilled at the thought that he was doing magic. He put his hand on Arondight at his side. For a moment he felt like the knight or the wizard he had wanted to be as a boy.

Osbert went forward and down, swirling the glowing feather in front of him, creating a tunnel through the rock. Bale followed behind with the lamp. The rock opened out and they were in a dungeon, a filthy place stinking of every noxious thing that could be imagined. Three bodies were in there, no one alive.

"Smell that rot," said Bale. "Wouldn't you love to have a feed in here, old Slurp?"

"I would that, Color Sergeant," said Slurp.

They were faced by a door.

"We've come down into one of the cells, just get us through that and we're in," said Gressil.

Osbert waved the feather again and the door blurred and buckled, a hole appearing in it big enough to crawl through.

"Allow us," said Bale.

The boar devils ran through the hole, Bale first, Slurp second, one turning left, the other right. There was a brief cry of "hoy!" and then silence.

"Come on," said Slurp, his head appearing through the hole.

Osbert ducked through, drawing the holy sword. He was beginning to enjoy himself now, a combination of alcohol and the effect of seeing such incredible magic at close quarters lifting his spirits considerably. He felt like having another drink to wash the taste of vomit out of his mouth.

"One dungeon keeper, dead," said Slurp, as if reading off an inventory.

"Which cell do you think he's in?" said Gressil.

"Well, there's only three," said Bale.

"He's in that one," said Osbert. "I put him in it."

Bale lifted the keys from the dungeon keeper as Osbert lifted the man's bottle of wine.

"Are you going to drink again?" said Gressil. "You need to sober up."

Osbert said, "You're right, I do."

"So why are you drinking?"

"Because I so rarely find what I need is what I want. It's a toss-up, isn't it? Want, need, need, want. Which is it to be? Oh, go on, want then."

"You need discipline," said Bale. "Drunkenness is a sin."

"Everything's a bloody sin if you listen to you lot," said Osbert. "Look, I'm English. Drinking is what we do. Blame the weather. Rain's more bearable when you're zonked." He swigged on the wine. Not bad. Maybe Philip had been in a good mood after the recapture of Montagu and had ordered the monks to hand out the good stuff.

Bale opened the door. Suspended from the wall, his hands above his head, was the sorry figure of Montagu.

"I hope he's not dead and you haven't got me out of bed for nothing," said Osbert.

"Unclasp him," ordered Bale.

"What, are the manacles holy? Can't you touch them either?"

"They're too high up, you bollock," said Slurp.

Osbert went over to Montagu, taking a stool. He stood on it and undid the first clasp. Montagu's left arm fell from the manacle, swinging all his weight onto the right. It dislocated with a crack.

"Whoops," said Osbert. Montagu cried out. Osbert was not happy to see the lord that way. He respected men like Montagu, was proud to tell their stories and feel they were the better of any French or German knight. To see him so beaten and broken was a shame, albeit that it was Osbert who had brought this about. He undid the other clasp and Montagu fell heavily to the floor.

"Give him drink."

"This is my wine," said Osbert.

"Water." Gressil came in, a cup in his hands. He put it to Montagu's lips, but the lord was too weak to drink. The demons lifted him between them and dragged him back toward the passages the feather had carved. They were gone, but with a swipe the pardoner renewed them. Out into the monastery. Still foggy, still silent.

They carried Montagu over to the woods near the curtain wall.

"Give him the letter," said Gressil. "Put it in his tunic. And the sword."

"Well, er, no," said the pardoner. "I'm in charge as long as I've got the weapon."

Montagu opened his eyes and lay looking up at the trees. "Devils."

"Devils who have rescued you—think on that," said Gressil.

"How?" he asked.

"A wave of my wand," said Osbert, flourishing the feather.

"Put that away; it's visible even through these trees," said Montagu. "Did you get that off the Templar?"

"Who? I got this off the angel," said Osbert.

"The man who came with me. Did he make it out of Caesar's Tower?"

"God knows," said the pardoner.

"Do you have my letter?" Montagu asked him.

"What letter?"

"The letter you took from me, along with my sword and my money, no doubt."

"Your tone is very aggressive for an unarmed and wounded man," said Osbert. "I—ah!"

Montagu reached over with his left hand, drew Arondight from the scabbard at the pardoner's side, and leveled the tip at his throat.

"Though your mood seems reasonable for a man in possession of a sword," said Osbert. He handed him the letter and the purse.

"We need to go back to the tower," said Montagu.

"No, no, no!" said Osbert. "Look, it'll be dawn soon. Despenser might have recovered by then. And . . ."

"Put my arm back in," said Montagu.

"What?"

Montagu lay on his back and pulled his arm over his chest. "Take the arm and pull it to the side of my body," said Montagu. "Do it sharply!"

The pardoner did as he was bid. There was a click, and Montagu swallowed hard.

"We will go to Caesar's Tower," said Montagu, "where I will get what I need. Then we will leave."

"This is suicide," said Osbert.

"For you it is suicide to stay. Follow me or die," said Montagu. "My arm is useless and you must help me search."

"Follow you and die, more like," said Osbert.

"Perhaps, but you'll find the 'or' takes places quicker than the 'and.' Let me be plain, low man. I intend to kill you. You attacked me and therefore you deserve a traitor's death. Make yourself useful to me and I may reprieve you. But know that, if we are frustrated in our mission, or capture looks likely, I will kill you in an instant."

Osbert looked Montagu up and down. The pardoner had long experience of men who issue idle threats. The Lord Marschal did not strike him as one of them.

Montagu turned to the devils. "This is Arondight, the sword Lancelot held. It is a holy blade and death to you. Only the noise that your slaughter would cause prevents me from using it now. Get back to Hell," said Montagu.

"Actually, I thought we might go to England," said Gressil. "There seems a good deal of employment for our sort there at the moment."

"What do you mean?" Montagu asked.

"Hell is going to make the king an offer."

"In a month the king will have his angels," said Montagu, "and he won't need Hell, free or otherwise, and you devils will be as vapors on the wind. Now you, merchant, go forward—we've got work to do."

38

E dward leaned at the window of his room in the White Tower of the Tower of London, taking in the dawn, the shame of compromise deep inside him. The capital had always been an unruly place, resentful of the rule of kings, indifferent to any concerns but its own. Now the streets were in ferment.

The poor were muttering against their masters and, in some places, there had been rebellion. Everywhere, according to Edward's advisers, people spoke of Lucifer as the true maker of creation, God as an imposter. The morning sun had a dark smudge across it. Edward shivered. More of those little demons. Numerous as locusts, they swarmed through the air, whispering in the ears of the poor and stirring them to rebellion.

He'd led a party of longbowmen out to face them when they'd hovered over Southwark one day, but the arrows had been useless, the creatures simply flying up out of range. It was like trying to shoot down a swarm of bees. After the second volley the bowmen had rebelled at firing at the demons, who had done nothing to them. Before Edward could have them arrested, the archers were gone into the stews. He'd caught and hanged four of them, but that was hardly a sufficient example.

Edward thumped the wall. How was he supposed to conduct a war with the French when he wasn't even secure in his own realm at home? He could do nothing against these creatures, nothing. In the stews there was talk of a preaching whore—a great fat-bellied creature who spoke alongside a fallen priest, turning the people to Lucifer and away from God. He'd ordered his men to search for them—even put a price on their heads—but the people had not yet surrendered them. Edward imagined Montagu by his side. What would he say? "At least the fact our enemies are demons shows we're on the right side."

Edward fancied he could still taste the smoke of the humiliating defeat at Tournai. The army had run, not even been put to the sword. They had just melted away. There had been grumbles of mutiny there. One group of Welsh bowmen had openly made the Fork of Lucifer sign when they'd been informed they'd have to wait for pay. Did it hurt them to starve a little for their king? That's what they did, the poor: they starved and they froze for the glory of greater men. That was their God-ordained duty.

Edward needed to pray. He wound down the stairs and through into St. John's Chapel, two bodyguards falling in beside him as he exited his private chamber. He told them to wait at the chapel door. Edward loved it in there—the close huddled pillars, the bright arches of light from behind and above the altar. It was not a public church, but a little place to which he could escape to be alone with God—if He were there.

Edward prayed, as he had always prayed:

"Dear God, I sincerely repent my sins. I have traded with darkness, but only seeking the light. Grant me your light now. Grant me your aid and your direction."

A thump at the door.

Edward ignored it.

Another thump.

"Go away! I am at prayer!" he said.

Edward tried to fight down his temper, aware it was not appropriate in such a holy place.

The door opened and young Tom Whitley, the squire, poked his head into the chapel, his face white as a priest's surplice.

"I said get out!" I will not have my most private chapel violated! Get out before I put you out!" said Edward.

The young man was still ashen. He said, "Majesty, there is a pressing visitor here to see you."

"I'm not seeing anyone for a week; now do as I say and get out of my sight! Tell them to wait, I don't care if it's the pope himself!"

"Lord, he is most insistent, he . . ."

There was a rumpus at the doors of the chapel, men shouting, a couple of loud bangs. Edward stood, picked up his sword. The pain in his thigh from the crossbow bolt at Sluys was still there, and he was stiff as a board from walking awkwardly.

He asked, "What impertinence is this?"

An enormous figure in a green hood had pushed its way past the guards, so hard that two of them fell flat unconscious on the flagstones. Three more men were attached to its neck, trying to pull it back, but it shook them off as a dog shakes off water. The men drew and came for the figure, but it threw back its head before letting out a roar like the fall of a city wall, sending all three to the floor.

The figure picked up each of the guards and threw them through the door. Then he closed the door of the chapel and put the wooden bar across it. Edward crossed himself. As the figure walked forward it became apparent that it was a good head and shoulders taller than the king, who was himself a tall man. It threw back its hood. It was not a man at all but a huge lion, the color of dull steel with a mane comprised of metal rods, straight as crossbow quarrels and, it appeared, a good deal sharper than most.

Edward again crossed himself. "Are you an assassin?" he asked it.

"I'm an ambassador. Assassination is just a sideline." Its voice was a metallic growl.

"An ambassador for whom?"

"We need to talk in private," said the lion. It bowed.

"About what? You have to tell me, then I tell the king," said Tom Whitley, who had been locked inside.

"Private!" roared the lion, right in Whitley's face. The squire collapsed to the flagstones as Edward instinctively covered his ears.

"You haven't killed him, have you?" inquired Edward.

"Don't know. Do you want me to?" said the lion.

Edward glanced at Whitley. He owed his family £5,000. It would be convenient to have him eaten, but he couldn't serve up all his debtors on a plate to devils. He doubted there were enough devils in Hell to eat so many. He said, "No, look, I still have another summer's campaign to honor my debt. You're here too soon."

"You haven't got a debt to us," said the lion. "Let me rest my paws—I've had to swim from France." It hopped up onto the altar and sat facing Edward.

Edward said, "You are of Free Hell?"

"I curse its name. I am Lord Sloth of Hell, plain and simple, the infernal pit, the lake of fire, Hades, Gehanna, a rough neighborhood, no matter how you slice it."

"I will not deal with demons!"

Lord Sloth said, "Sounds like you already have. I'm a devil, anyway. Satan is my master, not Lucifer, he who enforces order for God."

"Why are you here?"

"To offer you a deal. The way it is, is this. Your angels have deserted you and will not come to your aid, we can see that. It seems you've done some sort of deal with the other side, Free Hell. Boo-hoo, a pity, you hurt our feelings. Never mind, we'll get over it—but spare us the details so we don't have to worry too much about it. The fact is that Free Hell is breaking through into this world. We can't have that and we need to oppose it. I'm offering you help with putting down your rebellion. We'll lick the poor into shape, get your armies behind you again, put God's holy order back in place."

Edward asked, "Who knows about my dealings?"

Lord Sloth replied, "Well, Satan, that's rather his job—keeping score and all that. But the point is, we're offering you a deal. You are a king. It would be quite right for you to command me."

If Satan did know that Edward's father was alive, it seemed he had not yet told his minions.

"And what do I deliver?" Edward asked.

"A say in the running of your armies."

"Can you oppose the French angels?"

"I am a senior devil. I can control a fallen angel, with effort. And certain fallen angels can expose weaknesses in the real angels."

"But the angels do God's work too."

Lord Sloth said, "God likes us to vie for His love. Who is more deadly to the ambition of kings: their enemies or their brothers? So it is with us."

Edward replied, "But the angels would just destroy you."

"Not necessarily so," said Lord Sloth. "For a start, I hear that the French have their own problems with their angels. Beyond the one that died."

"I heard that. Its body went missing too."

"Don't count on it staying missing for long. For now, know that God is with you. Sort of. Well, we're with God and we're offering to be with you. I don't know what God would think about that, but he is notoriously hard to second guess."

Edward said, "If God is with us, why did the angel defect at Tournai? Why did it leave us in such trouble?"

"The angel didn't defect at Tournai. It was a simple lack of paying a bill, according to our spies. The Holy Roman emperor despaired of getting any more money from you and withdrew your Vicarship. Now Philip is making some interesting deals with his own factions of Hell. That's why you need us."

"Which factions?" asked Edward.

Lord Sloth replied, "Ambitious devils. Devils who would rather live here on earth than in Hell."

"And what do you want?"

"What you want—the conquest of France. God's holy order maintained under devil order, not angel, so we might show him how this world would look if ruled by devils, not angels. To beat the other side, of course. I want my devils up here, not some jumped-down fallen angels."

"You would put yourself above angels?"

"Nothing wrong with a bit of ambition, is there? You'd put yourself above the French king."

Edward said, "If I renege on my deal, I will lose more children."

"Not with devils on your side. Battling demons is our speciality."

"I need time to think about this."

Lord Sloth said, "Of course, of course. But let me offer you a bone, so to speak. God, I'd love a bone. Have you got any bones, meaty ones? Don't look so pale, man, I'm not talking about yours. Half a cow will do."

He replied, "You can be fed." Edward thought of how the creature had thrown his men down, how much more formidable it seemed than any human fighter. If Philip had sinned so, if he had risen up against God's order, if these creatures truly were on God's side, then perhaps . . ."

"I'll offer you a little something," said Lord Sloth. "You have a rebellion going on in your streets."

"Yes."

"Let me and my boys sort out the ringleaders. We'll find 'em, drag 'em in, and you can make some sort of example of them. I'll tear out their vital bits in front of a crowd myself if you like; that should give a few of them pause for thought. Hand this over to us—suppression of demons and the forces of Lucifer is our stock in trade. Let us sort out the domestic situation while you ponder what might be done in France when your truce ends."

Edward thought. He said, "Without obligation on my part?"

"Call it a sample," said Lord Sloth, "a neb of pepper to whet the good-wife's appetite."

"I am no one's goodwife," said Edward.

"An expression, Majesty!" The lion took an extravagant bow.

"Fetch the ringleaders, then," said Edward, "and let me consult my counselors. In the meantime, let me get some doctors to these men."

"They'll recover soon enough," Lord Sloth assured him. "Now might I request the cow, Majesty? I am very hungry and would eat before more of my troops arrive. I have a foul temper while hungry."

"Very well," said Edward, "you will be my guest. You may eat in the Great Hall while the ambassadorial rooms are prepared. How many of your troops are you expecting?"

"Oh," said the lion, "hundreds, eventually."

Edward looked at the bodies on the floor. The sooner he got this devil into a formal agreement the better, he thought. He didn't want hundreds of these creatures roaming around under no obligation to the crown.

"I'll summon my counselors and then we'll discuss terms," said Edward.

"Spoken like a lion!" said Lord Sloth.

Edward put his head into his hands. What it is to be a king, to stand balancing on a web of intrigues and alliances that could snare one as easily as one's enemy.

Edward drew his sword Clarent and looked at the blade. "Arthur pulled you forth in simpler times," he said. "What I would give for a clear enemy, a clear friend. Montagu, where are you?"

Then Edward drove the sword into the side of a bench, embedding it a hand's span into the wood. Then he wrenched the sword out.

"Strike anyway," he said. "Strike and fight. That is what it is to be a king."

39

M ontagu told the pardoner to make as small a hole in the base of Caesar's Tower as he could. The pardoner waved the feather and a hole appeared but nothing behind it. The tower was solid at the base.

He said to him, "Keep going."

The pardoner did as he was bid, but it became clear the feather was opening a way through solid rock. Montagu didn't know what to do. He didn't want to go around to the front of the tower where he risked being seen. But that was where Good Jacques had tried to get in. He could keep burrowing as the tunnel had been burrowed at Nottingham, but there was no guarantee he wouldn't go straight through the tower—bring it down on top of him even.

There was nothing for it: they had to go around to the front. Close to the wall, he prodded the pardoner ahead of him with his sword. Osbert slunk around. They were at a doorway, or rather what should have been a doorway. It was entirely bricked in. Fortunately the courtyard and grounds were deserted.

Montagu gestured to the doorway and the pardoner waved the feather. A gap opened, leading onto a staircase. They would have to be quick now; the breach might very quickly be discovered. Osbert went through first, Montagu swiftly following.

As soon as they were inside, Montagu began urging the pardoner on.

"I'm doing my best," said Osbert. "Ahh!"

He had clattered into another wall—the feather's scant light was not enough to warn him it was there.

A wave and there was a hole in it, small enough that anyone following would be very vulnerable when climbing through.

"Go on," said Montagu.

In the moony light of the feather, Osbert looked as though he might hesitate—but seeing Montagu's sword, available for use even in the other man's left hand, he did as he was bid. Montagu slid through right behind him, his hand on the pardoner's ankle to prevent any attack, his injured right shoulder agony against the stone.

Montagu needn't have worried. Osbert was not a brave man. Before he took on an English military hero, he would want better odds than his opponent already beaten up, his arm a wreck, on his knees, one-eyed, in a space so tight that a couple of stamps to the head could hardly fail to kill him. Montagu would have needed to have been unconscious for a week before Osbert would have summoned the courage to take him on.

"Do you know what you're looking for is here?" whispered Osbert.

"Whatever is here, they don't want people getting to it easily, do they?" returned Montagu.

They pressed on, and on. Another wall, this one sealed with a magic circle containing a drawing of the head of a devil, just visible in the dim light.

"Can the feather get through this?" asked Osbert.

"Find out," said Montagu. He hoped Good Jacques had not got there before him, but he didn't see how he could have. The courtyard had been swarming with men when the Templar had jumped. No, he was gone and should stay gone if he valued his life.

The pardoner waved the feather and the head of the devil disappeared, a gap opening up in the wall. Inside it was light. The pardoner crossed himself.

"This is as far as I go, threat or no threat," he said.

"Look in there or die now," said Montagu.

"Actually, it turns out it's only as far as I go, no threat," said Osbert. "With threat, I'm happy to proceed."

He stuck his head inside. "It stinks in here." He gave a low whistle.

"What is it?"

"The boy Navarre!" said the pardoner. He crawled inside a very small room. There, curled up in the tiny space, was Charles. He was sweating and shivering, a strong light coming from a cloak of angel feathers wrapped around him.

He said, "How, in the name of Christ's fat cock, did you get in here?"

"Think, pardoner," said Montagu. "If we can get in here with one feather, what can he do with all those?"

"He doesn't look well, does he?" said Osbert. "Look at his eyes."

Montagu peered at the boy. His eyes were more like those of a cat now, a bright green with dark vertical slashes as pupils. "Are you all right?"

The boy nodded. The space was no more than a cupboard, really. The boy was in there, the pardoner crammed beside him, but Montagu could only peer in from outside.

Beside the boy was a small chest, again marked with magical circles and symbols.

Osbert tried it but it was locked fast. He smiled and dabbed the end of the feather at the lock. It sprang open. Osbert removed it and was about to open the chest when Charles spoke.

"Mine." The word came with great effort.

"We're not starting that again, your lordship, are we?" said the pardoner.

Osbert passed the chest back to Montagu, who opened it. It had a number of letters within it, all their seals broken. He uncurled one and read. Yes, it was a correspondence between the Templars and Philip. The bottom half of the page was given over to magical drawings and an astrological chart. A quick glance revealed the others to be similar.

There was something beneath the letters too. A pouch in velvet on a cord, a sort of purse of the type designed to be worn around the neck. Montagu took it out. A little carved wooden box was within. He opened it. A fine, almost translucent key was inside, no bigger than a thumbnail. It was paper-thin and looked as if it might blow away in a light breeze.

Osbert crossed himself.

Montagu asked, "You know what that is?"

"I saw one at St. Olave's. It is a key to Hell," he said.

"A what?"

There was a clamor at the bottom of the stair. "A breach! A breach."

Montagu snapped the box shut on the key and put it back into the pouch. With difficulty he got it around his neck. He shook Charles by the foot.

"That cloak got you in here. Can it get us out?" he asked.

The pardoner went scurrying back down the stairs. "Up here, *mes amis!* I have apprehended the knave!"

The boy gestured for Montagu to bring him the little chest.

Montagu did, pressing it into his arms.

"Thank you!" whispered Charles. "If I survive, I shall repay your family."

"My family?" Montagu said.

"I think you are about to die," said Charles.

He took up the cloak, which glowed with a fierce light.

"No!" Montagu snatched at him with his good hand, but the boy disappeared, taking the chest with him.

Montagu had grabbed a handful of feathers from his cloak as the boy went. A man-at-arms was on the stairs. Montagu drove a kick into his face, sending him sprawling backward unconscious. Good, at least he would block the way.

He waved the feathers at the wall and saw lights beneath him. Torches and lanterns. The giant Despenser howled from the chapel and came crashing into the forecourt. Five feathers. Enough? Montagu didn't know. Only one way to find out. He jumped hard from the tower, clasping the bright quills in his good hand.

He didn't fall but instead went up, his jump magnified many times, carrying him forward from the tower, over the trees and onto the top of the perimeter wall. The giant had not seen him go and howled and beat at the tower, shaking it as if to knock it down.

Montagu did not look back. He jumped from the wall and ran south, into the blackness of the streets, heading for the Great Hall and the apartments of Joan of Navarre. He grasped the feathers as he ran. No! The light. A scream from the giant as it saw the feathers bobbing like a bright mackerel through the sea of the dark.

He told himself, *Faster, Montagu, faster.* He felt old and his arm was agony, but he laughed. Wasn't this what he'd dreamed of as a boy? The injured knight on a mission only he could fulfill, beset by the deadliest enemies. Yes, boys dream of such things: old warriors of repose and peace. Montagu would not die. He wouldn't give Despenser the satisfaction.

Soon he would encounter the wall and he needed to be prepared for that. He stuffed the angel feathers into his tunic.

Behind him the limping giant Despenser blundered and crashed through the houses. Montagu heard the cries of men and of devils, houndly barks, the call of great crows, grating and gurgling noises no earthly animal ever made, all distorted in the fog. Montagu kept running. The fog was thick but a watch fire near to the wall guided him. He ran toward it. He had to make the Petit Pont—the bridge that led to the Île de la Cité, where the Great Hall lay. Charles would have gone back there, he was sure. And if he hadn't gone there, then Montagu needed to impress on Charles's mother the importance of returning those documents.

He reached the wall. Two guards were outside the locked gate, warming themselves around a fire.

They both had spears and leveled them as Montagu emerged from the murk.

"Is the hue and cry for you?"

Montagu didn't bother replying, just ran off down the length of the wall. All along it people had built lean-tos—using the solid stone of the city's defenses as at least one good wall in their shelters. Some people emerged as the mob bayed for Montagu's blood; Despenser bellowed that he'd tear off Monatgu's arms and eat him like a leg of chicken.

He came to a rough turf lean-to. The guards who had followed him down the wall gave a shout. The first charged with his spear. Montagu had trained off-handed often enough, but the excitement of combat made him forget his bad arm. He sidestepped and instinctively brushed the spear aside with his right hand. Montagu felt as if his arm might be torn from his socket. He was sick in his mouth, but he had achieved his objective—the spear snicked by him and Montagu delivered a heavy backhanded blow to his opponent's head, flattening him to the ground. The second guardsman did not like what he saw and his charge faltered.

"I am Montagu," he said. "England's chief killer. Run while you can."

The man did as he was bid. Montagu knew it would not be long before he came back with many more men. He sheathed his sword and took out the feathers, cutting a hole in the wall just big enough to squeeze through. He cut a passage twenty feet deep before he made the other side. Then on through the cramped streets of Paris, down toward the water. He sensed it in front of him, a cold presence.

On he ran. The giant roared behind Montagu. It had clambered over the wall and was now smashing a couple of the city guard down. Clearly no one had told Paris's able defenders that a torn and bloody giant climbing over their walls was to be treated as a friend. Montagu got lost, turned down blind alleys, found himself running uphill when he should have been running down. All the time he could hear Despenser howling and roaring for his blood.

Finally, he turned down a street that fell into water. He made his way along the muddy bank, toward the looming stretch of the Petit Pont. The night watch had formed up all the way across it—twenty men, shields, mail, and lances forward, gray men in a gray fog. There was no way across. But there had to be. He got up onto the bridge. The spears bristled, ready for an assault.

"I'll suck out your marrow for what you've done!" the giant screamed through the fog.

Montagu summoned his best court French.

He cried out, "Prepare to repel this giant, men, prepare to repel it. Devils are on earth! Make way for the king of Navarre!"

He ran across the bridge as fast as he could, his arm a dead weight at his side, his sword in his good hand. He did not feel tired, though. Were the angel feathers making his body lighter?

The watch pointed their spears but the commander slapped them down. "Let him through, boys, let him through!" Montagu thanked God for the fog and the confusion that meant the men had no time to realize he was dressed as a pauper. They would not have let him through if they had—kings never dressed in rags, in any circumstances.

Montagu bustled through the line and got onto the island. He turned for the Great Hall. Now more men were pouring onto the bridge as the lumbering figure of Despenser loomed through the fog.

A guard challenged him at the door to the Great Hall and Montagu cut him down.

On into the building proper. No guards there, all having gone to face the giant, no doubt looking for a bit of glory to enliven the evening, rather than standing about doing their useful duty. It took him a moment to remember where the ambassadorial quarters were. He felt sure Joan would be there, along with her son.

To the back of the building and up four staircases. Now there were guards, four of them, too many to take on with his injuries. They came running for him but, as they closed Montagu reached inside his tunic with his sword hand to touch an angel's feather and he leapt. He soared over their heads and landed behind them, running to the spiral staircase that led to the solars at the top of the building. He made it through the door and bolted it behind him. Up and up. Then a corridor at the top. Two Navarrese guards.

Montagu said, "I've come to see Queen Joan."

"With a sword in your hand?" The guard presented his spear. The corridor was narrow and there would be no dodging here.

"Get the queen."

The guard replied, "Drop your sword."

Montagu put Arondight on the ground. The guard weighed his spear in his hand, as if deciding whether to charge. The man behind him said they should take Montagu to Le Châtelet and let the queen decide if she wanted to see him in the morning.

"Montagu!" Joan was in the corridor, dressed in a loose nightgown.

He said, "Queen Joan." Montagu bowed.

"Let him in."

"Do you need a chaperone, Lady?" said the guard.

"I have my ladies and my son."

Montagu picked up Arondight and went into Joan's solar. Two ladies-in-waiting barely acknowledged him; they were bending to tend to the little boy on the bed. Next to Charles lay the cloak of angel's feathers. He was soaked in sweat and moaned out as if in a tormented dream. But he was awake.

"Look at him, William," said Joan.

Montagu went to the boy. His eyes were as he remembered from Caesar's Tower—green, cat-like. And now that cat-like aspect was extending to his face. No substantial change had come over him, but Charles held his face differently, as if he'd been asked to do an impersonation of a cat. Beside him was the chest.

"What's happening to him?" said Joan.

The door opened and an extraordinary figure came in—a cardinal, with an iron collar about his neck. He swallowed a lit candle and shivered. Hadn't Montagu seen him beheaded in the chapel?

The cardinal said, "I think I have deduced it."

"What?" asked Joan.

"He is a devil," said the cardinal, "or a half devil. To travel as an angel is greatly stressing for mortal flesh. His mortal self is fading away and revealing what he is underneath. Who did you lie with, lady?"

Joan was pale in the candlelight. "Get out," she said to her ladies-in-waiting. They did, their eyes on the boy as they left, full of fear.

There was shouting outside. Despenser's voice boomed through the night, promising murder to Montagu.

"What is that?" she asked him.

"Another devil. You are not the only one who has been conjuring," said Montagu. He was breathless and needed to sit down, the exertions of the last days taking their toll now the rush of combat was over. He looked at the boy.

He added, "You always accounted your husband a weak man. Did you want a stronger father for your son?"

"The Capetian queens have certain arts," she said. "My line is broken. I could not see my husband's offspring bringing it back."

The boy shook and shivered on the bed.

Montagu said, "He took certain letters."

"That compromised Philip. They prove the usurper's guilt. I have looked at them."

"Yes. But they are of no use to you. The French nobles will not rally to you. Your claim has been dismissed and they fear you. My king claims the throne of France. Give him those letters and you may yet see the Valois fall."

"And how will you escape with them?" she asked.

"I will take the cloak."

"That is ours."

He said, "And yet it has brought you no good. How will you explain your son's condition? He is still required here at court."

"I will say an English sorcerer cursed him. You, Lord Montagu."

"You're very like your aunt when you are angry."

"Yes, and remember, when the women of House Capet are stirred to ire, kings fall. Sooner or later. Ffff!" She swiped at the air with her hand.

The window rattled. Something had gone past it. Despenser, Montagu guessed, crawling up the outside of the building, despite his injuries.

"Give me the cloak and the chest," said Montagu.

Joan said, "You could take it easily enough."

"I could, but you are a lady and I am in your chambers. I would not abuse your hospitality so."

A face at the window, the giant pressed his eye against the pane. "You!" roared Despenser.

"Take it," said Joan. She glanced to the window.

"No, Mama, there are spells there!" the boy cried out.

She said, "Not the sort princes should use. That is the magic of demons, who oppose and hate God's holy order. This family has always been scrupulous in restricting its dealings solely to devils."

The hand smashed through the window, groping for Montagu. Joan was still calm.

"He is too big to get in, I think." She showed no agitation.

Montagu said, "You know the king's troops will be here soon."

"Yes. I cannot command them to leave you alone. I am Philip's loyal subject, remember."

Montagu put the cloak around him. Immediately he felt light, his own weight nothing to him. He picked up the chest. Guards were on the stairs now.

Joan called to them, "You gentleman are too late: we have been robbed and assaulted by magic."

"What do I do?" Montagu asked.

"Wish to be away, sincerely," said the cardinal. "Think of a person in another place you might want to be with."

The guards crashed in, the giant keened, and Montagu thought he should reach for his sword. But nothing was easier for Montagu than to wish to be away.

"To Edward," he said. Despenser's face loomed momentarily as he shot through the window, out above the Great Hall, and up into the stars.

40

I t was Sunday at St. Olave's, and the rich merchants and minor nobles of the congregation filed up to take communion. The young under-priest Father Paul was surprised to see Edwin come in, halfway through the mass. He had often thought to complain to the bishop about Edwin's behavior—for his whole tenure he hardly took one mass in four on a Sunday and none in the week. In the last year he had not been there at all.

In the end, however, Father Paul had decided to stay silent. He had an easy life with no supervision, and he was free to take collections and dona-tions and allocate them as he saw fit—on necessities such as cooked goose, fine cassocks, or splendid furniture for his home.

Father Paul was a handsome young man with an easy charm and found it straightforward to collect money above and beyond the tithes the rich parish was owed. A stroke of genius had led him to provide benches in the church. This made the elderly of the parish very grateful and more likely to remember the church in their wills.

He had also found that the purchase of rich tapestries drew richer people to his church, who in turn drew more rich people. A Sunday at St. Olave's was now quite a sight as the merchants—and even nobles who might have chosen between three competing parishes—came to his church so its splendor might reflect on them. Paul had just lifted the rather fine new silver communion cup to the lips of a master of the Clothworkers' Guild when the door of the church was opened.

He looked up over the array of rich coats, houppelandes, dresses, and tunics to see the thin figure of Edwin in the doorway. Edwin had something under his arm, and a woman the size of a traveling bear was with him. Behind her was a mob of the lower sort in their tatters and rags.

"Father Edwin," Father Paul said. "The church is quite full. If you wish to favor the poor, then I'm sure some bread will be left for them after the service."

A merchant's wife raised a large loaf from a basket. It had been brought for just that purpose.

"No," said Edwin, marching up to the altar.

"Er, no to what?" said Paul. "I'm afraid you are a little too cryptic for me, Father."

A murmur went through the church. Paul had thought Edwin carried a bag under his arm. Now he saw it was a fat little creature with stunted arms and legs, a wide mouth, gray skin, and horns upon its head.

"No, I'm not Father Edwin," said the priest.

"Well, er, you are," said Paul. "Though I cannot help noticing that you have a devil attached to you."

"I am friend Edwin, not father. And it's a demon, not a devil."

"That would appear to be splitting hairs and not quite . . ." Paul gave up his attempt at eloquence. "It's a thing of Hell. You're a priest. What are you doing?"

"Your problem, Paul, has ever been that you don't use the ears Lucifer gave you. I am not a priest and I'm here to explain what I am doing," said Edwin.

He faced the congregation, the demon clinging to him, the fat woman at his side.

The paupers filed in beside him, surrounding the benches, mingling with those who were standing.

"This is an odd do, Father!" said a rich dyer who had been particularly generous to the church.

"I didn't come here to mingle with whores!" said a man's voice.

"Where do you go then?" said a rough-looking woman.

"The Woodbine stew," said another lady, prettier, but no more refined. "That's the weaver. Cock as big as a rye loaf—some of the younger girls won't go near him."

A woman standing next to the weaver thumped him on the shoulder.

"I am here to talk to you about God!" said Edwin to the crowd.

"We've had all that already," said a man in a fine fur coat, which he wore despite the warm day.

"He is evil, and he opposes the true nature of man as established by Lucifer at the making of the earth," said Edwin.

"I won't hear that!" A knight in a tunic embroidered with white doves tried to stride up to the altar, but a couple of big bowmen barred his way.

"Lucifer asked us to love one another," said Edwin. "He came to earth as Christ, but God tricked and killed him. God's followers, people like me, corrupted his message of love. We must return to it. See what is important. Do not follow blindly the mad instructions of a tyrant. Look into your own hearts for what you know is right."

Paul made a drinking sign with his hand and gestured with his eyes toward Edwin.

"I am not drunk," said Edwin. "Unless it's drunk on the knowledge and freedom that acceptance brings. I do not value gold. I do not value silks." The heavy woman took his hand in support and nodded to the crowd.

"Can we have them then?" shouted a wag from the back of the church.

Edwin said, "I am here to give them away. Take the tapestries. Take the cups. Sell them to buy bread for your children."

The bowmen pulled at a huge embroidery showing the passion of Christ and it fell from the wall. A young whore plucked the silver cup from the priest's hand.

"Now steady on there!" said Paul.

"You're a priest—you should be ashamed of yourself!" shouted the knight to Edwin.

"I have been ashamed all my life. That is what I have been taught, shame. Shame for being as I was made. I will be shamed no more."

He turned to Greatbelly. "Will you kiss me?"

"She won't. She doesn't do that!" shouted a young freeman's son.

"I will," said Greatbelly, putting her lips to Edwin's for a long kiss.

"Ahhh!" said Annie Rolfe, one of Greatbelly's girls.

"That is an abomination!" shouted the knight.

"I don't know; it wouldn't do if we all liked the same!" The wag was at it again.

"Call in the poor!" shouted Edwin. "Call them from everywhere. This is the first church of Lucifer and I welcome them in to hear the truth."

"We won't listen to you!" shouted a merchant.

"No," said Edwin. "You won't. No priests anymore. No high men. Listen to Joanna. Listen to Annie Rolfe or Rosie Ashe. Listen to Tom Trevalyn of the western archers or ask their children. And listen to the word of Lucifer!" He stretched out his hand. His ympe Know-Much gave a great caw, and the church was full of the fluttering wings of ympes.

"The king will hear of this!" shouted the knight. "The king will hear of it and then you will pay!"

"Let him," said Tom Trevalyn. "We have forty men of Cornwall here, friends of Lucifer and the bow. Let him, let the king come—because the poor are standing in the morning light and their shadows will be cast on him!"

41

M ontagu crashed heavily into the wet grass of the tournament camp not thirty yards from Edward's beautiful royal pavilion. He looked up at the sinuous painted leopards and the fluttering flag of St. George. He tried to stand, but it was as if he was drunk. Montagu felt very weak and, had he eaten anything in the previous two days, he might have been sick. Home. God's teeth, he could just sleep there on the grass.

Trust Edward to make a show of it. The banners were streaming in the Windsor breeze, pavilions in yellow, red, and blue lined up all down the bank of the Thames. The Thames! *My God*, Montagu thought—it felt good to be near an English river after that stinking Parisian sewer. And it looked as though the French campaign had been victorious.

"Hold!"

Six guards came running for him, polearms pointed toward him. One of them was not as Montagu would have expected for a member of the king's guard—he had the legs of a gigantic goat and short horns protruding from his head.

"Do not move or you will be cut down where you stand!" one of the men shouted at him, doing a little dance backward and forward with the polearm, unsure what to make of Montagu, wrapped in glowing feathers, materializing from thin air.

Montagu coughed and took in a big breath. He felt as though he'd been knocked from his horse by a lance. "Sorry to draw your attention to the obvious, but I'm not standing," said Montagu. "If I'm going to have any hope of doing so, then I may need a little support."

"Don't speak your magic at me, demon! . . . Or angel, or whatever you are!"

"I'm Montagu, Lord Marschal of England. So bring me to the king, sit me on a stool, and fetch me a leg of game and cup of beer," said Montagu.

"You're in rags. You're not Montagu!"

Montagu felt his anger rise. "Look at my eye. Look at *this*!" He drew Arondight, the magic sword sparkling like the waters of Avalon.

"He's drawn a weapon," said the goat-legged man. "Kill him."

"If you kill me, the king is going to be more than a little put out," said Montagu. *Always remain light, William, always careless and glib. Never let them see you desperate*, he thought.

A guard went running back into the tent. Then a huge voice boomed from inside it.

"Lead me to him! Get out of my way!" King Edward pushed his way through his guards like a destrier through surf.

Montagu tried to stand to greet his king. His legs wobbled like a man struck by a mace and he collapsed.

"William! William! What's happened to you?" Edward threw his arms around Montagu. "You're injured, my God! And in rags. Are you all right?"

Montagu smiled. He said, "Some mild inconvenience encountered in your service, sir."

A crowd had been pulled in and Edward rounded on them. "Has no one a drink for the lord? A seat? You useless dogs. Do I have to carry him myself? You, horn head, make my bed and fetch some clothes befitting my friend's status. I'd rather have this man on my side than a whole army of you useless, lazy cowards!"

Edward got Montagu to his feet, with others now piling in to help him. So many squires and knights came forward that Montagu feared he would be crushed. He said to Edward, "My arm, lord—I took a bit of a knock."

"Be careful with him, you oafs. Here's a man who carries the injuries of a noble fight, not like you shivering mice, afraid to bruise a finger!" The king turned to his squires, almost apoplectic.

"Fetch Lord Sloth," said Edward. "Bring him now."

"He's gone to London, sir, to quiet the rebellion; you sent him yourself."

"So send for him! My God, William, you've faded away since I last saw you!"

The throng parted as Edward supported Montagu into his tent. Edward lowered him to the bed, leaving the cloak of feathers about him. Edward stroked the cloak in wonder and gently unclasped it, leaving it beneath the lord like a blanket. Then his squires stripped the filthy and tattered gaoler's clothes off Montagu.

One squire took the letter from the tunic and placed it carefully on top of the casket Montagu had brought from the tower. The king slapped away another who brought out a scarlet shirt of fine lamb's wool, ordering him to give Montagu the king's very finest clothes. So they dressed him in satin and cloth of gold, set pearls at his ears, and put sapphires and ruby rings on his swollen fingers. When Montagu cried out as a page accidentally tweaked his arm, Edward struck the boy a fierce backhanded blow that sent him scurrying from sight.

He said, "Perfume, bring perfume for my lord—he stinks like a public shithouse. Bring perfume. And get out. All of you, get out!"

Edward didn't seem to mind issuing entirely contradictory orders. The tent cleared and Edward himself poured Montagu a cup of wine.

By God, that tasted good. French, clearly. Montagu savored it, taking the moment to gather his thoughts. "No good over there?" he queried.

"You haven't heard?" asked the king.

"No, but I can guess."

"A ruinous truce," said Edward. "We were outside Tournai. I would have had it but for a couple of shillings more from these penny-pinching merchants. But no. They need their money for their finery and their whores, aping gentlemen with furs and jewels. I tell you, they were sorry to see me come home; I made an example of some of them." He waved his hand, dismissing something, Montagu wasn't quite sure what. "We made our peace with the House of Valois—a five-year truce. Five years! How am I to pay my debts with five years of peace? The whole thing came to nothing."

Montagu said, "We still have Gascony?"

"We're fighting there. The truce only extends to France. And there is some hope of plunder in Aquitaine but beyond that, slim pickings. We may lose as much as we gain."

The goat-legged man came into the tent with a small stoppered bottle of perfume and a cloth.

Edward took the perfume and poured it onto the cloth. He dabbed it at Montagu's face, beneath his arms, onto his trousers. It smelled of primroses. Montagu was so glad to be back in ordinary civilization again. He could go back home, be with Catherine, watch the youngest children grow up, forget war. Forget Isabella—if that were possible. Yet a question troubled him.

"You are served by devils?" he asked Edward.

He said, "Hell approached me last month. An ambassador came. We have no angels, William."

"But we don't need them if there is no war."

"Rebellion stirs. The poor are rising up, some of the merchants too— more out of a desire to hold on to their gold than out of conviction."

"There are few convictions stronger than wanting to hold on to gold."

Edward said, "The situation is dire. My knights could kill the people, strip their gold, but the devils are experts at control. They will make the people fight for us, work for us."

He said, "What can be done by force can also be done by compromise or by more subtle means. Invite the rebel leaders to parlay and then kill them."

"Not so simple. They do not *have* leaders; little demons guide their actions. My eyes have been opened, William. The devils serve God and His holy order here on earth. The king at the top, the nobles beneath them, the merchants beneath them, the working men and the poor beneath them. The poor have a heresy—the cult of Lucifer. They would overthrow us and make a pig keeper or a beggar our masters."

"And we can't put down something like that?" Montagu's head swam.

"It's growing in strength. Half the longbowmen believe it now. Have you not seen this sign?"

He held up his three middle fingers. "Lucifer's fork. The sign of those who belong to Free Hell. Do you know—"

"I know the heresy," said Montagu. He was still terribly dizzy and wished the king would let him sleep, but you do not order monarchs from their own pavilions.

"It is not heresy. They lie when they say Lucifer made the world, they lie when they say he came here as Christ, but there is no disputing there is a war in Hell that is spilling over into our realm. With no angels we must choose sides."

"I know why there are no angels."

The king had been about to hold the wine cup to Montagu's lips again, but now he hesitated. "Yes?" Edward said.

Montagu said, "Your father is still alive."

Edward's tongue came to the tip of his teeth, but he said nothing, just waited for Montagu to continue.

"He is in the east. I don't know where. The Hospitallers have him. The French angel said he was in Lombardy. The answer may be in that casket."

Edward looked where Montagu gestured. "What is in it?" he asked.

"Evidence of House Valois's dealings with demonic forces to obtain the throne. I took it from the Hospitallers' most secret tower in the old temple of the Templars. Philip is a king killer and a usurper, and the history of it is within. There are also some certain spells that he used to do it. He traded with demons. You have enough to set before his allies to strip him of all support. You can bargain for lands in France. You can win what you want without bloodshed."

Edward's eyes lingered on the casket. Then they turned to Montagu.

"What do you know of my father?" The king's voice was a murmur.

"The Templars told me. Despenser was plotting to overthrow your father. He killed an angel to put certain ingredients into the hands of the Templars. They gave him a banner to help him stand against your father's angels."

"The Drago?"

Montagu replied, "Not the Drago. Something far worse. The Evertere. It is Lucifer's banner. The one he will use in his final rebellion against God. Despenser abandoned his plans to overthrow your father and tried to use it against you and your mother when you invaded. It drove off your father's angels and destroyed them. Your father battled, along with his angels, to put it back in the casket that stores it. When he did, he went east with the Hospitallers. I believe they may have captured him and be using him for their own ends. The funeral we attended was a sham. Another man was buried."

"You are telling me I wept over the grave of an imposter?"

Montagu knew Edward well enough to tell he was feigning surprise. So Edward already knew. It was as bad as Montagu had feared.

Edward was a man famous for his rage, but Montagu had never seen him so angry. All the blood drained from his face, his hands shook, and his eyes stared forward into nothing.

"Tell me that the Hospitallers deceived you—that you've only recently found out," said Montagu.

"There was no deceit. They told me the truth."

"Yet you allowed yourself to be crowned?"

Edward let out a great funereal groan. In all the years Montagu had known him, he had never heard the king express any weakness in the face of hardship. Now tears were in his eyes, though his knuckles were white.

"I did not know until after I was crowned. Even then, for years I was uncertain—but what other explanation could there be? The angels would not come!" His voice was a low whisper and he glanced to the walls of the tent.

"I have men seeking him out," said Montagu, softly.

"If he is found . . ." Edward's voice trailed off.

Montagu said nothing, just held the king's gaze. For a moment Edward's jaw set in rage as he clearly understood what Montagu planned. Montagu knew his friend was capable of killing him in a moment's temper—that he would spend a season of weeping and regret afterward would be of no consolation at all. Edward clenched his fist. Then he put his left hand to his right and used it to pry the fingers straight, as if his war arm could not be brought to peace any other way.

"Stop them," said Edward. He had to say that. To say anything else was to be complicit in a murder.

"I will try."

The king had said what he was required by God to say and then changed the subject. Edward said, "The Hospitallers are wise in magic. It is why I use them to contain my mother. Another devil's bargain."

At the mention of Isabella, Montagu eyed the letter by the chest. He said, "Your mother is a holy woman. Mortimer enchanted and threatened her as he threatened you . . ." Even as he said the words, Montagu didn't know quite how he had come to that conclusion, but he went on, compelled to represent Isabella to her son as he had promised to do. "I believe she would be a great asset to the country, were she released. She was strong enough to throw down your father. Why not use her strength against the French?"

The king replied, "She is the possessor of strange arts. If I want to rule the country in my own right and be free of her influence, I have no choice. She cannot enchant me, but weaker men fall under her spell. She would be a threat to my rule if I allowed her to be free. She would be queen and I a puppet once more!" Aware that only cloth separated him from the ears of the camp, the king did not speak loudly, but his voice was full of passion.

"I believe she has your best interests at heart."

"I know you saw her. You were lucky to get away, Montagu. A weaker man would have been made her servant." Edward's levity was a veneer on his anger. Montagu was thankful for it. The king was trying to keep his temper. That was what decades of service bought you—the king would try to remain calm. There was no guarantee he would succeed.

"She wants to be by your side, Edward; she would help you."

He said, "Because it was you, I overlooked that you had betrayed my command. I said no one was to go anywhere near her, and did not expect to be disobeyed, least of all by my closest friend and confidant! I thank God your noble heart allowed you to resist her."

"Welcome her back, Edward. England needs such a powerful ally."

Edward was stone, the last reserves of his will stilling his anger to utter immobility, as if any movement risked shattering his control.

Presently, he spoke, very quietly. "You have fallen into her snares."

"I have seen what she can offer the realm." Montagu wanted to be silent, but he had longed to talk of Isabella with someone, to have his passion recognized. Like Edward, silence, stillness, was his only option. He said nothing, but Edward read his eyes. His friend the king knew him far too well.

He said, "You love her."

Montagu, who could stare down any man in a fight, could not meet the king's gaze.

"That woman has overthrown kings by taking men to her bed. How has she charmed you—you, the strongest, the best?"

Montagu said, "She . . ."

Edward's voice was a murmur. "You have lain with her."

"Edward, I swear I did not." Montagu expected his tongue to swell, the gaping pit of Hell to open and for him to fall in. He was a coward. He had denied her. Montagu had lied to his king.

Edward nodded. He said, "Then any offense is forgivable. You're my friend, William. You act only for my good and you love me as a son loves his father, for though I am young that is the station God set us in. Like a son you stray, but the wise father knows that you are full of filial duty. You have labored greatly on my behalf and any hurt you have done me is as nothing." Edward knelt at William's side. "Embrace me, friend."

"My lord!" A squire came running into the tent.

"Do you not get announced before you enter?"

The squire dropped to one knee. He said, "My lord, I am from Lord Sloth. There is a riot in London. The devils are outnumbered and are facing blessed weapons. He requests you send some of the tournament knights."

"Send them! Now get out!" He threw the wine cup at the squire's back as he went. "Good God, so much for being king of France; I'll be lucky to be king of England by the end of the year! I can't go cutting down my own bowmen: I'll have nothing to fight with. We need more of these devils— they're the fellows to do it!"

Montagu crossed himself, then silently asked forgiveness of God, but stopped halfway through his prayer. Did he want forgiveness? He had dishonored her memory, dishonored himself with a filthy lie. He would at least complete the quest his lady had set him.

"I swore to your mother I would deliver this letter." He gestured to the letter on top of the casket.

Edward said, "I will not touch it. You don't know her tricks, William."

"I swore I would deliver it to you and persuade you to read its message. My king, I have suffered greatly for you. I have given my eye, my arm, and my blood. Allow me to fulfill my oath."

"You are an innocent, Montagu, for all your strategy, bravery, and guile. Armies fell down at my mother's feet. My father ignored her, sported with his favorites. He treated her badly, yes. He took her jewels and gave them to Despenser, I know. He left her to the mercies of the Scots, they who have no mercy." He glanced left and right. The noise of the camp was all around, horse hooves, cries, songs, and squabbles, but still he reduced his voice to a forceful whisper, leaning close into Montagu. "But she lay with his enemy! That was an offense against God and against me! My father a cuckold! How do you think that made me feel? She unmanned our whole line and then she overthrew him. I locked her away because I will not add matricide to my other crimes!"

Montagu felt shame building up in him. "She is gentler than you think," was all he could say.

"She tried to bewitch me," said Edward, "to confuse me and shape me, and she managed it for a time. When, by my royal right, by prayer and devotion, I saw through her guiles, I acted." He drove his fist into his hand.

Montagu feared to speak, though he did. He said, "You raised Hell."

"Bright rivers must mingle with dirty waters to reach the sea," said Edward.

Montagu crossed himself. Edward had repeated Good Jacques's phrase almost word for word. "Did you know, the man who helped you—he killed the Capetian kings, released the Evertere, and, in the end, overthrew your father?"

Edward simply tapped the embroidery on his doublet. *It is how it is.*

"I had no choice. I was a . . ." He hushed his voice. "A neutered king. No angels. Perhaps even a usurper, God forbid. I was desperate. To find one's way out of the dark forest it is sometimes necessary to go a little farther in. Though there is a cost to the unrepentant man." Edward laughed dryly. "We should employ the Luciferians. They could use the devils for us—you can't damn the damned."

"Perhaps you should write that on your doublet," said Montagu.

Edward pulled Montagu up from the bed and shook him.

"If you were not who you are, you would be dead for that impertinence," said Edward. He threw Montagu back to the bed. "Though what you say is true. I must atone. This war, this stuttering, half-arsed excuse for a war. This is how I would atone."

"We must all atone," said Montagu. Nausea gripped him when he thought about his journey in the cloak. "But read the letter, Edward. I swore I would deliver the message. She has some ideas on how the war might be won. You must give your mother that: she's a rare strategist."

"That's one way of describing her. Fulfill your promise, Sir Chivalry; you read it," said Edward. He sat down on a camp stool.

"I can't get up."

"Boy!" he called.

A page scampered into the pavilion.

"Pass that letter to the lord. And then get out! Have the drums sound. I have private business and want no spies listening at the canvas."

The page did as he was bid.

Montagu inspected the letter. There was that odd seal, still intact, the vellum stained but whole. He was proud to have done this for his great love and glad that he was now putting her out of his life. The drums beat, a thumping pulse slower than Montagu's heartbeat—but scarcely more powerful. Her words were in there. It was a connection to her, an evocation.

The seal broke with a snap and a smell of sulfur. He opened the letter and read aloud:

> Son and most high majesty of the English realm, rightful king of France, protector of the English people, and vanquisher of enemies. The seal on this letter was a magic circle, through which devils have issued, bound by ancient lore and the names of God to serve you. They will help you with your war in France, need no earthly pay, and will fight each as the equal of twenty men. There will be no more until I am released from this prison, though I pray to God I may have released myself by the time you read this. Deal with me, my boy; let me be your helper. Do not allow your temper or what has happened between us in the past to rule you. You must do this.

Montagu put his hand to his mouth. He had been the source of the devils. He had carried a magic circle out of Castle Rising for her, one fashioned in wax. He read on.

"Montagu . . ." He read the words but could not quite say them.

"You look pale, William," said Edward. "Do not read anything you think I shouldn't hear."

"I am sworn to deliver the message," said Montagu. No future now. No peace. No sunlit days with the children and Catherine on the river. It didn't matter. The words of the letter made any thought of tomorrow impossible. But good, he would no longer be a liar. He read: "Montagu will kill your father or have him killed. God demands his death for such a sin. Should tender thoughts stay your hand, know that I took him to my bed. Your father is twice a cuckold. Destroy Montagu."

Edward sat for a while staring at his boots. Then he stood. "Did you lie to me?" said Edward. "I can believe my mother is a liar, though it shames me to say it."

"She speaks the truth. I am the liar."

Edward's eyes were moist in the candlelight. "You have betrayed my trust. And she is right. You have cuckolded my father in the bargain." He was silent again, still.

Montagu had no words. No thoughts.

The king said, "You have labored greatly on my behalf, William Montagu. I reward you with the greatest honor. You will fight as my champion in the lists tomorrow."

Montagu tried to sit up but he was too weak. His useless arm shot pain through his whole body and his head reeled.

"It will take too long to send for your armor," said Edward. "You will wear mine."

He clapped his hands. "Squires!"

Three men came into the tent. "Remove Lord Montagu from my tent and see to it that he is provided with comfortable quarters of his own. When Lord Sloth returns from London, tell him we require that his name shall appear in the lists tomorrow. He will tilt against the king's champion."

"Thank you," said Montagu.

The king nodded. He came close to Montagu so the squires could not hear. Edward whispered, "I won't take your honor, though you have taken mine."

42

The Hospitallers' lodge was an enormous building outside the city walls in the Brolo di Sant' Ambrogio—a vast woodland that spread north out of Milan. It was built in pale brick and was relatively square and plain in the old Roman style, what you could see of the outside under the ivy. The commander of the hospital—a middle-ranking officer of the Hospitallers—was not there to meet Dow and Orsino, and no man could be admitted to the order without his say-so. So they waited and asked at the gate every day until, on a blazing afternoon in August, they were finally let in. It had taken them six weeks to get an audience.

They were led in through a side gate into a large square surrounded by a cloistered walkway. This was a poor hospital—or at least it had been at one time. There were few signs of the poor here, though many rich pilgrims sat in the sun of the main squares or walked among market stalls that sold clothes, sandals, cheese, and bread.

"Wait here." A stout soldier with the white fluted cross of the order on his black surcoat strode across the courtyard away from them, tapping the sword that swung at his leg. His tone was not over-friendly.

"I'm worried about the shield," said Dow. "It marks you as an angel killer if they've heard of what happened in France."

Orsino shook his head. He said, "I'm not a fool. Who knew that angels even had shields? I never heard of one taking flesh before."

"Are you sure?"

"Who is ever sure about anything? The sacred heart of Christ is a familiar symbol to crusaders. I've seen a dozen men with it on their surcoats and I've only campaigned with crusaders in Poland in the east. Those of us who don't come from noble houses often adopt such things on the battlefield, to be known by our own side."

Dow asked, "What if the other side does the same?"

"That's where the theory breaks down."

The soldier swung back across the courtyard, munching on an apple. "Nope," he said.

"Nope, what?" said Orsino.

"We're not taking men on. The way you speak is not that of a high man of this order. Your squire is a raggedy-looking idiot and, though you can doubtless fight, you would dishonor us by your common blood."

"Mark our equipment. This is a true knight," said Dow.

"Bollocks. One nicked shield doesn't make someone a knight."

"My honor does," said Orsino. "I don't stand for such remarks."

"You reckon yourself, do you, son?" sneered the soldier.

He stepped toward Orsino to push him, but the Florentine stepped into him, sweeping his foot and putting him to the ground.

"More than you." The soldier tried to get up but Orsino stood above him, tripping him every time he tried to do so until the man gave up. Three men came toward them, soldiers. Now Orsino's hand was on his sword.

Dow despaired—their chance of infiltrating this order was sitting in the dust. And Orsino had lost his temper. Dow had never seen that before.

Dow's eye was taken by someone marching toward them across the square. He was a small, dark man in the flute cross insignia of the Hospitallers. He bore no sword but carried a length of counting beads in his hand. The man waved to Orsino.

"Master Bardi?" said the Florentine.

The little man walked up to the group and nodded at Orsino in acknowledgment. Orsino offered him a deep bow and Dow, who was keen to avoid attention, did the same.

"I thought I'd find you here, Condottiere," said Bardi, "and my word, you've taught this ape to bow. Really, Orsino, they should beatify you. If ever I've seen a living miracle there it is."

"You know these two, sir?" said the soldier, who'd taken advantage of the pause to stand.

Bardi answered, "This is my man, gatekeeper. The soldier Orsino, one of the most deadly men ever to have drawn a blade, and his charge the stuttering little heretic. I was told they were here and I came to greet them."

"We had a misunderstanding," said the soldier.

"No," said Orsino. "I understood perfectly. Apologize and we'll say no more."

"Sorry," said the soldier. He bowed as he said it. He withdrew a little way, trying to maintain the illusion that he was still in charge of this encounter.

"Told we were here by who?" asked Orsino.

"Whom. All in good time. Really, gatekeeper, have you not offered these men a drink?"

The soldier said, "They were applying to join the order, sir."

"And very good monks I'm sure they'd make, one or two differences in dogma aside. Come with me, the both of you."

"You're convinced that's safe, sir?"

"I'm safer now than I was an hour ago," said Bardi. "Come, follow me."

Dow felt his familiar hatred of this rich man rising in him, but he bit it down. The order was where to find the old king, and through him the banner. This snake had wormed his way within it; he might be useful.

They stepped out of the heat of the day into the shadow of the cloister and then went inside the building. Straight stairs led up and the three climbed them. They went down a narrow corridor of rough stone, low enough to cause Orsino to duck. Bardi opened a door and went inside. It was a well-appointed cell.

"Close the door," said Bardi. He sat on the only chair. "Well, I've found you. And you haven't found . . ."

"Not yet," said Orsino. "Are you a monk now?"

"Yes, for the meanwhile. I thought the spiritual life might do me some good."

"You have no spirit."

"Oh, you know how to flatter, don't you?"

Orsino asked, "How did you finish up here?"

"A man of my financial skills is always welcome. Do you know the Hospitallers have riches that dwarf those of many kings, certainly of your king?" He jabbed a finger at Dow. "They need managing."

"And you had to take holy orders to do it?"

"The wise ship runs with the prevailing wind," said Bardi. "But look. This is the headquarters of the Lombard Hospitallers. The whole Italian tongue of the Hospitallers is headquartered in Rome. Considering how ineffectual you've been, I've had to act myself. All I need to do is to come up with some reason to see the accounts and we will have where Edward II is kept."

"How?" Orsino asked.

"Because kings eat money! These fellows can keep as quiet as they like, hold their secrets close, but money speaks. He will need a retinue, he will need keeping . . . Or, even if he is a hermit, they won't risk leaving him without a guard—there will be *some* unexplained expenditure. We will have him!"

"You've gone broke, haven't you?" said Orsino.

Bardi allowed himself a nonchalant pursing of the lips. "What makes you say that?"

"You don't deny it. And I know you as a man of pride. You would have commanded someone else to work this subterfuge for you if you were still in funds. The English king has reneged on his deal, hasn't he? Are you still paying me?" said Orsino. "What of my sister and mother?"

"Your family will be safe," said Bardi. "There are certain provisions within the law that have enabled me to retain a modest base of property. My grand house has been sold and the money gone to my creditors, but so far your mother and sister remain comfortable. If you wish them to continue so, then I suggest you prepare yourself to do what is necessary as soon as I have found the king."

"I will write to them," said Orsino, "and if I don't receive a reply that I like, it's your throat I'll be cutting, not that of a king."

"That won't bring absolution."

"I'll take the risk," said Orsino.

Something flitted across the window. Murmur, Dow knew, was roosting until nightfall when he could approach unseen. A fluttering—like a bat— and a tiny woman flew through the open window into the room.

"Who is this?" said Dow.

"I am Catspaw," said the little woman, "and I need to talk to you, man of perdition."

"Why do you call him that?" asked Orsino.

"The heresy that these creatures maintain is that an Antichrist is coming to earth, to lay low the high men and raise up the poor. That's your Antichrist right there," said Bardi. "If I didn't have so much riding on it, I'd cut him down and prepare for Heaven."

"I have helped this downtrodden man," said Catspaw, settling on the table, "but I fear I may have been misled by him. He has quickly clothed himself in the garb of the oppressor." The ympe's voice was reminiscent of the meowings of a cat.

"He is our enemy," said Dow, "but we must work with him until we get what we want."

Catspaw said, "I do not like his company anymore. I am sorry I told him where you were going."

"That banner is mine," said Bardi. He took out a small bottle of holy oil and anointed his hands, making the sign of the cross as he did so.

"We will see," said Dow.

"The ympe can still be useful to us, though," said Bardi.

"How?"

Bardi leapt forward and grabbed Catspaw with both hands. With a quick wrench, he broke the little woman's neck.

"Oil from the tomb of St. Claire," said Bardi. "I thought it would work!"

Dow drew his blade but Orsino barred his way.

"What was the point in that?" Dow asked him.

"It's important to find favor in these places. How better to announce one's arrival than with the discovery of a whispering ympe," said Bardi. "They're quite the pest around these parts."

"It was murder," said Dow.

"Not so," said Bardi. "It was the rightful elimination of a fiend. And, even if it wasn't, then it was practical. It moves us closer to our long-term goal."

"I'm going to kill you for this."

"No, you're not. Do you think I'm a complete idiot? This will bring me great respect in the order. I need as much of that as I can get in order to secure access to the right accounts so I can track this king. Doubtless you think you can steal the Drago and use it to your own purposes. You would not be with us if you didn't want what the king has as badly as we do. So, you will not kill me; you will help me and you will accept my help. You are a creature of magic, no doubt, and thus useful to me. Be thankful for it—it's kept you alive. Orsino, get him out of here. I will arrange your lodgings with the servants."

Bardi picked up the body of the ympe.

"Now," he said, "I'd better find the commander. I think this may get me sent to Rome for an interview with the prior."

43

M ontagu spent his last night on earth productively. He visited the chapel at Windsor to take mass and made confession of his sins. In normal circumstances he hated to do this, as it put him in the power of the priests. They were sworn never to reveal the secrets they heard, but he knew what their oaths were worth. The chapel shone with gold in the candlelight.

He thought of Good Jacques, throwing his purse back to him, telling him it could feed countless numbers of the poor. Unsteady on his knees in the chapel, Montagu knew the Templar had been right. All his possessions meant nothing now. It was as if he was naked before God, everything stripped away but the essentials of his life—the sword at his side the most essential of all.

He did not allow himself the indulgence of thinking too much of his family. Isabella had duped him into carrying his own death warrant back to Edward. He had done it gladly, keenly, as she knew Montagu would. Even now he still longed to see her. The thought of her was a fire, burning away all reason.

He wrote a letter to his wife and sons, as honest as could be without admitting his faithlessness. He bridled at his own cowardice. Montagu told his sons he expected them to grow to become true servants of the king, his wife that she had done her duty by him and that he had loved her. He did not say that he was to die, just that he had returned from captivity in France and had been honored to fight as the king's champion in the tournament celebrating victory over the French. Montagu did not say that it was an honor that never was for a victory that also never was.

He included some instructions, including that Arondight should be given to his son William. In another letter, this for Edward, he set out what he'd discovered, including details of the return of Despenser. Montagu signed himself Edward's loyal servant. There was still time, of course, for the king's temper to cool. He doubted it would.

Trumpets and shouting. People arriving at the camp after nightfall—remarkable. The halloos came nearer, accompanied now by a monstrous drumming. "Make way for Lord Sloth! Lord Sloth returns. The avenging hand of the Lord is here!"

Montagu decided that, since he would be spending a long time lying down very soon, he had no desire to spend his last night on earth in bed. He called for the king's squire young Tom, who had been sent to attend him.

"Help me here, boy, I want to walk the camp."

"You're sure, sir? You look as though you would be better off sleeping."

Montagu said, "No. I'm sick and it is my custom, when sick, to walk the illness out. Support me. I'd see this Sloth if I can."

The squire lifted Montagu using his good arm and the two made their way out of the tent, Tom supporting Montagu as if he was a drunk. The going was not easy.

"I can bring you a jennet if you wish, sir," said Tom.

"Yes, do that." It wouldn't really do to tour the camp on a lady's horse, but he thought the men would understand, given that he'd been injured.

The drumming was loud now and the cries almost hysterical. "Sloth, Sloth is here! See the prisoners he has brought, see how rebellion is punished!"

Devils burst past Montagu—squat, boar-headed men in red velvet livery bearing the image of a silver lion. They squealed and shouted as they ran, two at the front bearing drums banging out a heart-bursting beat, others behind trailing torches, still others dragging captives bound by ropes.

The pace was fast and the prisoners stumbled, some falling. The devils did not slow down—they just dragged their prisoners on. A priest careened past, dragged by his bound hands. The man was very thin and had a look of grim forbearance on his face.

Beside him was a woman, like his partner from a children's rhyme—"Big Fat Bess did burst her dress, Thin John couldn't fill his hose." She was impressively short and rotund, so much that Montagu almost expected her to roll rather than run as the devils pulled her on. The woman had bare arms like sides of ham and her breasts seemed to reach her knees. She was more scared than the priest, calling out "Alack!" and "For shame!" and crying a good deal.

Others were there too—some old men and maids, some children. Montagu did not look at them for long. Behind them, riding on a dust gray destrier, was a huge lion, itself the color of beaten steel. It wore a weathered mail hauberk and its mane rattled as it spurred its horse forward. Montagu marveled at the horse—bearing such a terrifying burden without fear. The lion carried a long whip in its paw and cracked it forward with expert precision to lacerate the backs of the prisoners.

Behind him, at a trot, came more boar men.

"Lord Sloth?" said Montagu to Tom as the procession tumbled by.

Tom replied, "Indeed, sir. The Iron Lion himself. He serves God. We've had it all explained."

"Indeed."

"If you want the evidence, see how he's taken the revolutionaries. That's the Black Priest, I'll wager, and his dame Greatbelly. They've been stirring rebellion here for months. It'll be good to see them hang. If he hangs them."

"What else might he do?"

"He ate the last one he captured alive. Took his time about it. If I had a choice, I'd let them draw and quarter me. A quieter death."

"Get me that horse."

"Yes, lord."

In a few moments Tom returned with the jennet. My God, it was difficult to mount. How would he get on one of Edward's destriers in the morning? He must, somehow, even if they had to tie him on.

The saddle had a very high pommel and cantle—a war saddle designed to be difficult to fall out of. He'd take that tomorrow. In ordinary tilting Montagu preferred a low back to his saddles—better to be knocked out of the seat than held firm against the lance. But he would be too groggy to sit in one of those. A proper battle saddle was designed to keep the rider in the seat no matter what. That would do for him.

Getting on was another matter; a mounting block had to be brought, and Tom had to shove Montagu from below. Finally he was on.

Sloth's drums were unceasing, dizzying, and loud, like a second heartbeat thumping in the chest. The devil wheeled his charger at the center of the prisoners—the terrified captives scattering from the stamping hooves, only to be pushed back by the ring of boar-men.

Sloth threw back his head and roared, "See, see how I have brought the rebels to pay! Tomorrow we'll hang 'em high and I shall suck on their entrails! Now pray with me, boys!" There were screams from the prisoners, some voices raised to call for help from Lucifer, others repenting and asking God for forgiveness.

Sloth dropped from his charger and kneeled. "Dear God, who made Heaven and earth and Hell, we have delivered these rebels to you. We will part their souls from their bodies so they may descend to the lake of fire where your punishment will be visited upon them. You, the great and mighty Lord, strengthen us to downthrow your enemies as you downthrew the imposter Lucifer. Amen!"

The boars all said amen and set about tying the Luciferians to one another. Sloth prowled around examining knots, crying out, "Good and tight boys—tie 'em good and tight!" and sniffing at the terrified people.

Montagu rode forward. Now he could see the Luciferians close up, they didn't seem nearly as frightening as Edward had suggested. Overthrow the king and upset God's order? They didn't look capable of overthrowing a plum pudding.

The lion looked across at him. Montagu was seated on the horse, but Sloth was at eye level. His breath stank of rotting meat.

"Lord Sloth," said Montagu.

"Lord Montagu, I take it, by your eye," said Sloth, bowing. "You are a servant of God, I know it well. I am honored to meet you."

"How did you find the rebels?"

"How one finds anything: by fear. Chew on enough guts and you get the answers you want well enough."

Montagu's head was spinning. The lion's voice had the quality of a cymbal struck close to the ear.

"The king bids us fight tomorrow," said Montagu.

Sloth licked at his lips, appraising Montagu. He said, "Then he wants you dead."

"I believe he does."

"I'll be glad to oblige him. Enough of talk, I'm going for food." The lion gave a little bow and strode off through the camp, a boar man leading his destrier behind.

Sloth chilled Montagu. It was as if he'd come back to a different world, where everything he'd known had been turned on its head. Montagu had never thought to ask why, if angels could walk the earth, devils didn't too. Now it seemed that they did. What had reduced England to reliance on these abominations? He thought of the mercenary in the east and the boy. How long would it take to find old Edward and to kill him? Young Edward would surely use his angels to rout this scum as soon as they came back to him.

His horse, led by the squire, took him through the camp. Men hailed him as he went. Already talk of his God-granted escape from the French dungeon was circulating the camp. Edward was nowhere to be seen.

"You'll put these devils in their place tomorrow, sir!"

A man-at-arms saluted him. It was all Montagu could do to incline his head in acknowledgment. So the word was spreading, he would fight in the tournament. He wondered where Edward was.

Montagu longed to see his friend, to talk of their struggles together. Who had he loved in his life? His wife, certainly. His sons, undoubtedly. His feelings for Isabella were not love, nothing as healthy. She was a fever and he was sick with her. But apart from that, who? Edward. Best friend. Confidant. King. Montagu always knew he would gladly have given his life for the king, should it have been demanded. And now it was demanded. So be it.

Montagu wanted to be useful to his friend, even on the eve of his death. The lion would never get anything of worth out of the prisoners. On campaign, Montagu had seen enough men tortured to prise out information on secret routes, supply lines, and expected dates of reinforcement. He thought it a useless practice. Such truths as were revealed were caught up in a web of desperate invention and willingness to please.

However, negotiation and bribes worked well. Offer a man a way out of a lifetime's toil if he would betray the lord for whom he toiled, and you had a good chance of success. Knights, despite their vows, could be bought as easily as any other man, grievances exploited, ambitions piqued.

"Let's go back to the prisoners," Montagu said.

The group were tied, fearful faces peering out in the light of the camp fires like the damned souls in Hell they were so shortly to become. Montagu had sometimes actually felt sorry for the poor who had been captured in war rather than being slaughtered on the spot. Not their war, not their quarrel, nothing more to gain from risking their lives than a few pennies' pay. But these were different: they were not content with their God-given station. They had ambition, and ambition was the preserve of high men.

The great fat woman and the thin priest were tied at the edge of the group. Montagu felt compelled to talk to them. "Get those two out. I want to speak to them in my pavilion," Montagu ordered the stinking boar man looking up at him with his piggy red eyes.

Montagu felt he might vomit. His head pounded and his hands shook on the reins.

"The prisoners are to remain here, so says Lord Sloth!" The boar man's voice was a squeak, like a swollen door on flagstones.

He said, "I am the Lord Marschal of England. I don't care what Lord Sloth says—if I want to interview a prisoner, I will. Bring me the prisoners."

"The prisoners are to remain here, so says Lord Sloth."

The squire asked, "Do you want me to kill this devil for his presumption?" Tom had his hand on his sword.

"That won't be necessary, Tom," said Montagu. "I'll kill it myself if I have to. I won't repeat myself. Do as I say."

Another boar man spoke. "The prisoners are to remain here . . ."

"So says Lord Sloth," said Montagu. "I am Lord Marschal of England, therefore second only to the king in God's appointed order. Lord Sloth is a devil of Hell, no more than one of God's menials, not, unlike an angel, of the same substance. In the name of the right invested in me by God on high, you will do as I say."

The boars glanced at each other. "He'll kill us for this," said one.

"But we must respect God's holy order," said the other, who wore a black-plumed helmet. The boars began to argue and squeak among themselves.

"Tom . . ." said Montagu, gesturing with his eyes to the prisoners. Tom slid past the quarreling boar men.

"Hey! We'll cut you down for that," said a boar man.

"Did Lord Sloth command that?" said Montagu.

The boar man hesitated, his tusks seeming to twitch. "He left no instructions," he said.

"Well, I don't see how you can proceed without orders," said Montagu.

There was a deal of head-scratching and miserable squeaking from the boars.

"Go and ask him," said one.

"He's at his feast. You can't disturb him during his feast—he definitely left orders about that," said another.

Tom freed the priest and the fat woman and led them through the ranks of the grumbling devils.

They had been badly beaten—both had swollen faces, and the priest had a large untreated cut across his forehead. Montagu, feeling slightly more steady, turned his horse for his pavilion. He didn't like the sensation of turning—it was as if a part of him stayed in the direction he had originally been facing, while most of him wheeled about, the laggardly part jerking back to join the rest with a dizzying snap.

At the pavilion he dismounted with difficulty and all but crawled back to sit on his bed. Tom brought in the prisoners.

He said, "Kneel before the lord."

Montagu said, "No need for that, Tom, no, no. They can sit if they find it more comfortable."

Both prisoners slumped to the ground, the woman clutching the carpet.

"Fetch them a drink, Tom, beer and a little bread."

The squire raised his eyebrows but left the tent to do as he was asked.

"You've caused us a deal of trouble," said Montagu. The eyes of the priest weren't on Montagu but behind him, where lay the angel feather cloak. Neither prisoner replied.

He said, "What do you want? We're all Englishmen in the best modern way now. I can speak a different language to you, but I am as wedded to this country as you are. Surely we should fight together against our common enemy, not be at one another's throats."

Again nothing.

"If you refuse to set out your demands, then your enemies have a clear field to insist on theirs. I ask again, what do you want?"

"Food for our children. Clothes, shoes," said the fat woman.

"You must labor for them. That is the station God appointed you."

"To have the lords take everything from us? To be taxed on top for wars we don't want to fight? Why has the king greater need of my wool than I? This carpet on which you wipe the shit from your shoes is finer than any bed my children have ever known." The woman was not cowed, Montagu noted. She spoke with passion and intensity, her great arms quivering as she wrung her hands. Beside her the priest glowered, his face like a skull in the flickering lamplight. Perhaps, thought Montagu, she took all his food.

"What is your name?" he asked her.

"Joanna Greatbelly."

"Joanna Greatbelly, lord," he corrected her.

She said, "I would once have called you lord, but no more. I have seen the truth of creation and I know that the one who will lead us to the promised land is here on earth."

"You have a leader?"

"Not a leader," interjected the priest. His head came forward, as if to butt the words into Montagu—he looked like a starving guard dog straining against its leash.

"I'm not sure I like your tone," said Montagu. "I've treated you civilly, now I'd thank you to do the same. What then, if not a leader?"

"A friend."

"And this friend will downthrow all God's order?"

"Yes."

"Who is he?" Montagu said.

"My apprentice, Dowzabel."

"The mercenary's squire? I wouldn't put your faith too strongly in him."

"He will go to the king in the east. He will take the banner that will overthrow the high men. Ask yourself why the skies fill with demons, why devils come to earth, why the angels are nowhere to be seen. Lucifer is coming and he has sent his harbinger," said the priest.

"Surely you must want to prevent this? What is it you want from us?"

"Your humility," said the priest. "Confess how you have leeched off ordinary men, stolen, and deceived. Confess. Learn the lessons Christ Lucifer gave you in the Bible—'But woe unto you that are rich! For ye have received your consolation. Woe unto you, ye that are full now for ye shall hunger.'"

Montagu said, "My remembrance of the beatitudes is that they encourage people to love those who hate them. Do you?"

"We do not seek your blood. Where are our soldiers? We have five hundred Welsh bowmen who would gladly fight for us, but we ask them not to."

"Why do you quote Christ?"

The priest replied, "Christ was Lucifer, come to earth. His message was peace and reconciliation. You turned it to war."

Montagu felt uncertain. Two years before he would have believed nothing of what the fallen priest was telling him. But so much of it had proved to be true. Demons were different from devils—he had seen as much, heard as much. He found it easy to feel that he sided with angels but not with the likes of Sloth, Despenser, and the boar men.

Montagu was no scholar, not at all, but what king followed Christ's injunction to poverty? Christ had said to a prince, "If you want to be perfect, sell everything that you have, and give to the poor, and you shall have treasure in Heaven, and come and follow me." The passage had always troubled Montagu. On the eve of his death, it troubled him exceedingly.

When had he been happiest? In the camp, among his soldiers, at a fireside or in the counsel of war, cajoling his men, encouraging the timid, and speaking wisdom to the foolhardy. The night before a battle hadn't the ordinary observations of rank and place melted away a little? It was as important to speak to the bowman and foot soldier as it was to the knight. No luxury there, no soft bed and fine wine. But Montagu had been happy, through his care for others, not himself. He wondered how George was. He'd forgotten to ask in all the night's tumult.

"All holy men tell us the king is the head of the body of the nation," he said.

"The same holy men who welcome in these devils with their whips and their knives. Sloth killed five men in the Smithfield market yesterday just by interrogating them. Then he took mass at St. Margaret's, welcomed in by the priest," said Greatbelly.

"He is God's servant."

"He is that," said Greatbelly, "but could Christ have sent one such as he?"

"How does God, who smites so many in the Old Testament, become so loving in the New? They are not the same being. Lucifer is love and compassion and forgiveness. God loves blood," said the priest. "Once it would have pained me to say that, but I have won this knowledge by hard study and sacrifice."

"No, Jesus removes our sins through His blood," said Montagu. "God so loved the world that He sent His only son to die for us. Sacrifice is a noble thing. I have seen it many times on a battlefield and it is never less than inspiring. Self-sacrifice is at the heart of our faith."

A great roar went up from the rear of the camp. Lord Sloth had been informed of his missing prisoners.

Greatbelly clung to the priest. Montagu didn't know why he wanted to help these two paupers. Was it that he sympathized with them? No. Whatever happened, kings were kings and the poor were the poor. That was the immutable order God had ordained. Was it that his broader faith had been shaken? A little. But maybe the truth was a little less noble.

Montagu knew what awaited him in the morning—that Sloth would kill him in the tournament. He despised the Iron Lion's coarseness even more than his brutality. Creatures like that had no place in ruling England. They were more suited to the German east. Yes, he could see Lord Sloth bashing heads for the Holy Roman emperor; he'd fit right in there.

Montagu's desire to help Greatbelly and the priest could have come from a simple wish to frustrate Sloth, to deny him a victory. In Montagu's youth, that would have been motivation enough: he'd have set free his prisoners and told Sloth if he wanted to argue about it he could do so with a lance in his hand the next day.

Above all these influences, however, was simply that Montagu had seen enough suffering. He'd spent his whole life killing and maiming and now, hours from death, he wanted to do something magnanimous before he died. This comical pair, one thin, the other bulbous—he couldn't regard them as a threat to anyone.

Montagu pointed to his cloak. He said, "Do you know what that is?"

The priest said, "No."

"It is an angel feather cloak. It will transport you anywhere you need to go. Choose carefully because you will be as weak as I am when you arrive. Wrap it about you both and wish earnestly to be gone."

"Why don't you use it?"

Montagu sat tall. "My king commands me to appear in the lists tomorrow."

The priest stood up and staggered toward the cloak, Greatbelly waddling after him. Sloth's roars were fairly blowing through the camp now, the boar men's squeaks and grunts making a foul music behind them.

"Take him," said the priest quietly to the woman.

"No, my love!" Greatbelly objected.

"Take him! They have captives, take him. They will not dare harm me while he is ours—we can get the release of all our people."

"Now hold on there . . ." said Montagu.

The priest bundled Greatbelly toward Montagu.

"I'm scared, my love," said Greatbelly.

"We are in the hands of the light bringer," said the priest.

"What's this?" Sloth was at the entrance to the tent, half the leg of a cow in his paw. "Grab them!" he said.

Five boar men sprang into the tent, but Greatbelly had the cloak around her and her arms about Montagu. Montagu grabbed for Arondight but was too weak to draw. The tent filled with light and the boar men shielded their eyes.

Only Edwin, the former priest, remained.

"I'll have your guts for this!" roared Sloth.

The priest's thin face was impassive. "If you ever want to see that lord again, I think that would be very ill-advised," said Edwin. "Now lead me to your king. I mean to negotiate."

44

No one dared wake the king to tell him the news, but at dawn a huge stoneskin gargoyle flew in on grinding wings to see him. It had a letter in its claws.

Edward saw his mother's seal upon it. He took the precaution against any spell by making the squire Tom read it. The youth did so in a halting voice.

"Son. My messengers tell me you have received Montagu's letter. I hope that traitor is now dead. I am my own mistress again. The Hospitallers have ceded control of Castle Rising to me and the devils God has sent to aid me. I am your mother, son. I do not seek to control you or usurp you, only to love you. I seek only to help you in your rule and send you this gargoyle as a token of my good faith. Summon your magicians, bring your wisest men, and let them ward you against all enchantment if you are worried about my loyalty.

"Though know that I am loyal. Send word to Nottingham Castle tomorrow. We will overthrow it as a demonstration of what we would bring to your war in France. All your troubles will be at an end if only you share them with me and let me, your mother, help you."

Edward tried to think straight. He had always known keeping her alive was a risk—but now, with the death of another child imminent, perhaps it was time for desperate measures. He would not meet her, not expose himself in that way. But his wife might do it for him. Women were not as susceptible to her charms, and Philippa was a holy, strong-minded woman.

Nottingham to fall. No, he couldn't afford that. Edward called for a scribe and told him to write a letter to Nottingham to tell them to open the gates to her. He wasn't wasting his resources on civil war. Then he dispatched the gargoyle and stood outside the tent, watching it laboring up into the gray summer sky.

Anger rose up in him again—Edward felt the heat in his face. This time he would make her chastity a condition of any deal.

Ten yards away he saw the Iron Lion watching him, crossing himself. Clearly he was not bearing good news.

He turned back into the pavilion and waved to the lion to follow him in. Lord Sloth said, "Bad news, lord. Montagu has left the camp."

He said, "Montagu's escaped?" Edward felt himself trembling slightly and struggled to hold on to his temper. He looked to his table, where Clarent lay in its scabbard. Who to blame? Only himself. He'd never thought Montagu would be so dishonorable as to run.

"No, Majesty," said Lord Sloth, his mane rattling as he spoke, "he has been kidnapped. The Luciferians—I curse their name—made off with him by magical means. They mean to bargain for him. Their priest remains here. I say we let them kill Montagu—does my job for me—and we tear out all the prisoners' guts as an example."

The king said, "We can't do that. He's an English nobleman. My God, he's *the* English nobleman. We can't surrender one of his rank to death at the hands of the poor. Where would it end?" Edward kicked over a stool with such violence that Sloth actually took a pace back.

He continued. "Of course he should die for what he's done, Sloth, but now I have to ransom him before I can kill him."

"Let's tear into the poor," said Sloth. "Let my devils get among the starvelings of London, rip a few to bits, and keep ripping 'em until Montagu's returned to be killed in the way you prescribed."

Edward tapped his finger against his front teeth. He kicked the stool again. Sloth flinched as it sailed past him out of the tent.

"No. Action against rebels and heretics can be understood by the people. Indiscriminate slaughter can't. My father tried it—or rather Despenser did on his behalf. Mortimer tried it. It ends the same way, with the ruler swinging from a gibbet. No—this must be considered. Bring my advisers in here. And this priest of the poor. He's some sort of magician, isn't he? They can be useful, those Luciferian fellows."

Sloth said, "You need no adviser but me, sire."

Edward replied, "I'll be the judge of that. Do as I say."

"Treat with your mother, sire. She opened the way for us to come here. She can furnish you with more legions."

"Get out and fetch my advisers!" The lion bowed its head, offering Edward the deference he owed him as a king.

Edward looked down at his mother's letter and thought of his children. He needed to conquer France. Otherwise, who would he lose next? One of the girls? Joan? Maude? Edward loved his daughters, but he felt sure the demons wouldn't take a girl. It would be the loss of a valuable trading commodity, a means of cementing alliances and a personal distress, but nothing like the loss of a son. The loss of a girl was terribly sad and an inconvenience, the loss of a son a catastrophe.

How to do it? How to meet all obligations and protect his family? He couldn't pay his soldiers and that was well known. So what was the solution? More devils. Edward would have to trade with his mother. She would not be allowed at court, not allowed to start casting her webs of influence, but she would be recruited to use her skills for England's good. But would devils be enough? Not if Philip managed to persuade his angels out of their shrines.

It is as it is. Get the devils, make what bargains you need to and see what shakes out in the end. The poor would be needed to fight—devils would not be enough on their own. The French chivalry owned so many swords with handles made from the bones, teeth, and hair of saints that it was more unusual to find a conventional sword. And there were rumors Philip had devils of his own—along with the aid of a giant. Despenser back from Hell, the spies said. Well, one of the great disappointments of Edward's life was that he had been too young to cut that dog's throat himself. Now he'd have the chance.

That morning, while convening his top nobles in council, Edward explained that his mother was to come to England's aid, using the considerable diplomatic skills God had given to her in England's favor. She would employ her God-given blessings to summon more devils to the English cause.

"Hear, hear!" Sloth was at the entrance of the pavilion, his voice like distant thunder.

Edward shot him a look to silence him. The king said, "I have sent her to Nottingham Castle. My wife, Philippa, will meet her there to discuss the terms of her new liberty. She is still to be kept from direct contact with men."

"She won't be happy about that, sire," suggested young David Lafage.

Before Edward could stop himself he had punched the knight, felling him. Lafage was unconscious; Edward's knuckles were already swelling from the blow.

"Any other man making insinuations about my mother may expect harsher treatment!" said Edward.

All the nobles looked at the pavilion floor.

"I'm aware of my lady mother's ability to sway the minds of men," said Edward, "and I can accept that—if it advantages us. But it is a courtly devotion she inspires, not base lust." He calmed himself. Feeling slightly ridiculous at this compulsion to explain himself, he persevered. "She is like Emaré in the romance—men fall in love with her. I'll grant you she can manipulate that, but it is a good thing, is it not, that knights offer their chaste devotion to a lady?"

The other nobles, mindful of the unconscious Lafage, agreed that it was.

"Get that fool out of here," said Edward. "I will tell you a plan that will go no further than this canopy."

The nobles gathered in, with Sloth visibly preening with the pride of being the king's confidant.

The king continued. "We will offer the poor what they want—or part of it."

"No!" Sloth roared, and the plume on Sir Peter Lavalenet's hat bent under the blast.

Edward said, "Quiet! We will offer them honey in the morning, so to speak. They will make concessions to us: we to them. The first is that the Luciferians will have part of some territory in France. We will give them their own state. Gascony is not covered by the truce. We will make war there and rid ourselves of these pests. That way they become France's problem, not ours."

"If they made a paradise there, then we would lose so many poor to them that England would crumble through want of labor."

"Is our faith so weak? Many of them will go, but more will stay. The Luciferians win some battles for souls but lose more. Our churches are still full. And this state they envisage is contrary to the law of God. They would set it up without a king!" Edward laughed at the very thought, and the nobles laughed too, until Sloth's guffawing gave them concern for the stability of the tent.

The lion said, "Men need masters!" Here Sloth nodded his great head.

"Now send in the Black Priest," said Edward, "and we'll see if his sense departed with his soul."

He sat back on his chair. Edward was never a man to rely on one plan. He knew the importance of contingency plans in battle. And giving Gascony to Free Hell had become a contingency plan after Montagu had brought him news of his father. The angels were close. Edward was sure Montagu had put in place plans to kill his father. A man had been sent. Should he require help, Edward could not send it directly—but his mother might be able to.

Edward could use the revolutionaries of Free Hell to fight the French, with the promise of reward or their own lands. That would weaken them, cut their numbers. Then, with angels and devils combined on his side, he could annihilate them, set up angelic protection for his sons as Philip had done and make his own peace with God. If the angels never came, well, Free Hell would have its lands after all.

How that would sit with the devils was anyone's guess, though he'd let them sort it out between themselves. Not an ideal situation, but better than giving up part of England, which Edward was charged by God to protect. He touched the embroidery on his jacket. *It is as it is.* Strive for the best outcome, prepare for the worst. These labyrinthine deals with competing forces were nothing new to any ambitious king in history.

Still, Edward hoped he would get a chance to see the Luciferians slaughtered. They were an abomination to him and to God, and he knew he would be doing God's work by putting them back in the place He had intended.

The priest was bundled into the tent.

"Stand there," said Edward. "You and I need to talk. Bow, man. My God, what sort of creature are you?"

PART V

1346

❧ · · ❧

In the year the great battle of Crécy was fought.

I t could not escape anyone's notice that Charles of Navarre had developed the appetites of what could only be described as, well, how would one say it? A cat. Those close to him tried not to mention it out of regard for the prince's feelings.

He did not look particularly feline, if one ignored his eyes. His fingernails were sharp and he had a funny way of holding his mouth, with the top lip dropped over the bottom, as did some cats. Apart from that there was nothing of the cat about him—though Charles had taken to climbing up on the palace roofs and lying in the sun and was given to stalking the kitchens in search of mice, which he liked to eat live and whole.

As none of the servants would ever presume to comment on anything a prince might do, it took his mother a month to find out about it. When she did, she immediately insisted it stop at once and, if he was to eat mice, he ate only fine white mice pulled from a jeweled box. Most people in the court agreed that, at fourteen, the prince had become a creditable young gentleman despite—some said because of—the feline aspect.

Charles himself, of course, questioned his mother about exactly why he might be feeling so "miggily moggily." At first she had tried to fob him off, saying many young men developed odd appetites around the coming of their maturity. Her cousin, for instance, had taken a great liking to cheese.

Charles, however, was an intelligent boy and questioned many people about his new hungers. Philip told him plainly he had never heard of such a thing, and the comte D'Évreux said that the only mice most boys of his age liked to play with were those to be found hiding up serving girls' skirts.

Then the palace cats started to follow him around, a minimum of eight, including some war-torn mousers from the kitchens. Again, Joan intervened and had those cats got rid of and replaced with pure Persians, the color of smoke. If her son was to be followed by cats, he would be followed by noble cats. When it proved hard to keep the inferior felines away, Joan insisted that her son only favor the aristocratic animals with titbits.

"Why do they follow me, Mother?" Charles said. "Uncle John says I must keep fish in my hose."

She tried to offer him the story that they had peddled at court—Charles had acted nobly in trying to defend the Sainte-Chapelle against the English devils and invaders, and then the sorcerous Montagu had cursed him. His cat-like appetites and irresistible charm to the animals were the wounds of a magical battle and deserved the same respect as any injury suffered by a prince in defense of his realm or that of his allies. Charles accepted the explanation at first, but eventually he worked out that it simply didn't make sense.

Charles said, "None of them cursed me, Mother, I'd have heard it. I'd have felt it. What's more, if an Englishman was going to curse me it would be with something worse than being liked by cats." He opened a dark wood box at his side and pulled out a wriggling white mouse by its tail. "Are you convinced that's the explanation?" He popped the mouse into his mouth and crunched its neck in his jaws in a way that always made his mother visibly blanch.

Joan, who hated to see her son so miserable, so stricken, thought she owed him the truth. She finally confessed—his father was not who Charles had taken him to be.

"You lay with a *cat*?" he asked her. Charles sat with a box on his lap.

"Yes."

"How?" said Charles, whose thoughts were habitually more concerned with matters practical than moral.

"A devil," she said, "invoked as we Capetian queens have always been able to do at times of great need." Nergal, in his usual place, gave a little smile.

"Why?" he meowed.

"I was given to my husband. He was not the man to restore our line to its former glory. I needed a father with more bite about him."

Charles, as if in illustration, drew another writhing white mouse from the box and dangled it by the tail above his mouth before dropping it in.

"I find it hard to credit," he said, his mouth full of fur.

"Don't look so shocked," she said. "Plenty of queens have had such lovers when they doubted their husbands. But for the cloak you would have retained your human appetites, I am convinced of it. That weakened your human side."

"Don't worry, Mother," said Charles. "I like being so catty. I can out-climb any boy in the court, outjump them too. No one is my master in swordsmanship."

Joan replied, "It's good to hear it, son, but restrain yourself with the mice. You will grow too fat for war."

"I shall never be too fat for that, ma'am!" He took out another mouse, tossed it to the ceiling, drew his blade, and impressively sliced it in two in midair. Its two pieces splatted to the stone of the floor. Joan's hand went to her mouth, but otherwise she kept her composure.

Charles's attention snapped back to his parentage. "How did you summon the devil?" he demanded.

"Not easily," said Joan.

"Did you open a gate to Hell? I would like to go back if I wouldn't be punished for failure," said Nergal, swallowing down his customary candle. He breathed out, but no more than steam came from his mouth. "I am sorely stricken," he said. "Time was I'd have been able to burn this entire castle down. I could project flame from my fingers when I was in the mood, too."

"Stop your complaining," said Joan. "It severely tests my patience. No, I did not open a gate, not even a postern gate by which a devil might slip through."

"I suppose there are devils wandering the earth at any time," said Nergal, "looking for queens to bargain with. I did in the days of my flame."

"Which queens?" said Joan.

"Can't remember," said Nergal.

"More idle boasting. Devil, I begin to wonder what you are for. What do you give us for the fortune we spend on keeping you in candles?"

"I have saved your son."

"And been well rewarded for it. I estimate I have allowed you to eat about five thousand candles and one cardinal since you stayed with us."

"Prince Charles," said Nergal, "defend me against your mother. Tell her how I have served you."

Charles licked at his lips—his broad tongue flashing pink. He said, "Times are tight, old Nergal. Mice of this quality aren't cheap, I tell you. And I wonder if you might not further our aim of destruction by fending for yourself. I daresay you'd get in a few scrapes stealing lanterns from fine ladies. I bet you might even kill a few if they came between you and a flame."

"I couldn't kill a kitten nowadays."

"The very idea!" said Charles, covering the ears of a fine Persian who sat on his lap.

Nergal said, "Don't mock me, lord. See what I have given for you." He rattled the collar on his neck.

Charles showed his teeth. "A grievous wound, but I am done sharing my chamber. You don't even warm the air anymore."

"Then find me another chamber."

"And risk my secrets being out among the servants of the palace? No, Nergal, it is better we part. If you can bring me any better servant, or regain your former power, you will be welcomed back."

"I was sent from Hell to track down the Antichrist. You were to help me in that endeavor or I wouldn't have been sent here."

Charles said, "I tracked him down. Had you kept your head, you would have been able to kill him easily after the angel fell on him and your mission would be done; Satan would have opened the gates of Hell to you himself, have welcomed you in, and sent me who knows what rewards."

"Please, sir, do not turn me out into the cold. I am bound to you."

"How bound?"

Nergal said, "You are a prince. I am a low devil. I am yours to command and swore service to you in the forest when I first protected you."

"It's been no sort of protection recently, has it? If you weren't with me when you walk the streets of Paris, a gang of starved urchins would beat you and rob you. Losing my patronage will focus your mind, Nergal. You've been sitting in here feeling sorry for yourself for years now and what has happened? England has made a tolerable inroad into Gascony, some stirrings in the south—but I want to see this land on fire. Time was I thought you were the man to deliver that."

"I am, sir, I am." The devil wept.

"Time was those tears would have sizzled on your cheeks," said Charles.

"Shall I have him expelled, son?" Joan asked.

"Oh, why not? Why not indeed?" Charles batted at the threads dropping from his mother's embroidery and she smiled at him indulgently.

"No, sir, no!" Nergal said.

But it was no good. Joan called for the guards and they dragged the devil away into the streets.

Charles rubbed at the window, looking out into the falling snow.

"Do you think he'll be back?" he asked her.

"Devils are wily," said his mother, "and he is not of this world. He needs you more than you need him. For all his whining he doesn't want to go back to Hell. Deprivation is good for the lower sort."

"I'll remember that, Mama," said Charles. "Now send for more mice."

2

She has a link to him, magician, a link, and this is the best way to find it."

Osbert crossed himself. Despenser was a terrible sight now—four years after he had come to the French court from Hell, he appeared more like something found on a gibbet on a city gate than the angel whose body he had inhabited.

They had taken over the crypt of the Temple chapel as a work space and now its walls were daubed with magical circles and inscriptions, pentagrams and triangles, the names of devils and angels and the many names of God. The wax of four years of candles dripped over the tombstones and the effigies of long dead knights. Despenser knelt in the flickering light, his corpse-face examining the body of the young woman.

He said, "She hasn't rotted. Why hasn't she rotted? I've rotted."

The pardoner looked down at Sariel's body. "I think it must be because God doesn't want such perfection to fade," said Osbert.

"Why do you always bother with what God wants? Satan is our master and the source of our prosperity. Concentrate on pleasing me so I might please him. Why can't you get me into *that* body?"

Osbert tapped his wand on the plinth and adjusted his conical hat. "I'm not a bloody magician," he was tempted to answer, but, as he was doing rather well out of people believing he was, he contented himself with a shrug. "We've tried, haven't we?" he said. "If you're willing to undergo the ritual, we can give it a go."

"You would tear out my heart to do it?"

"I don't make the rules," said Osbert. "That's how Lord Despenser thinks it will work and he's made inquiries with all the devils on this very subject."

"Rip out my heart and I'd be back in Hell in an instant."

"Or in an angelic body."

He wiped sweat from his brow. In the corner a little branding devil—basically a smith's hot ingot roughly shaped like a man—roasted nuts for Despenser on the palm of its hand.

Despenser shot Osbert a dark look and the pardoner sat down in the space between a sarcophagus and the wall. He'd discovered that he could just about wedge himself in there deep enough so that the giant's rotting hands couldn't reach him. He kept his head down until the lord had found someone or something better to vent his anger on.

The giant said, "If I can inhabit this angel's body, then others can too. We can draw forth just the fellow to do it if you can hit on a better spell. No one is desperate enough to allow you to rip out their heart, not even the lowest devil."

Despenser peered down at Osbert, seemingly still in an even temper, though Osbert had been caught like that before—emerging from his refuge, lulled by a smile or some small talk, only for Despenser to thrash him. Rotting had not improved the lord's temper. He was desperate to find the boy and seemed to be coming to believe that the sole reason for his inability to do so was Osbert's incompetence. In fact Osbert had proved himself a competent, even talented, conjurer.

"I have consulted all my learned books and can find nothing better," said Osbert. This was true. He had no learned books but had used his magician's allowance to buy some rather nonsensical ones at a market. The Hospitallers, he was convinced, had what Osbert needed, but they had been mightily annoyed when the care of Sariel's body had gone to the pardoner and Despenser, not them. They were even more annoyed that King Philip had granted Osbert the use of the crypt and a room in the Great Tower, so they were not about to open any more of their library to him than they had during their short-lived collaboration.

When the company of Despenser's devils had finally become too much for them, they'd appealed to Philip to have them thrown out. Instead the king had told the Hospitallers to leave and they'd taken everything with them.

"You drew me out, why not others with the same talent?" said Despenser. "Why can we only summon scum? Why these weaklings?" A bull-headed devil, no taller than Osbert's knee, ran for cover, being well used to Despenser's love of casual and arbitrary cruelty.

"It is a matter of the right ingredients, the right timing," said Osbert.

He had used up the angel's blood on Despenser's summoning and several attempts to cure Despenser by dripping the blood onto his wounds. Well, used up was putting it strongly. "Opted to keep the rest of his stash to himself" was perhaps a better description.

It did Despenser no good, anyway. Despenser's view was that an angel's body could not be cured by angel blood. Osbert's was that there was something inimical to the angelic body in Despenser's personality. This was based on the observation that Jegudiel's body was rotting with Despenser possessing it while Sariel's had remained untouched by time. Also, Despenser's personality was inimical to absolutely everything else, so why not angel flesh?

Before the Hospitallers had been expelled, Osbert and Despenser had benefited from servants bringing them drinks and food in the crypt as they worked—until Despenser had crushed the heads of two, one for the sin of spilling some wine and the other for bringing chicken that was inadequately seasoned.

In the four years he and Despenser had been working, at least five hundred devils had come through—until a rival faction in Hell had moved to seal his postern gate. Despenser had no doubts who was behind it.

"That bitch Isabella! I should swim across the ocean and drown her now."

"Except you seem unaccountably scared of her," Osbert definitely didn't say.

News of Isabella's release had done for the last of the Hospitallers in the Temple. Despenser went on a rampage with his gang of devils, smashing the chapel windows, tearing down a wall of the refectory, and killing three Hospitallers before Philip had come in and commanded him to stop.

One thing Osbert was grateful for was that kings seemed to be able to command devils. What happened when one king commanded devils to do one thing and another commanded them to do another, Osbert couldn't say. Pretty much what happened with angels, he guessed—the supernatural beings sorted things out among themselves.

Despenser turned his back to attend to some aspect of the circle. Then Osbert scuttled up the stairs, shouting, "I'm going outside for some air."

He said, "You'll stay here until the job is done!"

"I am mortal, lord, and cannot work like you. I will serve you better after a break," said Osbert. He doubted that Despenser would bother to follow him—largely because it was something of a squeeze for the giant to get out of the crypt. He'd probably beat him when he returned, but Despenser's beatings were losing their passion. He was despairing and had a marked tendency to sulk.

Osbert went out into the smashed church—Despenser hadn't wanted so much as a sniff of an angel in there. He steeled himself to face the courtyard. Spider devils had strung webs from all the towers. There were none at ground level, thank God, but he hated to see their thready legs and translucent bodies hovering above him. Only Despenser's crown sigil prevented them swinging down to eat him.

Despenser had adopted the crown as his sign to demonstrate his ambition. He had made it known that he would be king of England and do the homage to Philip that Edward had refused. The pardoner wasn't too sure that any homage would appear should Despenser be successful. Nor was he that sure Philip would be entirely happy to welcome in a King Hugh. *Still*, thought Osbert, *I'm all right, so that's what counts.*

He went out through the postern gate, lighting a lantern as he did. It was normally considered dangerous to sit outside in that quarter, but the presence of the devils had driven any potential roughnecks away.

He sat against the wall. It was cold and sleet was in the air, but the stone was pleasantly cool after the close heat of the crypt. The branding devils gave off quite a lot of warmth and Despenser had insisted on having them in the crypt—because he was insensible to heat and Osbert suffered in it, the pardoner suspected.

He pulled his cloak around him and, despite the cold, began to doze.

A creak at his side.

Osbert opened his eyes. In his half-asleep state the candle seemed to float in front of him. Then he realized someone had it in their hand. *Gulp!*

The candle went out. The moon was strong enough for him to see a tattered and torn face peering at him. The man opened his mouth and breathed hard at Osbert. Clouds of steam issued forth.

"Still not working," said the strange figure.

"Jesus Christ, is it you?" said the pardoner.

"Not a mistake many people make," said the devil glumly.

Osbert got up. He said, "You—you bastard—locked me in a magic circle for God knows how long and put me in the power of madmen, and then pulled devils from my belly!"

"I saved you from being murdered, I seem to recall."

"Well, you did do *that*. I never got the chance to ask you: what happened to all those people who were chasing me?"

"I ate one of them and the rest I sent outside. The smoke makes them quite suggestible. Or it did. Where is my flame? Where is my smoke? Oh, the days of my glory are gone."

"Do you mean you don't possess your former power?" said Osbert, who briefly considered giving the devil the benefit of the rough end of his boot.

"I am a shadow, the shadow of a flame," said the devil, and then—clearly catching a look he didn't much like in Osbert's eye—"but I'd still do for you any day of the week." He opened his mouth and a weak puff of smoke came forth.

The last time Osbert had seen the devil, their conversation had been a little rushed. Now he had the chance to question the devil. "Why did you lock me in there?" he asked.

"Oh, it's just we devils' sense of humor," said the devil. "It was more to get at the priest than you, sorry. And my name is Nergal."

"How did you end up in there?"

"He summoned me."

"From Hell?" said Osbert.

"From Shoreditch. I was walking the earth looking for someone to use to get at the boy Dowzabel. It had taken me forever to locate him and then I discovered that demons had managed to get a magic circle constructed around the whole of Bodmin Moor. I couldn't get near him. I heard this priest's chanting and spell making on the breeze and hopped up to see if I could enlist his help."

Nergal added, "Satan's a mysterious one—but he does put you in situations where you can be useful, or rather where he expects you to work out how you can be useful. So I disappear walking through the Shoreditch market and appear in that cellar, confined to a circle, and being asked endless questions about the nature of the universe. What do I know about that? I'm a devil—good at my job, but we have very narrow horizons. As long as I've got something to burn and candles to eat, I'm a happy fiend."

"You used to be able to change shape. Can you still do that?" The pardoner had a vague feeling Nergal might be useful to him.

"Appearance," said the devil, "but my encounter with the angel knocked that out of me. I would have stabbed her if she hadn't shone in time. That's fallen angels for you. Dozy as you like, no idea what day of the week it is, who they are, what they're doing. Show 'em a knife and they suddenly remember a few of their old tricks."

"And then—didn't you lose your head in the chapel?"

"Yes," said Nergal, "and I wish it had stayed off."

"It'd be a show stealer in the begging stakes," said Osbert, who was warming to the devil, despite the injustices he had visited upon him. Life hadn't treated him kindly either. They had a lot in common. "You'd go a long way to beat that for pity, but there would be significant drawbacks."

"A devil like me shouldn't beg," said Nergal. "I should be put to good use serving kings and God. I heard there might be some of that sort of work going here."

"Might be," said the pardoner, who by now had become quite used to devils. Several years in Despenser's presence—though Despenser was not technically a devil but a fallen, fallen, risen angel—had inured him to most things. "What can you do?"

"Steam a bit," said Nergal. "I used to be able to breathe fire in the days of my flame, but now that's gone." Again he breathed out a disconsolate puff of smoke.

"You can make a mask from a man's face," said Osbert, prodding at the ragged flesh around Nergal's cheeks.

"Yes," said Nergal.

"How do you do that?"

"Just tear the face off and stick it on," said Nergal, "not difficult. I still have sharp nails and the power of bonding. That didn't disappear when they cut off my head." He held up his hands so Osbert could see the filthy, claw-like nails on the end.

"So why not take the whole body?" said Osbert.

"What do you mean?"

"Why not make a more convincing disguise by bonding with the whole body?"

"It might be possible," said Nergal, "but it's a big step. I might never de-bond. I might be stuck in human flesh for good. And human bodies are weak and feeble."

"You don't look too strong to me."

"How strong would you look after being beheaded?"

"Fair point," said the pardoner.

He eyed Nergal up and down. No other devil he knew had been able to strip faces. It was a peculiar talent. When he'd first seen Nergal, the illusion of a human face was very good—a little frozen, a little waxy, but no more than a lot of soused up old churchmen.

Now the face was torn and slack and the raw flesh clear underneath. Could he, though, take over Sariel's body? She was some sort of divine being—would that make it easier or harder? He certainly wasn't going to allow Nergal to tear her face off.

Osbert said, "So, if you wanted to, so to speak, transplant your soul into another body, could you?"

Nergal hemmed and hawed. "I've never thought about it," he said.

"But it might be possible."

"I like being me," said Nergal.

"Doesn't look like it from where I'm sitting," said Osbert. "Come inside and have a candle on me."

"Is it warm in there?"

"There are six branding devils from the lake of fire. It's as warm as you like it and a good deal warmer than I do."

"Then lead on," said Nergal, "for I have been cold too long."

3

B ardi told his tale as he, Dow, and Orsino rode north, clearly proud of his cleverness in tracking down the king. Dow knew it well, but Bardi could not be prevented from reliving it, his one substantial success in life in the years Dow had known him.

Bardi had searched for years for the expenditure that would give Edward away. He had looked for thousands spent, rich clothes ordered, fine foods, even tournaments organized. A king living however modestly would require a retinue to be paid and old Edward must have left England without a penny to his name. But nothing. Although his access to the books was always tantalizingly restricted, every drop of revenue was accounted for, every expenditure logged. Nothing, nothing, nothing.

The accounts from twenty years before—when Edward would have arrived—were not in the Lombard archive. They'd been sent up to Rome as all records were when they were older than five years. So Bardi had waited, built his trust and his connections, and then had himself sent on a mission to Rome. It wasn't difficult to request to see his order's books. But there was nothing there. At all.

But one morning, four years after he had come to the Hospitallers, Bardi realized he had been looking for the wrong thing—a something. He should have been looking for nothing, literally—a hole in the accounts. Edward's keep would be covered up. He would need to seek an overpayment here, a tithe recorded but never paid there. It took him all his skill and wiles to get access to the right accounts, but he did it. Still nothing.

In the fourth year Bardi found what he was looking for right in front of him—or rather one hundred paces through the woods. He had been taking the air in the benefactors' graveyard. Those who were particularly generous to the Hospitallers were allowed to be buried in the graveyards in the woods where the monks prayed daily for the repose of their souls. Even those who preferred to be buried in their own lands were allowed monuments there.

On a cold day in March he went to sit and clear his head there among the cedars. Bardi read the great names of the holy rich of Milan. He had seen them all on the accounts, the Guelphs and the Visconti, the Grimaldi and the Gattilusio. It was then that the idea of tracing their money occurred to him.

The Doge's office kept records of bequests quite independently of the Hospitallers. If Bardi himself had been going to hide the money to pay for a king, reducing the recorded level of money left in wills would be where *he* would do it. It could even be done with sleight of hand on the valuation of jewels, paintings, or houses. Bardi spent a year going through every grave there and chasing it up at the Doge's office. Nothing. It tallied absolutely.

All but one name. Twenty years earlier the Ambrosini estate in the north had been left to the order. That was recorded at the Doge's office and in the Hospitallers' books, along with some minor upkeep. So far unremarkable. The only unusual thing, on the surface, about the whole transaction was that the name of the donor—Ambrosini—was recorded on a slab half a yard high by a yard wide in the graveyard. One word only—the family name—Ambrosini. "A very big slab for a bequest that hardly featured on the books," said Bardi to himself.

A visit to the graveyard steward told Bardi what he needed to know.

"I'd like to be buried here one day," he'd told the man—a surprisingly young and cheerful monk.

"For your name a span wide you'll need to leave us seven hundred acres," said the monk, "and I guess if you had that, you wouldn't be a monk."

"Some of us are called to serve," said Bardi. *Seven hundred acres for a span. How much then for such a large plaque?* he wondered.

Then Orsino made the inquiries in the north. The answer staggered Bardi. A chapel, more than a chapel, a whole huge estate of forests, lakes, and islands to the north of Milan, with a splendid monastery at the center, had been bequeathed to the Hospitallers and then vanished—from the books, at least. No income, no maintenance costs, no tithes, no works commissioned or requested. It was as if the estate had ceased to exist as a financial entity on the day the Hospitallers inherited it.

Now they traveled to see it on the pretense of checking anomalies in the books of some minor houses in the north.

Ghost villages—places burned by a forgotten war, put beyond use and never recovered. Churches smashed, houses charred to nothing and then overgrown, the rotted bones of animals and people still underfoot in the streets. The lake would have been no more than a day's ride from Milan to the northeast had the roads been good, but they were not good. The area was heavily forested and, though the road went within fifteen miles of Brescia, it bore no one on it and was overgrown and rutted.

"What happened here?" said Orsino.

"A tax dispute nearly twenty years ago now," said Bardi. "The lord of this place decided to teach his people a lesson. That's what was said, anyway. Amazing that a man at death's door should purge the lands he has relied on all his life shortly before bequeathing them, don't you think? Why render them valueless and then pass them on?"

"The Hospitallers still haven't resettled this place." Orsino clearly found this a great wonder.

"The edict banning it from habitation stands, though the lord is dead."

"Who is there to enforce it?" said Orsino.

"Us," said Bardi. "It belongs to we Hospitallers now."

"This land could be put to good use," said Orsino.

"You'd think so, wouldn't you?" said Bardi. "But it isn't. What does that tell you?"

They encountered no one on the tracks, if anyone could call them tracks. The forest was thick and the horses labored through deep undergrowth, briars, and bogs.

"We're making a . . ." Dow and Orsino began the same sentence at the same time.

Orsino finished it. "A fine trail should anyone want to follow us."

"Will people follow us?"

Dow whistled and Murmur came tumbling out of the sky. "Anything?" he asked the ympe.

Murmur said, "Nothing I can see." Dow had not told Murmur what had happened to Catspaw. There was no advantage in it. He needed Bardi, and he needed Murmur to work with him.

Bardi crossed himself. "Keep that ympe watchful," he said. "These forests are full of wild men."

"You've traveled enough to be braver," said Dow. He considered telling him he'd still have an ympe of his own to watch, were he a man of his word.

"Not so lightly attended," responded Bardi.

"Two men-at-arms are as good as twenty," said Orsino. "Bandits won't attack if they think they'll meet any resistance at all. Why not wait for some undefended pilgrims?"

"Because there aren't any here?" said Bardi.

"Which means there'll be fewer wild men waiting for us. What hunter waits for a deer where deer are never seen?"

Four days into the forest the hills rose up to distant mountains. They crested a slope and descended through pines. Through the trees, a flash like a blade. The sun on water but no island.

"Wrong lake," said Bardi. "That village down there has a herd of cows outside it. Which means a cowherd will be there. If Edward is somewhere guarded by angels, the Hospitallers won't have witnesses on the shore to see their lights."

They turned the horses around. It was another week before they found what they were looking for—a bright mountain dawn crystaling the water of a steel blue lake.

Bardi, Dow, and Orsino looked down from the hillside over Lake Iseo and its island Monte Isola. The island rose high out of the lake, like a mountain of the imagination. At the top was a fortress and next to it an imposing church. No villages surrounded it, which Dow knew to be odd for a monastery. All the ones he had seen had villages sprouting around them like gall apples on an oak—people flocking to offer services to the monks.

"You can't assault that," said Orsino.

"That's not where we're going," said Bardi.

"Then where?"

"There."

Another island lay in the lake alongside the island mountain, shimmering like a green jewel in the early-morning light. It was far smaller, no more than five hundred paces long and dead flat. It too was thick with trees—tall pines and broad cedars. A villa like those of Milan squatted at the water's edge. The tower of the chapel was just visible through the trees—bloody with roses. If there was anything else, it was obscured by trees.

Orsino said, "That's the monastery."

Bardi said, "The Cluniacs were thrown out of that twenty years ago when the Hospitallers possessed the land. It's never been used for anything else since—nothing I can find on the books anyway."

"It looks well maintained."

"It should be," said Bardi. "The bequest was enough to maintain half of Milan, let alone an island of this size."

"Can you see any men on the island, Dow? Your eyes are better than mine," said Orsino.

Dow squinted. "There's movement," he said. "Look, by the villa."

A small figure swept the steps by the water's edge.

"So how do you get on to it?" said Bardi.

"If this is where the king is, he will have his angels with him," said Orsino.

Dow wriggled, his falchion digging into his side as if to beg use. Now? Two blows would do it—or rather one. He could kill Orsino with his first strike and then take his time with Bardi. The little banker would run, but he would not get far. Dow had been a faster runner than Orsino almost since he'd known him. Dow suspected he'd been a faster runner than Bardi for a lot longer than that.

Not now. He still didn't know what opposition he would meet on that island. The more people on his side the better, though he couldn't think the banker would be much good in a scrap.

"We watch," said Orsino.

"We've been watching," said Bardi. "What else is there to see?"

"I don't know," said Orsino. "Which is why we're going to watch."

"For how long?"

"A week at least, I'd say," said Orsino.

"To what purpose?"

"To find out what we're dealing with. Are there food deliveries on the island? Do they feast at any time? Is there a night guard? Other questions I don't know I need to ask until I see what's going on there. Now, if I was you, I'd get back over the ridge to the horses and make yourself comfortable for a long wait."

"Boy, come with me and make a fire," said Bardi.

"No fire," said Orsino.

"We'll freeze in the night."

"Yes, we will. But better than inviting God knows what—or who—out of that monastery to butcher us in our sleep."

They watched for four days, the mountain nights cold but not unbearable. Bardi complained, but Dow didn't see why. The banker had two good cloaks to wrap himself in, as well as having four blankets on his horse.

The days were uneventful, but the nights were disturbing. Lights flashed within the chapel, and with colors no earthly lamp ever produced—golds and silvers, emerald and ruby. Dow heard songs in what he imagined was the voice of the wind, he heard flutes and cymbals and something else beneath it—a deeper, darker tone that boomed like the ocean.

"He is here for you. Turn to God."

"You have been lied to. Turn to God."

"Your salvation is at hand. Only welcome God into your heart." Dow knew the voices were speaking to him.

Bright figures were seen flitting and moving in the darkness of the trees—beautiful winged beings who disappeared when Dow stood to face them.

"Angels?" said Orsino.

"I don't know," said Dow. "Something."

"So they know we are here?"

"It seems so."

"Do they know why?"

"I don't know," said Dow. "They are not all-knowing—Edwin told me that."

"Only God is all-knowing," said Orsino. "All knowing and all powerful."

"Then he is a knave," said Dow, "to see the world's pain and never lift a finger to stop it."

"You're really quite tiresome," said Bardi. "Most of the priests I know don't find it necessary to go banging on about God every second breath, so why do you? You don't even like him. I don't like the duke of Guelders. That's why you never hear me talk of him—I prefer not to think of him. Broaden your conversation; you're a dreadful bore."

"You who have nothing to live for beyond yourself might think so," said Dow. "You, Bardi, you do not honor even your God, you do not make a friend of Lucifer, you do not fight or work for your fellows. You worship only idle comforts—you have more love for jewels and gold than you do for your king, for your friends, for any creature or man, and your aim is only ease and indulgence. Even when you had riches beyond the dreams of princes, you lived poorly. A beggar who shares his bread with his friend is a richer man than you."

"Still not got the knack of light chat, have we?" said Bardi.

"What are they saying to you, Dowzabel?" Orsino was spooked, it was plain to see. He crouched low and his eyes scanned the forest in fear.

"They want me to come to God."

"You should do that, before it's too late," said Bardi.

"For them or for me?" said Dow.

"They are being merciful. You're lucky to still be alive," said Bardi.

"In my experience the followers of your God refrain from killing for one reason," said Dow. "They are scared of inviting greater retribution on themselves."

"Shhh!" Orsino waved for them to get lower. He said, "A boat!"

A small fishing boat with a lantern on board made its way from the green mountain island, two men rowing a curve from an unseen dock toward the villa entrance. Orsino added, "What's in it, Dow?"

He said, "Food, I should say. There are barrels."

"So there can't be too many men on the smaller island. That's not enough to restock a sizable garrison," said Orsino.

"Could be a top up," said Dow.

"Yes. Wait a little more."

"I thought you were men of action," said Bardi.

"We're live men of action," said Orsino. "Which means that most of the time we look before we leap. Do you think we could take the boat, Dow?"

He said, "We could, but we don't know it's not watched from the bigger island, or who would greet us."

"You could kill the men on the boat and take their clothes," said Bardi, "or hide inside the barrels."

Orsino snorted. "You've listened to too many travelers' tales, Bardi," he said. "How do you expect us to fold ourselves up into wine barrels or even have time to do that? Getting to the big island will be as difficult as getting to the small one. No wonder you went bankrupt with reasoning like that."

"Then how will you get across?"

"We will get across," said Dow, "but when we are ready."

"You can't swim it, Dow; we need weapons."

"We won't be swimming," said Dow.

Another six days' watch showed only the little boat again. Orsino spent long hours gazing at the lake, as if he only thought hard enough then its waters would part.

"Any point in waiting any longer?" said Dow to Orsino. He never addressed his comments to Bardi unless he had to. It would be too easy to kill the banker in a fit of rage if he spent too much time talking to him, so Dow kept contact to a minimum.

"No."

"Then tonight?"

"How?" he asked Dow.

Dow replied, "The ympes will carry us."

"How so? They are too small."

"They will do it."

The sun sank beside them, casting the lake in a copper glow before the dark shadow of the hill pushed a deep cool blue across the water. A sharp crescent moon burned cold above the black of the mountains and the lights in the windows of the chapels began to move. The moon's light silvered the tower that rose out of the trees, the roses black in its ghost light.

"We'll drop into the cover of the trees and then make our way from there," said Dow. "We must kill the guards quickly and quietly."

Dow's ympe scurried among the needles of a pine.

Orsino took the angel's mail from his pack.

"Best carry that until you get to the island," said Dow. "The ympes may not like to touch it directly."

Orsino grunted, strapped on his sword and shield, shouldered his pack, and took up his crossbow, along with its quiver. "Now what?"

Dow checked all his weapons—his falchion, his dagger, his crossbow. He too carried his mail in a separate pack, not because the ympes would not touch it but because he wanted to make himself as light as he could. He called to Murmur in the trees.

Tiny wings raced across the moon, turning in a swarm like a flock of starlings. Murmur had done what Dow had asked him to and called the whispering ympes from all corners of France and Italy. They came down in a cloud, lifting up Dow's pack, his crossbow, and then himself.

He saw the uncertainty in Bardi's eyes and felt good about that, enjoying his instant of power over the banker. Then Dow banished the thought. Bardi was worthless. There was no glory or pleasure in discomfiting him. There would be no glory or pleasure in killing him—only justice. Hundreds of tiny hands plucked at Dow's body and clothes, seizing the thick cloth of his gambeson, the laces of his boots, his hose, even his fingers as the ympes pulled him precariously into the air.

He heard Orsino cry out, surprised as the ympes took him. Dow looked at the island. The flickering of the light in the church did not change; no alarm was heard from the shore.

Up into the moonlit air at the center of a fluttering swarm, lurching across the bay in fits and starts as the tiny demons pulled, tired, and let go, to be replaced by others and returned to their efforts anew. The silver path of moonlight stretched out, the stars spun and danced, the trees swung below him as he swayed out toward the island. Dow tried to use his vantage point to survey the island, but the ympes were all about him, thick as a cloud, their tiny breaths hot on his face and hands, their wings pattering like rain, and he saw only glimpses of where he was.

He began to drop, the ympe cloud taking him down to forest. Here Dow fell in stages as some of the ympes were forced to let him go as they descended into the trees. They released him, darted below him, and caught him again.

Finally Dow was on the ground, pine needles sharp on his hands. The ympes dispersed into the trees and he saw Orsino dropping above him as if trapped in a swarm of huge flapping bats. The ympes dropped the mercenary too.

Something was strange in the air—it smelled very sweet, like pine, but with an intoxicating feeling to it. Fireflies bobbed on invisible currents and the woods were full of birdsong.

Orsino crossed himself and opened his pack. Swift and practiced, he put his sword and shield on the floor and put on his angel's hauberk. He picked up his crossbow from where the ympes had dropped it and, without saying a word, was ready to go. Dow could see Orsino had been shaken to travel in that way, but he was now a soldier on a mission. It wasn't the time to express surprise or exchange impressions of the journey.

Dow, who had now put on his threadbare mail, put his helmet on his head and took up his weapons and shield. Orsino nodded toward the chapel. He nodded and the two men picked their way carefully through the trees.

Now Dow began to doubt—two of them against however many? Two mortals against however many angels. He put it from his head. Doubt was not useful to him—it would not change his course of action, only make him hesitate. *This is your purpose, this your choice*, he thought. *Honor it.*

The wood, being pine, was less dense on the ground than it had seemed from the air. They had agreed—Orsino would take the villa, Dow the chapel. Orsino could hold off any attack from the rear while Dow went for the banner. Could he face down angels, if they were in there? The question was pointless. Free Hell had set him the task and he was going to attempt it. His pack was heavy enough already without putting doubt in it.

Still, he was scared, no point denying it.

Orsino moved right, Dow following him. The plan was that they'd observe the villa at close quarters, and then Dow would sneak on to the chapel if it looked as though Orsino was capable of handling the garrison on his own. Dow glanced at his companion. In his angel mail, with the shield of the Sacred Heart on his arm, the angelic helm on his head, he looked as if he was capable of handling an army. They'd estimated six men on the island, to judge by the supplies that were going over. Where were they?

They descended the slope. The chill of the mountains had gone here and a pleasantly warm breeze drifted in off the waters. It was when Dow looked up that he realized something was amiss. The constellations he'd seen since he was a boy were not there—no hunter, no pan, no crab. The sky was shot with billions of stars, but he recognized not one.

Movement in the chapel. Lights playing on the inside of the windows, just visible through the carpet of roses.

"An angel?" said Orsino, crossing himself.

Dow didn't reply, he just crept down the hill, toward the dancing lights.

4

W hen the deal was done, when Edward had offered the Luciferians what he had already promised in secret to the demon—that they would have their piece of France—they let Montagu go.

Montagu was surprised the heretics didn't know they had been offered something they already had. Why had the demons not told their own followers? Now he saw it was simply practical. It was one thing to deal with heretics, another to deal with demons. Free Hell had not announced its deal because if Edward was known to have struck a deal with demons, his knights might have rebelled and refused to fight for him, making a victory and a new Eden for Free Hell on earth less likely. No honor anywhere any more. Just brutal realities.

Edward had sent a troop of knights and men-at-arms to fetch Montagu from Southwark. He'd been kept in the country nearby because the Luciferians had been outlawed from London and its surrounding villages. Edward might have promised France but he reserved the right to keep England under God. Edwin remained as the king's captive until Montagu was returned.

Southwark was like a country under occupation. Devils stalked the narrow streets—whips cracking, pitchforks jabbing. The sniffing devils were the worst—great eyeless hounds, slobbering and straining at the leash to scent God's enemies' blood and draw the constables of Hell to them. They could smell disbelief in all its shades—rebellion, doubt, apathy. All were caught and all were punished.

He was there a year, and all that time the people went about their business under curfew and assault. Church attendance had increased out of all proportion—in terms of bodies. People's souls, it was said, stayed elsewhere. Every time a spider-headed inquisitor bit into a poor man's flesh, it won another soul for Lucifer, and the slum was emptying fast.

Old habits die hard and Greatbelly had looked to Montagu for guidance. "Will Edward play us false or true?" she asked him.

"I don't know," said Montagu. It was the truth. "Though I should approach your dealings with the king with the greatest care. He hates you, and a king's hate is a terrible thing."

"But we have his promise."

"He will honor that," said Montagu. "But he will honor it to the letter. Take your bowmen and your demons away from him as soon as you can. Go to France, but expect no favors from the French king. There are enmities within France. Exploit those if you can. Normandy is endlessly disputed even by the French. Some lord may need your bowmen and, for that, offer you brief protection."

Greatbelly shook her great jowls. "I wish my Edwin was here," she said. "And Know-Much. They could advise and tell me if you're telling me lies."

The woman talked a great deal about this demon Know-Much, and while there Montagu did see some of the little whispering demons. Apparently they were trying to carry messages to the king's court—unsuccessfully, for it was guarded by men with the wings of flies who tore the demons from the air if they saw them.

Montagu hadn't enjoyed his time with the poor. Unsophisticated, their manners wanting, they lacked leaders though they had great need of them. They had even debated the morality of keeping Montagu prisoner. Lucifer made all men free, they said. How could they then abuse the perfection of his creation by locking men up? No wonder these people were popular with rogues and thieves.

Still, he felt some care for these people. Montagu had been raised to believe that he as a nobleman, stood in the relation of a father to them, as the king stood as a father to his nobles. Like a father with errant children, he feared for them, he prayed for them, and he could not hate them.

When they released Montagu, they let him take his cloak and his sword. They were his personal possessions and therefore no man's to steal. His lands and his money, however, were another matter. They returned one of his coins and kept the rest to buy bread for the poor.

Good luck spending them, Montagu thought. Gold ecus d'or of the French realm would be like a pennant to the devils, drawing them from miles around.

So, as Montagu waited at the edge of the woods on Streatham common for the king's men to pick him up, he was resigned to his fate. Though not quite. He felt he would see *her* again before he died. In the dungeons where Montagu had been shut, in the battles he had fought, and the hardships he had endured, her face had always been in his mind. Isabella. He feared to die because of her, and he hated himself for that. Had he given Greatbelly the cloak expecting to be kidnapped? Montagu couldn't be sure he hadn't, though he hadn't even had the guts to face his desire honestly and use it himself.

No, he had betrayed everything, his wife, his king, his God. Death was a luxury; God's mercy unfathomable. He deserved to be damned and would put himself beyond redemption. Montagu walked north at first. He would not use the cloak because of the sickness it brought and had hidden it in a sack he'd taken from Greatbelly. The poor were generous, though they had little. If he considered nineteen gold coins for a sack a bargain.

His clothes were truly rags now, and he could not identify himself to get into London. The city was far from Edward's camp, but some spy or ambitious sneak there would have reported his movements to the king. Officially there was a reward for information on his whereabouts so he might be rescued. Montagu did not want to be rescued; he wanted to be damned and knew just where to go to secure that fate.

So he skirted the town, around the marshes. He couldn't spend his coin, so he had no change to pay a ferryman. Montagu headed west on the Tyburn Road. He reflected wryly that he was walking away from Tyburn, rather than toward it—as Edward might still command. He mourned his lost friendship; Montagu remembered those times they'd traveled together on various mad missions to courts across Europe. Once they'd gone disguised as merchants to avoid the attention of their enemies—and to save a few quid, Edward had pointed out. Low men didn't need to put on a show when they traveled.

Montagu walked out to the bridge at Staines and pared the coin there. He sold the shavings to a money changer and finally had enough to buy an aged horse and a pair of decent boots. He took in the market at Oxford as he traveled north and bought some secondhand clothes that, while far from fine, were not filthy. Watling Street was broad and green, then he took the Icknield Way—overshooting toward Lincoln before some pilgrims redirected him.

The roads were busy, though Montagu attached himself to no group of merchants, no pilgrims, no band of players. He placed himself in God's hands. Half of him hoped he'd be attacked and killed before Nottingham.

The going, however, was pleasant, and the nearest he came to assault was a couple of insistent hedgerow whores near Leicester. Montagu had no intention of doing business with them—having spent much of the last year locked in what amounted to a brothel without having been tempted. The lack of money had helped, that and *her* memory. Isabella. Before whom all women's beauty was simple prettiness—gaudy and commonplace as a woodbine.

Nottingham Castle could be seen looming above the city from five miles away. On this bright blue day women were washing their clothes in the river and hanging them like the flags of an army on trees for miles about. The town was under devil control now, and gargoyles flapped their stony wings above the castle, surveying the land. She'd be watching from up there. Isabella loved to look out from high towers, owning the land like an eagle.

He'd approached this way before, by night, armed, sneaking. That too had been a mission of love—for his king—but she had been there.

Montagu wept, for his stupidity, for his neglect of his wife. Catherine was better neglected by a man like him.

He gave the horse to the ferryman on the Trent. The man was surprised at his passenger's generosity, but Montagu just waved his hand and said nothing. Crossing the Styx, the old Greeks gave Charon the only coin they had to convey them to the land of the dead. No thought of return. He'd done the same.

The tunnel was how he remembered it—filled in with boulders, impassable. He pulled off an angel's feather and pointed it to the rock. The stone shimmered, jellied, became as glass. And then it wasn't there.

He climbed, clearing his way with the feather. The sack was an encumbrance now and he cast it aside, putting on the angel feather cloak he had got back from the Luciferians. Montagu would not use it to travel, but it would armor him against devils, he was sure.

He emerged on the stair. This time a spider devil, not a man, was on guard. Its legs were as thick as a man's arm, straddling the corridor. It leapt for him, but Arondight struck true, piercing the great body, the dripping jaws snapping uselessly, a span from Montagu's face.

He kept climbing to the master solar. Now a stoneskin gargoyle bore down on him, its spear singing over Montagu's head. The sword made sure it was the last song that spear would ever sing as the creature ground its teeth and died. Three terrible figures—men, their limbs impossibly elongated with their hands full of cruel knives—descended. They stood between him and her and were as straws blown away in the wind. His rage, his love, could tear any enemy down.

Finally he was at that door, the one he'd been at so long ago to kill a tyrant and let his friend reign as the true king that Montagu had imagined him to be.

He opened it. She had her back to him, looking out of the window again. At her side was a little devil—a beautiful child with the wings of a gigantic bat sprouting from its back. It wore a long white shift and was playing a pipe for her.

Isabella said, "Hello, William. I see you've been consorting with your old friend Death again."

He said, "I did not choose." He was panting with the exertion of the fight. "What?"

"Any of it. Nothing. My whole life. You have enchanted me and I am here."

She turned to him, her blond hair like spun gold in the candlelight. Montagu felt a lurch inside him, like a push in the back, drawing him forward.

"No, William. I never did."

Montagu said, "You are a sorceress. A she-wolf."

"A wolf doesn't bite everyone it sees. I chanted no names for you, William, I drew no circles—nor took a lock of your hair to seal in a bottle that I might call your soul my own."

"You are a liar. You add that to your many crimes."

Isabella said, "I'm not a woman to waste effort, William. I could not gain anything by working my magical arts to enchant you. I'm afraid you were already enchanted. God wishes you to love she who hates you. He must hate you too."

"What do you want from me?" he said.

"You presume I want anything at all."

The bat-winged child smiled sweetly at Montagu, its teeth a row of jagged spikes.

Montagu sank to his knees.

Isabella now smiled too. She said, "If you're expecting me to cut off your head, my lord, you're going to be disappointed."

She went past him and closed the door. "Better take precautions against any of my devils leaping to my help," she said. "You know that I hate you."

"Yes."

"So I ask you your own question. What do you want from me? What can you want from me?"

"To be your servant."

"Why?" Isabella asked him.

"Because of what I am," he said. "For you I have betrayed my best friend and my king. For you I am here on my knees like a servant when I should be leading England's armies in war. For you I have betrayed my wife and my children, turned my back on a happiness that would satisfy a thousand men. I deserve to be damned, lady, and I can think of no surer way of achieving that goal than by offering myself to you to do your vile work."

Isabella looked at Montagu like a cat assessing a sunbeam. "Oh, William," she said, "you are the most useful of men and, on that condition, are welcome to my service. The Hospitallers have my husband alive— Mortimer was happy with that. I am not. I think you and I need to talk."

Montagu said, "I will do what you ask. I will hurry to Hell for you."

"Of course you will. Now come into my arms. You will stay with me tonight."

Montagu was dizzy. He said, "You hate me."

"But I am not unsubtle. Share my bed. I can think of nothing that will make you hate yourself more than to compound your offense to your lord, to cuckold your rightful king and spite his son. What enemy could ever defeat William Montagu, England's most famous fighter? It's you, William. You are the man to undo yourself. I appoint you to the task."

She opened the little window and the child devil squeezed through, flying out against the stars.

"So come," she said, "let me be your torturer and your damnation."

Montagu closed his eyes. Then he walked across the room. He put his lips to hers. She smelled of almonds and apples, of church incense and rue.

"What do you want from me?" he said as he broke from her kiss.

"What I asked for from Mortimer," she whispered. "I want my husband's heart, for that will give me England."

5

D espenser eyed Nergal as the tattered cardinal made his way into the crypt. The giant was still crouching by Sariel's body, his rotten face pale in the torchlight.

"I'm not sure I like the look of him," he said. "He's not of our faction."

"Is he of Free Hell?" said Osbert. Behind him was a creature like a devil in a painting, horned and bearded, bright red, his body glowing like a hot iron. This was the hottest branding devil, brought in by Osbert for the warmth he would lend to Nergal.

"No. But he's not someone I know. Who do you work for, devil?"

Nergal replied, "For Lord Satan."

Osbert saw something remarkable—an expression of nervousness, almost fear, crossed Despenser's face, the angel's rotted lips drawing back from its toothless gums. Behind him the body of Sariel lay pale in the flickering torchlight.

"None other?" Despenser asked.

"I am employed direct. Or I was. My situation may have changed since I came here, so unsuccessful have I been, so abused and mutilated."

Osbert lit a little oil lamp off a candle. How quickly he had become indifferent to horrors. This decaying giant, this torn devil—no more disturbing to him now than the faces he'd seen in the market places. He reminded himself what he always reminded himself when looking at infirmity or disease—physical collapse was just a symptom of spiritual collapse. One of the comforts Osbert took in his own good health was that it showed God favored him at least a little.

"Self-pity suits no one," said Despenser, "but if you had to suffer my toe or my shoulder, then you'd know what pain was. Why is he here, pardoner?"

He said, "I believe he might have a talent similar to your own, lord, in that he could inhabit the body of this fallen angel."

"I would prefer a devil of my faction," said Despenser.

"I am willing to be of your faction," said Nergal. "I will represent you to Satan as a very fine devil if you allow me to move out of this painful and threadbare body." He removed his collar to reveal a line of neat stitches. "My head aches terribly; these stitches allow me to live, but they are so stiff and the collar chafes me so."

"You know how that feels," said Osbert. "You had just such a thing when I first met you."

"Are you suggesting some similarity between me and him?" Despenser grabbed the pardoner and pulled him close to the sucking pink wound of his mouth.

"Far from it," said Osbert, "but surely you must see how grateful he would be, how useful too, should the proper devil's oaths be extracted."

"You would take an oath?"

Nergal said, "I cannot take an oath to obey you because I obey Satan. But I can vow not to harm you, to further your aims, and to give credit where it is due should we catch the Antichrist."

Despenser looked hard at the devil. "And you think you could possess her body?" he asked.

"Yes. Time was when every devil worth his salt could manage a possession. Now the old arts are being lost and few can do it—none of the outer circles at all."

"Why is that?"

"The younger breed are content to jab a few sinners in the arse and spend their days in idleness. Satan's attention is on the battles in the inner circles—he doesn't impose discipline like he did. Those young devils are in for a shock once the battle's won, though. The outer circles will have to buck up their ideas!"

Despenser said, "You are not of the outer circles?"

"Certainly not," said Nergal with a sniff. "I am an ambassador from Lord Satan. I am a devil of breeding, of quality. My powers are great."

Now it was Despenser's turn to sniff. He replied, "Not so great since you lost your head, I think."

"Perhaps I will recapture them if I possess this corpse. I could be of great service to you."

Despenser glanced at Osbert, his great dead eyes meeting the pardoner's.

"If it gives us a chance to know the angel's thoughts and locate the boy, then it's worth it," said Osbert.

Osbert had never asked Despenser why he hadn't used the angels to defend the old king when Isabella attacked with Mortimer. Maybe they were disgusted by his tyranny and refused to appear for him. For fear of Despenser's wrath, Osbert did not much fancy bringing the subject up. He said, "Shall we try the possession then?"

"No time like the present," said Despenser. "Have you run him through the form of the ceremony?"

"Yes and no," said Osbert. He turned to address Nergal. "It would involve some little discomfort on your behalf."

"In what way?" he asked.

"I think we'd have to call on the higher spirits of the east, west, north, and south."

"I can stand that."

Osbert said, "You'd have to be put in another magic circle."

"That might be claustrophobic," said Nergal. He stroked his pale chin.

"And, at the climax of the ceremony, you would have to have—er, there really isn't a particularly pleasant way of saying this—your beating heart ripped from your chest and squeezed over the body of this fallen angel."

Nergal *umm*ed and *ahh*ed. "I do see that might work," he said, "the heart being the seat of all the emotions and of the spirit. There would certainly be some discomfort involved. It's not something that would be undertaken by a less desperate devil than me. I've only done faces before. Hmm. Life is a walking misery, though. Hmm. Can I ask who would do the ripping?"

Osbert gestured to Despenser. "He has the nails, he has the strength, and, more than that, it's the sort of thing he's good at. Have you ever torn out a heart before, lord?" he asked him.

"A couple of livers, a tongue, and a spleen," said Despenser.

"Not very different. Practically an expert," said Osbert. "What do you say?"

"It is a very fine body," said Nergal, "and I have no doubt it may invigorate me to inhabit it. The lord here looks a quick and efficient eviscerator. Yes, I think I'll say yes. Nothing ventured, nothing gained, eh?"

"Indeed not," said Osbert. "Well, I'll draw up the chalk circle and we'll get to it, shall we?"

"Contracts first," said Despenser.

"In blood too?" inquired Osbert.

"Just the signature; there's no need to go mad," replied Nergal.

"I thought devils usually demanded contracts be written in blood," said Osbert.

"Only to piss the sorcerer off," said Nergal. "It's a bit of fun we devils allow ourselves."

Osbert drew up the contract and both Despenser and Nergal signed, or rather smeared, their blood upon it.

"Is the moon right?" The devil was plainly nervous.

"The moon is fine," said Osbert, "and the stars are in a good conjunction. I know what is needed, I studied nothing but magic for long years under a harsh master."

"The tides?"

"Have shit-all to do with it," said Osbert.

"Just testing," said Nergal.

Osbert drew the circle, modeled on the one on his belly. He dabbed on a bit of angel's blood from his little vial. Not much left now.

"You said you had run out!" said Despenser.

"A good job I hid it," said Osbert. "Or where would we be now? Your Majesty."

"When you are no longer useful to me, I will kill you," said Despenser.

"Then I hope to be useful to you for a long time," said Osbert.

The circle enclosed the plinth on which Sariel lay. Osbert almost hated to complete the possession. She had been kind to him, even told him he was made for better things. Well, serving fallen, fallen angels like Despenser, serving kings, those were better things, weren't they?

The names of the spirits of the east, the west, the south, and the north were inscribed; the names of God were inscribed, without whom resurrection would have been impossible; Osbert lit the incense and purified the four corners of the world; he set down salt for the element of earth, a saucer of water, a burning candle for fire, a fan to represent the wind. Nergal himself would be aether—the spirit substance. Despenser crammed himself into the circle too, ready for his part.

Osbert moved by instinct, his knowledge derived from long observation of Edwin. He set the objects in their places, he muttered the names of Christ and of the angels and then of God, He who made the devils and confined their souls to flesh, and again of the name of God, He who made the angels who fell, and who allowed his servants in Hell to find their forms where they might. Sweat stung his eyes and wet his tunic—the presence of the branding devil was increasing the heat to an almost unbearable level.

Nergal stood at the side of Sariel's corpse, his hands grasping the plinth either side of her as if he might kiss her.

Through the long hours of darkness Osbert invoked the spirits who had been there at the creation of Hell where devils were assembled from the offcuts of God's creation and life breathed into them. He called on God, who had kindled that life to take the flame of the devil's soul to light the fire that would move the fallen angel's body. He called . . . "Now!"

Mid-word Osbert brought his hand down quick as a headsman's axe and Despenser grasped Nergal by the scruff of the neck with one hand and sank his nails into the devil's chest with the other. The devil howled and braced itself against the plinth as Despenser tore through its belly and up into its chest cavity. There were sparks and crackles from the devil's skin and Despenser cried out that Nergal's guts were hot, but Despenser didn't relent, he burrowed out the sizzling, sparking fiery heart and held it above Sariel's body.

"By the blood of Hell and the blood of Heaven, I bid you live!" Osbert's voice was cracked with the hours of incantation. Despenser squeezed the heart as Osbert flicked the last of the angel's blood onto Sariel's forehead. It was as if the heart turned to molten metal poured from a smith's bucket—it flowed through Despenser's fingers steaming and sparking and down into the dead angel's mouth.

Osbert crossed himself, fearing she would be burned alive, but she was not. Sariel coughed and hacked, her body wrenched by convulsions.

"If this just brings *her* back to life, pardoner, we could be for it," said Despenser. "Get ready to behead her before she realizes she's awake—at my command."

"Why don't *you* get ready to behead her?" Osbert asked.

"She'll attack her assailant. You're dispensable; bring your sword or defend yourself against me."

Sariel gave a great cry, a keening funereal sob, and Osbert scrabbled for his sword. Despenser backed away like a court lady from a spider, crawling around to the stairs.

"Strike if she lives!" said Despenser. He repeated, "Strike if she lives."

Sariel sat up. She looked around her.

"Nergal?" said Osbert.

The fallen angel opened her mouth. It was a tiny furnace, full of a roaring fire.

"Yes," she said, smoke billowing from her lips as she spoke. "Yes. Nergal. The days of my flame have come again. This is choice, this is rich, I can feel her here. She wants the light, but she is here for the boy. When the boy calls for her help, I'll know where he is."

"Good," said the pardoner, "let me know when that happens. Now if you'll excuse me, I'm off to get drunk."

"It could be years before he calls her, a lifetime even," said Despenser.

"I'm quite prepared to be drunk for that long if I have to," said Osbert. He went to step out of the circle, but Despenser grabbed him.

"Sorry," said Osbert. "I nearly forgot."

He kicked a gap in the chalk he had drawn, walked past the simmering branding devil, and made his way out up the stairs.

Osbert felt Despenser's gaze on him as he left. Soon, he would no longer be useful to the lord. He would have to start looking for other patrons. He had had enough of working with devils. Perhaps it was time to see what more pleasant forces had to offer.

Something Despenser had said had triggered a memory. "Why do you always concentrate on what God wants?" Osbert recalled what Despenser had said when he first met him—that perhaps God does not want what Satan wants. Perhaps angels don't want what God wants. Which meant that he who found out what God wanted would be in a very powerful position. Osbert would go direct to King Philip; he now had an idea what might rouse the king's angels.

6

Charles had a dream of an arrow flying. It flew against a strong Iberian sun. It was the arrow of the future, flying from the walls of Algeciras in Granada, striking his father in the throat and sending him slumping from his horse.

"Mother!" he said.

Joan replied, "Yes, Charles?"

The boy had taken to sleeping curled up on her bed, a blanket of cats around him. His mother had terrible trouble ensuring that the noble cats slept closest and the fight-torn alley cats farthest away. One such cat had only one eye. That reminded her of Montagu. At least there might be some hope from England, one day.

He said, "Father is dead."

"How do you know it?"

"I know it," he said.

The queen rose up in a fever of anticipation. She said, "We must head south tonight. Let's get to the great cathedral and have it call you king and me your regent, before anyone can start casting aspersions on your parentage."

"You my regent? Am I not ready to rule in my own right?" Charles twitched and inclined his head like a cat who sees a ball of wool move.

"I am queen, Charles. I'm not quite ready to give that up yet."

Charles twitched again. He said, "But I am chosen of God."

Joan shooed her ladies out of the room. Then she put her hand on her son's head and whispered into his ear, "Yes, you are. But your descent, you see, is through me, not your father. It is me who would have to die for you to become king and, as you see, I am very much alive."

"So how can they stop you from going to your own kingdom?"

She said, "There are still questions about what happened to the angels. If they suspect your father is dead, we will be prisoners here. We must get to Navarre and consider our options."

Charles stood and stretched. "Does this mean we are free to ally with England?" he asked her.

"We need to be more subtle than that, Charles. England has armies of devils now. The French angels still cower in their shrines after the death of Jegudiel. There is a chance England could win once the truce finishes."

"France at peace?"

"Yes. A disaster. Remember, we are seeking no victors, just a grinding stalemate—a cup of gall for Philip. We will think clearly about where to place our favor and we will be able to think more clearly away from this court. They have no hold on us now your father is dead!"

Charles moved to the window and looked out over Paris. It had been his home for a long time now, the sprawling, smoky, stinking, beautiful town. He loved the way the low sun hung on the shoulder of the spire of the great church of St.-Germain l'Auxerrois, how the long shadows stretched toward him like arms welcoming him in to the church of the parish of the kings of France. Was it so much to ask, just to be lord and master of all this, the greatest king on earth? Of course not. It was his right. He drove some uncharitable and sacrilegious thoughts about God from his mind.

Charles asked, "Will the angel speak to me?"

Joan said, "Once you are crowned king, it must."

"It may reject me as the child of a devil."

"You are of royal blood. You will be crowned. That will be enough for the angel."

They left the palace without taking good-byes, without calling attention. By the time King Philip realized they were gone, Charles and Joan were aboard their ship, *St. Maria*, heading for home, their retinue making their way as best they could. The sailors on the *St. Maria* had never known it so free of rats—the prince brought his full entourage of cats with him.

It was a fair summer with a light wind and an easy sea and within two weeks they were docking at Bilbao—proudly flying their flags marking them as allies of the Castilian overlords. From there it was a race across country to Pamplona, scouts running ahead of them to announce the heir apparent's arrival.

Charles and his mother rode rather than travel by carriage, the quicker to be there. Still progress was slow—Charles was limited to plodding, calm horses, as more spirited animals refused to carry him since his journeys in the cloak.

The royal coach and entourage met them five leagues from Pamplona, and Charles and his mother changed into their real finery at a monastery just outside the city. Charles wore blue silk, and his mother a great dress of crimson satin. They rode into the city in their gold and bloodstone coach, with four white horses as outriders, four more behind with the king's personal bodyguard marching behind them—red and yellow plumes bright beneath the southern sun.

"Will they receive us?" said Charles.

She said, "They must. The people may have heard rumors about your, er, appetites and your climbing, but they will come to heel. They owe you a duty of loyalty no matter what you breakfast on."

"They will come to heel or be brought to heel," said Charles.

They entered the city's gates in a blaze of trumpets, the creamy white stone of the town brilliant in the sun. People were on the roadside and Charles looked out at them, these strange brown men and women he had been born to rule. On his knee a fine gray Persian looked out too.

A loud meow burst from the crowd, and laughter rippled along the hedgerows.

Charles turned back to his mother. "There are rumors. Perhaps they suspect the truth of my parenthood?"

Joan grabbed Charles by his velvet tunic and stared into his face. "You are your father's son. Remember that; never tell yourself anything else. And you *are* king of Navarre. When the angel speaks to you, people will see."

The carriage drew to a stop outside the magnificent cathedral that rose as a symbol of what his ancestors could achieve, what they owed to God and

God to them. The people of Bilbao had come out onto the streets—many out of curiosity as much as loyalty. Their curiosity was twofold. They had heard the king had been cursed, but they also wanted a good look at the man, however feline, who was likely to be leading them to war sometime soon.

Still, the crowd was not huge. Charles's father had been a good king, but there were those rumors about his son. The people of Navarre knew that, when you come to look at a king, there is a chance the king might look at you. This was all very well if you were an ambitious merchant or minor noble looking for preferment, but not if you were a shopkeeper who wanted a quiet life.

Joan got out of the carriage first, drawing a gasp from the crowd as her jewels burned under the Navarrese sun, her golden Capetian hair bright as a flame. She put out her hand to the carriage and prodded Count Ramon in the back.

He shouted at the top of his voice, "Charles, son of Philip III of Navarre, has come to claim his inheritance. Bow down before your new king!"

Charles crossed himself and stepped from the carriage, as haughty a look as possible etched on his face. He carried a blackwood cane topped with silver and wore an extravagant purple hat. The crowd drew in its breath as the cats spilled from the coach behind him—Joan had tried to get the boy to leave them, but he would not. Count Ramon, as an encouragement to correct behavior, ordered his guards to attention and this had the desired effect. The people began to clap and cheer. Charles waved a gracious hand and set off for the church.

"It's going well!" said Joan, "Very well."

"All hail, King Moggie! Catch us a royal mouse, Your Majesty!" a drunken voice called out, and the crowd teetered on the edge of hilarity, although no one dared to laugh.

Charles stopped and turned to look at the source of the comment. His cats all seemed to look too.

"Bring that fellow to me!" said Charles.

The guards waded into the crowd and brought out a red-faced man who was drunk enough to make no apology for what he had said. Charles looked him up and down, though mainly up as the man was a good head taller than him and it was difficult to look him in the eye.

"Put him on his knees."

A guard pushed the butt of a polearm into the back of the man's knee, forcing him to the ground.

"A sous for the man's wit!" said Charles. Count Ramon at his side reached into his purse and gave the drunk a coin. The man grinned idiotically and held up the coin for all to see. The crowd clapped and cheered at the generosity.

"And your sword for his impudence, Count Ramon."

The drunk came to a quick realization of the danger of his situation and started to beg, but it was no good—Count Ramon had drawn and put a good blow into the man's neck. Two more swipes and the head was off, the queen stepping back to avoid the gush of blood, scarlet on the white dust of the road, the cats leaping in to lap at it.

"Do we have any more wits among us?" shouted Charles. If there were, they had the wit to be silent. "Let it not be said I am not fair!" The crowd now broke into nervous applause and Charles's procession moved on.

Joan said, "You did well, my son, you did well. I often counseled your father he should be rougher with these peasants."

Charles bowed his head. "We'll bring the country to obedience," he said. "My father has been soft for too long."

He walked up the steps of the cathedral, his entourage trailing behind him, his mother in front of him, walking irritatingly slowly. Charles had never thought it before but realized now the woman was always, in some manner or another, in his way. He passed through the doors of the cathedral into the crystal light.

As Joan came in, the light deepened, the air sparkled. The angel had come to greet the queen. Already the service had begun, the priests swinging their incense, singing their songs of praise. Nobles—who had been waiting rather longer than they would have liked, judging by their expressions—thronged the space in their best clothing. They wore cloth of gold and of silver, their jewels sparkling in the burgeoning light, flashing green, blue, red, white, and amber as the angel inhabited them for an instant, before moving on.

The aristocrats were eager to meet Joan and the new king, but equally eager to get out of the cathedral to find a seat to rest their aching legs. People were introduced to him, but his mother waved them away. "Afterward, afterward," she said. "First the angel must receive him." One man had a silver cage and in it a little bird that jingled when you shook it. The prince found it fascinating and would dearly have loved to have played with it, but then the light changed and deepened; it was a firelight, now the green light of the sun through trees, now the noon light of an idle summer's day.

Charles watched as the angel sparkled from the long thin windows that cut their way into the massive walls with a light like sun on ice, like the most perfect winter day.

It had the form of a shining man, bearing a flaming sword, and it floated at the highest point of the ceiling. Charles felt a leap of nervousness in his stomach. His father had forbidden the angel to speak to him. *Would* it speak? The light from the windows split and twined. Odd thoughts were in his head—they were braids of light, streams, rivers. Charles was finding it hard to think, as he always had in the presence of angels.

He felt a longing in it. It was bound to this place but wanted somewhere more beautiful.

No wonder it had not deigned to make sense to his father. The old cathedral had stood for three hundred years. It was a dusty slab of a place. They should knock it down and rebuild something beautiful and fine, of tapering pillars and fields of blue glass, not this jumped-up castle keep.

He made his way up to the altar, the smoke curling through the light. It struck Charles as a clichéd effect. In the cathedral he would build, he would unearth a true beauty, not rely on these ancient tricks.

"Welcome to Her Majesty, Queen Joan, queen of Navarre, and His Highness, Prince Charles, her noble heir!" shouted a herald.

Trumpets sounded and Charles walked forward. "Will you speak to me, angel, will you speak?" he murmured.

"Let me talk to it, Charles," said his mother. Charles sensed the disapproval coming from the light. It was most odd. He felt a deep connection to this angel. He could deal with it, he was sure.

A verse from the Bible whispered in his ear, "I do not permit a woman to teach or to have authority over a man; she must be silent." This was clearly an old-fashioned sort of angel, the sort Charles felt might suit him very well.

His mother was still speaking. She was always speaking. What this angel needed was someone who understood it. It respected hierarchy, it respected the God-given rights of men over women; it would respect him as king and resented having to communicate with someone who should, by rights, be troubling herself with embroidery, not the fate of nations.

His mother lacked vision. England was ruled by devils—devils that loved God. Charles was clearly a devil, or had devil blood. He should be in charge of devils. If he was a devil, he should side with devils. And yet Philip had prevented him from meeting those at the Temple, and now his mother would not side with England. The French angel had said Charles would never ascend the throne of France. But what about England? With the right alliances, the right deceit, the perfect moment of treachery, he could have the English throne.

And yet, and yet, Charles would bring his angel to the field against the English. More could be done from inside the French camp as a false ally, than from outside, as an obvious enemy.

He put his hand out to the shining air. "Jophiel," he spoke the angel's name, "who drove Adam and Eve from Eden."

"Charles," said the angel. "King."

"You see!" shouted Joan. "The angel approves him. Charles of Navarre! Ordained by God!"

She seized his hand and held it aloft, the nobles clapped and beat their feet against the floor, and the cats howled in approval.

7

P hilip said, "Your work with Despenser is progressing."

"Yes, Majesty."

Osbert had joined the king at the abbey of St. Denis—beneath the sparkling light that was the nearest to a manifestation of the archangel Michael that had been seen since Jegudiel had been killed.

The pardoner was serious and severe, dressed in his court sorcerer's apparel of scarlet cloak and blue hood. There had never been an official uniform for a court sorcerer before—largely because the priests had resisted anyone being appointed to such a role. The spectacular success Osbert had enjoyed in raising Despenser and his attendant devils, however, had brought him a great deal of prestige within the palace, though Philip was notoriously nervous of his new infernal allies.

The king saw Osbert whenever the pardoner requested it—largely because he consistently expected some disaster and sought the magician's reassurance that none such had occurred. Osbert had suggested St. Denis as a meeting place to whet the king's appetite. The Oriflamme lay there on the altar—in plain sight but untouchable under the angel's protection. Well, Osbert had hopes of a way around that.

"And you think you can find this Antichrist?" asked the king.

Osbert said, "I think we have a way, yes. But I fear . . ."

"What?"

"It is indiscreet of me to say."

"I command it. Friends, cousins, stand back a little."

The great throng that was with Philip—sixty or seventy nobles and servants in varying degrees of splendor—retreated out of earshot.

He said, "Well, that removes all impediments to me laying this before you. I fear Despenser will take the credit with Hell, building his alliance with Satan."

"What's that to me? These devils seem to obey me well enough."

Osbert said, "Indeed they do. But what if you took the credit? Might that not secure the favor of angels?"

Philip mulled it over. "How could I take the credit?" he asked.

"It seems to me that you appointed me. I have found a way to locate the Antichrist. Then the credit is yours, not Despenser's. He will only gain credit if he kills this enemy of God, but I'm not totally sure that God wants him dead."

"Why would God want His sworn enemy to live?"

"You penetrate to the one flaw in my argument, sir. I do not know—other than to say that he still lives."

Monks began a plainsong chant and a gaggle of priests stood smiling ridiculously by the altar, waiting for Philip to stop talking so mass could begin.

He said, "Be plainer."

"If one examines God's record of dealing with his enemies, one inevitably finds that they are burned, afflicted with boils, killed, mutilated, mutilated and killed, mutilated and left to die, consumed in fiery pillars, or turned to salt. Salt that is very likely then mutilated."

"I don't follow."

"Our Antichrist hasn't so much as suffered a bout of indigestion for the last decade, as far as I know. I met him and he appeared in rude health. Why?"

"Why do you think?" Philip asked him.

Osbert said, "I really cannot guess. Now we know the angels would like a word with him. So what say we use the murderous Despenser to find him—one of his servants even now seeks him—and then we deliver him to you for the angel to examine? This plan, I believe, will find favor with the angels—they will see how you labor for them and they will surely hop forth and dance for you."

The king looked around him, with the air of a prior asking for a charm for a floppy cock. He said, "But Despenser thinks Satan will favor him if he kills this boy."

"Yes."

"Satan is God's servant."

Osbert said, "How many of your servants have your exact interests at heart, Majesty? Despenser is your servant, but do you think he labors more for you or more for himself?"

"Careful what you say, low man—you are talking about a lord."

"Sorry, Your Majesty."

Philip said, "You're concluding that Satan wants the Antichrist dead, but God wants him alive?"

"Yes. I think if God and Satan both wanted him dead he'd be dead with the firstborn of the Egyptians. Angel of Death. Whoosh. Arrrrghhhh!" He mimed the effects of the passing of the angel of death upon the unlucky families of the Nile.

The king played with his rings. "We should put this to the angel."

Osbert replied, "I think it wise, sir. And then you could dispense with Despenser, so to speak."

"He is your master."

"Yes."

"So do not speak in this way of him," said Philip. "You are a sorcerer and must treat with strange and unnatural powers. But do not allow them so to corrupt you as to dream of overthrowing God's order."

"Not likely, Your Majesty," said Osbert. "I know which side of the bed is comfiest."

"Both sides of my bed are comfortable," said the king, slightly puzzled.

"My point exactly," said the pardoner.

"I'll put it to the angel," said the king.

At his signal, the priests began to swing the incense to purify the air for the mass.

Philip knelt on a velvet cushion, his son John and the queen came and put their cushions beside his, with the constable and the higher nobles behind them. After that, there was an undignified mêlée as lesser men fought to put their cushions near to the king's. Philip seemed oblivious to it. The pardoner had thought to withdraw but he instead knelt beside the king on the stone floor. Philip said the words of the mass—both the priest's part and the congregation's—with great conviction and wringing of hands. Osbert could just about stay with the Latin.

"Do me justice, O God, and fight my fight against an unholy people, rescue me from the wicked and deceitful man.

"For thou, O God, art my strength, why hast thou forsaken me? Why do I go about in sadness while the enemy harasses me? Send forth thy light and thy truth, for they have led me and brought me to the holy hill and thy dwelling place."

The incense curled in the beams of light, twisting and turning.

"Why is my soul sad? Why am I downcast? Trust in God, for I shall yet praise Him, my savior and my God."

A voice like sweet trumpets, impossibly tuneful.

"Michael," said the angel.

The air seemed heavy. The pardoner was already kneeling but felt the urge to prostrate himself, as if under a great weight. For some reason the words of the Bible came back to him. "There was war in Heaven. Michael and his angels fought against the dragon, and the dragon and his angels fought back. But he was not strong enough, and they lost their place in Heaven." He'd always assumed that meant the dragon had lost. Had Michael been thrown out? *In the name of St. Peter's porker, Osbert, this is no time to be having sacrilegious thoughts!*

"Are you worthy of the saint's blood? What do you bring me for the banner?" asked the angel.

The voice was a fanfare. Osbert couldn't believe the king was willing to be this open—to allow the angel to be seen to favor France reluctantly. But perhaps it was his way of communicating his difficulties to his nobles.

Philip said, "We are laboring to bring you the head of the Antichrist."

"Where is he? That is hidden from my eyes."

"We can find him. I have instructed learned men . . ." Here the king gestured to the pardoner who crossed himself hard enough to hurt. Philip added, "They will find him. They will . . ."

"Bring him to obedience," said Osbert.

"You should be struck down for your presumption!" said the count of Eu, who took exception to a commoner, particularly a mouthy one, sitting next to the king.

The inside of the cathedral swam with a light like the sun on blue water, the vault above ocean blue, the decorations as red and gold as the bodies of bright fishes.

"Approach the Oriflamme," said the angel.

The king went to the altar. The tattered banner lay there, its sun motif dull and faded, the blood of St. Denis still spattered across the yellow—just a dark stain on the red. Philip picked up the banner, and the cathedral was no longer an underwater cave but a bright bubble of incandescent crimson as the banner shone over all the nobles. Their faces reflected the blood light and each man cheered, the count of Eu now slapping the pardoner's back.

Philip waved the banner and shouted, "All hesitancy is gone, as the mists of spring are burned away by the shining face of summer. As the season of the sun stirs the lightning and the thunder, so stir I! To arms, Frenchmen, and flood our green meadows with English blood!"

"Might this entail a promotion?" said Osbert.

"You are the Supreme French Sorcerer!" cried the count, who, thought Osbert, showed the same sudden change of heart whores show upon seeing the glitter of your gold.

"I was hoping for coin, rather than titles," said Osbert. "However, could you confirm that is an actual promotion—I could get several decent loans out of it." The constable did not hear him. He had gone to the altar to embrace the wild-eyed king.

8

D ow opened the door of the rose-covered chapel and let out the light in all its streaming colors. Orsino was beside him, the angel's rainbow mail on his back, the heart-shield and the holy sword in his hands, ready to strike.

There were roses everywhere inside the chapel, across the floor, across the wall, up onto the altar. At the center of the church lay what looked like a tomb, a stone king lying on top of it. But the king was not stone, he was a man, dressed in a fine white robe stained with blood.

Below the plinth sat two of the most beautiful creatures Dow had ever seen. They were people, a man and a woman made not of flesh but of light. It was as if a figure in a stained-glass window had come to life, shining blue, red, and gold—but substantial and solid, not flat like an image. Both had wings on their backs, but not like those of Jegudiel, who had fallen to flesh in the chapel.

It reminded Dow of looking into the body of a gem. These wings were many-colored, spectral, half-substantial. In one instant they looked like splendid feathers, in the next foils of light. Both carried spears in their hands. But they too were covered in roses, which grew from their shining skins in bright whites and reds.

Dow heard a name. "Afriel, angel of the newborn." He saw visions of a lush forest, of foals in the dawn, of a land renewed under rain. Another, in the woman's voice. "Aftiel, angel of the dying sun." He saw a red dusk, heard night birds and the call of frogs, had a sense of mist descending on the land.

Dow walked forward with the sword. The angels did not move. Yet he had a sense of them. They were tattered and torn, he now thought. They were neither one thing nor the other, and what he took for beauty, the rare light that emerged from them, came from where the rose thorns pierced their skin.

The angels regarded him. They spoke in unison. "You are the Antichrist. Half human, half angel. The opposite of divine. A mongrel, impure thing." The angels' voices bore no hatred.

Dow said, "I am a man."

"A servant of Lucifer," they said together.

"Not a servant. A friend."

"Then help us. We are fallen, trapped here by God."

Dow saw how the roses engulfed them. He looked at the man on the plinth. He too was covered—ensnared—in the flowers. The plinth beneath him was not a plinth at all, but a gigantic box, bound with the rose briars, marked with strange symbols.

"For what purpose?" he asked them.

"To feed the briar that holds in the banner."

Dow saw that the thorns of the briar were pricking into the angels and that the light shone ruby red where they penetrated. The man on the plinth too was pierced all over, big thorns sticking into his face, his torso, his limbs.

"I will cut you free." Dow hacked into the briars, but, as quick as he did, they regrew, rustling and hissing, snaking up to catch his hand. He jumped back.

"The only way to have the banner is to kill us, yet do not," said the angels. "Have pity on us."

Dow looked at the fallen angels. Could he kill such beautiful things? Not if they were friends of Lucifer.

"The struggle we're engaged in is a great one," said Dow.

"We fell when Lucifer fell, but God caught us and put us here."

"I need the banner."

"I was a sunbeam in the dawn," said Afriel.

"And I in the dusk," said Aftiel.

"Do not extinguish our lights."

Dow put his hand to his sword. He had not expected to find the angels so vulnerable, nor thought they would be allies, not enemies. He could not kill a friend of Lucifer's.

"I am the Alpha and the Omega. The first and the last." A youth's voice. Dow couldn't see where it came from.

The air darkened and swam and he saw the angels tremble.

"Who's that?" he asked.

The voice said, "I am the one who inhabits eternity."

Dow looked around him. Another angel? He didn't feel that headiness he'd felt in the chapel in Paris, nor the first-flush-of-wine feeling he had when he looked at the angels in the briars. Dread gripped him, his stomach contorting, his teeth clenching as if he beheld a dizzying vastness, stood at the bottom of some great tower looking up and wondering why it did not fall.

"Heaven is my throne and the earth my footstool."

Dow felt as if the top of his head was lifting off, as if his thoughts were a flock of birds, wheeling and turning in the dusk of his mind. His hands were clammy, his mouth dry.

He looked up and the ceiling of the chapel was no longer there. Instead, a huge sky, snowed with stars, spread out above him, the sickle moon sharp and brilliant, comets cutting trails across the heavens. A bright light fell from the heavens, blinding his eyes.

When Dow regained his sight, a dazzling boy of around thirteen stood next to him, clothed in an ermine cloak and with a magnificent crown of fire on his head. The pale skin of his face was marked with magical symbols, the rest of his body invisible beneath rich dark clothes shining with the brilliant light of the rare gems that studded it. His cloak was a cloak of stars. He was a being of such perfection that it was difficult to look at him.

The boy said, "Yours will be the vast heavens, yours the depthless oceans. You will play forever in the sunbeams and starlight. Lucifer fell. *You* might ascend if only you will worship me." The boy extended a hand. In it, impossibly bright, burned a little sun.

Dow asked, "Who are you to offer me these things?"

The boy closed his hand and the sun disappeared. Dow steeled himself to look at the strange being and when he did, he saw that the perfection was marred. A great fresh welt marked the boy's face, and a sword like a shaft of light was stuck through his body. His trembling hand was grasping the hilt as if he would pull it away but dare not. Still, the youth hurt to look at and Dow turned his eyes away. When he looked back again the youth was whole and beautiful, yet Dow sensed the perfection was an illusion.

He said to the youth, "You are Îthekter."

"I do not accept that name. Do not call me that for I am no horror."

"You put some men above others. You drink the blood of your martyrs. What else should I call you?"

"God." The boy stood tall. He said, "What do you want? What can I give you that you will bow down and worship me?"

"I would see the poor free and fed."

"I will show you how to make stones into bread. How many could you feed then?"

Dow replied, "Not so many as the kings can rob and kill."

"See my splendid clothes, cut from the cloth of the night and sprinkled with the stars of Heaven. Does the sight not thrill you? Bow down before me and you will be a king."

"Not while my fellows starve."

Îthekter said, "You cannot help them. I made some men to lead and others to follow. Given all the riches of the earth they would fritter them and be in rags within a year. You best help them by ruling them firmly in my name."

"We don't want the riches of the earth. Just the fruits of our toil."

"Those fruits will be yours to give. What a boon is the kindly master to his servants. If a man waxes poor, then he should be sold to his brother. Therein lies his protection. How many men have been saved from starvation by selling their families to the lord?"

"After the lord took the grain that would keep them free."

Îthekter said, "Your lords defend you."

"From other lords."

"I could protect you, set angels to guard you so that you would never strike your foot against a stone."

Dow repeated, "Not while my fellows starve."

"You could be their defender."

"Better they have no need for defense. Let us live as we lived in Eden, without masters."

The boy became angry, stamping his foot. He said, "Can't you see that I'm trying to help you? I was the master in Eden and it was in Eden that the first sin crept in when Adam bit the apple."

"You put the apple there for him. Why, anyway, should he not know what you know? It was the rule that was at fault, not the man."

The boy raised his hand and Dow was flying up, the air trailing from his fingers, so fast did he move. He saw out over the wide country of the night, over oceans and lands—to the east where the light smudged the horizon and to the west where the stars still hung in an inky sky.

"I will give you all this," said the boy. "All of it will you rule. No king but you, no courtiers but those you choose. Set up your friends as men of rank, open your granaries to the poor, abolish war. Only bow down before me."

Dow replied, "If all these things are in your gift, you have no need of me. *You* open the granaries. *You* make men as they were before you shut them out of paradise and set them at one another's throats. Do not put such power into the hands of a corruptible man such as me. Set me down, Îthekter, for I am friend to Lucifer, the one maker of things, and I call you to guilt and shame in his name."

"Bow down and I will release the angels from the briar."

"And the banner?" Dow asked him.

Îthekter said, "You will not want it if you bow."

"Release us!" the angels pleaded from the chapel below, their voices a beautiful harmony.

Dow said, "I will not bow. Take my hand and call me friend and equal."

"You are not my equal! I could destroy you."

"Then do. You kill so many, why not me?"

The form of the boy shifted and changed and Dow saw that sword again, driven deep into his belly. He understood. Lucifer had put it there. Only Lucifer could remove it. Or perhaps his most trusted friend on earth. The Antichrist—Dow. God strikes down his enemies. The only reason Dow was still alive was almost shocking—even to him, a Luciferian. God needed him.

Dow said, "Would you have me end your pain? Renounce your over-weening claims, accept you are no better than anyone else, repent your deeds and vow to live in peace with all men. Then I will remove the sword."

Îthekter replied, "Bow before me. Be my servant. Then take this sword from my belly and use it to rule the earth in my name."

Dow said, "I will not take it away while men must bow to you."

"I will destroy you."

"If you could, I would already be dead. You need me, Îthekter. That is no shame. Every living being needs another."

"I have a further power over you," said the youth, "one that may still see you kneel. Do you know where you are?"

"It is Heaven."

"No. This is the path to Hell I reserve for the worst of sinners. This is where they live, thinking they are forgiven, thinking that they will have an eternity among the pines and the flowers, waiting only for their loved ones to appear to make it perfect. This is Gehenna gate, the one to which only I have the key and through which the truly disobedient are pushed once they are used to a life of comfort. Let me open the gate."

God moved his hand and there was the sound of a deep, deep drum, so powerful Dow felt he was being punched in the chest.

A smell of sulfur filled the chapel and the air by God's side buckled as if a great fire warped and bent it. A face emerged, a man walking in a priest's cassock. He was ghastly pale and his eyes were no more than burned holes, a gag of forged metal about his mouth. In his hand he bore a pair of scissors. Dow flinched. It was the man who had cut him, all those years ago.

"This is Father Tregarn," said God, "a useful priest, but one who, as you see, sinned and needed to be punished. Sinner punishes sinner in Hell, and the devils find the terror to suit each wayward son, each ungrateful daughter. See whom he punishes."

Two more figures emerged. One was a squat little man with gray skin, his hands deformed and smashed. He had a rope about his neck, which was attached to a woman he pulled behind him. Immediately upon seeing her, Dow cried out. It was his nan.

"Tell him how you suffer," said God.

She said, "I used my tongue against God, so every day the blind priest comes to me and cuts it out, and every night it regrows. I hear him crawling and creeping for me among the flames and endlessly try to avoid him, but I am tied to this man, as I was tied to the poor in life and I cannot move away."

"She could be free," said God. "I would set her free if only you bend the knee. Take her hand and I will accept it as your homage."

"Nan," cried Dow.

She said, "Dow."

"I love you."

"And I you."

Dow was bursting with sweat, the heat of the open gate overwhelming, his longing just to touch his dear nan immense.

He said, "One day you will be free! I will take the banner. I will find the keys and free all those unjustly imprisoned by this tyrant!"

"Maria! Giannio!"

Orsino was behind him.

From the heat haze two more figures came, a woman and a child staggering, little devils like monkeys sitting upon their shoulders, pressing their hands over their eyes and ears. The mother and the boy reached out but, as soon as they caught a glimpse of each other, the monkeys moved their hands over their eyes, causing them to stumble and miss each other.

Dow was struck by the woman's resemblance to Sariel. They must be Orsino's wife and son, he thought.

"Here are two who loved each other more than they loved me," said God. "Is it not written that anyone who loves his father or his mother or his children more than me is damned? It says so in the Bible—I really don't see any grounds for complaint. Nevertheless, bow the knee and they too may walk free. I will grant them entry to Heaven where they may dwell forever in fragrant groves by sparkling waters."

"Dow!" said Orsino. "For all that I have done for you, for the times I have saved you, for the protection I offered, I beg you now, repent. Come to God, if not for yourself, then for me."

Dow saw the overwhelming love in Orsino's eyes, saw how he reached out for his wife and son, and he was moved. He owed his ability to maintain the struggle against God solely to the Florentine. Nan cried out as the priest found her face with his hand, reaching around swiftly to grab her by the hair. Dow could stand no more. He could endure any suffering inflicted on him, but not this.

"Release her," Dow said. "The woman and the child too."

God gestured to the priest and he let go of his nan's hair.

She fell gasping to the floor.

"You will bow?" said God.

Dow said, "I will bow."

God smiled broadly and the ceiling of the chapel burned with light before giving way to depthless stars.

"Then remove the sword," he said.

Dow saw the sword was made of light, he was made of light, as was the chapel and all the world. Only God, only God had a streak of darkness in him, shot through where the sword penetrated.

Dow tugged on the blade and it started to move.

"Dow, no!" Nan shouted.

"I cannot endure it, Nan," he said, "even if you can. We will do some good when I am a king of the world."

"If God can release me, he can release all those he has imprisoned. I have seen little children with their knees broken for refusing to say their prayers. I have seen . . ."

The priest grabbed her again and she screamed.

"I will never remove the sword unless you let her speak," said Dow. He took his hand from the hilt.

"Let the faithless harlot talk," said God.

Nan said, "I have seen poor men with their hands cut off for taking a hare from the lord's forest, I have seen men's skin shaved from their faces because, in life, they refused to grow a beard; women condemned to eternity in a shirt of briars for wearing clothes of wool and linen mixed, church gossips driven mad by chattering devils. Let him release all those."

"That I will not do, for those are my laws and they are holy," said God. "What use is authority if never exercised? What use the sword that lies eternally in its scabbard?"

"Save but a few, Dow, it's better than none!" Orsino was shouting, trying to reach his wife but forced back as if by a great wind.

"You will suffer forever," said Dow to his nan.

"Not forever! You, Dow, you will release me! God is stricken. He can be beaten!" she said.

Dow shook his head. He put his hand to the hilt of the sword again. God smiled.

"Bow! Bow! Save us all," cried the angels.

"She will change her mind in Heaven," said God. "She will see that mercy is not for everyone and is all the more precious for that."

"You speak the truth," said Dow. "As you judge, so are you judged. You have no power over me, Îthekter. I will take the banner and drive you from the earth."

The youth smiled, his eyes fixed on Dow's hand. He said, "To do so you will need to kill your father."

Dow touched his tunic where the fork scar lay. "Not so."

"He was the abomination—a king who was a friend of the poor. He wanted to abandon the place I had given him and live as a poor man, thatching, tending his flock, watching winter become spring, summer turn to autumn, sowing and harvesting and not troubling himself about the affairs of nations. He would have raised up the poor, so I offered a fallen angel a way back into Heaven to persuade him. I could not force him to my way, so I had him seduced by Despenser, to bring him back to his duty, impose order and control."

Dow said, "You're lying. You could have just killed him."

"I am infallible and to have removed him would have been to admit error in appointing him. No. I have bound the Evertere thus, so you might never remove it. Lucifer teaches you to never kill another believer. There lies a believer. You cannot take the banner and so cannot oppose me. Remove the sword and rule Heaven with me instead."

Dow could not accept what he was hearing—that he was the son of a king, a high man born to rule. "I defy you!" he shouted.

The air seemed to boil, great welts of light scarring the chapel, the ceiling invisible, fire streaking the sky. God stamped his foot.

"Well," he said, "shan't we just see about that? I shall bring my kings and angels against you. I shall see you smashed. I could destroy you now. But you will see your world in ashes, you will see all hopes cast down and you will reach out to me to beg to please me. Do you remember the devil girl in the woods? The one who burst?"

"I remember her."

"Remember her well. She did no harm to you, for you are of an angel born. But you carry a gift for humanity which I will allow you to inflict upon the earth if you do not come to obedience. *And the Lord said unto Moses and unto Aaron, Take to you handfuls of ashes of the furnace, and let Moses sprinkle it toward the heaven in the sight of Pharaoh. And it shall become small dust in all the land of Egypt, and shall be a boil breaking forth with blains upon man, and upon beast, throughout all the land of Egypt.* Do you doubt my power?"

Dow said, "I doubt it."

Now Îthekter began to rage, the heavens blazing, red and gold, his body radiating fire. "I will see you brought low. I will see you beg for forgiveness and declare me lord of creation! I will see you beg to be my servant, Antichrist! We will see how strong you are when the people suffer. You will remove the sword!"

"I'd say you'd got that wrong," said Dow, and, grasping the hilt, he thrust the blade in as hard as he could. A scream rang out that was so piercing it blew the walls from the church, echoing out over the island, throwing Dow down. When he opened his eyes the land around him was blackened and burned, the church a ruin, its walls no greater than the height of his knee. Only the plinth remained, the angels, the king, and the roses that ensnared them. Orsino, crouched behind the angel shield, weeping, unable to stand or unable to bring himself to stand. Dow could not tell. Îthekter had gone. Dow drew his falchion.

The angels were in front of him, begging from the briars. "Did you bow to save us?" they asked him.

"You are not fallen angels," said Dow, "for, if you were, you would not be afraid to die for this cause. You are deceivers, set there by God to stay my hand and keep me from the banner."

"No!"

Dow raised the sword and struck at Aftiel. The angel tried to come for him but the briars held it back. The angel screamed, bursting with a red light like the dying sun. He cut at Afriel, who died with the blue and yellow light of the dawn.

Orsino stood up, looking around at the blackened island. He had his hand on the knife at his belt. "You didn't save my wife and son."

Dow replied, "I will save them; they will be free. I will take the banner and raise Hell here. From there our demons will find the keys to Hell and all the sinners will walk out again."

Orsino approached the limit of the briars and looked down at the dead angels, now fleshy and bloody. The briars writhed and flicked toward him and he took a step back.

"And to think," said Orsino, "that I tried to teach you feats of arms. One of these would account for an army if the mood took him, yet you have killed two."

"It doesn't please me to destroy such beauty," said Dow.

"And a good job," said Orsino, "because if it did there would be no holy things left in the world. What are you, Dow?"

"I'm a man who would put things right."

"You should fear God. And yet I saw you spite him and walk free. My Maria, my Giannio. Why did you not save them?"

"Because I would have damned all the others," said Dow. "God fears me. Did you not see? He is the king of fear and yet he dare not strike against me."

"I loved you," said Orsino. "But now my love is turned to hate."

"Will you kill me?"

"No."

"Why not?" Dow asked him.

"Because I know what I saw. And if God will not release my wife and son from Hell, then perhaps you can. Know that I despise you, but I offer you my sword and my service."

He bent his knee before Dow.

"Stand up," said Dow. "I am no one's master."

"You are mine."

"Then I grant you your freedom. There. No cowering in the night praying for a tyrant God's favor any more, Orsino. I lost my hate for you long ago. You found yours for me. It makes no difference to us; we have worked together thus far and can do so in the future."

"You will not make me worship Lucifer?" asked Orsino.

"No. He has been a friend to you. But as we do not always choose our enemies, sometimes we don't choose our friends. You must follow your heart."

Orsino pointed at the king. "I thought his damnation was my absolution," said Orsino. "Now I must watch you kill him and cheer as you fight God?"

Dow stared down at the king. "What brought him here?" he said.

"What brought us here?" said Orsino. "Chance and desperation, stupidity and hope. The things that drive men anywhere."

"We should wake him."

"Why?"

"To see if God lied."

"What difference does it make?"

Dow said, "I cannot kill a friend of Lucifer's, Orsino. I think that is why God set him here. Give me your armor. I will wake him."

The Florentine he did as he was bid. When he was dressed in the rainbow mail, Dow took the angel's sword from Orsino and strode forward through the briars. They reached out to entrap him, but they could not grip or penetrate the angel's mail or helm, and when they did snake around his feet or his arm, he cut them back with the sword.

Still, progress was hard and Dow staggered and tore his way up to the plinth, to see his father's face for the first time.

He could see no similarity between himself and the king—Edward was tall and blond, his face a long oval, whereas Dow was much shorter and dark, his face round as Sariel's had been.

Edward's eyes were closed, his skin pale and waxy, the starved flesh clinging to his skull, his lips dry and drawn back from his teeth. He was breathing, but that was all that showed he was alive. The rose briar wound him tightly to the box beneath.

Dow looked up into the blue light of the chapel. "Lucifer," he said, "guide me now, friend." The briars still hissed and tried to ensnare him.

Dow held up his knife, red with the blood of angels. Then he smeared the blood to the king's lips.

All was silent, apart from the king's labored breathing. A cough, a sigh, and Edward opened his eyes.

"God says I am your son," said Dow.

Edward winced, now aware of the pain of the thorns. Dow smeared more angel's blood across his lips. The old man gulped. His lips were pale, encrusted in sweat.

The old king said, "He said you would come for the banner." His voice was weak.

"Who?" Dow asked.

"God, that terrible child."

Orsino crossed himself. "Where are your angels, Majesty? Are they not here to defend you?" he asked.

Edward said, "I sent them away when the box was sealed."

"Why?"

"Because," said Edward, "they would not fall. I believe in the Son of the Morning. I would not be a king, but an ordinary man."

The king groaned and tried to move his hands to his face where the thorns pricked him, but he was held fast by the writhing briars.

"How shall we release you?"

He said, "Kill me."

"That is against my belief." Dow suspected a trick. God had never played straight, but this man *had* been a tyrant. Devils lied, angels dissembled. Only demons had ever told him the truth.

"If you are a friend of Lucifer, then why did you replace the banner?" said Dow.

The old man closed his eyes. "I was born in the wrong place. I had no pleasure but to cut wood, to thatch roofs, and to work with my hands on the land. But I was born to fight, not to toil, though it did not stop me. I loved to make things, to see the beauty of creation in the handle of a knife, or to cut a stone just so to make a step or a lintel. It was there—working with men on my own estates—that I heard the word of Lucifer and determined that all men should live as I could live, free of conflict, by the work of their hands. But Heaven saw me and could not tolerate me. So it sent me a fallen angel to appeal to my weakness."

"What weakness?" said Dow.

"For beauty. For lust."

"Fallen angels serve Lucifer."

Edward said, "Not all. Some were drawn down by the love of the pleasures of the body and seek a way back to God. Piers Gaveston was one such, my first love. But he was corrupt and strange and led me to great abuses. My wife, Isabella, summoned spirits and worked magic to undo him and I was grateful for a time.

"But she saw that I was dangerous to her. Isabella was born to rule and thought I would set swineherds on the throne. And so I would have. She tried to control me, but I was too strong. Not strong against beauty, though. Heaven sent another fallen angel to me—Hugh Despenser. I loved him, but he enchanted me, made me rule as a tyrant. He could do everything but control my angels. They had fled me for my treason against God, but they would not go to him."

He continued. "When my wife moved against him, he asked the Hospitallers for a banner of great power that he believed to be the Drago. But many Templars, friends of Lucifer, had joined the Hospitallers in secret for refuge when the Capetian King Philip moved against them. They saw the harm Hugh was doing and sent him the Evertere instead."

"What does the Evertere do?" said Dow.

Edward said, "It eats angels and commands all demons to follow it. My angels returned to me when the throne was threatened, but the Evertere chased most of them away."

"So why did you agree to put it away? You sought to overthrow the angels, so you say."

"Because of Mortimer—the usurper, my wife's lover. I knew him to be a dangerous man, a far worse tyrant in the making. If he got his hands on it, he would have caused damage without limit. The Evertere is for the use of Lucifer on the final day—not for selfish mortals. I called God himself to help me, and we sealed it in its chest after a great struggle. The Hospitallers brought me here and then God bound me so, my sacrifice of pain like Christ's—to keep the world from sin, so he said."

"What were the other two angels doing here?" asked Dow.

"They were mine. They ran from the Evertere, so God put them where they could never run again. They sought to return to him and perhaps they have. This island is the nearest he can come to the world, the portal between Heaven, earth, and Hell. With his wound he would die if he set foot on the earth. This is why Satan and Lucifer think they can build their kingdoms there."

"I would build such a kingdom for Lucifer, where all men can be equal."

"Then it is the last days. You must kill me and take the banner," said Edward.

"I cannot. I am sworn to defend Lucifer's friends."

"Then let me," said Orsino. He took his crossbow from his back.

Dow drew the sword in the king's defense. He said, "My oath is inviolable, there must be another way."

"There is not," said Edward. "God set me with this rose to suffer, to sustain the rose, and be sustained by it. If you would kill it, you must kill me."

Dow tried to pull away the briars that pricked the king's skin, but they wound around his hand, lacerating it. He cut the clinging briars free with his devil knife. Already his fingers were swelling.

"This is no time to stand on fine principles," said Orsino. "Do, and repent later."

"There would be no repentance for killing a friend of Lucifer," said Dow.

"Lucifer would forgive you," said the king.

Dow replied, "I would not forgive myself."

"Hell must be opened!" said Orsino. "Dow, this must be done." He was trying to get a clear shot at the king, but Dow swayed in front of Edward, guarding him.

Dow came wading out of the briars, slashing them away with the angel sword, only for them to regrow and reach out to him again. Without the angel armor, he would have been engulfed. Even with it, his exposed skin was cut, itching terribly where the thorns tore it. Orsino fired his crossbow, but Dow leapt in front of it. A thump in his chest and snick as the shot was deflected off the angel's mail and Dow waded on. Behind him the king moaned and cried out as the snaking thorns moved over his skin. Orsino reloaded.

"Dow, don't. This is the only way."

"It is not the only way!"

Dow broke free of the briars, pulled the crossbow from Orsino's hand, threw down the helm, pulled off the coat of mail.

"There is an easy way out," said Dow. "Kill me. Any man can be the Antichrist with enough will. Years ago I heard a fire demon tell you Hell had a use for you. This must be it. Kill me. Then take the banner. Find the keys. Open Hell and kiss your darlings again. It should be easy, for you hate me."

"So you would die?" said Orsino.

"Better than dishonor."

"I've seen both and it really isn't," said Orsino. "You can't die, Dowzabel. You're a fanatic, as bad as the worst torturing priest. You couldn't let me kill you. You want to see this through to the end."

"Perhaps I do. It doesn't matter. I've brought you this far, Orsino. It's in your hands now. This completes everything. If I die, then I can never be tempted to pull the sword free. God's way back to power is closed. Maybe that was why Lucifer let them nail him up at Golgotha—because he would not forgive God. I will not forgive him. Kill me."

"You'd go to Hell. God would work on you there."

Dow said, "So why did he not kill me and torture me at his leisure?"

"I can't guess his mind."

"I can. He needs me alive or I'd already be dead."

Dow looked around him, at the blasted landscape—only the roses, bright red like blood from a wound, still alive.

"So what do I do?" said Orsino.

"Kill me. And then keep killing. That's what you do, isn't it? Kill the angels, kill the devils, find the demons to work the magic to find the rest of the keys to Hell. Then be a champion in the final war. Destroy Hell. Free your wife, your child, and every tormented soul."

"What of the murderers, the cheats, and the torturers who are deservedly in Hell?"

"Send them to their own place. We will build our Eden. They can build theirs."

"Isn't that what God said?" he asked Dow.

Dow looked around him. "There's far more good than bad in the world, Orsino. There are so few real sins. Let's bother about our friends and let our enemies look after themselves. Use the sword and let the fall of God begin. I will go to Hell, but you will free me. My dear nan, your family, are suffering greatly because of me. I would not ask something of others I would not give myself. Use the sword."

Orsino swung a great blow at Dow's neck, stopping the blade so late it cut the young man's collar. Dow did not flinch.

"You mean it, don't you?" Orsino said.

Dow said, "I have a vow to the friends of Lucifer. I cannot break it. This is the only way forward. Cut and be done."

Orsino swung again. He stopped, though this time the blade cut off the tip of Dow's ear. Still he did not shy from the blow.

"Last chance," said Orsino.

"Summon your hate, Orsino. Remember who suffers because of me."

Orsino gave a cry and pulled back his sword to strike. Dow knew that this time the blow would strike. The sword swung toward him, Dow spoke a word, "Mother," and Orsino burst into flames.

For an instant Dow thought it *was* her, Sariel. She had appeared like a trick of the light, a flash of green, a glimpse of white skin, the flicker of a candle. She took shape—beautiful against the roses on the plinth. But when she spoke, her word was fire, blasting from her mouth in a torrent, sweeping Orsino away, engulfed in her burning curses. Dow sprang up, but she had him by the neck, dragging him away from his father. Dow fumbled for his misericorde, but she snatched it from him.

The king looked out from the briars with peace in his eyes. "Am I to live?" he asked.

"The blood briar," said the devil possessing Sariel's body. "I've seen that before in the torture gardens of the fortress of Gall. No way of cutting you out of that, I'm afraid, or even burning it. And it's against God's holy order to kill you. I've bigger fish to fry. Well, not fry, not yet anyway."

Dow tried to break free, to get it to release its grip, but he could not. The light swam, danced in little points at the corner of his vision, and then was gone. He knew nothing.

+—+

When Dow awoke, he was on a cart, chained, his neck constrained by an iron collar. The blackened island was behind them, the mass of red roses seeming to smoke like a dragon's mouth.

"Where are you taking me?" said Dow.

"To Hell," said the devil, "via a trip to meet Hugh Despenser, who wants the pleasure of sending you there."

"What of the banner?"

"Not sent to get that," said the devil, "and I wouldn't anyway. Anyone releasing that will be damned to the lowest levels of Hell and believe me, damnation is doubly difficult for a devil. You can't look for sympathy from sinners you've been roasting alive ten minutes before. Heya!"

He cracked the whip and the horses lurched forward. Above him, Murmur wheeled away in the sky.

9

B ardi watched for a day before he decided to go across. He could see nothing on the island—just the green of the pines, brilliant against the glimmer of the lake. But where were Orsino and Dow? He could not call on his courage, so he called on his greed. His life as a monk was comfortable. But to Bardi, comfortable was uncomfortable. He had been used to riches and needed them again.

How to get across? Oh dear, oh dear, so how to get across? Swimming was a complete waste of time because he'd want to take the banner with him when he left. A boat, then. He finally hit on the idea of making the horses swim it when he saw the woman Sariel dragging the boy across by his belt, her body steaming as the water boiled about her. Where was Orsino? Must be dead. Sariel had no loot with her. The Drago still had to be on the island. Farewell, Antichrist, time to pay for your heresies.

It wasn't too far and, if Bardi lashed the banner to a horse, it should survive unharmed. The Drago was blessed by God and had withstood dragon fire in the hands of St. George. A little water wouldn't hurt it.

Into the shining water, the horse hesitant. Bardi was no great horseman, but eventually he bullied the animal across, heavy on the whip, then heavy on the reins as his horse panicked and thrashed so much that Bardi feared he would be unseated. The lake was deep at first, but a submerged sandbank halfway across allowed them rest, and then to walk for sixty or seventy of the five hundred paces. They made the little beach just in front of where the villa had been, the horse he'd been riding hacking its lungs up as it staggered ashore like a newborn foal.

Bardi too gasped, but not with exhaustion. Everything about him had been burned as he moved inland. There were no bright pines, no blaze of green grass, just desolation everywhere—the trees all burned to stumps, the sand black with ash. The sky itself was a pale dirty yellow and the air was thick with smoke. A verse of the Bible came to him: "The sky over your head will be bronze, the ground beneath you iron. The Lord will turn the rain of your country into dust and powder. It will come down from the skies until you are destroyed."

What sacrileges had taken place here? Bardi looked back behind him to the lake. He could not see the shore. It was as if a mist lay upon the water. On the island there was still one flash of color. A ruined and blasted chapel from which spilled roses, bright as blood. The roses had survived whatever had happened here. Perhaps they were holy and there was some value in them.

Bardi took his knife from his pack. Then he put it back and took his wood axe instead. He returned to the pack and took the knife as well. He still felt insecure and wished he had a third weapon to hold in his teeth—or, better still, Orsino to protect him.

He made his way up an ash-black shore, looking around him all the time. No birds, no insect noises, no voices. The ground was hot beneath his feet, almost uncomfortably so. Bardi walked toward the chapel. There was some sort of plinth there, he saw through the shattered wall.

The roses fell from the plinth, engulfing the ruins of the church. That gave him the shivers—it was never natural. Roses should burn as well as any plant, and there had been a mighty burning on this island. He climbed over the rubble of the chapel. He peered over the remains of a wall. Great, there were two dead angels ensnared in the roses. Hmm. No one had thought to strip them for relics. What kind of stupid bastard was Orsino? Bardi hardly had any bottles of any sort on him, but he'd a cup and he'd balance that back to where he could get a bottle for the blood if he had to.

Beneath the tumble of flowers, on the plinth, Bardi could see the body of a man. The old king? It had to be. God, he hoped the king was already dead and he wouldn't have to kill him himself. Bardi would kill him, of course, if the old king still lived, largely because he still had hope of calling in Edward's debts after a bit of legal wrangling, but Bardi still feared for his immortal soul. Murder was work for intermediaries.

He put his hand on the wall to climb over and the roses hissed and moved, snapping tendrils toward him. He recoiled. Oh, God, were those roses trouble? Would he end up trapped by them if he tried to dig the angels or the king out?

"Is that you in there, Your Majesty?" Bardi asked.

No reply. What to do, what to do?

He watched for a long time. Night fell, a starless black, and he went down to sleep by the shore to sleep. In the morning Bardi came back, buoyed by the fact of his survival, feeling braver. He found a way around the flowers into the church and approached the plinth. Yes, it was the king in there, just as he'd seen him in the last days of his court. And old King Edward was on top of a long chest. That had to hold the banner.

"Not so handsome now," he said out loud. The king was very pale, his skin terribly pierced. "You're a king, yet I'm better off than you," commented Bardi. He enjoyed these little victories. He tried the knife on the briars. Immediately they curled around his hand and he had to withdraw, his skin lacerated.

"Great, brilliant," he declared. This was the kind of trick God had in for him—his whole financial salvation right in front of him, but untouchable.

Bardi had nothing to burn, or he would have burned it to see if he could set fire to the roses. Orsino had taken his crossbow and that was now doubtless part of the blackened body that lay in the chapel—he recognized the Florentine's boots, or what was left of them.

"Well, Your Majesty, I'd kill you but I can't think of a way right now."

The horses? He could ride one at the plinth and stab down at the king that way. But that could be painful because the briars might ensnare his legs. On the other hand, they might just consume the horse and give him a free crack at the king. Could he guarantee that he'd be able to cut free the angels and the chest afterward? Clearly not. He resolved to sleep on the problem for one more night.

Bardi could not say what time he was disturbed, though the night was deep and dark.

A glow was in the chapel; someone cried out. He crept forward and peered over the crumbled walls, only the pearly light from inside the chapel to see by.

Montagu! Around his shoulders was a glowing cloak of angel feathers and in his hand that famous sword. He was stricken, terribly stricken, lying on the floor unable to move.

Bardi ran to him. "My lord!" he said.

Montagu said, "Bardi, you traitorous dog. Is there no loyalty you would not betray? Usurer, gilded ape, acting only for yourself!"

"The same, my lord."

Montagu coughed and hacked, a great spume of saliva and snot pouring forth. He said, "This will be to your profit. In my tunic. A vial. Open it and put it to my lips."

Bardi reached inside and took out the tiny stoppered bottle. He opened it and put it up to the lord's mouth. Montagu swallowed the contents. Was it Montagu? He looked younger. The lord coughed, breathed in heavily, and stood. He seemed instantly refreshed. Angel's blood, Bardi guessed.

"I never thought I could commit such sacrilege," said Montagu. "But I have and now I stand, whole and healthy."

Bardi asked him, "Did you get that from the angel you killed?"

"You are an evil man, Bardi, though I am glad of you. I had thought I would have the strength to open the bottle without you. Have you killed him?"

"Edward? No. My lord, I have care for my soul."

"Really?" said Montagu. "That's the most surprising thing I've heard since someone told me the king still lived."

"Everyone has care for their immortal self, sir."

"Do they?" said Montagu.

He weighed Arondight in his hand. "I once did. Not now," he said.

Montagu wrapped the angel feather cloak around him and leapt over the briars, floating up to land on the plinth above the king. The tendrils snaked up to engulf him, but Montagu would not be denied; he hacked and slashed, tearing the briars away from him with his sword. Twice he was dragged down but cut himself free to stand again, terribly wounded, his face bloody, his mail torn, his gambeson in shreds. Only the angel feathers afforded him any protection.

Montagu said to the old man, "You have lived beyond your time. God claim your soul and the devil mine!"

He thrust the sword down into Edward's chest. The king kicked, spat, retched, and died. Montagu worked the sword up under his ribs, cutting and pushing, his knee on the king's belly. He plunged his hand into the gaping wound, tearing out the heart and holding it up to inspect as a man might inspect a root he had pulled from the earth. The briars shook and rattled, shriveled, blackened, and died all over the plinth and ruined church. Bardi repeatedly crossed himself, flinching and cowering as if it was he who had been engulfed in thorns.

Montagu limped down to the dead angels, his leggings in tatters, his legs bloody. He took out a knife and two vials, worked the knife into an angel's side and bled it into the vials. He stoppered them, put them beneath his armor, picked up the heart and pointed Arondight at Bardi.

"I had thought to kill you, banker," he said. "But you have done me and England a service, which I said would be to your profit. Come to Queen Isabella for your reward."

And then Bardi saw something he thought he would never see in his life. An English baron, William Montagu—of the purest Norman blood in England, the foundation stone of God's England—put up three fingers in the sign of Lucifer.

Montagu wound the angel feather cloak about him, taking the bloody heart underneath it. "Isabella," he said. A white streak like a comet leaving the earth, he shot up into the heavens, leaving Bardi alone.

The banker crossed himself. Angel cloaks, enchanted briars, devils walking the earth he could deal with. But Montagu a Luciferian? Bardi simply could not believe it.

"Truly these are the last days," he said. But, as his father had always told him, in any disaster or crisis, there's money to be made. The end of the world might just be an opportunity, should he find something with which to invest. Bardi scrambled up to examine the chest.

10

*A*nother child had been taken. Free Hell had claimed little Maude; the child was revealed as missing from her crib with the morning light, then the flame demon visited to urge him to action. Philippa's howls had filled the palace and Edward had smashed everything about him. Vases, chairs, windows, tables, all took the brunt of his useless wrath. No good. They had his daughter. Edward was a sentimental man, so he mourned his bonny little Maude—but at least it was not a son.

"I am trying," he said, on his knees in the Windsor chapel. "God, give me strength. I will honor my vow to your enemy and then I will crush them."

Philippa was pregnant again. Edward could not lose another child. Another, harder push would need to be made. France must fall. The war was proving utterly ruinous. How ruinous? France was finding it expensive, the richest country in the world. Edward could pile up his IOUs to the sky. He was indebted to virtually every landowner in England, and still he needed more for his expedition. The devils had helped there. Lord Sloth was uncommonly good at extracting money from people, his violence and aggression yielded even better results than Montagu had achieved with his charm.

Montagu. Still the name made him boil. He'd told Edwin the Luciferian priest that he wanted him delivered up, but Edwin said he couldn't find him. Edwin was no longer really a prisoner, more of a leader of the bowmen who traveled in promise of their Eden in France.

Montagu had lain with his mother. His mother! Isabella had, by letter, suggested burning his manor house and imprisoning his wife to flush him out, if he was not captive, and to provide a lesson to others even if he was. Had he admitted her to his presence, no doubt she would have got her way. As it was, Philippa had begged mercy for Lady Montagu, and his wife's tears prevailed.

So many years of fighting, so much destruction, all to come to this. Edward knelt in the chapel, his armor on his back, his son Edward beside him, nearly a man now, he too in full armor, taller even than his tall father.

Little Edward, as his family still called him, wore a green and white caparison over his harness decorated with the royal leopards. Would the boy fight? Of course he would. He had held a sword as soon as he'd been removed from his mother's breast. At a tournament he gave the best knights in the land a run for their money. Little Edward would become just Edward today when they brought the French to battle.

The king thought back over the years of truce—years in which the fighting had hardly ceased. Brittany had been burned black, half held by the pretender to the dukedom, John de Montfort and his more able wife, half lost again. Edward remembered the walls of Quimper, the devils howling over the battlements, no need for siege engines or ladders. "There's a reason the fortress at Dis has smooth walls a mile high," Lord Sloth had said. "These little defenses are no more than country stiles to the legions of Hell."

Some stile Quimper had proved to be. The giant who claimed to be Hugh Despenser had marshaled his forces there. Lion fought spider, the boarheads of Dis fought the waspheads of Agana, while the Luciferians with their bows blackened the air with arrows blessed by the priest Edwin— blessed in the name of Lucifer. Edward had tried to insist they have their arrows blessed by God's priests, but this they would not do—promised land or no promised land. Without the blessing, the arrows were useless against the devils, so Edward, a man who had swallowed so much of his pride it was surprising he had not grown fat on it, had to swallow some more.

What a coalition. What a mess. But the French king still had not put his angels in the field, and his reliance on Despenser was encouragement that he could not.

No angels from France, no angels from England. Some said the age of angels was over. It was not over. Spies at Reims had seen the angel sparkling above the cathedral, at Chartres and Notre Dame too. Some said the archangel Michael had come to France's aid and sat in a great throne above Montmartre.

The English needed all the help they could get. Devils could fight the devils, the men the men but without angels, without angels! The Holy Roman emperor had taken his back, unsatisfied with his rates of pay. Charles of Navarre was known to have coaxed his from the shrine in Pamplona. Which way would that odd fellow and his mother jump? They'd had enough meetings with Navarrese representatives and nothing solid had ever come out of it.

The south, the Agenais and Aquitaine, had been at constant war—cities lost, cities gained, Bordeaux falling, recaptured, falling again. And yet the main truce—in truth a series of truces—had held, while Edward's children were threatened by fiends.

Now it was over and the ships ready to sail. Edward crossed himself.

"King." A voice hung above him, like the sound of a deep bell.

Edward looked up. Around him the light cut rainbows in the air, a curtain of diamonds seemed to drop from the ceiling of the chapel, falling soundlessly to the floor, not settling. A strange elation filled him and his head swam. He recognized the feeling immediately—he'd had it when his father had introduced him to the angel at Walsingham as a boy.

"Angel?" he said.

Floating above the altar was the figure of a man shrouded in light.

"I am Chamuel, an angel who keeps the law."

"You were one of my father's angels."

Chamuel said, "Your father is dead."

Edward crossed himself, fighting back the thanks to God. At last, after all the years of struggle, he was a true king, beloved of God. It was as if he didn't know what to feel. For the first time in his adult life he wanted to cry. Part of him wanted to shout his joy to Heaven, another part mourned his father deeply. Old Edward had been a great man, a great fighter, an example in many ways.

"How did he die?" he asked the angel.

"A great love overwhelmed him."

Edward stood, his heart drumming. His father dead. So long dreaded. So desperately longed for. He showed nothing on his face, by habit concealing any emotion that gave a hint of weakness. He wanted to press for details, but long experience of his father's dealing with angels told him that to do so was only to invite more confusion. Dead, dead. Oh, Father, so wronged, so wronging. Dead at last. God rest your soul and thanks be to Him that He has received you at last.

"Then God has granted me you. Where are the others?"

The angel said, "Fled or devoured."

"Devoured?" asked Edward.

"The banner of the evil one. Despenser had it at Orwell. We toiled to replace it in its chest."

"So you're the only one? I have no more angels?" Edward's temper rose in him again. He had stuck his kingdom together with glue and hope, waiting for the day the angels would appear to bond it properly. And now only this lesser spirit had come to him.

He'd seen the archangel Gabriel sparkling in Westminster Abbey as a boy, and the being in front of him, while beautiful, did not compare. Could he stay the power of Michael in the field? They had no choice. Could Edward simply call off the invasion? No, he had to take the war to Philip on his own soil. This angel could depart as quickly as it had come if it faced the French angels. So he was still dependent on devils, and still on the heretic bowmen.

Chamuel said, "I watched over him while the others ran. I avoided the briars and the thorns. I am here for you. Venerate me, pray to me, and bring me jewels so I might play in their light."

None of this made sense to Edward. He had that heady feeling that comes with talking to angels, like the first glass of wine on a summer's day. It was unwelcome. Edward turned to his son, the prince, who was staring up in wonder at the angel. He said, "Go outside, fetch me some monks. If this thing wants venerating, then we'd better venerate it." He looked back at the angel. "What can you tell me of the world? What is the disposition of my enemy's forces?"

"He has many allies. Michael and Adriel and Eremiel. From the south comes Jophiel. Devils attend him and fifty thousand knights."

"That's no good to me, my earthly spies can tell me that. I want more if I'm to keep you in gold and glass."

The angel shimmered and Edward's head swam, but he would not be cowed by this angel. It had been given to him as a servant by God and he would use it as one.

Chamuel said, "Philip fears the evidence in those letters Montagu brought you, but he knows you will not use what you have against him. To do so is to incriminate yourself."

"Is there a way back for me? Can I come to God?" Edward asked.

"Yes. There is a boy—your mother has heard tell of him."

"The Antichrist. Our French spies report that he has been mentioned over there. He isn't here or the Luciferians would be parading him around. Should I kill him for God's favor?"

"God does not want him dead."

Edward said, "What does God want?"

The angel replied, "His faith in Lucifer shaken. He wants the Antichrist to come to worship Him."

"How do I make him do that?"

"If you want him to come to God, you will catch him and find a way."

"Where is he?"

"He is with one of Despenser's devils, captured and heading for France."

"Where in France?" said the king.

"To Despenser. Despenser wants to kill him and win favor with Satan."

"And Satan, though he is God's servant, wants to kill this boy?"

Chamuel said, "The aims of the master and those of the servant are not always the same. God is wounded. Do you imagine Satan wants his master fully well? Politics are as subtle in Heaven and Hell as they are on earth."

"God is sick?" he asked. Edward knelt down again.

"The struggle with the evil one has been at great cost."

"He's still all right, though? He's still . . . there."

"He seeks the youth so he can return to his former glory."

Edward could hardly believe what he was hearing. God was dependent on a boy. Still, *it is as it is*. Analyzing and asking questions was for the monks. He had a war to conduct.

"I have a spy in Despenser's camp who knows of him. I'll send word to him," said Edward. "With luck he can intercept the boy and smuggle him away. Can you take the message to our spy?"

"The angel at Notre Dame forbids the presence of English angels in all of Paris."

"Fine, I'll sent one of my mother's flying devils. The skies above France are thick with them nowadays, I hear. I don't suppose they'll notice one more. Why don't the angels blast those?"

"They are persuaded they fight for the same cause. God is uncertain of the correct course. How much more so his angels?" said the angel.

An abbey monk opened the door.

"You," said Edward. "Get to venerating this thing here. Your best songs and incense. I'm off to get a chapel constructed on my ship. Well, good news, boys, good news, the angels are here in England again. Bring me a stoneskin; I have a letter to send!"

He tapped the sword at his side and strode from the church.

11

As the monks chanted to the angel at Windsor, Isabella watched the bright morning from her solar at the top of Nottingham Castle. The piping child devil was playing "May Is Merry," one of her favorite tunes and, at her shoulder, a little devil cracked walnuts for her and fed them to her on the end of its fork.

It had become impossible for Montagu to stay at Nottingham. She had admitted Salisbury to goad her son into coming into her presence, but it hadn't worked. Edward simply said they would do very well without her devils until Montagu was handed over. Well, she had no intention of doing that—contrary to her expectations when she had planned to have him killed, the earl had become far too useful. There had, however, been a certain satisfaction in banishing him from her immediate company, once he had become thoroughly intoxicated with her.

The king had been furious when Isabella had let Montagu go—spiriting him away on gargoyle's wings—and it had taken her sending Edward the Drago to placate him. That was one weapon that would come as a shock to Despenser's flying devils come the day of any battle.

Montagu had sent her a letter. He had seemed unusually keen to detail his crimes. He went to the Luciferians, who had captured him, and asked them to help find the old king. They had suspected his motives, so he had taken their oaths to Lucifer—after all, Montagu was seeking damnation—and lived among them as a poor man, finding no earthly riches of account now that he was gone from her presence. How sweet.

The Black Priest, Edwin, had used his creature Know-Much. All they had told him was that they were seeking the old king too—the whispering demon of the boy Dow reported as much. He was in Lombardy and, when the old king was found, the ympe Murmur would whisper it to the skies and the teeming demons would bring the message back to Know-Much. Then Montagu would have the old king, she would have his heart, and with it the ingredient to cast the spell to rule all England.

Now there was a light that seemed to split away from the morning sun—a meteor approaching from the east. Isabella opened the window. There was a flash and Montagu landed at her feet, wrapped in his cloak of angel's feathers. In his hand was a bloody tuber of slick meat. The heart.

She bent to take it from him.

"Oh, William," she said. "It's still warm! You really are a man to get things done!"

Montagu lay panting on the floor, clearly unable to move. She remembered how weak little Charles had been traveling with that cloak. The famed warrior Montagu seemed just as afflicted.

Montagu gestured to his tunic—rather a workmanlike affair, not fine cloth at all. Isabella reached inside to remove a small bottle.

"Angel's blood!" she said. "Monty, you naughty boy, what have you been up to? I must say, you *do* look younger. Well, now you know all my secrets." She unstoppered the cork with her thumb—her left hand still holding the bloody heart—and dabbed her tongue at the opening of the little bottle.

"Can you speak?" Isabella asked him.

"I can." Though with effort, it seemed.

"Oh Monty, so often I find myself able to kill you and yet unwilling to do so. Why? I think it must be just how very useful you are. I often said to myself, if only I had a servant like that Montagu, I should rule England. And now I do and I was right! With this gift it seems I shall, in just a few short years, providing we get the magic right. The heart of a godless king. What a prize for any devil! Keep your eyes off it, you!" Isabella spoke to the little winged child, who made a big-eyed face of exaggerated innocence.

"The question is: 'Shall I revive you?' I could leave you there while I invite in a succession of lovers. Robert the monk's quite the performer now, and he's even let his tonsure grow out a bit. But no, I shall revive you, of course I shall, and you can tell me how you intend to kill yourself. I'm going to banish you from my company forever now, so I expect you'll want to do that."

She put the bottle of angel's blood to Montagu's lips and he sipped.

"You really do look younger, William. Still, I'll never want you."

Montagu stood, his strength visibly returning.

"I had no hope of your favor," he said. "Rather the reverse. You have given me what I want. Your scorn, your hatred. It removes all doubt, you see. If you were wise enough to hold out even the slightest hope you might . . ." He stumbled over the words, looked up as if what he wanted to say might be written on the ceiling.

Montagu continued. "Not *love* me but indulge me. If you offered me a kind word that might spark my dreams of you then I might seek to live, and live in torment forever. But you have released me, cast me out completely, and I know I have no path to you. So thank you, lady. As you rightly guess, I can now go to die—whereupon I will pass on to another kind of torment, one that cannot be worse than what I now endure."

Isabella tilted her head again, the same pleasure in her eyes as when she received a rare gift. She replied, "Perhaps I was foolish and there is more entertainment to be had from you. But I'm not a vindictive person, William. I've had my revenge on you; I don't seek to polish the stars and bid them to shine some more. Enough. Go."

The winged child began to play upon its pipe again, "May Is Merry."

Montagu put the feather cloak over his arm and walked to the door. "Keep the remains of the angel's blood," he said. "I shall not want it again."

She smiled at him, and he had to turn his gaze to the floor. He still wanted her, it was obvious, still couldn't trust himself not to beg or wheedle for her love, though Montagu knew how useless that would be.

"How will you end it?" asked Isabella.

In one action Montagu strode forward, drew Arondight, and struck the child devil, half severing its head. It dropped lifeless to the floor. "In fighting," he said. "It has been my life, it will be my death."

Isabella hardly blinked. "For whom?"

"For Edward," he said, "to whom I gave my oath when he made me earl. And for Lucifer, to whom I gave my oath when you made me nothing."

Isabella looked down at the dead devil. She said, "Yes, it seems apt you should die in war, though I fear you are rather too good at it. Take care not to survive, William. I would not hear of you again."

Montagu sheathed his sword. "What did you give for the powers you have? What did you promise to overthrow Edward?"

"What do you think?"

"Your soul?" he asked her.

"Don't be melodramatic. I promised England to the devils, under my rule, that is all. Soon I shall honor my bargain. Now go and think of me as you die."

Montagu bowed and left the solar.

12

O sbert threw Edward's letter into the fire and watched it burn. He cradled his purse in his hand. It was full now, bulging like the devil's nutsack. Edward's devil had brought him a good pawful of gold. Life was good, life was very good.

At the French court Osbert had his salary as court magician, then he had his money for spying on King Philip from Despenser, his money for spying on Despenser for King Philip, and his money for spying on them both from King Edward. It hadn't been difficult to make contact with the English king now that Osbert had mastered the control of swarming devils—tiny breeze-borne creatures that blew on the winds. They were as reliable a way of delivering a message as any ship—and thank God the angels saw no reason to strike them.

Paris sparkled now, the archangel Michael floating above it like a second sun, a gigantic shining, winged man, arms outstretched, a sword in his right hand. It was good to see, but Osbert remembered the story of the fall of Jericho. Michael had been asked whose side he was on and seemed maddeningly noncommittal, according to the pardoner's recollection.

The devil that delivered King Edward's message—and, more important, his money—was not a swarming devil. It was a stone devil, flapping in on clanking wings—one of those that looked exactly like gargoyles and, when not employed, could often be seen sitting on the parapets of Notre Dame and other great buildings. The use of the clunking stoneskin showed that this was an important missive—not one to risk getting blown off course by a stray breeze.

Find the boy Dowzabel. Everyone wanted him. When Osbert thought of the efforts he had made to convince people they needed so much useless tat, it grieved him that the only thing of huge worth he'd had in his life—the boy—he had let go without a second thought. Was he even alive? Despenser had told Nergal to return with him in one piece, but a devil's idea of "in one piece" might be normal folk's idea of "dead"—stitched together at the neck or some such madness.

Osbert mulled the options. He could return the boy to Philip and convert him. That had seemed like a good idea when it popped out of his mouth at St. Denis, but on reflection it was clearly never going to work. The boy was a fanatic. So Osbert was going to disappoint Philip and he was well aware of how kings reacted when disappointed. Failure may even anger God. God had bolloxed up Osbert's life without even noticing him. What would He do if he came to His attention?

Despenser was still under the impression the boy was his property and had promised to find a way to kill Osbert if Dow didn't end up in his possession. And Nergal, swanning around in skirts so pretty, was a disciple of Satan. He wanted the boy dead and had sworn solemnly to Despenser to deliver him. So that just left Edward as a potential buyer, who should be pressed for as much money as possible before being incinerated in holy fire.

It would be difficult to get the boy to England but, from what Osbert heard, the English army was coming to France. There would be a way, there was always a way. He took a couple of low-value coins from his purse and then slipped the purse into a little chest, which he locked. The chest went into a hole he had kicked in the lower wall specifically for the purpose, and then the hole was stuffed back up with rags, as if it was just another repair on a rat run.

Osbert stepped out into the mist of the summer night, into the courtyard of the Temple. The great spider devil hung above him still, its webs glistening in the moonlight. Most of the other devils were gone out into the field with Despenser. Osbert was relieved that Despenser's position had become more tenuous since the raising of the angels.

The angels were willing to fight on the side of the devils, but Osbert knew, as Despenser knew, that the devils had become unnecessary with the raising of the fourth angel. One angel might abandon a battlefield to play in a rainbow, two might. Three, very unlikely. It would be unheard of for four angels to come from their shrines and none of them help the king in battle. The only reason Philip had taken the devils at all was so they could engage England's devils and minimize the French casualties until the angels decided enough blood had been spilled to step in.

For a foolish moment Osbert felt like doing nothing. He was the chief—and only—court sorcerer, living better than he had ever lived, dressed in fine clothes and eating fine food. However, ever since he had got out of the magic circle, a strange suspicion had grown in Osbert—that he might in some way be capable of influencing his own fate. It was such an odd feeling that he decided to actually make some decisions—even plan for the future, rather than waiting for it to come crashing in like a stone from a siege engine.

Mind you, riches and fine wines were all very well but what really mattered was . . . Hmm. What? Not being completely and utterly pissed on the whole time. The only problem was that, in order not to be one of the multitude of pissed on, one had to be a pisser on, so to speak. The more Osbert considered the metaphor, the more it struck him as being widely applicable to human behavior. Never piss up, for that piss only comes back down. Piss sideways and the pisser next to you may turn to see who is pissing on him, thereby pissing on you. Piss down, piss down, lad, he said to an imaginary son he'd acquired as he left the Temple. Piss down and piss hard.

Osbert passed down by the side of the Temple, heading through the suburban stink toward the river. He enjoyed the new freedom to ignore the curfew that his elevated status brought him and loved to wander about at night, though not here. The curfew didn't hold outside the city walls and all manner of men wandered the suburbs. He had his hand on his knife. Osbert needed to be out, though. The sort of men he was looking for were out at that time of night.

He would have preferred to have recruited a devil for the job, but the devils gave their loyalty to Despenser, and Nergal was doing Despenser's work. Devils could be stupid and could be fooled, but he wasn't ready to stake his life on it.

A low mist hung on the blackness of the river as he neared the water. Osbert was looking for the stews, although these whores were the sort who didn't bother with the niceties of washing you down. Flop it out, stick it in, pay your money, and don't forget to wipe your feet on the way out. Good value if you watched your purse while on the job—the whores had swarms of little kids and most of them were thieving little bastards.

He was looking for Wild Marie, a lady he had much patronized on his days off from devil summoning. She was a drab woman, ordinary as a turnip, and that was why he liked her—nothing of Heavenly perfection or devilish corruption about her. She also had six brothers who were useful sorts and it was them Osbert had come to see.

Through the squelch of the narrow streets, past dogs—with murder in their eyes—who were roped far too generously for his liking, arguments crackling into the night from low huts, laughter, the bawls of children, the songs of mothers. Despite his wariness he was quite enjoying himself. If he'd been more raggedly dressed, he would have felt at home here.

Osbert reached the house—a slanting, broken-down thing that looked as if it had been cowed under the blows of a prevailing wind. He knocked at the low door and it was opened by a ragged-arsed boy.

"Marie!" he called without really acknowledging Osbert. "Customer!"

Osbert wondered if he'd have time for a quick one. Probably not well-advised. He had use for Marie's rattish brothers and didn't want to antagonize them. No man wants the fact his sister is a whore thrust in his face, and even the most demure little fiddle might cause bad blood in business dealings.

The door was left open and Osbert peered within. During the day only Marie and a couple of other women were to be found at the house—though they made it known the men were near enough in case of any funny business. Now the house was stuffed to bursting, a good twenty people of all ages and both sexes in the tiny space.

Marie appeared, her slight frame squeezing through the press. She said to him, "You came, then."

"I did. Are your brothers here?" asked Osbert.

"Yes."

"Will they do my work?"

"They will. How many do you want?" she asked.

"How many are available?"

Marie said, "All six. They're good and strong, at a sou each for the work. They have three mates. That's ten sous and one for me is twelve."

"I have that money."

"One has a dagger whose handle is wound with the hair of St. Joan. You'll need that to take on the devil, so that will be an extra sou for the hire—fifteen."

"I have a couple of devil knives too. They'll be useful. We'll call it twenty and your men will split the extra."

"Good health, sir!" A thin, dirty man who looked as though he had never even seen good health to know what it meant, lifted an imaginary cup.

"And yours," said Osbert. He spoke to Marie. "Can they leave now?"

She replied, "For an extra five sous, yes."

Osbert knew he didn't have to pay the extra but almost gave in, just because this was small change to him now. He knew though that he needed to get the respect of the men and of Marie. Let them see you as a soft touch and there's no limit to the liberties they'd take.

He said, "We go now. I've already agreed to your five extra. Let's move before I decide to take my money elsewhere."

Marie looked back at him with her passive eyes—whore's eyes in which you could read nothing, not contempt, not disgust, not love, not hate. "Two extra."

Osbert said, "I'll go."

She said, "Twenty it is. Lads, the gentleman wants to leave."

The men got to their feet. "Not inside the city, then," said one, a black-haired rascal with a simpleton's lumpy face.

"Not inside the city. We watch the road from the east. Do you know any good vantage points?" asked Osbert.

"That's bandit territory," said the simpleton, who was clearly not as stupid as he looked.

"I thought *you* were bandits."

"Yes, but there are bandits and there are bandits. This is our home patch; that's theirs."

"A problem?" he asked the man.

"Not for another five sous . . . and what's to stop us taking it all now?"

Osbert smiled. "I do the work of the Temple giant. He knows where I am and if I don't return, doubtless he'll give you a visit. Would you like that?"

"Not much," said the man.

Osbert said, "Thought not. Now let's go." He was keen to curtail further conversation about money.

The nine men filed along the riverbank and out to the east. The moon was a good one above the mist and they soon found the ford to the north bank and the road. They followed it quietly through the fields and farmsteads, careful to wake no one by talk. Strangers on the road at that time of night would be assumed to be hostile and the last thing they wanted was to confront a bunch of well-fed country boys armed with forks and backed by dogs.

Very soon, the woods loomed. Now they had a choice—go on unseen but largely blind, or stick to the road and progress faster but risk discovery. They entered the woods—it wouldn't do to alert the Vincennes boys of their presence. Everyone was quiet and slow. The going was difficult and, when the dawn peeped through the trees, they tried to push forward as quickly as they could. The outlaws kept their dens deep in the trees, only venturing to the road to rob. Then they'd be gone, fearful of city guards or thrill-seeking noblemen and their retinues who would come looking for them.

The men camped in the forest, making no fire and eating no food—for they had none. They were accustomed to hunger. The next day they found a rise with a good view of the road.

"We'll make our camp here," said Osbert. "They will be coming this way."

"Who?" asked one man, who Osbert thought of as Lumpface.

He replied, "A woman and a boy."

"And you need nine of us for that? I thought you said there was a devil."

"Nine? Your sister said there were ten. Am I paying you too much?"

"Ten of us. What about the devil?"

Osbert said, "The lady *is* the devil. I'll talk to them while you sneak up. Kill her quickly and cleanly. Botch it and you won't live to see the next dawn."

He passed the two devil knives to Lumpface. Osbert added, "For your most able men. Do not harm the boy."

They waited by the road, waited a long time—weeks, living off the land as best they could. They were too near to the city to catch any lone travelers and most people moved through in big groups, many bearing weapons. Some groups of men-at-arms were on the road—crossbowmen with their baggage train, giant shields strapped to mules and donkeys, knights from the east taking a night in Paris before heading on to face the English in the north.

How much easier it would all be, thought Osbert, if the angels would engage without first seeing evidence of men's bravery? They could send the archangel Gabriel up to wherever Edward's army was, watch Gabriel engulf it in fire without the trouble or expense of discharging a single crossbow quarrel. God wanted too much from man, he thought.

It rained and was miserable, then it was sunny and more pleasant. The men trapped rabbits in the woods and became more complacent, building a fire. The Vincennes gang did not appear and Osbert guessed they too might have gone north to follow the army and grab whatever plunder was going.

It was night when they finally came, the cart creaking along the road. It woke Osbert, who lay half-toasted, half-soaked with his front to the fire. Rising, he looked down onto the moonlit road. A distance away Osbert saw them—she driving the cart on with a whip, something in the cart behind. It could have been a sack, but Osbert guessed it would be the boy. Something else was in there too—long like a coffin. The Drago?

One of Marie's brothers drew a bow, but Osbert waved him back.

"It will not hurt it," he said. "Get in close, attack with the knives."

"Where will you be?" asked the man.

"Coordinating from up here."

"What's coordinating?"

"It's a sort of cowering," said another man.

"At a sou a piece I think you can reasonably be expected to risk your lives," admonished Osbert. "The trouble with you people is that you want something for nothing. Now get down, attack, and if one of your fellows with the devil knives falls, pick up the knife and attack again."

He said, "Easier to kill you and take the money."

"The thought had occurred to me, which is why I took the precaution of bringing none," said Osbert. "Now please attack, before they drive straight past and are gone."

The man tossed the knife in his hand. "Come on," he said to his friends.

The men dropped quietly down the bank and Osbert briefly lost sight of them. Then a huge cry and hullaballoo, a flash of fire, screams, and silence. Osbert waited. Still silence. He feared the worst—that all his men had been killed and the cart had moved on. He scrambled down the slope to see the trees in front of him on fire, crackling away with a pleasant, piney smell.

"Sorcerer," said a cracked, female voice.

Osbert moved around the fire to get a better view. "Shit," he said. Nine humped bodies blazed away in the road, intensely enough for Osbert to take a pace back.

When Osbert had feared the worst, he had shown quite a lack of imagination as to what the worst might be. The worst was not that all his men were dead and the devil had gone on. The worst was that all his men were dead and the devil was still there, angry and out to roast him like a Lammas hog. The devil would not be moving on because he had, in the exuberance of his defense, incinerated his horse too.

"Nergal," said Osbert. "Thank God you're safe. You've rescued me!"

13

T he French angels blew the English fleet ragged for nine days, forcing it back from the towering white rocks of the Needles off the Isle of Wight to Portsmouth harbor.

Montagu observed the four angels on a lighted cloud above the fleet puffing their cheeks to blow the English invaders back to land. Michael was the hardest to look at, his great spear blazing from the clouds, his fearful beauty turning night into day.

Montagu knew what he would counsel Edward, had he been allowed near, and hoped the king's present advisers had said the same. Get out on the deck and convince them to allow the crossing. It would do the men good to see their king addressing such powerful beings; it would show them that God respects the courageous. From his place on his little fishing boat, hedged in among twenty cursing London archers, he saw the king emerge.

"Your God won't let us cross." Greatbelly was at his side.

He said, "Not my God anymore."

"I think he is. You are not happy here among us. You despise low men."

"I despise quite a lot," said Montagu. "That doesn't mark them out as particularly noteworthy."

Montagu fought his inclination to look down on this common woman. Had he not given up all right to rank and station to follow Lucifer, a being he hated with all his heart? God forgave, the priests said. Well, Montagu would test that theory, commit offense after offense against the Almighty, and secure his damnation.

He had seen his wife once since his fall from grace, his children too. He had kissed them and told them that he was effectively dead now, and to enact his will. Catherine had tried to hold him, but Montagu had repelled her.

He had told her, "I am become a serpent and must crawl in the dust."

Then he had returned. Something in the filth and degradation of the Southwark hovels suited his temper. Montagu was not welcome at first, but the little demon Know-Much had argued that he should be allowed to stay.

After two weeks, by the chalk cliffs of the Isle of Wight, the angels disappeared—Edward had won his argument with them in the short term—and the fleet of seven hundred and fifty ships, some great, some small, sailed out of Portsmouth. That was on a bright day, the sun on the water, the wind at their backs, devils in the half shapes of lions, leopards, wolves, and men, plunging through the white surf behind them.

Above them great wasp-men hung in the air in swarms, their four human arms clutching darts, their legs kicking as they flew under buzzing wings. There were other flying things too: gargoyles—stoneskins as the men called them—and bat-winged men; monstrous red birds whose plumage trailed smoke across the sky; fat droning flies with the faces of women hovering low above the sails. And there was the English angel too—like a man, but six-winged and burning in flame.

"Holy! Holy! Holy!" it called continually as the fleet went forward. Montagu was glad when the angel ascended on a cloud and he could hear it no more. He found it irritating.

"Why do you fight?" said Greatbelly as the ship sailed. The Luciferians had brought their women and children with them—they had no intention of going back to England under the yoke of kings and masters.

"Why do you?" he asked her.

"For my freedom."

Montagu brushed the patch that covered his ruined eye, a gesture somewhere between a scratch and a stroke. He did not reply, so she asked again.

"So why do you? You really have no love of our cause."

He said, "I was raised to fight."

Greatbelly replied, "But now you serve no one."

"I still serve Lucifer, as I vowed. And I serve the king."

"The man who is Lucifer's enemy. The man who would kill you."

Montagu smiled. He said, "Loyalties aren't thrown away over such trifles. I am still an Englishman and Edward is still my friend. I would see him prosper. Your aims are not exclusive, from what I hear."

"Aims are not exclusive . . ." Greatbelly repeated the words in a mocking voice. "You do talk lovely, don't you, for a murderer?" Greatbelly was less whorish now. She had abandoned the yellow hood that marked her for a prostitute and wore just an apron like any goodwife. Her daughter, a pretty girl of nine, huddled against her for warmth.

"Whom have I murdered?" Montagu asked.

"Plenty, I should say."

"If you don't believe I am in earnest, then why do you not tell your fellows to cast me from their ranks?"

Greatbelly stroked her child's hair, planted a kiss on the girl's head. She said, "Someone needs to see my lads through this battle and I should say of all the people I've ever met, you're the man to do it."

"So you need leaders, after all."

She said, "No. Sometimes we need leading. That's different from needing a leader, a man to call lord. We need a marshal in the field as we need a mason to cut stone. But the mason is not above his fellows when the stone is cut, nor the marshal when the war is done. When we set up Eden in France, there'll be days and weeks for talk, for debate. With a bunch of French knights trying to stick their spears up your arse, I should say now is not the time for discussion."

"You'd be right," said Montagu.

The woman's company was increasingly pleasant to him. Of course he'd been raised with farm boys and girls—all nobles took their playmates from every degree of man—but he'd never had a proper conversation with anyone of that rank since he was twelve years old. He'd talked more to his dogs than his servants. She was rude and rough and hideous to behold. Her education was nonexistent, but Montagu did recognize some native intelligence. And she was honest. She said what she meant. Only the very highest men in the land had done that in front of Montagu since he'd been old enough to attend court.

The English made it to Normandy and put a blight on the land, pillaging St. Vaast, Barfleur, and then burning the abbey of Notre Dame du Voeu. Montagu watched the flames with a soldier's approval; God had to see that the French were not defending His houses. Montagu saw little of the fighting—the Luciferians could not be persuaded to kill and burn their French "brothers and sisters" as they called the poor, but the godly men and the devils set to it with zest and the flames rose for a day's march all around the landing site and for a strip of land two hours' ride inland all along the coast.

The French had been fooled, their fleet and the majority of their troops all down in Gascony, and Edward made the most of their absence. Montagu left the Luciferians for a while and tagged along with the prince of Wales's division, chasing Marschal Robert Bertrand and the few defenders he could scramble together across the countryside.

All the time, Montagu watched the skies. Angels could stop the invasion. But he understood their nature now, from listening to the Luciferians and from the evidence of his eyes. The angels loved beauty but, like God, they loved suffering too. They would come when the French had suffered enough. Then there would be a reckoning.

The pillaging and the burning went on too long—evidently the devils enjoyed it too much. This was not the work the English army needed to be doing—it needed to take some strategic objectives and quickly—some place that could be captured and then defended. Caen was burned, the devils streaming over the walls of the new town. Montagu ran at their backs, watching as Robert Bertrand and the count of Eu staged a magnificent charge through the diabolic horde to reach the protection of the castle, hacking at a regiment of goat-headed devils who fell screaming beneath their blessed swords.

My God, those French could fight. Montagu felt himself itching to face them, as a lord—not skulking in his pauper's rags, trailing behind a pack of devils. The castle fell, hideous beetle devils swarming over the walls to overwhelm the few defenders. A priest was torn from the battlements and hurled to the moat as he blessed the defenders' arrows. The devils were targeting the holy men, he realized. Once they were gone, the arrows were no more bothersome to the devils than summer midges. The townspeople were slaughtered—five hundred tipped into a mass grave because of the stink.

The massacres were a luxury the army could not allow itself because time was running out, Montagu knew. Where was the strategy? The army veered across the countryside and all the while, Philip and his angels would be coming. And then the English would be running.

Edward abandoned Caen and struck north. The Flemings would be in the north and Edward needed to meet up with their army before facing the French. Paris was within Edward's grasp, but he pulled back. There could only be one reason, Montagu knew—it must be that Edward's flying devils had told him Philip was near. Edward the Fox had played havoc in the henhouse, but now Farmer Philip was coming with his dogs.

It was a race to the Somme now, but the army could not be focused. Men were drunk on pillage, the devils too. Montagu saw a great goat-headed devil sitting on a burning farmhouse, chewing on a man's head as a boy chews on an apple. Montagu had to remember his new station—that he was only a churl now, though he wanted to scream at them to rally, to move. Time was running out, running out badly.

News came in from the south. Carnentan, St. Vaast, and the other towns of the Cotentin peninsular so recently captured had been regained by the French—and this wasn't even Philip's main army. The way back was being cut off, the landing points on the Norman coast lost.

The prince of Wales knew the need for urgency, moving among the troops cajoling and shouting. The boy even shook Montagu by the shoulder. He said, "Get moving, man, or I'll cut you down myself."

Prince Edward—now a thumb taller than Montagu—was drunk with the thrill of command and the fight. He didn't see Montagu as anything more than another wayward commoner to be kicked and whipped into line.

"Very good, lord," Montagu acquiesced, and began calling to his fellows.

Columns were formed ready to march, but seeing a monastery on the hill, the troops and devils went whooping to sack it. A light in the south wasn't the sun. Angels. Would they act? Would they need to? The English were fifteen thousand strong, the French greatly outnumbering them.

Montagu saw a flight of gargoyles streaking in from the south on clattering wings, tearing into the wasp men with stony claws, the insect bodies slamming into the fields until Edward's angel began to shine and they peeled back toward the light on the horizon. Good, the men needed to hurry up. The attack focused English minds and the troops were easier to control.

They had to reach one of the bridges on the Somme before Philip. Squadrons of fly devils were dispatched to secure it, but when attacked by the men of Poix, the army could not be controlled, not until it had attempted to burn the town in revenge. King Edward himself went in to stop them, but the delay was fatal. The English abandoned their baggage train and hurried on, but the troops became hungry and stopped to pillage and forage what they could. Too late now; the light in the south was brighter.

The earl crossed himself as he saw the black horde wheeling away from the pursuing army, flying to meet them—hundreds of gargoyles clattering, night-born men with silver skins and the heads and wings of flies, smoke devils, all darkening the skies. They outnumbered Edward's devils three to one. There would be no crossing of the Somme, no meeting with the Flemings.

Blanchetaque! Edward must make for the ford at Blanchetaque. His angel might drive off the devils there and a ford was not like a bridge—it could not be demolished. Montagu, longing to counsel him, saw there was no need: the army began to head that way, skirting the Somme.

On the other bank he saw the galloping black horse banner of Godemar du Fay and the wagons of the Genoese, their great shields protruding from the open carts. How many? Five hundred men of quality and three thousand foot soldiers behind, many of them trained crossbowmen. Beside them loped a pack of dog-headed devils, their bald skin pied, their tongues lolling. They bayed as they ran. It would be a costly crossing, he thought.

Montagu gripped Arondight. He owed Du Fay and wanted to repay him.

The light in the south was strong now; the French with their angels couldn't be more than two hours away. Pushing through the ranks to find Greatbelly's Luciferians, Montagu cajoled them to run as quickly as they could.

His old squire, George Despenser, made the water first. So he had lived. Now George had his own red banner to announce his status as a leader; Cobham and Northampton were with him, their retinues at their side—twenty or so men each.

The horses charged into the ford as a volley of crossbows struck. Three horses went down, another two unseating their riders. Immediately another volley came in, and a third. The crossbowmen were well drilled, three to a shield, two loading while one shot, giving a near continuous rate of fire. Montagu saw George take two quarrels—one in the arm, another in the chest. The young knight kicked his horse onward. His mail and caparison had done their job.

The first volley went off, going largely long but the second flight of arrows found its mark, immediately making the crossbowmen wheel their shields and look for the source of the fire.

The English men-at-arms were massively outnumbered—only ten had made the bank—but they charged the French, lances leveled. Some crossbowmen panicked and fled, unable to deal with two sources of attack at the same time, though they stumbled into the oncoming charge of Du Fay's knights, forcing it to falter. The vanguard of the English foot soldiers stood uncertainly on the bank. Their lords had gone over on impulse and now there was no one to command them.

Well, William, if you're looking to die, this could be the time. Montagu plunged forward into the ford. He shouted, "England! England!" The other men hesitated as a huge dogman jumped in to oppose Montagu. It was a head taller than him, with deep black fur—and its teeth the size of spearheads. It carried a shield and spear and wore a great helmet that left its fierce muzzle exposed.

"God demands you fall back," said the devil.

Montagu replied, "Lucifer and my damnation demand I go on!"

The dog devil struck at Montagu with its spear, too sure of its speed and size. Montagu seized Arondight, one hand on the hilt, the other two spans from its end, using the sword to parry the spear aside before punching the sword's tip through the devil's chest. The dogman fell back, spurting blood, and Montagu called again, "England! England!"

Now the foot soldiers took courage and poured across the river on a great front. The crossbow fire was savage, but so was the retaliation. More archers had joined on the English bank and now it was a sharp hail indeed that fell on the French.

The dogmen came pouring in, but English devils were arriving—the pig-faced devils Montagu had seen in Edward's camp and more knights too, plunging their horses into the water, to strike home with lances blessed by archbishops or looped with the hair of saints.

On the bank he saw George Despenser go down—a charging knight's lance had missed him but the clash of horses had sent him sprawling. Montagu felt something snag in his gambeson. A longbow arrow. Someone needed to tell the English archers to stop firing now their men were on the bank.

Montagu reached George as a dog devil, jaws dripping spittle, jumped up onto a dead horse and stared down at the young knight. Montagu cut it down from behind.

He said to him, "You're all right, George, get up."

"Baron Despenser to you, you churl." George snapped to his senses. He said, "William?"

"Alive," said Montagu. Then he ran on, into the Genoese, joining the mass forcing them back. It was not long before the French were in retreat and the main body of the English army were looming under its angel. The army crossed, on a broad front, the tide rising. In an hour all the men were over and the French behind them cut off—at least for a while. Montagu had thought they might make a stand at the river.

Greatbelly was at his side. "You looked after the lads," she said. "Thank you."

"I don't need the thanks of a whore for doing what my duty and upbringing . . ." Montagu stopped himself. "Thank you," he said. "They'll come through."

"You seek damnation," said Greatbelly. "Is that part of it—treating us as equals, spitting on God's order?"

Montagu grimaced. "Yes," he said. "But I'm glad your boys are alive."

For a day they tried to goad the French across, but Philip would not be drawn. The English could stand in the field and starve, while the French were sustained by the baggage train the English had discarded. Montagu knew that Edward had to find food and his Flemish allies, so he was not surprised when the army moved on.

The Flemish were not there—they had retreated under a piffling French assault. Two weeks they marched north. Montagu's shoes were falling to pieces and he was not alone. They took more towns, but the people had spoiled or run off with their food and no supplies came from England. Had messengers got through or had angels torn the devils from the skies?

The French angels loomed above them now, Michael with his arms stretched wide, his sword flashing bright across the countryside, the French army close behind. They would not outrun them for much longer. The English were ragged men now, starving and tired.

Still they burned the land. Would the French angels engage? Would they need to?

In Cobham's force, Montagu made his way down the track of a wood out into a broad field that led uphill to a windmill. A small village seemed to tremble at the foot of the hill, as well it might. At the summit, Cobham planted the royal standard. "Here!" he shouted. "This is where we make our stand. This is Crécy, lads. Remember the name!"

14

In the Vincennes woods, Dow was tied to Nergal's cart by his hands and by a rope through the iron collar at his neck. Dow had failed utterly, he knew. God had been too clever for him, securing the banner in a way that He knew no true Luciferian—as the Antichrist was bound to be—could ever release it.

Dow thought of Orsino, of his father, of his nan, but most of all of his mother. Was she in there, still alive, possessed somehow by that devil? He tried to call down Murmur just to feel the little demon nuzzling against him, for the comfort it would bring. The demon did not come. He had not seen him since they crossed to the Island of Îthekter.

The devil drove on, night and day, taking fresh horses from the bandits they met on the road, or from farmsteads. In the mountains, a horse died from exhaustion, its back bloody from the devil's whip. Nergal took the yoke himself and pulled the cart onward. Dow was allowed to drink and, very occasionally, to eat and relieve himself, but only after he had explained to Nergal—the devil gave him its name—that Dow would die if he did not.

Dow suffered at seeing the low people's houses burned and their food and animals stolen. They went on at nightfall, Nergal never sleeping and moving always to the northwest.

"How do you know where to go?" said Dow.

"I smell fires on the wind," said Nergal, and sniffed. "France burning this way means the English king is ashore."

"You tried to kill me before, why not do it now?"

"And risk summoning your mother from inside me? I think not. Besides, I am serving two masters now. I'll secure your death, but without danger to myself. It will be quick and you will have no warning, so your bitch mother will not reclaim her body."

Dow was on the road for weeks, his bones aching from the restraints, and the jarring of the cart.

The angel's sword, mail, and shield were tied to the cart—Dow had tied them there himself, supervised all the time by Nergal with a lit candle to his mouth. The devil would not touch the angelic items.

"You are of Îthekter," said Dow. "How can they harm you?"

"We are imperfect," said Nergal. "Just as a knave should not go dressed in silk nor a merchant in ermine, God will not have the devils touch the things that belong to his angels."

"So a holy sword is death to you as it is to a demon?"

"Yes."

"Then why bring it?"

"My lord Despenser would trade it for favors. He is to be Satan's favorite when he kills you. I, as his obedient servant, can only profit from any trade."

Often Dow fell into something like sleep, something like death, the jolting of the cart banging his bones raw.

Suddenly he was awake. Bandits were whooping from the trees and from all sides. Nergal, who always kept a candle burning in a lantern, took out the flame and swallowed it. Heat and light, screams, the awful cry of the horse as it burned.

Dow could scarcely understand. Someone was in front of him on the cart. A man.

He heard the man say, "You can't treat the boy like this, Nergal; he'll die."

Nergal replied, "I have given him water five times now."

"Today?"

"Since we began."

"He needs more. There's a stream ahead."

Nergal said, "I have no love for water. He's lucky to have any at all."

Dow felt himself cut from the cart, light paining his eyes as the sack was pulled off, his face shoved into cool water. He gulped it in.

"Those men kidnapped you?" said the devil's voice, a cracked parody of Sariel's.

"And forced me to come here to find you. They were after the boy. Thank God you are such a stout defender, Nergal, thank God." Dow knew that voice too. Was it real? The pardoner. Well, that one was unlikely to forgive Dow, who had turned him out to fend for himself in the wilds.

←→

Dow was back on the cart. They skirted Paris. Despenser was not there, said Osbert. Days of more travel, not so tightly bound. Osbert wore the angel's armor—the sword at his side—with the high seriousness of a little boy dressed up in his father's gear. Dow found the sight ridiculous, even through his pain.

Soon they were traveling at the rear of an army.

"Make way for the king's men!" shouted Osbert, though many marveled aloud to see such a finely dressed knight on a cart. Osbert bought a hobby from the retinue of a southern chevalier and spent most of the journey trying to control it until he tied it to the cart to force it to step on.

With regular water, though still no food, Dow began to recover slightly.

Every sound had the pardoner flinching. Even a sudden blast of hail had him dropping beneath the shield, screaming about arrows.

"You know they intend to kill me," said Dow to Osbert.

"You don't know that. Look . . ." Osbert whispered. "Between you and me, it's no good to me with you going to Despenser. I'm going to try to get you to Edward. It's the only way I'll get paid from this." He spoke as if that might be Dow's chief concern.

"So *he* can kill me?"

"Well, he'll kill you later than Despenser, and we'll be on him in a couple of days according to this lot here. Look, there's one of his devils flying in the distance."

There was too—the size of a man, bat-winged, wheeling from the dark clouds. Up ahead was something more ominous. The clouds themselves seemed to glow and Dow thought he could see immense figures peering down from them, bright and haloed. Philip's angels. Four of them, painting the rainblack sky with gold.

"You couldn't just pretend to convert, could you?" said Osbert. "I could keep you in my office and you could be my assistant. Wine. Whores. Food. Everything a man needs for a happy and contented life."

Dow said nothing and the pardoner threw up his hands. He added, "All right, all right, I just thought I'd ask. Do you realize how inconvenient your attitude is for other people? Might it be time to think of them, for a change? This means Edward is my only option, and not a very good one looking at the size of this army."

Nergal sang:

God's blessing they have,
Holy fire they hold.
But they have not the Antichrist,
"More precious than gold!

Don't shout about it," said Osbert.

The press was too great now for the cart to make it through. They were on the army's baggage train and it blocked the road completely, the whole procession going at the pace of the slowest, most rickety cart, overloaded, pulled by the most miserable horses—the ones who were blown, tired, and sick. Knights trailing banners and pennants muscled their horses through, cursing the rabble, though the poorer people were content that the column should crawl. Ahead of them, they knew, were the English.

"If we don't get to Despenser soon, the battle's going to be over and he might even be dead," said Osbert. "We need to hurry up. We should ditch this cart."

Dow guessed Osbert had thought that he might be easier to liberate in the crush of the road. That seemed impossible now.

"I can't see the reward in this," said Osbert.

"Many men are to die," said Dow.

"Yes, but I'm rather concerned about what happens after the battle. I hope my position is secure."

"Shut up. We'll walk," said Nergal.

They pressed on, drawing comments and whoops of amazement as they passed—a slight, pale woman dragging a strong lad by the neck, a lit lantern in her free hand.

Dusk came down and now the angels were easy to see. Sometimes they appeared as a sunburst behind a cloud, sometimes as giant and beautiful creatures floating upon it. It was difficult to see how far away they were—the angels appeared near, but they were massive, and after an hour's walk they were still halfway to the horizon. The baggage trains were full of weapons now—giant shields for the crossbowmen, great sheaves of quarrels. No sign of the crossbowmen, though—all at the front of the column.

"Looks like England will have a new king by the end of the week," said Osbert.

"Or none," said Dow.

"Forget it; it all collapses without kings. Look, your only chance of survival is to declare for God. Convert and I can get you to Philip. I reckon Edward is a plucked goose."

"He's going to Despenser," said Nergal, tugging Dow along.

Dow said nothing. Four angels. He could have killed them, had he not stood on principle and failed to get the banner. He had done the right thing to spare the king's life. But now what? Would England ever hand over the lands to Free Hell?

The three took to the fields, as many did, as if the road was a river and they part of a human flood. It was a hot August but a close one, the dark clouds full of rain. To the front of the column they saw the winged devils wheeling in spirals under the angel light.

Dow had the impression of two darknesses—the clouds above, the writhing devils below, and between them a light at once fragile and mighty. The light was like the sun in her veil of rain on the moors, like the green light of the river pools he'd swum in as child, like the shifting blue light of the sea, and the lilac light of evening where the hawk hangs waiting, like the light of the stars and the moon, and the light of his mother's eyes—like all the remembered light that had ever comforted him or thrilled him.

They were arriving late in the day. Now there was a light from the south, a comet, a shooting star blazing through the sky to the head of the column.

They were nearly there, beneath the angels, their vast inscrutable faces staring down from the clouds.

"Let's hope they don't shit," said Osbert. "London pigeons are bad enough."

Knights were crammed into the lane here, fully armed and armored, clanking against each other in the press. Horses screamed and panicked, riders shouting at them, at one another, at their pages and grooms.

"They can't mean to attack today," whispered Osbert to Dow. "I need time to get to Edward."

Nergal strode on, tugging the boy behind him.

"Look, Nergal. Have you considered any other buyers for this Antichrist? Despenser is simply not offering you the best deal."

"Favor with Satan is the very best deal," said Nergal. "And look, there ahead is my master Despenser's red lion slouching on his banners!"

A shout came from the front of the line: "France! France!" Trumpets blew. It spat with rain, though it was hot and the sun shone strongly up the hill toward the English lines.

There was no way through at all now—knights pushed, horses kicked, one panicking, and in trying to climb the bank of the lane, sending its rider crashing to the floor. Those around him tried to make room, but it was impossible. So many colors, so many sigils and banners.

It was the most magnificent rabble Dow had ever seen. They skirted it by two hundred paces, through lines of squabbling crossbowmen. The rain came down hard—the crossbow captains were screaming at their men and Dow didn't need to speak Genoese to understand that the crossbowmen were not happy to deploy so late in the day in such weather. The captains gestured to the blazing angels and, Dow guessed, told them God was on their side. The men ran up the hill, forming into their lines before the English.

Nergal pushed on to the front of the line. Dow whispered for Murmur to release him, but Murmur didn't come.

"I heard that," said Osbert. "Your flying devil's likely keeping a low profile. The angels are keeping it away, I should guess."

Death, then, thought Dow.

Despenser's banner was twenty yards away now when the giant loomed into view—massive in mail and helm, a huge sword in his hand, attended by eight winged gargoyles. The rain stopped as suddenly as it had begun.

"Lord!" Nergal called out to him.

He said, "What? You have him, Nergal? You have the Antichrist!"

"Yes!"

Despenser strode forward, each step eating the ground between them. Dow trembled.

There was a noise like a great wind. The English longbows had fired. Screams and shouts from the Genoese. The crossbowmen were dying.

"This is he?" said Despenser, jabbing a rotting finger at Dow.

"Yes, lord."

Despenser, a walking corpse, stared down at Dow. "He is not as I imagined. I think you are wrong."

Nergal said, "No, lord, he was there with the old king. He invoked me in the name of his mother. It is him."

More sounds like the wind, almost constantly now. The screams were louder, shouting too. The crossbowmen had lost the encounter with the longbows and were running back into the French lines. A noble voice shouted a curse at them.

"He'll die, anyway," said Despenser. "I need Satan's favor before this battle begins, Edward's got legions of devils down there. Archers with blessed arrows too."

"The angels will take care of them," said Nergal.

"And maybe us too," said Despenser. He sniffed. "They'll probably just play in the lightning of this storm. Let's hope so. You, sorcerer," he addressed Osbert.

"Lord?" Osbert replied.

"What are you doing here?" Despenser asked him.

"I am your sorcerer, lord."

"When did you last summon me a devil? I hear talk that you've been scrabbling behind my back. Talking treachery!"

"No, lord! The little cracks we have opened in the walls of Hell have been sealed. I have been lucky to achieve what I have." He gestured to Nergal.

"You'll summon me a devil within a week of this battle ending or you'll die in as unpleasant a way as I can devise. At the moment I'm favoring crushing by pebbles—one extra a day for a year."

"That's really unfair!" said Osbert.

"Don't think you'll avoid my devils in Hell, either," said Despenser. "If you think life's unfair, you should try death!"

There was a disturbance at the front of the line. The trumpets of Navarre had sounded and its knights charged, howling. The men and devils around Despenser were caught in the excitement and themselves charged down the hill, the gargoyles lumbering into the air with a terrible sound of stone on stone. Despenser pushed down the visor on his great helmet. "Now, Satan, accept this offering and bring me victory!" he shouted.

"Can we not bargain?" said the pardoner. He stood in front of Dow, but Despenser's sword swung at the young man.

"Oh, God!" said Osbert as he realized what was happening. The Sacred Heart shield jumped on his arm and turned Despenser's blow aside perfectly.

Despenser screamed and hacked again, but the shield had a life of its own, moving to catch the blow and save Dow again. "No!" shouted Osbert. "This is entirely inappropriate, shield! Let him kill the boy!"

"Now you're going to die!" yelled Despenser. He lifted his sword once more.

"Get off me!" said Osbert, poking with the holy sword. Once more the shield took Despenser's blow, but the giant had leapt forward and the sword snagged in his coat of plates. His armor was nothing against the Heavenly blade and it went into his belly to the hilt.

"That was a mistake, lord," said Osbert. "And I hope it will not affect your view of the good work I have done for you in the past, nor the possibility of us working together in the future."

Despenser muttered, "I . . . I . . . I'm . . ."

If Despenser had any other words, then neither Dow nor Osbert heard them. Nergal swallowed his candle and—with a demented roar—breathed fire all over Osbert. Again the shield swung around, deflecting the flame.

Dow felt light building inside him, an enormous energy that leaked from his eyes, from his mouth, from the scar on his chest.

"Hang on, I didn't attack you, don't do this to me!" screamed Nergal at Dow. "Satan! Satan! Take me hence!" Nergal crossed himself and Dow erupted with light.

15

C an you persuade the French angels away?" said Edward. His angel shone above Crécy Wood, armored, bearing a shield, with a spear in its hand. Edward looked out from the top of the windmill that stood above the battlefield, gazing up at the shining creature.

"No. They wait to see the sacrifice of the French and then they will act."

Edward crossed himself. Thank God Philip had detoured to Abbeville on the way there. There had been time to dig pits in front of the archers to trip the incoming horses, to choose the best defensive position on top of the hill, to set the bombards, for whatever good they would do, to bless the arrows of the archers and the swords of the men-at-arms.

But Edward was sure Philip had reinforced at Abbeville—the black bat standard of Jaime of Majorca was visible, the white and red lions of blind King John of Luxembourg, the black and yellow chevron of Hainault, the arms of Savoy and of many German princes. How many in total? Maybe thirty thousand—among them six or seven thousand men-at-arms, largely mounted—and a similar number of crossbowmen. Outnumbered three, maybe four to one, similarly in angels.

And what of devils? Edward had his division of pig-men devils, a flight of gargoyles, about twenty flaming devils, and a crack squad of leopard men under Lord Sloth. The rest had got strung out across the country, absorbed in plunder, burned by angels, or fallen foul of raiding parties of Philip's stoneskins.

Edward concentrated on the angel. "Can you keep away the devils?"

The angel said, "The devils punish for God. Any who die by their hand are ordained to do so by Him on high."

Edward said, "He has five divisions of them. We have two."

"There is a fourth angel here."

"A fourth?" asked Edward.

"Jophiel of Navarre."

"So four oppose us."

"Perhaps not so."

Edward said, "How not so?"

"It seems unconvinced of the holy right of the French king."

"Can you draw it to our side?"

"No. But it may argue with our brethren to see more evidence of piety, a greater willingness to sacrifice."

He said, "Get it to make that argument. And if you can, get it to tell its men to charge us. We need an early charge from the enemy."

"You are king." The angel sparkled above the wood and stretched out its hands. The angels on the cloud above the French army stretched out theirs too. Edward guessed they were communicating.

He remembered the tales of Bannockburn where his father had fought the Scots. There the angels had wanted to see a great sacrifice of men before they would act, but they dithered so long that, by the time they deemed enough English blood had been spilled, the battle had been lost and they decided God had made His position clear. But at Bannockburn a large force of Englishmen had been defeated by a smaller Scottish army by provoking an early charge from the English horse. That was the model he'd use.

"Get the devils in the line to goad them too," said Edward.

"I will lead," said Sloth.

"Good," said Edward, "but don't goad them for too long. They have more devils and more angels than us. Taunt the line and retreat. And you, angel, can you make it rain?"

"I am the rain."

"Is that a yes or a no?" Edward's patience with angels was thin at the best of times, without having to listen to these nonsensical statements.

"Yes."

"Then do. They're the ones who have to move, we'll be staying still. Let's see it slippery for them. Give it a while for the Genoese crossbows to get a soaking, then get into them."

Edward watched as Lord Sloth mustered his leopard men. The rain started to pour and Edward couldn't help laughing. Fifteen years of chapel building, of prayer and donations to monasteries, of attempted crusades and reckless war he'd given God. What did he get for it? A rain shower.

The French army was still spilling from the road through the woods, fanning out across the field. There were a lot of them—banners of every description.

Edward saw a huge figure towering over the wagons and the horses. That must be Despenser, he thought. Around him swarmed smoke devils and above him a flight of gargoyles. Edward ordered the Drago unfolded to ensnare them. Who would attack first? The devils must guess that the English arrows would be blessed. Best soften up the line with crossbow fire before attacking. Through the driving rain, almost exactly as the thought crossed his mind, he saw the Genoese coming forward. No shields. He turned to Cobham.

The king said, "Fire only unblessed arrows at the crossbows. The devils can charge in under our own arrow fire."

He replied, "Very good."

The Genoese kept coming, the English army hurling insults through the rain, a few idiots loosing too early, their arrows falling short. One hundred and fifty paces, Edward knew, was the distance the crossbows would try to engage—at the limit of the longbow's power but well within their own range, sheltering behind their great shields to fire in turns at an impressive rate.

But they had no shields. And in this weather, with wet strings, firing uphill and . . . The angel lit up behind him, bright as the sunset. Yes! Now they would have to fire into the light and a crossbowman depended much more on aim than a longbow. The longbows dropped their arrows at a distance in a swarm. Each crossbowman picked his target.

Lord Sloth and his leopard men were astride their horses. They rode them not for speed but for protection. If the crossbowmen had blessed their quarrels, then the horse offered a formidable shield to the devils as they poured in. Behind them stood ranks of pig-headed devils—the 20th Legion of Dis. Behind them winged gargoyles clattered and chattered, ready to go. Edward was glad of such troops. They knew how to take an order.

Now they would need to. The crossbowmen formed up in scuttling ranks—impressive to see such trained troops at their work. Edward signaled to his bannerman and lowered the banner. It was the sign for the archers to fire. They did. Ten volleys and the crossbowmen were buckling. Another five and they were in flight.

Edward's bannerman held the banner aloft and a flight of gargoyles went cawing to the fight, Lord Sloth and his devils underneath them snarling for blood. Sloth caught a crossbowman and tore off his head, but the French knights charged into the arrow storm. Devils were impervious to the arrows, as were the men in their armor, but the horses suffered and died dreadfully. One horse tried to charge Sloth down, but he picked it up, rider and all, and hurled it into the air.

A flash from the French lines, an unbearable bright light. Had an angel materialized? No, but for some reason the French devils chattered and screamed, panicking, pushing out through their mounted men-at-arms. Shoved and jostled by loping stretched men, by dogmen and burning devils, the horsemen had no option but to charge.

Masses of French horses came down on the English devils. A lance went clean through a leopard man; a sword hacked off a swooping gargoyle's wing as it tried to rip the count of Foix from his mount. It traveled a little way before spinning wildly and crashing hard into the mud where a French lance ran it through.

Arrows fell in black sheets, horses screamed and fell beneath the knights. In the mud, those who could stand fought the devils—the ones with blessed weapons standing a chance, the others not.

16

O sbert got the boy up onto a cart. The devil had vanished when the great light had burst out of Dow and the battle had gone wild, but now Dow was unconscious. God knew what was happening down that hill. Osbert, had he ever imagined a battle, thought of it as orderly lines of knights and men-at-arms charging and retreating in a disciplined way.

This was chaos, people running everywhere, every direction, friend indistinguishable from enemy. Devils tangled in the skies—the buzzing night-born men clashing with stoneskins, swarms of insect devils fighting with monstrous birds. Osbert knew only one thing—he was off.

Osbert drove the cart as best he could away from the site of the mêlée. Who had started the attack? Osbert had heard "France! France!" The explosion from the middle of the French camp had been enough to send its men-at-arms crazy and they had spurred their mounts into the fight.

The sky poured rain, there was a dreadful screaming from down the hill—and then the cart had got stuck up against a ditch. How can you lose your way out of a field? In the panic, Osbert had managed it.

He had to get the boy away. Dow would fetch a good price from someone. First, Osbert had to make it to the English, and the English had to make it through the day. He looked up at the angels. They were gazing out over the battlefield. Across the rainy valley he could see another light—a shifting green and blue. The English angels? He put his hand to his eyes. Yes, he could see a giant face shining from behind a rain cloud, turning the air around it to stained glass.

Get out, get out! What to do? Christ's fat balls! Men were coming back up the hill, or something like men. The Genoese, arrows sprouting from their arms and legs, caught in the thick padding of their gambesons—so many hedgehogs running back through the lines.

"Navarre! Navarre!" Cavalry charged through them, spinning them around, trampling them down. Oh, God. Osbert looked up—the angels were still gazing down.

Screaming and crowing, a flight of gargoyles swept over him, arrowing into the English. Tendrils reached up from the English lines to snare them and then recoiled under a blaze of light. Philip was galloping his charger to the front of his line, with the sun on a pole borne alongside—the Oriflamme burning out its blood light.

Oh, God—the gargoyles slammed into other shapes floating in the air—monstrous birds, leaping devils with long legs like grasshoppers, springing up to fight the gargoyles in the sky. The English couldn't break through, could they? Not under four angels. Osbert couldn't make the cart move; it was rutted deep in the clay soil.

"Help me!" he called out as there was a rumble from his right. The knights who had mustered nearby had charged. Those who had not had charged too, everyone from the lane leading to the battlefield putting his spurs into his horse—some spilling out on to the field of combat, others just careening into their fellows. Osbert ran back to see if he could get a loose horse to help pull out his cart.

Christ! He'd never seen such bravery or such foolishness. Boar men charged from the English side, and Despenser's wasp devils flew down the hill to back up the French knights. The fighting was brutal and the knights quickly discovered whose swords bore the real teeth, hair and bones of saints and who had been sold something else.

Music was all about him, the notes like cold fingers down his spine. Osbert looked above him. An angel had a pipe at its lips and was playing a dizzying tune. The reason the devils had been held back was plain—the French needed to give their own knights a chance to prove their bravery, to sacrifice themselves, to prove to God they were worthy of his aid.

Above the English a single angel replied to the piping with a flute of its own, the music equally as giddying. *Smack!* A fat gargoyle hit the dirt beside Osbert, not four paces away. That could have killed him! It was huge, solid, its stony skin pierced by a barbed spear. Another gargoyle spun away. How they told friend from foe, Osbert didn't know. Philip rode the line, the Oriflamme burning in his hands, incinerating arrows fired from a cloud of tiny demons above him. What if Philip was killed? What if Edward was killed?

Osbert tried to enlist a couple of foot soldiers to help him with his cart, but everyone was transfixed by the battle. The knights charged and charged again, arrows raining down, horses dying, devils tearing off heads and themselves being torn. The ground was mountained with dead.

A blink. The English angel disappeared and an angel from the cloud above stretched out a finger. A division of English archers disappeared beneath a tongue of fire. The angels had negotiated and come to France's aid, which meant the main market for the Antichrist was about to go up in holy fire. Two hundred boar men, who had rallied—having been dispersed by a charge of crow-headed devils—were burned as they mustered for a charge.

Osbert had a living to make. Dow was all he had—one Antichrist, slightly worn.

Would Navarre buy him if the English lost? The French regarded him as their property.

A cry went up from the French line. "France! France! God is with France!" A road of fire appeared, burning through the stakes the English had in place. Still the archers stood, pouring down death on the knights. The English men-at-arms charged into the stricken horses, the enmired men-at-arms.

"See our valor! Come to our aid, angels; we are as worthy as the French and as willing to die for God!" Even at a distance of nearly six hundred paces, Osbert could hear the desperation in their voices.

Osbert had seen enough. He had to get his only treasure away, the battle would be won soon, and the men would begin to plunder. Without protection, he would lose Dow.

He ran to Dow to get him off the cart, standing up on it.

A streak of fire on the horizon, a shimmering in the light. There was a big thump on the cart and there in front of him was an extraordinary sight.

Wrapped in a badly stitched cloak of angel feathers—actually a horse blanket with the feathers just stuck into it—was the man he had seen in the priest's cellar, the little Italian banker. He was sitting on top of a long box marked with magical symbols and what Osbert guessed were the secret names of God—they looked like the stuff he carved onto his laminas.

Osbert looked up. Was this a gift from God?

The banker said, "I have wished to be with the chief sorcerer of the French court—he who procures relics and magical items."

"You're looking at him," said Osbert.

"I have here a magical banner. I have come to bargain for . . ." Bardi—that was his name, Osbert remembered—was heavily sick. Bardi tried to stand but looked like a stuck fly. He said, "I'm sorry, I am stricken by the manner of travel. The rags I have here are soaked in angels' blood. Put one to my lips."

An arrow smacked off the back of Osbert's angel helm.

"Are you having a laugh?" said the pardoner. He stripped Bardi of absolutely everything he had on him—including his rather well-tailored monk's habit—and slung him naked into the mud.

"That's mine!" shouted Bardi. He rolled over and screamed as an arrow fell limply from the sky to stick into his arse.

"Don't look like it from where I'm standing, son!" said Osbert. Bardi tried to reach up, but he was too weak.

The banner! The one all the fuss had been about! *Praise God!* But how to move it? Osbert just couldn't lift it from the cart. The chest was too heavy. But it was only supposed to be a banner. That, by definition, had to be portable. He used his devil knife to cut away the dead briars that were wound around the lid. Men were all about him, screaming, cheering, goading on the angels. There was a great roar and an angel came forward on a horse that seemed half smoke, all color, cracking the sky with light. Osbert banged the knife into the line between the body of the chest and the lid, working it free.

"Hey, what are you doing?" A fish-headed devil faced him, along with three foot soldiers.

Osbert said, "Just some worthless things, friends. I am a pardoner and hope to sell a few trinkets so our brave Frenchmen may have something to bless and thank God for the victory."

"There's trinkets in there?" said one.

"Nothing. The teeth of pigs, the hair of dogs. I am a pardoner, friends, you know our trade. A little comfort for a little money."

Another roar of fire from above. Osbert felt himself flinch, though he tried to look brave.

"I want to see," said a foot soldier. "I reckon you're a plunderer and an English plunderer at that. You don't sound French. And you don't look like a pardoner. You're an English knight, you bastard! Where are you from? A Breton?"

He said, "It's a banner, nothing more than a tattered old banner that I had knocked up on the Rue De St. Denis."

"So it was teeth and now it's a banner. Show me," said the foot soldier.

The angels above swayed and turned, their hands trailing fire. On the field men screamed—some exultant, some dying. Osbert wanted away desperately and feared the soldiers would snatch his prize from him. But holy banners never looked in top condition. He was sure it would be a moth-eaten old thing and that he could convince the soldiers it was worthless.

"Look," he said, and pried off the lid.

17

M ontagu told his men to hold firm, to keep shooting their arrows. He said, "The angels will not support dead men. Keep killing! Kill until you are killed!"

Fire was everywhere, among the men-at-arms, among the archers. The bombards on the right flank had ceased firing, consumed in smoke and the windmill where Edward had been was ablaze.

Edward charged down the hill, his guard around him, holding up his sword and screaming at the angels, "I am Edward, chosen of God! Rightful king of the English and a good man. I have built chapels, I have given greatly to the poor, I am here now to strike at my enemies and defend my churches where God dwells! Abate your fire!"

Still tongues of flame poured down but none touched the king. Men crowded to be near him, a rank of archers almost overwhelming the horses. Nobles were calling out their family names, telling the angels they were appointed by God, begging them to cease the fire. Cobham got in among the archers on the right, his men swinging their pennants up at the angels to get them to recognize their nobility, to give them pause. The fire faltered but, if France's divine powers were uncertain, its worldly ones were not.

To Montagu's left he saw the blue and yellow colors of Alençon go steaming in to the prince of Wales's division, five hundred men-at-arms charging straight at the prince's standard, the horses' caparisons billowing.

Still it rained, but the English angel was long gone. Devils were overwhelming the English lines. Montagu leapt to the defense of his archers, cutting down a huge crow devil as it tried to rip one from the ground to carry him into the sky.

In the middle of the battlefield a wedge of steaming devils—like those from a painting, goat-legged, red, and with horns—pushed toward the king's position. The Drago snapped and whipped at gargoyles in the sky, but it seemed to Montagu that it was taking devils indiscriminately, tearing down French crows, English gargoyles, then English crows, and French gargoyles.

Fire swept through Montagu's men again and he held up Arondight to deflect it. The angels would recognize someone carrying a weapon like that as blessed of God and the fire would not harm them.

Lord Sloth had taken up the prince of Wales's banner. The Iron Lion had a pawful of arrows and he bit off their heads to spit them into the charging French. Five men went down under his blast. He roared and roared again, felling horses, felling men. The prince of Wales was close by him, hemmed in, fighting off enemies on all sides. A jackal-headed devil, its body that of a lizard, leapt toward him—but the prince skewered it with his sword. He lost the weapon in the creature's body and drew his misericorde, the dagger his only weapon now.

Montagu charged in, hacking all around him. Alençon himself had his hands on the banner. If that went down, the whole flank would panic and run. More fire, more screams. The angels poured down death on the English. Montagu cut his way through a thicket of men to reach Alençon, Arondight shining white as it cut arcs of crimson.

Alençon threw the banner down but Montagu pierced, the sword cutting easily through the mail. As he died, the count recognized his killer.

He said, "I thought you were dead."

Montagu replied, "No, that's you."

"Then please give my regards to your wife," said Alençon, clutching the sword in his belly. "My daughters appreciated her kindness on our last stay."

"I shall if I see her," said Montagu. "You die a true and chivalrous knight."

He shoved Alençon off his sword and picked the banner off the floor.

"Montagu! Montagu!" he shouted. It was just reflex, just what he had always done, rallied his troops, shown them he was in the thick of the fight.

The prince of Wales grabbed a sword. How many enemies about them now? The angels would not use their fire against a royal banner and Montagu knew they must now stand or die on their own fighting skills.

A blast from the bombards as the smoke cleared. French horses screamed and whinnied. The horseman wheeled and charged the archers again, and again. How many charges now? Seven? Eight? If the angels eliminated all the archers then surely they would get through. Nine charges, ten—and the arrows still vomited forth. The angels' fire ceased, why, Montagu didn't know. Angels were unfathomable—likely the death of so many Frenchmen under the arrows had only bought so many favors. They must want to see more. They got more. The horsemen charged again and again. Fourteen charges, fifteen.

The prince of Wales was coming toward him. "You've been named a traitor, Uncle." He pointed his sword toward Montagu.

More French, men-at-arms on foot—ten of them.

"Montagu! Montagu!" Montagu screamed into the faces of the Frenchmen. Montagu was not a conceited man, but he knew his presence on the field was worth a little courage to his own men, a little fear to the enemy.

"The boar! The boar!" Prince Edward screamed his father's nickname as they closed with the enemy.

Montagu was hampered by the standard but he used it in place of his shield, to block blows. One Frenchman came running in with a greatsword above his head. Montagu dispatched him with a thrust to the throat. Another attacker behind him bore a spear, but Montagu flicked the standard toward him, obscuring his vision, before dropping to stab up underneath the hauberk into the man's groin.

Prince Edward flung away two men with prodigious strength, slew another, but lost his sword once more. A third—bearing a surcoat of a golden rabbits—ran at Montagu, slicing into his fingers. Arondight fell to the mud, but the Frenchman signaled his next attack too clearly, drawing back his sword. Montagu stepped under the blow.

Four French were on the prince of Wales. The Oriflamme had cast its blood light over the field. No prisoners were supposed to be taken, but these men weren't going to worry about that. They wanted young Edward alive—great fortunes could be made that way. Montagu's right hand was useless, but he planted the standard and drew his misericorde with his left and leapt at a man, punching the blade into his unprotected face. The man screamed, the prince kicked another. The prince stood. Montagu felt all the breath leave him. Something had hit him. He fell to one knee, supporting himself on the standard.

Cobham's men came charging down the hill, banners streaming, and the French fled, but the battle was lost. Everything was burning. The Oriflamme shone, the angels poured fire, arrows only picked at the enemy. Disarray everywhere.

Montagu said, "Blind John's ready to charge." That mad bastard, John of Bohemia, unable to see past the end of his nose.

Prince Edward said, "You're dead, Uncle."

"What?"

Montagu looked into the prince's eyes. They were an intense blue, more intense than he had ever seen them, as if the battle had drawn it forth.

The prince smiled and Montagu saw for the first time that his teeth were sharp and pointed, like a dog's. He'd asked Isabella what she'd given to ensure the help of devils—now Montagu knew. Her grandson. She'd allowed devils to corrupt the royal line.

The prince said, "A little needle has pricked your thumb."

Montagu realized he had a spear straight through him. He would soon die.

"Have you anything you'd like to say?"

He replied, "My wife, my daughters, you know the sort of thing. Love and all that." Montagu had never been comfortable with overbearing expressions of emotion.

"My grandmother?"

"I have given her one gift she craved. Now I give another. I go now to pay the price for loving such as she."

Devils at the court. It should never be, not in such a position. A devil to serve, yes. To rule? What would become of England?

A high, melodious piping from the French side and the angels spoke as one.

"God favors France. The English imposter is thrown back. God favors France! Great nobles of the great houses, aided by our fire, now sweep the rebel from the field."

"All over," said Montagu.

"All over," said the prince, "though sooner for you." He took out his misericorde. Then he thought better of it, apparently. "A longer death for you, I think. No point in disguising my nature now. I will let the spell fall a little further."

He stood and Montagu saw that the hands that grasped the sword were talons. A pointed tail flicked from underneath his hauberk and horns grew on his head.

Montagu looked around him, the smoking ruins of the English lines. John's horsemen were gathering not one hundred yards away down the slope. It would be slaughter. Montagu stood, forwarding the standard, intending to use it to dislodge a horseman if he could. The pain in his guts was immense, but he knew it would be stupid to remove the spear. That could kill him. Leave it in and he could fight maybe for an hour—as plenty had done before him.

The shaking of mail, the drum of hooves, John's line was. Prepare to die. Or don't. Prepared or not, the outcome would be the same. Montagu found Arondight, took it up, the worn grip unfamiliar in his left hand. He asked forgiveness for his sins, called on St. Anne—but St. Anne wasn't there.

The pipes of the angels sounded, fire was all around again, and then the dragon struck.

18

T he noise brought Dow around on the cart. In front of him, ten paces about, the grass was burned and the giant Despenser was dead on the ground. Dow felt cold and weak and remembered only the light leaving him.

Above him, night had fallen, but the sky was fire from horizon to horizon, and the sound was like the throat of a smith's furnace but many, many times louder. He saw angels, spears shining, shields gleaming, gigantic things that now filled the horizon, charging into battle—but caught in coils of fire that streamed up from the very bottom of the field. The heavens screamed and boomed and something turned above Dow—the head of a monstrous dragon, shaped in fire of gold and green, tearing an angel from the sky, crunching it and ripping it, the Heavenly creature dying in flashes of light.

The Evertere, it had to be the Evertere! The banner had been released.

An angel wheeled in the east, turning its horse of glittering smoke toward the banner, its spear a shaft of light, its armor shining emerald. Michael was facing the banner.

Up above him on the ground the English archers were reforming, taking advantage of the hesitation of the French men-at-arms who sat on their horses open-mouthed, gazing up at the burning sky. The French were no more than one hundred paces away, being driven down the hill by a standard-bearer who had a spear through him. Montagu, who he'd seen on the boat.

On the hill, the English reserve under the king's flag waited, Dow saw. The angels had burned the front lines of the English army, but a substantial number of bowmen had survived, along with a number of leopard devils. One—an enormous gray thing with a clanking iron mane—was roaring his devils into order.

The English, if the French did not act soon, would counterattack, but all the French nobles seemed transfixed by the sky. One hundred paces to his left, Dow saw the Oriflamme and under it the French king, utterly motionless. Even his devils stood crossing themselves as the angels were torn and died.

Where was Nergal, who had taken his mother's body? Nowhere. He had vanished in the light.

Dow needed the Evertere. If he could get his hands on it, he could summon all the demons of the earth to his side. For what, though? Nothing here. He wouldn't risk them in this meaningless conflict of kings. He should take the banner and run, call his army in secret and strike when the time was right, in Paris or in London, not in some sodden field.

Next to him on the cart, the tail of the great dragon was still pouring like a column of fire from the chest up into the heavens. It had an angel in its jaws and bit down, shattering its body in a burst of golden light that seemed to flow into, rather than out of, the body of the angel. The sky darkened and the French panicked, men streaming from the field.

The pardoner was next to the cart, sitting in the mud, a number of men-at-arms unconscious on the ground beside him, a fish-headed devil flat on its back and a man face down in the filth.

"Sorry!" said Osbert. "Sorry! I didn't think it was going to do that."

"What did you expect?" said Dow.

"That it wouldn't work! Clearly, that it wouldn't work!"

Dow saw now that the tail of the Evertere was not a tail nor a column of fire but, at its base, something like a torch holder. No angels were visible in the sky and the great dragon roared above the battlefield, belching fire into the unnatural darkness. Dow took up the holder and held it above his head, feeling the great flame body of the dragon writhing above him. He saw the French king along the line, under his Oriflamme, and a wave of hate sprang up in him.

"Attack!" he said.

The great dragon bent its head, snapping toward the king, but the king's standard-bearer fought back with the Oriflamme, keeping it at bay, a great dome of red light forcing the dragon back. The action brought the French men-at-arms out of their stupor.

"Bohemia!" Blind John roared, and the cavalry charged, but their devils did not go with them, still cowering in front of the Evertere. The sky was black with arrows and Dow instinctively ducked. An arrow struck him in the cheek. Still he clung to the banner.

"Get it back in the box!" The pardoner was at his side.

"Never!" Dow cried out.

Osbert said, "Get it back in the box. There are all sorts of sorcerers out there, and your good Luciferians are the ones sending down the arrows. They may kill you without knowing who you are. Get it back in the box and we will fight another day."

Another arrow scratched Dow and the pardoner grabbed onto him.

"Put it back. Do you want the high men to get this?"

Dow said, "God himself only just managed to contain it last time."

"That's mine!" said a voice like a cat's. It was an adolescent boy, with six cats behind him.

"Sod off, spotty," said the pardoner.

The boy leapt up onto the cart. He said, "I, Charles of Navarre, claim that in the name of Hell!" The creature made a grab for the Evertere.

Another flight of arrows. Osbert ducked behind the Sacred Heart shield, though one went penetrated through to his leg. It bounced away from the angelic hauberk. Dow, though, had been hit twice more. He sank to the base of the cart, grasping still at the Evertere.

"You," said Charles to the pardoner, "would be more tolerable as a corpse."

He went to seize Osbert, but the pardoner brought up something from his side and flicked it at the boy—it was a piece of blood-soaked rag.

The boy screamed and fell back off the cart. The horses, though shielded by the cart, were panicking and stamping. Osbert put the shield up above Dow as more arrows rattled in.

"See!" said the pardoner. "They'll have this from you and you're about to die. Let me steal it away. The English are coming. You've either killed or driven off all the angels. Put the banner away!"

The English devils were surrounding the French king but could not penetrate the light of the Oriflamme. Instead a party of men-at-arms charged the banner. The Oriflamme went down, the blood light dimming, and the tendrils of the Drago, unleashed by Edward, shot out from the English line to engulf the devils of France.

Dow remembered what Sariel had said of Osbert, how she had seemed to find something good in him. He said to him, "Shield me." Dow pulled down the banner, whirling it around and around; soon the fire dragon caught up in a whipping whirlwind, a great cone of fire, until it was a ball of intense green and red fire, spitting and shimmering on the end of the torch holder.

The French cavalry had fallen under the arrows, the English were running in. Dow put the Evertere back in the chest and the pardoner snapped shut the lid.

"If your lot want this banner, they can pay for it like everyone else! Here, never say I give you nothing! I nicked it off you when you cut the angel anyway!" said Osbert. He pressed a small vial into Dow's fingers.

"Now, farewell!" Osbert put his boot into Dow's side and kicked him from the cart. He prodded the horses forward and set off along the track, crying out, "England! England! Edward conquers the land!" as the French men-at-arms rushed in to make a last stand.

Dow felt his life ebbing away. "Mother," he said, "protect our cause."

19

T he angel led Montagu on. Around him the French knights were being killed, some dispatched by bowmen, some eaten by devils. He saw the hideous Lord Sloth, his hide hanging with arrows, devouring the corpse of Louis of Blois, the blue and white bells of the count's surcoat soaked in his blood as the lion swallowed his head whole.

Montagu was angry—Edward should not have allowed this. Prisoners should be taken. Many of these knights were personal friends of Edward's and had shared the tournament field with him. This was no way to act after a battle—the vanquished should be tended to and fed in the king's own tent. Montagu wanted to stop the slaughter but he couldn't; dressed in rags as he was, he'd never be taken seriously.

The spear through him hurt terribly now and Montagu knew he didn't have long to live—the appearance of the angel was enough to tell him that. She was an odd sort of angel, her green dress torn, her hair disheveled. Sariel!

She led him on through the slaughter field, out to the French lines. Philip had fled, it seemed, though his standard had been captured, and the Oriflamme lay on the ground. No one but a true king would be foolish enough to pick it up. The angels were all gone and Montagu was full of anguish at that. He had seen the dragon tear at them, seen Lucifer's victory blazing in the heavens. And now what? England given over to devils. Even if Montagu accepted they were on God's side, then they were gaolers, no more than guards. To think of such a lowborn thing on the throne of England filled him with disgust.

He staggered on, the angel leading him by his one good hand. There was devastation here. He found Greatbelly among the dead men and horses, holding a boy stuck through with a spear. Montagu could see by the pallor of the youth's face that he was as good as dead. "You said you'd keep 'em safe!" she said. Montagu had no words for her.

The angel led him on, Greatbelly trailing behind.

Up on the hill Lord Sloth had finished his feast and gave a great roar of victory.

"This is the cost of Eden," said Greatbelly. The boy was scarcely breathing, but he grasped at something in his fist that he fiercely defended when Greatbelly tried to take it away.

She said, "This was him, the sweet Antichrist. He is dying. Do our hopes die with him?"

"Your hopes were the hopes of fools," said Montagu. "Do you really think you could defend your lands against the king of France?"

"The king of France is beaten," said Greatbelly.

"Not so. This is no more than a raid. Edward will dump you here and go home. You cannot defend this. Edward cannot defend this. He can burn the land a while longer, plunder and kill but there are no supply lines, no defense. Philip will come again."

Montagu coughed up blood. He sat down on the wet earth. The angel knelt beside Dow.

"Mother," said the boy, "is it you?"

"You drove the devil from me," said Sariel.

"My life is gone."

"No."

She took the vial from his fingers and worked the arrows free from his body. Then Sariel undid the wax stopper and anointed his wounds with the angel's blood. She turned to Montagu, put her hand to the haft of the lance.

"Yes," said Montagu.

Sariel pulled it and Montagu fainted. He was floating in some strange space, he was a light among other lights, a sparkle on a wet leaf, a glimmer of sunshine under a dark cloud. He saw Isabella, saw Prince Edward, a prince all in black, with the tail and the horns. England was in their grip now and, though hers was the only name on his lips in his delirium, Montagu knew he must return, to live, to oppose her.

The true Prince Edward was dead, very likely. But if not, he must be found and restored. As a lord Montagu opposed usurpers and as Luciferian he opposed devils. He had a clear duty and he would do it.

When he came around, the arrow-struck boy was on his feet, the angel by his side. Montagu touched his belly. Healed—his hand too, though the fingers were a little crooked. The angel's blood had done no good to his eye. Perhaps it was a punishment from God.

"We need help," Montagu said. "We will be sold short."

The king was rallying his men-at-arms and his devils now, giving thanks to God. Bowmen stood apart from this, holding up the three fingers of Lucifer's pitchfork, claiming the victory for the Lord of Light.

A party of scavenging bowmen came past them. "Who's this? Are you a Frenchman?" said one.

Dow pulled aside his tunic to reveal a scar in the shape of a pitchfork. The bowmen all put up three fingers—Lucifer's sign. These were his enemies. But they were no friends of devils either. They could be useful.

"How many survived the battle?" said Dow.

"Hard to say, not many," said the bowman.

"What shall we do?" said Dow to Montagu.

He replied, "Edward has offered you a part of France. Offer him something he wants too. The best path now is Calais. Take that, hold it, and you have the basis for trade with England, you have a valuable port which, if you strike the right alliance with England, you will be able to hold."

"Be friends with the high men?" said Dow.

"Not friends, but allies. It's very different," said Montagu, "and, come the right moment, when you have gathered your strength, you may even strike against England or France and see what you want imposed."

If Montagu could expose the impostor prince, even find the true prince, then England could be delivered from the grip of devils. God would not allow a devil to stand in the place of an appointed royal.

"You don't want what we want," said Dow. "Why should you help us?"

"You're wrong. I seek to be damned for betraying my wife and my king."

Dow replied, "To be damned you can kill yourself or just miss church on a Sunday. Why go to this trouble?"

He said, "Because a Montagu fights. That is the motto of my family."

"Does he fight God?"

"*Now* he does," said Montagu. "Though he hopes to lose. I will not give up my life, but I will give up my soul. I can be useful to you. I'll tell you now, the devils won't want you to have Calais. You have to work out a way to deal with them."

"We need the Evertere," said Dow. "Osbert took it."

"You," said Montagu to Greatbelly. "Find Edwin and get him to negotiate for at least equal possession of Calais. It's the only realistic strategic objective now."

"Realistic strategic objective!" said Greatbelly. "That the same as any port being good in a storm?"

Montagu said, "Something like that."

Up the slope devils were already squabbling with bowmen and one had already drawn back his bow for the benefit of Lord Sloth, Edwin's Lucifer-blessed arrow no doubt chosen from the basket.

"And now?" said Dow to Sariel.

She said, "From Calais grow Lucifer's peace. The Evertere may find its own way home."

"Does the true prince live?" said Montagu.

"What true prince?" said Dow.

"Isabella has bargained with devils. One has taken the guise of the English prince."

"The true prince *must* live. A devil commits no crime against God by merely relocating a prince. He would sin if he killed a legitimate royal son," said Dow.

"Will you help me find him?" said Montagu.

"Are you not of Lucifer now?" said Dow. "What happened to your damnation?"

"Edward is still my friend, though he hates me," said Montagu. "I will not see England go to devils. I oppose God's servants, the devils. I spite God. I am damned. Is that philosophy enough for you, Joanna?"

The woman Joanna Greatbelly nodded. "We need your help, William. We won't win our land without you," she said.

He said, "You'll have it. But you must find your sorcerers to help me find this boy."

"Will you do it, Mother?" said Dow.

"I will go to the light and look," said Sariel. She kissed Dow on the forehead. Then the light was like a rainbow caught in a waterfall and she was gone. Montagu went to cross himself but thought better of it.

"We should move," he said. "I don't want to be found here by the devil prince if he thinks I'm dead."

Dow replied, "To Calais and something we can have and hold. The seed of freedom for all the world will be planted there."

Up on the hill there was a great cry. Edward's men were calling his name. The king went to the foot of the windmill tower, held up his hand, and said something to the warriors. They all sank to their knees in prayer. Then they stood and shouted as one, "Glory to God! Glory to God!"

"Lucifer! Lucifer!" shouted the bowmen. The English united to loot the corpses of the dead.

At Montagu's feet something he had believed to be a corpse moved. It was a naked man with an arrow in his backside. Bardi!

"Help me!" said Bardi.

Montagu bent to him. "You who have traded with powers diabolic and devilish, you who have sought only your own good. Where has it brought you?"

"I only seek to serve!" said Bardi.

"To serve yourself," said Montagu.

"Have pity on me!"

Montagu took off the angel feather cloak, still intact despite the battle. He said, "You may not survive the journey, but I know one who is in need of a man like you. Go to the old English queen, Isabella. Say that I sent you and that I hope she will find a use for you."

"God, I'm in agony. Will she have doctors to get rid of this arrow?"

"All your troubles will be at an end," said Montagu. "Now go, wish for Isabella, and she will find a use for you that rewards you amply."

"Thank you," said Bardi. He crossed himself and said "Isabella." There was a flash of white light and Montagu saw a comet heading northwest.

"Where has he gone?" said Dow.

"To reap the interest on his investment," said Montagu. "Now let's away, the victory's not yet won."

Dow held up his three fingers, the sign of Lucifer. Montagu held up the three fingers in reply.

"For Free Hell!" said Dowzabel.

"For Free Hell," said Montagu, as a cry went through the camp. "To Calais! To Calais!" but on the field of slaughter, the men were deaf to the call, lost to their plunder.

So on Crécy field did this Dowzabel
Treat with a lord for the good of Free Hell
And Lord Salisbury did swear most truly
To find Prince Edward, taken so cruelly.
To Isabella flew Bardi of the bank.
She could not find it in her heart to thank
That most gentle Florentine courtier
And took her pleasure in his foul torture.
Our tale of the morning's bright child is done.
The Son of the Night's must now be begun.

Acknowledgments

T hanks to Adam Roberts and Richard Hornby for their reading and perceptive comments.

"The lyf so short, the craft so long to lerne."